BEFORE I SLEEP

BEFORE I SLEEP

Cynthia Harrod-Eagles

SEVERN
HOUSE

First world edition published in Great Britain and the USA in 2023
by Severn House, an imprint of Canongate Books Ltd,
14 High Street, Edinburgh EH1 1TE.

Trade paperback edition first published in Great Britain and the USA in 2023
by Severn House, an imprint of Canongate Books Ltd.

severnhouse.com

British Library Cataloguing-in-Publication Data
A CIP catalogue record for this title is available from the British Library.

ISBN-13: 978-1-4483-0619-0 (cased)
ISBN-13: 978-1-4483-0621-3 (trade paper)
ISBN-13: 978-1-4483-0620-6 (e-book)

All Severn House titles are printed on acid-free paper.

Typeset by Palimpsest Book Production Ltd.,
Falkirk, Stirlingshire, Scotland.
Printed and bound in Great Britain by
TJ Books, Padstow, Cornwall.

ONE

If You Knew Sushi Like I Know Sushi

Jenrich stuck her head – all cheekbones and burning blue eyes – round the door. 'Mr Porson wants you in his room, guv. Right away.' She gave him a look of dispassionate curiosity, like someone driving past a car crash, and added, 'He's got Mr Carpenter with him.'

'Bloody Nora,' said Slider. The last thing you wanted to face of a weekday morning was Borough Commander 'Call Me Mike' Carpenter, Slider's boss, Porson's boss, everybody's boss, who had all the warmth, charm and empathy of Vladimir Putin with a toothache. 'I never really got the hang of Wednesdays,' he muttered as he set off down the corridor.

He tapped at the open door, and saw that Carpenter had occupied Porson's usual prowling space between desk and window. Porson, marooned against the filing cabinet, rolled his eyes at Slider in a look that said, *Run. Run like the wind, and don't look back.*

Carpenter was tall, well-built, with a suspiciously luxuriant head of hair – Slider suspected plugs. He was standing with his back to the door, hands in pockets, staring out of the window – purely a piece of theatre, since the windows hadn't been cleaned since the Thatcher premiership, so the view was of grime on grime.

He did not move or turn at Slider's tap. More power play. Well, they could stand there all day in Beckettian symbiosis, or Slider could say, 'Sir?' He went with that.

Carpenter turned majestically, like the *Queen Mary* in the Hudson River. 'Ah, Slider,' he said. He withdrew his hands from his pockets. He smiled.

Slider flinched. He had braced himself for a bollocking, but a smile was far worse. It boded no good – and in the Job you quickly became an expert at recognizing boding.

'I have a job for you,' said Carpenter.

'Sir,' Slider said again, but without the question mark. Discouragingly.

'It's concerning Henry Holland – do you know who that is?'

The name sounded vaguely familiar, but, 'No, sir,' said Slider.

'He's a writer. Of a series of novels, about a ship-captain in the Napoleonic Wars. I'd never heard of them, but apparently they're quite popular. He makes a living at it, at any rate. Lives in St Anns Villas.'

It was a street just over the border in Holland Park, a posh street on the unposh north side of Holland Park Avenue. On the south side of the avenue was the park itself and Campden Hill, with some very high-end residences; beautiful old early Victorian places, some of them detached, with large gardens. The north side of the avenue was really Notting Hill, and segued into the shabbier hinterland of Ladbroke Grove; and, if you were so pioneer-spirited as to keep going, Harlesden and Willesden, where the only posh they acknowledged was a Spice Girl.

'Anyway,' said Carpenter, 'Holland's wife went out yesterday morning to go to her pottery class, and she hasn't come back. He's worried sick. He telephoned the commissioner last night about it.'

The commissioner being the top bod in the whole Met, Carpenter waited for Slider to register amazement or curiosity. When it was clear Slider wasn't going to play, he went on, 'The commissioner told him to wait until this morning, and if she still hadn't come back or contacted him, to let him know. She hasn't. And the commissioner's now telephoned me to ask me to look into it, as a matter of urgency.'

This all smelled to Slider like the sticky end of something deeply undesirable. He made the obvious objection. 'Holland Park isn't our ground, sir.'

Carpenter had been waiting for that one. He made an impatient gesture, but there was satisfaction in the set of his mouth. 'Perhaps I haven't made myself clear. Mr Holland telephoned the commissioner of the Metropolitan Police *personally*, because they were at school together and the commissioner likes his books. And the commissioner telephoned *me* personally, and asked me to undertake the enquiry myself as a favour to him. Any little jurisdictional problems will be ironed out – don't you worry about that. I want you to investigate, Slider – you, yourself, in person. Use whatever personnel or resources you need. Just find this woman, and find her fast, before the worst happens.'

Porson was studiously avoiding Slider's eyes. That crack on the ceiling had never been so well scrutinized.

Slider had to ask for himself. 'Why me, sir?'

Now Carpenter looked uncomfortable. 'You're an effective officer. You've had some notable clear-ups. And you've been involved in some – shall we say – *sensitive* cases. Involving people who needed kid-glove treatment. You have a reputation.'

Slider knew what his reputation was among the Carpenters of the Job. He surprised himself by saying, 'You mean that if it all goes tits-up, you don't mind if it's me that gets thrown to the wolves.'

'I don't appreciate insubordination, Slider,' Carpenter said icily. 'Remember who you're talking to.'

Silence followed. Judging by Porson's concentration, he had mentally dug out that crack, brushed it clean, filled and sanded it, and was about to apply a coat of primer.

Carpenter blinked first. 'You do appreciate there is a woman's safety, quite possibly her life at stake here,' he said sternly. 'This is not a teenager or young person who might have run away from home, or got drunk at a party and be sleeping it off on a friend's sofa. This is a mature, married woman with a settled lifestyle who has gone missing out of all character and precedent. She is almost certainly in danger. The sooner you get on the track, the better chance you have of finding her alive – *alive*, Slider, do you understand?'

'Sir,' Slider said.

'Then get on with it. This is your number one priority. Go and see Holland yourself and get the details. Drop everything else until you've found his wife. Understood?'

He sat down at Porson's desk and picked up Porson's telephone as a sign of dismissal.

Porson followed Slider out into the corridor and said, 'Bit of a poisoned challenge, I'm afraid. Sorry you've got stuck with it. But he's not wrong, vis-à-vis the best chance of finding her alive. Sooner you get looking—'

'But it's not our ground,' Slider complained stubbornly. 'Notting Hill's just as capable – more capable, they know the area. Why doesn't Carpenter give it to Bleasedale?'

Barry Bleasedale was the borough commander responsible for the Notting Hill station, under whose jurisdiction Holland Park fell.

'Because Bleasedale's wife isn't shopping buddies with the commissioner's wife.'

'And Mrs Carpenter is?'

'Mrs Carpenter knows everybody. And she's related to everybody she doesn't. I bet the Queen sends her birthday cards,' Porson said sadly. 'When there's a string being pulled, Mrs Carpenter's generally on the other end of it. So there's no point complaining. You should take it as a compliment: hand-picked by the top nobs for an important task.'

'You really think so, sir?' Slider asked ironically.

'Well, no. It's a hand grenade with its pants down,' Porson conceded.

'And what do I do when toes get trodden on and Notting Hill orders me off their patch?'

'We'll burn that bridge when we come to it,' Porson said largely. 'But he's got a point, you know,' he went on, fixing Slider with a serious look. 'This woman's probably in danger. Someone's got to look for her, pronto. So just get on with it. The sooner you start, the quicker. Take Atherton with you – he's a proper egg-box, he's read books. He'll know how to talk to this Johnny and reassure him. Because the last thing we want is him complaining to the commissioner that we're not taking him seriously.'

'I always take a missing woman seriously,' said Slider.

'There you are, then. You *are* the right man for the job,' said Porson, his parting shot.

And if I don't find her, Slider thought, heading back to his office, or if I don't find her in time, or if she doesn't *want* to be found (the whereabouts of a missing adult once discovered could not be revealed to anyone without their permission), I'll be the right man for the chop. The chalice from the palace held the potion with the poison, all right.

He was slightly comforted by the idea of Atherton as an egg-box. Porson, in his tempestuous relationship with life and the Job, tended to throw words at meaning and see what stuck. He had gone for brain-box or egg-head, and the resultant portmanteau was oddly charming.

Detective Constable Kathleen 'Norma' Swilley was looking Henry Holland up on Wikipedia. 'I suppose you know all about him,' she said snarkily to Atherton. Like many in the Job, she was suspicious, if not contemptuous, of intellectualism.

'I know the name, that's all,' said Atherton, Slider's sergeant, bagman and friend. Well-spoken, well-read and well-dressed, he was a misfit in the Job. 'Never read any of his books. I've seen them on the shelf – naval yarns. The Hornblower genre.'

Jenrich, the other sergeant, was watching over Swilley's shoulder. 'The horny what?' she asked.

'Holland's books,' Atherton explained. 'Marine subculture.'

'There's a Subway in the W12 shopping centre,' McLaren offered. 'I like their marinara meatball sub.'

'I thought marinara was fish,' said Jerry Fathom.

'Nah! A fish sub would be shit,' McLaren said, making a face.

'You eat sushi,' Fathom accused.

'I go sometimes cos Natalie likes it, but I only eat the chips.'

'But marinara—'

'Marinara is American for tomato sauce,' said Jenrich impatiently.

Fathom was stubborn. 'It's gotta be fish. Marine means the sea, dunnit?'

'How many times have I told you, Jezza,' Swilley said, eyes on the screen, 'you have to stop pushing the Q-tip when you feel resistance. Here it is. The Captain Arbuthnot books. Adventure stories set in the age of sailing ships.'

'But, like, submarine means "under the sea",' Fathom insisted.

'They didn't have submarines back then,' McLaren objected. 'Day of yore.'

'Your what?' Fathom was puzzled.

'Henry Holland – it's a good name for a writer,' said Atherton desperately.

'It's got a ring to it,' Swilley agreed.

'Yes, but more importantly, it begins with an "H". That puts it on the middle shelves, near eye level. If your name begins with "A", you're up too high to be seen, and "W" puts you on the bottom shelf. No one ever bends down to choose a book.'

'Is that true?' asked LaSalle.

'Everything I've ever told you is a lie,' said Atherton. 'Including that.'

'Including what?'

'That everything I've ever told you is a lie. That's just not true.'

LaSalle waved it away. 'Well, but I'm thinking if it was true, every writer would change their name, and then they'd all begin with "H".'

'Then they'd have to go by the first name, wouldn't they?' said Lœssop with an air of academic enquiry. 'So someone called Andy Holland would be on the top shelf and someone called Zebedee Holland'd be on the bottom.'

'Then they'd change their first names as well, to begin with an H,' said LaSalle.

'So then you'd have to—'

'For Gawd's sake shut up, you twonks!' said Swilley, scrolling. 'Look at all this, all these books. There's twelve of them. How come, if he's written all these books, I've never heard of him?'

'There are thousands and thousands of writers,' Atherton said, 'and only a very few become household names.'

'Well, he can't be much good, then,' Jenrich said.

'Good enough to afford to live in St Anns Villas,' said Lœssop. 'That's pretty juicy.'

'Maybe the money's his wife's,' said Jenrich. 'Maybe he married a rich woman who could keep him.'

'Well, there's not much on here,' Swilley said, scrolling down. 'Grew up in Portsmouth, where his visits to HMS *Victory* sparked his love of wooden ships. Really?'

'It probably wasn't *only* that,' said Atherton.

'Went to Portsmouth Grammar School—'

'There you are. They've got lots of naval links.'

'Navel links? Is that like belly-button rings?' said Lœssop innocently.

'—then read history at Christ Church, Oxford,' Swilley continued. 'Joined the Civil Service. Wrote the first Arbuthnot book in his spare time. Its popularity allowed him to leave the Civil Service and write full-time. That's it. The rest is all about the books.'

'One every two years,' Atherton said, looking at the publication dates. 'So if he's fifty-nine now, he was mid-thirties when he started. What's it say about the wife?'

'Nothing. Nothing about his private life at all. It just says on the sidebar: "married, yes, children, no."'

'So he obviously likes to keep himself to himself.'

'Or there's not that much interest in him,' said Gascoyne. 'I mean, if he was a pop idol everyone'd want to know everything – what he had for breakfast, what hair gel he used. But a writer no one's even heard of . . .'

'Point,' Atherton acknowledged.

'There might be stuff about her elsewhere on the net, if we had something to go on,' said Swilley. 'A first name'd be helpful.'

Slider, who had just come in, heard her and handed her a slip of paper. 'This is the information given by the husband,' he said. 'For what it's worth. Felicity Holland, age fifty-three, five feet four, slim build, short dark brown curly hair, blue eyes. No visible distinguishing marks.'

'Might help if we knew her maiden name,' Swilley grunted.

'We'll find out more when we see him,' said Slider. 'For the moment, get this to the Missing Persons Unit.'

'We're supposed to wait seventy-two hours,' said Swilley.

'They can complain to the commissioner if they want. Meanwhile, let's go with the personal touch. Start phoning the local police stations, starting with the nearest and working outwards. In case she's had a blackout and wandered in, or been in an accident, or been reported behaving oddly. Fathom, McLaren, you can get on with that.'

'They won't like it, guv,' said McLaren.

'Use your charm. Use the commissioner's name. Ditto hospitals – Jenrich, Gascoyne, work outwards from the closest.

When we come back we should have more information, then
we can really get at it, but I want to show we didn't wait to
take action. Remember there are some pretty beady eyes on
us. Atherton, ready?'

'Yes, Kemo Sabe.'

On the stairs, Slider said, 'What was that for?'

'Obviously Mr Carpenter sees you as a sort of Lone Ranger,
carrying on the fight for justice whatever the odds. It means
Trusty Scout.'

'I was never a scout. It was all Boys' Brigade round where
I grew up.'

You wouldn't have described the houses in St Anns Villas as
semi-detached, but effectively that's what they were: each
tall, wide, Dutch-gabled building – three-storeyed with semi-
basement, red brick with smart white trim – was divided down
the middle into two substantial dwellings. The road was broad
and quiet, edged with pollarded lime trees, wide enough to
allow residents' parking on both sides of the road and still
leave two full running lanes.

'Nice,' Atherton concluded as they stood looking up at the
Holland house. 'What d'you reckon? Six bedrooms?'

'Yes, probably. Big rooms, too.'

'So you're looking at two and a half, three mill? Twice that
if it was on the other side of Holland Park Avenue,' Atherton
observed, 'but still he must be raking it in.'

'Not if they've lived there for a long time,' said Slider. 'It
wouldn't have cost a fraction of that twenty years ago.'

'Well, logically, anything it cost would be a fraction of some
sort.'

'Don't be pedantic.'

'Why is someone trying to be accurate always called
pedantic?'

'That's a very pedantic quibble.'

'I shall sink into a hurt silence. Are we going in?'

'He's expecting us,' said Slider.

Henry Holland was tall, late fifties, with the sort of lean,
fair good looks associated with English public schoolboys. He
had probably looked a lot like David Attenborough when he

was young. His hair now was a mixture of grey and blonde, but still nicely thick; his eyes were blue; his face was firm with the sort of lines of maturity that in a man only enhance attractiveness. Probably he had a charming smile.

Just now he was not smiling. His face was taut with tension, his eyes looked unslept. All the same, he was immaculately dressed, in wool trousers, proper well-shined shoes, shirt and, if no tie, at least a sports jacket. The proverbial Englishman who always dressed properly, even on a desert island. The sort who'd have a shave and polish his shoes before facing a firing squad. Only the strain on his facial muscles showed that he was not having a normal day. And that, when Slider introduced himself and Atherton, he said, 'Yes, come in, come in,' impatiently, waving them past without waiting to look at their warrant cards.

Inside, the house had the kind of cool hush that goes with high ceilings and low occupancy. The shining floorboards of the hall seemed to stretch into that distance where all points meet; the air was scented with lavender wax. Holland led them into the drawing room, which was so beautiful it made Slider gulp. The height of the ceiling, the proportions, the tranquillity; the polished floorboards covered in the centre by a handsome Persian carpet; the huge marble fireplace, with a gigantic gilt-framed mirror over it. The walls were painted a delicate duck-egg blue, a chandelier hung overhead, and the exquisite pieces of antique furniture had acres of space between them so that each was a little statement of individual perfection.

On the wall opposite the fireplace was a large oil painting of a sea battle between square-rigged ships. When they had investigated the murder of literary agent Ed Wiseman, Slider had learned a lot about the world of publishing, and in particular how little most writers actually made. Would Henry Holland's twelve books generate a fortune sufficient for these surroundings? But the style of the house, plus the age and quality of the furniture, and in particular that big oil painting, suggested old money. His, or hers?

In one of the alcoves beside the fireplace was a fine break-front mahogany bookcase in which there were books displayed face outwards so that you could see that the jacket illustrations were of more square-rigged ships in excitingly rumpled seas.

Reproductions, by the style of them, of famous naval oils. The twelve Arbuthnot books, then, given pride of place.

Holland saw the direction of his look and said, 'My *oeuvre*, yes.'

'You must be very proud,' Slider offered politely.

'Perhaps I was. But how trivial it seems now, when one's wife is missing,' said Holland. He had a good voice, rich and well-modulated, with a public-school accent. He waved them to seats. 'You must find her,' he concluded bluntly, sitting rather suddenly as though his legs had given way.

'We'll do everything in our power,' Slider said.

'So much time has been wasted already,' Holland said. 'More than twelve hours since I rang David. Why did he tell me to wait?' he mourned.

Slider saw Atherton's flick of the eyes that said, *David, yet?* Was this merely a bit of I-call-the-commissioner-by-his-first-name pressure, or were they really chummy? It could be crucial down the line, but it didn't change what they had to do now. 'Tell me everything that happened yesterday,' he said. 'From the beginning.'

Holland paused to assemble his thoughts; but narrative was his trade, and they could hope for clarity and coherence.

'We woke as usual at a quarter to eight,' he began, 'and had a cup of tea while we listened to the radio.'

'Who made the tea?' Slider asked. It could matter. If she had gone down to the kitchen, picked up a letter that had just come . . .

Holland looked slightly blank. 'We have a Teasmade in the bedroom,' he said.

Atherton, taking notes, was impressed that he said 'Teasmade' without a trace of embarrassment.

'Go on, please,' said Slider.

'We got up at a quarter past eight. We have separate bathrooms. I shaved, showered and dressed and went downstairs at a quarter to nine. My wife was already in the kitchen – she is quicker than me in the mornings. We had breakfast and read the papers.'

'Had any post arrived?'

'No. Our postman does two walks these days, and he

alternates them. On Tuesdays, Thursdays and Saturdays we don't get a delivery until the afternoon.'

'Did your wife take any phone calls?'

'No.'

'Go on please. You finished breakfast, when?'

'Half past nine.'

'You seem sure of that. Is this your usual routine?'

'Yes. Routine is very important to me,' Holland said. 'I like to go up to my study at half past nine every day. A disciplined environment is important to a writer.'

'So I understand,' Slider said helpfully. 'Where is your study?'

'On the top floor. There were three bedrooms up there which we had converted into one large space. With my desks and papers and reference books, I need plenty of room – for instance, I have a separate table to spread out maps and charts. And it's quiet up there, away from any street sounds.'

'And what did your wife do yesterday, when you went upstairs?'

'She was going to her pottery class – always her pottery class on Tuesdays.' His cheek muscles trembled for a moment with some emotion. He swallowed and went on, 'She said she would be lunching out. She generally had lunch with some of her fellow students afterwards. She asked me what I wanted for dinner – said she'd shop on the way home. Then I kissed her goodbye and went up to work.'

'And did you see her again before she went out?'

'No.' That seemed a hard word to say, and came out unelaborated.

'Or speak to her?'

He shook his head. 'That was quite as usual. Once I start work, I don't like to be disturbed. It's very important that my concentration is not broken. Felicity knew that – it was understood.' Another spasm of the cheeks.

Slider helped him along. 'So you went up to work. Do you work up there all day?'

'I like to do a solid four hours in the morning – it's my best time for concentrating. At half past one I take an hour to eat, relax, perhaps take a short walk. Then I might work again for a couple of hours in the afternoon, depending on what I have to do, what stage I'm at. Towards the end of a book, I may work longer. At the moment I am still in the research stage of a new book. Researching, making notes, compiling a timeline, sketching out a possible plot.'

'Did you and your wife usually have lunch together?'

'If she was at home, yes. But she often lunches out. If she did, she would leave me a sandwich.'

'So what time did she go out?'

'Her class was from ten thirty to twelve thirty, so she would leave a little after ten, I imagine.'

'You imagine? She didn't call goodbye? You didn't hear the front door close?'

'No, but that's quite usual. Once I'm up in my room, I'm not aware of what's going on below.' He looked down at his hands, his mouth taut. 'Believe me,' he said in a low voice, 'if I had known . . .'

Slider left him a tactful beat, then went on, 'Did she ring you at any time during the day?'

'No, but I wouldn't have expected her to.'

'She has a mobile phone?'

'Yes. Just a basic one. It makes and receives calls and texts, that's all. She only has it in case of accidents.'

'And you didn't ring her?'

A trace of annoyance crossed his face. 'Why would I do that? If I wanted to talk to her, I'd wait until she got home. We're not teenagers, to have to be chatting every five minutes.'

'Quite so. And it didn't worry you that she didn't come home after lunch?'

'I don't keep tabs on her when she's out of the house. We are autonomous adults. There are any number of things she might have been doing – shopping, going to the gym, visiting a gallery.'

'At what point *did* you become concerned?'

'At half past five I mix a cocktail. It's something we look forward to – a time to talk over our day, make plans, catch up with each other. I expected her to be back by then. When it got to six thirty and she hadn't appeared, I wondered where she could be. She ought to have been home by then to start the cooking. We eat at seven. She knows I like to keep to a routine. If she was delayed so badly, she ought to have called me. So I rang her mobile phone, but I got the recorded message saying that number was not available, which means she had it turned off. I didn't know what to do – I felt quite helpless. I tried the number again at half past seven, with the same result, and then, at my wits' end, I rang Sir David for advice.'

'You went straight to the top, to the commissioner of the Metropolitan Police himself?' Slider said. 'Are you and he very close?'

'I didn't know who else to ask,' he said defensively. 'One does not expect to find oneself in this position. I don't *know* any other policemen. He and I were at the same school, though not in the same year. He's three years younger than me. But I was his house captain, so there was a little – shall we say – hero-worship involved. We weren't in touch after I left school, but when my first book came out he recognized my name, bought the book and read it, and contacted me to say how much he'd enjoyed it. Since then, he's read all my books, and he's always written to me with very generous praise of each one. So I felt he would . . . *want* to help me. Old Portsmuthians are very loyal to each other.'

'Evidently you were right,' Slider said mildly. 'You didn't ring any of her friends before going to the commissioner?'

He looked helpless. 'She doesn't really have friends separately from me. We have friends as a couple, people I know through my writing, one or two old work friends from the Civil Service, people we play bridge with, and so on. She wouldn't have gone to visit any of them, on her own, without me. Without saying anything. And besides,' he went on with a touch of anger, 'if she was with one of them, she would have rung me to say so, wouldn't she? Or if something had happened while she was with them, *they* would have rung. She, or they, wouldn't have left me to worry like this. It's not normal. It's not *reasonable*. I *know* something has happened to her. And there's been enough delay as it is. If only you had come here last night . . . But David said to wait until this morning. What did he suppose was going to happen?'

'Sometimes news takes time to filter through,' Slider said soothingly.

'Well it didn't! And precious time has been wasted. So what are you going to do about it now?'

'We are going to make enquiries,' Slider said. 'You've given us a description of your wife, and I'd like a recent photograph, if you have one. And can you tell me what was she wearing?'

'When she went out? How would I know? I didn't see her after breakfast.'

'Well, what was she wearing at breakfast?'

'I don't remember,' he said irritably. 'I don't pay any attention to clothes. Besides, she'd have been sure to change before she went out, wouldn't she?'

'If you looked through her wardrobe, would you be able to tell what's missing?'

He scowled. 'Good God, of course not! She has a lot of clothes – hundreds of outfits. It amazes me how many clothes a woman needs for one small body. I mean, she can only wear one thing at a time. She's always smartly turned out, that's all I can tell you. People always comment when we go out together on how attractive she looks.'

'Well, perhaps we can have a look at her wardrobe later, and get an idea of the sort of thing she wears,' Atherton said. 'And see if there are any obvious gaps.'

'You can, of course, if you think it will do any good,' Holland said, giving him a look that Admiral Hornblower might have given an unpromising midshipman.

'The better the description we can give,' Slider explained, 'the more chance we have of tracing her. But first, can you tell us a bit more about her.'

'What do you want to know? *Why* do you want to know?'

'We're working blind here, Mr Holland. We need to know who we're looking for if we're not to waste time looking in the wrong places. Who *is* Felicity Holland?'

'She's my life,' he said, and put his hands over his face.

TWO

Hearts and Crafts

They first met at a launch party. 'Publishers still had them then,' he said. It had been held in the Holland Park Orangery. 'It was for my first book, *Arbuthnot and the Swiftsure*. She came with a friend, who was a colleague of the art director. Collingwood's – my publisher – were planning for a series, you see, and all the jackets were to be based on oil paintings of Napoleonic-era sea battles. The Collingwood art director had been consulting the curator of Marine Art at the National Gallery, and invited him to the launch. And he brought Felicity with him. The moment I saw her . . .'

He lapsed into a brooding silence.

'You were – thirty-four then?' Atherton prompted.

'Thirty-five.' He looked up. 'I had never been romantically involved before, not since one or two light dalliances at Oxford. I was quite content with a bachelor life. I had a pleasant flat in Park Crescent. My job at the Ministry of Defence was satisfying, my research into the navy of the Napoleonic era, and latterly my writing, occupied my spare time. I had no sense that anything was missing. But from the first moment I saw her . . .' His eyes were distant. 'It was as though I had been seeing in black and white all my life, and suddenly I could see colours.'

'That's very poetic,' Slider said. 'I can tell you're a writer.' Holland's focus changed sharply, as though he suspected satire. Slider hurried on. 'What was her maiden name?'

'Aubrey-Harris. Her father is Sir John Aubrey-Harris, the QC.'

Atherton flicked Slider a glance at the name. It was probably another reason the commissioner had got involved. Aubrey-Harris was a very eminent barrister, now retired, who had conducted prosecutions for the CPS. Some of his cases were still taught at police college.

'I couldn't have been more surprised when she seemed interested in me,' Holland went on, back in his dream. 'I've never been – er – what you might call a lady's man. And she was not only beautiful, but bright and vivacious, so full of life. I could see that everyone in the room was attracted to her. But when we were introduced, something seemed to happen, something clicked. We were married six months later.'

'Had she been married before? She was – what – twenty-nine then?'

'No, astonishingly, she'd never been married either. It was obviously "meant to be".' He looked apologetic at the senti-mental phrase, and put verbal inverted commas round it. 'It has been – it is – an extremely happy marriage.'

'Does she have a job?'

'Not recently. She trained as a dancer, and taught ballet as a peripatetic to various private schools around London. Then, for the last ten years, she worked for a dance agency – Marylebone World Dance Management, in York Street, just off Baker Street. But she gave that up three years ago, when she turned fifty. She went through a bad time with the –' he lowered his voice, squeamishly – '*menopause.*'

'I see.'

'She was quite depressed for a while. But now she has an active life. She does voluntary work, she does classes, she goes to the gym. We play bridge. She's always out and about. But in twenty-four years of happy marriage, she has *never* not come home.'

'Yes, I can understand why you're so concerned. Now, this pottery class – every Tuesday morning, you said? You didn't ring them to ask if she'd attended?'

He looked helpless. 'I wouldn't know where to begin, or who to ask.'

'Where is it held?'

'Somewhere in Notting Hill Gate. Some arts centre – I'm not sure of the name.' He frowned in thought. 'No, I can't recall. I think it's named after some prime minister or other.'

'I see. And the friends she had lunch with afterwards – their names?'

'They were just people she did the class with – they would

go off to lunch together afterwards. I don't think she ever told me their names specifically – it would probably be a fluctuating group.' He looked sharply at Atherton, who was making notes, as though he had said something critical. 'I don't interrogate my wife every time she leaves the house – or when she comes back. Why should I? I couldn't have expected this to happen, could I?'

'What do you think *has* happened?' Slider asked. Holland looked blank at the question, and he elaborated. 'Do you have reason to believe someone might mean her harm? Has anyone threatened her? Has she fallen out with anyone?'

'No! Everyone loves her! Why would anyone want to hurt her?'

'Has she seemed her usual self lately? Has she been moody, withdrawn, anxious? Has she seemed nervous or depressed? Has she had any unusual phone calls or letters?'

He shook his head each time.

'Anything that she seemed to want to keep hidden from you.'

He reddened, and his eyes sparked. 'Of course not! What are you suggesting? Why should she keep anything from me? If she was in trouble of any sort, she'd have told me, and I'd have helped her. That's what married people do.'

'Even so,' Slider said carefully, 'sometimes a person wants to keep trouble away from the person they love, to protect them.'

Holland waved a hand. 'Well, it's academic, anyway, because she has been completely her usual self. If I'd noticed any change in her, I'd have asked her what was wrong.'

'Very well. Now, I'm afraid I must ask you about money.' He frowned. 'What about it?'

'Did your wife come from a wealthy background? Did she have money of her own, or expectations of an inheritance?'

He didn't like the question. 'Her father is moderately wealthy. I told you he was a QC. What has that to do with it?'

'Money is so often at the bottom of things. If there's a lot of it, she could be a target – *you* could be a target through her.'

'Oh, that's nonsense! We live comfortably, but I'm not a

rich man. She has an income of her own from a trust fund, but it's not of the order to attract criminals – just enough to give her independence.' He was getting angry. 'I don't see the object of these intrusive questions. Why don't you do something about finding her, instead of wasting time interrogating me? It's obvious that she's been snatched by some random person – you read about it all the time in the newspapers. There was that woman recently, just walking home in broad daylight, bundled into a van by a strange man, held prisoner for days and then murdered. You've got to find her while there's still time!'

'I know that's the great fear when someone close to you goes missing,' Slider said, 'but I can assure you it's extremely rare for someone to be targeted like that by a stranger. In nearly every case, the missing person turns up after a few days, having been involved in some unusual but harmless set of circumstances. But,' he forestalled him, 'we will not be relying on that, of course. We will be making every possible enquiry, and putting every possible effort into finding your wife.'

'I wish I believed you,' Holland said, staring at him desperately. 'I wish I didn't think that – to you – she is just some meaningless statistic.'

'I promise you,' Slider said, injecting all the sincerity he could muster into his voice, 'that I am taking this very seriously indeed. In fact, I can promise you that I have put everything else aside until Mrs Holland is found. It is my sole concern.'

Thanks to Carpenter, that was literally true, so it sounded unexpectedly genuine.

Holland produced a photograph for them, from the previous November, of him and her in evening dress at the annual dinner of the Society of Nautical Fiction Writers (Guest Speaker: The Admiral of the Fleet) in the William Kent room at the Ritz. In a simple black sheath, with something modestly sparkly at her neck and ears, she looked a stylish and beautiful woman. She had, even in a photograph, one of those smiles that ought to be accompanied by a 'ping!' sound effect.

When Holland conducted them to the bedroom, so that they could look at her clothes, they found her looking down from the wall over the marble fireplace from a magnificent portrait in oils. Slider didn't know much about art, but you didn't have to have special training to see that the subject came alive in the painting.

Atherton beat him to the comment. 'Oh, is that a Laertes French?'

Holland seemed impressed. 'Yes. You know him?'

'I recognize the style. I saw an exhibition of his portraits a couple of years ago, at the Courtauld.'

'He *asked* to paint Felicity,' Holland said proudly. 'She volunteers at the National Gallery, you see, and he'd met her there. He said she had one of the great faces of the age. She didn't really want to sit for him – she said she didn't like the idea of being frozen in time on the canvas – but he persuaded her. It won the William Locke prize.'

The artist had represented her half-length, sitting in a chair, her arms resting on its arms, her hands relaxed. The light was coming from the side, as though from a window, and she was looking away from the viewer, as though looking out of the window. Though there was a faint smile on her lips, there was something in her stare that seemed to Slider not just thoughtful, but actually sad. But perhaps it was just boredom – what did he know? She hadn't wanted to sit. If she was a very active woman, as Holland said, she might find sitting still for any length of time a trial.

The bedroom, like the rest of the house, was spacious, quiet, beautifully furnished with well-kept antiques. Apart from Mrs Holland in oils over the fireplace, there were several pictures on the walls, all watercolours, all depictions of sailing ships in violently heavy seas. Slider supposed if you were a marine artist there was no challenge in painting a gentle swell. There was also a model of a square-rigged ship in a glass case on top of a side-table. She must have been a patient wife, he thought, not to mind all this nauticalia in the bedroom. He tried to imagine how Joanna would feel about a display of antique truncheons and handcuffs, and failed.

On the mantelpiece there stood a strange-looking lump of

clear Perspex, all angles, like a chunk chipped off an iceberg, affixed to a black base. Souvenir of the *Titanic* disaster? Slider wondered. But that was after Holland's time, surely.

'I see you're looking at my award,' Holland said.

'Award?' Slider queried.

Holland lifted it down and handed it to Slider. It was unexpectedly heavy – solid Perspex. Now, close to, he saw something was engraved somehow *inside* the block – it must have been made in two halves and sealed invisibly together, so that it appeared there was a three-masted sailing ship imprisoned in the ice.

'Nice, isn't it?' said Holland.

'HMS *Victory*?' Slider hazarded.

'*Bellerophon*. Given to me by the Society of Nautical Fiction Writers. Lifetime achievement award.'

'Very handsome,' Slider said. 'You must be proud.'

'Well, it was an honour, though whether one deserves it . . .' he said with becoming modesty. He took it back and replaced it tenderly on the mantelpiece.

Mrs Holland had a large mahogany wardrobe in the bedroom and, they were told, a second one in a spare bedroom, but there was nothing to be gleaned from them as to what she might have been wearing when she left the house. They were full of clothes, but without any obvious gaps. There were trousers as well as skirts, dresses and suits, shoes and boots carefully kept on trees, handbags in protective cloth bags, a drawerful of beautiful knitwear. Her taste seemed to be for plain, unpatterned clothes in expensive fabrics, in which she would be indistinguishable from any other well-to-do woman walking about the better parts of Kensington. Everything was beautifully kept, clean and pressed. There was even one item – it looked like a skirt suit in garnet-red wool – hanging up still in the dry-cleaners' bag.

They continued to ask questions as they examined her things. A battery of top-of-the-range beauty products in the bathroom. Hairbrush, toothbrush, curling wand, manicure set all present. Nothing to suggest she had done a runner.

'Do you have children?'

'No,' he said shortly. And then he expanded. 'I'd have

liked a family, but Felicity couldn't. I knew that from the beginning, before I married her. But it's quite all right – it's been quite all right. We are perfectly content as we are, just the two of us.'

'You mentioned her father,' Slider said. 'Is she close to her parents?'

'Not particularly. Her mother died – oh – it must be ten years ago now. Her father's retired, of course – he's in his eighties now. He lives in Buckinghamshire. We go down once or twice a year to visit him but there's no real contact otherwise. He was always a difficult man. He doesn't like *me*,' he added, as though in a blurted confession. 'Thinks I'm not good enough for his daughter. He calls me "the novelist".' He made the word sound withering. 'Of course, he wrote several books himself, on the law. He thinks non-fiction is the only proper writing. He regards fiction as something rather low and vulgar.'

'Any other family?' Slider asked. 'Brothers or sisters?'

'One sister. Thelma.' He pronounced it 'Telma'. 'She's four years younger than Felicity.'

'Are they close?'

'They talk on the phone a lot, but they're both too busy to see each other very often.'

'Where does she live?'

'In Hampstead. She's married to Joshua Wilbraham, who's also a barrister – much to Sir John's satisfaction. If she wasn't the favourite child before that, she was after she made the better marriage of the two.' It sounded quite sour. An Old Portsmuthian and well-known author might well resent being seen as a second-ranker.

'And have you contacted her, to ask if she's seen her sister, or heard from her?'

He looked a little confused. 'No, I – I didn't think of it. I told you, I just rang David. Besides,' he rallied, 'why would Felicity telephone her and not me? If she could ring at all, she'd have rung me. And if Thelma knew anything, she'd have contacted me, wouldn't she? You don't seem to be taking this seriously at all.'

'It's just the usual policy, when someone is missing, to check with all their usual contacts,' Slider said soothingly.

'Well, she has obviously been taken by a very *un*usual contact, so I suggest you stop wasting time fiddling about here and go out and look for her.'

'We shall indeed,' Slider said. 'One last thing,' he said as they trod back down the stairs. 'Does your wife have a car?'

'*We* have one,' he corrected. 'The silver Volvo parked outside. We don't use it much – it's more convenient to use the tube. Parking in London is so impossible these days.'

'So she would have used the tube to get to her pottery class?'

'Yes, probably, unless she walked. She likes to walk.'

'Or took a bus,' Atherton said to Slider when they were outside again, walking to the car. 'There's four or five that run along Holland Park Avenue. Or took a taxi.'

Slider glanced back. Henry Holland had seen them out, and was still in the open doorway, watching them depart. He looked somehow pathetic standing there, dwarfed by the large house, tall though he was. A life of permanent bachelorhood can be happy and fulfilling, but once a man is used to being married, an involuntary resumption of the single state leaves him at a loss.

Atherton was still talking. 'If she walked, it's mostly residential along the Avenue, except for that flight of shops next to Holland Park station, so no cameras. That's if she even went that way. We don't know where this class was held. Why do the words "needle" and "haystack" keep trying to connect up in my mind?'

'Let's not get ahead of ourselves,' Slider said. 'If she was at the pottery class as usual, we'll be starting from there.'

'It's odd – don't you think it's odd?' Atherton said, dissatisfied. 'If she'd run off and left him, she'd have taken her stuff, and probably left a note. If she was stuck somewhere, there'd have been a message to him via somebody, somewhere. Even if she'd had an accident and was unconscious, there'd have been ID in her handbag. Do you think he could possibly be right, and that she *has* been snatched? OK, it's the rarest of rare occurrences, but it *does* happen.'

'I don't know,' said Slider. 'It has to be a possibility. It's not as if she could have fallen down a quarry or a disused pit shaft. Unless she left London. But the car's still here.' He paused to look through the Volvo's window, but there was nothing to be seen inside except the resident's permit in the holder on the windscreen. They kept their car tidy and clean, though there was some old mud between the treads of the tyres.

'I knew someone who got stuck all night in the lavatory in a theatre once,' said Atherton helpfully. 'But they found her in the morning when the cleaners came in.'

'I read a story once where a tube train stopped in a disused station, and the guard absent-mindedly opened the doors, and someone got off, and got stranded there.'

'What happened to him?'

'I think he was killed by some supernatural entity that haunted the place. Or got eaten by rats. Something like that,' Slider said vaguely. He handed Atherton the photograph while he felt for the car key. 'She's a very good-looking woman,' he commented, plipping the door.

They got in. 'But Sir John Aubrey-Harris?' Atherton mused, fastening the seat belt. 'He must have made some enemies over his career. Maybe it's a revenge snatching.'

'What about this very sinister organization, the Society of Nautical Fiction Writers? The jealousies, the rivalries. The secret rituals in their bat-haunted Gothic headquarters. The shadowy mastermind of their chairman, pulling the strings of publishers and agents . . .'

'While slowly stroking a white cat? She must have had an Oyster card,' Atherton said, 'if they used the tube a lot. That would give us some useful travel data.'

'Excellent, Watson. You have learned my methods.'

'Named after a prime minister?' LaSalle said, buckling his forehead.

'Probably Churchill,' Gascoyne suggested. 'That's usually who things get named after.'

'But an old geezer, like Holland is, would remember *that* name,' said Jenrich.

'He's fifty-nine,' Atherton protested.

'There you are, then. Getting his bus pass this year,' said Jenrich.

'Well, there isn't a Churchill Arts Centre anyway,' Swilley said, at the computer. 'There's only three arts centres. The Acorn is for kids. The Kensington Arts Centre is actually a sales gallery. And the Godolphin . . . Was there a prime minister Godolphin?'

'There was a seventeenth-century one who was First Lord of the Treasury. It wasn't called prime minister back then,' said Atherton.

'Fount of bleedin' knowledge,' Swilley grumbled. 'Anyway, it's in Shepherd's Bush, not Notting Hill.'

'Try adult education centres. And social centres,' said Atherton.

'I already am,' Swilley said impatiently. 'There's a few of them. Nothing named after a prime minister. And . . . none of them does a pottery class.'

'I suppose you'd need special equipment,' said Jenrich. 'A kiln, or whatever it's called. That'd be expensive.'

'What's that?' said McLaren, leaning over Swilley's shoulder and blowing pastry flakes from his custard tart in her ear. 'Elizabeth Ferrier School of Ceramics. Ceramics is pottery, isn't it?'

'They do lessons, private and group. But it's in Hammersmith. And it's not a prime minister.'

'Well, the old boy was probably confused,' Jenrich said. 'You can't go on that.'

'I keep telling you, he's not old,' Atherton said.

'Not to *you*, maybe,' Jenrich said provocatively.

But Atherton had spotted something. 'There! Eden Dale Community Centre. Click on that.'

'There's no prime minister called Eden Dale,' Swilley objected.

'*Anthony* Eden.'

'Never heard of him.'

'That doesn't prove anything. You've probably never heard of Spencer Perceval either.'

'Who's he?' McLaren asked.

'Only British prime minister ever to be assassinated.

Actually in the House of Commons. He was shot in the lobby.'

McLaren winced. 'Sounds painful.'

'Eden Dale,' said Swilley. The website had come up and she was scrolling. 'There you are. Pottery. Every day at ten thirty. And it's in Notting Hill. Denbigh Road. Got to be it.'

Porson was not happy. 'I've had Mr Carpenter on the blower again, *and* the deputy assistant commissioner. That's the trouble with the Job,' he went on in a savage mumble. 'Too many cooks and not enough Indians. How's it looking?'

'He seems a nice enough chap,' Slider said. 'Obviously very dependent on his wife. A bit woolly—'

'You'd expect an author to be woolly,' Porson said. 'Living in another world all the time. You get any leads?'

'A sister she talked to. Her father's Sir John Aubrey-Harris—'

'Oh my good gawd!'

'—but they don't seem to have been close.'

'I suppose the Archbishop of Canterbury's mother wasn't her nanny, by any chance?' Porson said sourly.

Well-connected people were a pain in the arts. They complicated any investigation. 'So what are you going to do?' Porson went on.

'Try to trace her movements yesterday. Talk to the sister, find out who her friends were. By the time we've done that, she'll probably have turned up again back home, and we can get on with some proper work.'

'If she doesn't turn up, it will be proper work,' Porson pointed out. 'There's a lot of publicity these days about how women are treated by the Met. Make a good showing, it'll play well on the BBC. Skimp on it, they'll do a number on us.'

'I know,' said Slider with a sigh. 'It's just that I can't shake the feeling that we're being made fools of.'

He didn't say by whom.

'Eden Dale don't answer their phone – it's just a recorded message,' Swilley told Slider when he came back into the CID room. 'Telling you to go on line to book a class.'

'You'd better get down there, then. They've got classes on,
so there must be somebody around. We can't do much until
we know whether she was there and who she left with.
Meanwhile, someone get on to Transport for London, get her
Oyster card record, see if she went somewhere afterwards.
Nothing from hospitals or police stations yet? Keep on with
it. And this is her mobile number – keep monitoring it. And
get the call record from the provider. Atherton, you and I are
going to see the sister.'

'Thelma, now Wilbraham,' Atherton for the general benefit.
'Married to a barrister.'

'Look her up before we go,' Slider instructed. 'And her
husband. Quick about it! I've the feeling Mr Holland is going
to be breathing down eminent necks every ten minutes until
we get some news.'

On the way to the car, Slider said, 'You can drive.' He looked
sharply down at Atherton's feet, surprised. 'Have you got odd
socks on?'

'I'm afraid so,' Atherton said. 'Getting down to the bottom
of the drawer – haven't had time to do washing.'

'But you're always so well turned out,' Slider complained.
'You must have another pair, surely?'

'I have got one more pair – but oddly enough they're exactly
the same as these.'

Slider gave him a suspicious look. 'You're too perky. What's
going on?'

'Can't a man be happy?'

'Not that happy. When you came in this morning you looked
as if you'd eaten a banana sideways.'

They got into the car. 'Well, if you must know,' said
Atherton, 'I met someone last night. Of the female
persuasion.'

'You're always meeting people. Almost exclusively of the
female persuasion.'

'This one's different. She . . .'

He stopped, but as he was trying to ease out into the traffic
on Uxbridge Road, Slider assumed he was concentrating. Only
when he didn't resume did Slider prompt: 'She?'

'She's different.' Another long silence. 'Look, there's no way to talk about this sort of thing without sounding all Barbara Cartland. Just . . . I think you'd like her.'

'That's very generous of you, but I'm already suited.'

'Go ahead, trample on a man's most delicate feelings. What do you think *has* happened to Mrs Henry Holland?'

'I don't know. I've got a funny feeling about it,' Slider mused. 'Much as I hate to encourage the baseless paranoia of a member of the public, I think something may have happened to her.'

'You don't think she's just run off and left him?'

'Without taking a toothbrush?'

'You can buy toothbrushes. If she went out with her handbag, as we must assume she did, she could have every-thing she needed in there: money, credit card, even her passport.'

'But why would she leave him without a word?'

'Ah well. That's the question. He seemed like a harmless enough chap. Money, nice house.'

'And apparently all the freedom she wanted – he didn't exactly sound as if he was handcuffing her to the radiator. You haven't read any of his books?'

'I had a glance at one on Amazon – you know, the "Look inside" the book bit.'

'And?'

'It seemed competently written. Had full stops and commas and all that sort of thing. A bit turgid – but then it's not my genre. All that reefing the tops'ls and backing the mizzen . . . But if you like that sort of thing—'

'—then that's the sort of thing you like,' Slider finished for him; and then realized that finishing each other's sentences was what old married couples did. 'We have *got* to see other people,' he muttered.

'Come again?'

'Most likely she's just got stuck somewhere with no phone signal, and she'll turn up later today with a very boring story,' Slider said. 'But we've got to go through the motions.'

'Especially as he's got friends in high places.' Atherton changed to the inside lane to avoid a clot of buses, passing the row of shops on the north side of the Bush that had survived the apocalyptic Coming of the Mall. 'I've always wondered,' he said, 'why undertakers have such big shop windows when there's so little they have to sell that looks good in a display.'

'You keep thinking, Butch,' Slider said. 'That's what you're good at.'

THREE
Bridal Path

Hampstead was an ancient settlement up on the hills to the north of the Thames, once a spa village for its chalybeate springs, a leafy rural retreat where rich Londoners had had their country houses. But London had spread like a red wine stain on a white tablecloth, covering, though not obliterating, the villages in its path. Lofty Hampstead had been subsumed into the London Borough of Camden, which had something of a mixed reputation. Hampstead was still an expensive part of London, but you drove there at your peril: quaintness, in the form of steep, narrow, twisty cobbled lanes, made parking extra impossible.

The Wilbrahams, of course, had to go and live in the centre of Hampstead where it was at its quaintest. Their house was in Windmill Hill, one of the narrowest lanes, with double-yellow lines on both sides, and no front gardens to be paved over for car standing.

'I see now why you wanted me to drive,' said Atherton. Having squeezed, reversed, edged, backtracked, gone round again, and cursed volubly, he finally wedged the wheels on the corner of someone's drive somewhere, stuck the 'On Police Business' card on the dash, and they walked back. Much of Hampstead was Georgian and older, but here was a row of Victorian semi-detached houses, three storeys plus semi-basement, built in a brick of a deep, dark red – almost fruity. Handsome iron railings, which had somehow survived the melting down of two world wars, divided the property from the narrow pavement and protected passers-by from tumbling down into the area. Though it was much smaller than the house in St Anns Villas in terms of footprint and room size, it would probably, given the nature of Hampstead, be worth about the same.

Thelma Wilbraham answered the door herself. She was tiny, with a delicate-boned face of great beauty, large blue eyes, ash-blonde hair cut in a Twenties-style bob. With her short skirt and slender legs, red lipstick and perfect pointy red nails, she could have stepped straight into a film about Flappers, right down to the extra-long string of pearls round her neck. She didn't exactly look young, but she didn't look nearly fifty. She had found her look and was working it, and she was extremely easy on the eye.

Slider began introductions, but she interrupted. 'Oh, you're the policemen! Come on in.' She gestured them in and went before them into the front room. Apart from the very high ceiling, it was much smaller than her sister's drawing room, though still, for London, a handsome size. Instead of beautiful antiques, it was furnished for comfort: large, expensive, but worn-in pieces of varying ages; pictures on the walls crammed frame to frame in the manner employed by those who just love pictures; the jetsam of everyday life scattered about; and a trace of dust on the shiny surfaces.

She waved them to seats and perched on the arm of a sofa, flinging one leg over the other. All her movements were rapid and birdlike. She was smiling, as though enjoying the unexpected company. There was no wariness or hostility: she looked at them as if she expected to like them. It was quite refreshing.

'You said you wanted to talk to me about my sister. What's going on?' she said. 'Why all the mystery? Don't tell me she's committed some major crime!'

'Her husband hasn't spoken to you about it?' Slider asked.

'Henry? No. I haven't spoken to him in an age. Probably not since Christmas.' Her quick eyes were scanning their faces. 'Now you're scaring me. Tell me what's going on, right now,' she demanded.

'She didn't come home last night, and he's worried about her.'

She received the news blankly. 'She didn't come *home*?'

'I'm surprised Mr Holland didn't ring you to ask if you'd heard from her.'

'Oh, Henry is such a lemon, he'd never think of it. He lives in a world of his own, you know. Him and his silly boats –

only you must never call them boats. Oh, and never call it Nelson's navy,' she advised, 'or he'll tell you what he thought of Nelson. At length. I called Nelson a hero once. What happened wasn't pretty.' She caught herself up. 'But *you're* here. Don't tell me he rang the police! That's not at all his style.'

'In fact, he rang the Met commissioner—'

'Oh Lord! Isn't that just typical? Talk about a sledgehammer to crack a nut! He's terribly proud that David's a fan of his books. Probably glad of an excuse to bother him.'

'You don't seem to be worried about your sister,' Atherton said.

She opened her eyes wide at him. 'But you haven't told me anything yet to be worried about! She didn't come home? What does that mean? You mean she literally went out somewhere and didn't come back? But surely she rang Henry if she was in difficulties – missed the last train or something?'

She was still looking at Atherton, so he answered. 'He didn't hear from her all day, from the time she left the house in the morning to go to her pottery class. Did you speak to her at all yesterday?'

'No, as it happened, I didn't. But there's nothing strange about that. We talk on the phone several times a week, but it's not a regular thing – I mean, it's not ten o'clock every morning without fail or anything like that. She calls when she calls, and the same for me.'

'When did you last speak to her?' Atherton asked.

'Um – Monday, I think. Yes, it was Monday afternoon. I remember because I was having my nails done and I had to keep swapping the phone over from one hand to the other.' She glanced at the glossy scarlet ovals as if for confirmation.

'And what did you talk about?'

'Oh golly!' She laughed, and looked at Slider as if to draw him into the absurdity. 'As if I can remember! Just the usual stuff, you know. Girl talk. Though, to be fair, I expect I did most of the talking. I usually do.' She laughed again. 'She's more of a listener. Not that she *doesn't* talk – she's a great conversationalist – but she's not one of those people who have to impress their opinions on you, you know? If other people want to do the talking, she'll sit back and coast. Now, *me* – I never stop unless I'm asleep. And Wills says I even talk in my sleep.'

'Wills?' Slider queried.

'My husband. His name's actually Joshua, but everyone close to him calls him Wills. From Wilbraham, you know. One of those school nicknames that stuck. His family are terrible ones for nicknames. All his brothers have them. And he calls me Tink – after Tinkerbell. He even tried giving one to Henry once – called him Horry, after Horatio Hornblower.' She laughed again, which could have been annoying, but she was so pretty and vivacious and had such a sweet voice, getting annoyed would have been like kicking a kitten. 'But it didn't stick. Henry was a bit offended, to tell the truth. To be fair, I suppose it must get a bit wearisome, having the Hornblower thing brought up every time you have to tell people what you do. "I write naval adventure stories set in the Napoleonic wars." "Oh, you mean like Hornblower?" Grrr!'

Slider took up the thread. 'When you spoke to her on Monday, did she seem in her normal spirits?'

'Oh yes, of course. She's a very equable sort of person – not given to moods or tempers or anything like that. Always lovely, calm and loving and always interested in what one says. I'm the mercurial one, you know. But I can always go to her and tell her anything and she'll say something that will put me back on track.'

Slider caught Atherton's glance. If this were true, wasn't it more likely something had happened to her? A lovely, calm and interested person would surely not leave everyone hanging by disappearing without leaving a note. 'Can you think of anywhere she might have gone? Anyone she might have visited? Any reason she might not want anyone to know where she was?'

She seemed puzzled. 'No. I don't know. What do you mean?'

Slider let Atherton ask. 'Is it possible she was having an affair? I'm sorry to ask, but in our experience that's often what's at the bottom of a sudden disappearance.'

'She's disappeared?' It was less a question than a final

realization. She looked from him to Slider and back. 'You really think she's – missing? I thought it was just Henry being a fusspot, you know. But you – you think something's *happened* to her?'

'At the moment, we really don't know,' Slider said patiently. 'That's why we're trying to gather all the information we can from those closest to her. *Is* it possible she was having an affair?'

'No! Of course not. I'm sure not.' Despite her words, her tone was uneasy.

'Would she tell you if she was?' Atherton asked gently.

'Who else would she tell?' she countered, the blue eyes wide, but anxious. 'We tell each other everything.' They waited while she thought, and then she said, 'I tell *her* everything. She – well, as I said, she's a listener. She talks about ordinary things – what she's been doing, funny people she's met and so on. Nothing serious or earth-shattering. But she doesn't *have* anything serious or earth-shattering to tell me – that's what I've always thought. She has a lovely life. She has everything she wants. She's happy.'

The last word hung on the air as the missing woman's sister contemplated her missingness and how that fitted with complete contentment.

'She didn't come home. She must have had an accident?' She made it a question, and when they didn't respond, she thought about it. 'But surely someone would know, if . . .' More implications flitted across her face. 'You think someone's done her harm?' she said at last, pleadingly.

'We don't know anything at the moment,' Slider said soothingly. 'Most missing people turn up all right after a day or two. You say she was happy. In her marriage?'

She pulled herself together. 'Oh yes. Henry's a bit of a stick, he wouldn't suit me, but he was what she wanted, and they've been together now for – what? – over twenty years, anyway, with never a cross word as far as I know.'

'A stick in what way?'

'Dull, not much sense of humour, but he's very reliable, and absolutely devoted to her. I think that's what she wanted most of all – stability. And he certainly gives her that. She's always known exactly where he'll be at any moment. And pretty much exactly what he'll say in any situation. There's a lot to be said for that.'

'Yes, I can imagine,' said Slider. 'She didn't marry until quite late, I believe? Twenty-nine? But I expect she was very popular with the opposite sex when she was young.'

'Goodness, yes! She dazzled. I lived with her for a while, when I was at college. She was already working – I'm four years younger than her. We shared a flat in London, and there was always someone, always some gorgeous chap hanging around, absolutely gagging for her.' She smiled at the memory. 'Moths to the flame. I was terribly jealous.'

'It sounds as if she liked variety,' said Slider.

She missed the import of the question. 'Oh yes. None of them ever lasted long. They were mad about her but she never gave a fig for any of them.'

'So isn't it possible that she's been missing that variety?'

'Oh, but she wouldn't endanger her marriage for a mere fling.'

'She might have fallen in love?'

She shook her head with certainty. 'There was only one man she ever cared a jot about. That was the tragedy, really.' She looked at them thoughtfully. 'I suppose I'd better tell you the whole story, or you won't understand.'

'That would be nice,' said Slider.

When Felicity was eighteen she enrolled at Belsize University to do a BA in dance, and went to live in a flat in Bayswater. 'In Orme Square – lovely! Grandma bought it for Daddy when *he* went to uni, and he kept it on for anyone to use.' And when Thelma in her turn went to university – to study art at the Slade – she went to live with her sister. By then, Felicity had graduated.

'She was never going to be a performer. It's terribly competitive, and she just wasn't good enough. And, really, that was never the point. Like with me and studying art, it was something to do until we got married. Daddy never expected us to have a serious career. She was looking at going into teaching, but there was no hurry. She'd come into Grandma's money by then, so she could take her time and look round. Our grandmother left us each a sum in trust, to provide us with an income once we turned twenty-one. It's not a fortune, but it's enough to live on if you're not too extravagant. You see, Grandma didn't want us ever to feel pressured into marrying for financial reasons, that's why she left us the dosh. She was a bit of an early feminist, Grandma. So Fliss was doing odd bits and bobs here and there, voluntary work, looking around for a niche, but mostly she was having fun.'

'Going out with men,' Atherton suggested.

'Why not? I had a great time too, tagging along, catching the crumbs. And golly, what crumbs! She always had the best men hanging around her. And of course, I thought it was only a matter of time before she'd take her pick of them and turn up with a gigantic diamond on her finger. But after I bit I started to realize that she was *only* having fun, that none of it meant anything to her. She liked the chaps and they adored her, but it never went any further than that.

'Then one day I came home early when she wasn't expecting me. I'd gone to the theatre with a friend and the play was so dire we left at the interval. My friend had a bit of a cold starting and didn't want to go on anywhere, so we split and I went home, and there she was, Fliss, with a man. And then it all came out. Turns out she'd been seeing him all along, only in secret. The others were just a smoke-screen.'

He was a jazz musician, Josh Milo. She'd been seeing him for a long time. 'I don't know how long – looking back it's as if he was always there in the background. After that, of course he wasn't a secret any more, not to me, and I met him a few times. I couldn't help liking him. Everybody liked him. He was talented and funny and *gorgeous* looking. He was one of those people who are so full of life, they just light up the room.'

He was ten years older than Felicity, with the sophistication and self-confidence the extra years had endowed: catnip to a young woman. He was warm and charming. He was bad news.

He was married.

'It was a disaster,' Thelma said, her face solemn for once. 'She was insanely in love with him, but he was never going to leave his wife. She knew what she was doing was bad, in general and for her particularly, but she couldn't help herself. Once I knew about him, she talked to me all the time about the situation. She kept trying to break off with him, but she always went back. She went out with the other chaps in the hope that one day one of them would break the spell, but it never happened. She just wasn't interested in anyone else – and of course the chaps knew it, deep down. You do, don't you?'

Slider avoided the question. 'Why wouldn't he marry her? There's such a thing as divorce.'

She shook her head. 'You'd have to ask him that. I'm sure he loved her – seeing them together, you wouldn't doubt it – but he never so much as hinted he might. If you ask me, his wife was a sort of protection, if you like, against all the women making demands on him. Because Fliss wasn't the only one. You know what it's like for these people, performers: the late nights, the drinking, the buzz, the girls always hanging around. Too much temptation, too easy to get away with it. He broke her heart again and again. But even if she told him she'd never see him again, he'd come back, all apologetic, and charm her and make her laugh, and she'd just – fall all over again.' She shuddered. 'She was an object lesson to me, poor darling. The nights I sat up with her crying like a bucket.'

'How long did this go on for?'

'Oh, years and years. I got married soon after I graduated. I'd had Wills lined up for a while – he was in Daddy's chambers, you see, so I'd known him for yonks, and I always sort of thought he'd be the one, so I was just waiting until the time seemed right. But though obviously I left Fliss alone when I got married, we still talked nearly every day, and she came round a lot, especially when I was pregnant and stuck on the sofa and needed company, so I still got to hear about Josh and the state of her heart.'

'You have children?'

'Two boys. Both out in the world now. Jonathon's just done his bar course and he's about to start his pupillage. Rupert's just qualified as an engineer. They both love their auntie. They'll be devastated if anything's happened to her.'

Atherton reverted to the story. 'Did your sister continue to see Josh Milo after she married?'

'Oh, no.' Thelma seemed genuinely shocked. 'You see, she'd finally, finally broken off with him, a few months before she met Henry. It was terrible for her, like an addict going cold turkey, but she really meant it that time. She said to me she had to be done with him before she hit thirty, or her life would be over. She was really determined. If he rang her – and he did! – over and over! – she wouldn't speak to him, just cut him off. If he came to the flat, she wouldn't let him in. She tore up his letters. I told her to come and stay with me, where he couldn't get at her, but she said she had to do it alone, so that she knew she could. But I had her over as often as I could persuade her to come, and oh boy, I saw how she suffered! But she came out of it at last, and she was back on an even keel when she met Henry. He fell for her like a brick, but I never thought she'd go for him. But she told me that after all the years of chaos, what she really wanted was stability. She said, "I know if I marry him, he'll never be unfaithful to me. I'll always be able to trust him, and depend on him. And that's what I want most in life." Well, I saw her point, though it wouldn't have been for me. Wills and I fight like cat and dog, but we adore each other, and it's real life, red and pulsing. Living with old Henry must be like living in a mausoleum. But she was really just worn out with the whole business, she wanted a bit of peace. And it's worked out all right. You can see she's contented. And I'm sure she's fond of Henry – who, after all, is a jolly decent chap, and not too dusty in the looks department either. So all's well that ends well. And she's never been unfaithful to him. We've talked about it, and she says all that's behind her, she's got a safe haven and she's never coming out. So you see she'd never jeopardize what she has with Henry for the sake of a quick thrill. Which in fact wouldn't be much of a thrill anyway. She was completely over all that.'

'All what?' Atherton asked.

'Sex,' she said, without a hint of a blush. 'You can have enough of it.'

Slider didn't need to see Atherton's face to know he was thinking *um, no you can't*. He reverted to the standard questions. 'Can you think of anyone she might have gone to visit? Any place she might go – say, if she was unhappy and wanted to be alone for a while?'

'No,' Thelma said with genuine puzzlement. 'If she was unhappy she'd have told me. And she could always come here – she knows that.'

'What about your father? Would she have gone to him?'

'Well, you can ask him, but I can't think of anything more unlikely. She and Daddy never got on – not as long as I can remember.'

'Why? Did he disapprove of her relationship with Josh?'

'Oh, golly, he never knew about that,' she said, shocked. 'Of course not. But I think he expected her to get married to someone suitable, and he didn't approve of her staying single so long. And then when she did marry it was to an outsider. Someone not in the law,' she elucidated to his questioning look. She smiled. 'He was a bit miffed, actually, that Rupert went in for engineering, even though Jonathon's following in the footsteps. He's a bit dynastic, is Daddy. More so, since Mummy died. She was a solicitor's daughter, you know. And Grandpa was Attorney General, so it's in the blood. Henry just doesn't fit in to Daddy's template.'

'I see,' said Slider. 'Well, thank you, you've been very helpful. If anything occurs to you, about somewhere we could look for her, you will contact me?' He handed her a card.

'Yes, of course,' she said. She looked up. 'Where are you looking?'

'We're trying to retrace her steps of yesterday. And we've put out her description. It's not made easier by not knowing what she was wearing. Mr Holland doesn't seem to know much about her clothes.'

'Husbands don't,' she said, her eyes crinkling with amusement. 'I bet you couldn't say what your wife is wearing this minute?'

Slider couldn't, of course – though in fairness he'd left before Joanna was dressed for the day. He covered himself by showing her the photograph Holland had given him. 'Can you just tell me if this is a good likeness? That is, whether she's changed her hairstyle or hair colour or anything since it was taken.'

She looked at the photograph and said, 'Oh!' in a sort of pained voice, as if just re-remembering what all this was about. She touched the image of her sister's face with a fingertip and said under her breath, 'Where *are* you?' Then she looked up and said, 'No, she hasn't changed anything. This is a good likeness.' There were tears in her eyes. 'Please find her,' she said.

Walking back to the car, Atherton said, 'I think our work here is done.'

'It is?'

'S'obvious. The jazz musician, her One True Love – please note the capitals – came back into her life. Maybe the wife died and he was finally free to gallop up on a white horse and take her away.'

'It's possible.'

'And as it was an act of impulse and of unpremeditated madness, it did not qualify for the leaving behind of the traditional note.'

'Well,' Slider said at last, and reluctantly, 'it's a theory. I still think if she wanted to run, she'd have packed a bag.'

'No, but consider – Henry's at home all the time. A woman running away likes to do it while he's out, to avoid the fuss – packs the suitcase and leaves a note for him to find when he gets home. Imagine if she'd gone to him and said, sorry darling, I'm off with your sexual rival, thanks for the twenty-four years, and by the way, can I have the car? Oh, the shock, oh the pain – oh the arguments! What if he went through the suitcase and confiscated things she wanted to take? What if he tried physically to restrain her? No, no – the does run when the buck's eyes are elsewhere.'

'You could be right. It would certainly simplify things if that was it. We'll have to look into this Milo geezer. But if he was ten years older than her, that would make him sixty-three-ish now. A bit old to be the dynamic seducer.'

'If music be the food of love . . .'

'Be it?'

'Well, look at Mick Jagger, seventy-three when he fathered a child. Old rockers never die, they simply smell that way.'

'Thank you for that thought. Oh blimey, we've got a ticket.'

'Another traffic warden who can't read,' said Atherton in disgust.

Slider pulled it off and opened the door. 'It's the paperwork I mind,' he said, getting in. 'We used to just ignore them, now they all have to be documented and appealed. In triplicate. We might look up the Wilbraham chap while we're at it,' he said as Atherton slid into the driving seat.

'What do you suspect him of?'

'Nothing, necessarily. But if there *was* any kind of funny business – it's all a bit cosy, him being in the father's chambers. I wonder if he'd have been successful without the contact? And how grateful he might be?'

'You know what they say, the difference between a good lawyer and a successful lawyer? One knows the law, the other knows the judge. I liked the house, though, better than the St Anns Villas one.'

'It felt more lived in,' Slider allowed.

'St Anns Villas was like a museum. Or one of those antique shops where you have to ring the bell to be let in. Whereas this house was a home. Not too big. Not too small. Just right.'

'And formerly owned by a blonde lady and some bears,' said Slider. 'Home, James.'

FOUR

We Shall Not All Sleep,
But We Shall All Be Changed

Swilley assumed the Eden Dale Community Centre was named after an area, like Notting Dale or Maida Vale, but it turned out to be a person. Eden Dale was a bit of a local hero, a lad from the council estate who had made good, made a fortune in IT, and come back to endow the centre to help other youngsters do the same. It was housed in a small ex-factory, very 1930s, two storeys in red brick with Crittall windows. Pausing to read the placard in the entrance hall, she learned it had once housed a family-run business called Haylings that made grommets. It didn't explain what grommets were. Evidently the followers of Eden Dale understood.

Inside the entrance hall it was very Thirties as well, dark green glazed tiles to halfway up the walls and cream paint above, with scuffed green lino on the floor and stairs, and stair railings of black cast iron. There was a reception window in the hall but it was closed and the cubby behind it was empty of life. She heard a voice echoing somewhere and pushed through double doors into a hall and the daunting sight of a dozen women on mats doing downward dog. On Swilley's hasty enquiry, the instructor directed her down a corridor to a room at the other end of the building.

'It's Linda Coelho you want. She should be there now.'

The room was a long rectangle, smelling flatly of clay and sharply of acrylic paint and varnish. A number of people were working at large tables on lumps of clay. There was a potter's wheel in one corner, and two large galvanized bins, which Swilley presumed held the grog. At the far end the kiln squatted, flanked by racks containing fired and unfired items.

Linda Coelho was a short, round woman in a smock. She

was in her fifties, with startlingly black hair tied up messily on top of her head, and a soft, gently creased face like a balloon that had lost most of its air.

'Oh yes,' she said, perching on the edge of what was evidently the admin desk. Her brown eyes were steady and honest and just a little bit curious. 'Felicity was here. This is her second year – she's quite keen. Doesn't miss a week. Lovely person – gets on with everyone. Why are you asking about her? She hasn't done something wrong, has she? Surely not!'

Swilley avoided the question. 'Did she seem in her normal spirits?'

Coelho frowned. 'Well, I couldn't say, really. I wouldn't call it spirits exactly. She's one of the quiet ones. But as far as I can tell, she was the same as usual. She was on the wheel a lot of the time so there's not so much opportunity for chatting to the others. But she seemed all right. She smiled and said goodbye at the end of class just like usual. Why? What's happened?'

'I believe she usually goes out to lunch afterwards with some of the class members?'

'I couldn't tell you that. I don't know what they do when they leave here. I just go upstairs to the office and have my sandwich. I only get half an hour before my afternoon class starts, so I don't hang around. Is she all right?' The brown eyes were insistent now.

Swilley yielded. 'She didn't come home, and her husband's worried.'

'Oh my God!' Coelho put her hand over her mouth and her eyes above it were wide. 'That's awful. You don't think she's—'

'We don't think anything. We're just asking questions,' Swilley said discouragingly. 'Does she have a particular friend in the class? Someone she's closer to, that she might have confided in?'

'Well, she's friendly to everyone, but . . . I suppose . . . maybe . . .' Coelho said, thinking. 'I've seen her laughing and joking with Mia sometimes, Mia Barton. I've seen them walk out at the end of class with their heads together. You might try her.'

She had an ancient wooden clipboard on the desk with an

attendance sheet on top, and underneath a typed list of names and addresses, the paper worn soft and rubbed at the edges.

'Can I get a copy of this?' Swilley asked. 'I might need to ask some of the others if they know anything.'

'Yes, of course. If you wait here, I'll run upstairs. There's a photocopier in the office.'

A telephone call established that Mia Barton was working in a charity shop on the main road in Notting Hill Gate. 'I do ten till two,' she said, 'but Sylvia's here, so I could pop out and talk to you for ten minutes.'

She was a woman in her fifties, stockily built, with broad Slavic cheekbones and frank, pale blue eyes, greying blonde hair in a bun, and a faint accent, the last trace of something ineradicable, though her English was perfectly idiomatic. 'So what's happened to her?' she asked bluntly as soon as Swilley had introduced herself.

'She's gone missing,' Swilley said, equally bluntly.

Mia Barton frowned. 'No,' she said. 'I don't believe it. Not Fliss. She's so – stable.'

'She didn't come home yesterday, and her husband hasn't heard anything from her since she left in the morning.'

'What do you think's happened to her? An accident? But wouldn't you hear from the hospital if it was that?'

This was an intelligent woman, Swilley thought. 'D'you want to get a cup of coffee while we talk?'

There was a modern café a few steps along the road, the sort with big windows and bright lights and a goldfish-bowl feeling when you were inside. They got a table in a corner and two lattes; seeing that Mia was bursting with questions, Swilley got hers in first.

'How well do you know her?'

'We've been doing the class together for a year and a bit. We joined on the same day, and sort of took a fancy to each other. She used to be a ballet teacher, and I was mad about ballet when I was young, and that got us chatting. I wanted to *be* a dancer, but—' She spread her hands deprecatingly. 'God wasn't listening. He made me short and fat with stubby fingers, so that was that. But Fliss said I should never give up, and that

even Shetland ponies like me could still dance. She said there
were lots of ballet classes for adults – for returners and even
for complete beginners – and you just went along and did as
much as you were able. Well, I said I couldn't see myself in
a leotard, everyone would laugh at me, but she gave me a stiff
talking to and told me to buck up, and said she'd come with
me. So, long story short, we both joined this ballet-for-oldies
class, and it was a lot of fun – though of course she could do
stuff that would make your eyes pop. She was so flexible you
could have folded her up like a tea towel and put her in a
drawer. But there were a few others like me who couldn't even
touch their toes, and I wasn't the only one with a jelly roll
round the middle. So I didn't feel a complete mug. And I was
surprised how much I could do. But I only did one year – I
couldn't afford two classes, and I liked pottery more. And my
old man said there was a point to the pottery class because
maybe I could get good enough to make things to sell, whereas
I was never going to get paid to dance. So I dropped the ballet
– though I think Fliss maybe kept on with it, I don't know.
But we saw each other at pottery every Tuesday.'

'And you used to go out to lunch together after the pottery
class? A bunch of you?'

'At first it was a bunch of us, but after a few weeks it was
just the two of us. You know how it is with these things – you
sort out the people you want to be friends with. We went to
Romano's – d'you know it? Just round the corner in Portobello
Road. It's a family-run bistro – old-fashioned Italian food.
They make a pizza to die for.' She patted her hips, smiling.
'Don't get these free with washing powder! But we haven't
lunched at all this term. The first Tuesday I said, are we going
to Romano's or d'you want to try something else, and she
said, sorry I can't today – I've got to see someone. And the
next week she said she'd got a lunch date. So I left it to her
to say she wanted to start again, and she hasn't. Every week
she goes dashing off. Gives me an apologetic sort of look, but
that's that.'

Interesting, thought Swilley. 'So, how did she seem when
she said she had to see someone? Was it like a boring duty,
or a bit worrying, or a pleasure?'

'Oh, a pleasure, I think,' said Mia. She thought. 'Maybe the first week she was a bit anxious, but in a nice way – you know, like going on a first date? You're not sure if you're going to like the bloke, but you hope you will.' Her eyes widened suddenly. 'Oh my God, you don't think—?'

'Think what?'

'You don't think she was having an affair?'

'Do *you* think she was? Is that what it seemed like?'

'It never crossed my mind for a moment, she doesn't seem the type, but now you ask me . . . She was sort of . . . pleased about it. I mean, she always looked cheerful when she left.'

'She never told you who she was going to meet? She never said a name? Where they were meeting? Anything about the person at all?'

'No, nothing. She just said she was meeting someone. Not even if it was male or female. But she looked – happy. And a bit fluttery, the first time. After that it was just – as if she was meeting a friend.' She digested a moment, then said, 'You think she had a lover and ran off with him? You think that's why she didn't come home?'

'I don't think anything. I just ask the questions,' Swilley said.

'But surely, in that case, she'd have told her husband. Or left him a note. Unless—'

'Yes?'

'Unless she was scared of him.'

'Do you think she was scared of him?'

'She never said she was.'

'Did she talk to you about her husband?'

'Oh yes. She said he was a writer. I've never read any of his books, but my Darren says he's quite well known. All about old-time sea battles – not my cup of tea.'

'Did she say anything about him as a person?'

'Um – that he was very serious about his work, mustn't be disturbed when he was writing, that sort of thing. That he was very clever – knew a heap about these old ships. She said once they were at a party and there was a man there from Greenwich Museum – which is all about that sort of thing, old ships and stuff – and this man was an expert, like a professor or something, and he had a long chat with her Henry and he said he was impressed with how much he knew. She was quite proud of that.'

'She never hinted that she was afraid of him?'

'No, not at all. She seemed happily married. I mean, she didn't rave about him, but you don't when you've been married a long time, do you? She just talked about him in an ordinary way, like I talk about Darren.'

'So no hint that she was unhappy in the marriage and might be looking elsewhere?'

'No. Well—'

'Yes?'

'She did once say she couldn't have children and she was sad about that. She said she wished she could have had a big family, but it wasn't to be. She said it was hard for her Henry at first. But you have to make the best of things, and find other things to fill your life.'

'Like ballet classes and pottery classes?'

'I s'pose so. She was always busy. She did charity work as well as these classes. And I s'pose the books were Henry's way. Kids take up a lot of your slack – you don't think about it necessarily, but they do. Have you got kids? But I suppose your job isn't exactly nine to five, is it?'

'So when you saw her yesterday, was there anything at all different about her?'

'No, not that I . . . Oh—' She remembered something. 'She had a bag with her. Like, a carrier bag. I asked her what was in it and she just said, oh, it's a present for someone. Very casual, she was, but she didn't offer to show me.'

'The carrier bag – can you remember the name on it? Marks and Sparks? Tesco? Waitrose?'

'No, it wasn't food, it was clothes. Wait, I'll get it in a minute.' The thought. 'Something and Something . . . Um . . . Haynes and Carver, that's what it was!'

'Haynes and Carver,' Swilley said. 'That's a men's outfitter.'

'Yeah,' said Mia, solemn with significance.

'She said it wasn't bulky enough to be a jacket or trousers, but it could have been a shirt or a jumper.'

'So she suddenly starts having lunch with someone after class,' LaSalle summarized, 'blows off her old pal Mia and doesn't say who she's meeting, and then takes him a nice, personal present from a posh outfitter.'

'*And* hubby still thinks she's going out with the gals from the class. That's her cover for seeing him,' said Lœssop. 'S'obvious.'

Slider and Atherton arrived back.

'It's odds-on, guv,' Jenrich greeted Slider. 'She was having an affair.'

'And we know who with,' Atherton capped it. With relish, he told them about the One Great Love of Felicity's life.

Swilley was doubtful. 'But he'd be an old geezer by now.'

'Old rockers never die,' Atherton offered his own rationale.

'Maybe he was down on his luck,' LaSalle said, 'and that's why she had to buy him a shirt.'

'An old geezer down on his luck?' Swilley said. 'That's charity work, not an affair.'

'If she really loved him, it wouldn't matter,' said Atherton.

Swilley stared at him in scornful astonishment. 'If she what now? How's that job at Hallmark going?'

He made a scornful face back. 'Ontogeny recapitulates phylogeny,' he retorted.

'Bollocks is still bollocks even when you say it in Greek,' said Swilley.

'Well, we've got a starting place to work from now, at least,' Slider intervened. 'We know she was at the class, and where it was. Most likely she went from there to Notting Hill Gate – then road, I mean – to get the tube, or a bus or a taxi. It's a short walk, but there might be a camera on the way. Once we get her Oyster card log we'll know more. According to her husband, she had a Visa credit card from her bank – Swilley, get on to them, find out if there's been any recent activity. And get her bank statement while you're at it. That might tell us something.'

'Boss, according to this Mia Barton, she was wearing trousers, beige tailored trousers, ballet flats and a pale blue cashmere sweater. And she had a short camel pea-jacket.'

'Good, that helps. Get that out,' said Slider. 'And start

looking for this Josh Milo character. Start with criminal records
– he might have got done for cannabis or cocaine at some
point, and it would give us a shortcut.'

'Just because he was a jazz musician?' said Atherton. 'Pretty
cynical.'

'Etymology recapitulates musicology,' Slider said. 'As I
don't need to tell *you*.'

Of the messages that had accumulated on his desk, like flyers
for Indian takeaways on the doormat of the returning holiday-
maker, Slider picked out and responded to the one from Pauline
Smithers. She and Slider were old friends, though she had
shot up the ladder, leaving him behind. She was now a detective
chief superintendent in SD1 – Homicide – but in its slightly
less stressful Missing Persons and Abductions unit. After many
years in child protection, she had earned a change of tempo.

'Hello, stranger,' she said. 'I haven't heard from you since
my wedding.' She was now married to Bernard Eason of SD6,
the Cheque and Plastic Crime unit, but kept her maiden name
professionally.

'I thought your husband would appreciate my leaving you
alone,' Slider said.

'A man likes to know he's won a woman other men wanted
but couldn't have.'

'Then tell him I said Yowzer.'

'Thanks for that. How's your cute new baby?'

'Getting cuter. George is mad about her, tends to lug her
around by the armpits if not discouraged, but at least it saves
the cat. She never seems to mind, though – just chuckles, even
when she gets bumped.'

'Ah, a manipulator already.'

'That case you told me about at the wedding – the missing
teenager. You were worried about her. How did it come out?'

'Oh, she went back home of her own accord in the end.
Climbed in through her bedroom window. The parents heard
a thump upstairs and went to look. They found her in her
underwear—'

'But surely that's the first place they looked?'

'Her bedroom?'

'Her underwear.'

'I'll forgive you that one. But why didn't you come straight to me with Felicity Holland?'

'How do you know about her?'

'Had my ear bent by the DAC. Was I helping? Had I offered my facilities to you? Bit difficult when you hadn't asked for them.'

'I was told to handle it myself. But I *was* about to ring you.'

'Don't worry, I told him I was all in with it.'

'You lied?' he said in a shocked voice.

'It doesn't count as lying when it's people that much senior to you. Who *is* this Holland person, anyway?'

'Wife of a school pal of the commissioner.' He outlined the situation so far. 'So we've got nothing to go on, and no leads except for this jazz musician type.'

'It sounds to me as if she's done a bunk,' said Pauline tersely.

'Without a suitcase?'

'Well, (a) you don't know that she hasn't got one. And (b) she can always buy whatever she wants.'

'That's what Atherton said.'

'Atherton's a smart boy. No, if something suddenly snapped, she wouldn't stop to fold her undies and fill a sponge bag. If it was a planned abscondsion, yes – but then there'd have been a note. It sounds as if she'd suddenly had enough and bolted – which means she'll probably come back of her own accord. Married twenty-four years, you said, dull predictable husband, gave up her job three years ago? Boredom Central. She'll hole up somewhere like a cheap hotel in Paddington, then she'll start missing her comforts and her own shower and go home.'

'Shower?'

'Very important to a woman. Cheap hotel showers are just tepid dribbles with plastic curtains that stick to your wet body.'

'Stop it, you're exciting me! Well, I hope you're right. But meanwhile, I still have to look for her.'

'I know. Clear misuse of police facilities, but . . .' There was a shrug instead of the end of the sentence.

'But it won't be, if she really has been snatched. You don't think that's possible?'

'It's always possible, if unlikely. I'll put her into the system if you send me over everything you've got.'

'It isn't much, but it's yours.'

'OK. And you'll keep me up to date on any developments?'

'It'll be a pleasure,' Slider said, and meant it.

'Yeah, right. And if we pull this off, we'll run away together, you and I. Or maybe have a drink one evening.'

'Whichever comes first,' said Slider.

Slider rang Joanna. 'All serene?'

'What's happened?' she said.

'I only said two words,' he complained.

'I know that tone of voice. Someone is excreting on you from an eminence.'

'If only all marriages were like ours . . .'

'. . . you'd be out of a job.'

He told her about the missing person.

'Well, I suppose you have to take it seriously anyway, when it's a woman. There was that woman recently who was snatched in broad daylight—'

'Oddly enough, that was what the husband said. He's convinced she's been taken. But at the moment it's looking as though she's done a bunk with another man.'

'Oh. Well, let's hope that's it,' she said. 'Though why *you* have to be looking for her . . .'

'Because nobody likes me,' he said plaintively.

'The people who matter like you. Are you going to be late tonight?'

'I don't think so, unless something unexpected comes up. Everything OK there?'

'Except that Teddy wouldn't go down for her nap.'

'You should have called me. It's a criminal offence to resist a rest.'

'Ho ho. I had hoped to do a bit of practice, but she remained stubbornly wide awake.'

'Practice for what?'

'The concert on Saturday. *William Tell Overture*. What Beecham used to call the William T. Hell. All those sixteenth notes. And a shocking turn at letter L.'

'Do a bit tonight.'

'I might – if you don't mind.'

'Work away,' he invited. 'Oh, by the way, does the name Josh Milo mean anything to you?' Joanna was an orchestral violinist, but Slider reckoned music was music in the professional world.

'Hmm. Sounds vaguely familiar,' she said. 'Clue?'

'Jazz musician. Would be in his sixties now.'

'Oh. Can't say I know him. But I tell you who might – Bob Preston – you know, who was principal trumpet in my old orchestra. He's an absolute jazz fanatic. Whenever we were on tour, he'd find the local jazz club, tip up and just sit in with whoever was playing. What instrument did this Milo play?'

'Dunno.'

'Helpful. OK, I'll try and get hold of Bob and ask him. Oh, that's the door – it'll be George back from pre-school.'

'OK, I'll see you later. Give him a hug from me.'

FIVE
Degas Vu

Porson looked weary. 'Anything? I've had Mr Carpenter on again. And he's had Mr Holland bleating down his neck: what have you done, what have you found out, when are you going to bring her home, ecksetera, ecksetera?'

'It's not even been one day,' Slider protested.

'I know, laddie, but you can't say that to the husband – *or* the borough commander. So I hope you've got some progress I can pass on, or we're up a gum tree without a paddle.'

'We've established that she did go to the pottery class, and she was going to meet someone afterwards.' Slider told him what they'd got so far.

Porson brightened. 'That's something! You don't buy a shirt as a present for any old person. Sounds like an affair all right.'

'It won't be the answer Mr Holland is hoping for,' Slider said.

'Well, pickers can't be choosers. He wants her found, that's all. We're not responsible for the rest.'

'But if she left him for another man, it's odd she didn't at least leave a note, isn't it?' Slider said, unwillingly. He wanted her to have left of her own accord.

'Women *are* odd,' Porson said. 'Have you spoken to her father yet?'

'It wasn't my priority,' Slider said. 'Holland told me they weren't close.'

'Maybe not, but he's *Sir* John Aubrey-Harris and Mr Carpenter asked pacifically if we'd seen him. It won't look good if a leading barrister and legal eagle is the last to find out his daughter's missing.'

'Mr Holland could have told him if he'd wanted him to know. For all *I* know he may have by now.'

'All the more reason. If Holland's told him, he'll be wondering why we haven't been round. Next thing, he's asking the commissioner. So do it. Do it now.'

'Yes, sir. I'll send—'

Porson held up his hand in a traffic-stopping gesture. 'Go yourself.'

The Aubrey-Harris seat was just outside Denham, another place that had been a rural retreat but was now a commuter village, albeit a posh one with a gastro-pub, hanging baskets on the lampposts, and an outfitters that sold riding clothes. The house was down a lane without footpaths, where the houses stood a decent distance from each other – no point in being rich if you could still hear your neighbours. It didn't have a number, but a name – Field End House – and Slider missed it on the first pass because it had been further shielded from *hoi polloi* by a nine-foot-high beech hedge along the whole front boundary, and he didn't spot the entrance gate until he was already past it. Not fancy suburban wrought-iron, either, but a solid five-bar larch farm gate. The *dernier cri* in ex-urban posh.

Within the gate was a gravelled yard with an L-shaped house on two sides of it. It would probably be designated a cottage in Estate-Agentese, having the required wobbly red tile roof, tall chimneys and diamond-paned windows, to say nothing of an ancient wisteria clambering across the front; but it had evidently been much extended over the years – albeit politely – to make a substantial residence.

Slider parked and got out of the car. It was a typical April day, with a sharp breeze and a weepy-looking sky, bright when the clouds parted and the sun showed, darkly threatening when they closed up again. Around the edge of the gravel was a fringe of grass in which daisies gleamed like miniature fried eggs, and dwarf daffodils curtseyed daintily to the breeze. The air smelled coldly and quietly of damp ditches with just a faint spike of manure – poignant to Slider, who was a country boy born.

When the front door opened, an elderly black Lab wambled out and looked up at Slider with cloudy eyes, swinging its club of a tail, and was followed by a younger golden retriever, frisky and smiling. Slider straightened from greeting them to see an elderly woman in a lavender overall in the doorway. Before she could speak, what could only be Sir John appeared behind her and said dismissively, 'Thank you, Brigid.' She gave Slider one keen look, as though making sure she'd know him again, and went away obediently,

Sir John Aubrey-Harris was tall and still straight, with sparse silver hair brushed smoothly back, and a deeply lined, large-featured face that must once have been handsome. He was wearing beige cavalry-twill trousers with a lovat-green check Viyella shirt open at the neck and a worn-looking tweed jacket – so archetypally what a country gent would wear it was almost a parody. He had no smile of welcome for his visitor, but scanned him with keen, critical eyes, as though waiting for him to put a foot wrong – a look that would have put the bejaysus up the junior defence counsel in court.

'Slider?' was all he said.

'Detective Chief Inspector Slider,' Slider elaborated, and reached for his warrant card.

Aubrey-Harris waved it aside. 'Come in,' he barked.

Inside, the low ceilings and awkwardly placed beams gave away its seventeenth-century origins, though its other historical attributes had been smoothed into submission. Slider was led into a long, low sitting room with a vast inglenook at one end, in which a log fire was burning – probably needed, even in April, he thought, because these old houses could be damp, and with tall trees and hedges all around it wouldn't get a lot of sunshine. The furniture came somewhere in between the exquisite antiques of St Anns Villas and the comfortable quotidiana of Hampstead: old, slightly rustic items in oak and leather, suited to a cottage, with the odd finer piece here and there, well-worn but well-polished.

There was an odour of dog intermingled with wax polish. A vase of tulips on a side table had all bent over in the middle, as if they were trying to dive out. The thing that most caught Slider's attention was a painting on the wall, halfway along, with a brass-hooded light fixed over it. There were several other paintings – watercolours, they looked like – but only the one was illuminated. It showed two ballet dancers in what appeared to be a backstage corridor, seated with their big skirts lifted over the back of the chair so as not to crush them. One was just sitting, legs fallen apart in the disjointed manner of dancers, arms loose by her sides; the other was bent over, massaging her ballet-slippered foot. They both looked exhausted. He knew enough to guess it was by Degas, but could it possibly be an original? The light suggested it was. It gave a better indication than anything else could of how much a senior barrister earned.

Sir John took up a standing position before the fire with one hand in his jacket pocket, as though he were going to be photographed for *Country Life*; and, not invited to sit, Slider came to an awkward halt beside an armchair while the dogs pushed amiably past him to hog the fire.

'Well?' Sir John barked unhelpfully.

It would have been nice if he had been told how much Aubrey-Harris knew, Slider thought. It was like being on the other end of a police interview, where the felon was invited to drop himself in it.

'I don't know whether you have spoken to your son-in-law since yesterday?' he began.

'I have not,' said Sir John. His mouth opened and shut like a trap, emitting words and biting them off, while the sharp eyes never wavered from Slider's face.

I'm not on trial here, Slider thought irritably. *I don't even want to be here. Can't see it's going to help.* He decided to go with straightforward exposition. 'Your daughter Felicity Holland went out on Tuesday morning to go to a pottery class. In the evening her husband Henry Holland rang the commissioner of the Metropolitan Police to say that she had not returned and he had not heard from her, and that he was worried. We are making inquiries, and it was thought that I should call on you to see if you had any idea where she might have gone or who she might have been seeing.'

At that point he shut his own trap and waited for Sir John to volunteer something. *Two can play at that game*, he thought.

Was there just the slightest gleam of appreciation in his eyes? No, Slider decided it was the reflection of the flames.

'I see,' he said. 'I know Sir David, of course. And, in fact, I spoke to him this morning, so I was aware of the situation.'

So why didn't you say so and save me oxygen, Slider didn't say. 'Have you heard from Mrs Holland?' he asked instead.

'No. I haven't spoken to her since Christmas. We are not close – though that doesn't mean I'm not concerned for her well-being.'

'Of course,' said Slider. 'We are making all possible enquiries. Have you any idea where she might go, or anyone she might visit? Are there any relatives, for instance?'

'Some distant cousins on her mother's side, but as far as I know there has never been any contact with them. Her sister—'

'We have spoken to Mrs Wilbraham.'

'Then there's no one else. Surely her husband must know best where she might go?'

There was a definite curl of the lip on the word 'husband'.

'I gather you didn't altogether approve of her marriage,' Slider tried.

'Gather from whom?' he asked sharply.

'Her sister.'

'On the contrary, I was relieved to see her married at all. Henry Holland was not what I would have chosen for a son-in-law, but she was nearly thirty. We were simply glad to have her off our hands.'

'But I understood she was already living away from home?'

The answer seemed forced out of him by some tremendous internal tension, and it was not an answer. 'She had every opportunity to make a suitable match. We gave her every advantage of upbringing and education. But she flitted from one relationship to another, one activity to another, never settling to anything. No constancy of purpose.'

His eyes seemed to go past Slider and rest moodily on the painting of the dancers.

'You didn't approve of her wanting to be a ballet dancer?' Slider tried.

'If she'd been serious about it, if she'd devoted herself entirely to it, perhaps . . . But there was no question of her going on the stage, not after . . . not once she'd shown her true colours.' The last words were bitter, and he sank for a moment into his thoughts, then seemed to rouse himself. 'It would have taken far more self-control and discipline than she ever showed about anything. And in any case, what sort of a career would it have been? A few years, that's all – and at the end, nothing to show for it but a ruined body.'

'But you let her take a degree in ballet?'

'She thought she might want to teach. And girls have to do something to occupy them until they get married.' His gloom increased a shade. 'She was always wilful, even as a child, but you try not to crush your child's spirit. You try to guide it into useful channels. Do you have children?' He didn't wait for an answer. 'You do your best for them, you give them everything, and then they—'

Slider waited a moment for the conventional conclusion to the sentence – 'they break your heart'. But Aubrey-Harris seemed to have come to the end of the thread. There seemed to be a lot of bitterness here, Slider thought. What had she done, apart from general rebelliousness? Or was non-specific headstrength enough when your father was a top-flight public prosecutor with a ferocious intellect? Probably he was not a man to take 'no' for an answer with any grace.

He came out of his gloomy reverie and said sharply to Slider, 'What are you actually doing to find her? What enquiries have you made?'

'We are tracing her last known movements. It seems she may have gone to meet someone for lunch on Tuesday, but we don't yet know who.'

'I can't help you. I know nothing of her current friends,' he said stonily.

'What do you know about a musician called Josh Milo?' Slider threw in.

Stony got stonier. 'I don't know any musicians. If that's all you have to ask, Mrs Yeatman will show you out. I am rather busy.'

Slider would have liked to ask *doing what*? But his suicidal impulses were at a low ebb just then. Besides, Sir John had actually pressed a bell-button beside the chimney breast. Classy! Slider thought.

The elderly woman appeared in the door, and Slider

obediently trudged across the room towards her, and was shown out. She didn't speak, but she gave him what he felt was a sympathetic look as he passed her in the doorway. Probably knew Sir John was not a great one for visitors.

He paused at the car for another lungful of country air before driving back to London, so that the journey might not be a complete waste. A dark cloud bundled across the sky above him and a hatful of icy drops hit him in the face.

'I'm sorry I'm late. The M25 was wretched.'

'It's all right. You can't spoil a good shepherd's pie.'

He kissed her. 'It's always better when it's a bit crusty.'

'You may have the heart and body of a king, but you have the stomach of a peasant,' Joanna said approvingly. 'I'll put the vegetables on. You've got ten minutes to wash your hands.'

'Glass of wine with it?' he said hopefully.

'Way ahead of you,' she said.

He went upstairs to shed his suit jacket and shoes, wash his hands, and look in on the children. Teddy fast asleep in her cot, on her back, minute fists resting beside her moist, flushed face. George sleeping busily, bedclothes tangled from his energetic dreams, and Jumper the striped cat curled against the back of his knees. The cat lifted its head and gave Slider a long, speculative look, then lowered it again. *I'll let you off this time.*

And Kate was in her room with the door ajar, at the desk against the wall, studying, but with ear buds in. She looked up too, as assessingly as the cat. 'Have you eaten?' he asked. 'It's about ready.'

She removed one bud. 'I had some salad earlier.'

'Still a vegetarian, then?' he said.

'What d'you mean, still? It's not a whim, Dad. It doesn't change from day to day.' He forbore to point out that she'd been a vegetarian for two months when she was twelve, and relapsed over a Walker's pork pie. 'If you cared about the planet—' she began ominously.

He gave her a beguiling smile. 'I'm an omnivore from way back. Beyond saving.'

She snorted. 'Don't need to tell me!'

'Come down and talk to me anyway. I haven't seen you for days.' He turned away.

'Whose fault is that?' she called after him.

'The criminal fraternity's,' he called back.

Joanna was dishing up. 'Oh, by the way, I managed to have a word with Bob Preston. He remembered Josh Milo. Jazz sax and clarinet. Not bad. Played with a lot of different bands, did a lot of dep work. Hasn't heard anything of him recently – he disappeared off the circuit quite a few years ago. Doesn't know where he lives or anything.'

'Oh. Anything else?'

'Big drinker. Bit of a nutcase. Well, you know these reed players, always a bit bonkers. Pressure on the frontal lobes. And he was a devil for the ladies, apparently. The groupies couldn't get enough of him. He knocked 'em over like skittles. Not just a great looker but with a terrific line in charm. When I hinted that someone's wife might have run away with him, Bob said he wasn't surprised. Even at his age. Well,' she concluded, 'sixty is the new fifty, isn't it?'

'And fifty is the new forty,' Slider said. 'So Josh Milo could even be gunning for you.'

'I've never dated a woodwind player,' she said.

Kate came into the room at that moment. 'What's wrong with woodwind players?'

'They're a sort of bloodless compromise – neither fish nor fowl nor good red herring.'

'Eh?' said Kate.

'Neither string nor brass, just stuck in between.'

'So what was that about the fish?'

'That was just a red herring.'

'Quotation,' Slider rescued his daughter. 'Shakespeare.'

Kate lost interest. 'Oh. There's a boy I see at the tube station, he plays the clarinet. He's always got his case with him. He's nice. He's doing engineering at the college.'

'Engineering's perfectly respectable,' said Slider, sitting down at the table.

'I like that he's doing music as well,' Kate said. 'Sort of means he's a rounded person. Who's Josh Milo?'

She sat down too, and Slider told her about the case. 'But

why are you doing a missing person? You don't do those,' she commented when he'd told her the basics.

'I've got an uneasy feeling about it,' he said, rather than go into politics. 'If you ever run away from home, please be sure to leave a note. And leave your phone turned on.'

She grinned. 'I wouldn't run away from home. I'm waiting until I pass my driving test and you buy me a car. Then I can drive away from home.'

Slider went in early to get some of his other work done. Whatever Mr Carpenter said, it wasn't possible just to drop everything, or the paperwork would mount up and bury him. By the time Atherton appeared, he was ready for a break.

Atherton had done the run to Mike's coffee stall on the way in, and brought him a sausage sandwich on thick crusty white, with tomato sauce. 'Just the way you like it.'

Slider looked at him. 'What's happened?'

'What what's happened is that?'

'You didn't give a look of fastidious distaste when you described my sandwich. You didn't handle the greasy bag with your fingertips. You must be happy.' He studied him, while Atherton looked away insouciantly and pretended to whistle. 'You had another date with this wonder-woman, didn't you?'

'We met for a drink, and sat talking until closing time. Didn't even notice the time,' Atherton admitted.

'Oh my God, that's serious. You'd better sit down.'

'I feel fine. She's – look, I don't want to jinx it. I'd like you to meet her, but all the others you've met have come to nothing.'

'I don't have to meet her. I'm not your mother.'

'Come on, you know you want to. When I've had a few more dates. You'll like her. How did it go with the legal eagle? Learn anything?'

'Only that she definitely wasn't the favourite daughter.' He gave him a potted account. 'There was a lot of hostility there – definitely some history.'

Atherton shrugged. 'I don't see that it helps. If they didn't get on, he's the one person she *wouldn't* have gone to see. We have to find where she went, not where she didn't.'

Swilley came to the door. 'Don't hog the sandwiches, Jim – they're getting cold. Anything from the father, boss?'

'I was just about to say I thought it a bit odd that someone who despised ballet as Sir John seemed to should have a Degas ballet girls painting on his wall.'

'Not an original?' Atherton asked, impressed.

'Maybe. Probably.'

'Well, it would be a sound investment, if he was set on buying an Old Master. And Degas is decorative enough, surely – a nice thing to have in your living room.'

'But he could have bought any Old Master. He could have gone for a Stubbs or a Rope or a William Eddowes Turner, for instance. Horses are nice. And uncontentious.'

'Why do you think he despised ballet?' Swilley asked.

'He just seemed a bit disparaging about it, about his daughter's fancy to learn, said it was a worthless career anyway, over too soon and leaving your body ruined.'

'But she—' Swilley began.

'Studied it to degree level? He said girls had to do something to keep them busy until they married.'

Swilley rolled her eyes. 'How old *is* this guy?'

'He says she didn't contact him, and on the surface there seems no reason to suppose she did, so no shortcut there. I'm afraid it's going to be the old basic slog – unless she makes contact, or goes home of her own accord.'

'That one. I like that one,' Atherton said.

Jenrich came in. 'Where are the sandwiches?'

Atherton thrust the clutch of bags at her. '*You* hand them out.'

She took them, but stayed put. 'Morning, boss. I've got her Oyster card record.'

'That was quick,' said Slider.

'I spoke to a woman, laid it on thick about finding her before it was too late. Anyway, Tuesday morning she took the 94 bus from the Royal Crescent stop to Notting Hill Gate station. Got on the bus at ten oh nine. That's a ten-minute journey at that time of day. Five minutes' walk to the Eden Dale.'

'Just about right,' said Atherton.

'Next journey is by tube, from Notting Hill Gate. She goes in at twelve forty-nine.'

'So, given that the Eden Dale centre is only a five-minute walk away, and we're told she hurried off at twelve thirty, she did something else before catching the train,' said Atherton.

'Yeah, but it's not long enough to have gone somewhere else. She could have stopped to buy a paper or a KitKat, but that's about it.'

'Or waited outside the station for someone to join her,' Atherton put in. 'The Oyster registers when you go through the turnstile, not when you arrive at the station.'

'Where did she go?' Slider asked.

'She got off at Covent Garden, came through the gates at ten past one. I suppose she got the Central Line to Holborn and changed on to the Piccadilly – time's about right for that.'

'Covent Garden. Interesting,' Atherton said. 'Royal Opera House.' Jenrich gave him a boiled look. 'They do ballet as well, you know.'

'You're not trying to tell me she was performing at the Royal Opera House every Tuesday afternoon?' Slider said.

'They have a ballet school right next door,' Atherton said patiently. 'Maybe she was teaching there.'

'But why would she keep that a secret?' Slider said. 'Her husband and her sister both said she'd given up teaching.'

'And who teaches just one class a week? Unless you're Margot Fonteyn,' Jenrich said witheringly.

'You're saying it's just a coincidence that Covent Garden is the home of this major ballet hub?' Atherton countered.

'Why not? It's a major hub of a lot of stuff.'

'Maybe she just met someone there, as a convenient place they both knew,' said Slider. 'Like saying, "I'll meet you outside the London Transport Museum", without actually being a train-spotter.'

'All right,' Atherton conceded. 'But who was she meeting?'

'The bloke she bought the shirt for,' said Jenrich impatiently.

'To be exact,' Slider said, 'we don't know that she did. She had a carrier bag from Haynes and Carver, but that could have been from a previous purchase, just a bag she kept for future use. My wife has a drawer full of them.'

'I thought we were proceeding on the assumption she bought an expensive shirt for her lover and went to meet him to give it to him,' Atherton complained.

Slider shrugged. 'You have to start somewhere.'

SIX

Dunce Inane to Burnham Woods

In the hope of a shortcut, Slider rang Henry Holland. Did he have any idea why his wife would travel to Covent Garden?

No, Holland said irritably, he didn't. 'It's a tourist place, isn't it?'

'There are lots of shops and restaurants,' Slider conceded. 'And the Royal Opera House, of course.'

'Are you suggesting she went to a matinée?'

'I'm not suggesting anything. I'm asking if she mentioned to you at some point that she was meeting someone there, or had some activity in the area – a class or appointment or something.'

'Well, she didn't.'

'The Opera House has volunteer ushers, and you said she volunteered at the National Gallery. Would she perhaps have—'

'She didn't volunteer at the Opera House.'

'But perhaps she was thinking of it and went along to see.'

'Look here, I have no idea why she would go to Covent Garden in the middle of the day – if, in fact, she did. Why are you so sure about it?'

'We have traced the journey on her Oyster card.'

There was a brief silence. 'I didn't know you could do that.' Then, 'But anyone could have stolen her card and used it. Or she could have lost it and someone else picked it up. You don't know it was her at all. Can't you do better than this?'

'Mr Holland, since you don't know where she was going on Tuesday, we have to try and trace her movements from the last place we know she was, the pottery class. That is what we are doing.'

'Well try harder!' he snapped. 'With all the resources you

have to hand, this is pitiful! My wife is in danger. Find her. I want her back!'

'I know you're upset,' Slider said. 'We are doing everything we can.'

He let Swilley ring Thelma Wilbraham with the same question, while he rang McLaren, who was out trying to find cameras between Eden Dale and Notting Hill Gate.

'I'm at the Prince Albert, guv,' McLaren said over a distant background noise of moderate midday jollity. 'They've got a camera that covers the road outside, and if she went from Eden Dale to the main road, she'd have to've passed it.'

'You can leave that,' Slider said, one corner of his mind relieved at an excuse to get McLaren out of a pub. 'We know she took the tube from Notting Hill station.' He explained what they'd found out. 'But she did something before going down into the station – there's about ten minutes unaccounted for. She might just have been buying a paper, but it might mean something. Try along the line of shops on that section. See if you can spot her talking to someone.'

'On it, guv,' McLaren said. He had a pint of Pride and a bowl of crispy squid in front of him, while he waited for the manager to download Tuesday's tape for him. He was in no hurry.

Lœssop, whose nickname was Funky, bore a striking resemblance to Captain Jack Sparrow, and his locks and facial adornments had been allowed to remain in defiance of regs because sometimes it was useful to have a detective who looked like that. Slider had given him the task of looking up Josh Milo, on the basis that if you looked like someone who knew the music scene you might as well act like it.

'Josh Milo, guv,' he reported. 'No criminal record, so no help there. And there's virtually nothing about him on the net. He's got no Wiki page, so he wasn't that famous. No Facebook or Twitter accounts or anything like that. Too old, I suppose.'

'Sixty-three isn't old,' Slider objected.

'Well, not for a musician,' Lœssop allowed. 'But what I mean is, that generation, they don't always bother with online stuff. Anyway, the only mentions I've found so far are for jazz recordings, listing him among the players. There's a lot of those. But they're all pretty old pressings.'

'All right. Keep at it,' Slider said.

'Yes, guv. There are a lot of fan sites for jazz. I'll try those. It's the sort of place you get old-timers mentioned. They chat about each other, whatever happened to old so-and-so, you know?'

McLaren came back, bumping into Slider in the doorway. 'You smell of fried food,' Slider said suspiciously.

'I don't think you're allowed to say that, guv,' said LaSalle, looking up from his desk. 'Harassment.'

McLaren hastened to change the subject. 'I know what she was doing before getting the tube,' he said. 'She was taking money out from a cashpoint. There's a Barclays in that parade. I tried there first because they're the most likely to have a camera. Well, certain to have one. And there she was. Drew out £250. It was a busy time of day, she had to queue behind someone, so that uses up the missing time.'

'Right,' said Slider. 'Another dead end. We'd better get a team down to Covent Garden. Jenrich, you can organize it. Take everybody you can. You know the drill – ask in every shop and restaurant, show the photograph, check for cameras.'

Jenrich looked unexcited. 'It's pretty hopeless, boss. She could have gone anywhere. And thousands of people pass through there every day.'

'Nobody said it would be easy.'

'I'll start with the station, guv,' said McLaren. 'At least we'll see which way she turned when she walked out.'

'Big help,' Jenrich muttered.

'Henry Holland has already raised the phantom that she might have lost her card and somebody else used it,' Slider said, 'so we'd better make sure it actually is her coming through the gate. Lœssop, keep looking for Josh Milo,' Slider said. 'Census, electoral registers, the Musicians' Union—'

'Try Jazz South,' Atherton suggested. 'It's a jazz support organization. Even if they don't know of him, they'll tell you where else you can look.'

Swilley said, 'Boss, is there any mileage in asking at Haynes and Carver? That sort of shop prides itself on personal service. If she did buy a shirt there, she may have chatted with the assistant about who it was for.'

'All right, no harm in asking.'

'More likely Henry Holland bought a shirt there once and she was just reusing the carrier bag,' Jenrich said, heading for the door.

'Try having a nice thought now and then,' Swilley suggested to her back.

Slider rang Pauline. 'I'm stuck,' he said. 'I have to start by finding Felicity Holland—'

'You couldn't start by looking for her?'

'If I knew where to look.'

'Anything specific I can help you with?'

'I don't suppose you can use your influence to get the bank records for me?'

'Piece of cake. Ask me something difficult.'

'Really?'

'No, I'm kidding you. Don't ask me something difficult. But I will put a firework under the bank. With online banking, there's no reason you shouldn't have the records within hours. They just don't like parting with anything, certainly not money, not information. Tighter than a duck's rectum, your average bank.'

'I suppose you'd want them to be careful, when it's your own money.'

'Yeah, but we're the good guys. It gets to be a habit – Computer Says No. Give me the details.'

He dictated them. Then he asked, 'Do you know anything about Sir John Aubrey-Harris?'

'Apart from that he was a QC? What about him?'

'Anything to his detriment.'

'I've never heard anything, but I'll ask around. What are you suspecting him of?'

'I'm not really. It's just that he seemed not to have liked his daughter, and wasn't much worried about her. Or didn't seem to be.'

'You *are* desperate,' Pauline said pityingly. 'I'll ask.'

*   *   *

Ten minutes later, she rang him back. 'Blimey, that was quick,' he said.

'I haven't even rung the bank yet. Someone just rang me. Her handbag's been found.'

'Where?'

'Hold on to your hat,' Pauline said. 'Burnham Beeches.'

'Oh damn,' said Slider.

Porson didn't like it, either. 'That's a whole new kettle of fish,' he said. 'Hornet's nest.'

Burnham Beeches, a large area of natural woodland about twenty-five miles out of London, came under the jurisdiction of the Thames Valley Police, and there had been, to put it kindly, instances of friction in the past between them and the Met; as, perhaps, there might be between neighbours, about whose fence it was, and who had the responsibility to replace it when it fell down. But even if everyone was as friendly as could be, dealing with another force still meant administrative difficulties, extra phone calls and the requirement to tread daintily. It was like staying with your aunt instead of your mother: you could never quite relax.

The bag had been found on Wednesday morning by a dog walker, and since local police stations didn't open any more, he had had to drive in to Slough, the nearest town, after work that evening to hand it in. There, it was still awaiting due process in the lost property cupboard on Thursday morning when, by the purest good luck, Pauline's general enquiry filtered down from the top and reached someone who had booked in the bag and happened to remember the name.

The immediate fear, of course, from Slider's and Porson's point of view, was that large areas of woodland – Burnham Beeches was nine hundred acres or so – was where murderers traditionally (and there was no one more traditional than your average murderer) dumped the bodies of their victims. It was right there in the *Complete Idiot's Guide to Homicide*, around page 96. Finding the handbag raised by a large factor the likelihood that Felicity Holland was dead.

As Porson put it, 'If the bag's in there, she probably is.'

'I'm afraid you're right,' Slider said. You didn't easily

separate a woman from her handbag. In his experience they were pretty much welded together.

'Course I am,' said Porson. 'It's not rocket surgery. You'd better get down there, asap.' He sighed like a leaking radiator valve. 'I suppose I've got to pass on the bad news upstairs.'

Sooner you than me, Slider thought. 'There's nothing really to tell yet,' he said comfortingly.

Burnham Beeches lay between the two main routes westward out of London, the M40 and the M4. It was slightly closer to the M40, which in any case was more convenient from Shepherd's Bush, but Windsor Road police station in Slough was closer to the M4, so Slider and Atherton went that way.

The station was a modern building of more than usual awfulness – 'Don't look, guv, it'll burn out your retinas,' Atherton warned – but at least they didn't have to do any explaining when they went in. Words had obviously been had at a higher level, and they were expected. A civilian staff member – a chunky female in black slacks, striped jumper and ballet flats (she was probably going for Audrey Hepburn but it was coming off more onion seller) conducted them upstairs and into the office of Detective Chief Inspector Trevor Dalton.

He was standing, talking on the phone, when they appeared at the door; acknowledged them with a raise of the eyebrows, and continued the call for a few moments more before ending it. Power play, Slider thought resignedly. They were all at it. Etiquette dictated that he had to be received by an officer of equal rank, but nothing said the officer had to like it.

Dalton was tall and lean, but not in the flexible, feline way Atherton was, more in the manner of cloth stretched over a metal framework. He looked strong, but unbending. You could imagine him standing up and pumping barbells, but not, for instance, lying in a hammock sipping a Mai Tai – he wouldn't have the necessary curvature, of spine or spirit. He had a long face and a curiously tall head, its height emphasized by the fact that he shaved it. He'd have been a cinch for one of those episodes of Star Trek where the alien planet is controlled telepathically by super-intelligent humanoids with massive brains. He even had a rather visible vein on either side.

Phone call ended, he greeted them unsmilingly. He gave them each the sort of Exec-u-Like handshake designed to impress – ultra-firm and short, two pumps and that's-yer-lot – and got straight down to business.

'The bag was found on the grass verge a couple of hundred yards from The Stag car park on Hawthorn Lane. Dog walker, name of Colebatch. Seems a decent sort. Nothing against him.' He reached under his desk and plonked an evidence bag in front of them. 'This is it. It's all right, you can handle it – it's been dusted for prints.'

Slider took it out and opened it. It was dark brown leather – expensive by the feel and smell of it – with a shoulder-strap. Inside was a make-up bag, a small hairbrush, a packet of tissues, a pair of glasses in a case, a small manicure set, one of those miniature sewing kits they give away at hotels, and a mirror in a leather case. A perfume spray – *Souffle de Soie* by Dior – in a suede sleeve. There was a small, slim torch, several ballpoint pens and a bunch of keys jumbled up at the bottom. And one of those leather purses that had a section at the back for bank notes and credit cards.

'Is this everything?' Slider asked.

'That's what was in it when it was handed in,' said Dalton.

There was some change in the zip section of the purse, but no notes in the back section. And in the card slots were loyalty cards and membership cards for various organizations, but no credit cards. Slider looked up.

'So you see,' Dalton said, 'we had a name but no address. Our normal protocol when there's no address is to wait five days for someone to claim it before we go about trying to trace the owner. But then this morning we had a circular from SD1 Missing Persons Unit, so all that changed.'

'There's no mobile phone here,' said Slider.

'There wasn't one when the bag came into our custody.'

'I'd like to see where it was found,' Slider said, adding, 'We won't get in the way of your search teams.'

Dalton made a very slight, impatient movement. 'I'll take you there myself. But there's no search team.'

'Surely . . .' Slider checked himself. Tread softly, for you tread on my corns. 'It's better, isn't it, to start the search as soon as possible?'

'There will be no search,' said Dalton, 'not until we have more evidence that she was ever actually there. The Beeches cover three hundred and seventy-five hectares. We are not launching a major exercise over an area that size, with all the personnel and budgetary implications, purely on the finding of a handbag that could have been dumped any time, by anyone.'

'But you do know this woman is missing?' Atherton said.

'Missing can mean any number of things. She could well have absconded, and dumped the bag there to lay a false trail. There's no money, credit cards or phone in the bag – all the things she'd need to keep back for herself.'

'Also the things a murderer would take out before throwing the bag away.'

'You have evidence of a murder?' Dalton asked sharply.

'Not yet,' Atherton admitted.

Dalton didn't need to say *there you are then*. His eyes said it for him. He turned to Slider. 'I assume you're tracing her last known movements, and if she'd been heading this way you'd have said so. Even if there was foul play, and you don't know that yet, there's no reason to suppose the woman was ever in those woods.'

'Except that murderers do like to leave their victims in woods,' Slider said mildly. 'You do know that there's a lot of very high-level interest in finding her as soon as possible?'

'There always is,' said Dalton.

Slider fired the big gun. 'The commissioner himself is involved.'

And missed by a mile. Dalton merely shrugged. 'That's above my pay grade.' *Yours too*, said his look. 'If the commissioner wants to have words with the chief constable, and ask for a major search operation to be initiated, that's up to him. But I can't see that happening until you can produce something in the way of evidence that there has been foul play.'

'We are, of course, still pursuing enquiries from our end,' Slider said. 'But time is of the essence in these cases, as you know. Are you really not going to do *anything*?'

'I didn't say that.' Dalton could afford to be magnanimous now. 'We'll have a look at the traffic cameras and any CCTV in the area, see if we can spot any anomalies. And all our officers will keep their ears to the ground. Now, if you'd like to see the spot, can we get going? I'm sure you are a busy man.' Which meant *I'm a busy man, even if you're not.*

'Ready when you are,' Slider said, with a brisk but friendly smile.

It hit Trevor Dalton's carapace and slithered sadly off like egg down a wall.

Burnham Beeches made a shape roughly like a teardrop, and Hawthorn Lane formed the boundary of its curved bottom. It was a country road, tarmacked but narrow and unlit, and the grassy edge of the woods came right down to it on either side with no footpath – without even a white line. The woods were typical of mature beech woods, with a high, dense canopy and an under-canopy of yew, holly and whitebeam. *The woods are lovely, dark and deep*, Slider thought. He could never see woods without wanting to plunge in. But he had miles still to go in this case. And when it ended, if it ended, there would be another, and another . . .

The sky had clouded over again in fickle April fashion and thin rain was hitting the windscreen. Dalton drove too fast, in the manner both of the country-dweller and the man sure of his own ground. Slider was reminded of the story of the two traffic cops who took a bend too fast, went off the road and hit a tree. One turned to the other and said, 'Wow, that's the quickest we've ever got to the scene of an accident!'

Dalton didn't talk until he slowed and turned into a tarmacked area just off the road and announced, 'This is The Stag car park.' On the opposite side of the road was a very large, newly built house with an estate agent's board outside. 'Used to be a pub there, called The Stag. This was its car park. City of London owns this part of the woods, and they bought it for a public car park. The main car park's further round, on Lord Mayor's Drive.'

There was only one other car parked there.

'Doesn't get much traffic on a weekday,' Dalton went on.

Slider nodded – they hadn't passed any other cars since turning on to this lane. 'Weekends, you get walkers all year round, though not so many this time of year. Come the summer, it's busier, but never as busy as the main car park. I don't know if your bag dumper knew that, or got lucky, but of a weekday he could have come and gone without seeing anybody, particularly if it was after dark. No streetlights, of course.' He jerked his head towards the house opposite. 'Nobody living there. Finished a few months back, so the builders have gone, but it's not been sold yet.'

They got out of the car, and he led them along the lane a short distance to where blue-and-white police tape was stretched between three trees at the edge of the wood. There was a strip of rough grass, about three or four feet deep, between the road and the trees. 'Bag was there,' said Dalton, 'just in front of that middle tree. Near as Colebatch could remember. One tree being a lot like another.'

Slider hunched his shoulders against the cold rain that was trying to get down his neck, and stared hopelessly. Without an army of police, strung out in a line and doing a fingertip search, there was no chance of finding anything amongst the rough grass and the undergrowth, even if there was anything to find. Had the dog sniffed out a body, it would have been a different matter, but Dalton was not entirely wrong – though entirely snarky about it – that the bag could have been dumped without Felicity Holland's being anywhere near. On the other hand – it had to mean *something*. There must be *some* connection, surely?

Beyond the tape, the woods stretched away into their own interior: quiet, with that strangely brooding sense you always got in an ancient wood, as though the trees were watching you, waiting with primordial patience for you to leave. Was Felicity Holland in there somewhere: lying in the leaf-litter, raindrops falling from the branches on to her unseeing eyes, beetles clambering over her moveless legs rather than going the long way round, while the quietly breathing trees kept their counsel? His muscles clenched with a fierce desire to get in there and search, not just to stand here on Dalton's leash and ignore her. If she was there, how long before another dog-walker found her, and how much of her would be left by then? There was lots of wildlife in Burnham woods, foxes, badgers, stoats, weasels, carrion crows, not to mention all the patient, unsung clear-up workers who lived below, in the grass and under the soil, and did their bit for the ecology, tiny mouthful by tiny mouthful.

The rain eased, and the smell of the woods came to him, wet and green and lovely. Perhaps there were worse places to see out eternity.

Dalton interrupted his reverie. 'So, they could have parked in The Stag car park and walked along a bit.'

'Or,' Slider forced himself to say, 'they could have been deeper in the woods, come out here and dropped the bag there on emerging.'

'Possible,' Dalton allowed graciously. And then, extra-gracious, 'If you find any evidence that your missing woman came to the Beeches, I will be happy to extend my full co-operation.' Then he spoiled it by adding, 'Dependent on my superintendent's agreement, naturally.'

'Naturally,' Slider said.

'Seen enough? Shall we go?' said Dalton. He had a stout and venerable wax jacket over his suit jacket, and his shaved hair could not be spoiled by getting wet, but perhaps it was annoying to have raindrops pattering on your bald bonce.

'Thank you,' said Slider.

They were on their way back to civilization. They had read the statement of the dog-walker and talked to the constable who had taken in the bag. Colebatch seemed eminently respectable, a retired engineer, married with two grown-up daughters, had lived in the same house for twelve years, wife a retired schoolteacher. Good credit rating. No criminal record. 'I thought he seemed absolutely straight, sir,' said the constable. 'But we've got his details if you want to go and interview him.'

They had signed all the forms required to transfer the bag to their custody, and arranged for the fingerprints to be sent over. And there had been a brief royal phone call from Detective Chief Superintendent Felway, to say that Thames Valley would, of course, immediately share any further evidence that came to light – with the distinct subtext that there would not, of course, be any.

'Why Burnham Beeches?' Atherton said musingly, when they were on the motorway. 'We'll have to find out if the place had any significance for Felicity Holland, if only to rule out the inane suggestion that she chucked her bag there to lay a false trail.'

'Inane?'

'Why on earth would she want to? If she was running away with nothing but the clothes she stood up in, the last thing she'd do is part with her handbag. And what on earth would be the point? In the time it took to get out here and dump it, she could be on an express to Scotland and the Outer Isles, or the Eurostar to all points east. The man's a dunce even to suggest it.'

'I suppose he felt bad about refusing to start a search,' Slider said. 'Not that it was his personal decision.'

'But he didn't have to sound so smug about it,' Atherton complained. 'Still, if the commissioner couldn't get them off their arses, there's nothing we can do.'

'Only the arm's length searches,' said Slider. 'Check for sex offenders with any connection to the place, check, as you said, if the place meant anything to her. Most of all, trace her movements from Covent Garden station. She could be anywhere,' he concluded in frustration. 'Burnham Beeches, Bournemouth or Baghdad.' He just hoped she wasn't in Burnham Beeches and they were driving away and leaving her there.

'One thing we can be sure of,' Atherton said, 'she didn't drive out there on her own. Because the car was outside the house, and the car keys were in her bag.'

'There are such things as spare car keys,' said Slider, fairly.

'True,' said Atherton, and lapsed into silence. When they came down off the motorway at Hammersmith, he said, 'I'm starving. We didn't get any lunch. Fancy a pint and a packet of crisps?'

'I could force one down.'

They stopped at the Brook Green Hotel, where there was an old-fashioned bar and a decent pint on tap.

'So,' said Slider when they were settled at a table, 'tell me about this wonder-woman of yours.'

'Her name's Stephanie.'

'Nice,' said Slider. He'd thought of that name for his new daughter, but it didn't go with Slider. Too many sibilants. 'And?'

'She's in her thirties, good looking, intelligent. She's a doctor.'

'What sort of doctor?'

'A surgeon, actually. Ear, nose and throat. Works mostly in Charing Cross hospital. Lives in Palliser Road.'

'Handy.'

'Yes. She can just walk through Margravine to the Cross.'

'Bit of a hack to your place, though. Does she like cats?'

'She's not been to my place yet. But, yes, she does.'

'Well, that's a start.' Atherton had two slightly mad Siamese, Tiglath Pileser and Sredni Vashtar. Their habit of dropping suddenly on to unsuspecting visitors from the tops of things – pelmets, bookcases – had tested many a relationship of his. 'Are you seeing her tonight?'

'No, she's working this evening. Otherwise, I wouldn't be sitting here drinking with you, would I?'

'No, I suppose you'd be home shaving your legs. Well, a doctor's quite a step up for you—'

'I beg your pardon?' Atherton said in offended tones.

'From all the solicitors, I mean.'

'Oh.'

'And if she's a doctor, she'll understand about difficult work schedules.'

'Yes, there is that. Though two people on difficult schedules is double the trouble.'

'Well, Joanna and I make it work. On the subject of which, she's working tonight, Kate's out with friends, and my dad has the con, so if you fancied going for a ruby? We haven't done that in a while,' he concluded wistfully. There was everything to be said for marriage, except the absence of curries and male bonding.

'Sounds good,' Atherton said. 'Won't there be a wholesome meal waiting for you at home?'

'There'll be something, but I can ring Dad and tell him to turn the oven off. He won't mind.'

'OK, then. The Raj?'

'Fine. I could just fancy their Karai Chicken.'

'Finish up, then, and we'll—' Atherton's phone vibrated. 'Text,' he said, picking it up. He scrolled through the message and looked up apologetically. Slider saw his curry dislimning like a ghost at cockcrow. 'It's Stephanie,' Atherton said. 'Her list has been cancelled because of staff shortages. She's not working after all.'

'And you prefer her company to mine.'

'She has certain assets you can't compete with.'

'Go, then.'

'I can get a taxi outside and meet her at the hospital, and pick up my car later.' He looked wistful. 'Do you mind?'

'Of course not. Go do your thing. Really. It's all right.'

'But I don't want to leave you high and dry.'

'I've never been lower or wetter,' said Slider. 'Go!'

SEVEN

Asbestos You Can

'You're obscenely cheerful this morning,' Jenrich said as Atherton bounced in.

'It's the superior intellect triumphing over the petty vicissitudes of life,' he told her.

'What?'

'Mind over matter,' he translated.

'Yeah. Well, that makes sense. I don't mind, and you don't matter.'

'You wouldn't be so cheerful if you had my problems,' McLaren said, tossing a screwed-up greasy bag into the bin.

'Oh no! Not another national lard shortage?' Atherton asked kindly.

'Bathroom tiles,' McLaren grunted. 'They were coming off, grout all falling out. Natalie made me do them, 'stead of getting someone in, to save money. Now they're lifting again.'

'You should never try and tile yourself,' Jenrich ruled. 'Always get a professional in.'

'But how d'you find a good one?' McLaren complained. 'There's a load of cowboys around these days.'

'You look in their professional magazine,' Atherton said. '*What Tiler?*'

Evidently no connection was made in McLaren's brain. He wrote it down. 'Thanks,' he said.

Without looking up, Swilley said, 'I've told you before, don't tease the animals.'

Atherton smiled and carried on. 'I got an odd-job man in once, gave him a list, but he only did tasks one, three, five and seven.'

Slider came in, raising his eyebrows to Jenrich. 'Nothing so far, boss,' she said. 'We know which way she turned out of the station, and that's about it.'

'We know it *was* her,' McLaren improved. 'Got a good full face of her coming through the barrier. I took a copy of the tape, in case.'

'But beyond that it's like looking for a needle in a haystack,' Jenrich went on. 'My opinion, it needs a lot more manpower than we've got to do it this way. It'll take weeks.'

'Do the best you can. If there was another way, I wouldn't be sending you out there,' Slider said. 'Speaking of which . . .'

'Yeah, boss, we're just going.'

Slider offered her some comfort. 'I had a word downstairs when I came in. They're lending us a couple of uniforms. Pick them up on your way out.'

'Oh, that'll make all the difference,' she grumped.

Swilley appeared at his door. In beige slacks and a cashmere jumper, with her blonde hair and golden skin, she was a symphony in fawn. 'I've got the phone record, boss,' she said. 'It's a pay-as-you-go, and she really did only have it for emergencies.' She sounded amazed.

'People do,' he suggested.

She shrugged. 'I suppose it's the generation. Anyway, she hasn't made a call in three weeks, and then it was only a short one to her home landline. Probably calling hubby to say there was no haddock and would he like turbot.'

'I can tell you don't approve of the surrendered wife,' Slider said.

She favoured him with a tight smile. 'Surrender? I'd take half a dozen down with me.'

She would, too, he thought. She was the best in the firm at unarmed combat. 'So, no help there,' he sighed. 'Do you ever feel the universe is arranging things to thwart you?'

'No, boss,' she said.

'Of course not. Sorry I asked.'

'I have to ask you a question. It may seem a little odd,' said Slider.

'Ask away,' said Thelma Wilbraham. 'Anything I can do to help.'

'Does your sister have any connection with Burnham Beeches? Was it special to her in any way?'

'Oh, the Beeches!' she cried fondly. 'Dad used to take us there for a treat when we were kids, when we still lived in Kensington. You know – getting out into the country, fresh air, walk in the woods, picnic maybe. We loved it.' She sighed. 'Happy memories.'

'Didn't you have holidays in the country?'

'Not really. Dad worked such long hours we didn't go away much, apart from skiing at Easter, and Granny Erskine in Callander at Christmas. Kensington Gardens and Hyde Park were our big outdoors. So Burnham Beeches was exciting. And Dad wasn't a great one for treats anyway, so it was even more special, going out as a family. And he was always in a good temper there – at least, that's how I remember it.' She took a breath, then came the question he didn't want to hear. 'Why are you asking?'

So he told her.

'Her handbag. Oh my God. Does that mean . . . You haven't found her – her body?'

'No. Just the handbag. Nothing else.'

'But doesn't that mean she's . . .?' She couldn't say it. 'Something's happened to her?'

'I'm sorry, we just don't know. But I promise you we're doing everything we can to—'

'—to find her, I know. But if her bag's there, it means someone took her. Doesn't it?'

'Let's not jump to conclusions.' He sought for something to comfort her. 'She might have gone there on her own, and lost the bag somehow, somebody found it, took the valuables and dumped the rest.'

'Is that what *you* think?'

'I don't think anything, Mrs Wilbraham. Not until I have all the evidence.'

'Yes,' she said, in a dull voice. She didn't like the odds. 'You'll let me know—'

'The minute we hear anything. Of course.'

* * *

'Boss,' said Swilley as he passed through the outer office in search of tea, 'didn't you say Sir John Thingummy was a bit anti-ballet?'

'I didn't say that, exactly. Just that he seemed scathing about it as a career.'

'Well, here's a thing. I was just searching him generally, and I came across his name on the Chairman's Circle list of sponsors of the Royal Ballet. That's the top level – people who give serious dosh to it. So I looked into it a bit more, and I find he's also a governor of Sadler's Wells Ballet, and a Balanchine Friend of the New York City Ballet. The top level of patronage in each case. What d'you think about that?'

'I think it's something we ought to follow up,' said Slider. Along with Burnham Beeches. God knows, he thought, we've got little enough.

Porson tapped his lower lip with the biro he was holding. 'Thin,' he said. 'You've got nothing there.'

'I know. But if anyone asks, at least I'm doing *some*thing. Mr Carpenter told me to drop everything else.'

'Hmm. Well, you can't go asking a QC if he misled you. Let alone did he bump off his own daughter.'

'It's been known to happen,' Slider said bitterly, remembering his last case. As a father of four he'd had difficulty in coming to terms with the idea that a man could willingly harm – let alone cold-bloodedly kill – the child of his body.

Porson gave him a look of sympathy but said, 'All the same, you can't go prancing in like a bowl in a china shop. Especially not with the commissioner's eyes on this one.'

'I know, sir. I thought about that. There's a housekeeper – has the look of an old family retainer.'

'Old family . . .?' Porson began derisively, then shrugged. 'Fair enough. Go in by the back door, eh? Good thinking. But you still need to be tactful.'

'In case she's intensely loyal to her boss. I know.'

'Better make sure Sir John's not at home first.'

*   *   *

Brigid Yeatman opened the door in a lavender overall, with a duster in her hand. She looked sharply at Slider, then gave Atherton a slow once-over.

'He's not in,' she said at length, 'but I can take a message.'

'It was actually you I wanted to talk to,' Slider said. He tried a smile. It was intercepted and shot down by her ground-to-air disapproving look.

'*Me?*' she said, as if it was the silliest thing since sliced bread. '*I've* nothing to tell you.'

'You've worked for Sir John for a long time, I believe.'

'Forty years, give or take. With breaks to have me kids.'

'So you know him pretty well.'

'What if I do? If you want to ask him questions, ask him.'

'Sometimes, in a delicate situation, it's best to go a more roundabout route. Sir John is probably very worried about his daughter being missing, and I wouldn't want to upset him unnecessarily.'

Her eyes narrowed. 'Was it you rang earlier, about the interview?' Her hand all this time had remained holding the edge of the door, and now she moved it minutely, suggesting it was about to close.

Slider lifted his own hand placatingly. 'I just want some background information on the family. It might help us find Mrs Holland. And I'm sure you can help us as much as Sir John, but without ruffling any feathers.'

She smiled at last, but it was a grim sort of smile. 'Me feathers is plenty ruffled right this minute, Mr Detective Inspector. But if it's just ancient history you're after, I see no harm. You can come in. But I'll probably have to tell himself when he gets back that you've been. I've never gone behind his back. I'd be out on me ear pretty quick if he thought he couldn't trust me. He's not one to forgive if you once let him down.'

Slider had an instant vision of Sir John complaining to the commissioner about harassment, and the fragrant shower that would descend from on high in consequence; but sufficient unto the day. 'Thank you,' he said, stepping forward before she could change her mind.

She took them to the kitchen at the back of the house, which was large and handsome, and had either been installed at great expense in the 1930s or was an even more expensive modern replica, with eight-inch retro tiles and a vast range of panelled solid wood cabinets, painted heritage green. She gestured them to sit at the table, and put the kettle on so automatically she probably wasn't even aware she'd done it. Then she came back and sat down opposite them. Her face was brown and firm and very little lined, innocent of make-up, with sharp pale-blue eyes and short, fair, wavy hair that was going silver through the fairness so you'd hardly notice. Only her thick-fingered hands showed her age, and the effects of a lifetime of housework.

'Go on, then,' she invited. 'Work away.'

'You were with the family when they still lived in Kensington?' Slider asked, to get her going.

'I was. They had a cook as well, back then, and usually an au pair – not that you get much work out of that class of person, but at least it was someone to keep an eye on the kids after school and in the holidays, take 'em to their classes and so on. Because *she* wasn't a well woman—'

'She?'

'Herself. Madam. Mrs Aubrey-Harris. *She* couldn't mind 'em. And there was no way I was going to get pulled in to that kind of caper.'

She had come most conveniently to the point – or one of them. 'What classes were they?' Atherton asked, taking a glance from Slider.

'Oh, all manner and sort of things those girls did. Not as bad as it is nowadays – my grandchildren never have a moment to themselves, it's woegeous – but still they were out and about and back and forth. Hither and yon. Tennis, art, music. With Felicity, of course, it was the ballet. Ballet mad, she was. Never still, that one. Come in the kitchen to chat to me, and she'd be doing pliés on the back of the chair while she's talking. She did a grand battement once and kicked the cream jug right out of me hand.'

'You know all the terms,' Atherton commented.

'Could hardly avoid it, with the ballet talk there was day in, day out. All nuts about it – bar Thelma, she was more one for the ponies. Riding lessons every week in Hyde Park.'

'Sir John was keen on the ballet as well, was he?'

'He wasn't Sir John back then. They were just Mr and Mrs. But, yes, they were both dead keen on it – Himself maybe even more than Herself. All the arts, mind you – theatre, opera, paintings and so. Belonged to everything going. But it was the ballet that was closest to their hearts.'

'And Felicity was really good at it?' Slider asked.

'She'd want to be, the amount that was spent on her.'

Atherton noticed that her Irish accent, faint at first, was becoming stronger the longer she talked. And she seemed to have forgotten any reluctance to answer questions. He supposed when your whole life was spent looking after someone, you naturally found them a fascinating topic.

'No, but she was good, Lord love her,' Mrs Yeatman went on. 'And she worked hard at it. But she was full of fun as well. She was the lively one. And so full of love – ah, she'd come running up and fling the arms round you, just for nothing at all, the little dote! *Too* full of love, she was.'

'Why do you say that?'

'That sort of person, people can take advantage of them.'

'Who do you think took advantage of her?'

Despite his care to sound casual, she grew wary at the question. 'No one at all. T'was just a general observation. Ah, she was a lovely child, Felicity,' she reverted. 'Sweet-natured. And so good with her sister. She was four when Thelma was born, and often a child that age that's had all the attention will be jealous of the newcomer, and play all sorts of mean tricks, but Felicity, never. She was the little mother with Thelma, and Thelma looked up to her and followed her everywhere. She was the quiet one, Thelma. Mind you, that was then. They switched around as they grew up. Now Thelma's full of fun and bubble, and Felicity's the quiet one. You never know what she's thinking. Not that I see much of her these days.' She stopped abruptly. 'I was forgetting.' She looked from one to the other. 'This is a queer carry-on. What does it mean, "she's missing"? Himself seems to think she's run off with another man. Spoke quite sharply about it – not that he discusses family matters with me, as a rule, but a comment was passed, and a bitter one it was. But if that was it, you wouldn't be here asking questions, would you? It's news to me if a married woman having a bit of a fling is police business.'

Slider answered. 'There are elements to the situation, which I can't go into, that we are obliged to take seriously. Do *you* think she's run off with another man?'

'I do not, though Mr Holland is not what you'd call a live wire, and Himself could never stand him, but, no, I don't think she'd do that. Though you never can tell, can you, particularly with the quiet ones? There was the vicar's wife here a coupla years since, you'd think butter wouldn't melt, but didn't she up and run away with the estate agent from the village, last seen living it up with him in High Wycombe, new clothes, dyed hair, mutton dressed as lampshade? But Felicity, no – I'd not believe it. But Sir John is dead against anything like that, the hanky-panky, always has been, so I suppose that's what jumps to his mind. Very old-fashioned in his views, Sir John – and why not?' she added loyally. 'There's right and there's wrong, and there's no shame in saying so.'

'So the girls were strictly brought up,' Slider suggested.

'It'd be thought strict now, but back then I'd have called it just normal. You're supposed to give your kids rules and boundaries, aren't you? But they were happy girls, don't mistake me.'

'And Felicity – how did she get on with her father?'

'Well, he wasn't one to be soft and cuddly with his kids, down on them like a ton o' bricks if they stepped out of line, but she was his pet, there was no mistaking. He was so proud of her. It was the ballet, o' course – she was to be the next Margot Fonteyn.'

'He really thought she was that good?'

'Oh my Lord! If time and money and thought and care spent on it could make it happen, it would have happened. Wait'll I show you.' She got up and went out of the room for a moment, and came back in with a photograph in a silver frame. She handed it to Slider, who shared it with Atherton. It showed a dark-haired young girl of about thirteen or fourteen, in leotard, tights and ballet shoes, holding a large silver cup and beaming at the camera. Behind her was a much younger Sir John Aubrey-Harris in evening dress, one hand resting on the girl's shoulder, and an expression of enormous, proprietorial pride on his face.

'That's when she passed Grade Seven a year early and won the Dortmann Cup. He didn't stop smiling for a week.'

'So what happened to change his feelings towards her?' Slider asked. 'He doesn't speak very fondly of her now.'

She belatedly regained her caution. 'I don't know what you're talking about,' she said.

'You said you don't see much of her these days. Sir John said he didn't see her often. He said she was lacking in seriousness, flitting from one thing to another, lacking in self-discipline.'

Her face hardened progressively as he spoke. She said, 'Families have their disagreements. Doesn't mean they don't still love each other.'

'But something must have happened to change his view of his daughter.'

'You'd have to ask him,' she said stubbornly, looking away.

'Was it because she wanted to be a professional ballet dancer?' Atherton asked mildly. 'Maybe he'd wanted her to do something more serious, the law, maybe, follow in his footsteps?'

'I wouldn't know,' she said. 'You'd have to ask him.' If her mouth got any tighter, she'd suck her own face inside out.

Slider let it go. 'I expect it's a quiet house these days,' he said, 'with Sir John being retired.'

'Oh, we have our little moments,' she said, as though being called quiet was a disparagement. 'We still entertain now and then. And he's not sitting by the fire by any manner of means. He goes to meetings and reunions and such. Dinners. Meets old friends – or colleagues, if you will. Often gets asked his opinion on legal matters, by high-ups as well. Plays golf. Got very keen on golf since he's had more time on his hands.'

'Where does he play?'

'Burnham Beeches club. Supposed to be quite a challenging course – not that I know anything about golf, so don't ask. He's been a member for years. There's other courses closer, but he likes that one.'

'He plays there regularly?' Slider asked.

'At least once a week, though not always on the same day, if that's what you mean by regular.'

'Did he play this week?'

'Wednesday morning, since you ask. What's wrong with that?'

'Nothing at all. Does he still drive?'

'Of course he does.' She sounded indignant. 'He's not old! Drives a Jaguar. Had it ten years but he wouldn't change it. He loves that car. Funny how men are with their cars, be they high or low. Mine was out polishing his every Sunday, though t'was only a Ford Escort. Couldn't get him to church, God rest him, but he'd wash the car like a religion. Mary Mac, what are we talking about cars for, with Felicity gone missing?'

'I was just going to ask you,' Slider said, 'if you knew anything about her life recently – what she was doing, who she was seeing, and so on.'

'No, not really. She always comes and sits with me a bit and has a cup of tea when she's over visiting, but it's general chitchat. Asks me about my family, but she doesn't say anything about herself, not personal stuff. She'll mention a play she's been to, or a do of some kind, that class of thing. Talks about Mr Holland's books and how he's getting on.'

'Does she seem happy?'

'I suppose so. Not *un*happy, anyway.' Her expression changed.

'You've just thought of something,' Slider said quietly.

Mrs Yeatman debated inwardly, then decided to tell. 'Christmas was the last time I saw her,' she said. 'They were all together, Mrs Wilbraham and her husband and children, and Mr and Mrs Holland. She came into the kitchen, Mrs Holland did, to give me a Christmas present. And she seemed . . .' She hesitated. 'I thought she was a bit merry on the wine, at first. They'd started with champagne and gone on to the red stuff. She was sort of lit up. But it wasn't wine, I could tell when she chatted to me. She was like—'

'Yes?'

Mrs Yeatman looked at him reluctantly. 'Like someone in love. That sort of shiny, blissy look. I even commented on it, I said, "You seem happy, has something happened?" And she said, no, nothing. And I said, "Come on, you can tell me, I could do with some good news," or something of that sort. And she said, "I'm just happy. Isn't family a wonderful thing?" And she gave me a lovely sweater for Christmas. And she gave me fifty pounds as well, and said, "Get something nice for Des." Des is my youngest, Desmond. He's at home. Been out of work a while, so it was nice of her.'

'And you haven't seen her since? Or talked to her on the phone? Has Sir John seen her more recently? Or talked to her?'

'Not to my knowledge. But he wouldn't tell me necessarily.'

'Can you remember what Sir John did on Tuesday? Was he at home?' Slider asked.

'He went up to London to have lunch with somebody, and don't ask me who because he never said.'

'Did he drive up?'

'Sometimes he would, sometimes he'd take the train. He'd drive to the station in any case, so the car went. Beyond that I couldn't tell you.'

'And what time did he get home?'

'Not before I left for the day.'

'Don't you live in?' Slider asked, surprised. She seemed such a fixture.

'I do not,' she said. 'I've a perfectly good house of me own in the village, five minutes' walk away.' Slider nodded receptively and, encouraged, she expanded. 'The way it was, when the family first came down here, I came with them, and I lived in. But then I got married to a local man, my Tommy, he was a builder, so I came in by the day. He died ten years back, Tommy – it's a terrible strain on a man's heart, the building work – and it was about the same time that Madam popped off. Liver, it was, with her. She'd not been well a long time – a norful colour she was at the end. It was a merciful release when she went, poor soul. Well, there's no one in the world could look after himself worse than Sir John, and he wanted me to move back in, but I like my bit of independence. Besides, I'd the boys to think of. Liam, my eldest, he's in Australia now, married a nice girl, got two kiddies, Lord knows when I'll ever see them, though he's trying to get me to buy a Skype, whatever that may be, like a telephone with pictures. But Des, my youngest, he's never properly left the nest. Goes away and comes back again. Not married. So how it is now, I come up at eight, to get him his breakfast for eight thirty, and I go home once I've given him his dinner, which he has at seven if he's alone, so I'm finished about eight.' She inspected Slider's expression and said, 'It sounds like a long day, but I'm not working all the time, he just likes to have someone to answer the bell and the door and the phone. I pop home when I want, and do me own business in between. Course, if he entertains, then I'm here longer, but I don't mind. It's a change, and what'd I be doing anyway? Sitting at home watching the telly and nagging Des to get himself a job. Anyway, he's sort of like family now, Sir John, and you don't mind what you do for family, do you?'

'So what time did you go home on Tuesday?'

'Well, I could have gone any time, because Himself said he was lunching in Town and had some other business in the afternoon, and he said he'd have his dinner at the club so he wouldn't need me to cook for him. But I'd some ironing to do, and it's nice and peaceful here, so I took me time, and I didn't leave until about half past four. But Sir John wasn't back then, like I said, so I don't know what time he did arrive, whyever you need to know that.'

'It's just routine,' Slider said soothingly. 'We like to know where everyone was, so we can get a clear picture. He played golf on the Wednesday morning, you say?'

'That's what he said. He went off in the car about nine o'clock in one of his tempers and said he was going to the Beeches. I wanted to ask if he'd be back for lunch, but you don't bother him with questions when he's in a fouler, so I kept me mouth shut. I reckoned he wouldn't want much anyway since he'd eaten big the day before, so I made some soup and baked a loaf, and as it happened he did come back, about two, and he had that without a word and went to his study to work for the afternoon.'

'What was he in a bad mood about?' Atherton asked.

She raised her eyebrows. 'Now, how would I know that? He wouldn't be telling *me*. All I know is, he was over it by the next day. He was his usual self. He's not a cheery person, never was, even before Herself went, but most times he's what you'd call equable. He does a lot o' deep thinking, and that'd take the giggles out of a person, in my view.'

'And we never even got that cup of tea,' Atherton said when they were outside again.

'But we did get something to think about,' said Slider.

'I'll say. Burnham Beeches for golf? Hear a new word, and you'll hear it again within the day. I wish we could interview him properly,' Atherton said. 'Find out who he was seeing in London on Tuesday. Grill him and get the truth.'

'You can't grill someone like Sir John,' said Slider. 'They're asbestos.'

EIGHT
Dads and Dudes

Haynes and Carver's flagship store in Jermyn Street was typical of a high-end men's outfitters: low ceilings, mood lighting, bare wood floors, oceans of space. There was something vaguely cruise-ship-like about all the polished wood, and the brass-railed staircase. A quick goosey suggested to Swilley that there was not much difference in the merchandise from that in John Lewis (where she had occasionally bought her Tony something) except for the price – but then, what did she know? Tony usually bought his own clothes, like she bought *her* own. Just because you were married didn't mean you did everything together. And they rarely agreed on taste. She liked plain and classical, whereas he every now and then went wild with some pattern or colour that gave you a migraine.

A willowy young man approached her with a polite enquiry and an intimate smile, which dissolved when she showed her warrant card; and on closer inspection, he wasn't that young, either, though he really was willowy. His shirt strained at the buttons, but that was because it was the current fashion for men to appear to be wearing clobber two sizes too small for them, and not because there was an ounce of fat on him. His haircut was also modern, a sculpted, choppy top waxed into shape, a bit like the Sydney Opera House, with highlights; and despite being, she reckoned, nearer forty than twenty, he had a tiny little goatee. She thought he might be wearing slap, too, but the shop was too dark to be sure.

He said his name was Jeremy Hunter, and that he was the senior sales assistant. She produced a photograph of Felicity Holland, but he knew the name even before he looked at it. 'Oh yes,' he said. 'She's one of our customers. Nice lady.'

They prided themselves, he said, on remembering their

repeat customers, and giving them that little extra personal
service that makes all the difference. Swilley agreed privately
that it made a difference: in her case, the difference between
buying anything and walking out empty-handed. Her pet hate
was being approached by an assistant in a shop when she was
browsing. If she couldn't pick something up and look at it
without being bothered with, 'Oh, that would look lovely on
you, why don't you try it on?' she'd go somewhere else. Even
a simple, 'Can I help you?' tended to elicit a rude response
from her. But she didn't want to break Jeremy's heart by telling
him so.

At all events, he had chatted to Felicity Holland. She had
bought things several times before, and their chat had established that they were for her husband. Though, of course,
Swilley thought, anyone could *say* that.

'Do you remember when she was last in?' she asked.

'It must have been about a week ago,' he said. 'I could look
it up for you. I do remember she bought a cashmere jumper,
because it was a bit different from what she usually picked
out. It was a turtleneck, with a little zip just at the neck, and
the colour was Bermuda Coral: £295 on sale, reduced from
£350 – terrific value. There was nothing wrong with it, just
that we overstocked. But the style, and especially the colour,
were more modern than her usual choices. It was more a young
man's jumper, and I remember thinking, I wonder whether her
husband will really like it, given what she'd bought him before.
Because older men are usually terribly conservative, and it's
hard to get them to change anything.'

'Did you ask her?'

'Oh no, it wouldn't have been appropriate. But she must
have seen it in my expression, because she gave a little laugh
and said, "It's a present for somebody."'

'But she didn't say who?'

'No, but she seemed very happy, sort of shiny-eyed and pleased
with herself. I remember that, because I remember thinking to
myself, "Hel-lo! She's met someone!" Well, she's a very nice-
looking woman, amazing for her age, so why not? I expect her
husband is a bit dull. I was pleased for her, really. I wished I
could have asked her about him, because she probably didn't

have anyone she could tell, and when you've made a conquest, naturally you want to talk about it, don't you?'

'I wouldn't know,' Swilley said, which took the fizz out of him. 'Shall we have a look at the records, make sure it's really her. And what the date was.'

He didn't actually say, 'Spoilsport,' but it was in the hunch of his shoulders as he turned away.

Gascoyne was the only one of them who knew anything about golf. His father was an instruction officer at the police college at Hendon, where a certain amount of politicking has to happen, and you couldn't get anywhere hobnobbing with the nobs in the Job if you didn't play golf. As a lad, Gascoyne had caddied for his dad during rounds with some top bods from Scotland Yard, the sort whose names were spoken in hushed voices – or sometimes with crossed fingers. But the important thing was he knew enough about the game not to embarrass himself by asking what sort of bat Sir John used, or whether he'd scored any goals lately. In addition, he had a gentle manner and a nice face, the sort of face everybody instinctively warmed to. If he'd been a dog, he'd have been a Labrador.

However, as far as the golf club secretary was concerned, he might as well have had a face like a slapped bottom, because the very idea of the police asking questions about Sir John Aubrey-Harris – *the* Sir John – made him come over all unnecessary. It took a goodly amount of soothage from Gascoyne before he settled down enough to answer them.

Yes, Sir John had been there on Wednesday. Obviously one didn't know every member by sight, though one did one's best, but Sir John had been a member for many, many years. And naturally, the more eminent people were easier to remember.

'Was Wednesday his usual day?' Gascoyne asked.

'He didn't have a regular day. He came when he came.'

'And who did he play with?'

'Oh, I've seen him with a lot of different people. Generally, people arrange to meet other members at the clubhouse, or they bring guests with them, though sometimes they just drop in on the off chance and see if there's anyone about who wants a game.'

'But on Wednesday?'

A little frown of concentration. 'I think he came on his own. Did he meet someone here? No, I remember now, he went round with one of the professionals.'

'And how did he seem?'

'Seem?'

'What was his mood?'

'I only saw him as I passed through the clubhouse. He seemed just as usual, I suppose.'

'And what was that? What is his usual?'

The secretary seemed embarrassed by the question. 'Well, you know. He's Sir John Aubrey-Harris. The eminent barrister. He's a sort of Grand Old Man. You don't slap his back and swap racy stories. Anyway, he must be in his eighties, though he's very spry for his age. But that generation tends to be a bit – stately.' He found the right word belatedly.

'Perhaps I could speak to this person he played with?'

'Jim Peters? I'm afraid he's not in today. Though I can give you his phone number.'

So instead Gascoyne had a word with the barman in the clubhouse, a tall, skinny, hyperactive guy with startling wiry ginger hair and full Captain Haddock beard, coarse as a coir doormat, bright as the sun, but both neatly cropped. He turned out to be Portuguese, and named Antonio, 'But call me Tony – everybody does.' His English was excellent and only slightly accented. 'I been here ten years,' he said. 'I learn quick, anyhow – I speak French, Italian and German also, and a bit of Polish. I should work for United Nations.' He smiled, a flash of white, even teeth in the foxy underbrush.

Yes, he remembered Sir John being there on Wednesday. 'You always notice Sir John when he's here. He's like a monument, like Nelson's Column. Good golfer, too, they tell me. Very low handicap – that's good, right? I don't play, but I hear them talk. Pink gin, that's his drink. Not many people drink that nowadays. Mostly old guys, guys who've been in Africa, India – colonials they call them? Old-type guys, old-fashioned. Classy manners, posh accent. Nice clothes, expensive but not flashy, you know? Like tweeds.'

Gascoyne signified that he had got the point. 'Did he come in alone?'

'Wednesday? Yeah, I think so. Never saw anyone with him, anyhow. He come in about ten o'clock. I say, "Pinkers, Sir John?" That's what these old guys call it, pinkers. He says, "It's too early." I say, "Sun's over the yardarm somewhere, Sir John." That's what they say, that thing about the yardarm, so I say it to them, josh them a bit. They like it. Makes 'em feel at home. But he ignores me and goes through into the changing rooms. Looks a bit grumpy.' He shrugged. 'I don't mind. They come, they go, but I'm a fixture, management knows that. "You're an institution, Tony," these old guys say. That's what they call me. An institution.'

'You thought he was in a bad mood?'

He shrugged again. 'Maybe, a bit. He looked a bit grim, is all.'

'Did you see him again? Did he come for a drink after playing his round?'

'I didn't see him, but I was busy. Eighteen holes takes about three hours, and that brings it to lunchtime, when I'm dashing about. I don't remember him being there. I didn't serve him, that's all I know.'

Back at the factory, Gascoyne said, 'I rang the professional, bloke called Jim Peters, but he didn't add anything much. Said they went round in silence, but Sir John was never chatty anyway; he'd concentrate on his shots and otherwise pursue his own thoughts. So Peters didn't notice anything different about him. But before I left, I asked the secretary if they had a camera on the car park, and he said they did. They get some trouble in the summer with trippers using it when the public ones are full. So I got a copy of Wednesday's tape. You can see Sir John arrive in his Jaguar, all right, and he's alone in the car.'

'Well, that's—' Atherton began impatiently.

'Wait, though. I noticed something.'

'Get on with it, then,' Slider said. 'Never mind the dramatic pauses.'

'All right, sir: he got his golf clubs out from the back seat of the car. That's queer. I don't know a golfer who doesn't put them in the boot. And he loves that car – why'd he risk scratching his upholstery?'

'What's your point?'

'Why didn't he put his clubs in the boot? Because there was something else in there.'

'You think he had his daughter in there? All trussed up and gagged?' Atherton derided.

'No, dead, obviously. No, but listen,' said Gascoyne insistently. 'He went to London on the Tuesday. Said he was having lunch with somebody. She went to London on Tuesday and she said she was having lunch with somebody. It's a coincidence, right?'

'A lot of people have lunch,' Slider said. 'It's a national habit.'

'You think he snatched his own daughter?' Atherton said scathingly.

'He wouldn't have to snatch her – she'd get into the car of her own accord,' Gascoyne pointed out. 'He was her dad, she'd trust him.'

'But why would she get in? Where would they be going?'

'He's giving her a lift somewhere, or they're going to lunch somewhere else – out of town, maybe. Or they're going to see someone. Could be any one of a number of reasons. It doesn't matter. She gets into the car and he drives off.'

'And then he kills her,' said Slider flatly. 'His own daughter.'

'Not necessarily meaning to, guv. My idea is, it's an accident. They have a row about something – we know he was a bit off her recently – and something happens, a blow or a shove or something, and boom, she's dead, and he's got an embarrassing corpse on his hands.'

'He's a retired barrister, a man of the law,' Atherton reminded him.

'All the more reason to conceal it. He's got more to lose – his whole reputation. A man like him can't go to jail. And he knows the ins and outs of the law, and how investigations are carried out. If he can get rid of the body, even if it's found later, who'd ever suspect him?'

'Not me, for one,' Atherton said snarkily.

Gascoyne flicked him an annoyed glance, but carried on to Slider. 'He puts her body in the boot and drives home. Worries about it all night – what's best to do? Next day he tells Brigid he's going for a game of golf. Puts his clubs in the back seat. Drives to The Stag car park. Hauls her out into the woods somewhere. Goes on to the golf club to establish his credentials. He left home at about nine and got to the club at about ten, and it's only a half-hour drive at most. What was he doing for the other half-hour?'

'He took an hour coming back as well, according to the Yeatman woman,' Atherton said.

'Well, she only said "about". But anyway, he had to get rid of the handbag.'

'Yes, why didn't he leave it with the body?' Slider asked.

'Maybe he forgot it. Or didn't notice it until he was back in the car – maybe she'd put it on the floor, in the footwell. Women do sometimes. So after the game he goes back round Hawthorn Lane. He doesn't want to go right back to where he dumped her – too risky – so he leaves it by the road where it'll be found. But he takes out her phone, cash and credit cards first, because he knows that's what a villain would do. That's where his legal knowledge helps him.'

'Did he put the clubs in the boot after the game?' Slider asked.

'No, in the back seat again,' said Gascoyne. 'But maybe there was some blood or something and he didn't want to get it on the golf bag. Anyway, he goes home and shuts himself in his study for the rest of the day – well, it's a pretty upsetting thing to have to do, and it takes time for him to get over it. By the next day, according to Brigid, he's back to normal. A man like him could get control of himself in that time, enough not to show anything outwardly.'

'Hmm,' said Atherton. 'You've thought it out, I'll give you that. But if he was going to dump the body, why not somewhere really remote? Or somewhere he didn't have any connection with?'

'My thinking is, he wants her to be found eventually. I mean, you would, wouldn't you – want a proper funeral and so on. And he'd have to know the place, so as to know where he could park the car and where he could dump the body. *And*,' he added, 'if anyone sees his car in the area, or he's caught on an ANPR camera on the way there or back,

he's got the reason to be travelling in that area: he's going to
have an innocent round of golf. And he has it. QED.'

'Quite evidently daft,' Atherton said.

'Have you got a better idea?' Gascoyne asked, surprisingly
politely in the circumstances.

'Your story holds together, I'll give you that,' Slider said.
'But we've got no evidence to support it. We don't know for
sure that she's even dead.'

'Most likely she's just run off with another man,' Atherton
said. 'Wouldn't you, if you were married to a bloke that writes
Hornblower books without the Hornblower? At the moment she's
just a missing person, and we wouldn't even be investigating if
Holland hadn't gone to school with the commissioner.'

'Still, it's a possible scenario,' Gascoyne said. 'I wonder
what Mr Porson would think about it.'

'You'd better come and pitch it to him,' said Slider.

'It has its points,' Porson admitted, thoughtfully scratching the
top of his bald dome with the cap end of his biro.

'The problem is—' Slider began.

'Yerss,' Porson anticipated with a long-drawn-out agreement. 'You can make up pretty stories till the cows freeze
over, but it doesn't get you anywhere without evidence.'

'And we can't interview Sir John,' Slider concluded.

'Can't even investigate him, if it draws attention,' said
Porson. 'He's the sort, if he finds out we've been asking questions about him, he'll complain to the commissioner, the
commissioner'll tick off Mr Carpenter, and Mr Carpenter'll
go spare.'

'If we could only take his car in,' Gascoyne said wistfully.
'See if there's any traces in the boot.'

'Not without a pretty damn good reason – not just a nice
story you've cooked up from a pair of coincidences and golf
clubs on the back seat.'

'Could we just ask him who he had lunch with, sir, just
that?' Gascoyne persisted. 'Then we can check with whoever
it was. See if he turned up. What his timings were, at least.'

'How are you going to ask him without telling him why
you're asking?' Slider answered.

'If he's worried about his daughter, he ought not to mind. He ought to want to help any way he can.'

'"Ought" butters no parsnips, lad,' said Porson. He chewed the biro cap in thought. 'If we had some evidence she was ever there, even in the area, we could put pressure on Thames Valley to search the woods. But if they won't accept the handbag as sufficient cause, I don't know what's going to float their boat. All right,' he made up his mind, 'as it's you, Gascoyne, and I know your dad, you can have a look for Sir John's motor, see if you can trace it from the house Tuesday. If he went up to Town on the train, your theory's a crock anyway.'

When Gascoyne had gone, Porson said to Slider, 'Holland's been on again, agitating about the handbag.'

'Who told him about that?'

'Mr Carpenter. Can't keep that sort of thing from the victim's husband.'

'If she's a victim.'

Porson waved that away. 'Wants to know why we're not searching the woods, like he's seen on TV.'

'He'd do better to go and agitate Thames Valley,' Slider objected. 'Or better still, his old chum the commissioner. There's nothing *we* can do.'

'Well, I don't suppose Mr Carpenter told him that. But we have to be seen to be doing something. What do you think about Gascoyne's theory?'

'It's a theory.'

'Yerss.' He tapped his lower lip with the biro. 'If he did have lunch with his daughter, they'd have to have made the appointment somehow. Any phone contact between them?'

'Not on the mobile. If we have to get the landline records, it'll take a while – you know what BT are like. And we're waiting for the bank statements. Otherwise all we can do is scour Covent Garden cameras, and you know how long that takes.'

'I'll give you some more uniforms to help with that,' said Porson.

Swilley had downloaded a photo of the jumper from the Haynes and Carver website.

'I see what you mean,' Slider said. 'It's hard to imagine Mr Holland in that.'

'Not in that colour, certainly,' said Atherton. 'If I try to imagine him in a sweater – on a sailing boat, for instance – it comes out navy blue and Guernsey-like. Definitely not pink.'

'Bermuda Coral,' Swilley corrected. 'It's one of this season's colours. Coral and mustard.'

Atherton made a face. 'I may never eat again.'

'Let's not get over-excited,' said Slider. 'Who else might she have bought a present for? Her brother-in-law? Or one of her nephews – any birthdays coming up?'

'But she bought it on Friday. And took it with her to the class on Tuesday, saying it was a present for someone, and she was going to lunch with someone. If it was for her brother-in-law or a nephew—'

'Maybe she was having an affair with the brother-in-law,' Atherton said. 'You should check with Thelma if he's been sporting any unusual knitwear lately.'

'You're not taking this seriously,' Swilley said, giving him a look that could have removed warts.

'Settle down. We don't know what was in the bag,' Slider had to point out. 'But by all means check with the sister on the birthday front. And ask her if there's anyone else she might buy a jumper for. We're woefully short of leads. I'll take anything that's going, at this stage.'

Mr Carpenter blew into the factory like a small, evil whirlwind. 'What have you got so far?' he demanded. 'What leads are you following up? Mr Holland is seriously unhappy about the lack of progress. He's lost his wife, damnit!'

'It's not even been three full days yet, sir,' Porson defended.

'Three days, when someone's life may be in danger?'

'And we started out with nothing to go on.'

'Well, what can I tell him you've done?'

Porson gave a précis. It sounded thinner when spoken out loud.

'Why aren't we searching these woods?' Carpenter cried in anguish.

'Not our ground, sir. Not even Met ground – it's Thames Valley, and they don't think it's warranted.'

'So where are they, exactly, the woods?' Porson told him. 'Never heard of 'em.' Carpenter came originally from Nottingham. Lesser forests didn't impinge on his consciousness.

'If you wanted to talk to Thames Valley, sir, put our—'

'Mr Holland wants to go on TV,' Carpenter burst out. 'Make a public appeal. Of course, he's seen it done in other cases.'

They'd all seen it. A grainy black-and-white video take of the 'last known sighting' – a missing girl passing a kebab shop late at night on her way home from a night out, or seen setting out on a near-midnight crossing of some deserted common. Then the awkward, teary relative reading from a script, begging anyone with information to come forward. It never ended well. You'd almost think the TV appeal was a jinx, that without it the missing girl might have come home.

'This is different,' Porson pointed out. 'She went to Covent Garden station in the middle of the day. We don't know that's where she ended up. All we know is she didn't use her Oyster card again, but it doesn't mean she didn't pay for a ticket or take a taxi. Or a mainline train, for that matter. She could be anywhere in the country. Getting information in this case is like pulling hen's teeth.'

Carpenter had had to get used to Porson's cavalier way with words, and did not blink. When he was agitated, he probably didn't even notice. His own vocabulary leaned heavily on corporate-speak. Being feared was more important than being understood. *Oderint dum metuant*, he might have said, if he'd had the Latin.

Porson passed the ball politely back. 'Maybe it *is* time for a national appeal, sir. If it's what Mr Holland really wants.' He didn't say, it might get him off your back, but it was implied.

Carpenter viewed the golden landscape for one minute, then scowled. 'No, no, no. You know what it's like. Setting up a phone line. Dozens of officers tied up. Thousands of false sightings and prank phone calls. No, we're not there yet. It's only been three days, for goodness' sake! And for all we know, she's safely tucked up in a country hotel somewhere with a lover-boy.' His expression changed. 'Of course, if that's the

case, a TV appeal might flush her out,' he mused. And changed
again. 'But the expense! No, better Thames Valley does a
search than that. I'll see what I can do in that direction. And
try to put Mr Holland off the idea of TV.'

Publicity was a two-edged sword, as they both knew. Yes,
it might winkle out new information, but it also got the press
interested, and that could seriously hamper an investigation.
Not to mention the unwelcome spotlight on inevitably slow
progress and possible failures.

They had been lucky, Porson mused as Carpenter whirled
out again, in that the Hollands were not social media bunnies,
because these days the internet was worse than the mainstream
press.

Swilley checked with Thelma Wilbraham about the coral
jumper. She had never seen it, or heard Fliss talk about it. She
didn't think it was something Henry would wear. No, there
were no family birthdays coming up. But of course she didn't
know about any of Fliss's friends, whether she might have
bought it for one of them.

'It's an expensive thing to be buying for a casual friend,'
Swilley offered.

'You think – it might be more than a friend?' Thelma said
hesitantly.

'I couldn't possibly say,' said Swilley.

A pause. 'You do think that she's all right, don't you?'

'I've no reason to think she isn't,' was the best Swilley
could do for her. 'You'll let me know if you have any brain-
waves, about someone she might buy a sweater for.'

'Of course. And you'll let me know the minute you hear
anything?'

'Of course.'

Slider came through from his office with Atherton behind him,
to see Swilley still at her computer. 'You still here?' he said.
'That's dedication. Go home, Norma.'

She looked up. 'I've just found Josh Milo,' she said.

'Well done.' He examined her expression. 'You don't look
very happy about it.'

'He's dead.'

'Oh.'

'I found his obituary. It was a very old post on a jazz fan site, so it was on page one zillion of Google,' she said.

'Another fine theory goes west,' said Atherton.

'He died three years ago,' she said. 'There's a photo as well, but it's of when he was very young. Taken on some tour he did in his twenties, to Daytona Beach.'

She brought it up and they looked over her shoulder. A young man with a cheeky grin, wild dark hair, arm locked round the neck of a gurning companion. It was in black and white, but it looked as if his eyes were blue. Black hair and blue eyes, a fatal combination. It was the sort of snap a couple of drunk lads might take of themselves in a photo booth in the days before mobile phones and selfies – same impulse, different technology. A poor, grainy thing, it was, from before the age of computers, so not amenable to successful uploading.

'He looks cute,' Swilley offered. 'As far as one can tell. The ob is very enthusiastic about him. Great musician. Great guy, everybody loved him. Doesn't mention any wives or families, though. And of course, being an ob, it doesn't talk about girlfriends or tendencies of that sort. Not that it matters, he's definitely dead.'

'Damn,' said Atherton. 'I so wanted her to be going off into the sunset with her ageing rocker boyfriend.'

'Just because her sister said he was the only man she ever loved, doesn't mean it's true,' Swilley told him. 'This is real life, not a romantic novel.'

'Yes, but it leaves us with no leads in that direction,' Atherton said. 'So we're back at square one. Square minus one, actually.'

'It's a disappointment,' Slider said, 'but there's nothing more to be done tonight.'

'Tomorrow to fresh—' Atherton began.

'Don't mention woods,' said Slider.

'I wasn't going to. I was going to say fresh dudes and boyfriends new. But you've spoiled it now.'

NINE

Lunchtime Achievement

They walked to their cars, Slider frowning in thought. 'There's something off about all this,' he said.

'You mean, apart from the fact that we're involved at all?' said Atherton. 'Apart from being diverted from our lawful courses on the personal whim of our overlords?'

'Don't whine,' said Slider. 'You get paid just the same. But don't you think there's something odd about it?'

'Not particularly. I still think she's done a runner, even if it wasn't with the OGLL.'

'What?'

'One Great Love of her Life. Granted women like her don't generally come off the rails like that without prior notice, but we've only got her husband's word for it that there were no signs. Maybe it's been obvious for ages, even to a self-obsessed bore like Holland, that his wife's not happy, and he's covering up his guilt for not doing anything about it by pretending it's a bolt from the blue.'

'That's not comforting.'

'Wasn't meant to be. What do you find odd?'

'The handbag, for a start. Someone took her credit cards, but left the membership cards that were in the same section. Why would a murderer bother to sort them out? Wouldn't he just grab the lot, and throw away the useless ones later?'

'Yes. It sounds like an amateur. But why wouldn't a murderer be an amateur? And if it was her who dumped the bag, that's exactly what she'd do – take her credit cards and phone and leave the rest.'

'I thought you said that was an inane suggestion, that she dumped it herself.'

'Well, maybe she's not very bright. Can't be, if she hasn't

thought she'll be spotted as soon as she uses one of the cards. What else is odd?'

'I don't know,' Slider said, frowning. 'There's something nagging at the back of my mind that I can't put my finger on.'

'Oh well, there's nothing to be done now, anyway, as you so wisely said not five minutes ago. Are you doing anything tomorrow night?'

'Don't think so. Joanna's not working. Quiet night at home, other things being equal. Why?'

'Would you like to come over to dinner at my place?'

Slider curbed the immediate impulse to decline – a quiet night at home with his beloved being just about the pinnacle of happiness for him – because there had been an unusual diffidence in Atherton's tone when he asked. 'Well,' he began, leaving space for amplification.

Atherton amplified. 'I'm cooking for Stephanie. And I thought it'd be an opportunity for you all to meet.'

Slider hid both amusement and surprise. So he was serious about having him inspect her? It made him feel fatherly – not a welcome sensation. 'I'll have to check with Joanna,' he temporized.

Atherton picked it up as reluctance. 'I'll get out the good silver,' he urged. 'Proper wine, the sort that leaves the enamel *on* your teeth. Petits fives instead of petits fours.'

'I didn't say no, just that I have to check with Jo. And see if Dad can babysit.'

'I know you'll like her.'

'I expect I will. But why does it matter?'

Atherton didn't answer at once. He veered round his car, which was parked next to Slider's, and only as he plipped the door did he say, 'Dunno exactly. I just think it would seem . . . more real if you'd met her.'

'I'll ring you later with an answer,' Slider said. 'But I expect it'll be OK.'

As he drove away, he thought of a story he'd read or heard once, of a middle-aged woman who'd never had a boyfriend, who suddenly started talking to her sister and brother-in-law about the wonderful man she'd met. The romance continued at whirlwind pace, in no time they were engaged, and a date was set for her to bring him to meet them for dinner at their house. On the night, she and the wonderful man didn't turn up. She was later fished out of the river, and it turned out that the man had never existed. She'd made the whole thing up, and got so embroiled in the story she couldn't go back on it. In the end couldn't face the humiliation of admitting it was a fabrication, and jumped off Hungerford Bridge.

Obviously, that couldn't apply to Atherton, the babe magnet, the serial bonker, who'd been known to have two dates in one evening after getting a quick one in at lunchtime. Though, Slider thought, he *had* been behaving a little oddly lately. But he wouldn't suddenly make up a wonderful new woman who was the answer to his dreams, would he?

Any more than Felicity Holland would suddenly run off without warning with a strange man.

If they went to Atherton's on Saturday, and he met them at the door with a rueful look and said Stephanie had suddenly been called in to work, it would be awkward. He wished now that he hadn't thought of that story.

Joanna met him in high good humour, with the baby on her shoulder.

'That child looks wide awake,' he said as he kissed her cheek. Zoe beamed at him and put out a starfish hand to grasp his nose. He honked, and she giggled. There was nothing in life so satisfying as to be able to occasion instant delight in your child.

'She *is* wide awake,' Joanna said. 'And George understandably says he shouldn't have to go to bed while she's still up. So you have a choice. Take them both up while I get supper on, or vice versa.'

He took the children option. With the baby on his shoulder and George's hand in his, and Jumper the cat sauntering up behind as though he just *happened* to be going in the same direction, he mounted the stairs. George was full of the day's chatter. He'd had a dream about school. What were dreams? Teddy had got her porridge all over her face and in her hair and it was yuck but she'd just laughed. Dommie at school had got the biggest bogey in the world out of his nose. Why was it bad to pick your nose? They'd done about flowers and seeds at school, and Miss Goude said they had to bring an avocado stone in, then they could grow it into a plant. What did Easter mean? Well, but why did they do that? It was wrong to hurt other people. Walter had pushed over Namita in the playground and she'd cut her knee and got all grit in it. She cried. They were going to have an egg hunt next week. Why did you have eggs at Easter? Well, but why did you have chocolate eggs? When you died, was it like being asleep? Did you dream when you were dead? Did Jesus like chocolate? What did Jesus dream about?

Slider was glad, at least, that George had got over his boring obsession with dinosaurs; and the questions were all right when they were practical, like how did cars work. It was rather flattering to be seen as the fount of all knowledge. Didn't happen very often in a policeman's life. But the questions tended to get more philosophical and harder to answer the closer George was to bed. Slider had yet to decide whether that was deliberate, or some instinctive survival mechanism. He let George help put the baby in her cot – he loved demonstrating his mastery of the side-lowering mechanism – then walked him to his own bed through a patter of why were there so many different animals, and why couldn't animals talk, and if they all had brains, why couldn't they learn new things, and what if monkeys took over the world, would there still be cars?

By the time he got downstairs, he was ready for the gin and tonic Joanna was just finishing pouring.

'Congratulations are in order,' she said as they clinked glasses. 'Sid Saxon phoned today, and I'm booked for three John Williams concerts. Successive Saturdays, Albert Hall, Birmingham and Nottingham. Good money. We can postpone selling a child.'

'Congratulations,' he said, and kissed her again. 'They'll be hard work, won't they?'

'A lot of dots. Very fond of his soaring strings, John Williams. But divine to play.'

'Will you have to stay up there? Birmingham and Nottingham?'

'No, it's all right. Peter White and Archie Paul are booked as well, and Peter's driving up, and they'll definitely be coming back, so I'll get a lift with them. It'll be late,' she anticipated his concern, 'but I won't be driving, so you needn't worry.'

'I always worry,' he said. 'But I don't really *worry*. When's the first – not tomorrow?'

'Saturday after next. Why?'

'Atherton's invited us to dinner at his place tomorrow. I said I'd have to check with you.'

'What's to check? I love his cooking. As long as your dad can babysit.'

'I thought you might prefer a quiet night in, with just the two of us,' he said.

'We can have a quiet night in tonight,' she said. His elder daughter, Kate, went home to her mother at the weekends, going straight from school on Friday, so they were alone. 'Did he say what he'd be cooking?'

'No, but he did promise the good silver.'

'Why the reluctance?' She cocked an eye at him. 'Have you two quarrelled?' she asked with mock severity.

'He wants us to meet his new girlfriend, Stephanie.'

'I like that name. If your surname hadn't been Slider—'

'That's what I thought.'

'—I'd have liked that for Teddy.'

'Instead of Zoe, you mean.'

'She's never going to get called Zoe. You have to make your mind up to it.'

'She'll be Zoe at school, once she's free of George's orbit.'

'Why are you reluctant to meet Stephanie?' Joanna persisted.

'I'm not, really. I just think it's odd that he's so keen we should.'

She thought a moment, sipping. 'I suppose it means it's serious. We never met any of his fleeting conquests.'

'I just hope it works out,' Slider said.

She smiled. 'You're worried about him. That's sweet.'

'It's not "sweet",' he objected.

'Oh, in a very manly, macho, deep-voiced way, I mean. If he's really keen on this one, you don't want him to fail.'

'Of course I don't. Nothing "sweet" about that.'

'Look, I'm sorry I called you sweet. You're a hairy caveman. And don't worry, even if he's presenting her for your approval, you won't mess it up for him.'

'What if I don't like her?' he asked, amazed at how she read his mind.

'Not even then. If it's meant to be, it'll happen.'

'Thank you, Dr Ruth.'

'If he could be put off her by your not liking her, it wouldn't be the real thing, would it? And I was channelling my inner Claire Rayner, actually. Dr Ruth is all about sex.'

'So is Atherton,' Slider pointed out.

'True. Five minutes to nosh. Do you want to lay the table?'

When they were seated, she asked about the case, and he told her about Sir John's visit to the golf club, and Gascoyne's idea.

'But it's just a coincidence, isn't it, the Burnham Beeches angle?' she said at the end.

'Possibly. Probably. Sometimes a coincidence is just a coincidence.'

'What do you think has really happened to her?' she asked.

'There's no reason to think she's come to any harm,' he said. 'Three days isn't long to go missing. If someone has a mental crisis and goes into hiding, it can be a lot longer than that before they sort themselves out. And during that time, they're very unlikely to be contacting the people they've run away from. Alternatively, if it's a love affair, it might be five days to a week before their conscience pricks them enough to let the family know they're all right. Oh,' he remembered, 'we found out about Josh Milo.'

'The jazz musician?'

'It's not surprising he hasn't been heard of lately – he's dead. Died three years ago – of natural causes, seemingly.'

'I thought he was only in his sixties? That's not very old.'

'Possibly his life was shortened by a jazzy lifestyle.'

'Hmm. Didn't you say it was three years ago that she gave up her job and changed her own lifestyle?'

'Yes, but that was menopause, according to her husband. She was a bit depressed for a while, but then she came out of it.'

'Sometimes a coincidence is just a coincidence,' Joanna said.

Gascoyne was in before Slider on Saturday, and came to his door before he'd got his coat off. 'I've found something, guv,' he said.

'You've traced Sir John's car on Tuesday?'

'Not yet. But I've looked at the station car park cameras, and he didn't park there any time on Tuesday, so it looks as though he did drive up.'

'Unless he went from a different station. We still have to find some evidence he was in London.'

'Yes, guv. But then I had another thought. So I rang round some car wash places. I found the one nearest his house that he usually uses, called Diamond Hand Car Wash and Valeting, in Oxford Road, and he had it done last Friday. Expensive service. They come and fetch it and bring it back. He's not had it done there since then. Then I looked a bit further afield. There's one in Fulmer, which is between Denham and Burnham Beeches, called Clean Me, and when they checked their credit card slips, there it was. He had the car washed and valeted on Wednesday. Time on the slip is 1.42. He stopped on the way back from golf to get the car cleaned.'

He looked at Slider with the hopeful, tail-wagging expression of a Labrador that's just brought you the newspaper. Slider wanted to say, *good boy*.

'It's something, isn't it, guv?' Gascoyne urged. 'According to Diamond, he has the car cleaned most Fridays. But on Wednesday he goes to a different one that he's never used before. Wrong day, wrong place. There must be a reason.'

'I'll give you that much. It's suggestive. We can't ask Sir John about it, though.'

'Can I go to Fulmer, see if they noticed anything?'

'Yes, but be discreet. Remember he's a public figure, and if any gossip gets about, we'll get the blame.'

Swilley came to the door with a print-out. 'I've got the bank statement, boss,' she said.

'Anything interesting?'

'Couple of things. For one, she takes two hundred and fifty cash out every Tuesday lunchtime in Notting Hill.'

'Presumably she has to have some cash.'

'Yes, but I've looked back over the past year. She takes out cash five hundred at a time, only at random intervals. There's no pattern to it – it averages about once every three or four weeks. But just since January, there's this two-fifty *as well*, and always on the Tuesday from the same cashpoint.'

'Conclusion?'

'The Coelho woman said since January she's been dashing off to lunch, not going out with the girls. It's got to be something to do with that.'

'Two-fifty isn't enough for blackmail,' Slider mused.

'No, and anyway, she wasn't unhappy or worried on Tuesday, like she'd be if she was being blackmailed. Excited, rather.'

'On the other hand, it's a lot for lunch. Unless you lunched at the Ritz.'

'But she didn't,' Swilley said with satisfaction. 'She paid for lunch on Tuesday with her bank card at a restaurant called Polpo in Drury Lane—'

'Covent Garden!'

'Yes, boss. And she's done the same thing every Tuesday for the past nine weeks.'

'Thank God for that,' Slider said. 'Now we can stop searching the haystack for needles. I wonder who she met there.'

'Well, it wasn't Josh Milo,' Swilley said. 'Maybe it was her dad.'

A surprising number of restaurants in London were called Polpo. 'It's not as if it's an attractive name,' Slider said.

'Not an attractive thing,' Atherton said. 'You name me any octopus that's ever got into the final of Miss World. Or any beauty contest, for that matter.'

'There's the knobbly tentacles contest at Butlin's,' said Slider. 'But the prize for that is only six quid.'

Slider had worked in Central at the beginning of his career. The middle of London was such a tourist destination, and with such astronomical, Russian-oligarch property prices, that he had always marvelled at how many ordinary people still lived there: in tiny bedsits above shops, council flats hidden behind the main thoroughfares, and the many Trust blocks that had somehow survived from Victorian days. And to serve their needs, a surprising number of small shops had also survived. Polpo in Drury Lane sat next to an old-fashioned hardware shop that would have fitted right into any town centre anywhere in the land, while on its other side was a tiny chemist's. Polpo itself was small and shabby, and the fascia board looked hand-painted: on a dim green background, an anthropomorphized octopus in faded pink grinned and beckoned, as though being chopped up, fried and eaten was just *loads* of fun.

It was closed at this hour, but there was a light on some-where in the depths, and the sense of someone moving about. Slider rapped on the glass door, and after a pause a tall, dark young man ambled up. Slider held up his warrant card. The young man stared at it like a dog looking at a quadratic equation. Slider pointed to the word POLICE at the top, where-upon his confusion cleared and he fumbled the door open.

'Nothing to worry about, we just need some information,' Slider said reassuringly. 'What's your name?'

'Gino,' said the lad. He made a huge mental effort at deduction. 'D'you want to come in?'

The restaurant was small, and in need of refurbishment. The lino was worn thin in several places, the dull green paint of the walls needed a fresh coat, and the plastic ivy and roses that clambered up the panels of trellis affixed to them were faded and dusty, quite apart from being just awful. But it looked and smelled clean, with red undercloths on each table, fresh white naps, and sparkling glasses and cutlery laid for the next service. To one side was a small bar and service point. Everything there seemed neat and orderly, and the light they had seen on was over it, winking in the polished chrome of the coffee machine.

The lad saw Slider looking at the machine, and said, 'Get you a coffee?' Without waiting for an answer, he went behind the bar and turned the machine on.

'I'd like to talk to the owner, or manager,' Slider said. 'I'm guessing that's not you.'

'That's me grandad,' he said, relief in his voice. His accent was all London. 'He's upstairs. I'll get him.' And he disap-peared through a doorway at the back.

'Family business,' Atherton commented. 'That'll be how they manage to survive. Endless supply of cousins coming over to work for peanuts while they learn English and have an exciting time living in London.'

'And possibly good food?' said Slider.

'It's easy to do good Italian food,' said Atherton. 'Simple, cheap ingredients, readily available just about anywhere. That's why you'll find an Italian restaurant in every city.'

'I like Italian food,' Slider said.

'I wasn't criticising. Tomatoes, herbs and cheese – what's not to like?'

There was a sound of feet descending stairs, and a short, round man appeared with the lad behind him. He was wearing black work trousers, and a white shirt open at the neck, showing a little forest of white hair. He had a shiny dome with neat white hair round the sides, a wide, brown, large-nosed, much-lined face, and merry dark eyes almost hidden in the creases. He came down on them with hand held out, and if the smile was professional, it was no less attractive. His teeth were white and even, and he brought a whiff of a pleasant aftershave with him.

'Gianfranco Uberti,' he announced. 'Polpo is my restaurant. This is my grandson, also a Gianfranco, so we call him Gino for short. What can I do for you gentlemen? But first, some coffee! Gino, you didn't give the gentlemen coffee?'

Gino muttered something in Italian, and Uberti made a flipping motion with his hand as though rapping the boy up the side of his head as he replied. He turned back to his visitors. 'He's young,' he apologized, 'but he learns. And he's already a good barista. How do you like your coffee?'

Slider deemed it easier to go along with this than refuse and elicit protests and more invitations, so he said, 'Espresso, if it's no trouble.' Atherton nodded agreement.

'No trouble! Of course it's no trouble. The machine does the work. Cost me five thousand pounds, that machine, and that was second-hand, so it should be good.'

Actually, it was Gino who did the work, while Uberti urged them to sit at the nearest table, rolled himself into a seat at the end, and talked about traffic and parking restrictions and thanked God his lunchtime trade was mostly office workers. His voice was warm and pleasant with a rolling Italian accent. When the coffee was finally placed before them, along with a single wrapped Biscoff in each saucer, he placed his hands flat on the table in a gesture of getting down to business, and said, 'How can I help you gentlemen?'

'We are interested in a woman who we believe was a regular customer of yours,' Slider began. 'We know she had lunch here last Tuesday, because it appears on her bank statement that she paid with a debit card.'

Uberti beamed. 'Yes, we try to discourage credit cards. Why pay fees if you don't have to? Our regulars are usually willing to use debit card. We are a small, family restaurant, good food at low prices, we have to keep costs down where we can. Fifty years, Polpo has been here. People know what they will get when they come to Polpo. A warm Italian welcome, and home-cooked food, like Mamma used to make.'

Slider noticed Gino wince slightly at the promo, and gathered that it was something his grandfather said all too often for his taste. 'The woman we're interested in,' he said, as Atherton pushed the photo across, 'is Felicity Holland.'

Uberti took the picture and said at once, 'Oh yes, I know her. Beautiful lady. She comes here regularly. Beautiful, beautiful – a lady of class. Always has wine. Always leaves *una mancia generosa*.' His eyelid flickered in a ghostly wink. Then his face was serious. 'What do you want to know?'

'She was here last Tuesday?'

'Yes. For lunch.'

'Alone?'

'No.' He looked at them carefully. 'You are serious policemen, not private investigators? This is not about a divorce?'

Slider came clean. 'She is missing. We are trying to trace her last movements.'

Now he was all seriousness. The jolly host was set aside. 'Missing. That is bad. Every Tuesday, for many weeks, she comes. Maybe eight, nine weeks. Each time she makes the reservation for next week. The table in the corner, she likes.' He gestured to it. 'Always she meets the same man.'

'Describe him.'

'Medium height. Slim. Dark hair. Stubble on the face. A little untidy – not a smart dresser. Not like her. She is truly elegant. I wonder sometimes . . . But love, you cannot argue with it.'

'Love?' Slider queried. Uberti shrugged. 'Do you know his name?'

'No. I know her name from the debit card, that is all.'

'Do they arrive together?'

'No, she comes on time. He is always late. But she waits, watching the door for him, and when he comes . . .' He lifted his hands in an expansive gesture. 'A lamp is lit inside.'

Gino muttered something in Italian that caused Uberti to frown. Meeting Slider's enquiring look, he said, 'Gino thinks it is sad, pathetic, a woman of her age with a younger man. He is young himself. He will learn in time that age is a number the heart does not recognize.'

'The man's younger than her?' Atherton asked. 'What age would you say?'

'I would say – thirty-five to forty. Maybe he looks older than he is because he is not smart, not well dressed. She is beautiful and looks younger than she is, but I have been close when I have served her, and I believe she is around fifty-five. Am I right? Gino thinks that should not be allowed, an older woman loving a younger man. He would not care, of course, if it was an older man with a younger woman, but there is nothing so critical as youth. He will learn.'

'She's fifty-three,' said Atherton. 'What makes you think she loves him?'

'Oh, the way she looks at him. She can't take her eyes from him. Wanting to touch him all the time – a little touch on the arm or the hand. She listens to him with all her heart in her face, and laughs at his jokes. Yes, it is love all right.'

'And what about the man? Is he in love with her?'

Uberti smiled a little ruefully. 'I must confess I don't look at his face so much – too much I want to look at her! But yes, it is love. They are very close. They talk and talk, very interested in each other. But she always pays.' He shrugged. 'Toy boy. It happens. Does not mean to say it is bad. If there is happiness on both sides, who is to say it's wrong?' A grunt from behind him made him add, 'Except for Gino.'

Slider looked at the lad, and he felt obliged to defend himself. 'It's not like Grandad says. She's a nice lady, she's always friendly and nice, and she tips. I don't like to see someone take advantage of her.'

'You think this man's doing that?'

Gino shrugged, sliding his eyes away as if not wanting to get involved. 'You can see she's got money. And he's scruffy.' He drew a breath and added sotto voce, 'He ought to make an effort.'

Uberti put his hands flat on the table again. 'But why don't you see for yourself? They will be on the camera. The tape lasts a week before it records over itself.'

'You have a security camera?' Atherton said, in the sort of tone that suggested he might have mentioned that before.

'On the door at the front, and the back, in case of break-ins.' He used his hands to heave himself to his feet. 'Come, I show you.'

Through the doorway at the back was a narrow passage, with the lavatories on the left, leading to the kitchen at the back. A doorless opening on the right gave on to the stairs. Uberti mounted nimbly, only rolling a little. At the top was another dining room, with tables set out but not laid, and a further door at the end led into a small office. The security camera had its own flatscreen, with a split shot showing the front and back doors.

'You can't see the people at the tables,' Slider noted. The camera, mounted over the bar, showed the door and only the corner of the table nearest it.

'Customers don't want to be spied on,' Uberti said, with a hint of indignation. 'Anyone who goes in or out must use one of the doors. It is enough.'

Muttering to himself, he sat at the desk and pounded the keys, scrolled for the date, scrolled for the time, backed up, then froze the screen. 'There,' he said. 'Beautiful lady.'

It was obviously a good-quality system, because the image was clear, of Felicity Holland in the doorway, smiling in response, presumably, to the welcome. 'This is your lady all right,' he said.

'It is,' Slider confirmed.

'Now, can we see the man?' said Atherton.

Uberti advanced the recording until he had a clear image.

Slider and Atherton stared at a man, yes, in his mid-thirties, probably, with dark hair that needed cutting, an unremarkable face, light eyes, probably blue, wearing creased chinos, loafers and a navy sweater with the sleeves shoved back halfway up the forearms.

'Can you print that for me?' Slider asked.

'Sure,' said Uberti, and did a screen grab. The printer in the corner groaned into action. 'I do you two – one each.'

'Did they leave together?' Atherton asked.

'Yes. You want to see?' It was not such a good image, of course, being their back views. They saw Uberti holding open the door, the woman walking out first, the man after her, and turning left and out of sight. The time on the cue was 2.45 p.m.

'And you don't know his name, or anything about him? Where he lives?' Atherton asked. 'Did you hear what she called him? A name? Or just "darling"?'

'I never hear her call him anything. When I come to the table, she stops talking, which is correct. But I ask my other staff if they ever hear anything.'

'Yes, thank you,' Slider said. 'Please let me know if you find out anything else about him, or remember anything that might help.' He gave him a card.

Uberti escorted them downstairs, where they noted some more staff had come in, someone bulky and shaven-headed with his back to them in the kitchen, and a plump, dark young woman talking in a low voice to Gino in Italian. They were escorted by the patron to the door, where he said with a thoughtful frown, 'You say she is missing. But she has booked the same table for next week. Maybe she comes.'

'If she does, you'll let me know at once?'

'Of course. And if I see him again,' said Uberti. But he didn't sound as if he thought that were likely.

'A toy boy,' Atherton said as they walked away. 'Well, who'd a thunk it?'

'It happens. You've been known to date women younger than yourself on occasion,' Slider pointed out.

Atherton winced. He would never forget the first time a

young woman had dumped him, saying he was too old for her. Something had died in him that day. 'Gino's right,' he said, to cover up. 'He ought to have smartened himself up.'

'Well, at least he wasn't wearing trainers,' Slider said. 'That's something.'

'So, do we think she's holed up with him somewhere? Too blissed-out-stroke-ashamed-of-herself to let hubby know she's OK? Overcome with a sudden tsunami of passion on Tuesday and decided on the spur of the moment not to go home? Or is he the villain of the piece who's got her tied up somewhere? Although,' he answered himself, 'if she's his willing bed-mate, why would he want to capture her? It can't be for blackmail purposes, since he hasn't asked for anything. I suppose there could have been an accident – her elderly heart gives out mid-rumpy-pumpy and he panics and conceals the body.'

'Elderly?' Slider queried. 'I shall remind you of that when you're fifty-three.'

'Doesn't have to be heart. She could fall out of bed and bang her head. Or be doing it in some unsustainable place, like the edge of a cliff or the top branch of an ancient oak tree.'

'Have you finished?'

'Nearly. Or – and this is my least favourite option – her disappearance could be nothing to do with Toy Boy. We only know she had lunch with him in Polpo. We don't know where she went next.'

'That's sadly true. I really don't like that name, Polpo. Makes me think of polyps.'

'And it could still be Sir John. Maybe he found out about Toy Boy – could even have bumped into them if he *was* in town on Tuesday. We know he has strict ideas. He could have lost his temper and done 'er in.' Atherton gave Slider a darkling look. 'There, you got me all excited thinking we'd solved it, and it turns out it's not a solution at all.'

'It's a jumping-off point, is what it is,' said Slider. 'Now we just have to find out who he is, where he lives, and what he did with her.'

'Oh, is that all?'

TEN

Rather Fun and Wholly Toast

Pattering footsteps behind them and a call of 'Hello-o?' made them stop and turn.

The plump, dark young woman from the restaurant was hurrying towards them. She stopped in front of them and looked from Atherton to Slider. 'Detective?' she said.

Slider gave their names and showed his warrant card. 'And you are?'

'Maria,' she said. 'Maria Dellucci. I am waitress at Polpo. I am second cousin of Mr Uberti.' Her accent was Italian. She had a round face and a large nose, giving her a perhaps unfortunate resemblance to the patron, but her thick, shiny black hair and lustrous dark eyes gave her enough of the illusion of beauty to be going on with. She seemed to be about nineteen, dressed in waitress black skirt and white shirt, black stockings and sensible flat shoes with thick soles.

'You have something to tell us?' Slider asked.

'About the man – the man you ask about.'

'That's our car, there,' Slider indicated. 'Come and sit inside and tell us about it.'

He got into the back seat with her, while Atherton got in the front and swivelled round to face them.

'I am here on work visa,' she explained first of all, with an anxious look, as though expecting to be quizzed and perhaps hauled off to jail. 'My mother, Mr Uberti's cousin, she work here too when she was my age, and my aunt Paola, and cousin Vinnie and cousin Ellie.'

'That's all right,' Slider said soothingly, 'tell us what you know about this man. Did you serve him on Tuesday?'

'No, Mr Uberti like to serve that table himself because of the lady. But I was there. I see them every week, the lady and the man, and Mr Uberti, he like the lady, he talk about her very much, and this younger man who is her lover.' She made a little shrug. 'Mr Uberti is very romantic.'

'You don't think they are in love?'

'I think she is in love with him. I watch them as I work. But he – not so much. But you can see she is rich lady. I think he is nice to her for her money.' Another little shrug.

This was nothing new or useful. Slider caught Atherton's roll of the eyes. 'But can you tell us anything more about him? His name, or where he lives?' he asked.

'I don't know his name, but yesterday I see him come out of Ritchie's. Ritchie's is music shop down there.' She gestured back down the street. 'He bought something. He had box in his hand, small box like this.' She made a two-way gesture which seemed to imply something the size of a bag of sugar. Then she looked at them eagerly, to check if they got the point. 'It is not shop for everybody. Special shop for musician. So maybe they know him. Maybe he's musician. Musicians know each other, yes? My cousin Tino is musician, all his friends musicians.' She shrugged, and added in parenthesis, 'Tino never have no money. He would like rich lady to fall in love with him.'

'That's very helpful, Miss Dellucci. We'll certainly look into it. Thank you for letting us know,' said Slider.

'I go now?' she asked, and waved a hand. 'I must be working.'

'Yes, of course. And thanks again. We know where to find you if we need you.'

Ritchie's was several doors down from Polpo in Drury Lane, and stood out from its neighbours by having its surrounding stonework and all its woodwork painted a startling dark blue. In the window was a display of guitars, acoustic and electric, and other stringed instruments – Slider recognized a banjo and what he thought was a ukulele and . . . was that a *lute*? But behind the window in the brightly lit store was a wide range of goods: electric keyboards, sheet music, albums and CDs, playing and recording equipment, sound decks and a lot of obviously technical gear that Slider didn't recognize. On the fascia board was painted RITCHIE'S in large capitals, with the strapline under it, *Everything You Need To Get Playing!* Above it, on the first floor, there was a display window across the whole width, also brightly lit, so there was presumably more equipment up there, though they couldn't see anything except some music stands. It was plainly a serious shop, and Slider and Atherton exchanged a glance of hope.

The tall, gangling young man in charge had a neat royale beard, and dark hair shaved all round except for an elongated curly mat on the top, as though he had nodded off in the chair of a vindictive barber. He had three silver rings in one ear, and was dressed all in black, body-hugging T-shirt and jeans, the whole ensemble ending in large engineer boots that made his skinny legs look as though they might snap off at the ankle in a high wind.

'Are you Ritchie?' Slider asked, showing his warrant.

'What? No!' He seemed indignant. 'Ritchie is Ritchie Blackmore. Greatest guitarist who ever lived.' He didn't end the sentence with 'man', but it hung on the air unspoken.

'I'll never forget his playing of Beethoven's "Ode to Joy",' Atherton said, getting him back on side. Slider gave him a look, which he answered with one that said *don't go there*.

'What's your name?' Slider asked, and managed reciprocally not to end *his* sentence with 'son'.

'Xavier Thompson,' the young man said. 'My friends call me X.'

He said it so proudly that Slider was glad he was not a friend and therefore would never have to break his heart. 'Would you have a look at this photo, Mr Thompson, and tell me if you recognize this man?'

Thompson frowned over the photo for a good few seconds before saying, 'No-o, I don't think so. Maybe he looks a bit familiar. But it's so hard to tell from a photo, isn't it?'

'He bought something in your shop yesterday,' Atherton said.

But Thompson still looked puzzled. 'We get so busy, Fridays and Saturdays,' he said. 'Maybe Taylor served him.' He gestured to a girl with purple hair and a much ringed and studded face, helping a customer who was dithering over an acoustic guitar.

Despite the hardware, she seemed more on the ball than her boss. 'Yeah,' she said to the photo. 'It's that guy who comes in sometimes. He was here yesterday, X, remember? You served him. He bought a condenser mic and XLR cable. A good one.'

'Oh . . . yeah,' said Thompson vaguely.

'He talked like he's got his own studio set-up. I mean, he knew what he wanted. He's been in before,' she added to Slider, 'but I don't know his name.' Thompson made supportive noises, obviously still with no recollection, but she said intelligently, 'You can get his name from the credit card, can't you? That was an industry-standard Rode – hundred and fifty quid, so he must've paid by card.'

'Oh, yeah,' said Thompson, with purpose this time, and his giant boots twirled him round and carried him away to the office cubby-hole behind the counter, where eventually he unearthed the correct slip. 'This must be it.'

'That's it.' Taylor took it from him and handed it on to Atherton. 'I mean, all these numbers've got to mean something, haven't they? The credit card company'll be able to tell you his name, and stuff, won't they?'

'You're right,' Atherton said. 'Thanks. That's very helpful.'

She escorted them to the door, and Slider said, 'You say you've seen him in here before. Anything else you can tell us about him? Does he live round here?'

But she shook her head. 'I just recognized his face, that's all. People come to Ritchie's from all over – we're famous. We've got practice rooms upstairs and a recording set-up, people can make their own demo tapes and everything. There's tons of music shops in Soho, but everyone knows Ritchie's.'

'Even I do now,' Slider said. He gave her a smile that reconciled her to his extreme age and squareness.

She smiled back and said, 'Yeah.'

'Do you think he's a musician?'

'I couldn't say. Professionals come in, but then there's ordinary public too. He could be anybody.'

'So, it seems Felicity's got a bit of a thing for musicians,' Atherton said as Slider eased the car through the byways of

Soho. Having worked in Central in the past, he knew the back routes like a taxi driver.

'Why not?' Slider said. 'So have I.'

'No, you've a got a thing for one particular musician.'

'But as she said, we don't know that he's a musician.'

'True. He might just be a rich nerd who bought the mic to do his own podcasts, or host a karaoke party.'

'Rich?'

'A hundred and fifty quid for a mic just to mess around with?'

'People are always willing to spend on their particular interest. If he's rich, what's his interest in Felicity Holland?'

'A bit richer never hurts.'

'And why do they meet in that particular restaurant? Why not Rules or The Ivy or Frenchie's?'

'Maybe they like Italian.'

'Café Murano? Why that obscure place, practically a workman's café?'

'Well, if they're having an affair, maybe because it *is* obscure. She needs to be discreet.'

'But why Covent Garden at all?'

'It's central, easy to find, and she knows the area – must do, all the ballet she must have seen at the Opera House.' He looked sideways at Slider. 'You're not buying it?'

Slider sighed. 'Oh, I don't know. I'm probably over-thinking. Being stuck on this at all is damaging my sense of proportion.'

'I know what you mean,' Atherton said. 'Never mind, there's nothing more we can do until we get the information from Visa, so we can have the rest of the weekend off. You'll have a fabulous meal at my place tonight and meet the lovely Stephanie, and that will restore you to mental health.'

'I'm just hoping when we get back that we'll hear she's come home again.'

His wish seemed about to be fulfilled when they went in from the yard and were greeted by Nicholls, the uniform sergeant on duty, who said, 'There's someone upstairs waiting to see you, Bill. Mr Holland.'

'Upstairs?' Slider said, frowning.

'Couldn't leave him out there in the waiting room,' Nicholls said. His west coast Scottish accent was as soft as a Highland mist. He had a beautiful singing voice – he was the star of the Met Police musical society's operatic productions – and always claimed it was having his vocal chords marinaded in damp Caledonian air that had given it its quality. 'Mr Holland is best pals with the commissioner, so it seems, and doesn't mind who knows it. But two of your boys have got him bracketed.'

'Well, I hope he's come to tell us his wife's turned up safe and sound,' said Slider.

'He didn't look like the man who'd come to wring your hand with gratitude,' Nutty warned.

'No, I'm still waiting to meet that man,' Slider said patiently. 'I'm hoping he makes it before I reach retirement age.'

Holland was in the 'soft room' – the interview room for non-suspects – and first glance established that he was as relaxed as a bee in a bottle. He was pacing up and down, watched impassively by LaSalle and Fathom – both tall, but otherwise so disparate in their conformation that when standing side by side they looked like the number ten.

Holland whirled on Slider as soon as he appeared. 'I've been waiting here over half an hour, with these two idiots!' he exclaimed. The epithet slid off the detective constables like duck off a greased plate. The Job being what it was, it was hardly possible to insult a policeman with anything less than a four-pound lump hammer. 'They don't seem to know *anything*!'

'I didn't know you were here, sir,' Slider said. 'I've only just this moment got back.'

'Why are you gallivanting about while my wife is in deadly danger?' Holland demanded. He looked as though it had been a rough few days since they last saw him. His face was haggard, his eyes pouched with sleepless nights, and while you could not say he was exactly unkempt, there was a suggestion of un-ironedness about the collar of his shirt. 'Why haven't you found her? What are you *doing*?'

'We were out following up a lead,' Slider said. 'Normally

I would have been here co-ordinating matters, but as I was requested by Sir David to investigate your wife's disappearance *personally*, I went myself.'

'And? What have you discovered? Do you know where she is?'

'We are doing everything we can, sir, I assure you of that. We have so little to go on.'

'So you've done nothing since Tuesday? She's been missing for four days, and you're no closer to finding her? She's in desperate, mortal danger and you simply *don't care*!'

'I assure you we do care, very much,' Slider said with sincerity. 'We have traced her to Covent Garden, where she had lunch on Tuesday. We have identified the restaurant, but where she went after leaving it is still unknown.' He nodded to Atherton, who produced the photograph of the unknown man.

'Do you recognize this person, Mr Holland?' Atherton asked.

Holland took the picture with an odd reluctance – what caricature of a salivating monster did he expect to be confronted with? – and looked at it. For an instant, Slider thought he did recognize the man – there seemed to be the hint of a reaction in the wood of his face – but he handed it back, shaking his head.

'No. I don't know him. Who is it?'

'The man she had lunch with.'

'Well, who is he? One of her pottery class friends?'

'We are working on identifying him,' Slider said. 'Are you sure she didn't say who she was having lunch with? Did she never mention the name of anyone in particular?'

'No. What are you suggesting?' He seemed to reach for his anger like someone grabbing for an umbrella in the rain. 'Are you saying my wife was having an affair with this man?'

'I didn't say anything of the sort, sir.'

'I know how you people think. It's how your minds work. My wife would never do anything like that. Someone has snatched her, and they're holding her prisoner. I've been telling you that from the beginning. Someone took her, and if you don't find her soon it'll be too late. If it isn't already.' He made a harsh sound, like a sob, and covered his face with his

hands for a moment. From behind them, he said, 'Her handbag.'
When he emerged, his expression had lignified again. 'You
found her handbag in the woods. Why aren't you searching
for her there? Searching for her . . .' He evidently couldn't
say the word 'body'.

'These things take time, sir,' Slider said, rather than go
into it.

'But can you think of any reason her handbag would be in
the woods if she wasn't there?' he demanded. 'You must have
records of the men who do this sort of thing – why aren't you
investigating them?'

'We are looking into that and every other possible avenue.
We will inform you the moment we get any information, and
if you'll forgive us, we will get on with it right now. One of
my men will show you out.' Holland opened his mouth to
protest some more, and Slider, contrary to his usual instincts
never to touch members of the public, thrust out his hand,
forcing Holland to partake of a valedictory shake. 'And please
believe me,' Slider said, using the hand to turn Holland towards
the door, 'I won't rest until I find your wife.'

He was rather afraid that might be true.

'That went well,' Atherton said cheerily as they walked back
to Slider's room. 'He didn't like looking at that picture of Toy
Boy.'

'Well, would you?'

'He's been adamant from the beginning that she was
snatched by a random nutter. Do you think he knows deep
down that she's left him for someone more interesting and
he's subconsciously covering up?'

'It's possible.'

'Possible. Likely. Probable. What's the difference?' Atherton
said airily.

'There's the handbag, as he pointed out.'

'The handbag is weird,' Atherton agreed. 'The only scenario
it fits is her body being dumped in the woods.'

'If only we could find any evidence she'd been anywhere
near them since she was ten.'

As they turned in at the door, Jenrich came in from the CID

room, saying, 'Oh, boss, Mr Holland's . . .' She saw his expression. 'You've seen him.'

'Yes,' said Slider, and that was all there was to say about that.

She shrugged it off. 'So what's happening about the search? Are we on again tomorrow?'

'No.' Slider handed her the credit-card print-out. 'You can get this off to Visa with all urgency, but until we know who he is and have a chance to interview him, I don't think there's any point in more general searching. She may be with him, if she's having a torrid affair. Or he can tell us where she was going next, which gives us a jumping-off point.'

'Or if he's a sex fiend and he's holding her captive, it gets interesting,' said Atherton.

'Or if he's killed her,' Jenrich said flatly, 'at least we know where we are. And we can do some proper police work.'

'It's all proper police work,' he corrected her gently.

'Yeah. Just not ours,' she said, and went away to her desk.

'Well, I'll be off now,' Atherton said. 'I've got cooking to do. Eight o'clock?'

'Yes, fine,' Slider said. 'Can I bring anything?'

'Just Joanna. And an appetite.'

Given that there was nothing more he could do right then to find Felicity Holland, Slider got his head down at his desk and tackled some of the accumulation of other work. It was Gascoyne who called him back to reality, appearing at his open door with a polite knock. Slider stretched, aware of time having passed. 'What time is it?'

'Quart' to six, sir.' Gascoyne had come to them from uniform a couple of years ago and had never quite developed the 'guv' habit.

'Oh Nora, I'd better think about getting home. Why are you still here?'

'I got stuck in looking at car parks,' Gascoyne explained. 'You'd never think there were so many near Covent Garden, when you think how crowded it is, and the price of real estate.'

'I expect they make up for it by being expensive.'

'You're right, sir. You could rent a flat cheaper than a parking space, seems to me. Anyway . . .' There was a tremor of excitement in his voice.

'You've found Sir John's car?'

Gascoyne beamed. 'He *was* in London that day. He left the Jag in the NCP in Parker Street.'

'Parker Street,' Slider exclaimed, interested despite himself.

Gascoyne nodded. 'Which is a turning off Drury Lane, as you know, sir. And what's more, I've found out from the internet that his club – you know he told his cleaner he'd have supper at his club? – his club is the De Vere, which is in Wild Street.'

'Which runs parallel to Drury Lane,' said Slider.

'Yes, and there's no cut-through from Parker Street. To get to the club, he'd have to walk down Parker Street, left into Drury Lane and along it, left into Great Queen Street and right into Wild Street.' He looked to see if Slider got the point.

'So there is a possibility that he could have bumped into Felicity on that walk. Have you got times?' Slider asked.

'Yes, sir. His motor arrived at the garage at eleven fifty-nine, and left again at four-oh-two.'

'Mrs Holland left Polpo with her friend at two forty-five,' said Slider.

'He could still have bumped into her. He was in the area.'

'It's a big area. We don't even know where he lunched. He could have gone in the other direction from the garage and never seen her at all.'

'But if he lunched at the club,' Gascoyne urged, 'he could've been leaving it after lunch and bumped into her in the street, and taken her back to the car for some reason . . .'

'Cameras in the garage?'

'The barrier works on number plate recognition, so I only know the Jag was there. There's a camera covering the entrance, but it's out of order – has been for a week.'

'Wait a minute,' Slider said. 'You said the car left the garage again just after four?'

'Yes, sir. And never went back, not on Tuesday. He said he was staying in town all day and having supper at his club, but he didn't go back to the same car park, or any of the others nearby. I haven't been able to find out yet where he did go in the afternoon. If only we could ask him,' Gascoyne finished wistfully.

'Well, we can't,' said Slider, his mind busy tracing the putative route to the De Vere. 'You know what else is in Wild Street?' he said. 'On the corner of Wild Street and Great Queen Street.'

'Yes, sir,' Gascoyne said. 'Freemason's Hall.'

Trust Gascoyne to know that. He suspected Gascoyne's dad was a mason. If you played golf with top coppers, it was logical . . . 'The United Grand Lodge of England,' Slider said. 'I wonder if Sir John is a member?'

'A lot of senior lawyers are,' Gascoyne said. 'Maybe that's where he was meeting someone on Tuesday, having lunch there.'

'There isn't a restaurant in the Freemason's Hall, is there? Wouldn't that be too much like fun?' Slider said, though nothing would really surprise him about what they got up to.

'Not a restaurant as such, sir, but there's a café and bar. It's open to the public as well as members. Light snacks, wraps and paninis and so on.'

'I can't see Sir John Aubrey-Harris settling for a toasted panini.' Especially not with members of the public swirling round, staring and chattering like magpies, maybe asking questions. 'Not when his club's just a step away.'

'No, sir. But that's maybe why he joined the De Vere in the first place, and not the Athenaeum, say. Or the Savage. Or one of the other nobby ones.'

Slider drummed his fingers on the desk in thought. 'So he went in to town to have lunch with someone, parked from twelve till four, then drove off, we know not where.' He looked up at Gascoyne's fair, favourite-nephew face. 'I could bear to know where he went. There's probably nothing in it except coincidence, but he did say he'd be in town all day, and if he wasn't . . .'

'And there was that getting his car washed on the Wednesday,' Gascoyne reminded him. 'After being right in the area where the handbag was found.'

'Probably just more coincidence.'

'But could I just find out from the De Vere club whether

he went back there on Tuesday? Whether he met anyone there? If he did have supper there that night, why didn't he park at any of the nearby garages?'

'No room, maybe?'

'There's generally room at night. It's daytime you can't get a space.'

'Yes, and why,' Slider said, having a little revolt, 'did he take the car in at all? If he was going to be in town all day, it would have made more sense to go in by train. Granted he's not bothered by astronomical car parking fees, but still. All right, you can make discreet enquiries at the club – but I *mean* discreet.'

'Yes, sir. You can trust me.'

'And keep looking for the Jag. You can have some more help with that on Monday, since we're not searching Covent Garden shop by shop.'

'Unless she comes back home in the meantime.'

'There is that,' said Slider.

ELEVEN
Vere the Boys Are

In the hierarchy of London clubs, there were very posh and less posh, and the very posh ones tended to be the ones that had resisted allowing women to become members. Make of that what you will, but the membership fees of those clubs amounted to serious biccies, and you had to pay a one-off joining fee of a serious order as well, to prove that you wanted to join badly enough. You probably also had to know someone, since just about anybody nowadays could turn out to have money, and that wasn't the point of club membership, not at all.

Gascoyne had a wife and teenage daughters to go home to, but with college looming he could do with a bit of overtime, and in any case, it was his wife's evening for selling beauty products from home, and he'd as soon not be there for that. Women found him attractive, and their house was too small for him easily to avoid her friends and customers when they swarmed on it. His wife only laughed when they flirted with him, but he didn't think it was right.

So he had a toasted panini and a cup of coffee in the café in Freemason's Hall, just out of interest, and then went along to the De Vere.

It was, as he had taken the time to find out, one of the very posh ones. In the Wiki listing, under 'Affiliation', it had 'science, medicine and the law', and his father, whom he had given a quick ring, had added that most senior judges were members, along with the top coppers and both arch-bishops, and that it was also, in his words, 'a little bit masonic'. It was fortunate, therefore, that it had a kitchen entrance round the back, since Gascoyne would probably not have got far via the discretion barrier of the front door, the hall porter and the club secretary.

It was lucky, too, that he found a large individual in a sous-chef toque lounging by the kitchen door having a crafty fag, and was able to get into conversation with him. He was tall, hefty and swarthy – so swarthy it was hard to tell if he had designer stubble or just stubble – but despite his alarming appearance he turned out to be disarmingly friendly and easy to talk to. He said his name was Blagoy, he was Bulgarian, but he had learned cooking as a child from his mother, who was French, and had cooked both French and traditional Bulgarian dishes. There was not much call for the latter in his present incarnation, but his ambition was to save up and open his own French-Bulgarian fusion restaurant, where the central feature would be a *cheverme* grill on which a whole pig or lamb would turn slowly all day, filling the restaurant with wonderful smells. If he had his restaurant right now, with Easter coming, it would be lamb, the traditional . . .

Gascoyne let him run long enough to make him grateful for the sympathy, then gently turned him to his own concerns. Blagoy listened intelligently, said he would make enquiries, but said it would take a while, so Gascoyne should come back later, when he took his break about nine o'clock. Now he would have to get back to work. He stamped out his cigarette end and went in, only to stick his head back out round the door and say, 'Wait!' and disappear. A few moments later he hurried out to press a foil-wrapped something into Gascoyne's hands.

'My *kozunak*. Chef let me make some to try out. Special Easter bread, sweet, with walnuts and raisins and rum. You will like.' Then he was gone.

To pass the time, Gascoyne walked down to Agar Street, to Charing Cross police station, where he could go up to the canteen and get a cup of tea to go with the *kozunak*, which turned out to be delicious. He could also have a yarn with anyone there he knew, and his acquaintance in the Job, thanks to his father, was extensive. Coppers get all too familiar with the conversation of those they work with every day, and are always ready for a bunny with someone with a new perspective, so he did not lack for a companion, and time flew. He had to drag himself away in the end to get back to the De Vere for nine o'clock.

The yard was occupied only by a furtive-looking kitchen porter having an even craftier fag, who started like a gazelle at the sight of Gascoyne and attempted to hide the cigarette behind him with a danger of setting fire to his shirt. Gascoyne calmed him down and tasked him with discreetly telling Blagoy he was here. Ten minutes later, Blagoy came out, looking fraught, to say it was not yet time for his break and they were very busy with a member's retirement bash.

'But I got a name for you,' he said, and passed over a slip of paper. 'Your man had lunch here Tuesday with this one in the dining room. Did not come in in the evening.'

'You're sure? It's important,' said Gascoyne. 'You're sure he didn't come in in the evening?'

'I'm sure. Milenka, she's a waitress here, friend of mine – she's Bulgarian too, gets lonely for the old country, so we talk a lot. I did her a favour when she first came, helped her with some papers, so she did me one back, got one of the porters to look at the register they sign when they come in. Fire regulations,' he added with a shrug. 'Your man was here for lunch, not in the evening. Now I must go, or I get the chop.'

He was gone, in a swirl of slightly stained whites and a lingering aroma of gravy. On the piece of paper, in the careful but oddly-looped capitals of the middle European, were the words: SIR NIGEL MULVANEY, HIGH COURT JUDGE.

'Something smells good,' Slider said over Joanna's shoulder as Atherton opened the door to them.

Atherton gave a modest smile. 'It's me. But thank you for mentioning.'

Joanna mock-punched his shoulder. 'You big girl! What is it – chicken?'

'Bless your nose. Chicken with preserved lemons. Ottolenghi calls it Bird of Paradise. You roast it, but before—'

'Drink first,' said a voice behind him. A face looked over his shoulder with a comical expression. 'Jim somehow makes recipes sound like pornography, and I don't know about you, but pornography always makes me thirsty.'

'Couldn't say about that.' Joanna gave a polite-company smile. 'I'm afraid we don't have a pornograph.'

Atherton slithered sideways to bring his guest to the fore. 'This is Stephanie. Stephanie – Joanna and Bill.'

'I know who they are, dummy,' Stephanie said cheerfully.

'Well, *excuse me* for introducing them properly!'

'You're cute when you go all Emily Post,' she said giving him a flashing grin and peck on the cheek. 'How do you do? It's lovely to meet you.'

Hands were shaken, they were drawn in, coats were taken, and Tiglath Pileser wound an ecstatic figure eight round Slider's legs, while Sredni Vashtar did his favourite ambush greeting by leaping from the curtain rail, where he had been teetering in anticipation, to land on Slider's shoulder. The Siamese was a considerably larger cat than when he had perfected the trick as a kitten, so a shoulder wasn't a large enough landing zone for safety, and he was forced to drive all his claws in hard to keep his position. Slider, manfully suppressing his cries of pain, reached up and unpicked him carefully and held him against his chest. Vash purred like a Rolls-Royce engine and pressed his head under Slider's chin in ecstasy.

'They haven't forgotten you,' Atherton remarked. 'Drinkie?' He moved away.

'You took that very well,' Stephanie remarked to Slider. 'The first time he did it to me I gave such a yell—'

'But if you startle him he only digs in harder,' Slider said.

'Yes, I found that out the hard way,' Stephanie agreed. 'He drew blood. Good job I like cats.'

'Fricasséed or casseroled?' Joanna enquired, accepting a glass of champagne from Atherton. 'What's the occasion?'

'If you think there has to be an occasion to drink champagne,' said Atherton, 'it marks you out as an unsophisticate.'

'That's not even a word,' Joanna objected.

'I bet it is,' said Atherton.

'Not as a noun.'

'An adjective can be a noun. What about "The meek shall inherit the earth"?'

'That's a collective. You wouldn't say "a meek"—'

'Let's you and me talk,' Stephanie said, drawing Slider aside ostentatiously. 'Do they often go on like this?'

'Invariably,' said Slider. He was gazing at Stephanie with

appreciation, and some amusement, touched with faint anxiety. She was younger, taller, more slenderly built, and her hair was longer, but to the connoisseur she had a definite look of Joanna about her.

The chicken was roast chicken but tasting as roast chicken never had in Slider's experience. Atherton explained that you chopped the preserved lemon with garlic and thyme and mashed them into softened butter, then eased the butter under the skin all over the bird before roasting. With it he served truffled mash and stir-fried Brussels sprouts.

'I am going to be as fat as a pig if I don't break off this relationship,' Stephanie commented as she consumed the feast with appreciation.

'Oh, are we having a relationship?' Atherton said. 'I'll have to give the bill to you, then,' he added to Slider. 'Can't charge for food in a relationship.'

'Why not? I'd charge you for surgery,' said Stephanie.

'But that's your profession. Cooking's only my hobby.'

'It's an essential part of your seduction technique,' Slider said.

'Snap him up,' Joanna advised Stephanie. 'Mine doesn't really cook, but his dad does the most delicious simple English dishes – shepherd's pie, macaroni cheese—'

'No talking about other people's cooking,' Atherton decreed.

'What's for pud?' Slider asked.

'Wait and see,' said Atherton sternly.

'Those who ask don't get,' said Stephanie. 'My grandmother used to say that. It was maddening, because if you didn't ask she'd say, "Oh, I thought you didn't want any."'

'In our house it was "those who don't grab don't get",' said Joanna. 'There were five of us.'

'Five of you?' Stephanie said. 'Boys or girls?'

'I have four sisters. Four sisters and one bathroom. That's where I learned to dance.'

Slider caught Atherton's eye. It was all supremely easy.

Pud was a baked cheesecake with Armagnac-soaked prunes. 'How did you have time to do all this?' Joanna marvelled.

'I made the cheesecake last night. It's always better the next day. The chicken only takes an hour.'

'When I get home from work, I'm too bashed to want to cook.'

'Ah, but your work is creative. Cooking *is* my creativity. I hear you've got some John Williams sessions coming up?'

'Concerts, actually, but we hope there'll be sessions afterwards. It'd be a waste not to have a CD. More work for us – and more lovely lolly. And it's lovely stuff to play, too.'

'You like John Williams's music?' Stephanie said.

'It's the real deal,' Joanna said. 'If there was any market for classical music these days, he could have written symphonies and concertos. He could have been the Tchaikovsky of the age. As it is, he had to make his career in film.'

'Lucky for film,' Atherton said. The phone rang, and he got up to answer it. 'Hello. Oh, yes, hi. Yes, he's here.' He handed the phone to Slider. 'Gascoyne.'

While Slider took the call, Joanna explained to Stephanie that – though Gascoyne's father's name was Harry – he was always called Bob, because 'bob' was the slang word for an old shilling, and the shilling was the coin that used to get put into a prepayment gas meter – hence, gas coin. By the time she'd got through all that, Slider was back with them.

'Well, well, well,' he said. 'It seems the esteemed Sir John Aubrey-Harris is not above telling porky pies. He did not have supper at the De Vere club on Tuesday. He left there after lunch and didn't return.'

'The De Vere?' Stephanie said. 'A lot of senior medical people are members there.'

'I thought *you* were senior medical people,' Atherton said.

'But I don't have a penis, dear.'

'And thank God for it, say I.'

'My department head at the Cross is a member,' she went on. 'Sir Cyril Kinnear. We call him Sir Serial Killer.'

'Does he have bad outcomes, then?' Joanna asked.

'Not noticeably, but he has a serial killer personality with juniors. Likes to impress everyone under him with his greatness, and since everybody in the world is under him, he gets a lot of practice. Who's this Sir John person?'

'The missing woman's father. And a retired barrister of note. Haven't you been telling her about the case?' Joanna asked Atherton.

'We've had other things to talk about. And it's not really a case.'

'Getting to be more of one, the longer it goes on,' Slider said. 'Most missing persons come home after two days, or at least make contact.'

'So – what? You think something bad's happened to her?' said Stephanie.

'It always has to be considered.'

'A retired barrister – and his own daughter? You surely can't be suspecting him of anything?'

'Well, it's true that most people lie out of sheer dumb habit,' Slider said, 'but sometimes they are covering up something.'

'What are you going to do about him?' Joanna asked.

'Gascoyne will carry on trying to trace his car after it left the garage near the club on Tuesday. He's going in tomorrow.'

'On a Sunday?' Joanna queried, hoping it didn't mean he'd go in to supervise.

'He needs the overtime. McLaren will be on in the morning, so he can help him.' The department only had a token presence on Sundays, unless there was an emergency.

'How will tracing the car help?' Stephanie asked.

'Sometimes with an ANPR camera shot you can see who's inside it. And even if we don't get a shot, if he can find out where Sir John went, there's a chance of asking questions at his destination about whether his daughter was with him.'

'It all sounds terribly laborious,' Stephanie said.

'It is,' said Slider, 'but that's police work for you. For thrills and spills, you have to join the fire service.'

'Or become a surgeon,' Atherton said. 'Stephanie's going to be doing more facial reconstruction work. There's a new plastics guy at the Cross who wants to expand the department.'

'I've never quite understood why ENT and plastics are connected,' Joanna said, looking invitingly at Stephanie.

'It starts with the face, which is the area I'm in anyway,' said Stephanie. 'I already do quite a bit of nose and jaw work,

and I've given a child a new windpipe. It's the serious reconstruction I'm interested in, post-cancer, and burn and accidents.
You have the chance to give someone their life back.'

As she talked, and Joanna listened and asked intelligent
questions, Slider caught Atherton's eye, and Atherton grinned
triumphantly. *Got a good one, eh?* You have, Slider thought;
but do you see the resemblance? And if so, how much does
it matter?

They were alone together for a moment at the end of the
evening, when Joanna and Stephanie were upstairs. Atherton
gave Slider a whimsical raised eyebrow to cover up the
seriousness of the question, and said, 'Well? Do you like
her?'

'Yes,' said Slider, and left it at that. 'More importantly, do
you?'

The barrier dropped with a crash. 'I'm mad about her,' he
said. 'She's . . . I find her . . .' He searched for the right
expression, then said – shamefacedly, because men didn't use
that sort of language – 'She enchants me. I never know what
she's going to say next. It's never boring.'

'I know what you mean,' said Slider, who felt that way
about Joanna.

'I find,' Atherton said diffidently, 'that I want to be with
her all the time. I never felt like that before. Even with Emily,
I was glad to get away for a bit, have a bit of male conversation – you know? But now I feel . . .' He paused, thinking,
staring at nothing. Tiglath Pileser ambled up to him, squinted
up beguilingly and made a piercing remark about leftovers in
the kitchen.

Slider waited a moment, then said, 'Well, it's a promising
start.'

Atherton came back from his reverie and evidently felt
enough unburdening had gone on for the self-respecting male.
He scooped up Tig and said, 'Oh crap, did I cover up the
chicken carcase?' and hurried towards the kitchen.

In the car on the way home, Joanna said sleepily, 'I liked her.'

'Me too,' said Slider. 'Did you notice—?'

'What?'

'Nothing.' He decided it was a can of worms, and anyway, maybe it was only him who saw a resemblance.

'That chicken!' Joanna said after a while. 'I think I might try that, when it's my turn to do Sunday dins. Or tell your dad about it when it's his turn.'

'It's a bit exotic for dad.'

'You underestimate him. He likes trying new things.' A pause. 'He seems smitten.'

Married couples can follow each other's shortcuts. Slider knew she wasn't talking about his father now. He grunted assent.

'Do you think it'll stick this time?' she asked. 'It seems different.'

'I hope so,' said Slider.

The phone call came very early.

'Bill,' said Pauline Smithers. 'I'm sorry to spoil your Sunday lie-in.'

'I was awake. What's happened?'

'The body of a female's been found.'

His heart sank like a barometer on a Bank Holiday. 'In the Beeches?'

'No, on Hampstead Heath. Early hours of this morning. No identification yet, but preliminary inspection suggests she's been dead about a week. Given the pressures of your case, I thought you might want to send someone over to have a look.'

'Yes, thanks, Pauly.' He reached for a note pad. 'Let me have the details.'

Joanna had put on her dressing gown and gone downstairs as soon as he answered the call. He found her in the kitchen, along with his father, who lived with his new wife in the basement granny-flat.

'Morning, son,' said Mr Slider. 'I just came to ask what the arrangements are for lunch today.'

'How did you know we were up?' Slider asked.

'Well, *I* was up,' said Mr Slider, whose early rising habits, learned when he was a farm worker, had never been lost, 'and I heard Joanna walking about in the kitchen. So, how many is it today? Kate and Matthew are coming, right?'

'Oh Lord, yes – I'd forgotten. Kate'll stay over for school, but Matthew will be going back tonight.'

'Just them two? Irene's not coming? Well then, that'll be eight including the nippers.'

'I've got a big leg of lamb,' Joanna said.

'Reckon I'd better do the potatoes for you,' said Mr Slider, twinkling. 'Don't want to spoil your artist's hands with all that peeling.' He turned to Slider, serious again. 'Joanna was just telling me you had a phone call. No good ever comes of a phone call this early on a Sunday.'

'They've found a body,' Slider said.

'Oh, no!' said Joanna. 'Is it her?'

'No identification yet, but she's been dead about a week, so it could be.'

'Was it—?'

'No, on Hampstead Heath.'

'But doesn't that mean—?'

'There's a family connection with Hampstead. And it was only the handbag that was found at Burnham Beeches. That could have been misdirection. We don't know that she was ever there. So we have to consider it.'

Joanna had been studying his face. 'Well, you don't have to go yourself,' she said flatly.

He knew what a body that had been lying out in the woods for a week could look like. 'Well,' he said, and hesitated.

His father got it. 'Thing about going yourself,' he said unemphatically, 'is that nobody else has to do it.'

Slider knew that reasoning wouldn't appeal to Joanna. Women's loyalties were intensely personal. She'd have thought, to hell with anybody else. Let 'em!

He said, 'I've been told to investigate this case personally, I told you that. I think I had better go. It probably won't take long. If it isn't her . . .'

'If it is, you'll be gone all day,' Joanna said, and then swallowed her resentment. Irene, Slider's first wife, had made his life difficult during their marriage by constantly pitching herself against his job, and Joanna would never do that. 'You can have some breakfast first, anyway,' she said.

'Thanks, but I won't. I'd better get straight over there,'

Slider said. Better to view that sort of stiff on an empty stomach. 'Sooner I go, sooner I'm back.'

'You go, son,' said Mr Slider comfortably. 'We'll hold the fort. I got some of that bacon you like yesterday, from the butcher's,' he said, turning to Joanna to release Slider. 'Meant to bring it up before. I'll pop down and get it for you now.'

'Oh, thanks. And come to breakfast as well, why don't you? Both of you.'

'If it's no trouble.'

Released by this little show of all-is-well, Slider went.

TWELVE

It's a Long Robe That Has No Turban

Various creatures of the night had been busy in the days since the death, and there was not a lot of the face left to recognize, but Slider was pretty sure it was not Felicity Holland, for which he offered up quick but fervent thanks. The hair colour, for one thing: it was of that undistinguished fair shade that his mother had always called 'mouse', while Felicity's was definitely very dark, almost black. The body also looked to be too tall, though that was a tricky one to be definite about; and from the skin tone and musculature, he would have said – and the police surgeon agreed – that the deceased was probably in her early to mid-thirties, while Felicity was in her fifties, and however well-preserved she might be, there were differences.

'We'll send off a sample for DNA verification, of course,' said the doctor, 'but—'

'Yes,' said Slider. 'I'm prepared to say this is not the woman we're looking for.'

'Right you are. I don't know whether to say I'm happy for you or not.'

It meant, of course, that they still had to look for her. And, also of course, she may turn out in the end to have suffered a similar fate to this poor soul, raped and battered and left out for the weasels and foxes. But for now, he could go on hoping that she was hidden somewhere and still all right.

'Sufficient unto the day,' he said.

And the doctor gave him a sympathetic nod and said, 'Right.'

It was when he had left the mortuary and got back into his car that the connection with Hampstead reoccurred to him. He sat for a moment, thinking, then got out again, locked the car, and walked. Easier to leave it in the mortuary's car park, which though small was not likely to be much in demand on a Sunday morning, than to try to find a space in Windmill Lane when all the residents were at home and using their slots.

Of course, it decided to rain again while he was walking; and, in a playful mood, the breeze got up and drove the cold drops straight into his face with gleeful enthusiasm. *Isn't this fun? Look, if I swirl about a bit, I can get it right up your nose!* There was a lot of yellow about – daffodils, and forsythia just beginning to open – but the splashes of colour only made everything else look greyer. And now, of course, he was starving.

Thelma opened the door to him, swathed in a towelling robe much too big for her, with a towel round her head, and stared at him for a moment before recognizing him. Then she grinned apologetically. 'I was just out of the bath when you rang the bell and I grabbed the first thing to hand. This is Wills's. He's gone with the boys to rugby. Always rugby, every Sunday,' she added with a slight roll of the eyes. 'Do you want to come in?'

'I'll wait out here until you're dressed,' Slider said circumspectly. You never wanted to get yourself into a position where accusations could be levelled. Not that he thought she'd do that, but her husband could come back unexpectedly – rugby rained off, someone has a nosebleed, etc.

'No, come in out of the rain,' she cried hospitably. 'Can't leave you out there dripping.' She hauled the folds of towelling around her, revealing her bare, cherry-tipped toes below and gestured him in. Then, belatedly, she wondered why he was there, and a painful hope cracked her face. 'Have you—?'

'No, we haven't found her,' Slider said, stepping in. *Either way*, he added silently. The hall had its original small-diamond black-and-white tiles, so he was glad he was not going to drip on anything that marked; and they obviously had underfloor heating, because he could feel the grateful warmth rising to his face. 'But I have got something to tell you.'

'All right. Come into the kitchen, then.'

In the kitchen – it was expensively fitted-out, but every surface was crammed with the everyday litter of people who lived in the kitchen rather than in the sitting room – she went straight to the stove. 'Would you like a cup of tea?'

'Yes please, I'd love one. Look, I can make it while you run and put something on.'

She grinned. 'Don't care for my sartorial style, eh? All right. Won't be a tick. Make me one as well, will you? Milk no sugar. Tea bags are in that cupboard, spoons in that drawer.'

She was quick, and returned in grey leggings and pink hoodie top just as he was adding the milk. Her hair was combed out but still damp, beginning to curl upwards, like feathers. 'Oh, ta,' she said. She examined him as she took the mug from him. 'You still look frozen. You must have got up really early. Have you had breakfast?'

'No, I didn't have time.'

'You sit there, and I'll make you something,' she said firmly, and he couldn't bring himself to refuse. 'So, d'you want to tell me what it's all about?'

'I haven't got any positive news for you,' Slider said. 'I really came to warn you about something that might otherwise upset you. Later on today it's bound to be on the news, and it's probably already on social media, so somebody will probably put two and two together to make eight, and ring you up about it.'

'You're being very mysterious. What are you talking about?'

'The body of a woman has been found on Hampstead Heath.'

She turned her head sharply to look at him, hands poised above the frying pan in the middle of breaking an egg.

'I've been to the mortuary this morning to look at her,' Slider went on, 'and it's not your sister. I'm quite sure about that. So I thought I'd better come and reassure you before you heard about it.'

'That was kind of you,' she said automatically. Her face looked grey. 'You're quite sure?'

'Quite sure. It's not Felicity.'

She nodded soberly. 'But it's someone. Somebody else is waiting for news, for a person to come home, and they never will. I'm glad it's not Fliss, but I can't be glad about it, if you know what I mean.'

'I know what you mean,' Slider said. 'And you are allowed to be glad on your own account.'

Nothing more was said until she had put a toasted fried egg

sandwich in front of him. 'It's Wills's favourite,' she said apologetically. 'I forgot to ask if you like eggs.'

'Love them. Thank you.'

She sat down opposite him with her own mug. 'So, can you tell me anything? Have you got anywhere? Henry's convinced someone has snatched her. Is that what you think?'

Slider ate some of the sandwich first. 'This is perfect. Just what I needed. Thanks. I don't know, is the answer to that. I prefer to think that she went away voluntarily, and that she's safe somewhere.'

'But why would she do that, without telling anyone?'

'Any number of reasons. People can suddenly have a crisis in their life and react to it. Not necessarily something that's happening right now. It can be a build-up of stresses. Or some long-ago trauma suddenly makes itself felt, and they just have to go away somewhere and think things out.'

She gave him a steady look. 'Or they can run away with another man – that's the one you're not saying.'

'Is that what *you* think?' He gave her her own words back.

'It's better than her being snatched.'

'The sort of attack Mr Holland is worried about is very, very rare,' he said. 'Statistically, it's the least likely thing.'

'Well, that's a comfort, I suppose,' she said.

'But running, and staying away, is also unusual.'

'Now you've spoiled it,' she said with a wry smile.

'Though running is some people's preferred solution. They build up a pattern of avoidance, and usually we find it has happened before. For instance, did your sister ever run away from home as a child?'

'No, never. I mean, she went to live in Grandma's flat in London when she was eighteen, but that wasn't running – it was all arranged, for when she went to college. And before that she went to live with Granny Erskine in Callander for five months – that's my other granny, my mother's mother. I was at boarding school at the time, and I didn't know about it until I came home at Easter, but Mummy and Daddy knew all about it, it was all arranged by them. No,' she said, frowning in thought, 'I wouldn't say avoiding was her way. If anything, she's always been rather brave about standing up to things.'

'Well, there are still many avenues to explore,' Slider said, hoping not to have to enumerate them, 'and of course, she may come home of her own accord at any time.'

'So what *have* you found out so far?'

'That she had lunch with somebody in London on Tuesday. In Covent Garden.' He tried her with the picture of the man from Polpo. 'Do you know who this is?'

She looked at it for a long time, shaking her head minutely. 'No. I wish I did, but . . .' She adjusted the angle to get more light on it. 'No. I thought maybe he looked a bit familiar, but I don't think so. It isn't anyone I know. What's his name? Maybe she's mentioned him.'

'Ah. We don't have a name. Just that image from the restaurant's security camera.'

'And that's it? That's all you've got after a week's work?'

'It's difficult when we have so little to go on.'

'I'm sorry,' she said. 'I'm sounding like Henry. I know it must be difficult for you. I don't know where I'd start looking, and I'm her sister. Needle in a haystack. I just hope she didn't go to Scotland, because that's an even bigger haystack.'

'Your granny in Callander—' he began hopefully.

'Dead, oh, must be twelve, fifteen years ago. No relations up there now.'

Slider got to his feet. 'Well, thank you for breakfast. Saved my life. I'd better get going now.'

She saw him out. 'That handbag in Burnham Beeches – I assume, as you're not searching there, that you don't think that's where she is.'

He couldn't go into the politics of it, not with an anxious relative. 'If we had any evidence to suggest she'd gone there, we would be searching. I promise you we're doing everything we can.' And he took his leave, before she could ask why the handbag didn't qualify as evidence.

With the day ruined anyway, he went to Shepherd's Bush on the way home, and stopped at the police station. Gascoyne and McLaren were both there, diligently trawling through traffic footage.

'Nothing yet, sir,' Gascoyne said.

To his surprise, Jenrich came in, having just come back from the ladies'. 'I was in the area, I just dropped by,' she said. 'Nothing else to do today. I'm going over CCTV footage, see if I can spot anything.'

'Guv,' said McLaren, 'given these two are here, can I go home? Phil says he doesn't mind staying to the end of shift.'

'You can swap rota with him if you like,' Slider said. 'By the way, you'll see it on the news later, no doubt.' He explained about his trip to Hampstead and the body.

'Not her?' Gascoyne said.

'Not her. And I'd better go and ring Mr Carpenter about it before someone else does.'

Carpenter, while unimpressed at being disturbed on a Sunday with negative news, had the grace to be glad to know that Slider was hard at it on his day of rest. 'If you're not too tied up, you might want to pop down to Hammersmith, to the media suite. Henry Holland is recording an appeal to go out on tonight's television. He'll be there – oh, in about half an hour.'

'You decided it would do some good, then, sir?'

'More a case of keeping the victim's nearest and dearest happy,' Carpenter said evasively, with shades of Sir David behind his voice. 'And of course, you never know, it might trigger something, in someone, somewhere.'

'Are you not going to be there yourself?'

'No need, no need. Trevor will be there, co-ordinating everything.'

This was DS Trevor Carthew, Carpenter's bagman and one-man fan club, known among the ranks as 'Boots' Carthew because he was so far up Carpenter's fundament, that was all you could see.

'It occurs to me, Slider,' Carpenter went on, 'that perhaps you *ought* to be there, in case Trevor needs to know any of the smaller details of the case. Your perspective could be useful. And it might comfort Mr Holland to see you there, taking a personal interest.'

Of course, Slider thought, it was Sir David who told Mr Carpenter to tell Slider to investigate in person, and Holland was Sir David's chum and might report that it was not happening. Which would drop Carpenter in it.

'Yes, in fact, you *should* go,' Carpenter concluded.

Slider didn't bother to argue. As with the centurion in the Bible, when Carpenter says go, one goeth.

Boots Carthew decided to believe that Slider had been sent to spy on him and report back. Henry Holland took the attitude that Slider should be out tramping the streets looking for his wife, not hanging around indoors in the warmth doing nothing. The media team no sooner placed Slider out of the way in one position when they discovered he was now *in* the way and really ought to be standing anywhere else. And Slider certainly didn't want to be there anyway, so no one was glad about it. It was not a happy way to spend an hour and a half on Sunday.

Holland was not a natural in front of the camera, and proved deeply resistant to taking direction. He moved when he shouldn't have, cleared his throat when he oughtn't, looked in the wrong direction, spoke too loudly or too quietly, said things that hadn't been agreed on, and generally presented so wooden an aspect that Slider was afraid the make-up girl might get a nasty splinter. The general public, he felt, would be more inclined to want to slap him than help him. But at last they got a take that everyone was grudgingly satisfied with, and on the monitor at least it was clear that this was a man devastated by events. He might not be melting into photogenic tears, but there was no mistaking that he was shaken to the core, and possibly on the brink of disintegration.

When he had been escorted out, to be driven back to St Anns Villas, Carthew let his hair down with a rant about the nuisance and expense of setting up an operations room and manning the phone lines to deal with all the useless and crank calls, for which he seemed to hold Slider personally responsible.

Slider felt he had to defend himself. '*I* never thought a public appeal would do any good,' he said.

'If you'd found the damn woman by now, we wouldn't have had to do it,' Boots snapped back. 'How you can have so little to show for an entire week's work defeats me. If it was *my* case—'

Blah blah blah. *It's not a week, it's only five days. And it's not even my ground,* Slider complained to himself as he trudged back to his car. What a way to spend a Sunday.

On Monday, the April showers really got their act together and merged into continuous rain, marking their borders only by a slightly heavier or lighter downpour. The sky was pewter; the light fluctuating from dull to dim to crepuscular and back as the clouds shouldered across the background of more clouds. In the street, people scurried, hunched; depressed-looking pigeons lurked in the lee of chimneys; daffodils in window boxes and front gardens gave up hope and lay down flat on their faces.

Inside the CID room they had the lights on.

'Did you see Our 'Enery on the telly last night?' Atherton asked, of no one in particular. 'Give him an inflammable hat and you could strike him against brick walls.'

Swilley looked up, scowling. 'What?'

'Potassium chlorate and sulphur, I believe.'

The scowl intensified. '*What?*'

'What a match head is made of. I was referring to his generally rigid demeanour and wooden acting.'

'For God's sake,' Swilley said under her breath and went back to work, still going through Felicity's bank statements. Until they got an ID on the mic-purchaser from the credit card company, there wasn't much else to do.

LaSalle said, 'Give him a break, poor old geezer. He must be worried sick. Not everyone's an actor.'

Gascoyne broke the tension. 'Gottim!' he cried. 'Got a ping on the Jag, A41 Finchley Road. There's a speed camera just north of St John's Wood station, got him turning right into Queen's Grove. So he must be going somewhere local. If he was going out of London, he'd have stayed on the A41.'

'Any visual?' McLaren asked. 'Is she in the car with him?'

'No visual. Angle's not right. Just the index. But now we know where he was and when, we can look for more cameras in the area.'

'Try Avenue Road,' McLaren advised. That's the next main junction on Queen's Grove. It's a through route, runs from the park straight up to Swiss Cottage.'

'What's east of St John's Wood?' Atherton asked, trying to visualize.

'Primrose Hill,' said McLaren. 'Open spaces and some clumps of trees.'

'Not private enough for him to lamp her there,' said LaSalle. 'Not in the middle of the day. And how'd he carry her body back to the car without anybody seeing?'

'I wonder if he's got a property there?' Atherton mused. 'It's a nice enough area. Maybe he keeps a pied-à-terre that no one knows about.'

'What, a love nest?' said Lœssop. 'That'd be a joke, bashing his daughter for extramarital nookie when he's having it himself.'

'He's not married,' Swilley pointed out.

'Let's not get ahead of ourselves,' Atherton said. 'We need to find where he went, first.'

'There's no speed camera on Avenue Road,' Gascoyne reported. 'And no traffic camera on that junction. I'd have to go there to see what CCTV there is.'

Atherton followed him to Slider's room.

'Yes, go for it,' Slider was saying. 'Might as well – we've got no other leads.'

'The other thing we might do,' Atherton said, 'is ask our brothers in Roads and Transport if they've seen the motor in the area. If he has got a place, or regularly visits someone there, they might have spotted it on a previous occasion.'

'What part of "you can't investigate Sir John" were you unclear about?' Slider enquired.

'No need to mention his name,' said Atherton. 'You can just give them the description of the car and the reg number. Innocent enquiry. If it comes back that they know whose motor it is, that at least tells us something.'

'I'm not sure what. But go ahead. If the spit hits the spam, we'll just have to play dumb.'

'Easier for some of us than others. Shove McLaren to the fore,' said Atherton.

'I can actually hear you,' McLaren called from the next room.

Atherton came in with a bag. 'Doughnut or Eccles cake?'

'No contest,' said Slider. 'Dried fruit is my raisin d'être.'

Atherton passed over an Eccles cake. 'I think they're currants, actually. That went well on Saturday night, I thought. What did you think of Stephanie?'

Slider was not comfortable with this sort of talk. 'She seemed . . .' He hesitated.

'I can hear the word "nice" slouching towards this conversation to be born.'

'Irritable vowel syndrome, that's what you've got.'

'Seriously,' Atherton insisted.

'Seriously, she seemed nice.' Atherton made a sound of impatience. 'What do you want from me? *I'm* not going out with her.' Atherton started to turn away, and Slider added kindly, 'Joanna liked her, if that's any help.'

'Thanks,' Atherton said ironically. 'She can be a bridesmaid. You can both be bridesmaids.'

'You're thinking of marriage already?' Slider said in surprise. His bagman had always been determinedly single.

Atherton, in the doorway, didn't turn. 'I was speaking metaphorically.'

The phone rang, saving Slider from further squirmy stuff. He wasn't sure he liked this new touchy-feely Atherton.

'Detective Chief Inspector Slider,' he said.

It was Henry Holland. 'Did you see the appeal on the television last night?' he asked without preamble. 'What did you think?'

Loved your perf, darling, Slider didn't say. Another actor's ego to polish? 'I thought it was – effective,' he said, selecting what he hoped was a neutral word.

Turned out it didn't matter. Holland didn't really care what he thought. 'Several people have rung to say they were quite moved by it. Friends of mine, from the Society of Nautical Fiction Writers. They thought I presented the matter very clearly and sensitively. Of course, I am accustomed to public speaking, though the occasion is unprecedented.'

'Fortunately so,' Slider interjected, since something seemed to be waited for.

'And I am under an enormous amount of strain.'

'I can imagine.'

'I doubt that you can, unless something like this has happened to you. How soon before we get any results?' Holland demanded.

'It's really not possible to say,' Slider said. 'It depends if anyone has any information to give, whether they saw the appeal, and whether they're willing to come forward.'

'That's all very vague,' Holland said, with a frown in his voice. 'Have you nothing more helpful you can tell me?'

'I think our best hope lies with the man your wife had lunch with on Tuesday. As soon as we can identify him—'

'He's probably a business contact of hers. She has a share portfolio in her own name, and takes investment advice from time to time. Or someone to do with one of the clubs she belongs to. If he were anyone important, I would know about him. I doubt he'll be able to tell you anything you don't know. It's a blind alley, and I don't understand why you are wasting time on it. You should be searching Burnham Beeches and the surrounding area. Her kidnapper must know the place, he must have taken her there, or why was her handbag found there? Either he lives nearby, and he's holding her, or he's . . .' He made a choking sound, and went on in a low, reluctant voice, 'or he's used the woods to . . .' He stopped again. 'You *must* find her before it's too late.'

'We are doing everything we can, sir,' Slider said, but the words sounded hollow even to him. If ever he had been handed a poisoned chalice, this was it.

THIRTEEN
Ligaments of Fire

Slider was just back from an unsatisfactory shepherd's pie in the canteen – they *would* put carrot in it – when Swilley came to the door and said, 'Martin Henderson.'

'Is this a version of the Mornington Crescent game? All right, Timothy Taylor.'

She gave him the patient look with which parents repress offspring silliness. 'The man she lunched with in Polpo. Visa have just come through with it.'

'That was quick.' Slider wondered who had had a word with whom to get the info released.

Swilley sighed. 'He couldn't have managed to have an unusual name, could he? There are only about five million Martin Hendersons on Google.'

'But didn't they give you an address as well?'

'Oh yes. But I thought you'd want to find out something about him before you went round there. He lives right there in Drury Lane.'

The address was Flat 73, Totnes House.

'It's one of those Purnell Estate blocks,' Atherton said, as everyone gathered round Swilley's desk. 'You know, the Victorian social housing, like the Peabody Trust? There are two in Drury Lane – Totnes House and Barnstaple House. Purnell was a rich mine owner with a big estate in Devon. MP for Westminster in the 1870s. Started a charity to build model housing for the poor. The Drury Lane blocks were his first, I think.'

'How do you know so much about it?' LaSalle asked.

'I know a lot about everything.'

Swilley snorted.

'I read up about the Model Dwellings Companies when I did social history for A level,' Atherton went on. 'It's interesting.'

'Sorry I asked,' Swilley said. She tapped for a bit. 'He's

not on the electoral roll.' More tapping. 'He's not on the last census, either. Maybe he's new there.'

'Or he doesn't bother with that sort of thing,' said Lœssop. 'Any images? We want to know it's the same bloke.'

'Like I said, five million Martin Hendersons,' Swilley said shortly.

'But he bought a top-end microphone,' Jenrich said. 'Try "Martin Henderson musician".'

'Right,' said Swilley. A pause. 'There's a drummer – not him.'

'You're sure?'

'Too bald . . . There's a guitar player from Long Island. Too fat, too hairy . . . A trumpet player. Too black . . . Another guitar player, from Maryland. Too dead . . . A singer-songwriter – wait a minute, this one's from London. No, his name's Henderson Martin. Could be a stage inversion? No. No picture, but from the date of birth he's in his sixties.' She looked up. 'So you're going to have to go in blind.'

'If he's got her in there, holding her prisoner, we'll have to tread carefully,' Slider said. 'He might turn violent. On the other hand, if she's there voluntarily, or he was just an innocent lunch companion and doesn't know anything about her disappearance, we don't want to bash his door down and charge in bellowing "Police, stand still!"'

'A bit of surveillance?' Atherton suggested.

'Yes, but we're already a week behind the event. Our bosses won't stand for too many more delays.' He drummed his fingers a moment. 'I think we should scope out the place, see if he comes out, and ask the neighbours if they've heard anything, or seen anything.'

'Those Trust flats are solidly built,' Atherton said. 'You may not hear much through the walls.'

'But neighbours often have an idea of what's going on next door,' said Slider. 'They may have seen her coming and going. Or coming and not going. Jenrich, Gascoyne, you can go. Oh, and Lœssop – you look the part, if there's a music scene to infiltrate. But check back with me before you make contact – unless he comes out into the street. Then you can ask him to help with enquiries. Use your discretion.'

But before any of these plans could be acted upon, Slider's phone rang again. Even as he went to answer it, he had a bad feeling. Sometimes a copper's instincts were so finely honed, he was almost clairvoyant. Or it could just have been the shepherd's pie.

There had been a call to the incident room in Hammersmith. 'I'm surprised it happened so soon,' Slider said, heading out on the M4. 'Frankly, I didn't expect any results at all.'

'Another person tired of our lack of progress?' said Atherton. 'Well, it wouldn't be the first time a murderer was longing to be caught, so he could display his cleverness to the stupid police. As a dog returneth to his vomit—'

'Must you? I had the shepherd's pie.'

'I'm surprised too,' Atherton said. 'I was convinced she'd run off with a lover and we were wasting our time.'

'I was hoping for that,' Slider said.

'Well, this could still be a false alarm,' Atherton said comfortingly. 'They usually are.'

The caller had been brief and to the point. 'This is the murderer. The body's in the woods at Burnham Beeches, and you'll never catch me, ha ha.' He actually said the words, ha ha. The voice was heavily disguised, and so far the experts who had listened to the recording – all the calls to the incident room were automatically recorded – could only pronounce with any certainty that it was an adult man. As anonymous callers were almost always adult males, this was little help.

The reason it was taken seriously was that the caller mentioned Burnham Beeches, which was not information yet released to the public, though of course it was so widely known at Slough station it could have leaked out almost anywhere by now. More importantly, the call was made from the victim's own phone, as was verified by call tracing, and the caller gave the number to prove his bona fides. 'And just so you know it's really me, I've got her Visa card, too,' he had said, and gave the number of that as well, before ringing off.

Commander Carpenter had immediately rung DCS Felway at Slough, and before you could say structurally synergizing your core competencies, it had gone up the line to the chief constable and the commissioner and the fiat went forth. Carpenter had gone mission-critical and mobilized his troops, and Detective Chief Superintendents Felway and Porson were in lockstep going forward strategically, taking it to the next level.

Which meant it was all hands on deck. 'And I *mean* all hands,' Carpenter had snapped at Porson. 'We've lost enough time on this one, and even with valid excuses it's not going to look good in the press. Get every warm body in your team out to Slough for a fingertip search. Felway's co-ordinating under the chief constable, and we're staying there until we discover the body. There'll be no not finding it, do you understand me?'

'If he's got her phone and her Visa card,' Slider now said unhappily, 'it probably isn't a hoax.'

'But it could still be misdirection,' Atherton said. 'She and her lover, snug in their hotel in Bexhill-on-Sea, see the appeal on the telly. They don't want to be disturbed and she gets him to make a call to say that she's definitely dead so there's no point searching for her.'

'Having already dumped her handbag to give that impression. Wouldn't it have been much easier just to disappear with him? No need to leave false clues – to say nothing of depriving herself of her credit cards.'

Atherton shrugged. 'You don't expect the general public to be intelligent. This way, when she eventually does surface, she'll be prosecuted for wasting police time on a massive scale, rather than just having to face an angry hubby. So it's all good for us. She'll probably do time.'

Slider sighed. 'I hope she does. But it won't happen soon enough to save me from fingertip-searching a wood frequented by dog walkers, not all of whom clear up after themselves.'

'You only have to put in a token appearance,' said Atherton. 'It's us grunts who have to get our hands dirty.'

'True,' said Slider. 'Thanks. That's cheered me up.'

The press were there, and the senior officers were all required to put on a show for the cameras of joining the search. There was a canine unit – dogs were always good press – and a number of reliable local volunteers in welly boots had been brought in to swell the squad. It was, after all, a large area. The Stag car park was taped off for the various vehicles, including the tea-wagon, so the air was fragrant with frying bacon – no sustained police activity can go on without bacon sandwiches. And since it was assumed the murderer had parked there in order to transport the corpse into the wood, it was the jumping-off point, and the search fanned out from there to make sure of covering every inch.

Some Thames Valley uniforms had to be deployed to keep the passing traffic passing, to prevent people parking along Hawthorn Lane and getting in the way, and to control the shifting crowd of *un*reliable locals, who gathered to watch the fun and keep up a running commentary on police uselessness. Fortunately, or unfortunately depending on how you looked at it, it soon started to rain; cold, blowy, penetrating rain, which diluted the enthusiasm of the crowd to departure point. At least under the tree canopy you were sheltered from the blowy part, though you did have the additional hazard of vertical drips from the leaves and branches. A single raindrop, falling from a great height, gets up a surprisingly painful momentum.

Rigidly upright DCI Trevor Dalton, distinguishable from a tree trunk by his uniform, came up to Slider and said, 'My guv'nor says you can go. Senior officers don't need to stay any longer, now we've got things under way.' Behind the words, Slider sensed the tension between being glad of the Met's extra bodies, and resentful of its intrusion into Thames Valley's ground. We don't need *your* help, thank you very much, versus we need all the help we can get.

'I'd like to see her found. It's my case,' Slider said.

'It's a Thames Valley operation now,' Dalton said coldly. 'We've got this.'

'I'll go soon,' Slider said. 'I'm just keeping my people's spirits up.'

Dalton grunted non-committally – or rather, it was the 'if you want to behave like an idiot I can't stop you' grunt – but then his rigidity flickered a little. He looked away, and said, 'I'm sorry we didn't start this sooner. Lost a lot of time. But there wasn't enough to go on, not for this sort of deployment.'

It was close to an apology. 'I know,' Slider said kindly. This amount of manpower cost millions, came out of a budget already stretched, and would attract stringent value-for-money analysis. Luckily, it wasn't his responsibility. Not Dalton's either, now it had gone up to the very top level. But blame, like water, tended to trickle down to the lowest level. Slider was fortunate that his immediate boss, Porson, was protective of his underlings. Dalton might not be so lucky. Slider had only caught a glimpse of Detective Chief Superintendent Felway, but it was not reassuring. Felway was of massive build that brought the words 'brick' and 'shithouse' to mind, and had a face like a concrete bulldog in a bad mood. It didn't help that she was a woman.

'You are so sexist, Dad,' Kate said stridently when Slider related the day's events at supper, including his glimpse of Porson's opposite number – if you defined 'number' as 'that which numbs'. 'You think all women have to be cute and girly and helpless, just to please you, and make you feel like the big man.'

'I married Joanna,' Slider defended himself. 'You couldn't call her girly and helpless.'

'I notice you left out cute,' Joanna said.

'Well, *I* think you're cute.'

'I think you are, too.'

'You're both impossible!' Kate interrupted. 'The point is, this Felway person doesn't have to conform to some body-image dictated by the gender-fascists of the commercial hegemony, just so she can win approval from Neanderthal old rockers like you.'

'In America, they pronounce hegemony with a soft "g",' Joanna said. 'I thought they were talking about hedge money – you know, like from a hedge fund.'

'When did you hear an American saying hegemony?' Slider asked.

'I've been around. And Emily used to say it that way.'

'There's another example of a non-girly woman,' Slider said to Kate.

'Emily who?'

'Uncle Jim's previous girlfriend.'

'Oh, that Emily. And he's not my uncle, thank you,' Kate said, making a 'yeuch!' face. She had been half in love with him not that long ago. '*And* you're avoiding the point.'

'The point,' Slider said, unprovoked, 'is that the forecast is for rain all week, and this search is going to take many days, unless we're lucky.'

'Lucky which way?' Joanna asked.

'I suppose, ironic as it seems, finding the body would be lucky. If we find nothing, it doesn't mean she isn't dead, only that the murderer's toying with us, and we've spent x million pounds polishing his ego.'

'But if you do find the body,' Kate said, distracted for the moment from her mission of improving their characters, 'will you be any closer to knowing who killed her? I mean, you still don't know where she went or who she saw after she left that restaurant. Even with a body, you won't be any further forward.'

'They'll have a *terminus ad quem*,' Joanna said, from a memory of Golden Age detective novels.

'I don't speak French,' Kate said loftily. 'We do Spanish and Mandarin at my school. Look, you know who this bloke is that she had lunch with. Surely it's more important to get hold of him than to go tramping through woods full of fox poo.'

'You make an eloquent argument,' Slider said.

'Maybe he killed her. But if he didn't, if he's innocent, he'll be expecting to meet her for lunch tomorrow, won't he? So if he turns up, you'll know he's OK. And he might know where she was going next.'

Slider smiled. He had, of course, thought of all those things for himself. But Kate reminded him of a young cat stretching itself. And for once she wasn't clawing the furniture. He was not going to discourage her. 'You're absolutely right,' he said. 'I think I shall pay a visit to Polpo tomorrow lunchtime. It'll have to be me in person, because all my team will be out in the woods again until further notice.'

Kate looked pleased. 'There,' she said approvingly, having set him on the right lines.

It was better than being re-educated, Slider thought. He had heard the distant rumble of the gender dysphoria debate heading down the lines towards them.

Uberti recognized Slider's face and welcomed him back with Italian effusiveness, just before he realized why it was he recognized him, and became first sotto-voce discreet and then nervously depressed.

'I have seen on the news, the police searching the woods. That poor lady! So beautiful, so elegant! You think he killed her? One cannot imagine such a thing. He seemed so ordinary, not like a murderer. And so fond of each other. Oh dear, that such a thing could happen in my restaurant! And if he comes here today – *dio mio!* You expect him here today? My other clients! I cannot have unpleasantness, signore. Polpo is a family restaurant, we are all one big family here, the staff and the clients. There must be no disturbance.'

Slider did his best to reassure. 'If he comes here, it will be because he expects to meet her as usual, which means he is not the murderer. If he comes, it means he is just an innocent man caught up in a drama.'

Both Maria and Gino, who had come up behind him to listen, now broke into Italian, presumably explaining the situation to him in a lot more words. Uberti replied sharply and lengthily, and they re-entered the lists, this time with gestures. It seemed they had got the point across, for Uberti put his hands to his cheeks in a gesture of distress, and said, 'Oh, the poor young man! I hope, then, that he comes. But if he comes, it means he does not know, and you will have to tell him, and, oh then, his world will be shattered.'

Gino muttered, 'I don't think he loves her *that* much.'

But Maria, woman-like, went to the practicalities. 'Where would you like to wait? Out of sight? There is a storeroom back there – we could call you if he comes in.'

'There's no need to hide,' Slider said. 'I only want to talk to him. If I could just sit at the bar?'

'Of course. Please,' said Uberti, becoming expansive again. 'You will have coffee. How you like it? Gino, coffee for our friend. Gino makes the best coffee in Drury Lane. As good as one can get at home, in *Roma.*'

Slowly the restaurant filled up, and the staff bustled about their normal duties, too busy to pay much attention to the unobtrusive figure sitting at the bar, with the self-effacing stillness only a soldier or a policeman can sustain. The door jingled as it opened and closed, customers came in, were greeted, some with kisses, and shown to tables, menus handed, water poured. A warm bath of conversation filled the space. There was a slight breath of tension on the air as one o'clock approached and passed. Five past. Ten past. Slider thought, *he's not coming*. His heart sank. Did that mean he was the killer? But it was possible there was usually some contact, confirmation of the date between them, and not having heard, he assumed it was off. Nothing in this case was certain, except that he, Slider, had had no chance from the beginning of getting it absolutely right.

At almost a quarter past, the door jingled again, and a man came in, unwinding the muffler from over his mouth, his thatch of dark hair and the shoulders of his jacket beaded with rain. Uberti came forward with his usual greetings, again an instant before he recognized the newcomer. Then, for a fatal instant, a disconcerted look came over his face, and he glanced at Slider. The man glanced too, Slider began to rise from the stool, his warrant card at the ready, the man's face blanched, and he turned tail and bolted.

To chase the fleeing is as instinctive to a policeman as to a dog. Slider was away before he had even thought about it, but he was hampered by the door swinging shut in front of him, and the man had gained crucial yards before he was outside. Possibly he shouted, 'Stop!' Possibly even, 'Stop! Police!' But it was only once. After that, he needed his breath for running.

Henderson ran. Chariots of fire it was not. He ran like a man not used to running, arms swinging, putting too much effort into it in the wrong places, and Slider hoped he would outpace him before long. Straight along Drury Lane, along the glistening wet pavements, Henderson ran. The rain had eased off for the moment, though the sky was still a moody grey. Then he dodged left into Shelton Street. The buildings on either side were being developed, with scaffolding and plastic sheeting protection, turning the alley temporarily into a covered tunnel. Footsteps echoed clashingly. It was so narrow that if anyone had been coming the other way, it would have been all over. Unfortunately, no one was. They emerged from the dark where the tunnel ended and Shelton Street opened out from an alley into a street, albeit a narrow one. Still no other pedestrians. Straight across Endell Street Henderson bolted, swerving out of the way of a taxi and jerking back from the passage of a moped courier, who screamed abuse before accelerating on. Henderson had lost a bit of ground. But Slider had the same road to cross, and taxis were as thick as black beetles and far less inclined to scuttle out of the way. Honours even.

Henderson glanced back, and veered left again, down Neal Street. Now there were people – lots of them. This section of Neal Street was pedestrianized and cobbled and was replete with cute, tourist-attracting shops, the most brightly lit a cupcake emporium. Cupcakes? Death by sickly buttercream – a *caveat emporium* if ever there was one, he thought. Funny how the brain had a life of its own while the body was straining every cell. Lots of people, but no help. In days of yore you could have shouted, 'Stop thief!' and somebody would have; but people didn't like to get involved these days. And there was always the fear that the fleeing man might have a knife, or that he might be the innocent party and the pursuer might have a knife. So people backed out of the way and flattened themselves against walls. It slowed Henderson down, dodging them, but it slowed Slider down as well, as people turned their heads after Henderson and got in Slider's way. Henderson even gained a bit.

At the other end, Neal Street opened into the wide thoroughfare of Long Acre. Catty-corner to the right was the handsome oxblood-red-tiled façade of Covent Garden tube station. Blocked by pedestrians on the pavement to his left, Henderson veered right and then across the road towards the station. There was a large crowd gathered all across the junction outside the station: people who had just arrived and were finding their bearings, people converging on the station to leave, people studying maps, people just standing chatting, people unfurling umbrellas as a new spat of rain began, threatening each other's eyes. And straight ahead, in James Street, the usual street entertainers had set up, despite the on-off showers, each gathering a knot of spectators around him. If Henderson went that way, he could lose himself in the crowd. He was winded now and needed to stop running. But he glanced back again, saw how close Slider was and, apparently panicking, ran into the station. Slider's heart rose. Now he had him. The entrance hall to Covent Garden tube was tiny, and there was no other egress from it.

Henderson vaulted over the ticket barriers with a younger man's agility, aided perhaps by a touch of desperation. And then fate took a hand. The lift gates were open, revealing a crowded interior. Given there was no other direction in which to go, he shouldered himself into the lift, was stopped by the sheer mass of bodies, and turned at bay. Slider, not quite able to vault, had to climb over the barrier, and was on the other side just in time to see the lift doors close, shutting Henderson's desperate-eyed, gasping-mouthed face from view.

Slider could have taken the stairs, but the spiral staircase went down the equivalent of fifteen floors, and contained 193 steps. By the time he reached the bottom, Henderson would be on a train and gone.

A station official had come cautiously out from the Staff Only door, to remonstrate if it looked safe to do so about climbing over barriers. Slider showed his warrant card, and the official helpfully, and with a touch of relief, opened the gate to let him back out, saving him another embarrassing climb. He went round to the station exit, on the off chance that Henderson might, contrary to appearances, be a clever shit, decide Slider would come down by the next lift, and come straight back up, hoping to pass him on the way. He waited for half a dozen lifts, but Henderson did not appear. All Slider could do was to go back to Totnes House and call for assistance.

FOURTEEN

You Can't Teach an Old Dog Newtonian Physics

orson didn't smile, but it was a close thing. He rubbed a finger across his lips to control it.

'How long since you last did that?' he enquired.

'Couple of years,' Slider said tersely. In memory, running after somebody was a lot less heroic, especially when you didn't catch them. Less Harold Abrahams, more Harold Lloyd. Henderson was younger than him, but probably not as fit. On the other hand, he looked skinny, and if Slider weighed more, gravity would have had a hand in it. It was simple science.

'It was bad luck about the lift,' Porson said, still gravely.

'It was.'

'Nine chances out of ten the lift doors'd've been shut and you'd have had him.'

'Yes, sir.'

'So you've got some uniforms from Central watching his place?'

'Yes, but I'd like to get our own people on that. If he's nervous, seeing a lot of bobbies hanging around might put him off coming home.'

'I can get some of your team back from Slough tomorrow,' said Porson. 'Anyone can do a fingertip search. And even if they do find a body, you still have to work out how it got there, which still means tracking her movements after she left that restaurant. If he did it, most likely he did it in the flat, in private, but then how did he get the body out to the woods? Has he got a car?'

'We'll look into that.' A name check with the DVLA would tell if there was one registered to him.

'But a person can always borrow,' Porson pointed out. 'Still, you've got to nab the bugger first.'

'And until they find a body, we can't assume she's dead. I'd like our people to talk to the neighbours before he turns up. Find out if she's actually still up there. And if she is, there's the question of whether it's voluntary or not.'

'Him having it away on his toes like that makes him look guilty,' said Porson.

'People run for all sorts of reasons. They can have a guilty conscience about something else entirely. Or sometimes it's pure instinct.'

'And on the other hand, turning up at the restaurant makes him look innocent.'

'But he might be guilty and thought going there as if he expected to meet her would put us off the scent.'

'Or he might just not be the sharpest needle in the haystack. It doesn't do to underestimate the stupidity of the general public,' Porson said wisely. 'Innocent or guilty, he might just go there for lunch without thinking about it. Because it's what he always does of a Tuesday.'

Slider looked glum. 'I don't know which I like less, a clever murderer or a stupid one.'

'You're not required to like them, laddie. Leave that to the courtroom psychologists. Well, carry on. You've got my full backing, whatever you want to do. I wish we could close this whole bally thing down, and get back to normal, but there's no chance of that now the commander's got the bull between his teeth. If it turns out she's tucked up in some love nest somewhere, there'll be some red faces.'

And red faces meant red places, when your embarrassed superior administered a spanking to salve his dignity. On the whole, Slider thought, I'd rather be in Philadelphia.

He got his sergeants, plus Gascoyne, back on Tuesday.

'I don't care what we do,' Lœssop said, 'it's got to be better than those woods in the rain. Drip, drip, drip. Like Chinese water torture.'

They took over from the Central at eight. Slider was not entirely confident that the Central PCs would have been so dedicated to the surveillance as not to have cooped a bit during the night, in which case Henderson might have snuck home and be holed up there. So Jenrich, armed with a clipboard and list of fake donors, went and knocked on the door of number 73, ready to pose as someone looking for sponsorship for a charity walk. There was no answer to several knockings, so she pressed a handy little plastic Pinard horn to the door – part of the kit kept for the purpose – and had a listen, but heard no sound or movement within.

Then she and Gascoyne tried the flats to either side but there was no reply to the knock. 'People out at work, I suppose,' Jenrich said. 'I'll do the flat upstairs, you do the one straight underneath.'

Gascoyne struck lucky. A tiny, elderly lady, who obviously liked his looks, smiled at him and listened intelligently, and, having examined his warrant card carefully, invited him in. The flat was dark inside and full of heavy brocade-upholstered furniture, dark patterned carpets, thick velvet curtains, small polished tables and what-nots, and a critical mass on the walls and on every surface of framed photographs of what were evidently children, grandchildren and great-grandchildren. They all beamed at the camera, some in academic dress (graduation pictures), some in wedding clothes, some in school uniform; all – even the babies – with the same enormous teeth and plentiful dark hair. It'd give you the willies, Gascoyne thought, to have them staring at you while you sat watching *Pointless* or *Call the Midwife*, but she seemed a chirpy old bird so presumably she didn't mind it.

She sat herself in one elderly Cintique chair and waved Gascoyne to another facing it, and said, 'You want to know about the man up above? I think he must have bare floors, you know, vinyl or whatever it's called, like they do these days, because I can hear every footstep. I don't think it's fair in flats to have bare floors, but they all do it these days, don't they? I have carpets. Carpets make it much quieter for every-body, but young people think they're not hygienic. I say it all depends how often you clean. If you have a vinyl floor, you're more likely never to clean it because you don't see the dirt, and that's not hygienic, is it?'

'No, it's not,' said Gascoyne. 'Now, Mrs—?'

'Bloom, dear. Avril Bloom. It was Blom, originally, but my father-in-law changed it when he came over here after the war, to fit in. I think that's only polite, don't you? There's so many strange names about these days, you hardly know how to pronounce them, let alone spell them. Now yours, Gascoyne, that must be French, isn't it?'

'My father's from Hammersmith,' Gascoyne said.

'But originally it must have been French, from Gascony, that's in the south of France. My husband and I took all our holidays in France, lovely country, we visited every part, but I especially liked Brittany. Very like Cornwall, in many ways. Lovely sardines, they have there. My husband's not with us any more. He passed away – more than twenty years ago, can you believe that?'

Gascoyne could. There was twenty years of not having anyone to talk to bottled up here.

'Tell me more about your neighbour upstairs,' he invited firmly.

'Well, he's been here quite a long time, about ten years, I'd say. That's a long time by modern standards, isn't it? Though people do tend to stay on here, in these flats, once they arrive, because the rents are protected, and they're such nice big rooms, not like in a modern building. My granddaughter Rose-Anne bought a flat in Enfield last year and I won't tell you what it cost but it wasn't cheap and the rooms are *tiny* compared to these. And you're so nice and central here, everything just round the corner. I keep getting these leaflets through the door advertising retirement places, "protected living" they call it, and my son Gerald says I ought to consider it, but you'd have to go and live out in Hertfordshire or somewhere, right out in the country, nothing but fields all around, and where would be the fun in that?'

'No fun at all. So the man upstairs is noisy, is he?'

'Well . . .' She pursed her lips judiciously. 'I wouldn't say he's *terribly* noisy in the normal way, just that you can hear him walking about, because he's not light on his feet and as I said, I don't think he has carpets. So you can track him back and forth from one room to another. And then there's the music. That's always in the one place, over my spare bedroom, luckily, not over the living room, but it does go on and on. Not that you can hear a tune – it mightn't be so bad if you could, but it's just the . . . what do you call it, the bass line? A sort of thumping – and sometimes some sort of instrument that makes a wailing noise. I've thought it was a baby once or twice.' She smiled, showing the family teeth. 'Mostly it's in the daytime, so I suppose I should be grateful. He doesn't have noisy parties or anything, just this monotonous music, as if he's playing the same thing over and over. Then there'll be a gap, and then it starts again. It isn't that it's very loud, so I don't feel I can complain to the landlord, but it's not proper music, nothing you could listen to for pleasure. I tend to have my radio on all the time just so I don't hear it. Radio 4 – well, it's a bit of company as well, voices talking, so you don't feel alone. I'm very musical myself – we all were in my family. I go to the Opera House every season, as often as I can afford. If he played opera, I wouldn't mind. I think he might be a musician of some sort, though, because I saw him going into Ritchie's once, the music shop down the road.'

'How did you know it was him?'

'Oh, because I was coming in from the street one time, and Mr Casubon, the landlord's agent, was standing talking to him in the lobby, and he introduced me. He said, "I expect you know Mr Henderson, who lives upstairs from you." And I said, "I haven't had the pleasure," and I shook his hand. Nice-looking young man, nice dark hair, though he needed a shave. He seemed very shy, didn't smile or look at me. But since then, any time I've passed him in the lobby or met him in the lift, he's always said good morning to me, not smiling, but quite civilly, which is as much as you can hope for in a neighbour these days, isn't it?'

'Is he married?'

'Oh, I don't think so. There's not generally more than one set of footsteps up there. And if he's gone out, it's quite silent. Nobody else moving about.' She frowned. 'This is not about a divorce case, is it?'

'No, I'm not a private investigator,' he said with a smile. 'I'm a regular policeman.'

'Is he in a gang or something? A drug dealer? A receiver of stolen goods?'

'Nothing like that.'

'Well, he must have done something, for you to come asking about him.'

'We don't know that he's done anything. But it would help to know if he's had any visitors recently – say, since Tuesday last week. Anyone staying, I mean.'

'Are you wondering about the lady I see him with sometimes? Very smartly dressed older lady. I took her for his aunt.'

Gascoyne's heart sang, though he didn't show it. 'It might be. Where did you see them together?'

'The first time it was in the restaurant, Uberti's, across the road. It's called Polpo, but everyone knows Mr Uberti. It would be a few weeks ago. I was passing and I saw them through the window at a table together. Very nice-looking lady, in a very smart coat. Lovely hair. I'd say there was money there,' she added judiciously. 'And then another time, perhaps a week later, she was coming out of the lift as I was going in, so I thought she'd probably been visiting him.'

'What about last week?'

She paused, thinking. 'He did have a visitor one afternoon. I could hear footsteps above, in between the music. And at one time I could hear someone talking. It sounded like a woman's voice, too high for a man, and she must have been talking loudly or I'd not have heard it at all.'

'Did you hear what she was saying?'

'Oh no. I couldn't make out words, just the tone.'

'Were they quarrelling?'

She pursed her lips. 'I couldn't be sure about that. But the person I heard sounded upset – she was talking loud and fast, as if she was arguing with somebody.'

'And can you say what day that was?'

She shook her head regretfully. 'Last week some time, is all I can say. Not Monday, because I was out most of Monday, and not Friday, because I go over to Gerald and Joan's on Fridays. So it must have been Tuesday, Wednesday or Thursday.

No, not Thursday, because the chiropodist came to do my feet. Tuesday or Wednesday, then.'

'And have you heard any more extra footsteps up there since then? Or voices, or thumps and bumps?'

'Bumps? Like furniture being moved, you mean?'

'Anything at all,' Gascoyne said, in hope.

'No,' she said, maddeningly. 'Nothing like that. If anything, it's been quieter up there than usual.'

'It *would* be quieter, if he had her tied up,' said Gascoyne.

'Or if she was dead,' said Jenrich.

'They go there after the restaurant. A bit of hanky-panky, then a quarrel. He kills her – probably an accident. Panics, gets the body away to the woods on Tuesday night. Broods about it all week. Decides, come Tuesday, it'll make him look guilty if he doesn't turn up at the restaurant as usual, so he goes, sees the guv, panics again, and has it away.'

'He doesn't have a car,' Jenrich said. She had done the DVLA check.

'He hasn't got one registered,' Gascoyne corrected. 'He might have an illegal one. Or borrowed one from a mate. And it's dead quiet round here at night, in the early hours. Quieter than in the suburbs. He gets her arm over his shoulder and if anyone's around he pretends she's dead drunk.'

'How does he know about Burnham Beeches?' Atherton asked.

Gascoyne shrugged. 'It's not a state secret. Thousands of people go there every year. Or she may have talked about it.'

'Or,' said Jenrich, 'she could still be up there. Tied up – or not. We've only got the old lady's word there's no extra footsteps, and she's probably deaf if she's not daft. You can't go by that.'

So there was nothing to do but keep vigil. Slider and Atherton waited in the car, round the corner in Great Queen Street, opposite the Prince of Wales, ready to assist or spell the other two as necessary. Gascoyne lounged on the corner of Broad Court reading a newspaper. Jenrich was on the corner of Martlett Court engaged with a mobile phone – you could spend all day looking at a mobile phone without arousing suspicion.

The entrance to Totnes House was across the road, halfway between them. There was no back entrance, nor even a fire escape. They didn't have those in the 1870s, but those Victorian blocks were solid brick and granite so fire was not a great hazard. Henderson could not get back home without being seen, and Slider was sure he would come home – where else would he go? The man was obviously not a great strategic thinker. As long as the Central bobbies had done their job and not let him slip in during the night, it was just a matter of time.

He came home like a weary dog in the early afternoon, head down, moving by instinct. Slider actually saw him first, rounding the corner from Long Acre – probably coming back from the tube station. He radio'd a warning to the other two. Gascoyne let him go past before crossing the road and falling in behind him, while Jenrich, eyes on her phone and apparently texting, wandered convincingly across and into his path, and bumped into him.

'Sorry.'

'Sorry.'

And during this brief transaction Gascoyne came up behind him, laid a hand on his shoulder, and said, 'Martin Henderson? I'd like to have a word with you.'

He felt the shoulder tense, as Henderson turned a white and wild face to him. 'Don't run,' Gascoyne said. 'It doesn't look good.'

'We just want a talk,' Jenrich said, showing her warrant card. 'Shall we go upstairs?'

'Oh God,' Henderson said in despair. Then, 'I haven't done anything!'

'Then you've got nothing to worry about, have you?' Jenrich said without sympathy. 'Come on, chap, don't make a fuss, or we'll have to arrest you.'

'Oh God,' Henderson said again, his face sagging like a neglected soufflé. He didn't look like a man who hadn't done anything. But then, everyone's guilty of something.

The flat was very different from the one below, though of course only Gascoyne had the privilege of comparison. It was much less dark, without the heavy carpets and curtains, and did indeed have vinyl flooring – the sort that mimics polished floorboards. No wallpaper, but off-white painted walls, and very little furniture, which did nothing to mute the clashing. It was not a cosy pad – Henderson was clearly no home-maker. It looked much as it must have done when the developers had finished with it. The only difference was that instead of smelling of paint, it had the flat, mildly stale smell that single men generally manage to impart to their living quarters: an absence of cleaning fluids, plus a hint of damp towels and Arôme de Chaussette.

Henderson hadn't said anything on the way up. He seemed to be thinking, and Slider half expected him to try to bolt again, even with such odds against him. But he let them all in to the flat, and turned in the doorway of the living room, tense and wide-eyed, a little dishevelled and unshaven, and said in a slightly too high voice, as if he expected to be beaten up, 'What's all this about? What do you want?'

'We're looking into the disappearance of Felicity Holland,' Slider said, watching Henderson's face for his first reaction.

Interestingly, the first flicker seemed to be relief. Then he said, 'What are you talking about, disappearance?'

'She didn't come home on Tuesday night, and hasn't been seen since,' Slider said.

He stared in blank puzzlement. At last he said, 'Well, she's not here.' And then, 'I don't know any Felicity Holland.'

Not the most nimble of thinkers, Slider concluded. 'You don't mind if we take a look round, do you?'

'No. I mean, yes, I do mind. No, you can't. Have you got a warrant? You have to have a warrant.' He was going for aggressive but it was coming off more as anxious. 'I know my rights. You can't just come into a person's home. We've got Habeas . . . something. This is not a police state. You can't push people around like a load of . . .' He stopped short of saying Nazis, but it hung unspoken on the air.

'Mr Henderson,' Slider said, quite gently, 'if you don't allow us to look round, I'll have to arrest you, and then I won't need your permission.' He gave him a steady look. 'Come on, be sensible,' he invited. 'What is it you don't want us to see?'

Henderson just looked miserable. 'Nothing,' he mumbled. 'All right, then,' said Slider.

Atherton remained with Henderson while Slider, Jenrich and Gascoyne looked round. Apart from the living room, there was a decent-sized kitchen, which seemed mostly used for the consumption of takeaways and the making of coffee; a rather smeary bathroom; an untidy bedroom with an unmade bed and a wardrobe, chest of drawers and bedside cabinet from Ikea; and a second bedroom which, unlike the rest of the flat, was tidy and dust-free, and was filled with home studio equipment, including a professional-looking sound board, an electronic keyboard, a computer, a saxophone on a stand in the corner and two guitars leaning against the wall, one electric, one acoustic. It was immediately evident that Felicity Holland was not concealed anywhere, alive or dead, there being no cupboard large enough to hold her, but whether she had been attacked there was a matter for forensics, so they touched as little as possible. Gascoyne looked into the hall cupboard – CH boiler and meters left barely enough room for a broom and an ironing-board – and Jenrich looked inside the wardrobe, just in case. She also checked in the top drawer of the bedside cabinet, and triumphantly produced a small baggie of white powder which she handed to Slider with a pitying shake of the head.

Slider went back into the living room and held it up in front of Henderson, whose crest fell visibly further. His lower lip wobbled and Slider could have sworn tears came to his eyes. He seemed very young for a man in his thirties, and remarkably unprepared for life's vicissitudes, even those of his own making. Slider remembered the panicky, flailing-limbed running of the previous day, and felt an unwanted sympathy.

'Is this what you were afraid of us finding?' he asked. 'Is this why you ran when you saw me yesterday?'

'Where did you get that?' he said desperately. 'That's not mine. You planted it. You're trying to frame me. What is it, anyway?'

'Mr Henderson,' Slider said gently, 'I really don't care what you put up your nose – that's not my current concern. But since this *is* an illegal substance, I can make myself care if I have to. If you don't co-operate and answer my questions, I can arrest you for possession and we can continue our conversation down at the station. But I'd rather not do that. I'd rather keep this all friendly. So, what's it to be? Will you talk to me here, and tell me the truth?'

'Like I have any choice,' he muttered sulkily.

Slider took that for consent. He sat down opposite Henderson, while the others took up unobtrusive positions out of the immediate line of sight so as not to distract him.

'Did Felicity Holland come here, to this flat, on Tuesday last?' Slider began.

Henderson looked wary, as if trying to work out where the trap was. When he answered, he tried to speak without moving his lips, as if that would incriminate him less. 'She was here for a bit. Not long.'

'What time did she leave?'

'I don't know. I wasn't checking. It's none of your business, anyway.'

'It certainly is our business. Didn't you hear me say she didn't come home on Tuesday night, and hasn't been seen since?'

He still looked more bewildered than worried. 'I told you she's not here. What d'you want from me?'

'Are you having an affair with her?' Slider asked sternly.

An expression of distaste came to Henderson's face. His nose wrinkled and his mouth turned down. 'God, no!' he exclaimed. 'Are you sick, or something?'

For an instant Slider channelled his inner Kate and thought him unpleasantly, intolerantly ageist.

But then Henderson concluded his answer. 'She's my mother.'

FIFTEEN
A Tale of Two Ditties

The story unrolled slowly. Henderson was no more an orator than an interior design guru, and Slider had to select the right questions to keep him going. He started with the easy stuff.

'You've lived here a while?'

'About three, four years.' So much for Mrs Bloom's memory. 'Since my mum and dad moved to Reading.'

It transpired there was a benign arrangement with the tenants of the Purnell Estate, if they had been good tenants for a number of years: that they could pass the tenancy on to a close relative. His parents had been there for seven years (Mrs Bloom forgiven) ever since his dad had retired. Before that they had occupied a Housing Association flat in Paddington, while Martin had lived in a studio flat in Bethnal Green. That would have been a tight fit for a pair of Doc Martens, so he'd been grateful to move into such generous accommodation at a controlled rent. 'It meant I could set up my studio properly.'

'You're a musician?'

'Songwriter,' he said, then, 'mostly.'

'Is that how you earn your living?'

Henderson looked at his feet. When he was embarrassed, he appeared even younger: it was possible to see what he had looked like as an awkward teenager – and Slider had had enough experience of humanity to know that this teenager had been awkward. Everything about him said so: his skinny, hunched shoulders, hands clasped between his knees, his unpremeditated clothes, his half-intentional-half-not unshavenness, his rampant dark hair that did not even conform to the current fashion of brushed-forward shagginess, but was merely a head rewilded. 'Well,' he said, 'I do the odd gig. And I do some production work for mates with bands. But songwriting's what I really . . . I mean, it's what I want to do. But it's hard to . . . You know. You have to have the breaks. I mean, if you can do a song for someone like Adele or Ed Sheeran, you're made. But . . .'

'And have you had any successes?'

'"Come and Get Me", Next Generation. That was one of mine. And "Just in Time" for Lara Carey. That got to number two for three weeks.'

Slider nodded as if he remembered them. He'd ask Kate when he got home. 'So you get royalties from those?'

'Yeah. And I wrote the "Longing for Home" song for the Warboy's bread commercial. That's me playing on it as well – the tenor sax solo.'

'And that's enough to live on, is it?'

'Well . . . I used to work for EMI, in Film and TV Sync, but I gave it up to concentrate on my writing full time. It's been . . . tough.'

'Even with a controlled rent, it's a bit of a struggle?' Slider offered sympathy. Henderson nodded gratefully. 'You've run up a bit of debt, I expect.'

'Yeah. Maxed out on my credit cards.'

'So Felicity Holland gave you money.' He reddened, and didn't answer. 'Two-fifty a week, wasn't it?'

'Look . . .' he began awkwardly. The baggie of cocaine hung metaphorically on the air between them. 'I never asked her. She offered. She wanted to help. She said – she said it was the least she could do.'

'Least she could do because . . .?'

'You know. Not keeping me as a baby. Not bringing me up.' He looked up. 'I never minded,' he said with sincerity. 'I always knew I was adopted. It never bothered me. My mum and dad were great. As far as I was concerned, they were my real parents. I never wanted, you know, to find out about my . . . my birth parents.'

'So how did you first meet her? How did that come about?'

'Well, it was when my dad died last year. Well, my mum was already gone – she died two years ago. And when my dad died, I thought . . . Well, there's just me, you see. No brothers or sisters – that's why they adopted, because they couldn't have kids – and my dad was an only child, my mum as well, so no uncles and aunts or cousins or anything. And I suddenly felt – well, not suddenly, I suppose, but I started to feel . . .'

'Alone in the world?' Slider helped. He supposed Henderson must be able to express himself in music and lyrics, because conversation face to face was obviously not his forte.

'Yeah,' Henderson said gratefully. 'It was like . . . I had nowhere I belonged any more. I started thinking. And then, when I was going through my dad's things, there was a photo album, and there were pictures of me as a baby, and there was a sort of certificate folded up behind one of them, and it was from when I was adopted. With the agency's name on it and everything.'

'How much did you know about your adoption?'

'Not much, really. Mum and Dad didn't talk about it – not that they wouldn't have, if I'd asked, but I wasn't interested. Really. I was happy as I was. They just said my birth mother couldn't keep me, and that was all. But then there was the music thing, you see. Ever since I was a little kid, all I wanted to do was play. I started piano at five – my dad did extra shifts to pay for lessons. Then at school I did clarinet and then sax, and I was in the school band and everything. So when I was sixteen I started my own band with some mates. We practised in one of them's dad's garage. I taught myself guitar, and I started writing our songs. Then we started to get some gigs at pubs and clubs and things. Mum and Dad were really proud and really supportive, but neither of them was musical at all. So after I found that certificate, I started to wonder if I got it from my birth parents. So I thought about it for a bit, and so then I wrote to them – the agency.'

'And what happened then?' Slider had to prompt him, as the long exposition seemed to have run down his motor.

'Well, it was a funny thing.' He started up again. The funny thing was obviously interesting. 'They'd just had a letter from her, a week before mine, saying that if I ever expressed a wish to see her, she really wanted to see me. It has to come from the adopted person, you see – the birth parent can't ask for it. So, anyway, they set up a meeting.' He stared in thought. 'Last December. Under the clock in Waterloo station.'

'I suppose it must have been a bit awkward at first,' Slider suggested.

Henderson looked up. When he looked straight at you, his eyes were a kingfisher flash of intense blue. Slider was reminded of Atherton's Siameses. 'No,' he said, 'that was the funny thing. It was really nice, right from the start. She's so easy to talk to. I've never been, you know, much of a talker, but she's a really great listener, and everything just sort of – poured out. And then, she knows about music, she did ballet and plays the piano. My mum and dad were great, they really supported me every way they could, but they didn't understand. My dad, he worked on the railway all his life, he was a booking clerk at the end but he'd done tons of other jobs, all for the railway. He knew everything about trains, they were his passion. And my mum, she worked for John Lewis, sales assistant, they don't pay well but it's like a big family. She loved it there. But neither of them listened to music, they didn't know anything about it, it was like I was talking a foreign language to them. But Fliss understands. She knows music like a musician, and it's so great talking to her. That first day, we walked along the Embankment for hours just talking and talking . . . well, I s'pose I did most of the talking.' A rueful smile, peeping quickly and disappearing again like a mouse. 'I felt as if I'd always known her. It was as if it was just . . .' A long pause, and then, slightly shamefaced for the language, 'meant to be.'

'And you've carried on seeing her.'

'Once a week. It was her idea. We meet at that restaurant across the road every Tuesday for lunch. She said we had to go slowly at first, get to know each other. But right away she was interested in my career. It was her that said I should go big, go all out for what I wanted. You see, I'd written a couple of songs for Ayeesha . . .' He looked questioningly at Slider and met blankness.

Jenrich helped things along. 'You mean Ayeesha from No Compromise?'

'Yeah,' he said gratefully. 'She wants to leave the group and go solo, and they say on the grapevine that she's got a rich uncle or someone who's going to spend masses on publicity so she's going to be big. Well, I'd written these two songs and I was going to send them to her, but when Fliss heard them she said they were so good, I should go all out and write a whole album for Ayeesha, make a demo and send it to her agent, become her dedicated songwriter, blend our styles so no one else could muscle in. She gave me money,' he said with a hint of defiance, 'so that I could improve my studio and concentrate on the project. I'm just working on the last song now. It'd be better if I had a female voice for the demo, and there's a girl I could ask, she's pretty good and I know she'd do it, but then I thought, I don't want to risk someone else hearing them before Ayeesha does and it maybe getting out, and maybe someone stealing my ideas. It's a cut-throat business, you can't trust anyone. Anyway, I can just sing them down the octave, it's OK. Fliss says my voice is fine for them, especially the slow numbers – she calls them "the melancholy ones". And she knows people, Fliss does, or she knows people who know people, so when the demo's ready she's going to make sure the right person gets it to Ayeesha's agent so it doesn't just get dumped on a desk some-where and forgotten, they'll definitely listen to it.'

It was painfully obvious from all this that Martin Henderson was not the killer of Felicity Holland any more than he was her lover – though he did appear to have somewhat of a crush on her, but that was hardly surprising.

'I assume,' Slider said, 'as you've been meeting once a week since – December? – that you'll have found out a bit about her, too, in all this talking.'

He did the blushing and staring-at-feet thing again. 'Yeah, we talked about her, about how she came to, you know, have me. I was a bit angry at one point about why she gave me away – you know, we were getting on so well, and it seemed like . . .' Apparently he had no word for it. A betrayal? Slider thought, but he didn't say it aloud. Henderson resumed. 'Anyway, apparently she was only seventeen when she fell for a baby, and the bloke, my birth father, he didn't want to know. He was a bit of a wild man, and he hadn't got a steady job and couldn't have supported her anyway. He was a musician, so that's where that comes from. Well, and her as well, of course. But he was professional. Jazz, not classical.'

'How did they meet?'

'She – her family – they lived in Kensington back then, and she bumped into him in South Ken station. Literally. He was on his way down the station to go to a gig and she was coming up, going to the museums to meet a friend. He bumped into her and they laughed, and then they got talking. And – well, something just sort of clicked. She says they fell in love at first sight. Couldn't stop looking at each other and talking. They started seeing each other secretly. It had to be secret because her dad wouldn't have approved, her being so young, and him being a lot older than her. He was very strict, her dad. And, she didn't know then but she found out later, he was married. Her dad went mad when he found out.'

He looked unhappy at the memory, though whether it was at his mother's frailty, his father's depravity, or his grandfather's lack of understanding, there was no telling.

'I suppose that's understandable,' Slider said cautiously, to help him along.

'Well, he's some high-up lawyer, her dad – really posh and all that. Strict. And a bit of a tartar. She was scared of him, back then. Not now; I don't think anything scares her now. Anyway, when she told him, her dad, that she was having a baby, he went mad. All about how she would ruin his reputation, she would kill his career, like she was breaking her mother's heart and bringing shame on the family and everything.' A flash of blue. 'You can imagine it.'

'Yes,' said Slider.

'He swore he'd make the man marry her, but she wouldn't tell him who it was, or anything about him. He went on and on at her, but she wouldn't tell him anything. So he said it all had to be hushed up, and he arranged everything, made her go to this special place in Scotland, way out in the wilds, miles from anywhere, where nobody knows you, and as soon as the baby's born they take it away from you and get it adopted. So she had no choice in the matter. She said they just let her hold me for one minute, and then took me away. But she's never stopped thinking about me, she says.'

'Have you met any of her family?'

'No. She says it's too soon. She says she's got to work them up to it slowly, because they'll be upset about it, especially her dad.' He shrugged. 'I don't care if I never meet them. But obviously, she cares, so I just go along with it. She wants me to be accepted into the family in the end – and her dad's apparently mega-rich, and she wants me to be in his will like his other grandchildren. I've told her it doesn't matter, but I think she feels I've lost out on a lot of stuff because of her. Like, she feels guilty. I keep telling her it's all right.' He shrugged again. 'Anyway, I must never write to her or phone her or anything, because she's married, and her husband doesn't know anything about – you know. She and him haven't got any children, and she reckons he'd be upset by it, she's got to find the right time to tell him. So that's why we do the restaurant thing – she rebooks the table each week for the next week. Only,' his voice faltered, 'when I went in yesterday, I could see she wasn't at our table, and she's always there before me – and then you got up and started towards me and – and I panicked. I thought . . .'

Obviously he didn't want to name it. 'Did you think we were after you for the illegal substances?' Slider said.

'I'm not an addict or anything,' he protested a little sullenly. 'Maybe once a week, that's all, when I'm relaxing, just a bit of blow, it doesn't hurt anyone, maybe the occasional spliff at a party. It's a victimless crime.'

'I haven't got time to go into why it isn't,' said Slider. 'Forget that for now. Tell me about last Tuesday. You met for lunch as usual, and then you brought her back here?'

'Yeah.'

'Did she buy you a sweater?'

He blushed. 'It was my birthday. I'd forgotten that of course she must know the date. She'd know it better than anyone. It was a bit weird thinking that she was actually there on the day, you know, when I was . . . That she was . . . It made me feel a bit . . .'

'Squeamish?' Slider offered.

He looked away. 'I don't really like thinking about that side of things. It's a bit embarrassing. I mean, she's a woman, she's attractive, you don't want to imagine . . . Anyway, she bought me this jumper. Not my style, but it was a nice gesture. It looks expensive. So we came back here. I showed her how far I'd got and played her the latest stuff, and we talked about the demo a bit, and whether we could maybe make a video to go with it. She said there was a film course at this adult education place where she does pottery, and she wondered if there was anyone there with a bit of talent. But I said it'd cost a lot of money to make it, and I don't have the equipment anyway. And then we had a cup of tea, and then she went.'

'What time was that?'

'Not sure. I didn't really look. About quart' to four, four, maybe?'

'And did you have a quarrel before she left?'

He looked surprised. 'A quarrel? No, of course not. I would never—'

'Loud voices were heard,' Slider said.

He stared, as if about to ask *by whom*, but didn't. 'Well . . . She made a phone call. Asked if she could borrow my phone. And she got a bit . . . She sounded angry with whoever it was.'

'Why did she use your phone? Doesn't she have one?'

A faint smile. 'She's got this ancient thing, it only does calls and texts, no apps or anything, not even a camera. She says it's just for emergencies. Anyway, she asked to use mine, and I said OK. Maybe her batteries were low. Or, it's pay-as-you-go; maybe it was out of dosh, I dunno.'

'Don't you know who she phoned?'

'I didn't ask.'

'Did you hear anything of what she was saying?'

'I didn't listen. I just gave her the phone and went into the kitchen to put the kettle on. She was in the living room. I could hear she sounded angry or upset, that was all. When she finished, she came into the kitchen and gave me the phone back, and we had a cup of tea, and then she said she had to go.'

'Was that her usual time of leaving?'

'There wasn't really a usual time. It was whenever. She just said she'd be off, and see you next week.'

'Did she say where she was going next?'

He shook his head. 'I thought she was going home, like usual.'

'But she didn't go home last Tuesday night, and no one's seen her or heard from her since.'

He was shaken at last out of the cosy cocoon of reminiscence. 'You don't think something's happened to her?'

'I don't know,' Slider said. 'I hope not. But it's becoming harder to believe she's safe somewhere but choosing not to communicate, though that is still possible. People sometimes strike a crisis in their life and go away somewhere to think. But generally there are some warning signs, and this seems to have come out of the blue. Did she seem different in any way when you met her last week?'

'No, not at all. She was just like usual. She seemed happy. And excited about my songs and my career. She said that I ought to sign on with an agency and do more commercials and jingles and so on. She said it paid good money, and it wasn't a question of prostituting my art, because the more I wrote, no matter what it was, the better I'd be at it. But I said I had to concentrate on the Ayeesha thing at the moment, though I said I'd think about it after the demo was finished. She said my Warboy's bread song was real music and I should be proud of it, and she said something like that could live for decades, long after a pop song was forgotten.'

Slider nodded, remembering some jingles from his younger days that stuck in the mind. 'Can you just account for your movements for the rest of that day?'

'Um . . . I just messed around for a bit. I went down the Prince of Wales about seven, to meet a mate of mine for a couple of pints, then we went to another mate's house and listened to some sounds. I s'pose I came home about eleven-ish.'

'And those friends would vouch for you?' Henderson looked alarmed. 'I just want to be sure you're out of the picture,' Slider said reassuringly. Jenrich took down the names and addresses. Then Slider said, 'Can you give us the number she called?'

'I never asked her. She didn't say.'

'It'll be on your phone. Under outbox, or recents, something like that.'

'Oh,' he said. 'I never thought of that.'

It was a mobile number, and Jenrich took that down too. Then Slider got up to go. 'If she should contact you, by any method, phone or text or whatever, you will tell me immediately, won't you?'

'Of course,' he said, accepting Slider's card.

'And if you remember anything she said that might help us?'

'Of course. I want to help.'

At the door, Atherton turned back to ask, 'Did she ever mention Burnham Beeches to you?'

'No. What are they?'

'It's a place. A well-known beauty spot.'

'I don't think so.' He frowned.

'She used to go there as a child.'

'We didn't really talk about her childhood much. I'd like to have . . . I expect we'd have got round to everything in time – but what we mostly talked about was what I was doing, my career and my music, Ayeesha and stuff.' He looked bereft, as if suddenly realizing the opportunity he had lost. He swallowed, and seemed to be near tears again. 'Please find her. Please,' he said.

'Well, that was a bust,' Atherton said. 'Where does that leave us?'

'Up the proverbial,' said Jenrich moodily. 'All we've done is move the last time she was seen forward by two hours.'

The rain had stopped, and dusk had come on. The lights from windows, cars and traffic lights reflected prettily in the wet pavements, and a chill little finger of wind worked itself down inside collars.

'I think we can eliminate Martin Henderson, don't you?' said Slider.

'I agree,' Atherton said. 'I don't think he's bright enough to dissemble. He's not the sharpest sandwich in the tool box.'

'Anyone can lie,' Jenrich said.

'Not so you can't tell.'

'Apart from his character,' Slider said, 'he had absolutely no motive for killing her. Exactly the opposite, in fact.'

'Yeah,' said Gascoyne. 'Two-fifty a week's got to come in handy. I wouldn't mind it. And he sounded to me as if he really liked her.'

'Yes. She was all he had left,' Atherton said.

'Plus, she *got* him,' said Gascoyne. 'That counts for a lot. Well, we can find out who she phoned. That might be worth something.'

'I can't believe he didn't listen,' Jenrich said.

'It would have been rude,' Atherton said. 'Obviously he was properly brought up. I rather warm to the railway clerk and the shop girl.'

At home, Slider found Next Generation's 'Come and Get Me' on Spotify – how did they manage before the internet? he wondered – and listened to it, thought it was quite tuneful. He'd be interested in Joanna's rating of the music, whether this man could actually compose, but she was out, doing a session. Given what else he knew about Felicity Holland's life, he assumed this was Josh Milo's son. There was certainly a resemblance to the ancient photo he had seen. Could musical talent be inherited? Well, in Henderson's case it looked as though it wouldn't have been nurture, so it must have been nature.

He took his phone to Kate and asked her opinion.

'Next Generation?' she said scornfully. 'That's old people music, from, like, a thousand years ago!'

'Five,' Slider said – though at Kate's age there wasn't much distinction, was there? 'But this particular song, "Come and Get Me". Do you know it?'

'I think I've heard it,' she said doubtfully. He played it to her. 'Oh, yes, I have heard it somewhere. On TV maybe. But it's as old as the hills.'

'All right, what about Lara Carey, "Just in Time"?' She shook her head. 'That got to number two, apparently.'

'Nobody cares about the charts any more, Dad,' she said. 'You like what you like. The charts are just the global business kleptocracy's way of monetizing talent. They manipulate sales figures to keep artists poor and grateful so they can exploit them. Why are you so interested in this stuff all of a sudden?'

What a bleak view of the world her generation had, he thought. 'What about Ayeesha?'

'What, Ayeesha from No Compromise? She's brill.'

One out of three's not bad, Slider thought.

'She's like, totally wasted in a group.'

'I understand she's intending to leave the band and go solo.'

Kate's cruelly plucked eyebrows rose. 'How d'you know that?'

'I was talking to a songwriter today, who's writing a solo album for her.'

'Wow!'

It wouldn't last long, and two minutes from now he'd just be, 'God, you're so lame, Dad!' again, but just for a moment it was pleasant to bask in Kate's impressed attention.

'So you think Ayeesha could make it as a solo artist?' he said, to keep her talking.

'Oh, totally,' she said. 'No Compromise did this great number last month that was practically like a solo for Ayeesha anyway, the rest of them just like doing a backing group. I loved it. Look it up on Spotify. It's called "Lay With Me".'

'I bet that's popular at hen parties,' Slider said.

It took her a moment, lips moving, to get it, and then she said, 'God, you're so lame, Dad!'

Normality restored. It was almost comforting.

SIXTEEN
Edifice Complex

'Thames Valley are winding up the search,' Porson said, fiddling with a stapler. Slider tried not to look – any minute the thing could go off in his hand. 'They've not found dicky, and the chief constable said they can't afford to keep on with it. Mr Carpenter says he thinks they reckon it must have been a hoax call. There's a lot of walkers use Burnham Beeches, and DCS Felway reckons she'd have been found by one of them long ago if she'd been there.' He clicked the stapler a few times, moodily. Without wanting to, Slider saw the staples fall into his neglected mug of tea on the desk.

'That's all very well,' Slider began, 'but—'

'That's what I said. It's chicken and egg. Nothing to be done about it, anyway. We're on our own again. Keep at it. Something's bound to break sooner or later. If at first you don't succeed . . .'

Silently, Slider provided his own ending – *then skydiving is probably not for you.*

'It's a long road that gathers no moss,' he said aloud.

Porson grunted agreement, then gave him an odd look. 'Well, get on with it, then!' he barked, clicking aggressively.

Ten minutes later Slider was back. 'The telephone call Felicity Holland made from Henderson's phone – the number turns out to belong to Sir John Aubrey-Harris,' he said.

Porson looked up from wrapping a tissue round his left forefinger. 'The one she had a row with?'

'She sounded angry or upset, according to Henderson. And she spoke loudly enough for the woman in the flat below to hear her. So it must have been pretty heated. *Now* can I interview him?'

Porson's face went thoughtful. Slider knew he was

considering whether he ought to run it past Mr Carpenter first; and thinking that if he did, Mr Carpenter would probably say no. But eight days into this investigation, you couldn't afford to ignore leads, however frayed they might appear, and however mangy the dog on the other end. Slider willed him to say yes. You can't make bricks without breaking eggs, he urged silently.

'He lied about not having talked to his daughter in weeks,' Porson said. 'So he's got something to hide. Do it.'

'He left his club shortly before four o'clock that day,' said Jenrich. 'She left Henderson's pad somewhere about the same time. He took his car out of the garage at four. He'd have had to pass through Drury Lane to get to the garage. So even if they didn't agree to meet during that phone call, they could still have met by chance on the street. Then what's to say he didn't invite her into the car, offer to give her a lift somewhere, so he could continue the row.'

'Why would she accept?' LaSalle asked.

'Because she wanted to continue it as well. The sort of row you have with your dad is generally the sort that goes on for years, and neither side wants to stop before they win.'

'All right, so he offers her a lift, and then what?'

'Drives her out somewhere – we've got him near Primrose Hill. Maybe he goes there. He parks up and they take a walk to continue the argument. Maybe they're both trying to be reasonable by that time. They both think they can persuade the other. But it can't last. Before long they're hammer and tongs again. It gets so heated, he lashes out – I'm still willing to bet killing her was accidental. Maybe he pushes her away and she loses her balance and falls and hits her head on something.'

'And nobody sees any of this?' Atherton said disbelievingly.

'Maybe they're among the trees by then. There's a lot of wooded areas on the Hill. So he sees he's killed her, panics and has it away. Sits in his car, maybe drives around, fear and trembling. But nothing happens. No hue and cry, no phone call, no one feeling his collar. So after dark he goes back, and she's still there, undisturbed. He gets her back to his motor and hides her inside. Stops somewhere quiet on the way home and moves her into the boot. Next day he drives out to the golf course, and on the way back he dumps her in the woods at Burnham Beeches, stops to get the car washed and valeted in case there's any bloodstains or anything, and Bob's your uncle.'

'Hm,' said Atherton. 'I still can't believe nobody saw any of this three-act play as it unfurled.'

'Maybe somebody did, but you know how people are – they don't want to get involved.'

'And why Primrose Hill? There are much wilder places he could have taken her.'

Jenrich gave him an impatient look. 'He didn't take her anywhere intending to kill her, that's my point. It was just supposed to be a conversation, then it went bad.'

'But still – Primrose Hill?' said Atherton. 'It's not even on his way home.'

'It might be,' said Gascoyne, coming in. 'Has the guv gone yet? I've got some more info.'

Gascoyne had just heard from his contact in Traffic division.

'The motor you were interested in – the Jag?'

'Yeah. You got a ping on it?'

'I've asked around, and it's been seen parked up in Elsworthy Road.'

'Remind me?'

'Runs parallel with the north side of Primrose Hill. There's a turning off it, Elsworthy Terrace, which is like an access road, opens right on to the hill.'

'Oh,' said Gascoyne, with interest. 'How come the Jag was noticed?'

'There's a lot of big houses in Elsworthy, lot of important people live there, cabinet ministers and stuff, so we do a regular patrol, just to keep the taxpayers sweet. Take note of any suspicious-looking motors hanging around. Not that the Jag's suspicious, but it's noticeable, with that index number.'

'JAH 1,' Gascoyne said, remembering that Atherton had said scornfully, 'Vanity goes no further.' As a social commentator you could despise people who had personalized number plates, but as a copper you were glad of anything that made your job easier.

'That's it,' said his contact. 'Last Tuesday it was parked there when the patrol went past at around seventeen hundred, and still there on the second pass at twenty hundred. But of course, they've checked the index on the ANPR so they know whose it is. So they don't take any action. My mate wants to know he's not going to get into any sticky telling you this.'

'No sticky. I don't know anyone's name,' said Gascoyne.

'Fair enough. Anyway, he says he's logged the Jag on ten days this year, on Elsworthy, at different times of day. So maybe your bloke's got a place, owns a house or a flat – some of the big houses are divided up.'

'Did your mate say what number Elsworthy?'

'No, but I can ask him. I'll let you know.'

'I like this better than the open-air murder,' Atherton said. 'If he's got a pied-à-terre, he might take her there and do the killing in the comfort and privacy of his own home, then take the body out to the car after dark and so on.'

'If it was an accident,' Slider said, 'the sensible thing would have been to call the emergency services right away.'

Atherton shrugged. 'People do stupid things when they panic. And often, the more educated they are, the stupider, because they overthink it, try to second- and third-guess. Hence his not mentioning that he had a telephone row with her on the Tuesday. And drawing attention to the car by getting it valeted at a different car wash. If he'd let his usual place do it, a thousand to one they'd just have cleaned it and never noticed anything amiss. Those boys work so fast, they're not looking for suspicious stains as they spray and buff.'

'You're probably right. Well, I agree he's got questions to answer, anyway,' said Slider.

Sir John was in Town that day, and though Shepherd's Bush was much too far west to ask a person of his eminence to travel to, he consented to meet Slider at Charing Cross police station, which was in Agar Street, just off the Strand, and was housed in a handsome neo-classical building of white stucco with a Greek portico, the sort of edifice a gentleman wouldn't be ashamed of being seen to enter.

They even loaned Slider a proper office to meet him in, with panelling and carpet and a mahogany desk. Sir John came in, head thrown back so that he could look down his nose, and snapped impatiently at Slider as though he was the help.

'Well? What is it? I hope you have asked me here to tell me you've made some progress. Have you found my daughter yet? If not, why not?'

'We haven't found her, but we have made progress,' Slider said. 'And I have some questions to ask you.'

Sir John's eyebrows went up so high his scalp shifted backwards to avoid them. 'Ask *me* questions?' he said, as if it were the most outrageous suggestion he'd ever heard.

Slider was heartened. Only a guilty person would assume that the questions would need to be objected to. He might have been going to ask about Felicity's reading habits or shoe size. 'Yes, Sir John,' he said with renewed confidence. 'We have interviewed the last person we know to have been with her on Tuesday, and we know that, while in his company, she telephoned you.'

'Rubbish!' he said, reddening.

'And a conversation was had with you which became heated. I'd like to know the substance of that conversation.'

Sir John tried a sneer. 'Has it occurred to you that that person, whoever he is, was lying?'

'I didn't say it was a "he".'

'Oh, for God's sake! Don't try your childish tricks on me. He or she, why should you believe them? I was a prosecuting counsel, many people have reason to wish to get their own back on me. They were probably trying to incriminate me out of spite.'

'We retrieved your number from the mobile phone Felicity used. So we know she called you. I would like to know what you argued about, and why you told me you hadn't spoken to her since Christmas, when in fact you spoke to her on the very day of her disappearance. Rather important evidence to be withholding, don't you think?'

Sir John shifted ground. 'What we spoke about has nothing

to do with her disappearance. It was a private conversation, and I have no intention of telling you any more than that.'

'If it had no relevance, why conceal it from me? Why lie about it?'

'I didn't lie about it, I merely did not tell you. Because it's none of your damned business. It's a family matter. And if that's all you have to say to me, I have better things to do than stay here listening to you. After ten days, you seem to have achieved nothing, done nothing at all. The commissioner will be hearing from me about your gross incompetence, and if it transpires that any harm has come to my daughter as a result, the consequences to you will be very serious indeed.'

He was leaving. Slider said, 'Let me be clear about this. You are refusing to tell me what you spoke to Mrs Holland about on the day she disappeared?'

'Got it at last,' Sir John said nastily.

'And will you tell me where you went after you left your club that day?'

'I went home to bed, of course,' he said impatiently.

'No, I mean when you left the club after lunch. You didn't go back there to supper, as you told your housekeeper. You drove to St John's Wood and turned off the A41 towards Primrose Hill. Where did you go then?'

He grew even redder, and spoke with low fury. 'You have been checking on my movements? How *dare* you! Is this how you've been wasting your time, instead of finding my daughter? You have no right, absolutely no right, to spy on me in this manner. I shall be making a very serious complaint about you to the highest authority.'

'So you're refusing to tell me where you went?' Slider said sturdily.

'I most certainly am. Get out of my way, I'm leaving.'

Slider let him go.

At the door Sir John turned to say, 'If you value your skin, you'll find my daughter, alive. Nothing else will save you.' Then he was gone, with a puff of sulphur and a swirl of cloak.

Slider was quite accustomed to being threatened. Indeed, a

day without threats to have his job, or his arse, was like the egg without the salt.

The complaint reached Shepherd's Bush before he did. Porson intercepted him on his way to his office.

'So that went well,' he said. 'I've had Sir John doing his biscuits on the phone for the last half-hour. You put a bug up his rear end all right. Obviously he's got something to hide.'

'Have I still got a job, sir?' was Slider's response.

Porson almost grinned. 'He came straight on to me as soon as he left you. Not the commissioner, not even Mr Carpenter – me. Which proves he knows he hasn't got a leg to stand on.'

'Oh,' said Slider.

'Now he's let off steam, he'll have a little think, and realize he's not covered himself in glory. Next time you talk to him, he'll purr like a pussy cat.' He shrugged. 'Still lie his teeth off, of course, but he'll do it nicely. Do you think he did it?' he asked abruptly.

'We don't even know if there was any "did" for him to "do",' Slider said wearily, staring at nothing. 'But he's hiding something. There are too many knots for it not to be connected. The phone call, the quarrel, Burnham Beeches, the handbag, the tip-off by the murderer, if it was the murderer. But did he kill her? I don't know.'

'But you do think she's dead,' Porson said quietly.

Slider looked up. 'After all this time? Unfortunately, yes – I do.'

'Then it's a murder enquiry, and you go on, no matter what. Nobody's pulling this. Do what you have to, Slider. I've got your back.'

'Thank you, sir,' Slider said. He'd have preferred to be pulled – except that then he wouldn't have slept for wondering.

He rang Joanna.

'Hello! What's up?' she said.

'Can't a person ring his own wife?'

'It's an unexpected pleasure, darling. What's up?'

'This is a serenity call.'

'What are you serene about?'

'No, I need serenity. I've been threatened with losing my job.'

'And you're all shook up? Isn't it just a monthly ritual?'

'Why do people lie?' he complained.

'Globally? Or specifically? Because a lie sorts out the present, though it rarely has a future.'

'That's very profound.'

'We had some Christmas crackers left over. I've been at the mottoes. George wants a fish pond.'

'Good Lord. Why?'

'Dunno. He's looking to extend his menagerie, I suppose. He knows we can't afford a dinosaur.'

'Well, tell him no fish. Apart from Jumper and all the neighbourhood cats, there are foxes—'

'Not to mention the occasional heron flying up from the river and looking for an easy meal.'

'Exactly. The price of koi is eternal vigilance. When I was a lad, a boy at school had a grass snake,' he mentioned.

'No reptiles,' Joanna said firmly. 'I don't mind a white mouse.'

'You're a remarkable woman. Gotta go.'

'Feeling more serene?'

'You could sail paper boats on me without capsizing. See you tonight.'

Someone had fetched custard tarts from the Portuguese deli on Uxbridge Road to go with the afternoon tea round. Gascoyne brought Slider's to his office. He was looking amused.

'My traffic contact's come back, sir,' he said. 'He got the house number from his mate, where Sir John's Jag's been seen, and I've gone through the Land Registry for the owner. It doesn't belong to Sir John.'

'Oh?' Slider said, wondering why Gascoyne wasn't disappointed.

'No, sir. It is the domicile of Sir Peter Spencer, justice of the High Court of the Queen's Bench division.'

'I suppose there's no reason he shouldn't visit a High Court Judge, given he was a silk before he retired,' said Slider. 'They're probably chums from way back. In chambers together, or the old school.'

'Except that my contact's mate looked into it, and on that Tuesday Sir Peter happened to be sitting on a special committee at the House of Lords that went on until ten p.m. And he's checked a couple of other times the Jag was logged, and each time Sir Peter was at work at the time. He says it's easy enough to check on a High Court judge,' he concluded. 'You always know where they are. My contact's mate had his interest piqued. He's going to check all the other times as well.'

'Are you going somewhere with this?'

'Judge Spencer's sixty-five, and his wife is fifteen years younger. And even given that makes her fifty-ish, she's a hottie.'

'Are you suggesting—?'

Gascoyne grinned. 'I had a look online and found some images of her. Here's one, sir.'

Slider looked. Mrs Justice Spencer was indeed a hottie, a ravishing smile and a sheaf of honey-blonde hair atop a very decent figure.

'Old tunes and good fiddles, and all that,' Gascoyne said. 'HRT's got a lot to answer for. And there's a lot to be said for variety – though why she'd want to vary an old High Court judge with an even older retired silk is beyond me.'

'Availability?' said Slider. 'Sir John, being retired, might have more time to devote to her.'

'He's not a bad-looking old gent,' Gascoyne allowed, 'and maybe he's terrific where it counts.'

'You're quite sure this is the right house? Parking outside a house doesn't mean you're not actually visiting the one next door, or several doors down, even if there's not much space.'

'Actually parked on the gravel of the front garden – I did check.'

'Don't look so pleased. You realize this would give him his alibi, and leave us without a suspect,' said Slider.

'He might still have taken Felicity there,' said Gascoyne. 'Mrs Justice might have been out as well, and he just used the hard standing to park. Or if he's a regular, he might have a key.'

'Now you're reaching.'

'Anything's possible. We don't know what happened, sir,'

Gascoyne said with a shrug. 'People do mad things. There's no accounting for them.'

'Well, that's true, at least. And I still want to know why he lied about talking to his daughter.'

'And why he put his clubs in the back of the car instead of the boot. And why he had the car cleaned at a different car wash. I reckon it's all connected, sir.'

'That's just what I said to Mr Porson,' said Slider.

SEVENTEEN
Perjury in Motion

The housekeeper gave him a tight-lipped, I'm-very-disappointed-in-you look, but she said, 'Sir John will see you. You'd better come in.'

Slider stepped from the delicious scents of dusk – cold grass, damp ditches, a green hint of nettles – into the warm house, and got furniture polish and a recently lit wood fire instead. The dogs circled and smiled at him, then shoved unceremoniously past him to get to the fire first. Sir John, sitting by the fireside reading what looked like an official report – many pages, properly bound together in blue card covers – stood up and gave him a look in which disapproval and a sort of sick resignation collided.

'I knew you'd be back,' he said. 'I've made enquiries about you. You have a reputation. You mistake obstinacy for integrity.'

Mrs Yeatman, at the door, interrupted. 'I'll be in the kitchen, Sir John, if you need me.' Given that it was an unnecessary statement – where else would she be? – Slider took it to be a warning for him.

Sir John waved her away without answering, and waited until the door had closed behind her to say, 'Well?' in as unencouraging a voice as possible.

'As you must know,' Slider said, 'in an enquiry you have to tie up loose ends. Defence counsel are all too happy to make hay with them. You lied about talking to your daughter on the phone that Tuesday. Our witness says it sounded like a quarrel. I can guess what it was about, but I need to know from you.'

'Who is this precious witness of yours?' It was said with a sneer. He was not giving in until he had to.

'Martin Henderson,' Slider said. The name was met with

blankness. Interesting – she hadn't mentioned his name to her father? He tried the shock tactic. 'Her illegitimate son.'

Sir John stared, and in the reflected firelight you couldn't see if he paled, but his expression suggested pallor of the heart. He sat down abruptly, and waved Slider to the chair opposite. A dog groaned companionably as Slider stepped over it; the fire crackled and a log popped, sending sparks up the chimney; somewhere in the room a clock slowly ticked, dicing eternity into bitesize pieces.

'How in God's name did you find out about that?' Sir John asked in a mutter.

Slider didn't answer that. He said, 'You didn't know his name?'

'No,' said Sir John. After a pause he said, 'I didn't want to know. I never wanted to think about it again. That was the point of the whole thing. That it should be all over, for good.' He looked up. 'For her, as well as for us. She was seventeen. Just seventeen,' he said bitterly. 'So beautiful, so talented, full of innocence and freshness and passion. Her whole life before her. To see all that . . .' He searched a long time for the word. 'Smirched. Tainted. To see her potential, her opportunities, all ended for one stupid, venal, tawdry . . .' He ran out of words.

'Did you know who the father was?' Slider asked.

'She would never say. Only that she "loved him".' It was said with a sneer. 'Obviously, *he* could not care less. It was up to me to act, to salvage the situation, to save what could be saved, of her and of the family's reputation. Culburnie House . . . It was established for that purpose. Remote, hidden. Complete discretion. A new start – for both sides. No further contact: the most humane outcome. How in God's name did he ever find her?'

Slider gave him the short version. 'Chance,' he said. 'She wrote to them, expressing willingness to see him if he should ever contact them. And he did contact them, almost at the same time. So they put them in touch with each other. Didn't she tell you any of this?'

'No. She said only that she'd met him and was very happy and wanted him to be part of the family. Part of the family!' he repeated in withering tones.

'Would that be so very bad?'

He stiffened. 'Keep your weak, liberal, bleeding-heart comments to yourself. It's not your job to make running commentary on my actions. I've told you what we talked about, and that's all you need to know. It's private family business and nothing to do with you.'

'People lying in an investigation is always my business. You lied about not speaking to her for months. I think you lied about not seeing her, too. You left your club shortly before four o'clock and collected your car from the parking garage around four. To get there you would have had to pass through Drury Lane just at the time she was there too, and I think you met her, either by arrangement or by chance.'

'What in God's name would she be doing in Drury Lane?' It sounded genuine.

'That's where he lives. She was with him, at his flat, when she telephoned you.'

'God Almighty,' he said. One of the dogs lifted its head and looked up at him for a moment, as if objecting to the blasphemy. 'I didn't know. She didn't say where she was. I didn't know he was there, listening.' He looked a little sick. Of course, he didn't know whether she might have had the phone on speaker. Slider wondered what exactly he had said in that heated exchange that he wouldn't have wanted Henderson to hear. Probably everything. 'I didn't meet her. I didn't see her. I picked up the car and went home.'

'Please, not another lie. You drove to the home of Sir Peter Spencer. Despite the fact that he was not at home at the time, you remained several hours. Was Mrs Justice Spencer – Lady Spencer – there?'

'What business is it of yours? Yes, I know Lallie Spencer. If you *must* know, my late wife and I and the Spencers were bridge partners for many years.'

'You know Lallie Spencer? Yes, I think you know her very well. It's an odd thing that you seem always to call at the Spencers' house when Sir Peter's out. Why is that?'

He was on his feet so fast it made the dogs heave themselves up in alarm. 'Get out!' he shouted. '*Get out!*'

One of the dogs barked. Remarkably quickly, the door

opened and Mrs Yeatman looked in. Had she been listening
at the door? 'Is everything all right, Sir John?'

Slider met his eye and raised an eyebrow, which said, *I can
tell her. It's no skin off my nose.*

Breathing hard through his nose, Sir John took control. 'It's
all right, Brigid. I'll ring if I want you,' he said harshly.

She gave Slider a minatory look and withdrew.

Sir John said in a low voice that trembled, 'How dare you
presume to judge me?'

'Oh, I don't,' Slider said. 'That sort of activity is too common-
place to arouse any curiosity in me, let alone condemnation. I'm
only interested in why, if you see nothing wrong in extramarital
sex, you treated your daughter's lapse so harshly.'

He looked genuinely surprised. 'That's completely different.'

'Is it?'

'It wasn't harshness. She was only a child, I was her father.
It was my duty to protect her, to give her the best possible
opportunities in life. I salvaged what I could from a terrible
situation, set her on a clear path.' His face darkened. 'But
she was always wilful. Stubborn. I did everything in my power,
but how could I succeed when she insisted on working against
me? And then, after everything we'd gone through, the pains
I'd taken, the expense, to put it all behind us and save our
name and reputation, she has the . . . the *insensitivity* to propose
I should meet this person, embrace him, take him into the
bosom of the family! And when I merely point out the illogic
of her request, the harm it would do to all of us – and there
are others to consider, not only her: what about her sister, her
nephews? What about her innocent husband? – she flies into
a rage and screams abuse at me.'

'I can see you must have been shaken. No wonder you
rushed straight to your mistress for comfort.'

Sir John had been speaking with heat, now he turned icy.
'I shall be sure to report your impertinence and inappropriate
behaviour to the highest authority. In the meantime, you had
better leave.'

'Just a couple more questions. Why did you put your golf
bag on to the back seat of your car the next day, instead of
in the boot?'

The surprise of the question flipped the answer out of him before he thought. 'I always put it on the back seat. It's heavy. It's easier to slide it out from there than lift it out of the boot. Why are you—?'

'Why did you take your car to a car wash in Fulmer that day, instead of going to your regular place?'

'*Why?* Because it was splashed with mud. Hawthorn Lane is very muddy when there's been a lot of rain. I don't like a dirty car, and I was going to meet someone. Why in God's name are you asking me these things?' Before Slider could answer he worked it out for himself. 'You think I had something hidden in the boot? What on earth could I have—?' His scalp shifted again, and an expression of extreme distaste came over his face. His lips trembled even as he curled them. 'You think I did my daughter harm? My own daughter? You're disgusting!'

'I have to ask questions and tie up loose ends,' Slider said. 'You of all people should understand that, Sir John. It's nothing personal.'

'You think there's nothing personal in accusing me of—'

'I accused you of nothing.'

'Leave. Leave now, before I throw you out. You have not heard the last of this, I promise you.'

Slider walked towards the door, turning only to say, 'Just from my own curiosity, did you ever speak to your daughter about the child, after she came back from Culburnie House?'

'Never,' he said, without emphasis. 'That was the whole point of the exercise, that it should be forgotten.'

Slider nodded, thinking it was strange how many people over the centuries had thought that separating a woman from her baby could be the end of the matter. 'I am still trying to find her,' he said quietly. 'I want you to know that. I shall not stop until I do find her. But I'm afraid my gut feeling is that it's too late.'

His last glimpse of Sir John's face told him that his guts were telling him the same thing, and that perhaps they had been saying it all along. There was no better way of dealing with guilt than smothering it with self-righteous anger.

*   *   *

Outside, Brigid Yeatman reached him before he got into the car. 'Did you have to bring up all that old stuff and upset him?' she said reproachfully.

'You knew about it,' Slider said.

'Of course I did. I'd to help with the arrangements. I packed her suitcase, for goodness' sake. Nobody else, though – just her ma and pa and me. Thelma never knew a thing, so don't you go spouting it out to her. She was away at boarding school and it was all arranged and over between Christmas and Easter, and I know for a fact that Felicity never told her. Why would she?'

'Why indeed?'

'What good would it have served?' Mrs Yeatman argued. 'It was all over and done with, and there was no going back.'

'Was there never any discussion about alternatives?' Slider asked, of his own curiosity.

'What need? Culburnie House was a specialist place, designed for unruly girls. That's what they called them. It kept them out of harm's way until the time came: miles from anywhere, out in the sticks, Inverness was the nearest town, and even if they could have got there – which they couldn't, with no bus or train and they'd no money anyway for either – what mischief can you get up to in Inverness? Then into the local cottage hospital for the birth, the babby whisked off, and it was all cleaned up and tidied away. They could go home and start a fresh life.' She hesitated, not quite meeting his eyes.

'Yes?' he encouraged. 'There's something else?' She plainly was not as easy in her mind about it all as she was pretending.

'While they were in the hospital, there was a little snip they could do to make sure it never happened again. I saw it on a doccyment once when I was dusting his desk. The parents or guardians could request it, with a doctor's letter. Mind,' she added quickly, 'I couldn't say if they had that done in her case. But it was a fact that she never did have any more children, even with being married all these years to himself. And it's a fact that she'd ample chance to fall for a babby, with the carry-on of her in her young days. But I've sometimes wondered . . . Maybe that's why she carried on, if they'd had that done and then told her about it. Because she'd have had nothing more to lose, d'ye see?'

'Yes,' Slider said, an unpleasant churning in his guts at the thought. 'What about her mother? Didn't she have anything to say?'

'She wasn't a well woman, even then. And even in the whole of her health, she wouldn't say boo to a goose, that one. She was well under his thumb. Himself made all the decisions.' Mrs Yeatman seemed to have received relief from her revelations. Her expression cleared and she shrugged. 'Well, it was not how I'd have dealt with it if she'd been a girl of mine, but there. Water under the bridge now. And he did it for the best. The end of it was she'd been given a fresh chance, and it was up to her to make it work.'

'Well, thank you for your help,' Slider said, feeling less than thankful for the additional burden. A long bath might make him feel less grubby.

She gave him a curious look. 'When I saw her at Christmas, and she looked so happy . . .?'

'Apparently they met for the first time in December. She and her lost child.'

'God A'mighty.' It was a different exclamation in her mouth than in Sir John's. 'And I thought she'd taken a lover. But it was him.'

'It's possible that's why she seemed happy. They've been meeting regularly ever since.'

'But she's not with him now?'

'I don't believe he has any idea where she is or what's happened to her.'

Mrs Yeatman shook her head slowly, a tragic cast to her lips. 'Oh Lord. What a thing, for this to happen, just when she's got her baby back again after all those years.'

'Except that all those years later he's a grown man.'

'You're right, Mr Policeman. You can never get your babby back. What a mess! But don't come here again, upsetting Sir John. He's a good man.'

'I don't think I'll need to come here again,' he said.

When – if – they found Felicity Holland, someone else could break the news.

When he got home, he found Atherton sitting on *his* sofa, next to *his* wife, with *his* cat on his lap, drinking *his* gin and tonic.

'Well!' he said.

'I thought I'd better check up on you, as you'd gone on a Kamikaze mission,' said Atherton.

'Fat lot of good you'd be doing me, making yourself at home here.'

'I did think of lurking in Sir John's shrubbery and listening for your screams, but it looked a bit damp outside, and I'd pressed my trousers this morning,' Atherton said. 'Anyway, Kamikaze pilots never got rescued.'

'How did it go?' Joanna said anxiously. 'Did he get angry?'

'More importantly, did he tell you anything useful?' said Atherton.

'He said he didn't see her after that phone call, and I believe him. He didn't seem to know Martin Henderson lived in Drury Lane or that she was with him when she rang. He didn't even know his name was Martin Henderson.'

'Anyone can feign innocence,' Atherton objected.

'He's no actor,' said Slider. 'Feigning is not his forte. I think we can rule him out.'

'I'm glad,' Joanna said. 'You'd hate it if another father hurt his own daughter.'

'Speaking of which . . .?'

'Kate's gone over to a friend's to revise together. George and Teddy are in bed. G and T?'

She didn't wait for an answer. While she was out of the room, Slider filled Atherton in on the interview with Sir John. Joanna came back with his drink, and on a plate a couple of individual pork pies cut into quarters, 'To keep you going until supper.'

There was mustard on the side of the plate to dip the pieces in. 'What a woman!' Slider said. Atherton snaked one piece with long fingers. 'Oy!' he protested.

'Come on! What's yours is mine, surely,' Atherton said. 'Is this the same mustard as I had last time?'

'Of course,' Joanna said, puzzled.

'Ah. I thought so. *Dijon vu*.'

'This is not the time for joking,' she said.

'It's the perfect time for joking, when you're at a dead end and can't see any way out.'

She looked at Slider. 'Are you really at a dead end?' He shrugged, his mouth being full. 'Do you think she's dead?'

He swallowed. 'I hope not. I'd hate this to be one of those cases where the bones turn up twenty years later. People shouldn't have to live with that sort of uncertainty about those they love.' As Felicity herself did, for thirty-six years.

'So what do you do now?' Joanna asked.

'Carry on. Keep asking questions. Sooner or later, something will break.' He said it more confidently than he felt.

'Meanwhile,' Atherton said, 'perhaps we need to try coming at it from a different angle.'

'Yes,' Slider agreed. 'Like an ill-regulated cat.'

'Eh?'

'Think "outside the box".'

'Let's start by talking about something else, give your brain a rest,' Atherton said. He turned to Joanna. 'How was your session last night?'

'OK. Ancelotti was conducting. We call him Shirley Bassey, because whenever he addresses the lower strings, he calls out "Celli-bassi, celli-bassi!"' She shrugged. 'These little things keep us amused through a long evening.'

'Us?' Slider queried.

'I was sitting next to Mike Richards. He's always got something funny to say.'

'What were you playing?'

'Oh, a modern piece. Klaus Goldfarb.'

'Never heard of him,' Atherton said.

'Squeaky gate music. And lots of percussion, including half a dozen Siamese gongs. Bill Mitchell, who was playing percussion, knocked one by accident in a quiet passage so it rang, and Mike whispers to me, "Dinner is served." It's really hard not to laugh. Then later, in another passage when Bill's been knocking himself out playing the whole lot, Ancelotti complains they're too loud, and Mike says so everyone can hear, "Let

Thai gongs be Thai gongs." Of course, everyone cracks up. Except for Ancelotti.' She stood up. 'I'd better get supper on. Are you staying Jim?'

'No, thanks, I'll be getting home. Stephanie said she might phone me later.'

'I never thought I'd live to see the day, Jim Atherton hanging around by the phone hoping for a call,' she mocked.

She went out, not waiting for his explanation. 'It's not that. Obviously she'll call me on my mobile. I just want to be alone when she does, so I can talk privately.'

'What could you have to say to her that we couldn't hear?' said Slider.

'Almost everything. You look thoughtful.'

'I was thinking. We don't know where she went after she left Henderson's flat, but we know she didn't use the tube or bus. Assuming for the moment she wasn't snatched off the street by a random maniac, maybe she took a taxi somewhere. Holland said they often did use taxis. We should put out an enquiry.'

'Yes. And it wouldn't be an Uber because she didn't have apps on her phone,' Atherton said. 'So unless Henderson called a minicab for her – and surely he would have told us if he had; but we can check with him in case he did and forgot to tell us, the dozy wagon – we just need to ask the black-cab fraternity. You see, my diversionary tactic for the brain worked!'

'I owe everything to you,' Slider said solemnly. 'Now can I have my cat back?'

EIGHTEEN
Gits That Pass in the Night

One of the good things about the digital age was that you could communicate with all black-cab drivers immediately and simultaneously, and send them the image of Felicity Holland over the net at the same time. Slider remembered in the old days having to speak to each taxi garage separately, and to have the managers pass on the message to their drivers when they came in to the depot, and give them a photocopy of a photograph. Things were that clunky back when dinosaurs roamed the earth and Cliff Richard was a lad.

The driver who came in gave his name as Stefan Kowalski from Poznań, though he had obviously been in London long enough to have lost almost all his accent. He was a tall, strongly built man in his late thirties – he looked too big to be confined to a taxi's driving seat all day. Slider could imagine him driving an enormous combine harvester across wide, hedgeless continental plains of wheat – or even a team of horses, with the multiple reins gathered easily in his large, capable hands. He had a broad, pleasant face with a fresh complexion, light brown hair cut *en brosse*, and frank blue eyes. Everything about him said, 'Trust me'. Slider would have bet he had a couple of adoring daughters. He reminded him a little of Gascoyne.

He lived in Maida Vale, but preferred working in central London where, if you knew your Knowledge properly, you could make better money and bigger tips. On the day in question he had just dropped off an American couple at the Waldorf Hilton, and had turned the corner up Drury Lane with the intention of heading down Long Acre to see if he could snag a tired tourist by Covent Garden station. It was just before four o'clock. 'They've spent all day walking about and want to go back to their hotel. Their feet are killing them and they can't face going down the tube again, so they're grateful when they see a cab cruise past.'

He grinned.

'You've got it all worked out,' Slider said.

'Fifteen years on the job, I should have,' he said. 'So then this lady hails me from the pavement.'

'Was she alone?'

'Yeah, she's standing on her own outside that big block of Trust flats.' He had absorbed the habit shared by taxi drivers and police constables of speaking in the Extended Present. 'The lady you circulated the picture of.'

'You're sure it was her?'

'Oh yes, it was her all right. You'd not forget that smile. Nice-looking, middle-aged, very smartly dressed. Confident. Obviously well used to taking taxis – you notice a thing like that, the way they open the door and get straight in, like they've been doing it all their lives. And she says, "Holland Park, please. St Anns Villas." Well, I know where that is all right. I live in Maida now, but most of my family's still in Ealing – that's where I grew up, I went to St Benedict's school – so I know all round that way, Holland Park, Shepherd's Bush, Acton, Ealing. It's home ground.'

'I understand,' Slider said.

'Anyway,' Kowalski went on, 'just as we're coming up to Holland Park tube station, she taps the glass and asks me to stop. So I stop and push the glass back and she says, "I want to pick up some dry cleaning. Will you wait?" Very nice, posh voice she's got. You could listen to it all day. "Save me the walk," she says. Well, the road happens to be clear, so I do a quick U-turn so as to set her down right by the dry-cleaners on the other side of the road. You know the one, in that row of shops beside the station. Fresh Start, it's called.'

'Yes, I know,' said Slider.

'So in she goes, and then she's back out with the plastic bag over her arm. The dress or whatever inside was red. She gives me a smile – she's got a gorgeous smile – and gets in. I do another U-ey, and drive the last bit to St Anns Villas. She taps the glass again and says, "Just here," and I stop.'

'Do you know what number it was?'

'No, there was no reason for me to notice. But I could take you there again. I stopped on the left, o'course, but once she'd paid me she crossed over and went up the steps of one of the houses on the right.'

'What time was that?'

'It'd be about twenty past four. My log'll tell you exact, if you want.'

'Anything else you can tell me? Did you see her go into the house?'

'Yeah. I sat there a minute, filling in my log, and I see her go up the steps to the door, and she's fiddling with her handbag – getting her key out, I reckon, and trying not to drop the dry-cleaning. They're slippery, those bags. That's why I was watching, hoping she wouldn't drop it. But she gets the key out all right and I see her push the door open. Then I stop watching. But when I start off again, she's not there and the door's closed, so I reckon she went in all right.'

'That's very helpful,' Slider said. 'Thank you. You have a very good, clear memory.'

He shrugged modestly. 'Driving around all day, what've you got to do but watch people? Be dead boring if you didn't take an interest in the fares. And she was a nice lady. She smiled like a film star, and she give me a decent tip.'

'How did she seem?'

'Seem?'

'Her mood. Did she seem happy, or sad, or thoughtful, or worried – whatever?'

'She seemed all right. Whenever she spoke to me, she smiled. And coming out of the dry-cleaners, she walked like she was all right. You know, how unhappy people sort of slump over and hang their heads. She had her head up. And she walked . . .' He hesitated, staring at the memory, trying to analyse it.

'Like a dancer?' Slider tried.

He smiled. 'Yeah. Light on her feet. Graceful. I could imagine her dancing.' The frank blue eyes looked levelly into Slider's. 'Can you tell me what it's all about? She's not done something, has she? She was a real lady. I wouldn't like to think she was in trouble.'

'You haven't seen anything on the television?' Slider said.

'I don't hardly ever watch TV.' Now he looked anxious. 'Has something happened to her?'

'She's gone missing,' said Slider. There was no harm in telling him now. 'So if you ever see her anywhere, or if you can remember anything else that might help us—'

'Yeah. Course. I'll let you know. I hope she's all right. What could've happened to her?' Slider didn't offer anything, and he comforted himself. 'I read once where this man was knocked down by a car and lay unconscious in a hospital for three weeks, and nobody knew who he was until he woke up.' He looked to see if Slider would endorse the possibility. 'She was a really nice lady.'

It sounded to Slider uncomfortably like an epitaph. But as epitaphs go, it wasn't a bad one.

'So she went home,' Atherton said when they returned to the CID room. 'How come Henry Holland didn't know?'

Swilley, lolling in her swivel seat and swinging it a little from side to side, said, 'He worked up at the top of the house, and he said he never heard anything that happened down below. If she came in quietly and didn't call out to him, and he was deep in concentration . . . And you can bet he'd lectured her many a time not to disturb him,' she added. 'Genius at work and all that.'

'Yeah, why would she make a noise, and have him pound downstairs to tell her off?' said LaSalle. 'If it was me, I'd creep in and out.'

'"Out" is the salient point,' Atherton said. 'She must have gone out again. And that, I'm afraid, leaves us right back where we started. We've moved the last-time-of-sighting forward again, that's all.'

'She went upstairs,' Slider said. They looked at him. 'We saw something in the wardrobe in a dry-cleaner's bag, so she must have taken it upstairs and hung it up.'

'It could have been something from a previous time,' Swilley said.

'If she'd left it downstairs,' Jenrich said, 'hanging over a chair or something, Henry would have seen it when he came down. He'd have said something.'

Swilley looked scornful. 'Do you think he'd ever notice anything that didn't directly relate to himself?'

Slider said, 'Well, we can easily check whether the item hanging in the wardrobe was the one from that day. Even if she took the cleaner's ticket off, the description will seal it. We might have to pay another visit to St Anns Villas. But for now, assuming she went in quietly, went upstairs to hang up her dress or whatever—'

'As one does,' Atherton said. 'If you go to the trouble of dry-cleaning something, you're going to hang it up properly, aren't you? I know I would.'

'Not everyone's obsessed with their gear like you are,' said McLaren, shaking the last crumbs out of a packet of salt and vinegar crisps on to his palm and, incidentally, his lap.

'No. Interest in your appearance is not one of your foibles,' Atherton remarked.

'Foibles? What's foibles?' McLaren said derisively.

'What a New York cat coughs up.'

'As I was *saying*,' Slider interrupted, 'assuming she did those things quietly so as not to disturb her husband—'

'Where did she go next?' Swilley finished for him.

They looked at one another blankly.

'We've eliminated Martin Henderson as a secret lover,' Gascoyne said, 'but it doesn't mean she didn't have one. Maybe she slipped off for a tryst.'

'A tryst?' McLaren mocked. 'You mean a—'

'Don't say it,' Swilley interjected swiftly.

'At half past four in the afternoon?' LaSalle doubted.

'Why not?' said Atherton. 'Afternoon sex is very relaxing. And if you're married, you have to catch as catch can.'

'So now we're looking for another taxi?' said Swilley.

'Unless her putative lover had a car and picked her up outside. Or he lived locally and she walked.'

Slider spoke. 'Henry Holland told us that she'd said she would pick up something for supper on her way home that day. She took that cab immediately after leaving Henderson's flat, and only went into the dry-cleaners on the way home, so it looks as though she forgot. So it's possible that, having got home, she remembered she was supposed to shop for supper, and went out again to the butcher's or whatever.'

'She could have walked to any number of shops from there,' Swilley said.

'There's a Waitrose in Westfields, within walking distance,' Jenrich added. 'I bet she's the sort that shops at Waitrose.'

'If she went to Westfields, we've got a whole new problem,' Gascoyne said. 'Huge shopping mall, thousands of people. Needle in haystack. And if she met someone, or someone took her, there's car parking and the tube entrance all inside the building. He could have got her away easily.'

'It's a problem whether she went to Westfields or not,' Atherton said, 'because once she left the house we have no idea what she was up to, and no leads. She could be anywhere in the country. Like I said, we're right back where we started.'

'And we've been on it ten days now,' LaSalle said. 'Mr Carpenter's going to go Will Smith on our arses.'

'Something will break,' Slider said, with more confidence than he felt. 'It always does. Meanwhile, go back over everything, every detail, make sure we haven't missed anything.'

They dispersed to their desks. Atherton followed Slider into his room. 'So we're back in the land of "maybe she was snatched by a sex offender"? I can't tell you how much I hope that's not the case.'

'I hope more than you do,' Slider said. 'It was Henry Holland's idea from the beginning, and I would hate him to have been right all along.'

Jenrich came into Slider's office just as his stomach was beginning to tell him he'd missed lunch. Despite long hours hunched over a keyboard, she still looked bandbox fresh, when the rest of the crew was now slightly grubby and crumpled. Not a hair on her neat head was out of place; her shirt was still white and crisp, her trousers still had a crease. He supposed it was an army thing. Her lean, angular face looked firm and shiny; her cheekbones were so sharp she could have sliced carpaccio with them.

'Boss,' she said, 'I've got a friend in the Job, at Hammersmith.'

'A friend at Hammersmith? That's almost an oxymoron.'

Maybe she didn't know what an oxymoron was. More likely she didn't care. She just waited patiently for him to get it out of his system. 'Carry on,' he said meekly.

'Mary Keyes is her name. She's been helping man the incident-room phone lines after Holland's TV appeal. They've more or less dismantled it now, but she's just rung me to say a call came in ten minutes ago, and they put it through to her. It's a woman who lives in Hawthorn Lane – on the corner of Hawthorn Lane and Bedford Drive. Mary wasn't sure it was anything, the woman was a bit rambling, so she didn't bother her bosses with it, but she passed it on to me for what it's worth.'

'And what is it worth?' Slider asked. He trusted Jenrich's instincts.

'Sir, apparently they've had a spate of thefts of domestic heating oil round there. It's where people's tanks are next to the boundary hedge or fence or whatever—'

'As they usually are,' Slider nodded to the point. Your oil tank had to be accessible to the tanker for refilling.

'So the thieves just drive up, stick a hose over the fence and siphon off the oil. It's easy to buy or hire a small oil truck, a thousand, fifteen-hundred galloner, or even just a bowser you can tow behind a car, and with the price of oil these days it's worth the outlay. Stolen oil's getting to be big business. Sometimes these guys follow the legitimate tanker round, wait for it to fill a tank, then just empty it again as soon as it's gone. Anyway, this woman, Betty Moth, her husband's had security cameras put in. The house is on the corner, and they cover both roads.'

'Oh?' said Slider, with interest. The corner with Bedford Drive was just along the road a bit from The Stag car park. 'That could be useful.'

'Long story short,' Jenrich said, 'she thinks a car went past in the middle of the night, that Tuesday night into Wednesday.'

'Thinks?'

Jenrich shrugged. 'She doesn't know how to work the security system computer to run it back. I thought I'd go over there and have a look.'

'Why didn't she tell anyone before?' Slider asked.

'That's one of the things I want to ask her,' said Jenrich.

*   *   *

It wasn't really a corner: Hawthorn Lane bent itself round a right-angle at that point, and Bedford Drive joined it at the apex, so it came to the same thing. Both roads were semi-rural, skirting the edge of the woods on one side, while on the other a few detached houses were scattered, well-spaced from each other and sitting in substantial grounds. They were mostly mellow Edwardian villas, but the house to which Jenrich had been directed was a sprawling modern bungalow in brick of a particularly virulent shade of yellow.

Because of the name, Jenrich had been imagining Betty Moth as a round, pink, comfortable little old lady, possibly with lavender curls and glasses on a pearl neck-chain. The woman who answered the door, however, was probably only in her forties, was thin to the point of scrawniness, and had sallow skin and greasy black hair dragged back into a punishingly tight horsetail. She looked sharply and suspiciously at Jenrich, and scrutinized her warrant card at length before letting her in.

'You can't be too careful,' she said. She had a hoarse voice and wheezed between phrases like a pug with a sixty-a-day habit. 'There's scammers everywhere. My friend Jas that lives up the road in Farnham Common, she had a laptop delivered by this bloke from ParcelPlus that she never ordered, then this other bloke come round to collect it back, he's got the jacket and the ParcelPlus logo on the van and everything, so she gives it to him, right? Only it turns out it was a scam, they was both scammers, and her credit card got charged for it.'

Inside, the bungalow was cold and unwelcoming, with bare wood floors and minimal furnishing, the off-white walls marked by careless passage, and a faint smell of damp mixed with fried food and dog and cigarettes. From somewhere distant and confined came a monotonous barking. 'You've got a dog?' Jenrich asked.

'Just got it,' she said moodily. 'Cos of the oil thieves. Phil went down the Dog Rescue at Beaconsfield last Sat'd'y. He's gone on nights now for a month, he thought it'd make me feel safer when I'm here on me own, but the bloody thing just barks all the time, you'd never know if it was barking at anything or nothing. It'll have to go back, only Phil says give it a chance to settle down. All right for him, he's never bloody well here.'

'Doesn't he sleep in the day?'

'Mornings. He don't need much sleep. Afternoons he's got other jobs. He's caddying down the golf club this afternoon. Other times he works at the car repair in Farnham Royal.'

'Is it just the two of you here?'

'Yeah, 'cept when his kids come over. He's divorced, and she bungs 'em on to us as often as she can, while she goes gallivanting.' She pulled out a pack of cigarettes, tapped one free and lit it. She didn't offer one to Jenrich. 'Bleeds him dry with the alimony, that bitch does, and spends it on fancy clothes and holidays. Holidays! I dunno when the last time was that *we* got away. Can't afford it. She's a blood-sucker, that woman. That's why he has to work all these jobs, just to make ends meet. And oil going through the roof, and then the bastards come and steal it. It's enough to make you—'

The sentence might have ended 'sick', or possibly, 'want to kill someone', but a coughing fit obliterated it. 'I'm worn out,' she said when she'd got her breath again, folding one arm tight across her bosom and tucking the hand under her armpit. The other hand held the cigarette, and she rested the elbow on the folded arm to keep the fag in the operative position. 'I can't sleep at night, for listening for them thieving gits coming for the oil.'

'So that's why your husband had the cameras put in,' Jenrich suggested, to move her on to the point.

She grew enraged, in a feeble way. 'I told him, what use is that? Cameras won't stop 'em. They're as likely to give you the finger while they rob you, the dirty scum. He says, at least you can give the film to the police, but *they* don't want to know. This man on the Britwell, my friend Jas knows him, he had full film of these burglars that done his house, their full faces, and he even knew their names, because they're thieving little bastards that live on the estate and everyone knows 'em, and he give the film *and* their names and addresses to the police in Slough, and they turned round and said there was nothing they could do about it.'

She stopped, panting, and Jenrich got a word in edgeways.

'So you think there was a car went past in the middle of the night on Tuesday last week?'

'I'm pretty sure it was. I can't sleep properly for worrying, and if I do get off, every time I hear a car I wake up again. There's not much traffic down here of a weekday night, once everybody's back from the pub. It's not a through-route to anywhere, there's only the woods and a few houses. So you notice even more when a car does come past. And I remember this one, because it sort of stopped outside for a minute, like they were checking the place out. I thought for sure it was them. Phil, he looked at the tape the next day and said it weren't anything, it was a car, not a oil truck, but then when it turned out this poor woman was murdered and buried in the woods, I thought it could have been them, couldn't it? Because the murderer would have been in an ordinary car, and she could have been in the boot, her poor body.'

There was no point in going into the fact that they didn't know there had even been a murder. She'd be more willing to help if she thought there had been.

'So why didn't you go to the police about it before?'

'I said to Phil we ought to, but he said don't get involved, you just bring trouble down on your own head. But I did go along, down to The Stag car park, when they were searching the woods, and I spoke to this lady policeman, but she weren't interested, she just turned round and told me to ring the incident line. And Phil, he said if you ring that line they take down your name and address and every-thing and then you're on their records for ever. He told me to forget it.'

'But you didn't forget it,' Jenrich said, managing to sound a bit admiring.

Betty Moth took courage from the tone. 'It was when they called the search off. I couldn't stop thinking about that poor woman, lying out there in the woods and no one even searching for her any more. She could lie there for ever, for all they cared. And her poor husband wondering for the rest of his life – I saw him on the telly, and he looked like such a nice man, and really upset. So I rung the number and told them, and they said they'd pass it on. And now you're here. But I've never told Phil, so you can't let him find out, because he'd kill me,' she concluded anxiously.

The dog stopped barking, and the relief was bliss. The silence seemed to ring for a moment, and then settled like a gentle blanket over the room. It lasted for about thirty seconds, before the dog started up again. Betty Moth didn't seem to notice either the cessation or the resumption.

'You said you didn't know how to work the security system's computer?' Jenrich said.

'Phil did show me, but I couldn't take it in. I'm no good with that sort of thing. But you'll be able to do it?'

'Let's have a look,' Jenrich said.

They passed through the grim, cluttered kitchen – the units were a depressing dark oak finish that probably dated from the Eighties, and a glimpse of the inset hob showed it crusted with grease spillings – and into a utility room beyond. The dog's barking rose to a hysterical crescendo, from behind a closed door at the end of the room, and there was a desperate scrabbling of dog nails on the other side. Mrs Moth had the grace to look a little ashamed. 'I shut it in the lav,' she said, 'after it pee'd on the kitchen floor.'

On one section of the worktop stood a monitor screen attached to a small box and a mouse. The screen was dark, but Jenrich found the on button behind, and it lit with three views, looking in the three directions, with the oil tank centre stage. Using the mouse, Jenrich brought up the menu panel and manipulated it. The recording went back two weeks, so they were in time.

'You done this sort of thing before,' Betty Moth said approvingly.

'It's fairly standard,' Jenrich said. The dog stopped barking in favour of a pitiful whining, which actually was no improvement as far as she was concerned. She couldn't wait to get out of there. She examined the box and found that it had a port, into which she inserted the firestick she'd brought with her, and for speed's sake downloaded the lot. 'I can look at it on my own screen back at the station,' she said. Mrs Moth looked slightly disappointed, having perhaps hoped for a Eureka moment, and Jenrich added, 'It will be very helpful for us to see who passed along Hawthorn Lane that night – and subsequent nights. You may have given us the very information we need.'

'And if it was his car – the murderer?'

'We can trace him from the registration number, and we'll bring him to justice.'

It was what Mrs Moth wanted to hear. 'And you'll make him tell you where he put the body?'

'Of course.'

'Only my mum used to talk about those wicked Moors Murderers and how they wouldn't say where the bodies were, and those poor women whose kids they'd done in could never have any peace. I can't stand thinking that poor woman's out there somewhere, and nobody knows where. It 'aunts me.'

'It bothers us, too,' Jenrich said.

Mrs Moth showed her out. The dog was barking again, now they had moved out of its range.

'You'll have to take that dog back,' Jenrich said at the door, kindly but firmly. 'You can't leave it locked in the lavatory. That's cruelty.'

'I know,' Betty Moth sighed hopelessly. 'I'll tell Phil when he gets back.'

'If I come by again and find it still locked in, I'll have to report you,' said Jenrich, having no faith in her resolve.

'It's took all the paint off the door,' Mrs Moth said, as though that were a logical rejoinder.

NINETEEN
Him Indoors

McLaren, being the firm's proclaimed expert on all things automotive – he proclaimed it himself – took the firestick to his own desk and computer, and Jenrich was happy enough to let him do the boring bit of scrolling through.

Slider was hoping, but not with any confidence. The chances that it was the right night, or that a car passing at that time was unusual, or that it had anything to do with their case, seemed like three chances too far.

McLaren's grin, half an hour later, proved he had struck gold. Silver. Or possibly oil.

'One thirty-eight on Wednesday morning. A silver Volvo, only car that passes between eleven fifty-nine p.m. Tuesday and four thirty a.m. Wednesday.'

'Nice quiet place to live,' LaSalle said.

'That's why the thieves get away with stealing heating oil,' Jenrich said, 'because there's no one around to see them.'

'Country people must go to bed early,' LaSalle said.

'It was a school night,' Swilley pointed out.

'And Farnham Common is not exactly Las Vegas,' Atherton added. 'Even the Star of India closes at nine thirty.'

'So the old biddy wasn't dreaming,' McLaren went on. 'It comes down Hawthorn Lane from the east, stops at the bend in the road where Bedford Drive joins it, then drives on in the direction of The Stag car park.'

'Why'd it stop?' LaSalle said, finger on the map they had been using. 'Hawthorn Lane's the bigger road, it's got right of way.'

'Just to make sure there's no one about, I s'pose,' said McLaren. He lifted his head as Slider came through. 'That lead's come up trumps, guv. You said something would break sooner or later.'

'The car that passed in the night?' Slider said.

'A ten-year-old silver Volvo S40 diesel four-door saloon,' said McLaren. 'These middle-classes and their motors! You couldn't make it up.'

'Volvos are very reliable,' Gascoyne defended automatically, and then looked worried. 'You mean—?'

'We know someone intimately involved with this case who has an old silver Volvo, don't we?' said Atherton.

'Henry Holland,' said Gascoyne. 'But, surely . . .?'

'Just got to check the index to make sure,' McLaren said.

'It could have been her, running away,' said Gascoyne. 'Going to meet her lover.'

'But then, how did the car get back home? We saw it there, outside,' said Atherton.

'You can see someone inside, in the driver's seat,' McLaren said. 'You can't make out the face, but it looks like a man, a tall man. And there's no one else inside.'

'Not sitting up, anyway,' said LaSalle.

Slider shook his head. 'It's too much of a coincidence not to be significant. But there may be an innocent reason he was driving to Burnham Beeches in the middle of the night.'

'If it was an innocent reason, he'd have told us,' Atherton said.

'People don't tell us innocent things that they think might incriminate them,' Swilley said. 'They just hope we won't find out.'

'But he's the one who reported her missing,' said Gascoyne. 'And he's been pushing us to investigate all along. Why would he do that if he's not innocent?'

'We could ask him,' Atherton suggested. 'That would be fun.'

'What do we do, boss?' Swilley asked. 'Do we bring him in?'

'Not yet,' Slider said unhappily. He could sense Trouble, the roughest of beasts, slouching his way. 'This needs thinking about. First of all, let's check the index. Old silver Volvos are not exactly rare, especially in leafy Bucks. And then, if it is Holland's, you can start tracing its movements on Tuesday and Wednesday. Put together a whole picture. Rule number one of interviewing, don't ask the question if you don't already know the answer.'

'Gordon Bennett!' Porson said – quite mildly in the circumstances, given that a two-bar electric fire might just have been pitched into the hot tub of his career. 'Wait a minute, wait a minute, this needs thinking about.'

'That's what I said.' Slider gave him a minute, but nothing came out. 'I'm wondering, did he go out looking for her himself, and then didn't like to say so in case it made him look guilty? People hold things back all the time for that reason.'

'But guilty of what?'

'Well, if they'd had a row and she stormed out and then didn't come back, he might feel to blame if anything happened to her.'

'Then why Burnham Beeches? We weren't looking for her there at that point.'

'She might have said something to him about it at some time. It was a favourite spot from her childhood. Maybe she liked to go there to meditate.'

Porson snorted. 'Meditate! All right, the obvious thing is to go and ask him. But . . .'

'Yes. But . . .' Slider agreed.

They looked at each other, working out scenarios. 'If he done her in and disposed of the body in the woods, why would he draw our attention to that very place?' Porson said. 'No, it doesn't make sense.'

'And he insisted on making the TV appeal,' Slider said. 'After which there was the call from the murderer, self-named, pointing us in that direction.'

'Well, that couldn't have been him. Or could it?'

'Again, why draw attention to the place?'

'But then, what was he doing out there?' Porson shook his head. 'Something's screwy somewhere. Could somebody be pulling his strings? These writer types, they live in their own world, don't they? Easy to fool. Maybe she really has run off, and she's pulling the wool over his eyes. And ours.'

'It wouldn't be the first time someone's faked their own death,' Slider said.

'Insurance scam?' Porson mooted tentatively.

'I wonder how we can find out if she had insurance, without asking him. But then, she's got to be proved dead for the money to be paid out. And it'd be paid to him, wouldn't it? So he'd have to be in on it.'

Porson was staring at the wall. The wall stared back unhelpfully. 'Well, we've got to look into it, one way or the other, and that's a fact, given this new evidence. There's no smoke without straw. But let's just make sure of our ground first. Go through everything you've got so far, line by line, see if there's anything you've missed. And we'll keep this to ourselves for now.'

'Of course, sir,' said Slider.

They both thought about the alternative – telling Mr Carpenter and, through him, the commissioner – and it made them both blanch.

'Yes,' said Porson. 'Keep it schtum. No need to make a pavlova before we have to.'

Atherton had gone out somewhere, and the guv was closeted with Barry Bleasedale at Notting Hill – who had just realized that since the Holland business was on his ground, he might be called to account for it at some point, so he should probably get up to speed on it. So McLaren approached Jenrich.

He was a bit wary of her: not only was she new to the firm, but she was ex-military, and they could be a bit funny, with rules in places coppers didn't even have places. He treated her circumspectly and called her 'sergeant' when he had to address her directly. He wasn't sure quite how to take her: with that sleek head, those cheekbones and the blue eyes, you could almost call her beautiful, but there was something about her that warned him she probably wouldn't enjoy having her looks commented on. Not that he was interested. He liked a bit of meat on his bones, and he was perfectly happy with Natalie, who understood him, and unlike his previous women never tried to change him into something he wasn't (or as Swilley would have put it, into a member of the human race, but he was used to her sniping at him, and Swilley was OK, a good copper).

So he said, 'Sarge – come and have a look at this.'

Jenrich walked over, put her hand down on his desk to lean over, lifted it again to brush away the shortbread crumbs, leaned in again and said, 'What am I looking at?'

'The guv said to go back to the beginning, and this was the first day, when I was trying to track where she went from the pottery class. This was the pub's CCTV – The Albert. There she is, see?'

'Yes, that's her all right.'

'Wait, though. Wait. There. Does that remind you of anybody?' He froze the frame on a man walking in the same direction as Felicity Holland, perhaps ten yards behind.

Jenrich stared. 'No, I can't say it does. You can't see who it is, with that stupid hat.'

The figure was of a tall man, wearing a dark car coat and a brown trilby hat which, because of the angle of the camera, mostly obscured his face.

'Yeah, but just look at his general figure and that.'

'No, I don't recognize him.'

'This is from the camera across the road, same time.' He cued and ran it, and Jenrich saw Felicity Holland come round the corner, followed by the man. 'See how he's looking at her?'

'People generally look straight ahead when they walk.'

'All right,' said McLaren. 'Now look at this.' He froze the last frame and sequestered it in a corner of the screen. 'This is Covent Garden tube, the exit barrier that Tuesday. Look. Here she comes.'

Felicity Holland pressed her Oyster card against the reader, the barrier snapped open, she walked through, it snapped shut. Two strangers went through behind her, snip snap. And then—

'That's the same man,' said Jenrich, noting the car coat and hat. And then, as the subject came through the barrier, he looked up slightly, revealing his face: 'Good God. It's Henry Holland!' McLaren froze the frame and looked at Jenrich, pleased with her reaction. 'It's definitely him. He's following her?'

'Gotter be. Can't be accidental – he must have been in the

same lift with her, to come through the barrier that close behind.'

'Same lift? That must have been hairy if he was tailing her.'

'Well, he wouldn't want to lose her, he'd have to stay close.'

'How could she not spot him?'

'Well, those lifts, you exit from the other side to the side you enter, so people generally face the same direction, the direction they went in. As long as she didn't turn round for any reason, he's all right.'

'Some balls, anyway. Why d'you think he followed her?'

'Why does a man ever follow his wife? He thought she was playing away.' He shrugged. 'Stands to reason. Anything else, you just ask, don't you?'

Jenrich was thinking. 'Have you got any more recordings from Covent Garden?'

'I've got the whole day – why?'

'I'd like to see when he went home.'

'The entrance is separate from the exit, round the corner. It's a different camera.' He called it up then ran it through, slowing down when he passed the time the two Hollands had arrived at the station. Then they settled in to watch.

Finally, 'There he is. He's taken off the stupid hat now,' said Jenrich. Holland was striding through the barrier, moving so fast he almost hit it before it opened. His movements were jerky, irritable. 'Look at his face.'

McLaren froze the frame. 'He's not a happy bunny.'

'What time is that? Quarter to three. Felicity and Martin Henderson came out of the restaurant about twenty to, didn't they?'

'Yeah. So—'

'He's waited to see her go into Henderson's building with him, then he's left to go home, to be sure of getting home before her.'

'Could be. We can get the information from TfL, from his Oyster card, whether he went straight home or somewhere else.'

'He's waited outside the restaurant for an hour and a half, just to catch her out,' Jenrich said wonderingly. 'What is he like?'

McLaren looked up. 'If he got home before her, if he's waiting for her, maybe they have a big row soon as she comes in. Maybe she storms out. And then when she doesn't come back, Holland starts to get worried, he feels guilty cos he's driven her out. So he calls in the police to try and find her. And he says nothing about the stalking, cos that'd make him look weird.'

Swilley had come over and listened to the last few exchanges. 'So why did he drive out to Burnham Beeches in the middle of the night?'

'To look for her?' said McLaren. 'Maybe she had a favourite spot. He didn't call the commissioner until the next day, did he?'

'No, he called the commissioner Tuesday evening, and Sir David told him to wait until morning to see if she came back,' Swilley corrected.

'So he's too worried to go to bed, he gets more and more antsy, then decides he's got to have a go finding her himself. Might not only have been the Beeches. We don't know where else he tried. Anyway, nothing doing, so next morning he's back on the blower to the commissioner. But he don't say anything about his midnight ride in case it looks suspicious.'

'It holds together,' Jenrich said grudgingly. 'You'd better get on with checking his journey Tuesday night. Where else did he go? And I'd like to know what time he came back.'

'He didn't go back the way he came, we know that,' McLaren said, 'because he never passed Old Mother Hubbard's again. Not before four thirty in the morning.'

'If he was searching for her, it would have taken hours. He could have left later than that. Check the rest of the tape.'

'And if he's not on that, it'll take days scouring the area, trying to find places with cameras,' McLaren grumbled.

'But Thames Valley's already done that, haven't they?' said Swilley. 'When they told the boss they wouldn't do a search of the woods, they said they'd have a look at local cameras. I'll get on to them. They can at least tell us where they are, and if they've downloaded any tapes, I'll get them to shoot them over.'

'And I'll put the index through the ANPR. He's likely gone out and come back on the M40.'

By the time Slider got back, much had been done. McLaren had established that the Volvo had not gone past Betty Moth Corner again that night. 'If he went home, he went home a different way.'

'We know he went home, dummy,' Swilley said. 'The car was there, when the boss and Jim interviewed him.'

Swilley had got a dozen tapes sent over from Slough and every available bod was going through them. And an ANPR search was under way.

Slider rang home to say he would be late. It was lucky Joanna wasn't working that evening, because Kate didn't usually stay on Fridays, going home to her mother straight from school.

'So you're suspecting the husband now? Henry Holland? What of?'

'Only of withholding evidence. But given that the whole enquiry was prompted by him in the first place, it's a bit strange that he didn't tell us he went out.'

'If they had a row about something, he might not want to say. People get embarrassed about domestic quarrels,' Joanna said. 'Or maybe he went out to visit a mistress – have you thought about that?'

'He doesn't look the sort,' Slider began.

'You said that about Sir John Whatsis. Besides, what *is* the sort of man who wouldn't have a bit on the side if it was offered?'

'You married one.'

'True dat. I'm a lucky girl. But I think you're a *rara avis.*'

'I think men get an unnecessarily bad press. There are more of us around than you think.'

'All right. But bear in mind Henry Holland might not be one of them.'

'I always bear everything in mind.'

The ANPR picked up the Volvo on the A40 at junction one, and again at junction two, the Beaconsfield turn-off, where it turned south down the A355. 'Best of all,' said McLaren, 'the camera's got a good angle as he's slowing, coming up the slip road, and you can see it's him. It's definitely Holland driving.'

The A355 led straight through Farnham Common, and from the timings it could be assumed that the Volvo turned off at Kingsway, which led into Green Lane and thence into Hawthorn Lane. There wasn't enough time between the ping at the motorway junction and the passing of the camera at Moth Corner for it to have gone anywhere else.

'But here's the thing, guv,' McLaren said, 'We've got him coming back on to the M40 at junction two, heading east – back towards home – at one fifty-eight. That's only twenty minutes after passing Betty Moth's, only enough time to get back to the junction. He couldn't have stopped anywhere.'

'Which means he didn't offload a dead body,' said Atherton. 'Even if he dumped it rather than burying it, it takes time to manoeuvre an unco-operative corpse out of a boot. And stagger any distance with it.'

Lœssop, who had been going through some of the Slough tapes, said, 'I've got it in Farnham Royal, the Volvo, at one forty-nine. There's a big leisure centre on the corner of Farnham Lane and the A355, with a camera on its car park, and it catches him turning out of Farnham Lane and north up the A355.'

LaSalle had the map. 'There's lots of back roads he could have cut through from Hawthorn Lane to bring him out on Farnham Lane.'

'But the point is,' McLaren insisted, 'there's not time for him to have *done* anything on the way. He's just done a loop. So what was it all about?'

Slider thought he knew. But even if he was right, it didn't answer all questions – certainly not the most important one: where was Felicity Holland now?

'I think we had better go and have a chat with Mr Holland, clear up some points.'

'Now?' Atherton said.

'No, tomorrow. I'll need time to put everything together. It won't hurt him to stew another night.'

Atherton pricked up his ears at the word 'stew'. 'You think he did it?'

'What's "it"? He did something. And he's not been entirely truthful, which offends me.'

'It pisses us off, too,' Swilley said, translating for the hard-of-thinking.

'But as to *what* he did . . .' Slider frowned. 'I can't see how it's possible.' He pondered a moment. 'I suppose we'll find out tomorrow.'

Henry Holland was in – where else would he be? – but he'd gone downhill since Slider first saw him. He was still wearing trousers, shoes and socks, but the trousers lacked a military crease, the shirt above them looked crumpled, as if it had been worn for more than one day, and he had abandoned the jacket. His face was clean and shaved but he looked haggard, and if he had combed his hair that morning, he must have run his hands through it since, because bits of it were sticking up out of line.

When he opened the door to them, he looked at them blankly, as if his mind was far away; then his focus sharpened, and he said, 'Have you come to tell me you've found my wife?'

Slider considered him for a moment. There was something in the tone of that sentence that caught his attention – a sort of confidence. No, that wasn't quite the right word . . . It sounded like a 'num' question – a question that expects the answer, 'no'.

'I wish I had,' he said. 'May we come in?'

'Must you?' Holland said wearily. He passed a hand over his face and then on through his hair on the side of his head. That's how it got ruffled, Slider thought. 'I don't feel much like company, as you must realize, and if you haven't any good news for me—'

'I'm sorry to intrude on your anxiety,' Slider said, 'but there are some questions I must ask you, and I'm sure you want to do everything you can to co-operate, if it means finding your wife.'

'But does it? All this time, and you seem to have got nowhere. I'm sorry, but if this is just another time-wasting exercise intended to cover your own failings—'

'Oh, I wouldn't say we've got nowhere. We know a great deal more than we did at the beginning,' said Slider. 'And I wouldn't bother you if it wasn't important. May we come in?'

Holland sighed heavily. 'I suppose so.' He led them into the drawing room. It was the same room, beautiful as before, and there was no sign of neglect – no possessions scattered about or furniture out of place – but it had an air of abandonment. Or was that just Slider's imagination? A home without its woman is just a house. Probably he was projecting his own feelings on to it.

Holland turned to face them, without inviting them to sit. 'Well?' he said.

Slider decided to plunge in. 'Your wife came home that day.'

He stared, shocked. 'What?' he said.

'On that Tuesday, she came home in a taxi at about twenty past four. The taxi driver saw her let herself in.'

Holland didn't say anything for a long time. Then he said, 'I-I had no idea. When I'm working, up at the top of the house, I don't hear anything.'

'Would it not be customary for her to call out to you when she came home, to let you know she was there?'

'No. I mean, there was no rule about it. It would depend on the circumstances. If she knew I was working, she wouldn't disturb me, unless she had something urgent to say.'

'So you really had no idea she'd come home?' Atherton asked.

'Of course not,' he said irritably. 'I would have told you so, wouldn't I?' He thought for a moment. 'This taxi driver – probably he's mistaken. They drive hundreds of people every day. How would he remember one out of so many? Probably it was a different house altogether. Or he's just trying to make himself important.'

Slider's face, Atherton noted, had gone inscrutable, and his own pulse quickened. The guv was on to something. 'That should be easy to prove,' Slider said, 'if you'd just let us go upstairs.'

'Go upstairs? What on earth for?'

'I'd like to show you something,' said Slider.

'If this is some silly game, I warn you, I'm in no mood—'

'This is not a game to me, sir,' Slider said sternly. 'If you'd be so good . . .' He extended his hand towards the door.

'Oh, all *right*,' said Holland.

In the bedroom, Slider went to the wife's wardrobe and, with some trepidation, opened it. But it hadn't been removed. There was the dry-cleaner's bag, and inside a dark red skirt and jacket. He indicated it to Holland.

'This item was collected from the Fresh Start dry-cleaners by Holland Park station at about ten past four that day. The description is on the ticket: lady's red skirt suit.'

Holland frowned. 'I'm sure there's more than one lady's suit being cleaned at any one time. And I wouldn't call that red – it's more like maroon.'

Slider produced from his pocket, in its evidence bag, the ticket which Jenrich had gone to fetch yesterday: the other half, torn off, from the one that was attached to the hanger. 'You see, the number is the same. And if necessary, it can be examined microscopically and the perforations matched. But I think you must be satisfied now. Your wife picked up her dry-cleaning, came home, came upstairs and hung it up.'

'Well, well, what if she did?' Holland said impatiently. 'I don't see how it matters. What does it mean?'

'And you had no idea?' Atherton said, 'You didn't hear her come in? You didn't hear her come upstairs? You didn't hear her use the bathroom?'

'She didn't—' He stopped abruptly.

'Yes?' Atherton encouraged.

'She may have done,' he said. 'I told you, I didn't hear her. There's nothing unusual about that. I didn't know she came home. What are you trying to say? Even if you're right and she did come home, she must have gone out again. That's obvious.'

'And you went out yourself later,' Slider said.

'What? Why are you interrogating me like this? I'm not a criminal. In case you've forgotten, I am the victim here! My wife is missing. I called you in myself to find her, and a wretched job you're making of it.'

'Yes, sir,' Slider said soothingly. 'But just this one question

– where did you go, when you went out in the car on Tuesday night?'

'I didn't *go* out in the car,' Holland said angrily. 'I stayed in, in case – in the *hope* – that my wife would come home, or telephone me. I never left the house.'

If rooms could sigh, this one would have, part sadness, part relief.

'I would like to invite you to come with us to the station, Mr Holland, and make a statement.'

He whitened, but it could have been with rage as much as anything. '*Invite* me? What is this? Are you some kind of comedian? Are you arresting me for something?'

'No, sir. Would you like me to?' Slider asked equably.

'How dare you! Get out of my house. I shall ring Sir David and we'll see what he has to say about your conduct.'

'Do I take it you're refusing to come with us to the station to help with our enquiries?'

'Take what you damn well please! This is a witch hunt. My wife is *missing*, and you're persecuting her grieving husband instead of looking for her! No, I will not come with you. Leave this house immediately!'

'In that case – Henry Holland, I arrest you on suspicion of the murder of Felicity Holland. You do not have to say anything . . .'

TWENTY

Above Rubies

'Are you sure, guv?' Atherton asked when they were alone. 'You surprised the hell out of me. Murder? We don't even know she's dead.'

'After nearly two weeks? I think we do.'

'She could be being held somewhere. Or she could still have run away. What happens if she turns up?'

'Then I'll look very silly.'

'A bit more than silly. The commissioner will string you up by your credentials.'

Slider shrugged. 'I've got a hunch.'

'In my case, it's a terrified cringe.'

'The beauty of an arrest is that we can search the house without having to get a warrant. And if there's any evidence, it's in the house.'

'So you deliberately provoked him?'

'No, that just happened naturally. He was going to object to anything I said, you could see that. The thing you have to ask is, why. If he's really worried about his wife, he should want to help us.'

'He's the sort that's just born stroppy,' Atherton said doubtfully. 'Entitled. Arrogant. I don't think you can read anything into it.'

'Oh well, let's go and provoke him some more and see what happens. If I'm wrong, at least it's in a good cause.'

'I wish I had your courage,' said Atherton.

'I wish I had your height,' said Slider. 'My trousers would hang better.'

By the time processes had been completed and his solicitor had arrived, Holland had cooled down somewhat. The solicitor, a young, pretty Indian woman, was from Hardbottle and

Shirling, a firm specializing in publishing law, but it was the one Holland asked for, perhaps the only one he knew. 'I'm more used to scrutinizing author contracts and arguing about royalties,' she confided rather touchingly before she went in, 'but of course we all study criminal law as well.' She was shocked that they had arrested Holland at all, let alone for murder. 'But he's a famous writer! His books sell all over the world!'

'I can see he'll have an enthusiastic advocate in you,' Atherton said, well accustomed to buttering up female lawyers, though generally to other ends.

'Now,' said Slider in the tape room, when the preliminaries had been gone through, 'I'll ask you again, Mr Holland: where did you go on the evening of Tuesday April the twelfth?'

'I told you,' he said impatiently, 'I didn't go anywhere. I couldn't leave the telephone, in case she called, or any news came in.'

'Very well,' Slider said. 'If you'd care to look at the monitor screen.'

He showed them the journey as McLaren had assembled it. McLaren had also caught Holland both ways on the traffic camera at the West Cross roundabout at the end of Shepherd's Bush, which nicely tied up the trip virtually door to door.

Holland wasn't ready to capitulate. 'It wasn't me. Someone must have stolen the car, taken it joy-riding.'

'And brought it back to your front door? Joy-riders are not usually so thoughtful. They abandon the car when they've finished with it, if they haven't crashed it first.'

'Well, you can't say they *didn't* bring it back. Obviously they did.'

'Mr Holland, we know it was you driving.' Slider brought up the shot taken on the slip road, and enlarged it to show Holland's face above the steering wheel.

He looked surprised. 'I didn't know you could do that,' he muttered, with a writer's interest overriding the situation. Slider liked him for the first time.

'Now, will you please tell us where you went and what you did that night?'

He had evidently been doing some quick thinking. 'I went

out to look for her,' he said. 'I-I couldn't just sit there, doing nothing, when she was in danger. So I drove about, hoping to spot her.'

'So why that particular part of the country? Why Burnham Beeches?'

'I don't know. It was just . . . I wasn't thinking clearly. I was mad with worry, I wasn't rational. You couldn't expect it.'

'It seems a very specific kind of irrationality, to drive straight to Burnham Beeches, along a motorway and an A road. You could hardly have expected to see her walking along the hard shoulder. I ask again, why Burnham Beeches?'

'She'd talked about it,' he said in a desperate sort of burst. 'She used to go there as a child. She loved it. It was the only thing I could think of.'

'But you went there and came straight back.'

'When I got there, I realized how stupid it was – I could never search the whole place on my own. So I came home again.'

'And why didn't you tell us that you had gone out?'

'I didn't see that it mattered. I didn't find her, did I? What was the point of mentioning it? Anyway I-I felt a bit of a fool. You know, not having achieved anything. So I kept it to myself. It was my business, wasn't it?'

'Indeed. But from the beginning, you told me you were sure she had been snatched from the street by a sex maniac. Why did you think a sex maniac would take her to Burnham Beeches?'

'Oh, I don't *know*,' he said in profound irritation. 'That's a stupid question.'

'I don't think you have the right to harry my client like that,' the solicitor said. 'A person can't be held accountable for things they say and think when they're in a state of shock.'

'That's it, I *was* in a state of shock,' Holland said, grateful to be rescued. 'I don't think you people have given that any consideration. You get so used to terrible things in your job, you forget that ordinary, law-abiding people can't cope with the horrors the way you do.'

'Very well,' Slider said. 'Let's turn to the events of earlier on Tuesday. You told me that you stayed in the house, after your wife went out to her pottery class, that you were upstairs in your study working all day—'

'Not all day,' Holland interrupted quickly.

'Not all day? You went out somewhere?'

'No, I mean I came down to lunch as I usually do, and had a sandwich – ham and mustard if you want to be particular – and had a walk round the garden before I went back up to work again.'

'So you didn't leave the house in the daytime?'

'No.'

'You were upstairs in your study and didn't come down until cocktail time?'

'That's right.'

Slider sighed. 'Mr Holland, have you not learned yet that lying is not in your best interests?'

'Lying? How dare you!'

'Please look at the monitor.'

Atherton cued the tape. 'You went to Notting Hill. You followed your wife after she left her pottery class. You followed her to Covent Garden.'

'But I . . .' He seemed to have lost his words.

'You followed her so closely through the ticket barrier that you could almost have touched her. You rode up from the platform in the same lift as her.'

'No! I didn't see her!'

'So you admit you went out, then?'

'No, I didn't. That's what I mean. I didn't see her because I didn't follow her. It's ridiculous.'

'Then what were you doing in Covent Garden?'

'I wasn't. I was at home. That's not me. It must be someone who looks like me. They say everybody's got a double – a doppelgänger.'

Slider almost admired him for his persistence. 'And you had two, did you? One in Notting Hill and one in Covent Garden. And perhaps another who stole your car to go joy-riding, and kindly brought it back to your house afterwards.'

'I don't have to answer your questions,' Holland said, turning sulky.

'You certainly don't,' the solicitor put in, belatedly. 'But her

voice was distant and she was looking worried. Good evidence
will do that to a brief.

At that point they were interrupted by Jenrich, who looked
in and called Atherton out. Slider waited in silence until
Atherton came back, and indicated with his eyebrows that
something important had happened. Slider terminated the
interview and went out, and had Holland sent back to
the lock-up.

Jenrich showed him two evidence bags. 'In the top of his
wardrobe, boss,' she said. 'Just pushed under a pile of wool-
lens, hardly hidden at all – that's how confident he was.'

Two credit cards, and a mobile phone – a very old
Nokia, the sort you flip up to open, like Captain Kirk's
communicator.

Slider looked at them in silence, an unwelcome cold feeling
sliding down inside him like a dose of Milk of Magnesia. He
hadn't wanted what he had been thinking to be right. He had
hoped, stupidly, that there was another explanation.

'The handbag, you see, was misdirection,' he said out of
his thoughts.

'Boss?' said Jenrich.

Atherton had got it. 'That's why he didn't take any time
at all, driving around. He wasn't getting rid of a body. He
just drove past, and either stopped just long enough to put
it by the tree, or even, possibly, threw it from the moving
car, and went home again. I suppose he thought the quicker
he was, the less chance he'd be found out. But where, then,
is Felicity?'

'She came home,' Slider said. 'She'd been out all day. She'd
paid for lunch. She collected her dry-cleaning and paid for it.
She paid for the taxi. She went home. She went inside, and her
handbag went with her. We thought perhaps she'd gone out
again to do the shopping, or meet someone, but she wouldn't
have gone out without her credit cards and phone. At least,
certainly not without the credit cards.'

'So – you're saying she never left the house?'

'She never left the house,' said Slider.

* * *

It was a big house, and searching it took a long time, because all the documents had to be secured, and Holland's computer. You never knew what you might need at a trial. A separate team examined the garden, to look for newly disturbed earth.

Slider stayed, feeling guilty, responsible, depressed and vindicated by turn. Porson came, to offer moral support – he was a good old boy. Astonishingly, Carpenter turned up, looking pale and agitated. 'But are you *sure*?' he kept saying.

'I'm never sure of anything, sir,' Slider tormented him. Carpenter had had a run-down of the evidence already, so he ought to know where they were, but he kept trying to find an out. Maybe someone had brought the credit cards and phone back. Maybe the murderer was trying to cover his tracks and implicate Holland instead. Surely, *surely*, Holland could not be the culprit.

'Sir David's going to be very unhappy about this,' he lamented more than once.

Porson tried to comfort him. 'I don't know that they were that close, you know. They only went to the same school, and that was yonks ago. Once we've got solid evidence, he'll distance himself from Holland as quick as a bunny, you'll see.'

'But *have* we got solid evidence?' Carpenter moaned.

Slider went inside to get out of range. His main team were now down in the basement, where in the original layout there had been the kitchen, scullery, coal-hole, pantries and servants' lavatory – a warren of small dark rooms that modern taste had thrown into one large, light room and filled with state-of-the-art culinary equipment. Almost one room. The lavatory, down at the garden end of the kitchen, had been left, so that people using the garden wouldn't have to go upstairs. And the coal-hole at the other end, a windowless space, had been turned into a utility room with strip lighting, containing washing machine, dryer, and a large chest freezer.

Lœssop happened to be the one to open the freezer lid, and turning his head, saw Slider in the kitchen doorway and called him over.

Bags of frozen peas and frozen vegetable medley lay on the top, but even they didn't quite conceal what was underneath. Lœssop moved them out of the way carefully, quietly, and Slider looked down at the chilly shape of Felicity Holland, laid on her side in foetal position so as to get her legs in. She hadn't been that tall in life anyway. There was frost on her dark eyelashes, and a crust of blood on the edge of the teeth that showed between her slightly parted lips.

'Oh Felicity,' he said sadly. 'That was a rotten trick.'

Sometimes they went on denying right to the bitter end, and that could be disturbing, bringing you to wonder, against your own certainty, if you had missed something. Others, faced by the solid evidence, gave up, and seemed to get relief from the confession of the whole story. Slider had thought, by his behaviour so far, that Holland would be a denier; but presented with a photograph of his dead wife folded up in his freezer, he went very still for a long time. Then he said, 'I didn't mean to kill her.'

So he was a confessor.

Slider was glad, because he was tired, and sorry, because whatever he learned now was only of academic satisfaction, to show he had been right. It might save his career. It wouldn't save Felicity. It wouldn't bring her back.

'I was following her,' he admitted when the questioning resumed. He had washed his face, consulted his solicitor, been given a cup of tea, and now was composed, but pale, looking as though he was suffering from shock. However much he may or may not have felt of love towards his wife, she had been his wife for a long time, and people's roots grow down into each other, and are painful to pull out.

'Yes, I followed her,' he admitted. 'I knew something was going on, ever since Christmas. She was – different. She had a look about her, when she didn't know I was watching, as if she was hugging a delicious secret to herself. I knew what that meant. So I looked for clues. I narrowed it down to Tuesdays. She was always – excited on Tuesdays. As if she was going to some special treat. Like a child on Christmas morning.' He said it scornfully. 'Then on that Monday night I found the sweater. It was in a bag behind the kitchen door. We never close that door, so the space behind it – you wouldn't normally see into it. It was a good hiding place.'

'How did you come to see into it?'

'Because I was looking. I'd seen the item on her credit card statement. From a men's outfitters. My birthday wasn't until December, so I didn't think it was for me. It was for whoever she was buying lunch for every week. Yes, I saw that too, on her bank statement. She always tore them up after she'd checked them, but I'd been getting them out of the bin, sellotaping them back together. That started after Christmas, the lunches. She'd lunched with people from her classes before, but why would she suddenly start paying for someone else? I knew she was hiding something. Then I found the sweater – a vile colour and a worse style, not something I would ever wear. That's when I knew for sure she had a lover. And it gave me a good idea of the sort of low type he must be. She was betraying me for a man who wore clothes like that! After she left that morning, I went down to the kitchen, and the bag was gone. So I knew she'd gone to give it to him. Today was the day, I thought. So I went to the arts centre and waited for her to come out, and followed her.'

'You pretended to me that you didn't know where the pottery class was.' Holland shrugged. What did that matter now? 'And you knew the name of the restaurant already,' Slider pointed out. 'You didn't need to follow her. You could have gone straight there.'

'The bank statement doesn't give the address. Anyway, she might have gone somewhere else. If it was a birthday celebration, for instance. I had to be sure. I followed her to some tacky restaurant in Drury Lane. I waited in a sort of alley just along the road for them to come out. She held his hand as they crossed the road. He had the sweater bag in the other hand.' His lip curled. 'And they went into a block of flats – where he lived, of course. That was where they were doing it. I felt sick to my stomach, I can tell you. So I went home, to wait for her.'

'So you did hear her come in?'

'I was waiting for her in the hall. I couldn't settle to anything, knowing what was coming. She came in, smiling, pink cheeked, as though she'd had a wonderful day. I thought I'd give her the chance to come clean. I said, "Have you had a nice day, dear?" She started up the stairs.'

'Did she have the dry-cleaning with her?'

He looked confused at the interruption. 'I don't know. I didn't notice. I suppose so – probably. My mind was on other things. I followed her into the bedroom, thinking what to say while she pottered about, taking off her jacket and hanging it up, taking off her shoes, brushing her hair, just as if nothing had happened. That's what really goaded me, that she could act a part so convincingly. I said, "What did you do today?" She said, "Oh, pottery class, then lunch with some of the girls." "Is that all?" I said – giving her a chance, you see – and she said, "I looked in a couple of shops." I said, "You're lying," and she turned and looked at me, and I knew then I was right. I could see it in her face. I said, "You slut!" and I grabbed her. She said, "It's not what you think!" But they always say that. And it was *exactly* what I thought. It always is. Everyone thinks their tawdry little sin is different, special, noble, but it's just as petty and tawdry as everyone else's. And then, I don't know how it happened, but we were fighting.'

He stopped.

'Fighting?' Slider said. 'She was a lot smaller than you. It couldn't have been much of a fight.'

'She grabbed my award from the mantelpiece and started hitting me with it. So I had to defend myself. I got her—' He broke off. 'I got her by the neck. I think I was shaking her. She was saying something, I don't know what, something about children. Mocking me because we didn't have children, as if it was my fault. I'd always wanted a family, but it never happened. I believe now it was her fault, it was deliberate on her part. She denied me a child. I think I hit her then.'

'You think?'

'It's not clear in my mind. I was so angry, I don't remember all the details. I think I hit her across the face. At the same time I must have let go of her, because she went reeling backwards. I heard her head hit the edge of the mantelpiece. A sickening sound – like, like someone hitting a peach with a hammer. She fell down. She put her hand to her face, she mumbled something at me, I don't know what. She started to get up, and I grabbed her again, by the neck, and shook her. And then – I don't remember.'

'I think you do,' Slider said grimly.

'I-I may have banged her head against the mantelpiece again. I was so angry – it's all a bit of a blur. I know she went limp, and when I let her go, she collapsed to the floor, like a sack.' He lifted defiant eyes to Slider. 'I didn't mean to kill her. I swear it. I would never hurt her, I would never lift a hand to her, to any woman, but I was just – so – *angry*. She wouldn't stop arguing, you see, even though I'd caught her out. If she'd only been honest, admitted it, maybe I . . . But she would keep on saying it wasn't what I thought, and it just made me madder.'

He paused for breath, long ragged ones, growing calmer. He said in a quieter voice, 'She'd had lots of lovers before me, before I married her. I knew that. She'd been a party girl. But I married her anyway. I forgave her her past. And I gave her everything, a name, a beautiful home, respectability. Money – she could have anything she wanted, within reason. Fame, of a sort, as my wife. I never interfered with her little pleasures, her clubs and arts and so on. But she never loved me, not really. She didn't give me a child, and in the end she wouldn't even give me that one thing I had a right to expect, her fidelity. I tried to make an honest woman of her, but it wasn't in her. She was – not . . . She wasn't . . .'

The thought ran out of words. He stared bleakly at nothing, perhaps realizing that, as little as he thought he'd had, he had even less now.

'So you were left with a dead body on your hands,' Slider said. 'Why didn't you call the police?'

He looked up. 'Are you mad? It would have been the end of everything. My reputation, my career would have been in ruins.'

'So you put her in the freezer,' Atherton said, without expression.

'Temporarily. Until any fuss died down. Then I would have – I don't know. Given her a decent burial. Somehow. For the present, I knew she would be missed, so the thing was to make sure that no one thought of looking for her at home, that no one suspected me. I racked my brains for a plan.'

'Then you remembered you'd been at school with Sir David
– the commissioner.'

'He was a tremendous fan of my books. So I had a reasonable excuse to contact him. And I thought if I was the one
to report her missing, especially to someone like him, I'd
never be suspected. And it worked,' he added stubbornly.
'Didn't it?'

'For a time. But it could never be more than temporary,'
Slider said.

He shrugged. 'I had to think what might have happened to
her. And there was that case a few months ago. That woman
snatched off the street by a serial rapist. I couldn't manufacture
evidence to prove that's what happened, but I could suggest
it. So I took her handbag and left it somewhere it would be
found, somewhere a rapist might go to bury a body.'

'Why Burnham Beeches?' Slider asked, the one he'd been
longing to put.

'They were woods, they weren't too far away. I'd no idea
where to go, but when I got in the car I remembered her
talking about them, and when I turned on the satnav they
were already in there. I remembered she'd gone there for a
walk with her sister not long ago. So I went there. I took
her credit cards and phone out of the bag, because I knew
that's what villains do, and I left it by a tree where someone
would find it.'

'And the TV appeal?'

He frowned. 'I suppose I got a bit carried away. But I
thought that's what someone would do in the circumstances.
I wanted to behave as naturally as possible. I thought I did
that pretty well. Thinking about her brought tears to my eyes,
so I didn't have to act. But then nothing happened, nobody
seemed to be doing anything, no one was even searching for
her in the woods, despite the handbag. I was angry on her
behalf. They weren't taking her disappearance seriously. So I
– made the phone call. Pretending to be the murderer.'

'Pretending?'

He winced. 'You know what I mean.'

'You used her phone. That was a clever thought.'

'Well, otherwise you might have dismissed it as a crank

call. But you couldn't ignore a call from her actual phone. Only the murderer would have that.'

'Yes,' said Slider.

He looked hurt. 'But I didn't murder her. I've told you, it was an accident. I never meant to hurt her. It was an accident.'

'Not entirely,' Slider said. 'If you'd called the police straight away, and explained everything frankly and openly, then we might have accepted it was an accident. But you've plotted this whole thing like an episode in a novel, treating her death like a factor to be worked into the plot. But this was her life, Mr Holland, her one and only life, and you took it from her. And she can't ever have it back.'

Anguish suddenly filled his eyes. 'I know,' he said. 'I can't bear to think about it. After . . . When she was – dead . . . When I saw her . . . You don't know what it's like. It was the only way I could cope, to work it out like a plot, as if it was a character in a book, and not my – not Felicity. Not . . .' He gasped for breath through a sob. 'I loved her. She was so beautiful and she was my wife, but she never loved me, and in the end she betrayed me for . . .' Another gasp. 'I saw him. He was younger than me. A lot. That was cruel. Younger than her, even. I couldn't stand that. She betrayed me for a common young lout. A *toy boy*!'

Atherton caught Slider's eye, and in it was the request, *let me be the one to tell him.*

Slider nodded, cold and sick. He'd had enough now of other people's emotions. Time to pull himself back from the brink.

'He wasn't a toy boy, Mr Holland,' Atherton said precisely and clearly, to get Holland's attention. Holland looked up. 'He was her son.'

Utter incomprehension. 'What?'

'She'd had a child when she was just seventeen. Illegitimate, of course. Her father made her give it up for adoption. That was who she'd been seeing. Not a lover. Martin Henderson, the baby taken away from her – lost to her, she thought, for ever. But he'd found her again. He was back in her life. That's why she was so happy since Christmas. She was planning how she could introduce him to the rest of the family. She wanted it all to be open and joyful, nothing concealed, no secrets any more. She probably thought that, in time, you'd be able to be glad for her. Since, as you say, you loved her. She wasn't unfaithful to you. She *was* an honest woman – just an unlucky one.'

Slider thought he might not have put it exactly that way, but it was certainly effective. Comprehension came to Holland at last, and the pain was appalling to witness. He looked as if nothing worse could ever happen to him now.

TWENTY-ONE
The Road Not Travelled

'I think,' said Slider much later, 'that what he couldn't stand was not so much the sin as the bad taste. If she'd erred with someone he approved of, he might not have taken it so badly.'

'Who *did* he approve of, other than himself?' Atherton said. 'Another author? Maybe one even more successful than him?'

'At any rate, to be upstaged by a shaggy-haired, sloppily dressed nonentity . . .'

'Do you think he really feels remorse now?' Atherton asked after a pause.

Slider thought about it, and shook his head. 'I think he still doesn't *really* think he did it. He enjoyed the ecstasy of a brief rage, of letting go control completely – something most of us never do our whole lives, even though we sometimes want to. Surrender to the scarlet surge of primal anger.'

'Nifty phrase. You should be a writer. Sorry – carry on. It must have felt almost like a sexual release.'

'Yes, exactly like that,' Slider said. 'Delicious, overpowering, profoundly satisfying. That's why it's so dangerous. When people discover its joys, it's addictive.'

'Hence domestic abuse,' Atherton said.

'He'd have had a high. But then there's the come-down – a short period when he really realized what he'd done. And by his own account he couldn't stand thinking about it. So after that he planned it like the plot of a novel, so that it was not really him. What would this character have done, what would this character have said, how would he have reacted. That's how he kept it up so well – being the worried husband, indignant at the police lack of progress.'

'He was acting a part.'

'Yes. And doing it pretty well.' Slider shrugged. 'Fortunately, like most criminals, he's fundamentally stupid. Because he's so invested in himself, he can't see how things look from the outside.'

'We've got a good case,' Atherton said, after a pause. 'Do you think he'll go down? Or will the old "It's all a blur, I dunno what come over me, Your Honour" get him off?'

'He'll do time,' Slider said shortly. 'Just not enough.'

'He'll have the rest of his life to regret it.'

Anger had sustained Holland – righteous anger. Now he had looked truth in the face. But humankind cannot bear too much reality; they're all too likely, sooner or later, to reach for the comforting lie. 'I'm just afraid he'll think himself out of it again, like he did before,' Slider said.

Porson was more relieved than pleased. 'So it did turn out to be a murder investigation after all. And you got him. That's worth a lot of points.'

Slider tried to be gratified. 'I can't see my desk for the piled-up backlog of work,' he mentioned.

Porson countered. 'I had the commissioner on this morning. Sir David, in person. To give us an attaboy.'

Now Slider smiled. 'That must have been embarrassing for him.' Sir David had pushed the investigation on to them as a favour to an old school chum, and made a fuss about personal service. Now the old school chum had turned out to be a dirty murderer, who'd taken them all for fools.

'Yerss,' said Porson, pulling out his lower lip thoughtfully. 'If you've got any sense, you won't push that aspect of it when you speak to him. Least said, soonest mentioned.'

'When *I* speak to him?'

'I told him it was all your bon, told him he ought to thank you in person.'

'Why?' Slider said wildly. 'Why would you do that?'

Porson actually grinned. 'Cos I knew he'd hate it. Come on, let me have a bit of fun!'

'But what am I supposed to say?'

'He'll do the saying. You just have to be humble and grateful for the fine words.'

'Fine words butter no parsnips,' Slider grumbled. 'They could at least give me a raise.'

'Don't count your horses,' Porson advised succinctly.

He took a phone call at his desk. It was Thelma. 'It is very wrong of me, to ring you?' she asked timidly.

'It's not . . .' He was going to say, normal procedure, but he remembered the toasted fried egg sandwich, and changed it to, 'It's all right. Didn't you have a visit from the family liaison officer?'

'Yes. She seemed very nice, she tried to be nice, but I couldn't help feeling it was just – I don't know – routine to her. All in the day's work. She said the right things, I suppose, but . . .' A pause. 'I need to hear it from you to really know it's true. I mean, I know you, sort of. Is she . . . Is Fliss really dead?'

'I'm afraid so.'

'You saw her?'

'Yes.' He waited. Nothing. 'You'll have the opportunity to see her, if you want to. The body will be released to the next of kin.'

'The body. She's just the body now.'

'I know it's hard for you,' he began.

'It's not hard, it's *impossible*. After Mummy died, it was just the two of us, really. Dad was never . . . He cared for us, but he was always – distant.'

Slider was thinking of the old adage, that girls always end up marrying their fathers. Felicity's father had been remote, emotionally unavailable, reproving, controlling; and she'd married Henry Holland. Perhaps something in her had needed the smack of firm government. And both relationships had ended in disaster for her. Had she been doomed from the start? Could her life have turned out any different? For his own sake, he needed to believe it could.

Thelma went on, 'And Henry – it was really Henry who—?'

'I can't discuss that with you, for legal reasons.'

'I suppose I'll read all about it in the papers,' she said miserably. 'I always thought he was a stick, but I always thought he loved her, in his own, dreary way. It's hard to believe he would . . . Did he admit it? Can you at least tell me that? Did he confess?'

'He has been charged, that's all I can say.'

'Oh God. I'm sorry. This is inappropriate, isn't it? I should go.'

'I know how much she meant to you,' Slider said gently. 'I spoke to Mrs Yeatman, and she told me how close you two were when you were children.'

'I never knew anything about the baby.' It burst from her. 'I went to school after Christmas and came back at Easter and it was all over and they never told me. Fliss never said a word. It was Josh Milo, I suppose? And she went on seeing him, in spite of everything.'

'He died three years ago,' Slider said, in case she thought of hunting for him.

'Oh God! Three years ago? That's when . . .' A silence full of realizations. 'That was when she was so depressed. I thought it was the menopause. She must really have loved him.'

'I think if you went to see Mrs Yeatman, she'd be willing to talk about it all now.'

'I suppose it can't do any harm any more,' she said drearily. 'And this man – this Martin? What must he be feeling? To have found his . . . To have found her after all this time, and then lose her again. I'd like to get in touch with him. Could I? Maybe I can help – maybe he'd like to talk about it to someone who knew her. Can you give me his address, phone number?'

'I can't, I'm sorry. But I can give yours to him, if you like, and tell him that if he wants to talk to you, you'd be happy to hear from him.'

'Thanks.' She sighed. 'And then there's Dad – what must he be feeling?' A pause. 'There's no end to this, is there?'

There never is. Evil casts a long shadow, Slider thought. 'There's nothing to stop you seeing him.'

'I'm not sure if I want to,' Thelma said. 'When I think what he did to Fliss.'

Slider didn't need to wonder what Sir John might be feeling, because he had spoken to him already. It was when Mr

Carpenter had been filling in Sir John on such details of the case as he was allowed to pass on. Slider and Porson had been in the room – they were at the first debriefing at Hammersmith when the call came through. Sir John had been contacted by Sir David to tell him the bare facts – that Felicity was dead and Holland had been charged with her murder – and he had immediately rung Carpenter to expostulate. Carpenter had listened and made non-committal sounds for some time, and finally had turned his head and fixed Slider with a lepidopterist's pin of a look. 'Yes, he's here.'

'He wants to talk to you,' Carpenter said, proffering the receiver, hand over the mouthpiece.

Slider had taken it reluctantly. But Sir John said, 'I think I owe you an apology.'

'Not at all, sir,' Slider said automatically. 'I was just doing my job.'

'And I didn't make it any easier for you,' Sir John said. Not humbly, not apologetically, just matter-of-factly, but it was more than Slider could have hoped for. 'I've served the law all my life, I've dealt with thousands of these cases, but when it happens to you . . . There's no way to prepare for it.'

'I understand,' Slider said, wishing it was over.

'Do you? Perhaps you do. You probably see things from both sides, in your job, the victim and the perpetrator. I never really saw . . . Just tell me, does this bastard really know what he's done? Does he suffer?'

Slider didn't answer.

'I suppose that's not a fair question,' Sir John said after a moment. 'I hope he does. I hope he lives a long, long life, and suffers every moment of it, thinking about what he's done. I just wanted *you* to know that I am suffering.'

'I'm sure you—'

'No, I don't mean like that. Not just over my daughter's death. Of course, that. But I can't help thinking that all of this comes back to me. I made certain decisions. I made them for the best reasons, and I don't repent them. Not given the context. Consequences followed which I couldn't have foreseen. I can't be blamed for that. But still, I can't help thinking that if I hadn't been so . . .' A pause while he searched for the right word. '. . . so sure of what was right – if I'd been more flexible – things might have happened differently.'

'Every decision marks a crossroads,' Slider said, as neutrally as he could.

'I can only say that in the same circumstances, if they arose now, I would probably make a different decision. I wanted you to know that.'

Will this day never end? Slider thought. 'Yes, sir,' he said.

'That's all,' said Sir John, and rang off.

Slider handed the receiver back to Carpenter, who looked at him with burning, not to say impertinent, curiosity.

'Well? What did he say?'

Slider hauled himself up from the depths. 'He said he wished it hadn't happened.'

Carpenter opened his mouth to protest, and closed it again, baffled. Porson looked at him with intense sympathy, and a certainly amused admiration.

On the way back to Shepherd's Bush, in the leather embrace of the back of the car, with the police driver in the front – such luxury! – Porson said, 'I'd never ask, you don't have to tell me, but what *did* Sir John say?'

'That it was his fault. Sort of.'

'Bloody Nora! To think I should live to see the day.'

'He didn't exactly apologize, but he said he thought he *owed* me an apology.'

'"Thought"! Well, I suppose that's as close as you'll get. He was practically Attorney General once, you know. Those buggers don't say sorry to anyone.'

'I know. I'm *deeply* grateful,' Slider said, with enough irony to shift the earth's axis. 'Like one of those poor sods who live through the war, end up with no legs and only one arm, and get given a medal.'

'That's right.' Porson patted Slider's arm briskly. 'Sometimes you have to wade through the shit to get to the gravy.'

Hallmark's loss was the Met's gain, Slider thought, closing his eyes.

It was customary to have post-case drinks at the Boscombe Arms, guv'nors and above paying. Even if you were tired –

and Slider always was at these times, his soul worn thin by the repeated friction of other people's sorrows, rages and stupidities – it was right to celebrate a victory over the forces of chaos. And, as Atherton said, everyone had worked their little bottoms off this time. Pints of the good stuff were soaked up with platters of pork pie, Scotch eggs and triangle sandwiches (egg and cress, cheese and tomato, and ham and pickle was the usual selection). It was the least they deserved.

It was arranged for Monday. Joanna was coming, which would help him be as cheerful as he needed to seem.

'Your dad's willing to hold the fort,' she told him when she phoned him back to confirm. 'Because Kate would really love to come.'

'Kate? How does she even know about it?'

'I rang and told her about the result. She wanted to be kept up to date on everything. It won't go on very late, will it?'

'No, but there might be unseemly language,' he worried. 'But why would she want to come anyway?'

'She wants to see how much you are loved and respected. I've told her often enough, but she thinks that's just me being a wife.'

'I'm not sure it's the right environment for her,' he said, still doubtful.

'Teenagers are a lot older than you and I were at the same age. And I promise to keep a close eye on her. Do say she can. It's been great these past months having her living here and getting to know you. A girl needs her father, in some ways more than a boy does.'

A girl always ends up marrying her father, he thought. What sort of man would he want his daughter to marry? One who would let her come to his celebration drinks? Or try to protect her from police canteen language?

What would he do if, God forbid, Kate came to him now, pregnant? Well, he wouldn't send her away, that was for sure; but the world was a different place now from when Felicity was a teenager. To be right, or to be popular? And how to know the difference? Blimey, this dad-business was a hot potato.

He thought about what Kate was really like, and somehow

Blue Moon Bay

**Center Point
Large Print**

*Also by Lisa Wingate and available from
Center Point Large Print:*

Beyond Summer
Dandelion Summer

**This Large Print Book carries the
Seal of Approval of N.A.V.H.**

Blue
Moon
Bay

LISA
WINGATE

CENTER POINT LARGE PRINT
THORNDIKE, MAINE

The text of this Large Print edition is unabridged.
In other aspects, this book may
vary from the original edition.
Printed in the United States of America
on permanent paper.
Set in 16-point Times New Roman type.

ISBN: 978-1-61173-322-8

Library of Congress Cataloging-in-Publication Data

Wingate, Lisa.
Blue moon bay / Lisa Wingate.
p. cm.
ISBN 978-1-61173-322-8 (library binding : alk. paper)
1. Texas—Fiction. 2. Large type books. I. Title.
PS3573.I53165B57 2012b
813'.54—dc23

2011044460

For Mary and Emily
And their awesome grandparents,
The Douglases

The future is a blank page, but not a mystery.
—Tinker's riddle
*(Written on the wall of wisdom, Waterbird Bait
and Grocery, Moses Lake, Texas)*

≈ Chapter 1 ≈

Is it possible for nine months and three days of your life to haunt you forever? Can memories become like restless spirits—their long, thin fingers always reaching, and tugging, and grabbing? Their fingernails, in my case, would be some variation of floral pink and nicely manicured. Perfectly matched to a shade of lipstick and possibly a purse or some other accessory. Undoubtedly, this is not the norm for personal demons, but try telling them that. They won't listen, I promise.

There is no escape from those graceful Moses Lake ladies, with their embroidery-adorned pantsuits and their languid Southern drawls. When they whispered in my mind, their sentences rose and fell and rose again, filled with long vowels, padded and powdered with cheerfulness they couldn't possibly be feeling all the time. They became the stuff of my darkest recurrent nightmares—the kind that reprised the most awkward teenage years and found me wandering the halls of Moses Lake High School with no idea where I was supposed to go, suddenly aware that I'd arrived in my Pooh Bear pajamas. Or even worse, I'd forgotten the pajamas altogether. Yet, somehow, I was just then noticing. . . .

Even from thousands of miles away, after the passage of season after season, the high school dream lingered, along with the feeling that somewhere in the tiny town of Moses Lake, Texas, the ladies were still talking about me. *Such an odd little thing,* they were saying, a purposeful twang morphing the last word into *tha-ang. All that eyeliner and that tacky, tacky purple lip gloss. Why, those black T-shirts didn't help her figure one little bit, I'm tellin' ye-ew. But how much can you expect, considerin' what happened?*

I wondered if their conversations turned darker, then—if the women whispered behind their hands about things I was never allowed to know. Did they debate theories or did they discuss facts as they sat at Lakeshore Community Church, making greeting cards or knitting scarves for orphans or boxing cans for the food pantry? Did they *know* what happened?

In my dreams, sometimes I was running toward a door. I heard the ladies on the other side, whispering amongst themselves. I recognized the door—large, white, with intricate molding. A double door. It was made to open inward, to allow the crowds to funnel through.

Then the door grew smaller, and it was a cellar door. It was plain and brown. There was a spider on a web in the corner. I reached for the handle.

I'd awaken in a sweat at that point, still hearing the echoes of the ladies chattering in the dusty corners of my mind.

Their voices found ways to carry into the daylight, sometimes. Occasionally, I heard them talking *to* me, those Moses Lake ladies. *Suga', now, sit up straight,* they'd admonish as I hunched over the table in some meeting, bleary-eyed while watching a computer render a building in 3-D from an electronic blueprint I'd been tweaking all night. *Oh, Heather, hon, put that foot down. A lady never crosses her legs at the knee. Darlin', don't swing your toe like that. Some boy might think you're a hussy. Mercy! Didn't your mama teach you any-thang?*

How, I wondered, is it possible for such a small part of your childhood to linger so persistently? Do we choose the ghosts that haunt us, or do they choose us? And if we choose them, shouldn't we be able to banish them?

The questions were scrolling through my head again as I sat in a meeting room, watching Mel generate a virtual walkthrough of a big-box retail store. He was explaining how customer traffic would flow, how the layout allowed for excellent point-of-sale potential. He laughed and said, "It's about capturing those impulse buys."

Leaning across the table, he inclined his head toward the Japanese contingent on the client side, as if he were sharing valuable trade secrets with them. "Of course, we all know that sixty-six percent of buying decisions are made in the store, and of those, fifty-three percent are pure impulse buys. Our research shows that with this layout, your percentages could increase to . . ." He paused, looked down at his notes, tapped the tabletop with his pencil.

I was only vaguely aware of the glitch in his presentation. I'd had the Moses Lake dream again last night. The past was floating in front of me like a cellophane overlay, scenes dripping and blending with the reflections from the conference room windows. It was raining outside again, typical for Seattle. Not the best weather for a critical presentation that could mean millions.

I'd dreamed all the way to putting my hand on the cellar doorknob last night. I'd curled up on a yoga mat behind my desk to catch a couple hours' sleep before the office came to life, and suddenly there were the doors. The white ones, then the brown one.

It had been a while since I'd seen the door. Maybe a year or more since I'd awakened with a start and moved through the day wondering what really happened at the bottom of those cellar steps.

"Heather, did you pull together the rest of that

research?" Mel glanced my way expectantly, as if he hadn't already been given the numbers. My boss was slipping. Seven years ago, when I'd started at CTI, Mel was a lion.

"Sure. Of course." I flipped through the paperwork to save face for Mel. In reality, the numbers and I were on intimate terms. "The consumer research indicates a potential seventeen percent increase in impulse purchases, as compared with your existing stores. Considering that we're discussing stores that are already running at a brisk average of three hundred and fifty dollars in gross sales per square foot, that increase would be . . ." Mel caught my eye and gave me a look that warned me not to start running calculations in my head and spouting figures. This was *his* meeting. Letting the papers settle back into place, I finished with, "Significant, of course."

Mel took over again, but two of the principals were clearly more interested in hard facts than Mel's sales talk about *Environments that perform* and *brand iconography*. Mel was pushing hard, borderline desperate, but after seven years of paddling in the man's wake, I understood his nuances. It was hard to know how to feel, sitting there watching him struggle to revive the old magic. On the one hand, he had plucked me off the bottom rung of the ladder. On the other hand, every time I tried to climb the ladder, Mel's foot was squarely on my head. I wanted to move up, to eventually achieve what he had achieved—project leader, junior partner, partner. I'd never get there with Mel in the way.

My cell phone vibrated in my pocket. I slid it out and glanced while everyone was watching virtual customers move through checkout lanes. The customers started at a normal pace, then gradually sped up, buzzing by like bumblebees exiting a hive, having sacrificed nectar for shopping carts filled with fifty-three-plus-percent impulse buys. They were moving so fast, they never even knew what hit them.

The text message was from Richard. *Problem. Call me ASAP.*

The phone vibrated with an incoming call as I was tucking it away. Surely that wasn't Richard. He knew how long these meetings could take. One advantage of dating a guy who was in the real estate business was that he understood. When clients come to town, the clients come first.

I took a peek at the screen. I didn't recognize the number, but I knew the area code. 510. California. My mother, undoubtedly. Suddenly Richard's text message made sense.

My foot vibrated under the table as the meeting worked toward a close. When it was over, I gathered my files and politely excused myself from the room. Somehow, Mel and I ended up on the elevator together anyway.

"They left quickly." He leaned into the corner,

his head falling against the wall as if he couldn't hold it up one more second.

"It was a long meeting." But we both knew what a quick exit usually meant. "They won't find a more comprehensive proposal than ours, though."

"Let's hope." His eyes slowly closed, like he was already trying to figure out how he'd survive if we didn't get this Itega contract.

The doors opened. Watching him there, crumpled against the wall, I felt the need to say something more. I held the doors open with the button, so as not to be ferried to the executive suites along with Mel.

"It's a good proposal," I offered. "We've got a slick design. Perfect fundamentals."

He didn't react.

Like a puppy, I stood there pathetically waiting for a pat on the head, for some acknowledgement of the countless hours I'd put into the proposal, of the devotion I'd given to managing all aspects of the design package. Finally, there wasn't much choice but to step through the door onto my floor. The one nicely above the designers in their Spartan cubicles and squarely below the posh executive level.

"What's going on with that thing in Texas?" Mel's question followed me.

I turned and pushed the button to open the doors again. "What?"

"The thing in Texas. The processing plant . . .

Proxica Foods. What's happening with that?" Mel cracked an eye open. "*Your* project." Was it my imagination, or did the emphasis on *your* come with an underlay of resentment—an insinuation that I was overstepping my bounds by insisting that, if I could bring this project in, I would be the project leader.

"Everything seems to be right on target. The principals at Proxica are happy with the design concept. The property deals are in the final stages. They're looking at a state-of-the-art processing plant and eight corporately-owned production farms—six for poultry and two for grain crops." The phone message from Richard crossed my mind, and an uncomfortable sensation settled underneath my favorite blue blazer. The biggest event in my career, and I was banking on something that involved my mother. . . .

Mel's lips pursed, smacking slightly, as if he were tasting the potential of the deal. Maybe now that the Itega bid had soured a bit, Mel was looking to take over my Texas project. Would he really do that?

"Keep me apprised," he said, rubbing his chest as I exited the elevator.

"Aye-aye, Cap'n." The words were a thin attempt at lightness. The second the elevator doors closed, I raced toward my office, muttering to myself and thinking of the Texas deal and my mother.

A pair of interns, chatting as they ferried mailing tubes, stopped talking and sidled to the wall as I passed, clutching the tubes like Roman shields. I had the momentary pang of regret that comes from knowing someone finds you humorless and slightly frightening, but it quickly passed. Interns rotated through the firm constantly. If they were here to learn architecture and design in the real world, they might as well see how things really were. No point filling them with the warm fuzzies. It was a long, hard climb before you got to take on a project of your own. Those fresh-faced college kids were better off seeing the truth now and then deciding how badly they wanted it.

I dialed Richard's number while rounding the corner into my office. "Hey, what's up?" I asked, an odd little singsong in my voice. Maybe I just felt the need to be girly and cute, so as not to send him scurrying, like the interns. In the dating world, intimidation is not considered a desirable quality. Normal men tended to see me as slightly work-obsessed and hyperfocused. Or, as my friend and former roommate, Trish, liked to put it, *married to my iPhone.*

But Richard was as normal as they came. Normal and successful, and he liked me. He didn't have a string of failed marriages behind him, and he was with a respectable law firm. An especially rare find among the over-thirty set, where pickings became slim.

He sighed, and I knew the news was not good. I loved him for hesitating a minute, as if he felt the need to break it to me gently. In general, Richard hated conflict, which was probably why he was in real estate law and not prosecuting murder cases. "Well, I know you said she was unpredictable, but . . ."

I didn't even wait for him to drag through the rest of the sentence. "What happened? Did she sign the offer?" Poor Richard. I should never have brought him into this. My mother was probably lighting incense in his office, hanging crystals, or reciting dark, dramatic, obscure poetry by some writer only English professors had heard of.

"She's not here. Not coming . . . Well, not today, anyway."

"What?" My voice echoed into the corridor, and I closed the office door, keeping the conversation inside. No one knew about the Texas project except Mel, Richard, and the commercial broker who was quietly shopping for land he would then resell to Proxica for their new facilities. Proxica had insisted that their expansion plans be kept confidential. Strange things happen when communities find out that a company with deep pockets is sniffing around. "You've *got* to be kidding."

"I wish I were." Richard sounded frustrated, tired, and uncharacteristically irritable. He'd put in countless extra hours on this real estate deal and managed to get my family an offer of more than the property was worth. He'd sorted out the convoluted deeds for the land that had been in my father's family since just after the Civil War. Once the property was in Proxica's possession and the feasibility studies were finished, my part of the project came in—designing Proxica's new flagship facility, where big pieces of raw meat would become little pieces of cooked meat, neatly sliced and packaged in deli bags for people like me, who don't like to think about where meat actually comes from.

"Where is she?" *Within reach,* I wished. If my mother were within reach, I would . . . I would . . . What? What, exactly, would I do? Talking to my mother was like talking to one of those gauzy, diaphanous scarves the street vendors sell in India. Anything I said would go right through, my breath barely creating a ripple in the fabric.

"In Texas, apparently." I could hear Richard typing on his computer as he replied.

"In *Texas?* Why?" My mother hated Texas—especially Moses Lake and the portion of the family farm that had passed into her hands after my father's death. "Is Uncle Herbert all right? Uncle Charley?" A mental scenario materialized in which my dad's uncles had driven to the family farm, fifteen miles outside Moses Lake, and were holed up with shotguns in hand. Even though they both now lived at Uncle Herbert's place in town, they had grown up on the farm and were still sentimental about it.

"As far as I know, your uncles are fine. Your mother is down there with them, apparently. She said they are 'talking about some things.' "

"What things?" Inside my brain, I heard the high-pitched whistling sound of a pressure cooker about to blow. No wonder Richard was irritated. He'd worked so hard to convince the broker to take not only the farm property, but to make a package bid for my uncles' other properties, as well. Altogether, they owned four plots of land and two businesses. Uncle Herbert ran the Harmony Shores Funeral Home in town, and Uncle Charley was famous for the fried catfish at his floating restaurant, Catfish Charley's.

Now that both of my great uncles were in their eighties, the family farmland and businesses had to go. That was all there was to it. Uncle Herbert and Uncle Charley had made plans to relocate to Oklahoma to be near Uncle Herbert's son Donny and his progeny. Selling the property all at once would allow them to leave Moses Lake behind in one clean sweep.

Why had my mom suddenly decided to swirl her big toe in the pool, muddying the waters? She couldn't possibly have gotten wind of Proxica's plans to acquire the farm property, and quite frankly, I couldn't imagine why she would care. She'd hated Moses Lake even before we lived there, and she never wanted to see it again after we left. If my father's portion of the family farm hadn't been squarely landlocked between Uncle Herbert's portion and Uncle Charley's, it would have been gone shortly after my dad's passing sixteen years ago. Now the old dairy farm would be quietly recommissioned as a Proxica location, I would get my first design project, and the town of Moses Lake would see sorely needed new jobs. It was a win-win, if you didn't count the fact that everything hinged on my mother's cooperation.

"I'll call and talk to her about it," I said, and then apologized profusely to Richard, privately admiring his composure. He was accustomed to issues like this. I'd met him while testifying as an expert witness in a case. He was a lawyer for the opposition. My side won. He didn't hold it against me, fortunately.

"I'll take care of it. I'll have her here tomorrow." My words brought on that feeling you get on your first ski trip when you realize you've accidentally turned onto a double black diamond slope.

"The drop-dead date is eight days away. The broker offer expires February fifteenth."

February fifteenth. February fifteenth . . .

The day after Valentine's Day. Valentine's Day was a week away, and Richard and I hadn't even talked about it? That was odd, considering that Richard was a planner, and in Seattle, restaurant reservations on Valentine's Day were a must.

Maybe this little silence wasn't purely accidental. Maybe Richard had something special in mind, a surprise.

Could there be a certain little trinket attached to the hush-hush Valentine's Day . . . maybe something that comes in a little ring-sized box? We'd been dating six months. Having turned thirty-four last month, alone in my apartment with a cat that wasn't even my own, I was feeling the nudge. Richard was six years older than me, ready to find someone and settle down. He'd said so sometime early in our relationship. It was one of the things I liked about him. Neither of us had time to play the games that went with dating.

I found myself staring out the window, idly picturing an upscale apartment, two kids. . . . Would they have dark hair like Richard's, or auburn hair like mine? My caramel-brown eyes, or Richard's gray ones? Short and stocky, like Richard's family, or lanky like mine? Wavy hair like mine, or straight hair like Richard's? They'd be good at math. Both Richard and I were good with numbers. . . .

I realized he was waiting for me to reply on the broker issue. "So the offer expires the day after Valentine's Day, then, right?" *Hint, hint.*

He didn't pick up on the nuance, unfortunately. "Yes. Right. February fifteenth."

"Got it." First things first. Right now both of us were focused on the property deal. Between all the confusion about easements, ancient surveys, and my mother's failure to update the deed after my father's death, we'd come way too close to letting the offer expire.

I took a deep breath, then exhaled. "Don't worry." Which, of course, is what people say when they are worried. "If I have to go down there and drag my mother back here myself, I'll do it." The words held the false bravado of a schoolyard bully who's really afraid to fight. The last, last, last part of my life I ever planned to revisit was that terrible high-school year in Moses Lake. I'd shaken off the Texas dust sixteen years ago, and nothing short of the apocalypse would ever drag me back there again.

Truths are first clouds; then rain,
then harvest and food.
—Henry Ward Beecher
(*Left on the wall of wisdom by Andrea
Henderson, new Moses Lake resident,
and Mart McClendon, local game warden*)

≈ Chapter 2 ≈

Famous last words—nothing like planning a last-minute trip to Texas to make you eat them. One should never underestimate the power of twisted family ties and well-meaning church ladies bearing casseroles. Apparently, the Moses Lake ladies had discovered my mother at Uncle Herbert's place, and they'd pulled out the frozen funeral casseroles and the slice-and-bake cookies. They had shown up at Harmony Shores armed with food, ostensibly because widowed men like my uncles shouldn't be trying to cook for company. In reality, of course, they were there to figure out what, exactly, was going on at the former funeral home, and in what way it involved the town's ex-pariah, my mother.

The story, as my mother related it on the phone, grew more bizarre from there. Apparently she'd flown in on a whim, after arranging for a graduate assistant to cover her classes. It sounded like she'd been in Moses Lake overnight with the *uncs* (suddenly she was using the family pet name for my great uncles, to whom she had never given the time of day before). I wanted to ask her what she was thinking, taking off for Texas the day before she was supposed to be in Seattle. But trying to understand her thought processes was like contemplating infinity. It tied your brain in small, painful knots. Her actions were typically based on vague feelings, a sense of karma, or the advice of some spiritual advisor she'd met on the Internet.

When I called, she was walking along the lakeshore, ". . . just thinking," she said, as I rummaged around my office, stacking the Itega files all in one place, just in case I had to fly out of town to round up my mother. "Uncle Herbert found some boxes in his basement that were ours. Apparently, they've been stored here all this time. I wanted a few days to check it out, and then there's the estate sale issue. It's not easy for the uncs, having so many memories tied to the place. . . ."

She trailed off, and I thought we had a dropped connection, but then she started talking to someone who was there with her. I gathered that the pastor from Lakeshore Community Church had just dropped by to say hello and to pass along the phone number of a mortician who might want to buy the surplus caskets, casket stands, skirts, and various other funeral equipment in Uncle Herbert's basement.

"But . . . I thought all of that had been cleaned out. Uncle Herbert and Uncle Charley are supposed to be moving this week." *Right after the papers are signed.* It was a sad fact of this entire process that Uncle Herbert and Uncle Charley had to relocate closer to younger members of the family. They seemed to be handling it well enough, though, and as people age, difficult decisions have to be made. I needed to get my mother out of there before Uncle Herbert's son Donny found out she was meddling and a family war ensued. Donny and my mother had practically come to blows over the Moses Lake property numerous times in the past.

"Listen, Mother, the plans have already been made. You said you didn't want to handle your portion of the paperwork via fax, so Richard made arrangements for you to do it here, in person. He waited all morning for you to show. I don't understand why you're holding things up. You know that Uncle Herbert and Uncle Charley need the money, and you know they can't stay in Moses Lake by themselves any longer. You're just making things harder for everyone."

"Oh, they're fine. We played Chicken Foot last night." As usual, Mother was floating around somewhere in the fluffy cumulus nimbi. She sounded alarmingly relaxed. Not at all like someone about to head for the airport. "They're enjoying the casseroles. We've been writing down a few of the family stories, even."

"You're doing *what?*" The last thing we needed was everyone hanging around the funeral home, waxing nostalgic about the good ol' days. "What do you mean, you're playing dominoes? There's supposed to be almost nothing left in the house, and . . ."

I was momentarily at a loss for words. I imagined my mother camped out with my uncles in the massive Greek Revival house, where back in the day, you could turn a blind corner and unwittingly bump into coffin stands and body boards. My mother hated Uncle Herbert's place on Harmony Cove as much as she hated everything else about Moses Lake, which was why she'd fought like a banshee when my father had been offered the opportunity to supervise the con-struction and implementation of the Proxica plant upriver from Moses Lake, near the little Mennonite town of Gnadenfeld.

Mom had finally given in and let my dad accept the transfer—but only because my grandmother was in a nursing home, in the final weeks of her life, and my grandfather had been diagnosed with congestive heart failure. My dad was needed in Moses Lake, and so we picked up our lives and went. For me, a math-and-art-class-loving chick accustomed to a big-city high school in

Philadelphia, it seemed like the end of the world. I'd long since lost interest in going with my father on his cross-country trips to visit his family in Texas, and all of a sudden I was being told I'd have to spend my senior year of high school and graduate from tiny, podunk Moses Lake High. I hated my father for subjecting me to such a hideous reality. I made sure to communicate that in every selfish, immature way I could.

Sometimes, life turns upside down, and you never get the chance to say you're sorry.

"Listen, the offer on the property expires next week." I pointed out.

"I know," Mom answered, and I wondered at the strange, melancholy rhythm of her voice. Was Moses Lake wrapping its watery veil around her again, dragging her down the way it had in the months after my father's death? "So there's not any rush, really."

"Except that Richard did a ton of the work on the deeds as a favor to me, and he was expecting you today."

Mom exhaled. "Oh, Heather, men are always doing you favors. They love to do favors for you. It makes them feel like they might have a chance of cracking that shell."

"Richard is different." I refused to slide into yet another relationship conversation with my mother. I really did. She was the one with men bobbing in and out of her life like horses on a carousel. She was always holding court—discussing art, or literature, or theater with men from grad-student age on up to those with full professorships. She'd been in and out of love more times than I could count, the only constant being instability.

Just as she was working up what, undoubtedly, would have been some critical analysis of Richard, formed during their limited phone and email conversations over the real estate deal, I heard laughter in the background. A man's laugh. A familiar laugh.

"Mom, who's there with you?" My mind raced through the connections. My mother wasn't in Moses Lake alone. "Is Clay there? Is that Clay?"

Mom didn't have to answer. Suddenly the trip to Moses Lake made some sense.

Clay was there. He'd found out about the sale of the property and seen fit to involve himself, and now he was in Moses Lake, hanging out and giving Mom advice. My stomach clenched at the thought. Clay's involvement in the deal could be a game changer, and not in any good way. My little brother had been floating idly through college and law school for a decade, while taking occasional breaks to climb Mount Hood, or get his scuba-diving certification, or spend a semester in some tiny South American country, working with an earthquake relief team. So far, Clay seemed perfectly happy to move at his own aimless, relaxed pace, while Mother contributed financial support from the nest egg left behind by our dad's life insurance policy. At twenty-seven, Clay didn't seem in any rush to take care of himself.

"I'm coming down there," I said, but the show of bravado was intended only to make my mother snap to her senses. Surely she knew that Moses Lake, in terms of emotional stability, wasn't the best place for her to spend time. "Really, Mother. It isn't good for you to be there. What could you possibly be hoping to accomplish?"

"Maybe putting some ghosts to rest." Suddenly the lightness was gone from her tone. She sounded gravely serious. "They don't just go away on their own, you know."

A sick feeling leeched from the pit of my stomach, darkness spreading over me like a splash of ink. How was it that she could still do this to me? It was as if she knew where the painful spots were, and she could probe them whenever she wanted. "I'll be there tomorrow. I'll help you ship whatever boxes you want to ship, and then we're coming back here and doing the deal as planned."

A long pause left me hearing my own pulse thrumming, and then she finally answered, "Well, if you must know, there's another offer we want to look at, Heather. There's really nothing you can do here. I'll call you in a day or two."

My insides were rolling now, my mind whirling ahead. "What offer? An offer from whom?" There was no way that could be true. No one else was going to come along and pay the price the broker was offering.

"I really can't explain it all. . . ."

"I'll be there in the morning." Rubbing the ache in my forehead, I tried to think through the details. It was Wednesday. I could tell Mel I needed a couple personal days to see to the family matters related to the land sale. Mel wouldn't be happy about it, as *personal* wasn't really in his vocabulary, but I had enough unused vacation stacked up to last me until spring.

I mentally fast-forwarded through the Mel confrontation, then considered the practicalities. I'd have to book a flight, arrange for a rental car, look at a map, and figure out the route from the airport to Moses Lake. It would probably be easier to fly to Dallas and drive from there, rather than taking a commuter flight to Waco. . . .

"You're not bringing Richard along, are you?" Mother's question collided with my thoughts like an asteroid, leaving a fiery trail. Why would she care whether Richard was coming along? Unless . . . Unless she'd already made up her mind to bug out on the land sale, and she was afraid I might use Richard to try to strong-arm her into it. Maybe my brother was giving her some sort of amateur legal advice. Exactly how far had Clay gotten in law school before his last side trip on the highway of life?

The question nagged and nipped as I reiterated

29

that I was coming down there to straighten things out, then said good-bye.

Within an hour and a half, I'd cleared my impending absence with Mel, booked a flight, returned to my apartment, and thrown together a carry-on bag.

I ran into Trish as I was lugging my carry-on and laptop case down the stairs. She was ferrying a pizza box to the three-bedroom unit she'd moved into after she fell in love with the guy down the hall and got married. Now she was on the fast track to family life, having had three kids in four years. Since she'd given up ergonomic building design for mommyhood, we had most of our conversations in the stairwell at odd hours.

"Whoa, where are you headed?" she asked, holding the pizza like a platter.

"Texas," I grumbled, feeling pathetic and like I needed someone to feel sorry for me. I would never have let anyone see that but Trish. We'd met while working long hours at our first jobs out of college. She'd ridden the merry-go-round of family issues with me before.

Leaning against the stairway railing, she rested the pizza on the banister. "Your mom didn't show, huh?"

"Of course not." I gripped my forehead. I already had a headache, and my mother was still hundreds of miles away.

"I don't know when you're going to learn not to

expect anything from her." She punctuated the sentence with a disgusted smack. "Can I do anything for you while you're gone? Want me to water your plant?"

"I've already killed the plant. I watered it. Really. I mean . . . I think I watered it."

Trish rolled her eyes and opened the pizza box. "Here, take a slice of pizza, so you don't end up like the plant."

I thanked her, we hugged good-bye, and I transported myself to a flight bound for Texas, by way of several irritating layovers. Oddly enough, I didn't even think of calling Richard until I was high in the skies over Idaho. I dialed his number during a layover in Denver. He took the news well, which actually disappointed me a little. I was tired, frustrated, and irritated, and I suppose I wanted him to get manly and protective, maybe tell me it was brave of me to try to deal with this alone but he was hopping the next flight out.

Then again, why would he? Richard had no idea of the history that lay in Moses Lake because I'd never told him. No one in Seattle knew, except Trish. The best thing about living halfway across the country from the past you'd like to forget is that you're not obligated to reveal it to anyone. You really can leave it all behind. As far as Richard knew, Moses Lake was just an ancestral family place to which I had little attachment, sentimental or otherwise.

"I have a boatload of work to catch up on this weekend, anyway." Richard's words brought another unexpected letdown—as if I were dangling over a cliff, sinking a little lower and a little lower as he let out the rope. Maybe it was the whole Texas thing, but I was feeling uncharacteristically needy. The sensation was foreign and unwelcome.

I cradled the phone on my shoulder, juggling my laptop, purse, and carryon as I took a seat at the gate for my next flight. Outside the window, a Colorado moon shone on new-fallen snow. I wanted to walk out the door, catch a cab, and head for the mountains—lose myself in their cottony peaks and have a vacation. "I know. I'm sorry my mom wasted your time today. It's her world, and we're just living in it."

Richard chuckled, and I fell into the warm sound of it. He had such a nice laugh. "I like your mother. She's . . . artsy. A free spirit."

I was momentarily silenced. *I like your mother?* Traitor. "Thanks for being so nice about it." He wouldn't like her if he knew her better, would he?

"It's fine, really. I can understand her attachment to the family home."

He could? Richard understood my mother? "It isn't even her hometown. It was my father's. She never wanted to spend time there when I was a kid. She and my grandmother hated each other." I sounded like a harpy, like one of those bitter family members on Dr. Phil.

"Well, you know, the older people get, the more sentimental they feel about things. They have that sense of time slipping away."

I blinked, watching snowflakes swirl in the pocket of protected space near the Jetway. This didn't sound like Richard at all. "Are you okay?" I leaned away as a guy in a rumpled business suit took a seat next to me.

"Yeah, it's the birthday thing, I think."

Birthday . . . Oh, smack, I'd forgotten all about Richard's birthday. Friday. The day after tomorrow. Forty. Six years older than me. We'd talked about it, like, a month ago while watching the waiters at Chili's bring out a birthday cake and sing to an embarrassed customer. Richard made me promise I wouldn't take him anyplace with singing waiters on his birthday.

"Ohhh, your birthday. I'm sorry. I should be there. If I didn't have to get to Texas and straighten out this family thing, I'd turn around and fly right back." Forty had to be hard. I was glad I was a long way from forty.

"It's all right."

"No it's not." In all the talk back and forth about the land deal this week, I hadn't even mentioned his birthday. Because I hadn't thought about it. "I'm a really bad girlfriend." A flight attendant moved to the microphone behind the service desk, and a line began to form in anticipation of boarding. I stood up, grabbing my things.

"You're just you, Heather." There was a flat quality to his voice, a matter-of-factness, like *The grass is green* or *The air is invisible.*

It stopped me where I was.

The flight attendant announced that due to wind sheers associated with a storm moving over the mountains, all flights had been delayed.

I sank down in my chair. *Is that me? The girl who forgets people's birthdays and kills house-plants, and it doesn't even surprise anyone? They just expect it?*

Plans flashed through my mind—a tidy little suitcase of them that I'd been unpacking during these past months with Richard. Richard and I had a lot in common. We got along well. We were both nearing that age where it seemed like it was time to . . . well . . . fish or cut bait, as the uncs in Moses Lake would have said. Not having settled down hadn't bothered me in my twenties, but at thirty-four, you feel the fork in the road coming on. . . .

Some of our conversations had clued me into the fact Richard felt the same way. Maybe that was the reason for the melancholy sound in his voice when he mentioned the birthday. I wanted to believe it was, but really, I was afraid that I was the cause. Who wants to be dating the girl who takes off for another state right before your birthday and doesn't even realize it?

"Well, listen, I'd better let you go," he said, and I felt myself sinking lower.

Don't, I wanted to say, *Don't let me go.* But the words felt too vulnerable, too raw. I'd never been good at hanging my heart on my sleeve. But this was where so many relationships ended—with the old, *You're an amazing person, but we just want different things* conversation. Sometimes I was on the delivering end of that line, sometimes on the receiving end.

"Hey, Valentine's Day is next week." As soon as I said it, I felt pathetic, like I was pushing— fishing to see if he had something planned. The ring box I'd been contemplating earlier suddenly seemed miles away. "We could do dinner at the Waterfront Grill, take a walk through the sculpture park if the weather's all right."

"Let's talk about it when you get home. I haven't really thought that far ahead."

Let's talk about it when you get home? That wasn't the response I wanted, not at all what I expected.

Or was it? Maybe I'd been feeling the cooling air around us for a while—like evening setting in, but when you're busy, you don't notice. Then you look up, and suddenly it's almost dark. Chilly. Was that why I was trying to superimpose visions of a Valentine's surprise—because I was afraid yet another relationship was dying for lack of regular watering and feeding? "Oh . . . okay. We can figure it out when I get back."

"Have a good trip, Heather."

"Richard, are we okay?" As soon as the words were out, I wanted to stuff them back in. What was wrong with me tonight?

His hesitation was an answer, even if it wasn't. "Let's talk when you get home."

A wound, raw and deep, cracked open. On an architectural rendering, it would have been on Layer 1—the layer upon which everything else is built. "I'm sorry I asked." The words were bitter, hard-edged. "But you could have just told me . . . if there was a problem with you and me. You didn't have to pretend."

He sighed. I pictured him leaning forward, his short, thick fingers wrapped over his forehead, rubbing, trying to drum up the right words, trying to avoid a confrontation. "Listen, I know you've had a lot going on with all the family and the property sale. I didn't want to add any more . . . stress."

"I'm fine," I said. "It's fine." But, really, my head was ringing like I'd just had a hard right cross to the jaw. The fact that he was trying to be kind about it only made it worse. Is a gentle smack in the head better than the abrupt kind? It's still a smack in the head. "It's not like we were engaged or anything, Richard. We were just dating, right? It's not like there was any commitment."

36

He didn't answer at first. Clearly, I'd shocked him by being so blunt, but it was like a knee-jerk reaction, impossible to control. It's so much easier to reject than to be rejected.

"Sure," he said, and he sounded like I'd disappointed him in some way.

"I'd better go, okay? It's time to board my flight." It wasn't, but the rip inside me was widening. The only thing to do now was pull it back together before anyone saw.

We said good night, leaving things strangely open-ended, and I dropped the phone into my purse. Beside me, the guy in the business suit ventured a sympathetic glance. He'd heard the relationship drama, of course. He looked like he might be conversational, and there was a dangly fish-shaped luggage tag—the Christian kind—on his carry-on bag, so I grabbed my things, headed for the bathroom across the hall, and locked myself in a stall. The last thing I wanted at that moment was well-intentioned counseling— spiritual or any other sort. I just needed . . . a few minutes alone.

To figure out why.

I could never get.

This one thing.

Right.

After twenty minutes of standing with my back to the stall door and my eyes closed, I still didn't have the answer—what's the likelihood of a profound personal discovery happening in an airport restroom, anyway—but I had pulled myself together. After all, Richard hadn't exactly said we were breaking up. He'd just said we needed to talk, and then he hadn't argued with what I'd said.

I went back to the waiting area by my gate and took a seat along the windows, away from the man with the Jesus tag on his luggage. He looked my way a couple times, but I just leaned my head back against the metal frame and closed my eyes, letting the cold of the Denver night seep through my body as the stewardess announced an indefinite delay.

Be not forgetful to entertain strangers;
For thereby some have entertained
angels unaware.
—Hebrews 13:2
(*Left by Ruth, who's seen the proof*)

≈ Chapter 3 ≈

Greyhound isn't so bad . . . until you've been on one for sixteen hours, driving through the plains of West Texas in blinding snow. What idiotic notion had possessed me to climb into a taxi with the Jesus-tag man—Gary from Fort Worth, dentist, two kids, married twenty-nine years—to head to the Greyhound station, I couldn't say. He'd awakened me when all flights were canceled, an extremely kind thing to do.

"Hated to just walk off and leave you here sleeping." The slow Southern cadence of his words had comingled strangely with the fact that I was on my way to Texas, creating the feeling that I'd arrived there already. "Heard you say you had to get to Texas. No more flights going out tonight, and who knows what the backlog'll look like tomorrow? By morning, they could be socked in here for days." He'd smiled, his round face friendly, welcoming, sympathetic. "Greyhound's still moving, if you want to take a chance on it.

I'm headed to the station. Tomorrow's my thirtieth anniversary, and I'm gonna be there if I have to walk in on snowshoes."

There's something irresistible about a guy who would combine snowshoes with a business suit and walk through an impending blizzard to get home for his anniversary. I grabbed my stuff, and within minutes Gary from Fort Worth and I were partners on a journey of a thousand miles—the kind that binds you together like two tourists clinging to the same tree as a tsunami washes through.

By the time we reached Fort Worth, I knew all about Gary. Fortunately, he was a talker, so I didn't have to be. He owned a chain of family dental clinics that was expanding through Texas and the Deep South. He was interested in learning about how ergonomic design might make his clinics more efficient. I gave him my card, even though, honestly, his project didn't require a fully-integrated solutions firm like ours. Any licensed architect with an office in the back of a mini-mall could handle it. He asked where I was going; I told him. He knew about Moses Lake. He'd been there for a conference at the resort just past the dam. Small world. Amazing coincidence, if you believe in coincidences.

Gary's wife and teenage daughters were there to greet him when we reached the Greyhound station in downtown Dallas. Seeming completely oblivious to the cast of strange characters that typically inhabit a downtown bus station, Gary introduced me, and all three of his best gals hugged me. Theirs was probably the warmest welcome I'd get in Texas. Things would not go so well for me in Moses Lake, I felt certain. I found myself taking in Gary's family reunion like Scrooge watching the Cratchit family Christmas through the window.

Finally, I stepped back and blinked the bus station into focus, trying to ignore the creepy sensation that it was not the safest place to be on my own. The sooner I was out of there, the better. I'd have to find my way to a cab and then a rental car place, but really, I wanted to be where Gary was, turning the details and the luggage over to take-charge family members.

I leaned close to one of his daughters. "Tell your dad thanks for the help, all right? Tell him he's got my card, if he wants to get in touch about the dental clinics."

"Sure," the girl, Kylee, looked up from texting on her cell phone, and smiled. "Have a nice vacation."

"Thanks." Juggling my stuff, I went to get a cab. In short order, I was loaded up and ready to go—until the cab rolled away from the curb, and I reached for my purse to see how I was fixed for cash, and there was no purse on the seat. I picked up my coat, my laptop bag. Nothing. Panic swirled through my tired brain, lighting up circuits that had been lazily flickering a moment before.

My purse! My purse! Where was my purse?

"Wait!" I screamed. Where? When had I seen it last? I remembered looking at my cell phone as we pulled into Dallas, wishing there would be a text from Richard. . . .

The bus! It's on the bus! While I was gathering my belongings with Gary, sharing the euphoria of having survived our trip, I'd left the efficient-but-fashionable little Dolce purse tucked between my seat and the wall.

My money, my iPhone, ID, credit cards, everything. . . .

"Take me back to the bus station," I gasped. And as soon as we'd made it to the curb out front, I threw open the cab door, abandoned my stuff, and ran down the sidewalk. One peek around the corner confirmed that the bus was gone. My identity was headed to Texarkana . . . or possibly to some shady computer lab in Russia or Nigeria by now.

My mind whirled as I ran back around the corner to the cab, begged the driver to wait with my things for a moment, then burst into the lobby and scanned the crowd for Gary and family. But they'd moved on. Outside, the cabbie was unloading my stuff on the curb, and a couple of bystanders in soiled overcoats were already checking out the spoils. I hurried out and laid

42

claim before anything else could disappear, and then headed back inside, trailing two homeless guys, one of whom told me I was a dead ringer for Julia Roberts.

Despite assurances that I wasn't Julia, he called me Julia and insisted on aiding me in finding my way to an official bus station employee, who could help me. He and his friend stood guard while the counter clerk called the bus, now en route to east Texas. My purse was nowhere to be found.

A desperate search of my pockets failed to turn up any folding money for phone calls, but who would I call anyway? All of my numbers were stored in my iPhone, which was who-knew-where at that moment. My fingers settled on something cardboard, and I knew what it was before I pulled it out. Gary's card.

Oh, thank God. The thought came with an echo of surprise. I'd long since given up attributing much in my life to divine intervention, but right now, the fact that I'd stuck the card in my pocket instead of my purse seemed like a miracle.

The clerk had pity on me and let me use her cell phone, and in short order, my new friends, Harley and Doyle, were walking me to the curb and helping to load my suitcases into Gary's wife's Lexus. Gary thanked them and gave them each five bucks to go buy some lunch. Noticing that Doyle's teeth were in bad shape, Gary dug through the door pocket of the car and produced a brochure for a mobile cost-free dental program, which Gary's clinics helped to support. Doyle stuck the brochure in his ragged coat, shook Gary's hand, offered a blessing my way, and pronounced this to be an example of the mysterious workings of the Lord.

I left the Dallas bus station, sandwiched in the backseat with Gary's daughters, Kylee and Grace, all three of us waving good-bye to Harley and Doyle. There was an odd, tender feeling in the pit of my stomach, and Doyle's broken smile lingered in my mind as we rolled out of downtown. Despite my lack of confidence in divine intervention, I couldn't help thinking that if not for a snowstorm, a bus ride, a lost purse, an impatient cabbie, and a business card haphazardly tucked in my pocket, Doyle might never have found out where to get new teeth. Occasionally, luck and coincidence doesn't explain things as well as you'd like.

After a short conversation, during which I was unable to come up with any good option as to where Gary and his family could drop me off, they made it clear that, no matter what I suggested— the mall, a hotel, a bank location where I could attempt to gain access to my accounts—they were not about to abandon me in a strange town with no money, no phone, and no ID. They would be driving me all the way to Moses Lake. Everyone was surprisingly cheerful about it, and I determined this to be the kind of thing that happened often. Perhaps it was the kindly look of Gary and his family, or the skill that dentists develop for carrying on one-way conversations with unhappy clients, but they were like the Griswolds of mercy meet-ups.

I borrowed Grace's cell phone and called Trish—one of the few numbers lodged in my memory—so she could take the emergency file from my apartment and call my credit card companies and my bank. I didn't even bother to tell her the whole story. I was too tired to repeat it, and Trish's kids were screaming in the background. "Sorry it's such a disaster so far. Just call me if you need anything else," she said, and we hung up.

As we rolled southward under a cloudless Texas sky, sharing takeout food on the way, Gary's family entertained me with stories of past family vacations buffeted off course—or *blessed,* as they put it—by strangers in need. The day outside was clear and perfect, the sky painted with the long white strokes of winter clouds. I found myself oddly taken in as the countryside slowly changed from rolling plains to hills dotted with live oaks, their green boughs stretching heavy and thick over amber tufts of last year's grass. Here and there, we passed fields where cattle grazed happily on expanses of winter wheat, the lively

45

green pastures and frolicking calves seeming to promise that the startling color bursts of a Texas spring were right around the corner.

I leaned against the window, my mind traveling back in time. I was curled up in the backseat of my father's car, gazing out as wildflowers drifted by like spatters of paint on a bright green canvas—the deep azure of bluebonnets, the bright red-orange of Indian paintbrush, the purple of wild phlox, the yellow and crimson pinwheels of Indian blankets, the pale pink and white of primrose. Beside me, my little brother was asleep. Up front, Dad was driving and Mom was popping a new cassette tape into the player.

We were headed off on one of the trips Dad lovingly called Sunday-ventures. Those trips always occurred after church, which we attended only when my father was not away on business. Generally, following the service, we would pick up my mother at home, and then there was no telling where we'd end up. Sometimes Dad was checking on a Proxica facility, or doing an inspection on a locker storage plant, or taking a look at one of Proxica's massive farms, where rural families raised turkeys, chickens, hogs, and various produce to fulfill Proxica contracts.

Many of those trips took us far into the country, where Dad spied tractors or cattle in the field and told us stories of his childhood on the family farm in Moses Lake. Along the way, Mom would talk him into stopping so she could climb rocks, hike off down a state-park trail, photograph buildings in some derelict small town, or sit in a stranger's cow pasture, writing in one of her ever-present journals. I never worried about how long she would be gone when she disappeared into the woods. I knew that my father would be there taking care of us, making a game of her flighty, unpredictable nature.

Of all the things I remembered about him, that one was foremost in my mind. He was a really great dad.

My eyes fell closed as I drifted between a dream and reality, between Gary's car and my father's. Finally, all of it faded away, and the long Greyhound bus ride caught up with me.

"We're here! Wake up, Heather!" My father's voice probed the darkness, and pulled me away. I snapped upright, smelled water and cedar and the chalky scent of wet limestone.

Outside the window, a sign was passing by. It was old, made of earthy, weathered wood suspended between rock pillars. The etched letters had been newly-tinted with gold paint, seeming incongruous against the burnt umber background.

Welcome to Moses Lake
If you're lucky enough to be at the lake,
you're lucky enough!

47

"Hear that, kids?" My father's voice echoed through the interior of the car. "We just hit it lucky. Anybody bring a swimsuit?"

He laughed, and my mind stumbled into the present. It wasn't my father's laugh, not my father in the front seat, but Gary from Fort Worth. The kindly dentist. My rescuer, without whom I'd still be at the Denver airport.

Next to me, Gary's daughters tucked away their cell phones and stretched in their seats as we rolled into the sleepy little burg of Moses Lake, Texas.

It was just the way I remembered it: a convenience store selling bait and gas at either end of the strip, and in between, a row of brick and limestone buildings with high false fronts. A few new antique stores had gone in, but everything else seemed to have been frozen in time—the Variety and Dollar, the pharmacy with the soda fountain in it, the Wash Barrel Laundry, the chamber of commerce, the little rural medical clinic that was only open a few days a week, the community center, the little brown stone church with the white steeple, a squatty brick building that belonged to the Corps of Engineers.

Not much had changed. Moses Lake was still the same, right down to the little Moses Lake Hardware store at the end of the strip, near the church. Same wooden barrels out front, filled with fishing poles, shovels, and on-clearance tackle. In the summer, blown-up beach balls, air rafts, kites, giant squirt guns, and old tractor inner tubes converted for floatable fun would be stacked there, as well. Tourism in the winter was scant, of course, the place only appealing to fishermen and bird watchers hoping to catch a glimpse of the bald eagles.

Uncle Herbert's place, Harmony Shores Funeral Home, was only a few blocks farther, just past the post office and the Ranch House Bank.

"Let me off here, okay?" I said, suddenly not ready to face my family.

Gary glanced over his shoulder. "Here? At the hardware store?"

His wife swiveled in her seat, giving me a quizzical look. "We can drive you all the way."

"It's all right. My uncle's place isn't far." Somehow, I couldn't imagine pulling in with Gary and family in tow. Harmony Shores was a stately old estate, a classic example of nineteenth century Greek Revival architecture, but strangers tended to find the idea of a combined residence and funeral home rather odd.

When Mom, Clay, and I had moved into the gardener's cottage out back following my father's death, there'd been no end to the whispers. Couple that with the dark, drab, chain-laden and somewhat vampirish style of dress I'd adopted as a protest when my father had moved us to Moses Lake, and I'd looked way too much like I might

49

be sleeping in one of the coffins myself. Kids can be merciless, and when your mother is the reason the prodigal son left town in the first place, so can adults.

Gazing at the hardware store now, I remembered passing by on my way to the pharmacy and wishing Blaine Underhill would come out to help some customer with an inner tube or a fishing pole. In my teenage imagination, Blaine would look my way, and against all social mores and at risk to his reputation, discover his undeniable attraction to the skinny girl in the dark clothes and ridiculous goth makeup job.

It was an insane fantasy with which I both entertained and tortured myself throughout my senior year of high school. It kept me tromping back to chemistry class, day after day, and it broke my heart night after night. I wanted Blaine Underhill to love me; he didn't even know who I was.

Such are the twisted dreams of teenage girls.

It didn't occur to me until I was actually on the hardware store sidewalk, hugging Gary and family good-bye, that Blaine Underhill's family might still own the hardware store. The Underhills had been in Moses Lake since long before the Corps of Engineers ousted a settlement of Mennonites from the farms in the valley, then dammed the river and created the lake.

Blaine had been a prince in this small town; his

stepmother was the queen and his dad the banker. When I could get away from home long enough, I used to stand in the convenience store, catty-corner from the hardware store, peeking out the window while I pretended to peruse the magazines. I'd watch Blaine there in his football jersey, his dark brown hair curling on his suntanned neck as he sorted through the inner tubes for kids in swimsuits, or carried bags for little old ladies, or flirted with girls in bikinis. If there'd been a pin-up poster of Blaine Underhill in *Teen Time* magazine, I would have bought it and tacked it on my wall in some secret place.

". . . that okay?"

I realized that Gary was talking to me, and I hadn't heard a thing.

"Sorry," I answered, noticing that he'd unloaded my suitcase and laptop on the sidewalk. I whirled a hand by my ear, rolling my eyes apologetically. "Had my head in the past there for a minute. This town hasn't changed at all."

"There's something comforting about a place that doesn't change." Gary couldn't have known how wrong he was about that. My sweet memories of childhood visits to Moses Lake had been permanently painted over by the blackness of that senior year in high school. I'd spent the first three months of our stay trying to punish my father for marooning us on the family farm outside town, and the other six months living in the tiny gardener's cottage behind Uncle Herbert's funeral home, mired in the grief and guilt that followed my father's death.

Standing in the middle of town now, I sensed that those emotions could be as potent as ever if I let them, so I concentrated on expressing gratitude to the Good Samaritans who'd spent their anniversary saving me from disaster. "I really don't even know how to thank you. If there's ever anything I can do to pay you back—advice on the clinic designs, anything, really—please let me know. When I get back to Seattle, I'll send money for the gas."

Smiling pleasantly, Gary lifted a hand. "No money needed. It's a blessing to be a blessing. That's what my mother always said. Just pass it on to someone else when you get the chance. Can we pray for you before we go?"

Gary's wife smiled expectantly, and his daughters extended their hands, ready to form a prayer circle on my behalf.

I felt the momentary culture shock of having been asked that question, of being back below the Mason-Dixon line, where such an inquiry was considered perfectly natural. Nine years in the city —and not that I hadn't met plenty of passionate churchgoers—but I'd couldn't recall anyone coming right out and asking me that. Typically, I didn't run in those sorts of circles.

"Sure." I could hardly say no after all they had

done for me. Slipping in somewhat awkwardly between Gary's daughters, I closed my eyes and bowed my head, and for some reason, thought of Trish. She was actually quite spiritual herself, in the broader sense of the word. She thought it was ridiculous when I told her that I'd grown up in church with my father and didn't have issues with it, but I just didn't want to go anymore. *That's like saying you believe fatty foods cause heart attacks and then eating fried chicken all day,* she pointed out. *I mean, if what you do and what you believe are two different things, it's a guilt trap, right?*

Trish would have loved the sight of me standing on the sidewalk, hand in hand with the dentist's family as they prayed for my journey.

When the prayers ended, I did feel better, in a strange way—as if perhaps some special blessing had been called down and might ease my return to Moses Lake. Nearby, the white wooden steeple of Lakeshore Community Church glistened in the late-afternoon sunlight, as if in punctuation.

Gary's wife looked up at it and said, "It's a gorgeous day. Let's take a drive around the lake before we head back home. We can do the anniversary dinner tomorrow night."

Gary agreed, and even the girls looked toward the lake, placid in its deep blue winter coat.

"What a pretty little town," Gary's wife remarked, and I was startled by the chasm between their perspectives and mine. To me, this place would never again be beautiful.

Even so, I took a moment to describe some of the sights they might see on their drive—the cliffs above Eagle Eye bridge; the historic marker that told the legend of the Wailing Woman, whose voice could be heard moaning through the cliffs; the spire-like rock formations north of the dam, where tourists pulled off at the scenic turnout to watch bald eagles nesting. I finished by telling them about Catfish Charley's, my great-uncle's floating fried food Mecca, where they could eat batter-crisp fish while being watched by Charley, the hundred-pound primordial catfish who'd been greeting diners from his tank for as long as I could remember.

"I think they're only open on weekends in the winter, come to think of it, but if you want some dinner before you head back, the food is good at the Waterbird, over by the dam," I added, and then I realized that the Waterbird might not even be there anymore. It's funny how the mind believes that the places of your childhood will always be waiting for you to come back to them. "I mean, I guess it's still around. Anyway, the view of the lake is beautiful there, and it's sort of a tradition—people go in and sign the back wall of the store, sometimes leave a favorite quote. The legend is that if you sign the wall of wisdom with someone, you'll return to Moses Lake together again."

A lump rose in my throat. My father and I had signed the wall together when I was a girl. Every time we visited after that, we went by the Waterbird to look at our handiwork, touching the quote like a talisman. When we moved to Moses Lake that final year, I'd refused to visit the wall with Dad. I'd broken the chain. . . .

As I told Gary's family good-bye and watched them drive off, the blessing they'd pronounced over me seemed to fly away with them, rolling down the main street of Moses Lake, growing smaller, and smaller, until it drifted out of sight, and I was once again all alone, with no ID, no phone, and no money, in the last place I ever thought I'd find myself.

The man who troubles the water
might soon enough drown in it.
—Fisherman's proverb
(*via Catfish Charley,*
feeding lakesiders since 1946)

≈ Chapter 4 ≈

I'd barely been in Moses Lake ten minutes, and I could already feel the place winding around me, quietly and efficiently, a spider twisting silken threads about an errant moth before it can break loose and fly away.

The bells on the hardware store door jingled, and my mind tripped over itself. "May I help ye-ew?" The question traversed the parking lot in a long, sticky-sweet Southern drawl, and for an instant, I was like an astronaut being pulled into a black hole, lost in time and space. I turned to find Blaine Underhill's stepmother, a ghost from yesteryear, standing in the hardware store doorway, wearing a peach-colored pantsuit, her puffy hair still the same brassy shade of blond, pulled back in a pearl-toned headband. "Do you need directions to someplace, hon?"

The word *hon* took me by surprise. Even though some of the Moses Lake ladies had attempted to adopt me as a somewhat lost cause after my father's death, I was never *hon* to Mrs. Underhill. She couldn't quite forgive me for being the product of the unwelcome union of my father and the freewheeling out-of-towner who stole him away.

Clearly, she didn't recognize me now. I hadn't considered the possibility that, while the people of Moses Lake still loomed large in my mind, they might not even remember me. It was strangely pathetic to think that I'd been reacting all these years to people for whom I was just a temporary blip on the radar.

"No, I'm fine," I answered, and then started walking, conscious of Mrs. Underhill staring after me, no doubt wondering why I was dragging luggage along the side of the highway. She was probably thinking, *What an odd little thing. . . .*

I headed out of town, past Lakeshore Community Church, its brown stone walls warming in the winter sunlight beneath a patina of dust and moss. The doors to the squatty low-ceilinged fellowship hall were open, a half-dozen cars parked out front. An elderly woman in a red coat was trying to wrestle a wheelchair from the trunk of her car. After glancing back and forth between her and the door a couple times, wishing someone would come out and help her before she hurt herself, I parked my suitcase near the road and jogged across the gravel parking lot. The suede boots that had set me back a week's salary squished in a layer of creamy, limestone-colored goo as I skirted puddles left behind by a winter rain.

"Here, let me help you," I said, and unfortunately startled her off-balance. She caught herself against the car, with a bug-eyed look. Such was usually the way with my awkward attempts at random acts of kindness. I wasn't meant to be folksy and friendly, but I had promised Gary that I would pay it forward. If not for an act of kindness, I'd still be standing at the bus station, or worse yet, sleeping in an airport chair in Denver.

"Oh!" the woman gasped, catching her breath and squinting at me through glasses thick enough to make me wonder if she'd driven herself here. Something about her was familiar, but I couldn't decide what. "Oh, well, all right. Aren't you sweet?" She pulled and stretched the words, adding extra syllables on *ri-ight* and *swe-eet*. Scanning the parking lot, she tried to figure out where I'd come from.

She motioned to the sidewalk in front of the fellowship hall. "Just set it up there, hon. It's my cousin's. I was tryin' to make room back here for the casseroles."

Casseroles. Why did it not surprise me that the casserole ladies were on the move again today?

A blue piece of cardboard tangled in the spokes of the wheelchair as I pulled it out, and I rested the chair against the trunk rim for a moment, wiggling the paper loose and dropping it into the trunk. It flipped over and slid partway under a folded navy-and-gold Moses Lake High stadium blanket. I found myself cocking my head to read, from the bottom up, the bold, white letters on the royal blue sign. *Precinct 4. County Commission. Underhill. Blaine. Vote for.*

Huh . . . Looked like Blaine Underhill hadn't strayed far from the hometown. "You shouldn't be lifting this thing on your own," I said, noticing that there was a rather large stack of Blaine Underhill signs wedged against the side of the trunk.

The woman noticed that I was staring. "That's my grandson." Reaching into her oversized purse, she whipped out a flyer printed on red paper. "Are you a resident of the county?" A brow lifted with a hopeful look, and I gathered that my vote was about to be solicited.

"Just visiting." Now I knew why she looked familiar. This was the infamous Mama B. When I used to walk by the football stadium on my way home from school, she was always perched on the bleachers next to Blaine Underhill's father, the two of them watching practice, making sure their golden boy was getting the kind of treatment he deserved. If she wasn't telling the coaches what to do, Mama B was checking up on the teachers, shuffling through the school halls with a pug-nosed pocket pooch in her handbag, pointing out girls whose hemlines were too short and boys who had hair over their collars.

More than once, she'd cornered me and let me know that my oversized black T-shirts were "unbecoming on a young lady," and that if I'd drop by the variety store, she'd be happy to help me look for something more appropriate. Perhaps in a nice shade of blue or mauve. She felt sure there was a cute figure underneath my misguided wardrobe, and she wondered if I'd ever thought about entering the Miss Moses Lake contest.

Thank goodness she didn't recognize me now. I didn't bother to introduce myself as I carried the wheelchair to the sidewalk and set it against the front of the church.

"Thank ya, sweetie." She held out the Vote for Blaine flyer. "Here. Pass this along to someone while you're here. Tell them Blaine Underhill's their man. It's about time we cleaned up that county commission."

I felt obliged to take the pamphlet, and then I quickly backed away, folding it and stuffing it into my jacket pocket.

I could feel Mama B's curious stare following me across the parking lot. "Where'd you say you were stayin'?" she called. A propane delivery truck passed by in a *whoosh,* and I pretended not to hear. Swirls of asphalt-scented air skittered across the parking lot in the truck's wake, and I made a hasty exit, my suitcase bumping along behind me. Mama B hollered at the propane driver, informing him that the speed limit through town was thirty-five.

Dry winter grass crackled under my feet as I left the pavement and moved into the ditch alongside the rural highway, traversing the short distance to the tall limestone pillars and rusting iron gate that marked the entrance to Uncle Herbert's drive-way. The sign hanging in the shade of lofty magnolias still read *Harmony Shores Funeral Home and Chapel*, even though the place had been closed since Uncle Herbert's health problems had forced him to shut down the business. It was a beautiful old place, if you didn't find sleeping in the bedrooms above the funeral chapel strangely morbid. Unfortunately, I did, and the usual chill accompanied me through the gate and followed me up the long, tree-lined drive. A shudder gripped me like a fist, squeezing the air from my lungs. A voice in my head was urging, *Run, just run.*

Pulling in a fortifying breath, I veered off across the grass toward the memory gardens, my suitcase bumping over twigs and pecan shucks. Dampness from the soil seeped through my suede boots, making them soggy and chilly by the time I reached a stone path, where holly bushes and magnolias provided secluded alcoves in which grieving families could reflect privately.

Pausing, I gazed at the treetops and did a poor

imitation of the yoga breathing I'd learned from a fitness-guru-slash-boyfriend who'd tried to convince me that meditation would help my tension problems. At the time I'd laughed flippantly and told him I couldn't imagine what he was talking about. Me, tense?

Now I wished I'd paid more attention. The muscles in my back were as twisted and knotted as a string of used rubber bands in the corner of a junk drawer. I jerked at the sound of cars coming up the drive, and a charley horse kicked up its heels near my spine.

That odd temptation to bolt for the woods stirred me again. Instead, I did the mature thing and ducked behind the holly bushes, peeking through the limbs as three cars rolled past. I recognized the one in the lead, and I knew whose little gray head that was peering over the steering wheel. Mama B. That would be the church ladies behind her. Apparently, they had arrived on another reconnaissance mission, with food in hand, of course. The fact that the casserole ladies were so interested in what was going on at Harmony Shores was not a good sign.

The third car pulled in, and I peered through the leaves, undercover-agent style. The silver Cadillac rolled to a stop behind the first two vehicles, and doors opened on both sides. The puffy blond hair and peach pantsuit were unmistakable. The venerable Mrs. Underhill, whose stepson I was supposed to help elect to the county commission. She came bearing a foil-wrapped plate, and she had someone with her.

The holly bushes combed my hair as I leaned closer. Who was that with her? Someone young, svelte, and blond in a perky above-the-knee skirt and high heels. Blaine Underhill had a couple of half-sisters, as I recalled, but they didn't look like that. The Underhill girls had the misfortune of having the same figure as their father. They were stocky, muscular, and athletic. When we graduated from high school, they were entering middle school, and Mrs. Underhill was still cramming them into ruffled gowns and making them stroll the catwalk at beauty pageants, and attend cotillion classes. The kids at school used to tease Blaine about it, and ask him if his stepmother expected him to make a bid for Cotton Queen one of these days, too.

The girl with Mrs. Underhill today was definitely not one of Blaine's half-sisters.

She trotted up the steps, the dress swaying back and forth across her knees. My brother, of all people, answered the door, his dishwater blond hair sporting a bad case of bed head. I noted, in the split second before the newest visitors reached the porch, that Clay didn't seem to have changed much. Same rumpled look—khaki shorts, washed-out T-shirt, flip-flops. Mom's soft, slightly curly hair and hazel eyes, a green tone where mine were brown. His face had matured a little in the . . . how long had it been since I'd seen him, other than on his Facebook posts from the far parts of the universe?

Three-and-a-half years. He'd called on the Fourth of July. Just called me out of the blue. He was a hundred miles from Seattle on a bicycle tour—not the organized kind with other people, but a solitary, unplanned journey of his own making. He'd been rained on for three days, was running a fever, and wanted to know if I'd like to come get him. He wasn't complaining about the conditions, really. It was more like he was offering me the opportunity, and he was fine, either way. Maybe the choice between biking in the rain with a fever and visiting with me was pretty much a toss-up. He probably knew I'd ask why he was out of college for the summer and not working anywhere.

The girl in the cute dress tackled Clay with an exuberant hug. I watched in fascination, my mouth dropping open. What in the world was going on? Who was the girl, and why was my brother . . . slipping an arm around her waist and lifting her off her feet?

The casserole ladies twittered, giggled, and seemed delighted—*even* Mrs. Underhill. They politely pretended to be commenting on the condition of the memory gardens, as Clay gave the girl a peck and then set her down again.

Suddenly the ladies were looking in my direction, pointing, and I was cognizant of the idiotic position I'd put myself in, hiding in the bushes, spying on the funeral home. Another thought followed—something petty, and immature, and born of sibling rivalry. It wasn't fair that I was hiding in the bushes while Clay was getting hugs and cookie plates. Moses Lake had always loved Clay. The year we lived here, he was a cute, gap-toothed fourth grader—goofy, precocious, innocent, a little charmer who was easy to like. After my father's death, Clay had slipped neatly under the sheltering wings of not only his school teacher, but his Sunday school teachers and a half-dozen adopted grannies around town, including Mama B. They loved him then, and apparently still loved him now.

"There's someone over there," one of the ladies observed. "In the bushes . . . Look!"

"Where?" That was Mrs. Underhill's voice, the sound shrill, all traces of sugar-and-honey sweetness gone. That was the voice I remembered—the one that sent chills through me, back when there were secrets to hide. Mrs. Underhill loved nothing better than to ferret out people's secrets and spread them around. In particular, she wanted to find out what was *really* going on in the little cottage behind the funeral home. She was certain that, in some way or another, the authorities needed to be involved. She would've liked nothing better than for child welfare services to swoop in and take us away from my mother. It would have proven her right about everything and proven that my father should have married *her* years ago, instead of my mother.

"Yeah . . . you know . . . you're right, I think," Clay concurred, and then added, "Hey, Roger, come'ere. Come'ere, boy. What's out there, huh? You see somebody out there?" Of all things, Clay still had the goofball mutt-slash-golden retriever that was riding with him on the ill-fated bike trip. Roger traveled in a pull-behind bike trailer, the kind made for babies. He'd been an inconveniently manic houseguest in my no-dogs-allowed apartment building for a week, while Clay recovered from pneumonia. I'd come within a whisker, literally, of getting kicked out of the complex, and my Persian rug has never been the same since.

"It's just me. It's just me." Squeezing from the bushes with one hand in the air, I surrendered without a fight. "Everybody calm down." My suitcase wobbled over clumps of grass and loose twigs, threatening to tip over as I started toward the driveway. The casserole ladies squinted, and Mrs. Underhill took a couple of steps my way. Detaching himself from the blonde, Clay trotted down the stairs as his dog sprinted across the lawn, heading in my direction.

"Roger, hey! Roger, wait!" Clay called, and of

66

course Roger didn't listen. He tackled me with the momentum of a linebacker, and we did a clumsy backward waltz as I tried to avoid falling over the suitcase. Roger swiped his long, lolling tongue across my mouth before I could get my balance and push him away. By the time I did, Clay had caught up.

"Heather's here," Clay announced, in case anyone was still confused. One hand caught the dog, and one gave me a shoulder-hug, but I got the distinct impression that my brother wasn't thrilled to see me. "Hey, Sis," he said.

The casserole ladies regarded us with curious, somewhat uncertain expressions, as we walked to the porch. A few uncomfortable greetings passed back and forth, and I was actually relieved when Mrs. Hall shoved a casserole into my hands. It was still warm on the bottom, which felt good. I remembered Mrs. Hall from the pharmacy where, after Dad's death, I'd picked up the prescriptions that were supposed to *fix* my mother, but didn't. Mrs. Hall was always nice about it. In truth, she probably wasn't supposed to be handing that stuff off to a minor, but she let me take it, always with the kind admonition that they'd be happy to deliver next time.

I set the casserole on one of the porch tables and wiped my mouth, still contemplating the gross-out factor of having been kissed by Clay's dog.

Mrs. Underhill gave me a suspicious look, then

stated the obvious, "Well, Heather, my goodness, you're a wreck. Was that you outside the hardware store earlier? You didn't walk here all the way from Seattle, surely?" She batted a hand, peppering the artificially sweetened question with a sharp-edged giggle.

I did. You know, I'm on a new exercise kick, and I thought walking from Seattle would be a great way to start, was on the tip of my tongue. Heaven help me, but Mrs. Underhill obviously still held the strings to the broken, bitter, smart-mouthed teenager I thought I'd buried years ago. Even that was disconcerting—as if she had control of me, rather than me having control of myself. "It's a long story," I replied, instead. "Weather problems." Let her ponder that and draw her own conclusions as to how that equated to appearing in town on foot.

She was right about one thing, though. I was a wreck. No wonder the girl who'd just put the smooch on my brother was eyeing me uncertainly. She butted Clay in the shoulder, as in, *Introduce me, already. Who's this Heather person?* Apparently she didn't know anything about me. Strange, considering how familiar they'd looked a few minutes ago.

Another vehicle rattled up just as Clay was about to begin the introductions. The hearse was a dead giveaway, even from the end of the drive. As it passed through the tunnel of live oaks, I recognized three people in the front seat—two tall, one short. Two gray heads, one sandy brown with the hair loosely pulled back, fly-away strands swirling around her face.

My mother, Uncle Herbert, and Uncle Charley. Clay waved enthusiastically, in a way that said, *Hail, hail, the gang's all here!*

The hearse had barely skidded to a stop before my great uncles were grunting and creaking their way out of the car, then heading for the porch in stiff-legged shuffles. Mother, sliding over from the middle, was one step behind them.

"Well, praise the Lord and phone the saints. There she is!" Uncle Charley made a beeline toward me, outdistancing Uncle Herbert, who had to hold on to the handrail to make his way up the eight steps to the porch.

Uncle Charley pushed past the casserole ladies and swept me into a meaty hug. "We just been to the sheriff's department, finding out how to report you for a missing person."

The ladies gasped.

"Huh . . . wha . . . oof!" I stammered and grunted as Uncle Herbert moved in from behind and I was momentarily the filling in an uncle sandwich. The scents of Borax, axle grease, and musty leather flicked at my senses, pulling threads. Memories were tied to those smells—childhood visits to the old family farm with my father, where Uncle Charley gave me pony rides. The dark

69

days after my father's death. My high school graduation, when all I cared about was getting away from here. I didn't want the memories that were tethered to these two old men. I wanted to leave this place and everything attached to it.

Now I felt it all pulling at me again, leaving me confused and lost.

"Heather, where in the world have you been?" My mother's admonition came from somewhere outside the circle of scents and memories. "We had a call from a man in Dallas who discovered your purse in the trash that was cleaned off of a bus, but you were nowhere to be found. We were scared to death. He said he'd FedEx the purse, by the way."

The casserole ladies gasped and twittered and asked questions as I rushed to share the odd saga of my trip to Texas and the lost purse. No telling how big that story would get by the time it circled town a few times.

Uncle Charley brushed a sandy-sounding something off my jacket. "Looks like Roger got the besta you. Clay, you gotta teach that dog not to mug the comp'ny. He almost knocked Reverend Hay in the drink when we were takin' the lights off the restaurant after Christmas, and the UPS man is afraid to even come by here. He's been catching us at the Waterbird when we go for coffee in the mornin'."

Uncle Charley took my shoulders and held me

away from him. "Let me get a look at ya." He pulled me into a patch of sunlight and announced to the crowd, "My cow, look at our little Heather! She growed up to be a pretty thang!"

I was too confused to be embarrassed. Clay and his dog had been in town long enough to frighten off the UPS man and help take down Christmas lights? What in the world?

Mrs. Underhill wasn't the least bit interested in admiring my growth or my natural beauty. She regarded me with the fisheye, as if some frightening life-form had invaded the casserole circle. "My word, you got on the bus with a . . . a *man* you met on the *plane?* It's a wonder he wasn't after more than your purse."

I blurted out the first thing that came to mind. "He was a *dentist.*" As if that explained every-thing. "Anyway, I was never in any danger. I just forgot my purse."

"What sort of purse?" one of the ladies asked. "Nothing expensive, I hope?"

"Land sakes, what's that matter?" Mama B snapped, then turned and hobbled toward the car. "Let's leave these folks to their reunitin'. We got more deliveries to make."

Even the members of the Moses Lake human telegraph knew better than to refuse a direct order from Mama B. Reluctantly, they backed away, having ferreted out enough details to successfully add their own and come up with an account of my arrival in town. In closing, they offered a few sympathetic, but pointed, comments about the burden of my two widowed uncles being forced to provide for *all this company*. Then they handed over more food before following Mama B. Clay's apparent girlfriend kissed him on the cheek and whispered, "We gotta drop off a meal for a funeral." Adding a meaningful look, she told Clay she'd see him later.

An uncomfortable silence descended on us as the crowd departed. I was conscious of everyone surreptitiously watching me and maintaining their positions, in the way members of the bomb squad might gather around a suspicious package.

My mother broke the stalemate by peeking under the foil on the CorningWare pan. "Still hot," she said, her tone overly light and falsely cheerful. "Let's go around back and eat on the sun porch. Clay, maybe you can give Heather a ride over to Catfish Cabins after that."

"The cabins?" I glanced at the house. Despite the presence of the funeral office, parlors, and workrooms, as well as the chapel in what had once been a grand ballroom, Harmony House was still quite large, the entire second floor and both ends of the main floor remaining in use as personal residence space. There was also the small gardener's cottage out back, which meant there was plenty of space for me to stay here. So why was Mom trying to ship me off to the rental cabins, halfway around the lake by Uncle Charley's restaurant? With no car to drive, I'd be stranded there.

Maybe that was their plan. Maybe I was being given the bum's rush—while they were happy not to have to report me as a missing person, they didn't want me around, either. "I thought I'd stay here."

"Oh . . . Well, it's sort of . . . crowded. . . ." Mom hedged as furtive glances darted between the relatives. "Uncle Charley has been living here for a while now, since Uncle Herb shouldn't be alone. It's somewhat crowded with Clay and me in the house, too, and now the mess of getting ready for the estate sale. The place really is a disas—"

"I can bunk out back in the gardener's cottage." I didn't wait for her to finish. I wasn't about to let them warehouse me off-site while they continued with whatever they were doing. I'd never seen a group of people looking so culpable. I was going to be on them *like fleas on a back-porch hound,* as Uncle Herb's Mennonite housekeeper, Ruth, used to say.

Glancing at the house momentarily, I wondered what had happened to Ruth. During those terrible months of my senior year, she was the one who'd saved me. She hadn't tried to convince me to snap out of it, or stop skulking around in black T-shirts and too much makeup, or keep a stiff upper lip, like Uncle Herb and Aunt Esther had.

Nor had she echoed the geriatric pastor of Lakeshore Community Church, telling me how much God still loved me. Ruth just baked cookies, washed laundry, and occasionally laid a comforting hand on my shoulder as she passed by in her old-fashioned-looking dresses and sweaters, and a hair covering, as was typical of many of the Mennonite residents upriver in Gnadenfeld.

Uncle Herb rubbed the back of his neck, glancing toward the backyard and then toward my mother, his brows lifting in a way that seemed to say, *Uh-oh . . . Now what do we do?*

"Well . . . but . . . Blaine Underhill has things stored out there," Mother shrugged, dismissing my suggestion. "Signs and whatnot. He's running for county commissioner."

There was that name again. *Blaine Underhill.* Why was my family suddenly so tight with the Underhills? I'd never before in my life seen my mother speak the Underhill name without sneering.

"I don't mind," I pressed, calling their bluff, but there was also a painful little pinprick inside me. Nobody was happy to have me here. "All I need is a bed and enough space to put my suitcase, and maybe a plate of casserole. Why is the benevolence committee bringing food by here, anyway?"

Mom shrugged, her lip curling slightly, flashing an eyetooth. "Oh, you know those women.

74

They're always looking for an excuse to take a casserole somewhere and stick their noses in."

"Stick their nose into what?" The attention of the church ladies was never completely for naught. They believed in Christian charity, with a purpose.

Mom flipped a hand through the air. "Who knows? Heather, don't you think you'd be more comfortable at the Catfish Cabins? The gardener's cottage is a mess."

The sting of rejection put me back in my high-school shoes, when no one other than Ruth seemed to want me around. *I will not let them get to me. I will not.* "No. I'll be fine here. I don't plan to stay long. As soon as we get the hitch in this real estate deal taken care of, I'm gone." *And never coming back. Ever. You won't see me darkening your doorstep anymore.* "In fact, since we're all here, why don't we go on inside and hash it out? What's this malarkey about a competing offer on the properties? When did this come up and who made the offer?" *As if there really is one.*

Mother rolled her eyes. "Really, Heather. You've barely arrived, and all you can talk about is business? Let's have something to eat on the sun porch. The man who found your purse said he'd try to get it to FedEx today. You're stuck here until it arrives, anyway. You can't fly without identification. I think you're safe taking a little time for family niceties."

Irritation crawled over me on sharp little legs, digging in claws. A snappy retort was on the tip of my tongue, *Who are you to lecture me about family anything?* Squeezing my lips tightly over my teeth, I fought to keep the venom at bay.

Uncle Charley, looking embarrassed, nudged Uncle Herbert and started toward the front walk. "Well, I'm starved. Let's head around the back way. No sense traipsing through the house."

I was conscious of more covert glances and a collective holding of breath, but I'd also caught the scent of casserole, and I was hungry, weary, and lost. Every muscle in my body seemed to be liquefying. The afternoon had started to cool, and I just wanted to sit down someplace warm, so I followed the uncs and the casseroles off the porch. Clay grabbed my suitcase and walked along behind me as Uncle Charley talked over his shoulder, pointing out the growth in various trees, a new rose bush on the corner, an old lamppost that had been removed after it became too unstable, and other things he thought might have changed since I'd last seen the place.

By the time we reached the sun porch, it was all just a buzz. I couldn't concentrate on the words. The cold had pressed through my jacket, and my suede dress boots were wet all the way to my socks. On the sun porch, at the urging of Uncle Herb, I took a seat on the faded floral fainting couch that was nearest the old wall-hung propane

76

heater. Mom and Clay headed to the kitchen to get some plates and glasses, and to make a pitcher of iced tea.

"You look plumb wore out," Uncle Charley observed as he turned up the heater. "I'm gonna go put on a pot of good hot coffee."

Despite my insistence that he didn't need to make coffee on my account, he speedily quit the room and was followed by Uncle Herb. I heard the whisper of voices in the kitchen. The last thing I remembered was letting my head fall against the sofa pillows, then catching Blaine Underhill's name again and thinking that I should tiptoe in there and see what they were whispering about.

A life all turbulence and noise may seem
To him that leads it wise and to be praised;
But wisdom is a pearl with most success
Sought in still water . . .
—William Cowper
*(Left by Ben Murray,
retired—no longer in a hurry.)*

≈ Chapter 5 ≈

Family arguments should not be postponed until first thing in the morning, particularly on a gorgeous February day, when the winter sun slips over the water in a hush, biding its time before filtering through the canopy of live oaks into the rocky nooks and misty valley floors. *No rush today,* a morning like that says. *It's the off season, remember?*

I woke to the sound of ducks landing on the water and a cardinal chirping in the winter-bare climbing rose outside the window. My heart was pounding and I couldn't catch my breath. I'd just had the dream about the door. I'd gone farther than usual, this time. The knob had started to turn in my hand, but then the spider dropped from its web in the doorframe and landed on my fingers. I screamed, jerked back, awakened bolt upright in the bed. . . .

Now I sat clinging to my knees, my mind slowly settling into the fact that I was in the gardener's cottage behind Uncle Herbert's place. Frigid morning air chilled the heat from the dream as I gazed out the window at the cardinal, a bewitching splash of red, like a drop of blood among thorns. Beautiful, yet out of place . . . Somewhat noisy and demanding, as if determined to steal my attention.

The perspiration on my skin quickly turned to ice, and I grabbed the coat I'd thrown over my feet last night after piling the bed with dusty quilts. The collar of the coat was cold against my neck, and even the insides of the pockets were stiff and chilly. Something crisp bumped against my fingers, and I pulled it out, then vaguely remembered Mama B handing me the flyer from her suitcase-sized purse.

I unfolded it now, blinking the sleep from my eyes in morbid fascination, trying to bring the first few lines into focus.

Elect Blaine Underhill
County Commissioner
Precinct 4.

The man was everywhere.

Below the name was a list of bullet points, espousing Blaine Underhill's worthiness for the job of county commissioner.

Lifelong county resident
Experienced leader

Proven businessman—not a politician

Avid fisherman and outdoor enthusiast (now there was an important qualification for office)

Sixth-generation Texan (I sort of admired that one. Being estranged from my mother's family and perpetually conflicted during visits to my dad's hometown because of the in-law wars, I felt an absence of the ties that bind. Occasionally, it bothered me.)

A unifier, who would strive to work across party lines (These days, you had to wonder if anyone could make that claim. Maybe the county surrounding Moses Lake was an island unto itself, where people with differing opinions actually found ways to discuss things like rational, civil adults. Despite the fact that he had ignored me in chemistry class, I liked Blaine Underhill better already.)

A man called to serve, with the county's best interests at heart (Well, he was cute in high school, but I remembered him as kind of a goof-off who got by largely on football talent and an A-list family name.)

A half-dozen endorsements followed. Everyone from the county farm co-op to the local labor union, mostly comprised of employees of the Proxica plant and Proxica poultry farms in and around Gnadenfeld, were squarely in favor of Blaine Underhill's candidacy. Why wouldn't they be? He was an Underhill, and besides, if they didn't support him, his stepmother would borrow a broom from the barrel out front of the hardware store, fly over their houses, and zap them with one of her evil hexes.

It was hard to imagine the goofy, somewhat intractable boy—who'd once kidnapped a neighboring school's mascot costume—now being qualified to make decisions that affected the entire county. A guy who would show up at a pep rally wearing a contraband buffalo costume along with a pink tutu and ballet shoes couldn't really change that much, could he?

I turned the paper over, compelled to read whatever was on the back side, which, as it turned out, was actually the front. There were live-and-in-person photos of Blaine Underhill—one of him coaching a pee-wee baseball team, one of him visiting with a young family in front of their home, one of him holding a rather large fish, and one smiling for the camera.

My first thought was, *Whoa* . . .

The ring of metal striking metal outside tugged my attention away. The noise traveled at light speed through the synapses of my brain, quickly pulling data from dust-covered files. It sounded like someone was moving Uncle Charley's rental canoes, which in the off-season were stored in an old cotton barn at Harmony Shores.

Why would anyone be down by the lake with the canoes on a frosty February morning?

Sliding from the bed, I pressed my face to the glass while shivering and shifting between freezing sock-feet. The corner of the cottage and a bare crape myrtle blocked all but a glimpse of the weathered board-and-batten barn that had seen its heyday when the valley was a fertile river basin.

Uncle Herbert's wife, Aunt Esther, occasionally talked about the days when Harmony House was the toast of Central Texas. Aunt Esther herself had been Cotton Queen of 1942, and she didn't let anyone forget it. Harmony House had been her inheritance, and she never really appreciated the fact that Uncle Herbert had moved his funeral business there in order to help support the expenses of the massive house. Aunt Esther liked to pretend she'd allowed the funeral business into Harmony House as a service to the community, not because her family had spent all the money allotted to them when the Corps of Engineers took their farmland through eminent domain and built the lake.

My teeth started chattering, the cold forcing me away from the air seepage around the wooden windowpanes. I'd forgotten how chilly the place could get at night, even with the heater running on the window air unit. I should have started a fire in the wood stove before going to sleep.

Stiff-limbed and chattering, I did the Frankenstein run to the bathroom and considered the tiny turn-of-the-century propane heater on the wall. A faded box of Diamond Strike-Anywhere matches sat atop, and surprisingly, I could recall exactly how to light the heater. Leaning close, I blew the dust off, then entertained the fleeting question, *How long since this thing's been lit?* A vision of myself and the cottage going up in a small mushroom cloud convinced me to forgo the heater. Instead, I hopped and shivered my way through pulling on some sweats, my coat again, and the cute little suede boots that were somewhat bedraggled and still damp after yesterday's adventure.

The metallic noises stopped as I headed out the door and rounded the cottage, gaining a view of the other side of the barn, where the canoes were stacked under the shed roof on the end nearest the lakeshore. I could just see their brightly-painted tips sticking out—yellow, green, blue, red. Maybe someone was looking them over, deciding how much to pay for the lot at the estate sale.

A nippy February breeze wafted off the lake—not frigid but just cold enough to make the idea of hanging out by the water seem less than pleasant. Even so, I wandered closer, tempted to take a walk along the shore to clear my head before going up to the house. On this morning's agenda was the family meeting that had been derailed last night after I fell asleep in the chair on the sun porch. Conveniently, no one had awakened me until it was time for bed, and the lights in the main house were already off. Mom had given me some coffee and muffins in a ziplock bag, and said that Clay had readied the cottage for me while I was dozing on the sun porch. I'd headed down the hill, too tired and foggy-brained to protest.

This morning, I had to get down to business and dispel this craziness about a competing offer on the property. Someone was trying to throw a monkey wrench into the plans here, and I had to find out who and why. Surely Uncle Herb's son didn't know about this. If my iPhone wasn't somewhere in a FedEx box, I would have called him already. If Donny was aware of this situation, he'd be having a fit.

Wouldn't he?

I knew there had been some hard feelings between Uncle Herbert and his kids in the past, but now that plans for the move had been made, things seemed to be reasonably civil. Donny obviously cared for his father's well-being, and Uncle Charley's, as well.

Water splashed behind the barn, and I moved a few more steps, catching a glimpse of Roger-the-dog frolicking along the water's edge, his tongue lolling and ears flopping as he ran. Someone was on the water in a kayak. . . .

Clay? He was paddling out from the shore with long, even strokes, his orange parka and the royal blue kayak making for a pretty picture. His paddle touched the surface of the lake in perfect rhythm, *left, right, left, right,* bending and shaping the water into swirls pink-tinged with morning light, drawing the froth upward with each stroke, suspending it in air temporarily before it ran down in glistening streams.

For a moment, I could only watch in awe, breathing in the serenity of the single kayak slicing soundlessly through the waters of Moses Lake. Clay looked perfectly at home there, perfectly at peace, despite the chill of the morning and the solitude on the lake. Looking at him I thought, *That's my baby brother, all grown up.* I remembered teaching him to swim during those months we lived at the lake. He was almost ten, and all he could do was dog paddle. Some little girl in his class was planning a swim party for her birthday, and a couple boys had made fun of Clay because, being Clay, he had come right out and admitted that he didn't know how to swim underwater.

I'd found him on the playground after school, crying his eyes out because the kids made fun of him. I wanted to find the little snots and beat them up, but Clay already had enough to deal with. He was small for his age, sort of a gump, way too honest, his dad was dead, his mom wouldn't get out of bed, his sister was the town weirdo, and he couldn't sign up for baseball or soccer because we couldn't afford it. My father's life insurance company was too busy investigating the death to care whether we could put food on the table while we waited for them to pay off. The last thing Clay needed was snotty little rednecks picking on him.

Instead of finding the boys and doing them bodily harm, I took Clay to the water and taught him to hold his breath and go under. It was late April, and the lake was still cold, but we did it anyway. By the time we were done, we were laughing and shivering. The next weekend, I walked Clay to that little girl's birthday party and ended up having to stand at the corner of the patio like a dork, because once we got to the house, all the parents were there and Clay was embarrassed to go in by himself.

Now I watched him alone on Harmony Cove, and I couldn't believe he was ever the clueless, wimpy little boy who was afraid of the water, the dark, snakes, and (oddly enough) big dogs.

What was that little girl's name? Clay had such a crush on her. He'd cried when, at the end of the summer, Mom decided to get out of bed—she had to, since I was leaving home for college—and announced that she was going back to college herself. She'd contacted a friend, a grad student at Berkeley, and she and Clay were moving there to share an apartment with the friend. Fortunately, my father's insurance policy had paid off shortly after that, and Mom had a way to finance her portion of the apartment and her higher education.

A flash of movement caught the corner of my

eye, shattering my reverie. I'd been spotted by Roger, and he was headed my way in a dead run, droplets of water spewing from his coat, catching the light, and giving him a wet, glistening halo.

"Roger! Roger, no!" I scolded, trying to abort another mugging. "Stop! Heel! Stay back!" I hurried to a nearby fig bush, putting it between myself and the galloping water sprinkler. I'd only brought two outfits and a pair of sweats in my carryon. This was one of my few clothing options.

Unfortunately, Roger was not the least bit intimidated by fig trees. He went right through the narrow V in the middle and landed on me anyway. I ended up flat on my rear in the wet, dewy grass.

"Oh, my gosh!" someone screamed—a woman's voice, young with a soft Texas drawl.

By the time I tossed Roger off, Clay's friend from yesterday was looking down at me, her hands over her mouth. "Oh, my word," she gasped between her fingers. "Are you all right?" She had a very nice manicure—pink, with little yellow smiley faces on the thumbs. "Roger, no!" she scolded, grabbing the dog's fur in two big handfuls and holding him away from me as I climbed to my feet. "I've never seen him do that to anybody before. He's usually a perfect lil' gentleman."

I blinked at her in disbelief. Gentleman? The dog who'd eaten my sofa, a Formica countertop, and the six-hundred-dollar Gianmarco Lorenzi shoes I'd splurged on during a business trip to Sicily—all in one week at my apartment? Roger was no gentleman, but what I really wanted to know was why this girl seemed to be so well-acquainted with Clay's dog. And why was she at Uncle Herb's at seven fifteen in the morning, all dressed for work?

"Are you oka-ay?" she asked again, her drawl stretching and softening the end of the word. She watched me with the sort of expression you might have when an elderly person slips on a spill in the grocery store. Once I'd righted myself, she let go of Roger and stuck a hand out to shake mine. "We didn't really get to meet one on one yesterday. You probably don't remember me. Amy Underhill? I was just little when y'all lived here."

I suddenly felt old and rather frumpy, standing there in my sweats. Amy Underhill? Blaine Underhill's toddler cousin? The one who attended day care across the street from the school? She used to bolt across the playground when Blaine passed by with the football boys on the way to fourth-period athletics. I'd watched them any number of times from algebra class as he jumped over the day-care fence and she tackled him with hugs. He'd pick her up, swing her onto his shoulder, featherlight, then open the gate and jog off while she laughed and squealed and the daycare-ladies playfully admonished him.

She was all grown up now—nineteen, maybe

twenty years old, I guessed. Workin' it in a small-town sort of way: cute skirt, high heels, white faux leather jacket.

"Great to see you," I said, self-consciously smoothing fly-away reddish-brown hairs into my ponytail. "Where's Clay going?" I pointed toward the water, where Clay was almost to the end of the cove. A black boat with a glittery silver rim had just stopped out there, and Clay was paddling toward it. I couldn't imagine why anyone would want to be on the water in the morning chill. It also wasn't normal for Clay to be up before nine, at least as far as I remembered. "Is he meeting someone out there?"

Amy swiveled, watching as Clay glided to the boat and the driver threw out a rope, with which Clay proceeded to tie up his kayak. When Amy turned back to me, she shrugged innocently but averted her eyes and looked at the house. "Oh, that's my cousin. Do you remember Blaine? He was in your class, I think. Anyhow, they go out and fish sometimes."

Tires screeched in my mind as my thoughts did a quick one-eighty. Blaine Underhill? My brother and Blaine Underhill had become fishing buddies? Since when had Clay started cultivating connections in Moses Lake—girlfriends and now fishing pals? Why hadn't my mother mentioned any of this during our talks about the real estate sale? It was as if my brother had a secret life, and no clues to it had ever filtered to me.

You shouldn't be surprised, the voice of conscience admonished. *It's not like you keep in touch.*

But I had been in touch lately, quite a bit with my mother and some with Uncle Herbert, Uncle Charley, and Donny. Why all the cloak-and-dagger stuff? Why was Clay's personal life such a big secret?

"I didn't realize they knew each other," I muttered, and Amy gave me a nervous look, her gaze shifting to the ground, searching the frost-tipped grass for a good answer.

"Oh, well, they got to be friends after they started talking so much. Blaine runs the bank now for his folks. He does business with a lot of people. . . ." She let the sentence drift, then quickly pulled her lips to one side.

"My brother's doing business at the bank?" I squeezed my arms around myself, trying to ward off the cold and the idea at the same time. I was afraid to know where this was leading. "What kind of business?"

Amy took the opportunity to glance at her watch. "Oh, mercy, look at the time. I better head for work." She sidestepped me and was off like a rabbit, headed toward the driveway. "It was really great seeing you, though. You have a good visit with your family, okay?"

I didn't answer because there wasn't time. Amy

was out of there as fast as her size-five heels would carry her. I watched my brother exit the kayak and climb into Blaine Underhill's boat, then motor out of the bay with the red kayak trailing forlornly behind like a leftover Christmas decoration.

When they were out of sight I went back to the cottage, got dressed, and headed for the main house, my mind finally fresh and alert, and my determination renewed. Time to unravel the tangled web of family secrets and sort out the sudden appearance of a supposed competing offer. I needed to get my mother to Seattle as soon as possible to sign the papers that would complete the sale of the family properties. Considering what I'd just seen and heard, maybe the competing offer wasn't so sudden, after all. Maybe Clay had been planning this hijacking for a while.

When I entered the house, Mother was in the kitchen, sipping coffee at the breakfast table. The uncs were nowhere to be seen. That was fortunate for me, because the person I really needed was Mom. Alone.

"The delivery man usually comes around three," she offered, just as pleasantly as if we sat down to coffee every morning. "It's a good thing today is Friday. They deliver on Fridays."

"What?" As usual, we were on two different astral planes. Opening the cabinet to search for a coffee cup, I noted that all the dishes were still in place. In fact, everything in the kitchen was more or less where it had been sixteen years ago. There was no sign of an estate auction having taken place or the packing up of any personal items.

"Your purse," Mom answered pleasantly. "I'm sure you're missing your cell phone and all those gadgets."

I poured a cup of coffee and sat down. "I just hope some guy in Hackensack isn't stealing my identity."

Looking out the window, Mom sighed, as if my presence were a black cloud over her morning. "Terrible, to be in your twenties and be such a cynic. Have a little faith in people, Heather. He was a very kind man. A good spirit. I could tell it when he called on the phone." Her eyes, a soft, mossy color in the morning light, turned my way, filled with disappointment.

"I just wish you'd told him to take my purse to the nearest police station, or the bus company. Someone official." Maybe I was being cynical, but losing your ID, your money, and your iPhone a thousand miles from home was about the most vulnerable feeling in the world. I didn't do vulnerable well, especially not in Moses Lake. "And I'm *thirty-four,* Mom. Clay is the one in his twenties."

She lowered her head into her hand, groaning. "Ugh, don't remind me. Where does the time go, anyway?" Pausing, she looked at me as if I were a stranger she was trying to cipher. "Thirty-four . . ." Her brows drew together.

In some families, I suppose it might have seemed strange, even offensive, for your mother to not know how old you were, but it felt normal enough for us. Mother could have discussed any writer from Aristotle to Maya Angelou ad nauseam, but she couldn't tell you how old her daughter was.

"Seems like yesterday we were here." She breathed the words softly, turning to the window again. There was a melancholy tone to her voice that drilled deep into me and lit a fuse I feared had the power to reach the bedrock of my soul and blow things apart. "The four of us," she added.

I felt sick, then angry. All the emotions from that year came back—every day of watching her slowly fade after my father's death, of wondering whether she would disappear completely, pass through the bed sheets by osmosis, and be gone. Every long night of listening to her moan in her tranquilizer-induced stupor and call my father's name, until my baby brother, frightened and distraught, came into my room and crawled into bed with me.

I felt the heat of teenage anger, long dormant, volcanic, rising to the surface, hot and fluid. I hated my mother all over again. "Why are you here?" The words were sharp. "I want the truth."

She swirled her coffee in the cup. "I just . . . needed to be. Here."

"Why is Clay here?" The absolute worst thing for Clay was to be offered one more distraction from finishing law school and beginning a stable, self-supporting life. Didn't Mom ever get tired of paying his way? Didn't she get tired of rescuing him from his mishaps—wrecked cars, tuition payments that came up short because of impromptu ski trips he couldn't afford, the time he missed taking his finals because campus police found rolling papers and a Baggie of marijuana in his dorm room. . . . He claimed those things were left there by a friend, but still. He wouldn't ever grow up if Mom didn't stop treating him like a kid.

She smiled, even laughed a little, staring down at her coffee, reading the blobs of creamer like an oracle. "Oh, Clay loves to come here. He comes all the time."

"What do you *mean* he comes all the time?" Clay and I might not have kept in touch particularly well, but I did have some idea of where he was and when. He'd never mentioned spending time in Moses Lake.

"Roger lives here some of the time," Mom said simply.

I studied her—took in the loose-fitting plaid shirt, the khaki pants that were just as likely to have come from Goodwill as L.L.Bean, the carelessly plaited brown hair, tinseled with strands

94

of gray. She was dressed in her usual garb for rambling around the English department, discussing quatrains, iambic pentameter, and Haiku as an expression of self. Her appearance was normal enough this morning, but maybe she really was having some sort of a breakdown. "Roger the *dog?*"

"Do you know another Roger?"

I bit my lower lip. If I'd had my money, ID, iPhone, and car keys, I would have walked out the door right then. Even the prospect of being project manager on the Proxica facility design wasn't worth losing my mind. I was starting to rue the day that Mother had contacted me to ask if I could remember where the deeds to my father's portion of the family farm had been stored after his death. She was practically gleeful at the news that Uncle Herbert and Uncle Charley were finally ready to sell out. Shortly after that conversation, I'd happened upon an article in the Proxica shareholders' magazine that said the company was planning major expansions in Texas. I'd asked Richard to quietly make some inquiries, and that had started the ball rolling. I should have known it would swerve badly off course and compact me into the soil before the deal was done.

The insanity of this sudden shift, combined with the ghosts in this town, was too much to bear. I couldn't stand it. I couldn't sit in this house, talking about Roger the dog over coffee. "I want. To know. What. Is going on. There isn't any competing offer for the real estate, is there? No one in their right minds would pay the price Richard got for us—not with the economy the way it is. Even if we hang on to the property until the economy improves, we'd never get that kind of money."

Her eyelids held calmly at half-mast, regarding me with a measure of coolness that hurts coming from your mother. "Which would make you wonder why this broker is offering such a sum, wouldn't it? Presumably he has to then resell the property for an even higher price. Who, exactly, would he sell it to, if the price we're getting is so astronomically out of line?"

"Why do you care?" I threw up my hands, let them slap to the tabletop, and affected the look of being completely and thoroughly offended. But an inconvenient smidge of conscience landed on my shoulders, squawking in my ear like a magpie. I had been keeping secrets, too. But that was part of the deal with the broker. I wasn't at liberty to divulge any information. "When we started this process, you couldn't wait to be out from under the place. You were tired of having to keep up with the accounting on the farmland and figure out how to divide up the property-tax payments with Uncle Herb and Uncle Charley. You said you wanted to be able to give Clay and me the money from the land, because it was our inheritance. You said that Clay needed the money to pay off some loans. What, exactly, about that has changed?"

Pausing to take a bite of her English muffin, she tipped her chin up and chewed slowly. "We've rethought it, simply enough. Uncle Herbert and Uncle Charley have owned the farm all their lives, for one thing. They and your grandfather grew up there." Her gaze met mine in a way that seemed intended to stab. "And so did your father."

Emotion balled in my throat and dripped downward, burning like acid, threatening to eat away the steely coating of anger and morph it into something raw and unpredictable. *My father died there,* I thought. There were two houses on the farm—the two-story white clapboard that had been built by my grandparents in the forties, and the modest stone house beside it. The basement of that little stone house was the scene of the accidental shooting that had changed all our lives. Among other memories, the question of whether the word *accidental* really applied haunted that house. It haunted me.

Even now, sitting here at Harmony Shores, I could feel the proximity of that place, fifteen miles down the rural highway. I could feel the house where my father's life had ended, where my nightmares took me again and again. I'd never set foot on the farm after the week my father died, and I didn't want to now. I just wanted that place to be gone. Maybe then the nightmares would stop.

97

Stay focused. Don't let her get to you. Don't let any of this get to you. "Uncle Charley and Uncle Herbert aren't the problem here, Mom, and you know it. Both of them realize that they have to move closer to Donny. This is about you and Clay, and as much work as I've put in on this deal, I deserve the truth."

She sent a narrow look my way, her lips tightening. I'd finally broken through the layer of serenity, found a nerve. "It's always about work for you, isn't it? Your whole life is about work." She frowned as if she simultaneously pitied me and wondered how I could possibly be her offspring. "You'll have to talk to your brother about it. Clay can explain everything more clearly than I can. He has a better business understanding."

Business understanding? My brother? Clay couldn't even be counted upon not to end up stuck out in the middle of nowhere on a bicycle, with pneumonia. "What business?" Maybe Clay thought he was going to somehow arrange a competing offer on the property—something on which he could turn a dime, perhaps. But as textbook brilliant as my brother was, he was out of his league in this situation. There was no better deal out there to be had. "I don't want to ask Clay. I'm asking you."

Mom stood up, took her coffee cup to the sink, calmly rinsed it out, and squirted a little dish soap into it. "Simply put, we're considering our options, just as I told you on the phone. I know you thought that by coming here you could change things, Heather, but you can't."

"What *options?* What?" I threw up my hands, shook them in the air like a crazy woman. I have never in my life, personal or professional, met anyone else who could bring out that side of me.

"Well, if you must know, your brother thinks we should keep the place in the family." She smiled as if I should be happy to hear of Clay's epiphany. "He's interested in living at the old farm. The renter who was staying in the two-story house has moved out. The place is empty and available. Clay adores the old tractors and the feeling of being close to the land. It suits him. I've never seen him so happy."

"What in the world is Clay going to do to support himself financially, living on what's left of a dairy farm, fifteen miles outside in the country?" A sarcastic laugh tailed the question. I couldn't help it. The idea of any of us living on that farm again made me sick. The little stone house had been locked up since my father's death, and the two-story clapboard next door had been occupied by a series of renters over the years.

Mother shrugged, her shoulders stiff. She hated being challenged. She was accustomed to reigning supreme over underlings and dewy-eyed

99

graduate students. "He is looking into taking over the restaurant and the canoe business. It worked well enough for Uncle Charley all these years. He made enough of a living, and . . ."

My head spun as Mom went on, the insanity growing exponentially, like the 3-D virtual image of a skyscraper, building layer upon layer from the electronic blueprint, the windows and doors filling in, the walls extruding and becoming real. But this entire building was leaning off-kilter. My mother was supposedly considering moving to Moses Lake, too.

"I'm ready for a change," she asserted. "I've been looking for an opportunity to step off the carousel of teaching and lecturing. I could pursue my writing, maybe teach some classes online. These days there are opportunities, and with my credentials . . . Well, it's perfect, really. Uncle Herb doesn't want to leave his house, and this way he wouldn't have to. I could live here in Harmony House with the uncs, and Clay could live out at the farm. It's crossed my mind that Harmony House would make a lovely bed-and-breakfast. It's already licensed for public occupancy."

"Public . . . what . . ." I stammered. "You have got to be kidding." Bracing my palms on the table, I stood up. There are times when, despite all attempts at keeping things at a rational level with my mother, the fact is that if we stay in the same room any longer, a Jerry Springer moment will erupt. Chairs will fly, claws will come out, and hair will be pulled.

I was conscious of some sort of emotional fault line giving way within me, the tectonic plates sliding and making the ground shake. One more nugget of craziness on my mother's side of the divide, and things would break wide open, allowing ugliness of epic proportion to spew forth. The only thing to do in a moment like that is walk away before chaos breaks out, and keep walking for however long it takes.

There is indeed, perhaps, no better way to hold communion with the sea than sitting in the sun on the veranda of a fisherman's cafe.
—Joseph W. Beach
(*via Pop Dorsey, proprietor,*
Waterbird Bait and Grocery)

≈ Chapter 6 ≈

The entire conversation had repeated twice in my head by the time I found myself at the picnic grounds behind Lakeshore Community Church. Doves fluttered from branch to branch overhead, their voices incongruously sweet, waves lapped at the shore, and squirrels dashed about gathering leftover pecans as I paced between the picnic tables, muttering and hissing like an alley cat caught in a box.

The situation with my mother and my brother was crazy, even for them. Mom was hardly suited to running a bed-and-breakfast in the country. Who would want to stay in a former funeral home anyway? And Clay had no way of getting the money together to buy Uncle Charley's restaurant and the canoe-rental business.

Unless . . . unless Mom was bankrolling it with whatever was left of the nest egg that had come from my father's life insurance. She'd hated it when Clay left with the disaster relief team. She was scared to death something would happen to him. Now that he was back, was this her way of trying to make sure he didn't wander off to the far parts of the globe again? Was she going to tie him down with fried catfish and canoes? All the money he'd borrowed and not paid back, all his starts and stops in law school were forgotten, and Mom was ready to take care of him, just like always?

Why was it always so easy for him? Why could Clay do whatever he wanted—consume her funds, consume her energy, wander aimlessly through his life—yet remain the object of her adoration? Why didn't I ever get that kind of consideration? Why did she criticize my life while approving of his, no matter what he did? It had always been this way. From the beginning, I was Dad's and Clay was hers. But Dad was gone, and I was on the outside looking in, while Mom and Clay flitted through life, two birds of a feather.

Tears came out of nowhere, and I sank onto one of the picnic benches. Trish was right—I'd be better off if I could stop expecting things from my mother. But no matter how old you get, no matter how hard you try, you can't give up wanting your mother to love you. Somehow, though, I had to find a way to let go of that hope, that expectation. It was hollowing me out little by little, like water dripping on stone.

Taking a breath, I swallowed hard and pushed the tears away. Our family relationships were complicated, confused, upside-down—and they always would be. I had to learn to work from that basis of knowledge. Given a little time, Mother would come down to earth and see that Clay running the restaurant and her turning the funeral home into a bed-and-breakfast was a pipe dream. Surely, I could find ways to help open her eyes and get her to Seattle before the broker offer on the property expired. I could still salvage this thing and save the uncs from certain disaster. . . .

"A little brisk out here for a picnic." A voice from behind startled me, and I jerked upright, feeling like I'd been caught someplace I shouldn't be. But I knew why I was there. I felt close to my father in this place. One of the last things we'd done together was go to Sunday morning service. I was cranky about it, of course. The pastor was boring and the music old-fashioned. There were no projection screens. There was no five-piece band rocking out modern worship music, like we had in our church back home. In tiny Lakeshore Community Church, there was only the pastor droning on while babies made noise, the casserole ladies gave me disapproving looks, and Mama B sang off-key, her voice crackling high above the rest.

I glanced over my shoulder, expecting the pastor I remembered, the one who'd tried to placate me with the usual platitudes as I struggled to comprehend the loss of my father. Instead, a thirty-something man, tall and lanky, with a thin, hawkish face, was headed down the hill.

"Want to come inside?" he asked, thumbing over his shoulder with an amiable smile.

I stood up, the back of my legs now fully chilled from sitting on the frosty stone bench. "No, I'm fine. I just . . ." His gaze met mine, and for an instant I had the weirdest urge to tell him everything. He seemed like the sort who would listen. I wondered if he knew my brother and my mother. Maybe I could gain some information about how long Clay had been hanging around town. I wiped my eyes and introduced myself. "Heather Hampton. I used to live here. I was just taking a walk around town, remembering."

His face brightened, and he held my hand captive between both of his for a moment. "Reverend Hay. Good to meet you. Any relation to the Harmony Shores Hamptons—Charley and Herbert?" I noted that he didn't mention my mother or my brother.

"My great uncles," I answered.

"We're sure going to miss them around here. Moses Lake won't be the same without the Hampton brothers. Tell your uncles I'll get by to see them before they go. I'm a little behind. Been gone three weeks on a mission trip with my fiancée's church."

105

He flashed a quick smile that was somewhere between giddy and bashful, and I decided two things: I liked him despite the preacher suit, and he knew absolutely nothing about what was going on with my family. As far as he was aware, the uncs were packing up and leaving. So . . . all of Clay's Moses Lake connections and his plan to live here permanently had developed in the last three weeks?

A horn honked up the hill by the road, and both of us turned to look. Uncle Charley's Ford pickup, Old Blue, was rolling along the shoulder. The window cranked down, and he waved us closer. "Hey, there you are!" he called, and Reverend Hay and I started up the hill. "Been lookin' for you, Heather. Your mom said you went out for a walk. C'mon, I'll take you to breakfast. You, too, if you want, Hay."

"Got a building committee meeting in twenty minutes," the reverend answered as we walked toward the road. "Promised Bonnie I'd pick her up at the office in Cleburne and take her to lunch, so I'd better stay here and get everything set for the committee, try to keep things moving along. When lunch hour hits, Bonnie's ready to get out of that counseling office and go somewhere else for a while."

Uncle Charley smacked his lips and shook his head as we traversed the ditch. "Well, sorry I can't be on the buildin' committee. They get things set with Blaine Underhill about the loan for the new addition?"

New addition. Glancing over my shoulder, I winced. I hoped they found someone who could design the add-on space in a way that would preserve the historic character of the building. So often, these little jobs out in the middle of nowhere were poorly done architectural eyesores.

I noted that Blaine Underhill was involved here, too.

"For the most part," Reverend Hay answered. "Blaine can't make the meeting. Said he'd be back in the bank about eleven, so I'll take everything by there for him before I head for Cleburne. He's gone to an appointment this morning."

Appointment? A sardonic scoff passed my lips as I circled the truck to get in on the passenger side. Blaine Underhill was out on the lake with my brother. Fishing. On a workday morning. I couldn't imagine taking off fishing while the rest of the world was at work.

Actually, that brought up the question of why, if my brother was in such a hurry to relocate to Moses Lake and take over Catfish Charley's, he was out fishing. Shouldn't he be at the restaurant, learning the ropes from the manager there, and getting the place ready to open for lunch? A little greasy spoon like Charley's wasn't exactly the kind of high-profit place where the owner didn't have to put in hours. Until his health had declined,

Uncle Charley had worked from morning through lunch, taken care of his cattle at the family farm for a few hours in the afternoon, then returned for the supper rush. His wife, Aunt Fea, had worked every day at the restaurant until shortly before her death. They'd lived on a houseboat docked behind Catfish Charley's, and between the restaurant, the canoe business, and the cabins, they were always busy.

Yet Clay had time to spend the morning fishing with Blaine Underhill?

Then again, maybe there was more to the fishing friendship than just dropping a line in the water. What had Amy said earlier? Something about my brother and Blaine becoming friends after talking so much at the bank.

Hmmm . . . How does a guy with no life plan and no money take over ownership of a restaurant? He makes friends with the banker. When Clay was on fire about his latest plan—whatever it happened to be—he could be incredibly alluring. He didn't even have to work at it because his beliefs were genuine. The problem was that Clay's focus was like a butterfly—bright, intense, beautiful to look at, unbelievably compelling . . . but likely to flit off at any moment. Blaine Underhill had no idea what he was being sucked into. Someone needed to clue him in, and it looked like that someone would be me. As much as I loved my brother, I couldn't let him create a situation that could leave a financial mess behind in Moses Lake.

Uncle Charley and Reverend Hay continued their conversation as I climbed into the truck. Uncle Charley suggested that the church should hire me to design the new fellowship hall, since I *drew up buildings and such*. Rather than telling them that this project was too small for our firm, I wrote my email address on a feed-store receipt from the mound of dashboard clutter and handed it out the window. Maybe I could do the job pro bono— a gift to my father's hometown. It would be worth it to see the church building, with its European lines and the decorative stone masonry of the original German pioneers, properly preserved.

Uncle Charley and I discussed the new fellow-ship hall as we wound our way around the lake, headed, I surmised by the direction we were driving, to the Waterbird Bait and Grocery. The local crowd of fishermen and retirees had been gathering there to sip coffee and solve the world's problems since shortly after the lake went in. I found myself picturing the Waterbird now, remembering my father taking me there when I was little. We bought lemon drops, cartons of squirmy worms, and dips of ice cream. Scoops of ice cream and scoops of worm-filled dirt came in the same white waxed-cardboard containers, so when you reached into the sack, you had to be careful which one you grabbed.

A laugh tickled my throat as I remembered squealing and tossing dirt all over the car once when I opened the wrong container. I was twelve or thirteen then, a sophisticated city girl, convinced that worms were not for me, but the lure of an afternoon alone with my dad was irresistible. We were visiting my grandparents for some holiday—Easter, maybe. The bluebonnets were out, the roadsides everywhere awash with sprays of vibrant azure that rivaled the water in the lake. My brother must have stayed home, because it was just Dad and me.

"Somethin' funny?" Uncle Charley asked as we rounded the corner and I saw the Waterbird's tin roof peeking through the cluster of overhanging live oaks ahead. For an instant, I heard my dad.

"I was just thinking about coming here with Dad," I answered, and I was surprised that, for once, the mention of him didn't trail dark threads behind it.

Uncle Charley chuckled. "Your dad liked this old store. Used to be when he was little, if I ever passed by here with him in the truck, he'd beg me to stop, so he could get at the penny candy counter. That boy did like his sweets.

"Wasn't too many years after that, he would've hung around here all day long, if he could've. It was where the young folks went to look at each other, and all them girls liked your daddy. Back when your granddaddy was farmin' cotton at the old place, if we ever had a tractor or a truck break down and we made the mistake of sending your dad to town, it'd be an hour later, and we'd say, 'Where in the world is Neal?' Sure enough, we'd call up to the Waterbird, and he'd be there— stopped in for a Coke and ended up flirtin' with some girl."

"Really?" I said, trying to imagine that side of my dad. He'd always been the responsible one when I was growing up. He had to be.

"Oh, sure." Uncle Charley chuckled as we drifted off the shoulder into the gravel parking lot. "Your dad was a corker. Gave his mama and daddy more than a few gray hairs. I ever tell you about the time he and some other boys found a little ol' possum curled up in a dead tree during the cold weather? They put it in the choir closet at church on Sunday mornin', thinking they were gonna get it later and use it to play a joke on somebody. That thing got all warmed up durin' service and went to growlin' and thumpin' around in there, and you never seen a bunch of boys sitting so straight in the pew, trying to look like they didn't hear a thing. Ended up, those boys had to work the rest of the winter to pay for a new set of Christmas choir robes."

Uncle Charley and I laughed as we exited the car to go into the Waterbird. Suddenly I was glad I'd come. I'd never heard that story about my father, never known that side of him. When we'd

111

come to Moses Lake to visit my grandparents during my childhood years, my mother had poured on the guilt long-distance, until we felt bad for enjoying anything.

As we entered the Waterbird, old men gathered in the red vinyl booths on the left wall waved and called out greetings worthy of an episode of *Cheers*. They observed that I was much more attractive than Charley's usual traveling companion, Uncle Herb. Already positioned in a seat along the wall with a cup of coffee, Uncle Herb pretended to take offense.

The Waterbird was exactly as I remembered it: the café, deli, and cash counter along the right side of the room; the booths and a pay phone on the wall at the far left; three aisles of indiscriminately mixed groceries, fishing tackle, doughnut cases, and candy in the middle. Beside me, the minnow tanks burbled in strangely close proximity to the drink machine and the freezer case. Along the far wall, a bank of tall windows afforded a view of the lake below, complete with docks, boathouses, and a waterside gas pump for boats.

As Uncle Charley ordered coffee for the two of us, I moved across the room to look at the wall of wisdom. I wondered if Gary and his family had signed it while they were in town. It wouldn't be easy to find their entry, if they had indeed made one, among the countless signatures and bits of Sharpie-pen lore that stretched from the front counter, circled the windows, and went all the way back to the bathroom. Without even intending to, I followed a rhythm of remembered steps, moving toward a place I hoped would still be there, just to the left of the windows. And then I was in front of it, reading the quote my father and I had jotted on the wall together.

You are braver than you believe, stronger than you seem, and smarter than you think. –Winnie the Pooh.

We'd signed our names after the quote—Neal Hampton, Heather Hampton—and then the year. I was nine, my father still a young man. We'd read the Winnie the Pooh books together so many times we could recite them by heart. It had never occurred to me that this place, Moses Lake, was my father's Hundred Acre Wood, and he wanted me to love it as much as he did. Maybe he'd had a premonition when we wrote that quote on the wall. Even now, I knew the rest of the quote—the part we'd left out, so as to save space. Touching a hand to words, I heard my father and me reciting the last part together, giving each other a high five after adding our entry: *But the most important thing is, even if we're apart, I'll always be with you.*

My father hadn't chosen our place on the wall at random. He'd picked a spot directly underneath a wooden plaque left behind by a German tinker who passed through Moses Lake back in the days when tinkers drove from town to town, sharpening knives and sheep shears, and fixing leaky kettles. The tinker's riddle had been the beginning of the wall of wisdom. Looking at it now, I remembered standing with my father as I read it. *The future is a blank page, but not a mystery.* The riddle had eluded me then. I'd complained to Dad that it didn't make any sense; I didn't see how it could be his favorite. He'd only laughed, scrubbed a big, brawny hand over my hair, and said *No sense trying to cheat a riddle. You have to figure it out for yourself, or it's no fun. Keep thinking on it. It'll be clear one of these days.*

Unfortunately, the tinker's riddle was no more logical to me now than it had been then. A page is either blank, or it's not. If it is blank, the possibilities are endless, the end result a mystery.

"Better come fix this cup the way you like it, darlin'," Uncle Charley called from the coffee counter.

I turned away from the wall and crossed the room, feeling unburdened, rather than weighed down, by the memory of that day with my father. The quote we'd written seemed almost a message from him, a promise that even though I hadn't been the person I'd wanted to be during our last turbulent months together, he realized that inside the melodramatic teenager there was still the little girl who loved him in the Winnie-the-Pooh sort of way—always and no matter what. The same way he'd loved me.

One of Uncle Herbert's fishing buddies vacated a seat for me as I finished preparing my coffee and walked to the table. A round of greetings came my way, along with some comments about how I couldn't really be related to Charley and Herb, because I was too pretty. I laughed and blushed at the banter circling the table, a few anecdotes about my father livening up the mix. A warm feeling washed over me as Uncle Herb reached for my coat and threw it into an empty booth like we owned the place. I had the sense of being right at home.

Two of the men sharing space with us looked familiar, although it took a minute for my memory banks to dredge up the information. They'd aged since my time here, but I knew who they were—Nester Grimland, who'd kept the Moses Lake school busses running, and Burt Lacey, the high-school principal, apparently retired now, since he was sitting in the Waterbird midmorning on a Friday.

"Hey, Missy, I ever tell you that your dad worked for me one summer milkin' cows?" Nester Grimland offered, wiping coffee off his thick gray moustache and directing a wink my way. He looked like one of those skinny cowboy statues you'd find for sale in a roadside tourist trap.

"Really?" I asked. "Dad never talked much about his dairy work." Actually, my dad had said that growing up on a dairy made him want to get a college education.

Burt Lacey frowned sideways, squinting through glasses that had gotten thicker since his days as a principal. "What are you talking about, Nester? You never had milk cows." I remembered them arguing just this way any number of times when I'd passed by the bus barn after school.

"I sure did," Nester insisted, seeming offended. "Neal Hampton worked milkin' cows for me." Adjusting his cowboy hat, he flashed a covert glance my way, a brow lifting conspiratorially. "Bet your daddy told 'ya about workin' for me, didn't he?"

I felt compelled to play along. "You know, I think he did say something about that . . . uhhh . . . once or twice." Both of the uncs swiveled toward me, cocking their heads, confused.

"See there," Nester held up a weathered hand, serving me up as proof. "Her daddy milked for me. Only problem was, every time a pretty girl drove by on the highway, that boy would come all unfocused. Ruined a whole batch of milk one time. He ever tell you that story?" Nester aimed a quick head-twitch at me.

"Ummm . . . yes. Yes, I think he . . . did."

Burt Lacey rolled his eyes. "Well, let us have it, Nester. You're not gonna hush up until we've

116

heard the whole thing. How'd the batch of milk get ruined?"

Reclining comfortably now that he had the conversational floor, Nester hooked an elbow over the back of his seat. "Well, see, it was like this. One day, that there boy was a-milkin', and he had him a good rhythm goin' along—playin' a little tune in the bucket. 'America the Beautiful,' I think it was. Must've been close to the Fourth of July." Pausing, he stroked his chin, pretending to think.

Burt Lacey snorted, Uncle Charley added sugar to his coffee, and Uncle Herb scratched his bald head, quiet as usual.

"Anyhoo, so there's young Neal Hampton, milkin' along, and a load of cheerleaders drives by, and he ain't payin' no attention at all to what he's doing. Right about then, a big ol' horse fly comes along and starts circling that milk cow . . . just buzzin' around and buzzin' around. Which ain't really a problem, since there's always flies in a cow barn, but that boy didn't even notice when that fly went right in that old milk cow's ear. The kid just kept watchin' them cheerleaders and milkin' along, tryin' to finish, so he could chase after them purdy girls. He didn't hear that fly buzzin' round and round inside that milk cow, looking for a way out. Didn't notice a thing. Finally, that kid was milkin' so fast it created a vacuum inside the whole cow and sucked that horsefly right out the udder. Landed smack in the milk bucket and ruined the whole batch."

Uncle Charley groaned and pulled his hat low over his eyes, and Uncle Herb shook his head. Burt Lacey slapped the tabletop, air whistling through his teeth. "Nester, that's not one bit possible. Even she knows that."

I shrugged and, quite wisely, kept quiet, not being an expert on milk cows.

Nester drew back against the wall. "She don't know any such thing, do ya, young lady?"

I shook my head again, and Nester took a sip of his coffee, then swilled it while all eyes remained focused on him. "Just goes to show, that boy took after the rest of the Hampton men. Why, you ask any of their wives and they'll tell you that it ain't the first time someone in that family's—" he paused for dramatic effect, the corners of his moustache twitching as he finished with—"let somethin' go in one ear and out the udder."

A chorus of laughter followed, and from his wheelchair behind the counter, Pop Dorsey joined in. I laughed along, having the fleeting thought that it felt good to be here, just sitting and watching the world go by on a Friday morning, taking a little time for coffee and conversation. When was the last time I'd done that?

Ever?

Gazing out at the water glistening in the morning sunlight below, I had the weird thought

118

that I might miss Moses Lake after all of this was over.

The conversation turned to spinner baits and fat bass, and Burt Lacey went to the coffee counter and commandeered the pot to refresh everyone's coffee. As he was returning the pot to its resting spot, a little dark-haired girl wandered from behind the deli counter and walked down the center aisle between loaves of bread, bags of charcoal, and a smattering of plumbing supplies. Studying the shelves, she picked up imaginary items and put them in a miniature shopping basket. The attention of every "grandpa" in the room quickly gravitated to her.

"Hey, Birdie, you gonna come serve us up some tea?" Uncle Charley motioned her over.

The little girl smiled shyly, her wide blue eyes twinkling.

Uncle Charley leaned back in his chair. "I'm tellin' ya, I'm just about dry as a baked horned toad on a six-lane stretch of blacktop. Sure could use me some tea."

Her smile widened, and she skipped on over to us, standing on her toes, so that she could look into his cup. Her lips twisted to one side, and she braced a hand on her hip. "It ain't empty."

I had the fleeting thought that it was a shame Uncle Charley and his wife hadn't been able to have kids. He'd been one of my favorite Moses Lake attractions when I was little. Every kid in

119

town loved him. "Aw, that's just that old black coffee," he complained, giving the cup a disdainful look. "I need me some of that good ol' magic tea. You got any of that in yer basket?"

As Birdie fished around in her basket of random toys and produced a little plastic teapot, I felt a twinge of remorse at the thought of the kids I didn't have never meeting the great-uncle I wouldn't see again after this weekend.

Watching Birdie serve pretend tea, I wished life were different than it was.

The banter started again after Birdie had filled all the cups and then scampered off. A buzzer above the back door interrupted the conversation, and Uncle Charley stood up, peeking out the back window. "Looks like you need to turn on the gas pump down there, Pop. Put it on the Underhill's bill. I'll tell you what, that's a nice fishin' rig Blaine's got. He could win some votes with that thing, sure enough."

Before I'd even given it any thought, I was excusing myself, slipping from my seat, and grabbing my coat. I headed out the back door to discern—from the source—what business was going on between my brother and the local banker.

A brisk February wind whipped over the water and raced up the hill. Swinging the coat over my shoulders, I stuck my arms in the sleeves and quickly realized that I'd grabbed someone else's outerwear from the pile on the empty booth. This one was large enough for me and my two best friends, and it was a camo color with roadstripe-orange western detailing. I pulled it on anyway, the bottom falling halfway to my knees, surrounding me like a puffy tent as I strode down the rock steps toward the lakeshore and the dock, where Blaine Underhill was nonchalantly gassing up his boat, one foot braced on the dock railing, the collar of a khaki-colored barn jacket turned upright against his neck, hiding his face. There was no sign of my brother or the red kayak. Apparently this morning's fishing trip was over.

A strange tangle of past and present swirled in my thoughts, a fruitless attempt to mesh the memory of the boy from high school with the banker of today, my brother's new best friend. If Blaine Underhill was the moneyman behind Clay's plans, did he have any idea what a mistake he was making? Did he know that, sooner or later, their plan would result in disaster for the uncs and leave Clay responsible for not only financial obligations, but most likely the reality of once again going from hero to zero in the eyes of the family? With Clay's history of chaotic life shifts, there was no telling where things might lead. Clay might join some mission trip to Bora-Bora and never come back. In the meantime, the property that had belonged to Uncle Herbert, Uncle Charley, and my family for generations would end up in foreclosure, in the hands of . . . the bank?

Potential motivations began taking shape in my mind, even though I didn't want to entertain them. Would Blaine Underhill finance my brother's flight of fancy, knowing that Clay would fail and the bank would end up with the property and whatever down payment my mother was putting into this unholy partnership? I tried to imagine the object of my chemistry-class crush, now playing the part of the heartless, shifty-eyed banker—the sort with the handlebar moustache and the evil laugh. The kind who would toss widows, orphans, and helpless old men out in the snow. Could he have changed so much from the prankster who had the ability to answer teachers' questions but typically chose to go for a laugh instead?

Of course he could have changed. Haven't you? After sixteen years, who could say what kind of person Blaine Underhill was? In truth, the Blaine I remembered was a schoolgirl fantasy. Even back then, I had no idea who he really was behind the high-school mask.

It didn't matter now. If he had any intentions of taking advantage of my family, he had another think coming.

Every ounce of nostalgic sentiment evaporated from my thoughts, and I welcomed the empowering rush of righteous indignation. It was easier to handle than leftover puppy love and mushy gushy thoughts of an unrequited adoration. Blaine Underhill was about to find out that the wimpy, quiet, messed-up girl who let everyone push her around in high school had grown up and gotten a backbone.

He hooked the nozzle back on the gas pump as I hit the dock, the wooden heels on my suede boots making a hollow *ping-tap-ping* on the half-frozen wood. I took note of the cracks between the boards. The boots didn't have high heels, but they did have heels, and those cracks were wide enough to create a misstep that would entirely ruin my entrance and put a kink in the strictly-business and slightly dragonlike persona that had served me so well in a male-dominated career field. The banker was about to see that not everyone in the Hampton family was filled with impractical dreams.

Wiping his hands on a rag, he looked up, blinked, and cocked his head to one side, as if a woman in dress boots, skinny jeans, and a giant camouflage coat weren't an everyday sight on the dock.

Employing a strategy I'd long ago learned from Mel while dealing with difficult clients, I opened the dialog and got right to the point. "I'd like to know what, exactly, is going on between you and my brother."

His expression went completely blank, and he backed away a step as I made it to the platform near the gas pumps. The decking rocked slightly in the current, causing me to spread my feet like a

123

gunfighter about to draw down at the O.K. Corral.

"Ma'am?" A dark brow lifted, and his chin drew inward a bit, the little cleft there growing more pronounced. I'd forgotten about that cleft in his chin. . . .

I admonished myself to remain focused. It was harder than I'd thought it would be. His appreciative look, and the lanky southern cadence of his words lured me in some way I didn't want to contemplate. "Please don't insult my intelligence. He may be falling for this, but I'm not. Let's be honest, shall we?"

Blaine finished wiping his hands and set the rag aside. "All right." His eyes narrowed, black lashes fanning over the brown centers. His dark hair was shorter than it used to be, windblown right now, curling just a bit over his ears and on his collar.

I took a breath, paused a moment to get my thoughts in order, and remembered watching those lashes drift toward his cheeks as he rested his chin on his hand in chemistry class. "Have you checked my brother's credit rating, looked into his background, investigated his history?"

Crossing his arms over his chest, Blaine leaned against the railing, the barest hint of amusement playing on his lips. I realized I was looking at his lips. I quit looking and focused on his forehead.

"That's not really the way I like to do things. I don't see the point."

"Don't see the *point?*" I threw my hands up, and

the ends of the oversized leaf-print sleeves flopped like tree branches in the wind. "Are you serious?" Maybe Blaine Underhill really was still the goof-off he'd been in high school. Maybe his parents, aging and unable to figure out what else to do with him, were letting him use the bank as his personal play toy. Maybe he was more like my brother than I'd thought. Weren't there federal regulators who prevented bankers from doing stupid things with other people's money? "What kind of sense does that make?"

He shrugged nonchalantly, his response annoyingly calm. "I think it makes perfect sense. Some things just aren't right to do." He had the same drawl as Clay's new girlfriend, Amy, though Blaine's was less pronounced.

"What?" My tree-branch sleeves flopped up and down once, twice. Talking with my hands was one of those nervous habits I had yet to overcome. *Some things aren't right to do.* Give me a break. How can you possibly operate like that?" This innocent country-boy act had to be a way of toying with me, trying to throw me off track. Maybe I should report him to some kind of . . . I wasn't sure who . . . the FDIC, or the board of banking, or someone.

"A man's background is his own business." He brushed a scrap of what looked like hay off his sleeve, and I noted that for a guy who'd just been out fishing, he was strangely neat and clean—

pressed jeans, fairly new cowboy boots, and a white collar peeking around the top button of his coat. He looked like he was dressed for a barn dance or a night at the rodeo, rather than an early-morning fishing trip.

I rolled my eyes, irritated with the runaround. He needed to be upstairs telling milk-cow stories with Nester Grimland and Burt Lacey. *No* bank —not even a little redneck bank like the one across the street from the Moses Lake post office—loaned out money without checking the applicant's background. "Pah-lease. Do I look stupid to you?"

"No, ma'am," he answered, his eyes twinkling. "A little fashion-challenged, maybe, but not stupid." His lips spread into a grin that went right to the pit of my stomach and did something strange there.

"This is *not* a joke." And how dare he think that I'd be weak enough to fall for the class-clown act. I wasn't used to people blowing me off, not taking me seriously. I hadn't gotten to the position of senior manager with a major firm by being the simpering little wimpkin I was in high school. "I guess maybe it's a joke to you, or just business, or whatever, but as much as my brother drives me insane, I do care about his future. A lot. I don't want him to end up falling flat on his face and taking the rest of the family with him. As brilliant as he is, he's like a big . . . teenager, basically. He has never managed to stick with anything in his life, and he won't stick with this. He'll be into it just long enough to dig a great big hole, and then something else will catch his eye." My arms, lost within the voluminous sleeves, beseeched him to look at Clay objectively.

"I hadn't heard that about him, but it's good to know."

I had the sense that I might be getting somewhere. Maybe I could sway him and end this whole thing. Clay wouldn't be happy with me, but he'd tack in a new direction soon enough, and then he'd be glad he hadn't entangled himself in Moses Lake. So would my mother, actually, and the uncs would be rid of the burden of properties they could no longer take care of. I would continue on to be the project manager, and Moses Lake would have over three-hundred badly needed new jobs. Everyone would be better off.

"So, you can see that the best thing to do is just . . . not help him."

Uncrossing his legs and then crossing them the other way, the banker blinked, cocking his head back a bit, as if he were trying to make sense of me. "I'm not trying to help him. I plan to come out a winner in this thing."

My mouth dropped open, and I felt like one of those cartoon characters slowly turning red-hot from the chest, upward. Any minute now, my ears would go off like a steam whistle. He was actually admitting that he planned to take advantage of my brother and my entire family? *How dare he!* "You're going to stand right here and tell me that? You're not even trying to hide it?" *The nerve of this guy! The arrogance.*

Did he have reason to be so confident? How involved were he and Clay? Was this situation already beyond salvaging?

"It's no secret," he said, and I felt sick. "I don't play to lose."

A lump rose in my throat, and for a mortifying instant, I had that I'm-not-going-to-cry feeling. I swallowed it and rode another wave of anger, instead. "You know what? You have to be the biggest jerk I've ever met. If you think you're going to just . . . take everything my family has worked for . . . for generations, and use my brother to do it, you'd better think again. That'll happen over my dead body."

His lips tugged at the corners. "That'd be a shame." He watched me with a look that could only have been described as *hot*. And, sue me, but for a moment, I liked it. The mini-grin morphed into a full-fledged smile, and he shook his head, chuckling under his breath.

"What in the world are you laughing at?" An insistent foot-stomp confirmed that my toes were prickly cold. The suede boots were cute, but dysfunctional in this environment, unfortunately.

Lifting his chin, he uncrossed his legs and

128

pushed away from the post. "I think I just figured out that we're chattin' out two different sides of the barn here. I don't have any idea who you are or what you're talking about."

I felt my mouth dropping open again, my chin just hanging there against the flame-orange collar, my mind running like a hamster on a wheel, around and around in circles. Perpetual motion but no forward progress. "Wha . . . but . . . you . . ."

I could see it in his face. There was not one hint of recognition in his eyes. "You don't . . ."

"I wish I did." He delivered another smoldering smile, then wiped it away. "You're not related to that idiot who's running against me for county commission, are you?"

"County comish . . . What?" All I could think was, *Blaine Underhill has no idea who I am. He's looking right at me, and he has no idea who he's looking at.*

I wasn't certain whether to feel wounded or pleased. How should a girl feel when confirming her belief that the object of her high-school crush never even gave her a second thought?

He was thinking about me now, though. That much was obvious enough, and even though I didn't want to, I felt my ego purring like a kitten. Right now, he was clearly waiting for me to melt under the heat of that smile. I was tempted to, but of course that was a juvenile impulse. Somebody

129

in my family had to act like an adult, to get down to business before it was too late. "I don't know what *you're* talking about, but I'm talking about my brother, Clay Hampton. I know he and my mother have some wild idea about getting the financing to buy Catfish Charley's, the funeral home at Harmony Shores, and the thirds of the family farm that belong to Uncle Charley and Uncle Herb. They've been talking to you about it, haven't they?"

He didn't answer at first. He was staring at me, his expression one of pure, unmitigated shock. "You're . . . Heather Hampton?"

Once again, I wasn't sure how to feel. I had, at least, managed to completely eradicate my high school self, as well as to wipe that smug look off his face. While I had him off-balance, I decided to go in for the kill. "Yes. And I don't want you doing business with my brother—bankrolling him or in any other way encouraging him or my mother in this idiotic fantasy they've hatched. I don't know what's going on with them, because the last time I checked, neither one of them wanted anything to do with Moses Lake. But this needs to end now. I can promise you that any business they open in Moses Lake would be a bad investment. My brother has a history of starting things and not finishing them, and my mother is . . . Well, let's just say she's no different than she's always been."

Blaine Underhill shook his head, trying to clear the fog, apparently. "You're Heather Hampton." An eyebrow squeezed low over one brown eye.

"Yes." Enough already. This was getting a little irritating, really. "And I suppose you see my point . . . about the bank loans."

He scratched the back of his neck, looking down at the dock. "Ma'am, I can't discuss someone else's financial business with you."

"This is my *family* we're talking about." Why did he have to be so obtuse? "I have a right to know what's happening."

"You'll have to talk to your family about that." He lifted his palms in a way that said, *Hands off, sorry.*

I clenched and unclenched my fingers inside my sleeves, a half-dozen broken fingernails from yesterday's adventure pressing jagged teeth into my skin. "You're the one behind this supposed *competing offer,* aren't you? You're helping my brother."

"Your brother and I are friends," he answered cautiously.

"You know what? A *friend* doesn't help you do something stupid. A friend doesn't set you up for a fall, so the *friend* can make a profit."

He drew back as if I'd offended him. "That's what you think I'm doing?"

My thin thread of patience was unwinding at a frightening pace. My feet were ice cubes, the cold

131

had penetrated my jeans, and the damp wind off the lake had changed directions, striking me head on and slipping inside the collar of my oversized jacket. "I don't know *what* you're doing. That's why I asked." Pinpricks stabbed my left foot and traveled up my leg. An unsteady backward step sent a bootheel sinking between the icy boards, and the next thing I knew, I was staggering off balance, my hands flying in the air, the floppy sleeves flailing, slapping me, then swatting the railing, then some other solid object, which I realized was Blaine, because suddenly the jacket was tighter on one side. He used it to pull me upright and stop me from landing on the deck.

Once I was safely on my feet, he pulled his hands away as if he feared that keeping them there any longer might result in the loss of a finger or two. We stood for a moment at a stalemate. I felt my cold cheeks going hot.

"Look, all I can tell you is that you need to talk to your brother," he said finally.

Humiliated, angry, and realizing that I'd accomplished nothing other than tipping my hand and refreshing his memory of the uncoordinated, awkward girl he hadn't thought about since high school, I did the best thing I could think of.

I just turned around and walked away, taking care to avoid the gaps in the dock.

The water downstream ain't clear,
if the water upstream is muddy.
—Len Barnes, veteran, proud grandpa,
and Moses Lake resident

≈ Chapter 7 ≈

After having tried to reason with my mother, confronting the highly-irritating banker on the Waterbird dock, and finally attempting to get some straight answers from the uncs during our drive back to Harmony Shores, I decided to attack the problem at its source: my brother. Clay was at the center of this debacle and obviously had been for a while. The frustrating thing was that he would waste time involving himself in Moses Lake at all. Clay was brilliant, talented, personable —amazing, really. He was three times as book-smart as I could ever hope to be. He would be a great lawyer, if he would just buckle down and get through school.

I found my brother by the lakeshore, unstacking the canoes and setting them upside down on the lawn, apparently checking for condition. I remembered the uncs doing that in the past. My dad and I had helped a time or two when I was little. The uncs had engaged in heated discussions as to which canoes needed to be scrapped and which could go another season.

It was fairly cold to be working down by the shore. I'd zipped up my coat all the way to the neck, but Clay had on shorts and a rugby shirt, the sleeves pushed up over his elbows. Daubs of paint dotted his skin, and there were stencils lying on a long, skinny shipping crate that had probably held a casket at one time. Roger was sitting in a nearby canoe that was right side up, his tail brushing back and forth across the aluminum seat, as if he were anticipating an adventure. I was careful not to make eye contact, lest he decide to launch himself at me again.

"So what's all this?" I asked, stopping in front of Clay.

He glanced at me without standing up, his mouth quirking to one side. "I'm . . . painting . . . canoes?" He answered slowly, as in *Duh, what does it look like?* "And checking them out."

"I can see that. Why are you painting and checking the canoes?"

"Because they . . . need it?" He stated the obvious in the same intentionally clueless tone. Long curls of straw-colored hair, bleached on the ends by the sun, fell over his neck as he turned his attention to the boat again and began sanding some sort of patching material he'd applied over a hole.

After my three previous unsuccessful talks today, I willed myself not to tumble into an emotional exchange. I would remain calm this time, logical. Logic was on my side, after all. "You know what I'm asking, Clay. Why are you here, hanging around Moses Lake, getting Uncle Herb and Uncle Charley all stirred up?"

"They don't look like they're all stirred up." He shrugged toward the house, where the uncs were crossing a shady veranda that had served as an overflow location for many a funeral gathering over the years.

"Stop toying with me, Clay. This isn't a joke." My voice rose slightly, and I willed it back down. "You know what I'm asking, and you know why I came here."

In the canoe, Roger stopped wagging his tail, dropped his ears, and cast a worried look from me to Clay and back.

Clay continued with his work. "I figured you came to see us—have a little visit with the ol' fam."

I heard myself snort, an ugly, cynical sound I instantly felt guilty about, but Clay knew that we never got together just to visit anymore. Actually putting that into words seemed sad, though. "Come on, Clay, be realistic," I pleaded.

Clay chuckled and shook his head. "You know me better than that, Hessie."

The pet name, *Hessie,* pushed past my crossed arms and heavy coat, and plucked a heartstring. He'd given me that name, a combination of

135

Heather and *sissie,* when he was still toddling around in diapers. He thought his big sister hung the moon back then.

Looking up from the canoe, he smiled that precocious, frustrating, boyish smile that had always accompanied excuses about lost home-work, forgotten chores, and times when he neglected to let us know where he was going before he wandered off to play. The difficult thing about Clay was that he was always so darned cute and he earnestly never meant to do any harm. He never intended for me to end up staying awake until midnight, doing grade-school homework he'd forgotten about, or to leave me running up and down the lakeshore, scared to death that he'd drowned. It just happened, because he was such a dingbat. A sweet, hapless, adorable dingbat with a huge heart that got him into trouble time, after time, after time.

Despite all of that, I fought the urge to smile back at him. "Don't even try to get cute with me."

"I don't really have to try." He grinned again and went back to sanding the canoe. "Cute just oozes out of me. Can't help it." He lifted his green-tinted hands, helplessly.

I wondered if the adorable little country girl he was now courting—Blaine Underhill's cousin—had any idea that she was stepping into a mess way deeper than her cowboy boots. Clay's history with women wasn't any better than his history with college degrees or jobs. Some poor female, usually the older and more mature sort, was always taking him under her wing, and they sailed along blissfully for a little while—Clay was one of the most fun people I knew—until the wind changed and blew him onto another new path. He'd left a trail of broken hearts behind him over the years, but never intentionally.

"Can you please just cut it out? You know, when you go off on these kinds of schemes, other people end up getting hurt. People who can't just go flit off to work at some ski resort or run away with an earthquake relief team. The contracts for the land sale have to go through before the broker offer runs out *next week*. Uncle Herb and Uncle Charley need this money. It's not like either one of them has a pension plan. Everything they have is tied up in property. They don't have time to waste."

"Why?" Clay sat back on his heels, finally listening. He set the sandpaper on the boat and rested his green elbows on his hairy knees. "What's the rush? Don't you even want to take a little time to look around the old place before you throw everything on the auction block?"

His eyes met mine, his gaze a soft, sensitive green, the color so like Mom's. He looked at me the way she always did, seeming somehow disappointed in who I was. In truth, I guess, we were perpetually disappointed with one another, all of us. "Not at someone else's expense. Not if it causes problems for the rest of the family, Clay."

I *didn't* want to look around the place, though. I didn't want it to grow on me or speak to me, or call me back to the past. I wasn't seeking any reason to miss it when it was gone from my life. Perhaps that was an advantage I had over Clay. I wanted to be rid of all ties to Moses Lake and the things that happened here. How could he not feel the same way? How could he look at this place and not think of what happened to Dad? "The broker won't wait forever. That's the way brokers are. If one deal doesn't work out, they just invest elsewhere."

Roger sidled out of the canoe and moved timidly to Clay's side, his large, brown eyes rolling upward as he nudged under Clay's arm. The two of them seemed remarkably, painfully alike—two lost puppies, looking for something they never could quite find.

I didn't wait for my brother to come up with an answer, but pressed on instead, driving the point home. "I know it's hard for Uncle Herbert and Uncle Charley to let go. I know it's hard for them to move. But it's reality, Clay. It's what has to happen. There's no one here to take care of them."

"There can be." Clay tipped his chin up defensively, and I had the sense that he meant well. As usual, he wanted to come to the rescue, but he hadn't thought things through.

138

"Clay, come on. What about law school? How many times have you applied for an extension on your thesis? You're just lucky the school has been willing to work with you. And they did that because you're so incredibly, amazingly smart that they couldn't stand to see you drop out. But this is the real world. People's lives are involved. Mom doesn't need to be here, either. You know what a mess she was when we lived here. What if that happens again? What if she gets all . . . wrapped up in the past, and she starts to act the way she used to? This sale needs to go through."

"So they can take the land and . . . what . . . develop it or something?" His hand, which had been running through Roger's fur, paused, and for an instant we were locked like a pair of players in a chess match. "Stick some golf course or resort on it?"

"What gave you that idea?" I asked carefully.

"Amy works at the Proxica plant in Gnadenfeld. That place is a gossip mill. She hears things."

"Well, what exactly did she hear?" Disquiet crept up my spine, clingy and stealthy, like a tick looking for a place to burrow in. Amy worked for Proxica? What were the odds that Clay would just *happen* to be dating a girl with ties to Proxica?

Clay nodded, oblivious to the connections spinning forth in my mind. "She heard that the broker guy's been all over the county, looking at land.

Why does he want our place so bad? What's he going to do with it?"

I couldn't come right out and lie to my brother, but the confidentiality agreement wouldn't allow me to reveal the truth, either. "You know what, Clay, why does it matter? What matters is doing what's best for our family."

"Forget what's best for the town, I guess, huh?" He stood up, a paintbrush still dangling from one hand. "What's best for the area."

I took a step back, dumbstruck as much by the out-in-left-field remark as by the gravity in Clay's voice. "How do you know what's best for the area? You don't live here, Clay. And if you're looking at this as one of your save-the-world social causes, how about taking a glance at the poverty rate on the other side of the lake, up in Chinquapin Peaks? A broker thinking about development would be a good thing. Look at Gnadenfeld. Look at how much it's grown in the past sixteen years. There are real stores, restaurants, new housing. I checked out their Internet site the other day. The school has a great big gorgeous performing arts center and a new multi-sport stadium."

Clay squinted into the distance, toward Chinquapin Peaks and the river channel. "Yeah, look at Gnadenfeld." His voice held an undertone that I couldn't read. Maybe my brother was on some kind of back-to-nature kick, ready to throw himself in front of the bulldozers to keep

140

anything from changing around Moses Lake.

"You know what, Clay, if there's something you want to say to me, just say it." I squeezed my arms over my chest, shivering.

He seemed to think about that momentarily, and I had the sense that we were finally about to excavate some nuggets of truth.

The sound of a car rattling up to the house caught Clay's attention just as he was about to speak. Casting a curious glance toward the driveway, he moved his paintbrush to a coffee can and started up the hill. I followed, frustrated by the diversion. My irritation sharpened and took on shape when I recognized the dark head, tan barn jacket, and cowboy boots visible above and below the truck door as the driver exited the vehicle. *What is* he *doing here?*

By the time we made it to the driveway, with Roger cavorting happily back and forth in our path, Blaine Underhill was headed up the front walk. The uncs had come around to meet him, and my mother was poking her head out the front door, looking curious.

Everyone greeted Blaine warmly, as if he were a long lost friend rather than a potentially greedy, unprincipled robber-baron wannabe bent on ruining my family. Roger ran across his path and nearly sent him sprawling into the flower bed. Good for Roger. Blaine shook a finger at the dog playfully. "Yeah, I know where you've been,

141

buddy," he said, and Roger stopped frolicking, then sat down and cocked his head, his ears drooping and his tail scrubbing the ground tentatively.

"Anybody here expecting a FedEx?" Blaine asked, and from behind, I could just see the corner of a FedEx box between his sleeve and the side of his coat.

"Me," I answered. Blaine turned around on the path, seeming to realize for the first time that Clay and I were there. Cradled in his arm, he had the FedEx box—the one that would bring me my credit card, my ID, my iPhone, and my favorite red leather purse. Oh happy day! At least something was going right.

What was Blaine Underhill doing with my FedEx, anyway? "Thank goodness," I breathed. "I've been waiting for this all day." I reached for the box, and, oddly, Blaine pinched one corner between two fingers and lifted it from his arm, as if it weighed nothing. The box stretched accordion-style, slowly unfolding, until it was one long string of mangled red, white, and blue cardboard, dangling from his thumb and index finger.

"What in the . . ." I muttered, as family members moved in from all sides, the group of us gathering around the remnants of the box like monkeys in a zoo.

"Uh-oh," Clay muttered.

"Roger!" Mom gasped.

"I told ya that dog chews things," Uncle Charley added.

Uncle Herbert nodded in agreement. "I dig stuff up in the flower beds for months every time Roger comes here for a visit. Probably got that box right off the porch," he added in his dry, unassuming way.

"The delivery people aren't supposed to just leave packages on the porch, are they?" Clay retorted, by way of defending Roger's honor. "Isn't somebody supposed to sign for it?"

"Depends on how you send it," Uncle Herbert answered. "I've had whole boxes of supplies left out here, sometimes."

"I found it tangled in your gate out front," Blaine offered, studying Roger's free-form artwork. "Probably blew out to the road after the dog got done with it."

I just kept staring, unable at first to accept the magnitude of the disaster represented by the pile of cardboard. "The dog *ate* my FedEx?" I questioned numbly, touching the box, then pulling my hand away. It was slimy, covered with teeth marks and dog hair. "Where's my . . . my stuff?"

"He buries things," Uncle Herbert repeated.

From the corner of my eye, I saw Roger slinking away, disappearing behind a holly bush. "My checkbook and my wallet . . . my credit card . . . my iPhone . . . that was a Dolce & Gabbana purse.

A seven hundred dollar . . ." I'd treated myself to the Dolce last year, after Mel and I closed a design deal for a high-end sporting goods store. Granted, I'd bought the bag online at a discount, but still . . . I turned to my brother, vaguely aware that my eyes were flaring and my lip was curling. "Your dog ate my Dolce & Gabbana and my iPhone."

There was a rustling in the bushes, and a quick flash of blond fur between the holly leaves as Roger, quite wisely, exited the area.

My shock swirled into full-blown panic, picking up speed, sweeping away my orderly existence, breaking it into pieces of tornadic debris. "My life is in that iPhone."

Clay lifted his hands, indicating that this was hardly his fault. "Who knew the delivery guy was just gonna leave it on the porch?" He gave the front door a disgusted look. "He could've put it up high, at least. How's Roger supposed to know not to mess with it?"

Something primal and sibling-related happened to me at that point. With no prior warning and no way to control it, I reverted to being a thirteen-year-old, stuck in the backseat with my little brother while he sang Sesame Street songs over and over and over, just because he knew it would drive me crazy. "How's Roger supposed to . . . Are you *serious?*"

"All right, all right!" Mom stepped in. "For

heaven's sake, Heather, don't be melodramatic. Obviously, Clay didn't mean for the dog to chew up the box. Let's just get busy and find your things. Roger can't have taken them too far."

"I'll grab some garden tools," Uncle Charley offered enthusiastically.

"I'll get some gloves," Uncle Herbert added.

The rest of the day was like a family Easter egg hunt. We even had help. Blaine brought over a metal detector from the hardware store, and Amy showed up after work. We combed the gardens, the roadside ditch, and the lawn. In the front flower bed, thanks to the metal detector, we unearthed a lipstick tube and my key ring. The uncs even broke out flashlights as dusk set in, but it was getting colder by the minute, and everyone was shivering. Mom started coughing and sniffling, and Amy's hands turned blue despite the fact that Uncle Herb brought out coats and hats for all of us. The only one who wasn't cold was Roger. He was having a grand time running from person to person and acting as if he had no idea why we were pointing at the ground and trying to get him to show us where the bodies were buried.

Finally, we called off the search. Mom thought everyone should come in for cocoa, and Uncle Herb wanted to feed us and stoke up the fireplace. "We got plenty of casseroles," he pointed out. "And pie, too."

I hung back, leaning against a porch post and

mourning my iPhone, as the group filed into the house. I'd been here a whole day and accomplished absolutely nothing. I was no closer to getting the papers signed for the property deal than I'd been when I left Seattle. Meanwhile, back at the office, Mel probably wondered what was going on. Work-related calls and emails were undoubtedly stacking up in my inbox. By now, maybe Richard had called. I wouldn't even know it. I was stuck in a communications black hole, living the primitive life. No cell phone. No wireless Internet. Outsmarted by a golden retriever.

How much worse could the day possibly get?

I wanted to tell someone about it, to describe the family digging, and raking, and hoeing, the uncs shuffling around wearing baseball caps with built-in flashlights, searching underneath holly bushes, cheering each time they spotted something shiny buried in the leaves. We'd found several soda cans and a Rhode Island license plate from 1955, but nothing else that belonged to me. Roger had hidden his bounty well.

Even if I had found my phone, I didn't have anyone to share the story with, I realized as I stood staring at the yard. Trish would be busy getting her kids fed, bathed, and ready for bed. And Richard . . . Well, Richard probably hadn't called, to be honest. I could call Mel, but he would just want the work-related update, short and sweet.

Sighing, I let my head fall against the porch

post and tried to move my frozen toes inside my soggy boots. A cold, lonely, miserable feeling crept over me. I wanted to be someplace else, but I didn't know where. Not home, necessarily. At work, maybe, with my head in a project, hyper-focused to the point that time passed without my even noticing, without my wishing that things were different. That I was different.

"Food's in here." The voice startled me, and I realized that Blaine was in the doorway.

Swallowing the prickly, teary lump, I blinked the moisture from my eyes. I was being foolish, standing here feeling sorry for myself, feeling as if my life somehow didn't measure up. I had everything I'd ever wanted: a good job, a cool place to live, enough money for all the stuff I wanted—a Dolce & Gabbana handbag . . . Well, not anymore, but I could buy myself another one. "I'm waiting for my iPhone to ring," I said, without turning to look at him. "I'll track it down by the sound."

"The battery's dead by now." The hinges let out a long, loud complaint, and the door clicked shut. Blaine's footsteps crossed the porch, then stopped.

"Maybe not," I countered, but we'd trekked all over the yard using Clay's phone to call mine, to no avail. "My iPhone loves me. It'll find its way home."

Blaine chuckled, the sound warm and nice, his breath forming a cloud of vapor, so that I knew he was close behind me. He took a few more steps and stood at the top of the stairs, gazing out into the night. "You ever read any of those self-help books about people who are obsessed with their gadgets?" He glanced sideways, the hazy glow from the gaslights illuminating a grin.

"I don't have the Kindle app on my phone," I said blandly. "I'll have to look into that. Maybe then I can read the books."

He laughed again, rubbing a finger alongside his nose. "I think that would defeat the purpose."

"You could loan me your phone," I suggested. Clay, I noticed, had been careful to take his phone away from me after the yard search. No doubt, he was afraid I'd call Uncle Herbert's son. "I could check in at work and leave a message for my boss, at least."

"It's Friday," Blaine pointed out. "Tomorrow's the weekend."

"He works on the weekends, believe me." I felt Blaine's gaze on me. I had a feeling I knew what he was thinking—that I looked like the type who spent the weekends chained to a desk.

"Anyway, I don't have one with me." His comment seemed to come out of the blue.

"One what?"

"A cell phone."

An indignant cough pressed from my throat, and I gaped at him. Surely he was kidding, making an excuse not to provide me with a communications device. Maybe he really did spend his days out fishing. How could anyone do business without a cell phone, these days? "What kind of a banker doesn't carry a cell phone?"

"This kind." He leaned forward slightly to catch a glimpse of the moon. "When I'm off work, I'm all the way off. The mobile phone stays in the office."

I studied his profile, trying to decide whether he was putting one over on me. "That doesn't drive you crazy?" The few times I'd ever forgotten my phone while I was out on a date, it made me insane. All I could think about was the backlog that was probably building and the fact that if Mel called, wanting to set a meeting or to ask for some numbers, he wouldn't be happy I was out of touch.

"Having that stupid phone going off all the time would drive me crazy," Blaine countered. "If you don't have it with you, you don't have to answer it." He turned my way, his features hidden in shadow, except for the chin with the cute little cleft in it. "You oughta try it sometime."

"I shudder at your ridiculous logic," I countered, and he snort-laughed. I bit back a chuckle, reminding myself that no matter how much fun he might be to trade quips with, Blaine Underhill was not my friend.

"There's a time to work and a time to play." He coated the words with a melodramatic tone that

149

coaxed another laugh into my mouth. I coughed to cover it up.

"My iPhone is out there, cold and alone, and you give me platitudes."

"I know it's hard to continue on, considering what you've been through." He patted my shoulder, and instead of sympathy, I felt electricity. "But you have to remain strong for your iPhone."

I couldn't help it, I chuckled in spite of myself. "That's so not funny."

"You laughed."

"It was a courtesy laugh."

Letting his head fall forward, he grinned, the light catching his face. "How about some casserole? You need your strength."

I pushed off the porch post and took a step farther away from him, my mind clearing a bit. I couldn't help but wonder why he was on the porch buttering me up. Come to think of it, why had he spent his whole afternoon tromping around the lawn with my crazy family, searching for Roger's buried treasure? Surely a guy who looked like Blaine Underhill had better things to do, or perhaps a wife and kids out there, waiting for him to come home? Back in high school, there'd been no shortage of local girls looking to fill that role.

But as we started in the door, he followed amiably along, whistling under his breath, the sound filling the vestibule and the front hall, where in the past crowds of mourners had gathered, exchanging greetings in hushed tones as they filed into the chapel for final rites. Blaine's song echoed off the paneled walls as we passed through the commercial area, where a casket stand still stood under the bay windows in Uncle Herbert's office, and into the private quarters, which on this side of the house included a ladies' parlor, a dining room, a den for watching television, the sun porch, and the kitchen.

All of a sudden, I recognized Blaine's tune as a medley of common cell phone ring tones.

"Stop that," I snapped, glancing over my shoulder at him.

He only winked, then changed to another tune. Behind me, I heard his bootheels on the wooden floors, accompanied by the haunting melody of taps.

He that will learn to pray, let him go to sea.
—George Herbert
*(Left by Bradley Breal, ministry student
headed for the mission field)*

≈ Chapter 8 ≈

In the morning I slept late, and by the time I woke, everyone—including Roger—had vacated the premises. On the kitchen counter of the main house, I found a vague note from my mother saying that she and the uncs had gone to Waco to pick up restaurant supplies for Catfish Charley's and they wouldn't be back until sometime later in the day. There was no explanation as to where Clay and Roger were, but after a sweep of the personal quarters, I pretty much concluded that I was on my own. No doubt the family had decided to avoid me as a way of putting off further conversation about signing the real-estate papers.

The note in the kitchen had been weighted down with the old milk-glass canister that had always served as Uncle Herbert's repository for loose change and an occasional crumpled dollar bill. When we'd moved into the gardener's cottage after my father's death and money was tight, five- and ten-dollar bills had started appearing there— Uncle Herbert's way of quietly making sure

Clay and I had what we needed for lunches and groceries. Aunt Esther would've had a fit if she'd known he was funneling funds to us. She felt that my mother needed to get out of bed and get a job, or at least work cleaning Harmony House and cooking meals along with the housekeeper.

Looking at the milk-glass canister now, I remembered Ruth quietly taking money from the jar and tucking it into my palm. Sometimes I suspected that she put cash from her house-keeping salary in there, too. Mostly, I liked Ruth because no matter how angry, depressed, uncommunicative, or withdrawn I was when I came home from school, she had oatmeal-chocolate-chip cookies, or Mennonite specialties like zwieback double buns, waiting. Ruth repaired a lot of damage that way, all while washing dishes and barely raising an eyebrow. She was exactly what I needed: someone who did not feel the need to turn me into a perfect Southern lady. She quietly shook her head when I was forced to sit in with Aunt Esther's bridge-club crowd—the theory being that social engagements and a change of wardrobe would cure whatever was wrong with me.

No matter how critical the ladies were in the parlor, or how much Aunt Esther didn't appreciate my lack of cooperation, Ruth extended grace to me. She was willing to love the little mess that I was, rather than trying to instruct, guide, and fix me. Whenever I was finally able to escape from the parlor, I knew I'd find her in the kitchen, a baker's apron protecting her modest flowered dress, her hair neatly plaited beneath a scarf-like head covering, her hands busy at work.

I wished Uncle Herbert were home, so I could ask him whatever happened to Ruth. She'd sent notes and care packages for a while after I'd headed off to college, but I'd moved after my freshman year in the dorm and probably never sent her the new address. Moses Lake had seemed a million miles away by then, and I wanted it to be. As much as I adored Ruth, it was easier to just leave the past behind.

Now I felt the past closing in on me again, voices whispering in the house, boards creaking and settling, a branch scratching the windows on the sun porch, a groaning noise from the vicinity of the front parlor and Uncle Herbert's office, as if someone were leaning back in his old leather office chair. A bird twittered outside, and the sharp, uneven sound reminded me of the ladies in Aunt Esther's gossip circle. I had a sense of not being alone in the house.

A shiver ran across my shoulders, convincing me that the prudent thing to do would be to borrow a few dollars from the canister, grab my laptop from the cottage, and head to the one place I'd seen in town that advertised an Internet hot spot—the combination convenience store, pizzeria, and Chinese food hut on the edge of town. It was a nice enough day for a walk, and considering that I hadn't officially checked in at the office since I left, Mel was undoubtedly not a happy camper. Getting in contact via email and offering a few details about the lost phone would be a good way to buffer things a bit. I could spend some time taking care of whatever I could handle long-distance and lighten next week's backlog of work.

It seemed like a good plan . . . until I actually got to the Chinese convenience store and opened my email. Backlog didn't even begin to describe what I found. Mel was in a tailspin because Itega wanted some tweaks to the design and corresponding cost analyses, and they wanted them now. If it weren't for the fact that it would have taken all day for me to fly home from Moses Lake, Mel would have insisted I come back right then. He wasn't interested in hearing about lost cell phones or anything else happening in Texas. He'd called our project crew in to work, even though it was Saturday.

I spent the rest of the day talking with various team members via Skype, working like a mad-woman on my laptop, transferring spread-sheets and AutoCAD files back and forth, downing egg drop soup and crab rangoons, and breaking open fortune cookies. Meanwhile, the owners of the convenience store tried to corral the gaggle of

155

kids who were obviously accustomed to playing in the restaurant when no one was around. On some level, I knew I was imposing, but I was in work mode. The world and everyone in it was outside the bubble.

By the time we put the design changes to bed, I was exhausted both mentally and physically, my eyes were blurry and grainy, and the poor people who owned the convenience store were sweeping floors and washing pans, glancing my way and hoping I would get the hint. I thanked them profusely and made a mental note to drop by with a huge tip when I had funds of my own again. The purchase of a pack of super migraine-killing headache powders seemed like the best way to spend the rest of my canister money, for now. A massive tension headache was pounding in my brain, and all I wanted to do was find someplace quiet to lie down. I didn't even bother to see who was at the house when I returned to Harmony Shores; I just staggered to the gardener's cottage, took my headache medicine, fell across the bed, and closed my eyes.

Sometime after dark I snuggled under the quilt, and on Sunday morning, I woke early, with my mind squarely back in Moses Lake. Lying in bed, I made plans to dig up gardens until I'd either razed the property or unearthed my cell phone and wallet. I'd been at Harmony Shores for two days now, and I had accomplished exactly nothing—and in the meantime, I'd almost been AWOL during an important crunch time at the office. Somehow, I had to bring the Moses Lake issue to a satisfying conclusion and get back to my real life.

I'd tried applying logic and reason with Mother, Clay, the uncs, and the banker responsible for encouraging my brother's flight of fancy. Blaine Underhill actually seemed like kind of a decent guy. He and my family were clearly on friendly terms, but how could he, as a financial professional and president of his father's bank, possibly condone my brother's plan, or my mother's? Was Blaine such a nice guy that he just didn't have the heart to point out the truth to my family?

Or was he a heartless small-town shyster?

The question chased away the morning drowsiness. This good ol' hometown boy, help-a-buddy-out thing of Blaine's had to be a façade, didn't it? You couldn't run a bank, even a little country bank, and be a pushover. Blaine was out to make money—out to win. He was, after all, the guy who'd mowed over players twice his size on the football field and given himself several concussions, because he had to win. What were the odds that he'd suddenly turned into a teddy bear? Not very good.

At the same time, another image swirled just overhead—tantalizing, like the sweet aroma of an apple-pie-scented candle. I remembered the guy who made me laugh on the porch as I mourned my iPhone, his smile flashing in the dim light, his eyes a deep, dark liquid. His laughter brushed across my ear, sending a prickle over my skin.

"All right, that's it." Tossing the covers aside, I swung my legs around and hit the ground running—literally. The floorboards were like ice again. If I stayed in the cottage any longer, I'd have to bring some firewood down from the woodpile at the main house. My teeth were chattering by the time I got to the bathroom, where I turned on the hot water and hopped from one foot to the other until finally the small space fogged up. My morning routine was rushed and uncomfortable, with little slices of February air sifting through the floorboards and pressing past the gaps around the narrow wood-paned window. My last pair of jeans and a blue sweater helped to cut the chill, and toasting myself with the hairdryer felt like heaven. While I was basking, I plugged the gaps around the window with crispy tissues from an ancient, yellowed box.

I finger-brushed wavy auburn curls and proceeded to the door, where my coat and my dirty, bedraggled, perpetually damp suede boots were like blocks of ice. I pulled the boots on and curled my toes inside, shivering as I started out the door and hoping that both the coffee and the heat were on up at the big house. A trio of cardinals flitted away, surprised by my passing, and a squirrel darted from the lawn, skittering up the hill ahead of me to climb an ancient live oak tree.

A flash of movement near the shore stopped me halfway across the lawn, and I turned, expecting to see Clay down there again. Instead, a tall, slim figure with dark, curly hair was just disappearing behind the corner of the barn. Blaine Underhill? What was he doing here so early in the morning . . . on Sunday? In fact, what was he doing, prowling around our barn at all?

Pulling my coat tighter around myself, I hurried back across the yard and slipped down the hill, staying close to the tree line on the way to the massive weathered-wood-and-limestone barn. When we'd lived at Harmony Shores, the barn had been my hiding place, my private cathedral. Among the narrow streams of sunlight and shade, I could lie on my back and listen to the coo of doves nesting in the rafters and pretend that the upside-down world outside didn't exist. I felt close to my father there, as if he might suddenly walk through the door, once again a hapless teenager bringing hay to be stored for the winter.

The barn wasn't even in use anymore. When we'd talked about the real-estate deal, Uncle Herbert had pointed out that any new owners would have to make some decisions about either repairing the barn or tearing it down. Why would

Blaine Underhill be poking around the place when the morning was still frosty and cool, the winter sun just casting pink light over the hills of Chinquapin Peaks?

A hinge squealed as I reached the corner of the barn and peered through the crust of dirt and paint spatters on a wavy, plate-glass window in what had once been the tack room. Beyond the tack room doorway, Blaine was a backlit shadow in the cavernous barn aisle. Resting his hands on his hips, he looked up at the ceiling, turned in a slow circle, walked out of view.

I moved down the barn wall, peeking through knotholes and cracks in the weathered boards, trying to locate him again. Where was he? What was he doing?

A faint, metallic sound rang out—the ping of gravel bouncing off one of the canoes that Clay had left lying around. I tiptoed to the corner and peered around it but couldn't see anything. Frost-covered grass crunched under my feet once, twice, three times, until I spotted Blaine. Rubbing his chin, he walked around the canoe, tipped it to one side, looked under it. The banker was dressed in sweats this morning—in a horrible orange color, actually—along with a ball cap and running shoes. Apparently, he was out jogging. Jogging, and investigating my uncle's canoes. . . .

Just as I was about to duck behind the barn again, Roger barked from somewhere in the woods. Blaine looked up, and I pretended not to have been hiding there, stalking him. "Oh, I . . . uhhh . . . didn't know anyone was down here."

He seemed unsurprised by my presence and not the least bit worried to have been discovered prowling the property. "Mornin'," he said, and smiled like we were old friends. Apparently, the family phone hunt and casserole feed had convinced Blaine that he and I were on amicable terms. That was probably just as well. Best not to let him know I was trying to figure him out.

"Good morning." I returned the smile. "Kind of early for a walk."

He nodded toward the water, a deep blue-gray in the morning light, and as slick as glass. A flock of mallards had landed near the shore to paddle aimlessly about, oblivious to the icy chill rising off the surface. "I like to get out when it's still quiet, before there's anyone on the water. Kind of nice just to look at it the way God made it."

"It's a man-made lake," I pointed out, and he smirked sideways at me.

"Well, now, that's a cynical observation." He licked his lips, worried one side between his teeth, like he was trying to make sense of me. That made two of us. I was studying him, as well. He seemed to know that but appeared comfortable with it, perhaps because we were on his turf. This was *his* town, after all. It always had been.

"Sorry." The apology was hollow, really.

There's no point apologizing for who you are. "It's my nature."

"To be cynical?" He raised a brow.

"Analytical," I rephrased. *Analytical* sounded better. Maybe *practical* was really the right word. "I imagine that bankers are analytical, too." *They probably don't show up at someone's place first thing on a frosty morning for no reason—just happening by.*

He cocked his head to one side, his thick, dark lashes narrowing slightly, casting a shadow over his brown eyes, making them earthy and warm, the kind of eyes that pull you closer. "That's not how I remember you."

A little puff of laughter pushed past my lips—a reflex action, like jerking a hand up to block an incoming object before it hits you. "Please. Like you remember me."

He blinked, appearing surprised. "You're making me feel old. There were only seventy-four in our graduating class, and it hasn't been all that long."

"Since high school? Yes it has." *And thank goodness for that.* "I hardly remember anything about the year here." Such a lie. Does anybody ever really forget high school? People like Blaine probably wanted to remember. He probably stood around at the first football game every year, recounting the glory days. Why wouldn't he? He and his friends were always into some kind of fun—making dates for the school dance, jumping off the rocks at the Scissortail, paddling out to the island beneath Eagle Eye Bridge, or having parties in the secluded park on Blue Moon Bay.

"Huh," he murmured contemplatively. "Well, those were some pretty bad times for your family. Guess it makes sense that it'd all be a blur." His eyes caught mine empathically, and I felt an odd little tug. *Those were some pretty bad times for your family.* What I wouldn't have given for someone, for him, to have said those words, made that observation during the horrible months after my father's death. How many times had I walked the halls dreaming that one of those people who looked right through me would suddenly see me, suddenly smile and offer friendship when I so desperately needed it?

Just like all the rest of them, Blaine never had. It was silly for me to still be dwelling on that all these years later, sort of pathetic, even. Old wounds are the slowest to heal.

"So, how *do* you remember me, then?" The words were out of my mouth before I had time to think about them, and a blush tainted my cheeks. What a stupid thing to ask.

He looked me over, as if he were trying to decide how far toward honesty he should go.

Lie to me, I thought. *I really don't want to know the truth.* Something about this place took me

163

right back to high school, turned me into that insecure, lost little girl again.

He pressed a knuckle to his bottom lip. I watched it stroke back and forth while the suspense inside me built to a ridiculous degree. Somewhere outside the bubble of unfinished high-school business, there was the vague realization that my toes were freezing and the wind was slicing through my jeans as if they were curtain sheers. The smart thing would be to leave him to whatever he was doing and head to the main house for breakfast. Blaine Underhill wasn't going to reveal any of his secrets. Not this easily.

But for some reason, I stood there waiting for his answer, rooted to the spot, like a doofus.

"Artistic. Quiet. Little bit of a temper." He assessed, letting his hand drop and bracing it on the bottom of his hooded sweatshirt. His lips spread slowly into a grin. "Guess things have changed a little. You're not quiet anymore."

I couldn't quite decide how to react. He had been generous enough to leave out *dorky, intro-verted, generally morose,* and *completely lacking in fashion sense.* "Meaning I'm still artistic, with a bad temper?"

"Well, Clay tells me that you're an architect. Creative stuff." He lifted a hand, waving it over the grounds as if to display them as Exhibit One. "And on the temper front . . . Well, you'll notice that Roger is still in hiding after the other night."

164

"I didn't *do* anything to Roger," I countered, but the words ended in a protest laugh. I could imagine the picture I'd made, keeping all of the family out in the dark, muttering idle threats against Clay's gooberheaded dog.

"But you wanted to."

"Roger and I have a love-hate thing. He loves to destroy my stuff, and I hate that." I shifted from one foot to the other in an exaggerated display of petulance, and tiny needles stabbed my frozen toes. I sucked in air, then did a full-body shiver, shaking the numb foot in the air. Despite the chill, I didn't excuse myself and head to the house.

"Cold?" Blaine stated the obvious.

"Just my feet." Which wasn't really true. I hadn't ever gotten warm this morning. "I'm staying in the cottage, and that place is polar in the mornings. There's no propane in the propane tank, and no firewood for the wood stove. I keep forgetting to bring some down from the big house during the day, and I'm *not* going out to the woodpile at night." I remembered that duty from our time in the cottage. Mom would let the fire die during the day, and it was freezing when we came home in the afternoons. I'd find her lying in bed, ashen-faced and hollow-eyed under a mound of quilts, oblivious to it all. Clay was afraid to go to the woodpile when dusk was settling over the tree line, so the duty always fell to me.

"Your shoes are wet," Blaine observed, motioning to the soggy suede boots.

"I know."

"Kind of cold for wet shoes." He pointed at the boots again. "Suede isn't too good around the lake. Too damp here in the winter, soaks through."

I curled my toes to warm them. "It's all I have with me. I wasn't planning to be here long."

With a backward step, he shrugged toward the lake. "C'mon."

"Yeah, I don't think swimming will help," I joked, but part of me was oddly in favor of following along with whatever Blaine Underhill had in mind.

A lopsided smirk indicated that, of all things, he found me funny. Go figure. "I'll open Dad's hardware store for you. We can walk over the back way."

I paused to consider the offer. Other than the dollar store, the hardware store was the only place in town that sold shoes. A nice pair of combat boots —something waterproof and fleece lined—would be pretty close to heaven right now. I might even sleep in them. I was so tired of having frozen feet.

Come to think of it, the hardware store sold heaters, too. A little electric heater would go a long way toward remedying the temperature problem in the cottage. At the rate things were going with getting Mom to agree to sign the land paperwork, I might be in town a few more days.

Some woodsy garb was definitely needed. But . . . "I don't have any money. I'd write you a check, but the dog ate my checkbook."

"I've heard that excuse before." He laughed again. "You can put it on account. I know where to find you." He started walking backwards toward the old path that led through the woods, past the park behind the church, and across an ancient rope bridge to the back of the hardware store. I remembered that path.

The logical part of my mind conjured up reasons to say no. *You don't want to owe him anything. What are his motives here, anyway? You still don't know why he was skulking around the barn this early in the morning.*

No telling what shape that rope bridge is in by now. . . .

On the flip side, Blaine Underhill was being nice to me. There's something irresistibly charming about having the attention of the guy you dreamed about in high school. Besides, I could imagine how displeased his stepmother would be when she arrived to open the hardware store tomorrow morning and found a big, fat charge with my name on it. I would send her a check as soon as I got back to Seattle, of course, but in the meantime there would be some guilty pleasure in knowing she would hate the idea of Blaine letting me help myself. Whenever I went into the hardware store after my dad died, she'd always stalked me like I might steal something.

"All right. Thanks." Perhaps I could use this opportunity to ferret out a few more of Blaine's secrets. "So why were you down by Uncle Herbert's barn so early?" *Casing the place for future repossession? Counting the canoes, perhaps? Major monetary value there. Not.*

He slowed, waiting for me to waddle up beside him on my ice-block feet, before we started along the shore. "Crossed my mind that we hadn't looked in the old barn last night, when we were hunting for your stuff. Your uncle's old dog, Sadie, used to steal eggs from the chicken coop across the road and bury them in the center aisle. I stacked hay in that barn one summer when I was fourteen, and, man, we busted some rotten eggs in there."

"Eeewww." I felt like such a cynic. Blaine Underhill had gotten up this morning and walked all the way over here to look for my stuff? The idea was bright and alluring, like a glint of sunlight on water, as we moved from the lake-shore into the murky shadows of live oaks and winter-bare pecans. "I didn't know you'd ever worked for my uncles."

"Oh, sure, off and on," he said, as we walked along the old wagon trail, leaves crunching underfoot, the fog off the lake muting every sound. "I think just about every kid in town did at one time or another. I was in shape for football that fall, I'll tell you."

"Was there ever a fall when you weren't in shape for football?" I joked, then realized it sounded like gushy schoolgirl admiration. "I mean, I always figured you jocks spent all summer waiting for the season to start."

The Underhills practically had stadium parking with their names on it. Mama B's bearcat roar was legendary, and even Blaine's normally dignified stepmother was an insane sports mom. She and my dad had been homecoming king and queen together, back in the day—the couple most likely to marry and produce little football stars.

Blaine reached down to toss a fallen branch off the trail. "Yeah, not so much. Football wasn't really my thing."

"Oh, come on." I rolled a who-do-you-think-you're-kidding look his way. "You were the 'pride of Moses Lake.' " My tone mimicked old Hack, the local volunteer fire chief, who'd doubled as football announcer since back when my dad was in school. My senior year, all the talk was about whether Blaine would get a football scholarship. Shortly after we'd come to town, his stepmother had cornered my father at the church door and prattled on endlessly about Blaine's accomplishments. My father probably felt like an idiot, standing there with his own progeny, me, in a Van Halen T-shirt, my hair dyed stark black with the garish red streak I'd included as a particularly potent protest over the Moses Lake move.

"You get to a point where you figure out some things are more everyone else's idea than your own," Blaine said, his gaze turned upward. A whippoorwill was calling somewhere in the trees.

The conversation lulled as we walked through the picnic grounds behind the church, then slipped into the little ravine beyond it and crossed a new wooden bridge where the old rope structure had been. I found myself watching Blaine, contemplating him, wondering if he could really be so different from the image I'd always held in my mind. "So, why did you quit playing football?"

A shrug indicated that it didn't matter now. "By my second year in college, I knew I wasn't really fast or big enough for pro ball. The funny thing was, I didn't feel all that disappointed about it. I was tired of waking up flat on my back on the football field, not knowing where I was. Like I said, it was never really my thing."

I looked over at him to make sure he really was Blaine Underhill. Not that we'd ever been friends, or anything, but I had known him from afar. He'd certainly given the appearance of eating, living, sleeping, and breathing football. "Why did you play all those years, then?"

A sideways glance flicked my way, catching my gaze. I fell in for a minute, my mind slipping into the past as we climbed the hill to the hardware store. "I thought I needed to," he answered, dismissively. "The trouble with expectations is that you feel like you have to live up to them."

Breaking the link between us, I looked at the ground, picking my footing as we stepped over a retaining wall and reached the stairs at the back of the limestone hardware building. I led, and he followed me up, keys jingling as he fished them from his pocket.

"You know, I always admired that about you," he said, leaning around me to unlock the door. For a moment, I was conscious of his nearness, of his breath ruffling the hair by my ear. "You didn't seem like you cared what anybody thought."

"Me?" A gush of warm air slid over me, pulling me inside the store. I wanted to turn and look at Blaine, to see what sort of expression went along with those words. But I didn't. A flush crept over my cheeks, and I felt the need to deflect his compliment with a joke. "Come on. Admit it. You really didn't even know who I was." I added a sardonic cough, resorting to what Trish would have referred to as a *defense mechanism,* using self-deprecating humor to keep people at a distance.

"I knew who you were." He was close behind me again, the two of us hemmed in by piles of boxes. Against the stillness of the building as the door fell closed, his voice was soft, intimate. I tried to brush aside the ridiculous desire to let down my guard. The temptation was almost overwhelming. *Grow a spine, already, Heather.*

You're here to do a job, a voice in my head insisted.

Unzipping my coat, I moved from the back hallway into the main part of the store, where things were less crowded. If it hadn't been for the fact that Blaine's wicked stepmother was always in it, this would have been one of my favorite buildings in town. Two stories, with cavernous ceilings, beautiful oak moldings and fixtures, and an ancient Otis freight elevator that, as far as I knew, still worked, the building whispered of the craftsmanship of early German settlers. They'd taken the time to create perfect dovetailing on the wall cabinets that held a myriad of tiny drawers filled with nuts, bolts, and plumbing supplies. In the center of the room, the open rotunda glowed with light from the tall, arched windows on the front wall. Moving into the warmth of it, I tipped back my head and gazed upward into the waterfall of light slipping through the ornate banisters.

I remembered standing in this very spot with my father, long before I was old enough to understand why the woman behind the counter always snorted and headed for the stock room when we came in. I was holding my father's hand, watching the shadows play over the well-worn wooden shelves, waiting for Dad to take me on the elevator. I was certain that he would. He knew all of the building's secrets. He'd worked there as a teenager.

I wasn't aware then that, until my mother swept through town one summer, my dad had been engaged to one of the girls he worked with. He was going to marry her as soon as he graduated from college, but my mother stole him away from his hometown sweetheart, Claire Anne, and from the rest of the town. A few years later, my father's jilted fiancée had married Blaine's father, the recently-widowed owner of the hardware store, the bank, and a huge ranch outside town. Mr. Underhill was twelve years Claire Anne's senior, but he had more money than my father could ever hope to accumulate.

"Are the clothes and shoes still upstairs?" Emotion cracked my voice, and I cleared my throat, wiggling out of my coat. I felt Blaine's hand grasping the hood, helping me slip free. His fingers brushed the wispy hair on the back of my neck and sent an electric tingle down my back. I stiffened against it.

The coat swished softly as he tossed it over the long, glass-front counter along the west wall. "Same as always," he said, and I had the sense that he was talking about me, rather than the store. For a moment, I wanted to be *not* the same, not the reserved, walled-off girl he expected. I couldn't do that, of course. I had to remember why I was here. Business. Just business. And a pair of shoes.

I started up the stairs, watching from the corner of my eye as he set his keys on the counter, slipped off his coat and laid it over mine, then followed. Beneath the low, eight-foot ceilings of the upper balcony, the space felt cozy, steeped in languid morning light.

"What'll it be?" He swept a hand toward the floor-to-ceiling shelves, crowded with shoe boxes, some of which looked to have been there since slightly after the turn of the century. "We got your steel toes, your stacked heels, your Mary Janes, flip-flops, wool socks, boat shoes, whites, browns, and blues. What's your pleasure?"

My mind jumped back in time again. I remembered Blaine's grandfather repeating the same singsong sales pitch when my father had brought me in for a pair of pink wading shoes with little cartoon fish on the toes. Looking up at Blaine now, I could see a bit of his grandfather in him. They had the same warm, brown eyes and slightly lopsided smile. What would it be like to have your present and your past so closely interwoven, a tapestry in which threads didn't begin or end but meshed so completely that there was no way to know where one ended and another began? Clay and I never had ties to anyone or anywhere. There were the issues between Dad's family and my mother, and Mom's mother and father were divorced and remarried; the family an odd mishmash.

I was jealous of Blaine. In truth, it wasn't the first time.

He grabbed a box from an upper shelf, blew off the dust, and pulled out a cowboy boot that must have been there since the days of *Hee Haw*. It had a silver eagle emblazoned in the vamp, and a ghastly long, pointed toe. "How 'bout some cricket killers?" He fanned a brow and gave the one-sided grin of a snake-oil salesman. "I can get you a discount. These are closeouts."

"From what year?" A chuckle-snort pressed from me. Very unladylike. I slapped a hand over my nose.

Blaine studied the boot, straight, brown brows drawing together in the center. "Not sure. Give 'em a try. They might grow on you."

"That's what I'm afraid of."

He sighed, indicating that I was difficult to please. I remembered now why every girl in high-school chemistry class had been gaga over him. He was charmingly goofy up close. His attention was like a flame you couldn't help wanting to stare into. "Come on, live a little," he urged, extending the boots my way. "When are you ever gonna get the chance to slip your feet into fine footwear like this again?"

"This side of the Grand Ole Opry, you mean?" Even as I said it, I was reaching for the boots, consumed with the odd notion that if I didn't put them on, I'd be sealing my fate as a mindless gerbil running endlessly on the same, boring wheel—missing some weird, once-in-a-lifetime

175

opportunity: The chance to wear silver cricket-killer cowboy boots on the second story of a hardware store.

Kicking off my bedraggled footwear, I pulled on the garish boots, stood up, and walked the length of the balcony, feeling like Dolly Parton—on the lower half, anyway.

Blaine crossed his arms, rubbing his chin appraisingly. "They've got . . . attitude."

I rolled a look at him, then leaned over to observe the boots.

"You'd be the only one in Seattle with a pair," he urged. "You could start a whole new trend."

"Yeah . . . tempting. But maybe something a little less . . . silver." It occurred to me that he'd mentioned Seattle. How would he know that, unless he and Clay had been talking about me?

The thought was strange. I wasn't sure whether to embrace it or be afraid of it.

He pulled out a pair of tall mud boots, the black rubber kind the Mennonites used in the mucky corrals around their dairy farms and in the Proxica poultry barns over in Gnadenfeld. I remembered borrowing similar boots when Clay and I went home with Ruth and visited her family's dairy. We did that occasionally when Aunt Esther was planning social events at Harmony House and didn't want us in the way. "Tempting . . . but . . . no. I remember those things from my short stint as a cow milker."

176

"You were a milkmaid?" Blaine's look of interest followed me as he leaned against the shelf.

I sat down on the bench to release the silver Dolly boots into the wild again and told him the story of my one and only attempt at helping the Mennonite kids with milking chores. Ruth and her husband lived a few miles away on a Proxica poultry farm, but they maintained an interest in the dairy, and Clay loved to visit there. My ill-fated milking career had ended when I sucked cow parts and my own ponytail into the vacuum end of a milking machine. The cow kicked, I panicked, and things went downhill from there. I was saved by a brawny Mennonite boy who was somehow related to Ruth. It was embarrassing. He was only seven.

Blaine laughed goodnaturedly at the end of the story, and we continued perusing the footwear. Finally, I selected a pair of hiking boots, along with some warm wool socks, two pairs of jeans, and a couple of fleecy Moses Lake sweatshirts from the stack near the counter. The only thing I didn't score was a new electric heater. They were out.

As Blaine wrote up my charges, I caught myself thinking it really was too bad that he was potentially in a position to ruin my family financially. He was kind of likable, otherwise. Fun.

But you don't get to the senior manager stage by being drifty-minded. I knew how to stay focused on a goal, how to tune out distractions like Facebook, office chatter, funny email videos of dogs who could dance the cha-cha while wearing ruffled skirts and sunglasses . . . cute guys who want to lure you in, so you won't wonder why they're cultivating your family's good graces.

He offered to walk me back to the cottage after we finished shopping. I told him I was fine. I knew the trail well enough. I used to walk it all the time, back in the day.

On the way back to Uncle Herbert's, my feet warm inside the new hiking boots, the bedraggled fashion footwear and a sack of new clothing swinging at my side, I tried to keep my mind out of the past. I thought, instead, of the silver boots. Maybe I'd go back and buy them tomorrow—well, not tomorrow, because, come to think of it, the hardware store was always closed on Mondays. Trish would think the boots were a riot. I could keep them in my apartment as a conversation piece. A memento from my unplanned detour to Moses Lake.

Then again, I wouldn't be around when the hardware store opened on Tuesday. I wasn't supposed to be, anyway. Somehow, I had to wrap up this mess and get back to work before Mel went postal and my best chance at leading a design project slipped through my fingers. I couldn't let myself forget everything I had to lose if this project fell apart.

I returned to Uncle Herbert's house with that thought in mind, determined to get the whole family into one room so we could get to the bottom of this mess and hash it out. Surely, with enough injections of reason, everyone would have to wake up to reality. A nice, quiet Sunday morning would be the perfect time to do that.

But the house was anything but quiet when I went in. Mom was in Uncle Herbert's kitchen, cleaning up from breakfast and, oddly enough, wearing a dress, which my mother rarely did. The rest of the family was bustling around upstairs. I heard doors opening and closing, feet moving, pipes rattling. Mom quickly informed me that I'd better hurry up, if I wanted to ride to church with the family.

She made the suggestion without missing a beat, and after I reeled my chin off the floor, I said, "Since when do you get up on Sunday morning and go to church?" That was rude, of course, but I couldn't help feeling that they were all playing some sort of game, with me as the patsy. Maybe they thought that by putting on a show they could confuse me into giving up and going home.

Aside from the fact that my mother getting dressed for church on Sunday morning was about as believable as a hippo in toe shoes, I found it slightly offensive that she would choose this particular means of creating shock value. I'd always prided myself on the fact that my occasional church attendance—holidays mostly, with Trish at a historic downtown church, where the architecture of the building was in equal parts inspiring and distracting—was to some degree better than my mother's flavor-of-the-month spiritual existentialism. At least I knew what I believed, in the official sense. Most of the time, Sunday morning found me heading for the office to either meet Mel and prep for a presentation, or get in a little extra time, shoveling at a workload that piled on as fast as I could dig it out.

Mom had the nerve to give me a *you're crazy* look and say, "Well, both of the uncs are deacons, and now Clay and I are going into business here. How would it look if we sat home on Sunday mornings?"

I was speechless again. Twice in one conversation. The fun, relaxed feeling that had bloomed during my footwear safari quickly faded.

"Besides," she added, and I sensed that she was coming in for the kill—putting my battered and bleeding sanity out of its misery. "I feel close to your father there."

The blood drained from my cheeks, flowing downward through my body, abandoning me to a hollow numbness. My mother had been through more boyfriends and live-ins over the years than I could count. How dare she stand there, acting like she'd been pining for my father all that time, particularly considering what I'd seen her doing right before he died. I opened my mouth to say something venomous, then closed it, opened it again.

Mother took advantage of the conversational lull. "And this afternoon, we're driving over to Gnadenfeld. It's Ruth's birthday, and they're having a little get-together for her at the dairy. She lives with one of her nieces now. You know that her husband passed away several years ago, and she's been diagnosed with cancer, right? She can't live on her own anymore."

My head swirled. I leaned against the door frame, my vision of Ruth shifting. All this time, I'd been imagining her still dividing her time between the Proxica poultry farm she ran with her husband, and the family dairy. I knew she'd quit working for Uncle Herbert shortly after I went away to college. She'd told me about it in one of the letters my freshman year of college. Her husband was experiencing some health problems, and she was needed at home. "Ruth has cancer? Is it bad?"

Mom nodded, the first honest look of the morning passing between us. "Yes, it is. Which is reason enough to go get ready for church, right?"

"I don't have anything to wear." It was a stupid thing to say, but I was still stunned, just babbling out words with no real meaning.

"Oh, anything will do," Mom insisted. "Just go get ready. Ruth will want to see you, especially considering the shape she's in."

I quit the kitchen and left her there. Grabbing my things in the utility room, I went out the back door and walked down the hill. The bracing air pulled tears from my eyes until I found myself inside the cottage, looking at my carry-on bag, my new clothes, my laundry pile. I had the urge to throw everything into the suitcase, force the zipper around it, and leave for the airport, to return to a world that was only big enough for one. A world where nothing else, especially anything that happened in Moses Lake, could affect me.

I dressed for church instead, and we headed off in one of the funeral sedans, Mom driving, Uncle Herbert in the passenger seat, and me sandwiched between Clay and Uncle Charley in the back. Clay and Uncle Charley talked about fishing. I thought about Ruth.

Amy was waiting on the small porch outside the church when we arrived. She walked in with us, and I heard whispers around the room. Blaine Underhill's stepmother stiffened in her seat, pretending not to see us sliding into the row across the aisle. I noticed Blaine at the far end of the Underhill pew. A blonde was whispering in his ear, tapping him on the shoulder. I couldn't decide, from this angle, if I remembered her from high school or not.

Reverend Hay took the pulpit and began the announcements by pointing out his new fiancée, Bonnie, in the front. The congregation twittered approvingly. I was glad to have their attention diverted from us, but it quickly returned in the form of covert looks, whispers, little notes jotted in the corners of bulletins, a nudge here or there.

What are they doing here? The question was like smoke in the room, making it difficult to breathe. Sun streamed through the squares of colored glass in the arched windows, choking the air, stirring the voices of the church ladies in my mind. *Sit up straight, hon. Don't slouch like that, you'll get a hump in your back. . . .*

I thought of my father's funeral. I'd overheard Blaine Underhill's stepmother and my aunt Esther whispering about the fact that my mother hadn't made me wear a dress. Aunt Esther had snorted irritably, then pointed out that my mother was impossible to deal with and if it weren't for the fact that there was no way we could continue to live at the farm with my mother completely dysfunctional in her grief, Aunt Esther would never have allowed us to move into the gardener's cottage at Harmony Shores.

Now, glancing across the room, I saw Blaine's stepmother eyeing me coolly from the Underhill pew.

I wanted to get up and leave before the choir even made it to the choir loft.

183

You don't drown by falling in the water;
You drown by staying there.
—Edwin Louis Cole
(*Left by Jim, teaching grandkids to swim.*)

≈ Chapter 9 ≈

The sermon wasn't bad, actually. Reverend Hay was a low-key sort of guy, and being newly engaged, he spoke from the heart when he talked about love and the nature of it. "In modern culture, we tend to think of love as something soft, frilly, and lacy, like the edging on a valentine," he said, smiling at his future bride in the front row. "And love is beautiful like that, intricate in the ways it changes you, grows you, makes you want to be more than you were before. Love sees in you the best possible version of yourself, and makes you believe it. . . ." I tuned out for a moment, only vaguely conscious of the sermon continuing. I caught myself looking across the room, watching the blonde watch Blaine. She flashed smiles and eye-commentary at him as the sermon went on.

I studied his responses, cataloging them without really meaning to. He laughed when she made cross-eyes at him during some reference to teenagers bouncing in and out of love at the drop of a hat. He returned a couple of smiles, and she winked at him. I still couldn't decide who she was, but her face was familiar—undoubtedly from high school. She flashed a couple glances my way, thinking the same thing about me, I supposed. Each time, I pretended to be studying the colored glass in the windows behind her head.

Farther down the Underhill pew, Mama B swiveled a narrow glance over her shoulder, and caught the blonde flirting with Blaine. Mama B's silent message to the blonde seemed clear enough. *Mind your business.*

Hmm . . .

The blonde turned her attention to the sermon again, and I did, as well.

". . . and so much of that is true about love. It's the best feeling in the world. It's glorious, but Hollywood teaches us that love is weak and fickle, that evil doesn't have a very tough time overtaking it. If you watch enough movies, you'll end up believing that sooner or later all love is doomed to fail, that a broken, wicked, sinful, hate-filled world is just more than love can stand up against. That when a marriage fails, we shouldn't be surprised. That when a family falls apart, or a neighbor hates a neighbor, or a kid bullies another kid in school, or a church body divides into factions, we should accept that as part of life, because the world is imperfect—so imperfect, in fact, that it's more than love can combat. But what we don't realize—what the writers of the Bible

185

knew that we've lost track of—is that love is the very essence of God, and God is powerful. In fact, He is all-powerful."

Pausing to let the point sink in, Reverend Hay moved from behind the pulpit, stood at the edge of the steps and held up his long, thin hands. "Brothers and sisters, don't let anyone convince you that love isn't strong enough to combat temptation or hate or prejudice or past hurts or misunderstandings or drugs or alcohol or culture clashes or self-loathing or any other form of evil that may afflict your life or the lives of those around you. Love doesn't need us to protect it from those things. Love *is* our protection. Great, big, crazy, extravagant, confident love, like the love God has for every one of us. Love that accepts us just as we are.

"If we only love people who are exactly like us, why, we're really just loving ourselves, aren't we?" He paused, gathering murmurs from the audience and a disinterested look or two from the casserole ladies. I glanced sideways at my mother and my brother, thought about all the ways I'd been frustrated with them over the years, all the decisions I'd criticized. Was I really just pointing at the mirror and saying, *If you'll be more like me, I'll love you more?*

A thorn poked somewhere inside me as Reverend Hay went on, the audience now hanging on his hook, ready to be reeled in. "But when we put on that great, big, godly love and go out into the world, we're ready to do battle with evil, with prejudice . . . yes, and sometimes even with ourselves. Sometimes the armor of love is heavy. Sometimes it's cumbersome, uncomfortable, and unwieldy. Sometimes it'll make you sweat, or keep you from having the knee-jerk reaction that'd be satisfying in the moment but would leave blood on the battlefield.

"Divine love is the key to churches that cleave together, to marriages that last and families that overcome, to friendships that forgive insult, and hands that reach out to those who are different from us. We've got to love each other more than we love our own reflections in the mirror. When we can do that, love is both a sword and a shield. No matter where we go, or what kind of battle we're facing, it's all the armor we need."

Reverend Hay moved to the head of the aisle then, and the pianist played an invitation song. A man and wife came forward to join the church—retirees, from the look of it. Reverend Hay introduced them to the members.

As the service wound down, my attention moved to a survey of the exits and who was sitting near them. I tried to gauge the quickest path out, the one that would allow me to vacate the premises without being stopped by curious church ladies, trying to ferret out information on our family's plans and my mother's reasons for suddenly taking up residence in Moses Lake. If the ladies' drop-by visit to Uncle Herbert's house the other day hadn't clued me in to the fact that we were the current topic of small-town speculation, the plethora of whispers and glances in church would have.

I felt like I was suffocating on a combination of the curiosity in the air and random memories of my dad. He was everywhere in this building, frozen in time. During our visits to Moses Lake, we'd come to church for Christmas pageants, Easter egg hunts, potluck suppers, a wedding or two. Every time we entered this place, people gathered around my dad as if he were visiting royalty, and I could see how much he missed Moses Lake. I always wondered if he resented my mother for putting him in a tug-of-war between his hometown and her.

Just as Reverend Hay was about to end the service, a little boy popped out of his seat and walked the aisle, loudly declaring that he wanted to be baptized. I thought about my dad. The day I was baptized along with a group of friends in our mega-church back home, he'd told me the story about getting up and walking down the aisle all by himself here in this little church. Now, looking at that little boy, I saw Dad. I wondered if, up in heaven, he was looking down and remembering. My dad, I realized now, showed us the kind of love Reverend Hay was talking about. He accepted people the way they were, even my mother, even when her inconsistencies caused him embarrassment, or inconvenience, or pain. If only I had inherited that trait from him, along with his hair and eye color. I wanted to be less like the casserole ladies and more like my dad; I just didn't know where to start.

When everyone stood up to go forward and hug and congratulate the newest members of the church, I whispered to Uncle Charley that I was going to walk home, and I ducked through an exit door into the parking lot. The air outside was brisk, but it felt good. Moses Lake glistening in the midday sun brought memories of my dad, and the thoughts were good thoughts, not painful spears with which I tormented myself. I felt as if my father were walking the path through the woods beside me, glad to see me in the place that he loved.

How would he feel about the land sale? Would he be pleased to know that something was happening that would provide jobs and much-needed income for Moses Lake, or would he be unhappy that the farmland would be developed? I wished I knew.

The family was already back at Harmony Shores by the time I made it there on foot. As we gathered food to take to Ruth's house, I began mentally preparing to start up a discussion in the car, where I would have a captive audience. While I understood this strange, nostalgic idea of Moses Lake as the idyllic family homeplace, in which Mom and Clay would happily settle while seeing the older generation through their senior years, I still knew it was impractical. Mom would never survive without her university dinners, her meditation classes, and the throng of graduate students, smitten by her knowledge of everything from Chaucer to Pope. And Clay couldn't even look after his poor dog properly. Case in point, I'd found the dog dishes empty on the back deck when I arrived at Harmony House after my walk through the woods. Roger was on his hind legs, trying to claw the lid off a metal trash can filled with dog food. I scooped out a helping and put it in the bowl, and Roger ate as if he hadn't seen kibble in a week. No wonder he'd felt the need to commandeer my FedEx package. If he got hungry enough, at least he could use my iPhone to call for a pizza. A twenty-seven-year-old man who couldn't feed his own dog regularly had no business taking on the care of two old men and a restaurant.

I rehearsed the conversation, making plans as to how I would gently hammer the point home while we were driving to Gnadenfeld. Somehow, I would figure out a way to do it as my dad would have—without being hard-edged and critical. When he gave advice, you knew he meant it for your own good, even if you didn't want to hear it.

I would channel Dad's wisdom, be calm, yet determined. Businesslike.

Unfortunately, before I knew what was happening, Mom and the uncs had filled the backseat of the funeral sedan with secondhand casseroles. They took off while I was in the bathroom, leaving Clay and Roger waiting for me on the porch.

"Guess you're in the second wave," Clay informed me, seeming cheerful enough about the idea of making the thirty-minute drive to Gnadenfeld with me riding shotgun.

I squinted down the driveway, my feelings oddly bruised. "They just took off without me?" It's pretty bad when you get ditched by people who don't mind riding to a birthday party in a car with *Funeral Procession* written on it. I had the old high-school feeling for a moment. Was I really that unpleasant to have around, or were they trying to avoid the in-transit conversation I'd been carefully planning? "I can't believe they just took off and left me here alone." *How rude.*

"What are we, chopped liver?" Clay and Roger sent smiles my way in unison—two shaggy blondes seeming completely oblivious to any undercurrents in the day. It really is true that people resemble their dogs—or vice-versa.

"Of course not." *But I can't reason with you, and you know it.*
Clay bounded to his feet on the top step and jumped down the other three in one carefree hop.

191

He hadn't gotten the nickname Tigger for nothing. He could have earned a college scholarship in pole-vaulting, but he was just as apt to ditch high-school track practice as to show up. "I'll go get our ride." He jogged off toward the back of the house, and Roger scrambled from the porch to follow.

I waited, wondering what cars were left back there. I hoped we weren't taking the hearse. As far as I could tell, Mom didn't even have a rental car, which meant that Clay must have picked her up at the airport. Did Clay even own a car? He'd sold the last one Mom bought him to finance his flight with the earthquake relief project.

I heard a rumbling and chugging out back that didn't sound like the hearse or Uncle Charley's pickup, so Clay did have a ride of some sort. Moving down the steps and along the front walk, I tried to catch a glimpse of whatever was headed my way. It sounded like a cross between a motorcycle and a street sweeper.

A white Toyota pickup with a crooked front fender rolled into view, the blinker cover broken on one side, an orange light bulb bobbing like a loose tooth. Something was letting out a dull squeal with each rotation of the wheels, and the entire truck listed to the left. Roger had taken up residence in the passenger seat, his head hanging jauntily out the window as the vehicle drifted to a stop. A string of doggie drool dripped from his mouth onto the door, sliding downward over some sort of badly-decayed decals that remained in bits and pieces all over the vehicle. Bugs, I decided, on further inspection. The truck was covered with partial decals of red-and-black bugs. Moving closer, I read the shadow of decal letters that had long since disintegrated or been removed under the passenger-side window. *Ladybug Pest Control.*

"This is it!" Clay announced cheerfully, not the least bit embarrassed to be piloting a vehicle that looked like it had driven through a swarm of locust and collected body parts. "Hop in!"

I couldn't help it—I laughed. I knew Clay wouldn't care. One thing about my little brother. His ego was all his own. No one else held sway over it. I envied that about him. I always had.

On the other hand, I wondered at the odds of the ancient Toyota making it twenty-five miles down the road to Gnadenfeld.

"C'mon," Clay said. "She runs better than she looks."

"That's not saying much," I quipped, and my brother smirked at me as I studied the truck. The engine sounded a little like the old crank-start Oliver tractor that Uncle Charley had always lovingly referred to as Betty. Come to think of it, I wondered what had happened to Betty when the family farm was cleaned out for sale. The massive estate auction out there had been scheduled for right after Christmas, as I recalled. Hopefully, Betty had gone to a good home.

Opening the truck door, I stepped back so that Roger could exit.

"C'mon, Rodge, scooch over," Clay ordered, hooking an arm around Roger's neck and pulling him into the small space behind the gearshift.

"We're taking Roger?" Surely Roger was not on the guest list for Ruth's birthday party.

Clay stretched, so that we could converse over Roger's head. "Yeah, if you leave him home, he eats stuff."

"Too bad we didn't think of that before he eviscerated my FedEx."

Clay shrugged in acquiescence. "Yeah, but just look at all the entertainment we would've missed. Family bonding and all."

Shaking my head and trying not to laugh, I climbed into my seat and closed the door so that Roger and I were nicely snuggled in. I had the odd thought that Clay was right about the family treasure hunt. All of us tromping around the yard with flashlights and gardening shovels was a postcard moment, the kind of insane family-visit story you'd tell your friends about when you got back home—great fodder for coffee conversation. But who would I tell? I couldn't picture Mel and me chatting about the homeplace while we prepped for a presentation, Trish was always busy with the kids, and who knew what would happen with Richard?

Strange . . . I'd hardly thought about Richard since arriving in Moses Lake. Too much else on my mind, I guessed. But even that seemed wrong. You shouldn't be fantasizing about making a life with someone one day and forgetting about him the next, should you? If a relationship mattered, it wouldn't be so easy to put it out of mind, would it?

What was wrong with me? Was I so screwed up, so damaged that I'd never be able to make the kinds of connections normal people made? Would I always be living in my own private space—running like a hamster in one of those plastic exercise balls, a see-through shield around me, so I could look at the world but not touch it? Would I always be that person Reverend Hay talked about—standing there looking in the mirror, only feeling safe with my own reflection because it didn't challenge my priorities or my choices?

"You've got to admit our impromptu treasure hunt wasn't *that* bad." Elbowing Roger out of the way, Clay put the truck in gear, and we rumbled up the driveway, the Ladybug singing a cheerful song of squeaks and squeals as it bounced over chugholes. "Kind of nice just to chill with everybody for a little while, right?"

I felt the sting of an open wound, and I closed off the tender place as we rolled along the rural

195

highway to Gnadenfeld. "Sorry to kill the fun, but somebody has to take care of business." Deep inside Clay's happy-go-lucky exterior there was a guy with a perfect ACT test score who had to know that what he was doing was wrong. He didn't want me around because he didn't want to hear it.

He shook his head, then rolled his gaze upward in a way meant to indicate that I was totally off base. "Sometimes it's not all black-and-white, you know. Sometimes there're people involved, and you can't just run it all through some spreadsheet. You're just like Dad. You're just like he was. It's all about whatever makes the most money."

I drew back, stunned that his feelings about Dad were so different from mine. How dare he say that. How dare he even think it. Sure, our dad had worked hard—even overworked a lot of the time—but he kept a roof over our heads. He kept our family together. He took care of us when Mom was too busy doing her thing, and he never complained about it. He held down the fort while she flitted off on every passing whim, leaving us to fend for ourselves while she indulged in self-obsessed ramblings in a spiral notebook.

Dad didn't deserve this from Clay, and neither did I.

I felt Reverend Hay's armor of love crumbling piece by piece, clattering through the floorboards and bouncing noisily in our wake as we drove along.

The vulnerable place inside me opened again, bled a little. I turned away and looked out the window, wishing I were anywhere but trapped in a car with my brother. "You know, Clay, why don't you give me a little credit? I'm trying to do what's best for everyone." A lump rose in my throat, and I swallowed hard, overwhelmed with a tangle of emotions I couldn't identify, much less catalog or control. *Stop here,* I wanted to scream. *Let me out. Now.* But if I said anything more, if I opened my mouth, I knew the dam would break and tears would rush forth, draining a lake that had been filling for sixteen years. There was no way of knowing what would be left afterward.

Silence descended over us, leaving an impasse, a broad, dark chasm between us. I focused outside the window, watching pastures drift by, the winter-brown fields dotted dusky green by live oaks and cedars. Roger wiggled around and lay across my lap, his head on his paws. He licked my hand. Maybe he sensed that I needed it. His fur felt soft beneath my hand as he nuzzled underneath it.

Finally I let out a long breath, took in another, and thought about Trish and all the secondhand advice from her therapist. *Deep breathing slows the heart rate. Think of something beautiful and pleasant to produce beneficial endorphins. . . .*

Why did everything have to be so hard? Why couldn't the property sale be quick, clean, painless? Just a business deal with a side benefit of putting the past squarely in the past, now and forever? Why did everyone have to keep bringing it up, to keep harping on it? My dad was a great guy. He died too early, instantaneously, without suffering. A gunshot victim. We would never know if it was accidental or intentional, or what my father was doing with the old shotgun in the first place. The gun had been my grandfather's, used for hunting. My dad could simply have decided to clean it, having no idea that it was loaded after all these years.

Or, his taking the rifle to the basement could've had something to do with the packed suitcases in the master bedroom, the man I saw my mother sneaking around with, and the change in my father's demeanor during the last week of his life. Clay didn't know about the suitcases and the man, and I wasn't going to tell him. What possible good could come from causing someone pain over events that couldn't be changed? Clay was better off writing his own version in his memory book and turning the page.

I wished everyone else would let me do the same.

The Ladybug chugged and jerked, coughing like a chain smoker as we rolled along the rural highway, now ten or twelve miles out of Moses

Lake. I turned to Clay. He was frowning at the console, his lower lip pooched over his top one. He tapped the cracked plastic covering over the gauges. "Aw, shoot."

My anxiety perked up. The calming voice of Trish's therapist vaporized and more pieces of the armor of love flew out the window. "What? What's *Aw, shoot?*"

The truck lurched, and Roger slid forward, his front half landing on the floorboard. He turned and eyed me with a frown, as in, *Well, look at what's happened to me.* I pushed the other half of him onto the floor, so that he was sitting on my feet.

Clay downshifted. "Yeah, we're low on gas."

"We're what?" I pictured being stranded in the cold on the side of the road and missing Ruth's birthday gathering, which I was looking forward to.

"The gauge sticks," Clay said, as if that were an explanation.

I sat up straighter in my seat, gripping the armrest on the door, though I wasn't sure why. A bailout wouldn't help at this point. Roger whined, indicating that he, too, was worried. Perhaps he remembered the bike trip, when Clay stranded them both in the mountains. "Well, if the gauge sticks, don't you keep some kind of track of how many miles you've driven since you filled up?"

Clay shrugged. "I knew we'd be going past the

199

farm. I figured we could pick up some gas there, if we needed it."

The logic of that was dazzling. "But . . . how do you know if you need gas, until you, like, run out?"

"It'll chug a mile or two."

"But what if the chugging *begins,* and we're *more* than a mile or two from the farm? Ever think of that?" That sealed it. My brother would never grow up and start to think like a normal human. He would always be some strange combination of Winnie the Pooh and my mother. *Oh, bother.*

"We're not." He motioned calmly toward the window. "Look."

I surveyed the surrounding territory, and it did look familiar. Some things had changed, but I recognized a few of the landmarks that had always told me we were nearing the family farm. While this was great luck, Clay's sense of planning still stunk.

"Have a little faith, sis," he said, as if he knew what I was thinking. Perhaps he could see my white-knuckled grip on the door handle as we chugged along the shoulder of the road, the vehicle gasping, wheezing, threatening to give up, then catching another burst of fumes and lurching forward. In the driver's seat, my brother was perfectly calm. I was envious of him, in a strange way. What would it be like to be so completely unaffected by fear? When I was with Clay, I couldn't help but feel like I was in a straitjacket, barely breathing, missing some grand adventure because I was afraid to strike out without first studying every inch of the map.

But intangibles like faith just weren't my strong suit, and I guessed they never would be. Faith was a blind journey, a path you couldn't predict or dictate. It was giving yourself over to the control of someone who might or might not necessarily agree with your plans. Faith could just as easily dictate that the chugging and the farm gate *wouldn't* occur at the same time, and that you'd end up standing on the side of the road, at the mercy of strangers. That wasn't something I wanted to experience. Clay, on the other hand, would look at it as an event that was meant to happen, an opportunity for an intended side trip of some kind. He would seek the meaning in it. He had learned that kind of thinking from my mother.

Which was exactly why I rejected it.

If you tried to erect a building based on faith, you'd end up with a mess. That was why you needed to create a blueprint ahead of time and follow it.

We ended up rolling into the farm, crawling and staggering up the dusty, gravel lane just as the gas gave out. The Ladybug came to rest in the center of the farmyard, the tall, hip-roofed barn on the left, and on the right, the two-story clapboard house my grandparents had built. Next to their house, the smaller stone house, the original dwelling on the farm, squatted silent and shadow-filled. I turned away, so that I wouldn't have to see it. I'd been there a thousand times in my dreams. My father died in that house. No one had lived in it since.

Turning toward the barn, I searched for happier memories as Clay put the pickup in park. I remembered my grandfather, a quiet but gentle man, showing me how to whittle and how to find caterpillar cocoons under milkweed leaves. I remembered playing pirate ship with Clay on the horse-drawn hay wagon that was slowly rotting in the sun.

Just looking at the barn made my mouth water for one of the RC colas my grandfather always kept in a refrigerator out there. Uncle Charley's old Ford tractor, Betty, was still sitting in the doorway, seeming to indicate that the refrigerator and the RC colas would still be there, too.

"Oh, hey, there's Betty," I observed, anxious to distract my mind from darker things. Didn't it bother Clay at all, coming here, seeing the house where Dad had died? "I didn't know Betty was still around."

Clay glanced my way enthusiastically, stopping halfway out the door. "You'd be surprised what's here. Want to take a look?"

"Nah," I said quickly, wrapping my arms around

myself. "I'll just wait while you gas up. It's cold out there." The cold wasn't the problem, of course; the memories were. They were an assault of roses and arrows, some sweet, some painful. My father used to take me for rides on Betty during our visits. I loved it when he did that. Sometimes we would drive all the way to the lakeshore, through the wooded hills on the back of the farm. He'd sweep a hand over the water and talk about how the whole valley used to be filled with farm fields—cotton, sorghum, corn. There were even a couple of small towns, now buried under thousands of acres of water.

I remembered looking at the lake and trying to imagine what was underneath.

Strange, I hadn't thought about those tractor rides with my father in years. The memories came back now, fresh, sweet, and fragrant, smelling of grease and diesel smoke, dry grass and caliche mud. I rested my head against the seat and breathed in the memories as Clay fetched gas from the barn, fueled up the Ladybug, did something under the hood, then slid back into the driver's seat.

"Remember when Dad used to take us down to the lake on the tractor?" I asked.

Clay turned the key and pumped the gas pedal. "He did more of that with you than he did with me." The Ladybug roared to life, sending out a cloud of black smoke that sailed past us on the breeze. "You were the one who liked the tractors and stuff."

"Guess I was." Relaxing in my seat, I smiled out the window as we circled the farmyard and left the place behind. "You were always too busy coming up with strange costumes and pretending to be a dinosaur hunter or Batman." Even in childhood, Clay's imagination was amazing. He only lived part-time in the real world.

"I haven't changed much." He echoed the thought I'd been forming.

I felt a rush of tenderness toward my brother as we turned onto the highway and rolled toward Gnadenfeld. Whatever else happened, however imperfect we were at loving each other, Clay and I would always be tied together by memories, a shared past, an understanding that no one else could duplicate. "Maybe change is overrated."

He blinked, then snickered, like he couldn't believe he was hearing that from me. The words did taste a little strange coming out, but they were heartfelt. I did love my brother, despite all his impracticalities.

The rest of the way to Gnadenfeld, we talked about some of the imaginary characters Clay had created as a kid. Off and on, I'd served as a bit player or cameraman during his fantasy productions. We were laughing about his Star Wars obsession as we passed through Gnadenfeld, its pristine antique shops, Mennonite bakeries, quilt stores, and mom-and-pop restaurants speaking of a healthy economy and plenty of tourism. *Guten Tag*, the sign read. *Good day*.

Judging by the look of the town, Gnadenfeld was enjoying good days. When I was little, the place had practically withered away, the Mennonite families moving off, finding it difficult to make a living farming in this hardscrabble country. Now the town spoke of prosperity, a symbiotic economy having developed between residents who worked for Proxica, the Mennonites who'd left the family farms to operate corporately-owned poultry production barns or to work in the processing plant, and those who still farmed and lived the old-fashioned way, selling their wares in roadside stands and the bakeries in town. The Mennonite residents of Gnadenfeld ranged from highly conservative to those who lived fully modern lives. They existed harmoniously, other than some differences in philosophy about mindless entertainment, like television. There seemed to be a place for all of them.

I imagined the economy of Moses Lake booming like this, the town thriving rather than scraping along on tourism dollars and dealing with a school in which half the population lived below poverty level in Chinquapin Peaks. I considered pointing that out to Clay, but I couldn't bring myself to spoil the pleasant mood in the car.

Memories—fresh and powerful, like a summer

rainstorm—surrounded me as we turned into the gateway of Ruth's family dairy. I knew this place. I remembered coming here with Ruth several times over the years. She'd brought us here the night after my father's death. She'd taken Clay and me home with her, and we'd stayed in her sister's house at the dairy, where we were surrounded by kids, animals, activity. Distractions.

Ruth had led us into the big, white two-story house, given us fresh milk and oatmeal cookies. She'd stroked my hair, kissed the top of my head, told me everything would be all right. That night she knelt with me by the bed, and we prayed together. But I was praying for something that couldn't happen. *God, please don't let my dad be gone . . . please . . .*

I'd never thought about the specifics of that night until now. The moments, the days after my father's death were a blur of family, dark clothes, dark thoughts, stark little rooms with police officers asking questions. *Heather, were there any problems between your parents that you knew of? Did you hear any arguments? There were packed suitcases in your parents' room. Do you know why your mother was packing . . . ?*

The questions burned again now, demanded answers I didn't have. I couldn't remember anything after hearing the shot and running to the cellar door. I didn't know what happened next. I didn't know how much I'd seen or what I'd seen.

Mom said she'd come into the cellar from the outside door when she heard the gun go off. She told the police she'd caught me on the stairs, turned me away before I made it to the bottom, before I could see anything.

Had she? Was that true?

Did Ruth know what had really happened that day? Did she know more than I knew?

The trip up Ruth's driveway took on a strange sense of urgency, an eerie feeling that chased away the beauty of the dairy farm, where various members of Ruth's family lived in three different houses, generations alternating through as elders passed on and younger members married. Beyond the green fields and tall white-washed stone dairy barns, a collection of toys in the yard—a wooden teeter-totter, a homemade swing set, a carousel of a sort, made by cabling a ring of wooden seats to a tall center pole—testified to the fact that there were children living on the farm now.

The swinging carousel had been there even years ago. I remembered pushing Clay on it the day after my father's death, trying to distract him. The sheriff's deputies came to talk with me, and then they wanted me to go with them. Somehow, I gathered that they'd been questioning my mother all night, and they thought I might know something. Clay and the carousel had slowly grown smaller and smaller in the yard as we drove away.

Closing my eyes, I tried to tame the flood of memories. It was ancient history. The police had ruled my father's death an accident. Our lives went on, but barely—the struggle becoming more and more difficult as my mother sank into darkness, her eyes hollow, distant. Her behavior only helped to fuel the speculation of community members uncertain whether to believe the police reports or the gossip. My mother had never been well liked in Moses Lake, so the gossip was tempting, popular among the ladies in their bridge circles and garden club meetings. The men wondered how someone like my father, who'd grown up around rifles and hunting, could have accidentally shot himself while cleaning a gun. There were whispers, of course. Looks.

But not from Ruth. Ruth had stood by us steadfastly. Perhaps it was easier for her. Being from Gnadenfeld, she didn't have to live in Moses Lake, but she had always been devoted to Uncle Charley, Uncle Herb, and the family. She'd stood by my dad through the funeral of my grandmother and through moving Grandpa Hampton to a nursing home within two months of our arrival in Moses Lake. When our family faced another funeral, sudden, tragic, unexpected, impossible to understand, she was our rock. I couldn't even begin to count the number of times she had stayed over at Harmony House in the weeks following my father's death, when all of us, including my uncles and aunts, were wandering through life in a fog.

I'd never realized how deep Ruth's connection to my family was, but she'd saved us in those dark months—pulled us up by a string, quilted the tatters together with her silent, even stitches. I'd never properly thanked her for that. As soon as high school graduation was over, I couldn't get out of Moses Lake quickly enough. If nothing else came of this trip, at least I would have the chance to thank Ruth for all she'd done to help Clay and me. It shouldn't have taken me so long to say it.

I prepared the words in my mind as we entered the largest of the three farmhouses and walked through the utilitarian but comfortable interior to the sun porch out back. We found Ruth settled in a chair, entertaining a come-and-go crowd of friends, relatives, and community members. It was an eclectic group—the attire ranging from Old-Order cape dresses and mesh prayer caps to jeans and sweatshirts.

In Gnadenfeld, the Mennonite population had always been in a strange state of flux, many of the younger members of the community gravitating toward the more liberal church on the outside of town, and the older people, like Ruth, tending to fall closer to the practices of the traditional church on Main Street. Even so, there seemed to be no hard-and-fast rules as to styles of dress and head covering. For as long as I could remember,

Ruth had usually worn modest, floral print dresses and a small scarf-like covering fastened over her braided and coiled rope of hair. Today, she was just as I remembered her, except that her hair was thinner, fully gray now, and her cheeks, in the past always round and plump, had a hollow quality. Her dress hung loose, as if she'd borrowed it from someone else.

Her smile was as welcoming as it had always been, her eyes still a sparkling blue, her hug exactly as I remembered. When Ruth took you in her arms, you knew she meant it. You felt her hugs through your entire body. She held me away from herself afterward, her hands cupping my cheeks. I hung bent over her chair, unable to rise and move back so that the rest of the family could come closer.

"You've been away too long," she said.

I couldn't help feeling that she was right.

Remember ye not the former things,
neither consider the things of old.
–Isaiah 43:18
(*Left by Mildred and Millie Millfast,
twin sisters letting go of the past*)

≈ Chapter 10 ≈

Our visit with Ruth was sweet, and relaxing in a way I couldn't quite explain. Ruth's family and friends were easygoing people who loved to laugh. Other than the work involved in cooking and basic farm chores, they didn't believe in laboring on Sunday, so it was routine for them to spend the day visiting.

I couldn't remember the last time I'd been in a roomful of people who weren't in a hurry to rush off somewhere. Not a single cell phone rang. Nobody pulled out an iPod. Nobody was huddled in a corner, texting away on a Droid. I sat back in a chair and just enjoyed listening as Ruth and my uncles laughed and recounted old times, sharing somewhat off-color funeral stories that delighted Ruth's family and friends.

While we talked, two little red-haired girls in long flowered jumpers, Mary and Emily, sat at Ruth's feet, listening. Mary, whose thick red hair had been carefully plaited and secured with a blue ribbon in the back, couldn't have been more than five years old, and Emily, whose hair escaped her braid in wispy red corkscrews, seemed only slightly younger. They sat with their dresses tucked around their white stockings and tennis shoes, their attention moving from speaker to speaker around the room, as if they weren't the least bit disinterested.

I couldn't help being fascinated, not only by the fact that they were adorable, but by their ability to quietly sit and listen. Trish's twins had just turned three, and we couldn't even carry on a conversation with them in the room. They were cute and sweet, but they moved constantly from one form of entertainment to another, and when they were around, they demanded attention.

Emily, the smaller girl with the cotton-puff hair, finally yawned and crawled into Ruth's lap. Whispering something in her ear, Ruth nestled the girl under her chin, smoothing the flowered jumper around her legs, then gently patting her thigh as Emily relaxed against her. Mary, seeming a little lost on the floor by herself, shimmied into the armchair beside me as if it were the most natural thing in the world. Twisting my way, she smiled, and I moved my arm, so that she could wiggle back in the seat. Her hair tickled my neck as she snuggled in, and I found myself resting my chin on her head, drinking in the soapy, grassy scents of childhood and feeling the tug in my chest that had caused me to imagine a future with Richard when there really wasn't one. As much as I loved my work, some primal part of me wanted this. At moments like these, it stood inside me, screaming, *You're thirty-four! You're thirty-four and you're still alone. Time is running out!*

I hated that voice. I hated it because it made me question everything about my life, and really, I liked my life. I liked the excitement of it, the travel, the sense of accomplishment that came from seeing a project I'd helped design take shape in the real world and become something massive and lasting. The feeling of little Mary in my lap ran in direct contrast to all of that. If I had kids right now, with the demands of my job, a nanny would be raising them. What kind of sense did that make?

Ruth glanced my way, her eyes meeting mine with a knowing look, as if she sensed what was going on inside me, as if she could read me like a book, just as she had in the old days. I was grieving again, whether I wanted to admit it to myself or not. Not grieving the breakup with Richard, but grieving the life I might never find. I wanted the sense of connection I felt among Ruth's family. I'd always wanted it.

I tried to put away my painful self-analysis and focus instead on the ongoing story in the room— something about a fiendish escape of Proxica chickens and a run for freedom down the highway. Uncle Herbert and Uncle Charley were red-faced, laughing as one of Ruth's neighbors described his wife and other Proxica plant employees, trying to round up the chickens. The poultry stories continued from there. Before long I was laughing, too, my problems temporarily whisked away, as if one of the hand-tied brooms on the wall had swept them under the carpet where they couldn't cause trouble.

When it was time for us to leave, Ruth rose slowly from her chair and walked with us through the house to the front door. Her steps were labored as she moved along, her fingers clasped around Uncle Charley's elbow, clinging like the roots of a withered tree. Uncle Herb assured her that she didn't need to walk us to the door, and she insisted that the exercise would do her good. Mary and Emily escorted me to the porch, holding my hands, until finally they released me and bolted after some puppies playing on the lawn.

"You're not to start coddling me." Ruth swatted a backhand at Uncle Herb. "I'm fine. These young people fuss over me too much."

Clay's cell phone rang as he stepped onto the front porch. He moved off to answer it, and I strained an ear in his direction. Call me nosy, but I couldn't help it. The phone call was from Amy, and I was still trying to figure out their relationship. Not that Clay wasn't adorable in his own rebellious way, but a sweet, conservative, hometown girl who was by my estimation barely out of high school wasn't the sort I would have pictured him with. Usually Clay wound up being a project for girlfriends who viewed his scruffy surfer-bum look and aimless nature as evidence that he just needed a good woman to shape him up and mold him into perfect husband material.

Amy, on the other hand, seemed somewhat clueless herself, and in need of Clay to take the lead in their relationship dance. Right now they were on the phone trying to coordinate a date. Listening to them attempt to come up with a meeting place, figure out what to do with her car, and decide between options for Roger—take him on the date, leave him here at Ruth's during the date, lock him in Amy's parents' garage, try to sneak him into the movie theater by pretending he was a seeing-eye dog—was somewhere between funny and painful. Clay practically had smoke coming out his ears from the pressure of it all.

Finally, he looked over and caught my eye, then performed a little pantomime of me taking Roger—who right now was having a grand time with Mary, Emily, the puppies, and various dairy dogs—to the Ladybug. Clay's imitation steering-wheel motions indicated that I was being asked to transport Roger home, presumably while Clay and Amy went on their date in Amy's car.

I rolled my eyes and nodded—don't ask me why. After spending the afternoon laughing,

215

talking, cuddling little Mary, and listening to stories, I guess I couldn't help the continued yearning for family harmony.

Clay gave me the happy thumbs-up, then went on with planning his date. I wondered, as I listened, if Clay might have finally found the perfect woman for him. Maybe, by being unwilling or unable to take the parental role in the relationship, Amy would manage to force him to grow up. . . .

It crossed my mind that I was actually thinking about my brother's love life, straining to hear the rest of the conversation as he trotted down the porch steps. How pathetic. Was it because I had no prospects of my own? Sadly, it probably was.

I felt that lost, somewhat pitiful feeling seep over me again, and I pushed it away, determined not to dip my toe into the blue waters of Lake Oh-Poor-Me, as Ruth used to call it. Funny, I hadn't thought about that saying in years. She had some funny little song about it. I couldn't remember the words now, but it had always made me laugh, even on the worst of days.

One thing I remembered about the Mennonites I'd met around Moses Lake was that they loved to sing. They were musical in all ways, in fact. Ruth said this was because, in the more conservative Mennonite churches, art for art's sake had always been discouraged as a vainglorious pursuit. Things like music and quilting had a purpose, and thus provided an acceptable outlet for artistic expression.

A melancholy overtook me as the uncs finished their good-byes. Today's visit was over. I wanted to get Ruth to tell me the words to the Oh-Poor-Me song, among other things. It struck me then that I might never know the words. Once I headed back to Seattle, I probably wouldn't see Ruth again. Her cancer and her thin, frail, fragile appearance had been the elephant in the room all day. No one wanted to bring it up on such a happy occasion, but we all knew that there wouldn't be another birthday gathering.

I watched her hug Uncle Herbert, her eyes closing as she rested her chin on his shoulder. The two of them hung on to each other, the moment seeming private, intimate enough that it surprised me. In all the months I'd lived at Uncle Herbert's and Ruth had helped to take care of us, I'd never seen Ruth hug either of the uncs. Of course, Aunt Esther was around then, and to her, Ruth was *the help*. Aunt Esther believed in the traditional, formal Southern rules about such things. One did not become overly familiar with the help, which at the time included Ruth, a retired man who tended the gardens, and a young guy named Lars, who did heavy lifting around the funeral home and took care of setup for services. Ruth, Lars, and the gardener ate at the breakfast table in the kitchen, while the family ate in the dining room, even on days when there was no one home except my aunt and uncle. Clay and I tended to be AWOL on purpose during dinners at the big house as often as we could. We preferred to eat in the kitchen while Ruth washed dishes.

She smiled at me as she released Uncle Herb and rested a hand against the doorframe, steadying herself.

"Hey, Ruth, I'm gonna change clothes in the dairy room, 'kay? I'm headed over to see Amy," Clay called from the driveway, and I realized he was shopping for date clothes in the rusted metal toolbox in the bed of his truck. What a romantic.

"There's no heat on in the dairy room!" Ruth's voice crackled like the old phonograph disks she used to let Clay play in Uncle Herbert's parlor, when Aunt Esther was gone to her teas and her meetings at the church.

"Not a problem," Clay answered, waving his clothes over his head as he started toward the largest of the barns, a massive hip-roofed structure that was neatly painted and picturesque.

"You come on in the house!" Ruth leaned out the door, looking concerned. She lost her balance a little, and Uncle Charley caught her elbow.

Clay turned and walked backward, cupping a hand around his ear in a gesture meant to indicate that he couldn't hear her. He grinned as he wheeled around and trotted off to the barn. No doubt he knew that if any of us went back in the house, we'd be here another hour, trying to break away again. Already, Ruth looked exhausted, and the niece who lived in the house, Mary and Emily's mom, had gently suggested that it was time to wrap up the birthday gathering.

Ruth frowned at me and shook her head as my goofball brother disappeared into the frigid dairy barn to get dressed for his date.

"Don't look at *me*," I said. "I can't tell him anything. He doesn't listen." I moved across the porch in her direction, while the uncs and my mother excused themselves and headed toward the funeral sedan.

Ruth's hand settled on my arm, her fingers trembling. "He has always listened to you," she said quietly.

I lost myself in the pale, cloudy blue of her eyes. It was hard to imagine never seeing her again, knowing that she had moved on from this world and *unpacked her suitcase in heaven,* as she had often referred to it when there was a funeral at Harmony House. Ruth not being on this earth was an impossible thought, like trying to contemplate the contents of a black hole in space.

"He reminds me of your grandfather," Ruth said.

"My grandfather? Really?" I'd always thought of Clay as being just like my mom—her spitting image in word, deed, and opinion, if not in looks. I was like Dad, and Clay was like Mom. Together, we were an odd couple, like Oscar and Felix.

"Ohhh . . ." Ruth's eyes rounded. "I could tell you stories."

That's just it, I thought, *you could.* But I wouldn't be around to hear them. I wanted to hear the stories. I wanted to know how Clay was like my grandfather. But in another way, I was afraid. I was afraid to bring up the past. I'd worked so hard to exorcise all the family tragedy from my life, to rid myself of the ties to this place, that time. To leave behind the depressed, withdrawn, frightened girl who had wandered through her last year of high school and her first year of college under a black cloud, desperately trying to find a way out.

Who would I be, if I let the past come to life again, allowed it to put down roots and grow leaves, renew its colors? Would I sink into the shadow that had consumed me after my father's death? Would I be even worse? Somewhere deep inside me, was there the potential to become like my mother had been—practically catatonic, completely dysfunctional?

I didn't want to take that risk, to allow it in. I'd changed my mind about even asking Ruth if she knew more about my father's death. What was the point in revisiting it? I had a good life in Seattle, a satisfying life, a job I'd worked hard for, an existence that was . . . was . . .

"Come on, Heather," Mom called, halfway into

the passenger's seat of the funeral sedan. "Aren't you riding home with us?"

"I'm driving Clay's truck home," I answered. "With Roger." Mom gave me a surprised look, then glanced at Roger, rolling on the lawn with Mary, Emily, and a sheepdog. I added hopefully, "Unless you want to take Roger with you." It was worth a try, but Mom was quick to shake her head and slip into the sedan.

I turned to Ruth. "Or unless you want to keep Roger here. It's just like having Clay around, only with four legs and a drooling problem."

Ruth swatted me softly and clucked her tongue. I could almost hear her quoting one of her special proverbs, as she so often had. *The man who speaks ill of others, foremost speaks ill of himself.*

"It's true," I defended playfully, and she swatted me again, then reached up and fixed the hood of my coat, where it was balled inside the neck. Her fingers were like ice against my skin. I slipped my hand over hers, held it. "Go on inside and rest. It's too cold to stand out here. I can wait for Clay by the car."

She nodded wearily. "You come to visit me tomorrow. I have a story to tell you."

"I'd like that." But in the back of my mind, I was thinking, *Tomorrow is Monday.* I needed to be back at work. But so far I hadn't accomplished what I'd come here for. I hadn't convinced Mom to return to Seattle and sign the papers. Now, by agreeing to drive Clay's car home, I'd missed another chance to corral the family. What was Mel going to say when he learned that I wouldn't be in Seattle Monday morning, and I still hadn't settled the business about the land deal? *He'll decide that if I can't even take care of this little detail, then I don't have any business taking the lead on the Proxica project. He'll use it as an excuse. Whatever confidence he has in me will be completely undermined. . . .*

I felt stress heating up inside me, working toward a boil, a strange contrast to the cool touch of Ruth's hand. If I hurried home, I could work on my mother and the uncs while Clay was busy with Amy, try once again to make them see reason. "I'm not sure if I'll be here, though," I said, and Ruth's hand slipped away. I pulled my jacket closer over my shoulders.

"You'll call in the morning, then?" Ruth pressed, which for Ruth was unusual. She was never pushy; only kind, strong, and tolerant.

"Of course I will." I glanced over at her, and in the space of an instant, felt a shift in my thoughts. *What is wrong with you?* The voice in my head demanded. *This woman kept you on your feet during the worst time in your life and now she's dying of cancer, and you're worried about taking an extra day off of work?* "You know what, let's just plan on it," I said as Clay exited the barn in rumpled jeans and a sweatshirt, then stuffed his other clothes in the toolbox. Now that the day was cooling off, he'd finally donned a heavier shirt and long pants. "What time should I come? What's best for you?"

Ruth's lips lifted at the corners, pleating her skin like a puckered quilt. "Come for lunch. We'll sit on the sun porch and watch the cows go out on the winter wheat. They're so happy out there."

"That sounds wonderful." Only a farm wife would consider watching cows graze to be entertainment. "Can I bring anything?"

She mulled the question, then raised a finger, indicating a sudden and pleasing thought. "Bring some of that wonderful bratwurst from the Waterbird store—the ones in the natural casings. Do they sell those any longer? Come at eleven, and we'll bake *bauernbrot* to go with it."

A fond memory danced through my mind—one of Ruth and me in Uncle Herbert's kitchen. She was trying to teach me to make something—some dish with dumplings on top. I didn't want to learn. I wanted to wander off by myself, not talk to anyone, not be around anyone, just hide away and not think of anything. But Ruth insisted that I help her cook. In reality, she knew I would be no help at all—Ruth could handle a kitchen completely on her own—but she wanted me there with her, singing the song about Lake Oh-Poor-Me, rather than hiding in some dark corner, drowning in it.

"How about if I just bring lunch?" I suggested,

thinking that she probably didn't need to be cooking and no doubt her niece had plenty to do, taking care of kids and farm chores. "I'll bring enough for everyone and just buy some potato salad and beans from the Waterbird. How many do you usually have here for lunch?" Around the dairy, the numbers were always changing, depending on what combinations of family were living in the various houses and which boys or girls from nearby families were working there.

Ruth patted my hand, her attention turning momentarily to Mary and Emily, who were at present trying to boost Roger into the lowest branch of an oak tree. Oddly enough, he was cooperating with their efforts. "We'll cook. Mary and Emily will be disappointed if we don't. You can supply the bratwurst. . . . And will you do something for me? I wondered if you might bring something from your uncle's house?"

"Sure." My curiosity piqued, but I was suddenly aware of apprehension nibbling at the edges of my mind like a mouse trying to breach a cereal box. Was I jumping the gun, making plans? What if I called work, and Mel went postal about my taking a few more days off? I had plenty of vacation stored up, but that didn't mean that Mel intended for me to actually take it. "What do you need?"

Ruth glanced toward the lawn again, as if to make sure the girls couldn't hear us. "There may be some things . . . some . . . sketches of mine at Harmony House—tucked away in one of the closets or in the basement, perhaps. Your uncle probably doesn't even remember them. They may have been thrown away years ago, but will you look?"

Curiosity and something else . . . a tender sense that I owed Ruth this much and more pushed aside the looming dread of contacting Mel. I remembered Ruth sitting on Uncle Herbert's back deck with a drawing pad late in the afternoons when she was waiting to carpool home with a couple of ladies who did the cooking at the Waterbird store. Somehow, I'd gathered that Ruth's sketching time was private. She seldom showed me what she was drawing. When I asked her about it, she bought me a drawing pad of my own—a sketchbook and a journal. *It helps to put your troubles on paper,* she'd said in that cheery, simplistic way of hers. *Not to look at over and over again, but just to throw away.* She'd lifted a mixing spoon into the air, and I knew a Scripture was coming. Ruth loved quotations of all sorts, but she'd always stopped what she was doing when a Bible quote was on the way. *"Remember ye not the former things, neither consider the things of old."*

"Of course I'll look for your sketches," I told her now. "I'll ask Uncle Herbert if he knows where they are."

She shook her head quickly, then pulled her shawl closer around her shoulders. A sharp breeze rounded the corner and sliced its way along the porch, and she moved back a step in the doorway. "No, just look for them. Bring them to me if you can, but don't say anything to Herbert." The request had a mysterious quality.

"I will," I agreed, then told her good-bye.

Clay was headed toward the dairy barn with Mary and Emily when I reached the Ladybug. The girls were giggling and hanging from his arms with both hands, jumping and swinging through the air every time he yelled, "Look out! Alligator!" or "Oh no, it's a tarantula!"

"Do you need a ride to Amy's?" I called after him, the truck door squealing in protest as I opened it.

Clay spun around, slinging the girls like fins on a pinwheel, as they curled their feet into their skirts. "Nah, Amy's coming to get me. If she doesn't show up pretty soon, I'll just start walking that way until I run into her."

"Okay," I said, then left him to play with the other kids and climbed into the Ladybug, praying for a chug-free journey. As I wheeled around in the yard and started out the driveway, something bolted into my path, and I hit the brakes, causing them to squeal long and loud. Near the dairy barn, a teenage boy in jeans, a barn coat, and a hat stopped to look at me. He pointed to the front of my vehicle, and I stretched upward, catching sight of ears and a fluffy blond head. I'd almost forgotten Roger. Putting the truck in Park, I opened the door, and Roger scrambled across my lap before I could get out to allow him access.

As we rolled down the driveway, Roger yipped at Clay and the girls, now investigating something underneath the edge of the barn. Roger smelled like he might have been crawling around under there himself, and I hated to imagine what he'd left behind on the girls' dresses. Rolling down the window on his side to create a vacuum seemed the most prudent decision, so I leaned over and took care of it before we headed for home, me saying silent prayers for the Ladybug's continued health, and Roger happily lolling his tongue in the flow of fresh air before finally settling down for a nap, all worn out from playing with dairy dogs and cute little Mennonite girls.

When we returned to Uncle Herbert's house, the place was empty. There was no note and no explanation as to where everyone had gone. My frustration over being ducked by the family again inched up, but since I'd already decided to stay an extra day to see Ruth, there seemed to be no point in agonizing over it. I decided to take advantage of the quiet time to go down to the cottage, gather my laundry, and throw my things in the washer, so I'd have some clean clothes for tomorrow. The phone in the kitchen reminded me that a call to Mel was an absolute must-do tonight, and sooner was probably better.

I picked up the receiver, put it down, then picked it up again, only to set it back in the cradle. Around me, the house creaked and groaned, as cold and stiff as an old man climbing out of his chair on a winter night. My skin tingled with chills that had nothing to do with the drafts around the window sashes. I'd always hated being alone in this house. From the time I was big enough to understand that Uncle Herbert was in the business of handling final remains, I'd made any excuse I could not to come to Harmony House whenever we'd visited my grandparents out at the family farm. Usually, it was just as well, because Uncle Herbert's house was tied up with the funeral planning sessions, services, and visitations, as well as Aunt Esther's social engagements. Plus, Aunt Esther didn't really seem to like kids. Children running around weren't conducive to the peaceful, somewhat sophisticated atmosphere she was trying to cultivate.

That last year in Moses Lake, Clay had come home from school with countless ghost stories about the place. Legend had it that a young belle had hung herself in the stairway after her beau left her for someone else. Uncle Herbert said no such thing ever happened. I hadn't been upstairs since, and I'd always known what happened in the mortuary rooms in the basement, so I avoided that

228

area, as well. That didn't leave much territory.

Now even the kitchen felt spooky.

I heard Roger outside, and thought about the clothes that Clay had shoved in the back of the truck. Maybe, before making the Mel call, I'd grab those few things from the toolbox along with my laundry, then start a batch and bring Roger into the house to curb the creep factor. Roger could provide moral support while I called Mel.

The thought had barely begun to process before I was in the utility room, turning the heavy glass knob. When I opened the door, Roger was on the veranda, happily gnawing on something that may have been leather at one time, but now had the pockmarked, slimy consistency of a rawhide chew bone. It looked suspiciously like my wallet.

"Give me that!" I squealed and made a lunge. Roger leapt to the right, and we played a rousing game of keep-away on the frozen decking. Finally Roger bolted into the house, where we toured, at high speed, many of the rooms I'd never liked. I was reminded, while hunting for him upstairs, that Harmony House was filled with beautiful architectural details: ornately carved mantels gracing every room and gorgeous pilasters lining the halls. It was a grand house, if you didn't think of it as a funeral home.

By the time I finally cornered Roger in an upstairs bathroom and pried what remained of my wallet from his jowls, some of the creepy feeling had dissipated. If there were any ghosts watching, they were probably either laughing their heads off or feeling sorry for me by now. The exercise had helped me to pull my head together a bit, too. It was silly for me to be scared of a house. I wasn't a child anymore. *It's no different than any other house,* I told myself as I went downstairs with Roger trailing behind me, looking defeated. He sat at my feet, watching the emptying and towel-drying of my wallet and its contents. Miraculously, everything was still inside.

The newfound sense of empowerment from regaining my stuff made me feel almost whole again, except for the hollow spot in the center of my being, where my iPhone should have been. Trying not to think about it, I picked up the kitchen phone and reinstated my credit cards, then made my call to Mel. Fortunately, he didn't answer, so I was able to leave a voice mail explaining that the loss of my purse and some family issues were going to keep me in Moses Lake a couple of days longer. I left the funeral home number in case he needed to call me, and I promised to check in.

Now that I had my wallet with the little card that explained how to dial into my voice mail from another phone, I decided to check. There was a message from Gary the dentist, of all people. He wanted to tell me what a nice time his family had during our visit, following the rescue from the Dallas bus station. He also wanted me to get in touch sometime soon regarding designs for his new clinics. He and his partners were talking about building at least three more in the next year.

I mused on that as I slipped into my coat and went to the cottage in the thickening darkness to get my laundry. Then I headed to Clay's truck to gather the dirty clothes he'd deposited there. Maybe designing dental clinics wouldn't be so bad. It wasn't a state-of-the-art commercial production facility, but it was something. Maybe Gary really had the kind of money it would take to engage our firm. I could talk to Mel about discounting our fees. The man had saved my life, after all.

The Ladybug's toolbox seemed to be rusted shut when I attempted to open it, but muscle and determination finally won the battle. I pulled out Clay's frayed khaki cargo shorts first and quickly realized that his wallet and cell phone were in there. Apparently Amy was not only driving on the date, but she'd be paying for it, as well. Dropping the pants into the basket with my laundry, I reached into the toolbox again to grab the shirt. Something glass slid out of the pocket and clattered against the bottom, then rolled to one side. Behind me, Roger barked, and I jumped backward, the shifting moon shadows having set my nerves on edge.

"Roger, cut that out."

He answered with a growl that was surprisingly menacing, for Roger, and he homed in on something near the corner of the house. The branches of the bushes moved in the breeze, and for a moment I thought I saw someone there. A man in a dark coat and a fedora hat. Heebie-jeebies crawled over my skin, drawing forth an uncontrollable shudder.

"Stupid dog," I muttered, reaching into the toolbox and fishing around for whatever had dropped out of Clay's shirt. My fingers touched something small and round, roughly the size and shape of a prescription bottle, and a disquieting thought slid through my mind, fluid like the shadows. Why would Clay be carrying medication? Despite his reluctance to wear a coat and his strange eating habits, he was just about the healthiest person I knew. The object rolled in my palm as I lifted my hand and held it in the dim light fanning from the kitchen windows. It wasn't a prescription bottle, but it was a bottle of some kind—small and round, made of glass, with a plastic screw-on lid. There was a residue of something loose and silty inside.

Slipping it into my other hand, I reached in again and searched the floor of the metal toolbox. My fingers slid over a jumble of hammers and screwdrivers, some rusty nails, and a rubbery blob that felt like melted fishing worms. There was something else, but I couldn't quite reach it. . . .

Roger barked again, and nearby in the woods, a coyote howled. Roger took off to give chase, and it quickly became evident that no amount of hollering from me would bring him back. A sense of being watched slid over me again, causing me to give up the toolbox search and hurry inside. On the table in the laundry room, where casket draperies and curtains had always been folded, I laid out Clay's clothes and felt something in the baggy side pocket of his cargo shorts, then pulled out a dirt-encrusted ziplock bag. The plastic felt grainy, like it had sand on it or in it. Laying it on the table, I flattened it and looked closer. The residue inside the bag was powdery and white. A search of the other pants pocket turned up a small glass vial with a lid on it. The bottom of the vial had been charred. I held it to the light, looked inside. Empty.

A cold feeling traveled from my fingertips, through my arm, and into the center of my body. Setting the vial on the table, I pushed it to the corner near Clay's cell phone, raked all the clothes into the washer, dumped in soap, pushed the button, then stood with my hands gripping the corners of the washer, my back to the folding table. I didn't want to turn around. I was afraid to. I'd been living in the big city, in a high-pressure career field long enough to know what ziplock bags of powder and burnt test tubes meant.

What if that incident with Clay, the campus police, and the marijuana paraphernalia wasn't so innocent all those years ago? What if it was actually the beginning of something?

Was Clay into drugs? Was he using? Was that why his behavior was even more unpredictable lately? Could that be the reason he'd come to Moses Lake in the first place? Had he come here looking for an escape, a change of scenery, a chance to detox, far from whatever company he'd been keeping since he'd returned from the earthquake relief in the jungle? Could the problem have worsened there? Drugs were readily available in South America.

If it was true, did Amy know? Did she have any idea? Did Mom? Did the uncs? Did Blaine?

I turned around, looked at the bag and the vial. Clay wouldn't do something like this. He wouldn't. There had to be another explanation.

But the possibility that he had a problem could explain everything—his sudden hairpin life turn, my mother's willingness to support it, the uncs going along with some crazy plan for Clay and my mother to take over the restaurant, the canoeing business, and the house at Harmony Shores. Even Mom's willingness to be here made perfect sense now. She would do anything for Clay. Even pour all of her money into an ill-conceived business venture and a move to Moses Lake, especially if she thought his life depended on it.

I picked up Clay's cell phone, paged down the list of contacts. Blaine was on speed dial. So were Amy and my mother. The phone numbers for Harmony House and Catfish Charley's weren't even in Clay's address book. If you were really planning to take over a business, wouldn't you have the phone number logged into your cell? Wouldn't you be spending time there? A lot of time?

Was it possible that Clay didn't have any intention of following through with this deal? That all of this was some sort of scheme to take the money and run? I couldn't imagine my brother doing a thing like that. Clay had always been the kindest, gentlest person I knew. He never wanted to hurt anyone. I could picture him bringing about the family's downfall accidentally, through lack of planning, inadequate foresight, his usual pie-in-the-sky attitude . . . but on purpose? My brother didn't have that in him.

But people feeding a habit did strange things. Terrible things . . .

I heard the door slam in the foyer, and I jumped, my heart bolting into my throat, my body caught in a moment of indecision. Should I leave the evidence on the table, confront Mom and the uncs about it? Should I wait and ask Clay in private? If I kept it private, would I be helping Clay to hide it, enabling him?

Uncle Charley was turning the corner into the

kitchen. Sweeping Clay's things into a towel, I folded it up and tucked it on the top of the dryer behind a laundry basket.

"Well, there you are." Uncle Charley set a Styrofoam container on the counter. "We stopped off at the restaurant for a bite. Didn't have any way to get ahold of you, but we brought you some fried catfish and hush puppies. Good eats." Pausing, he directed his full attention toward me, scratching his head as if I'd confused him in some way. "You all right? You're pale as a Sun-dey shirt."

"I don't feel so well." I caught the scent of fried food either coming from the box, or wafting off Uncle Charley's clothes. My stomach roiled. "I think I'm just going to head down to the cottage and get ready for bed early. I started some laundry, but I can finish it in the morning."

"We could put a movie on while you wait," Uncle Charley suggested. "Sit up a little till you're feelin' better. Your mama's got a whole bunch of them teas she makes. Her and Herbert'll be here in a minute, I reckon. We ran by the church, and I picked up my truck. Must be they got tied up talkin' to somebody. The associational music meetin' was just letting out. I scooted before all them old hens could waylay me. Good-lookin' single fella like me has to be careful."

He winked and smiled, but I could only shake my head and stumble back a step, my mind on

Clay. "I think I'm just tired. It's been a long day."

"A good day, though." Uncle Charley's soft brown eyes, so like my father's, met mine, and for an instant I imagined my father standing there. He would hate seeing our family this way. He'd be worried to death about Clay. "It's good you're here, Heather."

"Thanks." Emotion choked the word. I hugged him, and he held on for a minute, rocking me back and forth. I closed my eyes and imagined I was hugging my dad. What would he do, if he were here right now?

"Good to have family back in Moses Lake." His voice was rough and gravely against my ear, his hands so dry and weathered they scratched over the fabric of my T-shirt like sandpaper. "The older you get, the more you realize that's what matters. I love you, darlin'. You're the spittin' image of your daddy, and I always loved all my brothers' kids, since I couldn't have any of my own. I love you younger ones, too."

I felt sick again. Did Uncle Charley have any idea what was going on with Clay, what was hidden in the towel just a few feet away? "I love you, too, Uncle Charley." I meant it, but all I could think was, *Grab the towel. Don't forget to grab the towel.*

The tender moment ended as quickly as it had begun. Uncle Charley handed me the Styrofoam container and a to-go cup of iced tea, just in case

I wanted it later. I slipped the towel with Clay's belongings on top of food, then escaped out the back door and hurried down the hill. Overhead, an owl hooted in the trees and the wind clattered among the branches, sending a shudder across my shoulders. I didn't catch my breath until I'd rounded the corner of the cottage and stepped into the glow of the porch light.

A small stack of freshly-split firewood had been left in the rack by the steps. On top of it was a box. I picked it up and recognized the picture of a woman in a snuggly blanket toasting her feet in front of a brand-new electric heater. A note had been tucked into the edge of the box.

Cold night ahead, it read. There was no signature, but I knew who'd left the heater and the stack of wood there on my porch.

If there is magic on this planet,
it is contained in water.
—Loren Eisely
(*left by Kat and Rhee, gal pals on a
girlfriend weekend in Cabin 3*)

≋ Chapter 11 ≋

When I woke in the morning, a solitary loon was singing to the rising sun. In the misty hinterland of sleep-waking, I realized I was baking alive under my pile of quilts, thanks to last night's load of firewood and the new handy-dandy electric heater, which wouldn't have to remain a freebie now that Roger had returned my wallet. Throwing off the covers, I peeled my pajamas away from my sweaty skin. Outside the window, the pile of firewood was just visible, and with it came a warm feeling that had nothing to do with the temperature in the room. It really was nice of Blaine to bring the firewood and dig up an electric heater for me while we were gone to Ruth's . . . thoughtful.

Now, did I want to admit that to him, or not?

I pictured him giving me that wickedly confident smile—overconfident, really—those big, boyish eyes twinkling. How many times, while slaving over the high-school-yearbook layout, had I dreamed of those eyes? I gave Blaine the prime spots on every page—in the feature about the guys who had lettered in more than one sport, in the article cataloging debate team awards, on the page with the homecoming court, and the section about the Fellowship of Christian Athletes. He became the poster child on the page listing football stats. I added him and his Hampshire hog to the feature about the county fair, bumping some other kid and some other pig, who had actually won the blue ribbon.

I wondered if Blaine ever noticed that he was the center of yearbook fame that year, if he knew who was behind it, or if he was even aware that the quiet girl in the dark clothes worked on the yearbook. I was only in the journalism class because I had to be somewhere, and it was a good place to hide out. Journalism was during the athletics period. The room was filled with nerds and misfits who didn't talk to anyone. It was a fairly comfortable way to spend the hour, and I could moon over pictures of all the kids to whom I was invisible. I could fantasize that, because I'd put them in the yearbook, they would suddenly decide to invite me to their secret parties at Blue Moon Bay and ask me to share lab tables in chemistry class.

There was no end to the rock-star status of Blaine Underhill back then. He was always the center of a crowd, cracking jokes and handing out high fives. Too cool for someone like me. Too self-important to even look my way. Could it be that, all that time, he really was a genuinely nice guy, and I was the one with the attitude problem? Had I been largely the cause of my year of Moses Lake High School misery—the big, fat chip on my shoulder and the secrets at home causing me to reject everyone before they could reject me?

Was I still doing it?

Was that why my life was stuck in the same place? Was I really still the girl who lived in the shadows, coming home and locking myself in my room so that I would never again become close to anyone, because people could be gone in a heartbeat? Had I forgotten Richard's birthday, maintained unusually long lag times between our dates, resisted calling him on nights when I actually could have . . . because I was trying to establish a certain separation? Was it all a subconscious effort to keep my distance, even as I fantasized about engagement rings and told myself I wanted a life with him?

Was I really that big of a coward? That much of a mess?

Sighing, I rested my elbows on my knees and combed a mop of tangles from my face. I felt like my hair looked—twisted up, tied in knots. Either the heat in the cottage or this place, Moses Lake, was making me insane.

The towel and yesterday's clothes stacked

nearby on a wooden chest caught my eye, breaking the morning reverie. It looked harmless enough, an innocent still life of sloppy housekeeping. But through the white terrycloth, Clay's cell phone flashed lazily, and of course, I knew what else was wrapped in the towel. Evidence. Hints of something terrible.

The reality descended on me, heavy and hard to manage so early in the day, like a death you forget about overnight, and for the first few glorious moments of waking, it doesn't exist. Then your mind engages, and it hits you like a slap, turning life upside down again.

There was no way I could leave Moses Lake now—not considering what I'd found in Clay's pockets last night. I had to get to the bottom of things, make sure my brother received whatever help he needed. I'd have to call Mel and let him know I'd walked into a family crisis. I would need a few more days.

Just a few? What if it took longer? I couldn't imagine hopping a plane and going home without proof that my brother was all right, but part of me wanted to run, to retreat to my own life. Anything could happen with the Itega project next week. Beyond that, the problems here, this issue with Clay, were far beyond the scope of my experience, far beyond my control.

Back home in Seattle, life was structured, manageable. In Seattle, I didn't wake up freezing, or sweating under a pile of quilts that smelled like old fabric and humidity off the lake. I didn't find strange things in people's pockets. My apartment was a peaceful shrine to furniture designed by some of the masters and procured from eBay. There were no dusty corners or leaky windows plugged with wads of Kleenex, or people doing things that were unpredictable, dangerous, impossible to face.

I loved my life in Seattle. I loved my apartment. I'd always loved that apartment. It was modern, clean, spacious, located in a concept building I'd helped design. There were retail stores on the bottom, then two floors of income-assisted apartments designed to help homeless families get back on their feet. From there on up, the higher you went, the nicer the apartments got. I was about three-quarters of the way to the top. Not bad for a girl only thirty-four years old.

My days in Seattle were mine to manage, mine to control, mine to schedule. Here in Moses Lake, the days tacked back and forth with the whimsy of a poorly-rigged catamaran, buffeted by the winds and the water, propelled by forces I could neither anticipate nor direct. This place, my family, made me crazy. Challenged everything I knew about myself.

Crawling to the edge of the bed, I leaned across and reached for Clay's cell phone. In an hour or so, I could call Mel and try to beg off for a longer stay. Mel was always in a better mood first thing in the morning, before the office came to life. Not a good mood, especially lately, but he was slightly less likely to breathe fire and render me to ashes.

The phone was cool in my hand, chilled by its proximity to the window, where the war of hot and cold air had formed diamond-like patterns of frost on the glass—tiny masterpieces that caught the morning sun in a dazzling array of facets. The surface felt grainy beneath my fingertip, the frost slowly melting, a dewy hole forming.

A memory struck me, old, and misty like the frost. Dad and I were studying the crystals on a windowpane, watching the sun illuminate its intricate designs. I was fascinated by their complexity, their beauty, their geometric structure. That so much detail could be laced into something so small, so insignificant as frost on a window-pane stretched my mind, pulled me toward a belief my father shared that day, in his quiet, unassuming way. The very proof of God's infinite power was in the details of life—those things we often looked past. His work was everywhere. In people. In nature. In the sensations that traveled through human contact, in the pleasantness of a loved one's voice.

We sometimes don't see God because we're so busy looking for something more complicated than frost on glass, my father had told me that day. *If God could put that much effort into something that only lasts a few hours in this world, think about how much He pondered you.*

A sigh pressed my throat. I couldn't remember the last time I'd studied the frost on a windowpane—given it, or God, any real thought. These days, I got up on Easter and Christmas and went to church because it was something I'd always done with my dad. I was afraid he'd be disappointed in me if I didn't, and showing up at church a few times a year was a way of apologizing for the wretch I'd been before he died.

Last Christmas, Richard and I had even gone to midnight mass at one of the historic churches downtown, but that was about as deep as my thoughts went. Most days I had enough on my mind. I was running on too little sleep and too much caffeine. The rush of daily existence didn't leave time for contemplating frost. But sitting here in Moses Lake, I felt the lack of connection in my life, the lack of contemplation of something larger. In the years of working for Mel, of trying to earn my stripes under his tutelage, I'd become like Mel. Mel had no life. His wife had left him. His kids never called. He was living in a big house. Alone.

At the very least, I had to be sure that my family was all right before I left Moses Lake. At the very most, I might find some of what was missing inside me. A connection. But how could I explain that to Mel? Spirituality and emotion meant nothing to him. Family was not a permissible excuse for lack of work performance. A day or two extension of this trip was bad enough, but a potentially open-ended leave to see to the care of a brother who might be struggling with a drug problem? There was no way.

If I wanted to keep my career intact, I had to find a solution to my family issues—and quickly. The real estate papers that had been so important a day ago hardly seemed to matter now. That issue paled in comparison to my little brother's future.

Setting the phone back on the windowsill, I decided to opt for a detailed email later that morning. I exhaled a warm breath to create a fog on the glass, drew a little heart in it with my fingertip. Somehow everything would work out. It had to work out. . . .

Please, God, show me how all of this works out . . .

A movement on the porch pulled me close to the glass again. Barely visible in the bottom corner of the window, a blond tail lay curled over a rubbery black nose.

Roger was sleeping on my doormat?

The chill of morning slipped over my legs as I found my slippers and crossed the cottage to the other side, to look out the kitchen window toward the house. It was awfully cold last night; not very nice of Clay to leave his dog outside.

Rolling my eyes, I went to the front door,

opened it, and surprised Roger, causing him to scramble on the icy decking. The tips of his fur were covered with frost, and miniature icicles clung to the ends of his whiskers.

"What are you doing out here?" I whispered.

With a soulful look my way, Roger walked past me into the cottage like he owned the place.

"Oh, for heaven's sake," I muttered as Clay's dog proceeded to investigate the living room, his tail sweeping and swatting various pieces of furniture, stirring up dust moats.

"Where's Clay?"

Roger paused to look at me again, both brows lifting, as in, *Search me?*

Crossing the room to the cabinet filled with free promotional mugs and treasures from estate sales, I took down a '40s-era jelly glass with yellow flowers and a picket fence painted on it. It reminded me of my grandmother. She'd had an entire collection in the house at the farm. I loved to look at the various designs. Grandma was, in general, particular about her things, but she always let me select my own glass, even the ones from her good china. She was trying to build a rapport with me, I understood now, but in general, I resisted her offers to teach me how to crochet or can pickles or bake nut bread. I'd heard countless arguments between my parents about visits to *that house* with *that woman.* I knew I wasn't supposed to like it there.

Filling the jelly glass with water, I poured some in a bowl and put it down for Roger, and he drank like he was dying of thirst. Either his water dish at the house was empty again, or it was frozen over. Poor thing. Maybe even he didn't feel like traversing the frozen mud at the edge of the lake to get a drink. I was tempted to take Roger's water dish, march it into the big house, and put it in bed with Clay. If he was going to be out until all hours of the night, the least he could do was to make sure someone looked out for Roger. . . .

Headlights pressed through the murky fog on the driveway, slowly growing brighter in the mist. I watched as they drifted closer, cutting the fog, disappearing into the low area where the driveway crossed a small watershed, then appearing again. Who would be visiting so early? Grabbing a dish towel, I wiped the condensation from the window and leaned close to gain a view of the parking area beside the house, where the family cars were kept. The approaching vehicle looked like Amy's, but it was hard to tell in the dim light. I watched as the passenger door opened, and Clay climbed out. He stood talking a moment, his hand on the door-frame, then he leaned in one more time, like he was going for a good-bye kiss before closing the door.

A blush traveled down my neck. I felt like a voyeur.

He stood in the driveway watching as the car

made the loop and retreated into the fog, then he tiptoed toward the house and, of all things, stole down the cellar stairs like some sort of miscreant. I wanted to go up there, catch him sneaking in, and smack him. Twenty-seven, and he was staying out all night, then slipping through the cellar door? How involved were he and Amy, anyway? Did she have any idea that he had ziplock bags and unmarked vials hidden in his pockets?

Another possibility entered my logic stream, and the data byte was disturbing in a new way. How could she not know, if she and Clay were spending this much time together? What if it was *okay* with her? Surely, whatever he was into, they weren't into together. She didn't seem the type. She had a job, a decent car. For a girl barely out of high school, she seemed fairly stable, living somewhere in that hinterland between childhood and adulthood, still in her parents' house, doing what people from Gnadenfeld did if they weren't headed to college—working for Proxica, where there was decent pay and health insurance. How did Amy's parents feel about her staying out all night with a guy who was eight or nine years older and worldly, in comparison to her?

Theories buzzed in my head, landing just long enough for me to swish them away and dismiss them. It couldn't be true—but there was only one way to know for sure. Clay, and probably my mother, held the answers to these questions, and I needed those answers. I had to know what I was dealing with. If Clay did have a substance-related problem—it was hard to even think those words in conjunction with my brother—I couldn't leave him with my mother. Her friends smoked weed in the name of inspiration, and she seemed to have no problem with that. There were good treatment facilities around Seattle. I could take Clay home with me and work with him to find the right kind of program. If he did need help, Moses Lake, a teenage girlfriend, and my mother weren't the solution.

The issues tumbled in my mind as I showered, dressed in jeans and one of my new Moses Lake sweatshirts, and mentally prepared for a trip up the hill and a conversation about Clay's issues. Roger was scratching and whining in the entry-way, ready to be let out as I took one last look at the towel with the vials wrapped inside, then grabbed my coat, tucked Clay's cell phone and wallet into a pocket, and proceeded to the front door.

My wristwatch caught a thread on the coat, hemming me in momentarily as I attempted to knee Roger out of the way and work my arm loose at the same time. "Roger, quit." For whatever reason, he was determined to dig his way out rather than moving, and finally the sacrifice of a few threads or the wristwatch seemed worth it in order to grab the collar and manhandle the dog. "Move out of the . . . Come . . . on . . ."

The moment the gap was wide enough, Roger lurched forward, taking the collar and my fingers with him. We staggered out the door in a tangle, each growling for different reasons, and the door slammed shut behind us. Canine momentum carried us halfway down the porch before I found my feet and brought the situation under control. Roger, intent on something near the corner of the cottage, continued straining as I leaned over, catching a glimpse of the dull, wintery shadow of a crape myrtle tree shifting and the branches snapping against the house, as if someone had just brushed by. Fine hairs rose on my skin, and I felt a prickle that had nothing to do with the cold. Just like last night, I had the feeling that someone was nearby.

"Clay?" I whispered. Maybe he'd seen me in the window and realized I'd noticed him coming home in the early morning hours.

No answer. Roger sniffed the air, his throat rumbling.

"Is someone there?" Pulling Roger along, I crept across the porch and down the steps. I couldn't see anyone in the yard, along the shore, or near the barn. Nothing out there but the quiet morning shadows and the waters of Moses Lake, blue-gray in this light, lapping at a ribbon of ice along the shore. A flock of mallards circled, honking and chattering, in search of a landing place.

Roger stopped growling and turned his attention

to the birds, yapping and wagging his tail. The minute I let go of his collar, he was gone, and I wrapped my coat closed, hustling up the hill, my breath coming in quick, smoky bursts. The lights were on in the kitchen, and the scent of coffee bid a cheery hello, dispelling the sense of uneasiness that had come over me at the cottage.

Mom was on the sun porch, wrapped in a quilt, watching the lake and sipping her morning coffee while reading a copy of Charlotte Brontë's *Villette*.

"Oh, you're up," she observed, like she wasn't entirely thrilled about it. "There's coffee in the pot."

"I'll grab some in a minute." Leaning against the doorway, I glanced over my shoulder, making sure no one was sharing space with us. This was probably as good a time as any to feel Mother out about Clay and drugs. I had to be subtle. If I just bluntly asked, she'd jump to his defense and if she did know what was going on with him, she'd feel like she was doing him a service by hiding it from me. Clay had been gone on the earthquake relief mission for weeks before she'd even admitted to me that he'd left, and that was only because I'd gotten an email newsletter, soliciting donations. The notice had Clay's email address on it, and he was pictured with the crew, helping to convert shipping containers into emergency housing. Mom hadn't told me, because she knew that I'd complain about his taking another detour from law school and hocking the last car she bought him.

"Where is everyone this morning?" That seemed like a suitably innocuous opening line.

She shifted the half-moon-shaped reading glasses lower on her nose, so as to get a better look at me. "Haven't seen the uncs, but you know they usually get up and head straight to the Waterbird to drink coffee and do political commentary with the docksiders. They could be gone already. I'm not sure where Clay is—still in bed, I suppose. Guess he and Amy made a late night of it."

So late that he just got home, I thought, but I didn't say it. One issue at a time. "Amy seems sweet."

"Yes, very." Mom took another sip of coffee, eyeing me with obvious reserve. She was wondering where this conversation was headed.

"Is it serious—this thing between Clay and Amy?"

Mom's head tipped to one side. "A little, I think. Why?"

I shrugged and reached across the doorframe to brush a smudge of dirt, but it didn't come off. "I don't know. I just wondered how Clay could be so close to someone in Moses Lake. I mean, he just got back from South America a couple of months ago."

"They knew each other back when Clay was in

253

school here. Her brother was in Clay's class. Clay remembers going over to their house a few times." She acted as if that explained everything. Of course Clay and Amy could be dating seriously —they were playmates when Clay was in elementary school and Amy was barely out of diapers.

I found myself searching for the path from dating Amy to, *So . . . does my little brother have a drug problem?* Unfortunately, my mother was an astute woman. She understood language. She'd spent a lifetime dissecting it, manipulating it, analyzing the fine points of character motivation. I reminded myself to watch my body language, so as not to tip her off. Thank goodness for those Dale Carnegie classes. "You don't think it seems a little odd . . .?" *That they're out all night, and he's ditching Roger for her?*

She shrugged. "I think it's fine. Your father and I met one month and ran away to get married the next. It wasn't anywhere in my plans or his. It just happened."

And look how that turned out. I drew back at the thought, and she must have seen it, because she stiffened, her lips pursing. She pulled her glasses off and set them in her lap. "People fall in love, Heather. Sometimes at first sight, even."

I blinked hard. I couldn't help it. Now, on top of encouraging Clay to give up law school for frying catfish, Mom was in favor of my little brother falling into a relationship with a girl he barely knew? "So you think it's, like, love at first sight?"

Mom licked her lips, and I could feel a debate coming on. Her eyes brightened and sharpened, like a cat's when it spots a tempting movement in the grass and it's contemplating a little sport. "Don't you believe in love at first sight, Heather?" My mother had the most annoying habit of answering a question with a larger question—broadening a simple, concrete discussion into the sort of nebulous, intellectual debate she and her crowd lived for. This topic was obtuse, even for her.

"What does it matter what I believe? We were talking about Clay."

Mom watched me with a closed-lipped smile that conveyed anything but pleasure. "There's someone for everyone, right? Maybe she's his someone. Isn't that the way it is with you and Richard?"

My stomach dropped through my shoes. I swallowed hard, an uncomfortable, tingly feeling in the back of my nose. Did she know about Richard and me? Had she said that just to land a blow, to shut me up?

"Is Clay all right?" I blurted out.

Mom jerked back, her chin tucking in. For just a flicker of an instant, I saw a crack in the calm façade, a hint that there was more going on here.

My mind once again spun the scenario in which Clay, under pressure in college and impulsive by nature, had experimented with drugs, then perhaps broadened a habit in some third-world country where the hard stuff was easy to get. Was that really it? Was she convinced that she could fix the situation by moving to Moses Lake, by letting him take over the restaurant and the canoe and cabin business?

She crossed her arms, the copy of *Villette* sliding off her knee and landing soundlessly in the chair. "I've never seen your brother more centered. It's *you* I worry about, really. You seem so uptight, Heather. So . . . unhappy."

Maybe that's because everything is upside down and backward and nothing makes sense, and no one will tell me the truth. "Does Clay have a drug problem?"

I'd done it. I'd gone too far, spilled the beans.

Her reaction was exactly what I expected. She blinked at me like I was the crazy one, then gave a sardonic little laugh. "Really, Heather. That's going too far. Why would you even say that?"

I bit my tongue, knowing better than to tip my hand again. I'd revealed too much, but something in her reaction told me I'd struck a nerve, scratched close to whatever they were keeping hidden.

She masked any initial shock with a sympathetic, slightly sad look. "I know you have some rivalry issues toward your brother, but honestly, why not just be happy for him? Not everything in life is a competition, Heather. Not everything is a race. There's something to be said for learning to just . . . be."

I swallowed hard, pinched my lips between my teeth, felt my eyes bulging with the pressure of the things I was biting back. *Me? Competitive toward Clay? Puh-lease! In what way, and for what reason?* "I'm worried about him—that's all."

A hand swat dismissed the notion. "Don't be. Your brother is fine. Everything's fine. Just because things aren't happening according to your plan does not mean anything's wrong. Perhaps the rest of us are entitled to want something com-pletely different. Perhaps, Heather, you should leave the ruling of the universe to bigger hands than your own."

I didn't bother to delve into the meaning of that sentence. There was no point. My mother was just spinning words that were, like much of her poetry, intended for shock value. My only choice was to retreat, sufficiently burned, and leave her to Brontë.

Passing through the family rooms, I found my brother sacked out on an antique brocade parlor settee, his head and shoulders askew against a pile of needlepoint pillows Aunt Esther had probably purchased at various church bazaars. A trail of drying mud-and-grass footprints led across the room from the cellar door. The path ended at Clay's feet, which were hanging off the sofa, as if he'd sat down to take off his shoes and simply crashed. I stood over him, watching him breathe. His nose and cheeks were still red from the cold. A piece of a dead oak leaf had tangled near his ear, its brown color slightly darker than the sandy strands around it. His hands were dirty, grime pressed under the fingernails, and the cuffs of his pants hung wet and sloppy over his shoes.

I tried to imagine where he'd been. Maybe he and Amy went parking in the woods? Back in high school, that was what local kids did. They knew all the out-of-the-way spots at the Ice Hole, Seven Springs, and Blue Moon Bay, where they could hang out and party without getting nabbed by the sheriff's department, rangers from the state park, or the local game wardens. Wasn't Clay a little old for that? Then again, he was dating a girl who was not far out of high school.

"Oh, Clay." I sighed, trying to see through him, to understand what was going on. Finally, I leaned over and shook his shoulder, attempted to rouse him, but I knew it was probably an exercise in futility. Once Clay fell asleep, a freight train could speed through the room, and he wouldn't notice. He only moaned and pulled away, his head falling off the pillows. Finally, it seemed hopeless to do anything more than cover him with a lap quilt and move on. Uncle Charley passed through the room just as I was about to walk away.

"Looks like he didn't make it to the bed last night." Uncle Charley jingled a set of keys in his hand.

"Guess not." I didn't have the heart to point out that Clay had come in only a short time ago. Apparently, Uncle Charley hadn't noticed the damp shoes or the tracks on the floor.

"I'm headed down to the Waterbird." He thumbed over his shoulder in the general direction of the driveway. "You could come along and class up the joint."

I was tempted for a minute. Morning banter with the docksiders and a funny story or two seemed like just what I needed. Maybe I'd run into Blaine there. . . .

The thought was appealing in some way I was afraid to analyze, especially first thing in the morning, not yet into an initial cup of coffee. "I'd better not." In terms of what I needed to take care of in Moses Lake, I would accomplish nothing by hanging out at the Waterbird. "I'm supposed to go see Ruth for lunch. By the way, can I borrow one of the cars this afternoon?"

Uncle Charley nodded, patting me on the shoulder. "Sure, help yerself to whatever's out there. The keys are on the pegboard by the washin' machine, where Herb always keeps 'em." He thumbed in the general direction of the kitchen. "I'm glad you're gonna see Ruth. She can use the company. All the young folks are out working the dairy during the day or in school—or runnin' around after the chickens, like little Mary and Emily. As you get old, you sit by yourself too much, seems like."

The words had an unusually somber quality, and I realized something I hadn't before: Uncle Charley was lonely, despite all of his connections to the community in Moses Lake. He had no kids of his own, his wife was gone, and the nieces and nephews he'd helped to raise were living far away now. Clay, my mother, and I weren't much of a substitute. Clay did his own thing, Mom kept her nose in a book, and I was only in town for a few days.

I couldn't come up with the right thing to say, so I changed the subject. "Listen, Ruth asked me to look for some sketches of hers. She didn't want them to end up in the estate sale, I think."

Uncle Charley chuckled. "Oh mercy, if you find any of her pictures around here, don't tell Herb you're takin' them back to her. Ruth used to draw them things and then put them in the trash. Herb would fish 'em out and hide 'em away. You know that Herb can't stand to see anything good thrown out. One of the few fights I ever saw the two of them have was over those sketches. I don't know why Ruth didn't just take them home to throw away, but Mennonite folk can be kind of funny about pastimes like art. The older, stricter folks don't always approve. Guess maybe that's why she did her sketchin' here, and why she was a little embarrassed about it. Anyway, if there's any of her drawings still around, Herb would've tucked them away someplace where Ruth wouldn't know. You'll just have to look around."

We said good-bye then, and he headed for the Waterbird. I made a cup of coffee for myself and began canvassing the house. Since I didn't want to go into the basement, particularly not first thing in the morning, with the light still dim, I concentrated on closets and bedrooms and did my best to ignore the creaks and moans of the old house. Footsteps passed by in the hall as I searched bedrooms. I assured myself that it was the floor joists creaking as the morning warmed.

In a quilt trunk in the bedroom where my mother was staying, I found a sketch pad. The cover lay crinkled with age and had been snacked on by a mouse, who quite fortunately was no longer present. An odd feeling settled over me as I slipped the pad from its hiding place, closed the lid of the trunk and sat on it, and then ran a finger along the edge of the pages. Only a few remained, just a sheet or two of paper tucked between the covers. If Ruth's sketches were private enough that she wanted to make sure they weren't left in the house, maybe I shouldn't be looking.

But I couldn't help it. I lifted the cover anyway. The first page was blank, a faint image in charcoal having bled through from the page behind it, the ghost of a stranger, the hint of body.

I lifted the sheet, watched it flip over, saw the face of a young woman. She'd been captured, frozen in a moment in time, her eyes filled with life, her dark hair swirling around her waist in loose waves. She'd turned to look over her shoulder, as if someone had surprised her from behind. A friend or a lover.

Her essence had been preserved in charcoal, in confident strokes of gray.

Her floral print dress and her eyes were blue. Pastel.

I watched her, tried to imagine the moment Ruth had recorded. Who was the woman? Her dress was vintage, perhaps from the forties, but form-fitting and stylish—not Mennonite garb by any means. The barest hint of a smile played on her lips, as if she were toying with someone.

I wondered what secrets she'd been keeping all these years as she lay in the quilt trunk.

In this house, everyone had secrets.

But whosoever drinketh of the water
that I shall give him shall never thirst.
—John 4:14
(*Left by Jack, glad to be back,
found God on a battlefield in Iraq*)

≈ Chapter 12 ≈

I finished searching out-of-the-way places upstairs and netted nothing beyond the picture of the woman in the blue floral dress. When I came back down, Clay's cell phone was vibrating in my coat pocket in the utility room. Tucking the drawing pad under my arm, I slipped the phone out and took it to the family parlor, where Clay was still crashed on the settee. The phone buzzing near his head didn't seem to bother him in the least. An incoming text from someone named Tara was on the screen. Tilting my head, I read the first few words. *Hey, babe. I miss u bad . . .*

I blinked, sidestepped, and touched the phone with one finger, swiveling it toward me. This technically amounted to snooping, but I couldn't help myself. Who in the world was Tara?

. . . come home soon, K? Not fair leaving me here alone for Mimi's party, BTW. . . .

The text went on from there, but I resisted the urge to scroll down. The area code was 817—Fort

Worth, like Gary the dentist. Clay had a girlfriend in the Metroplex? One who expected him to go to *Mimi's* party with her? Who was Mimi? Who was Tara? She was waiting for him to come home sometime soon? Where was *home?*

He'd left some girl behind and not even told her he planned to move to Moses Lake?

My stomach sank. The cell message lent credence to a theory I still didn't want to entertain —that my brother really was scamming everyone in Moses Lake, and he had no plans to stay. What about poor little Amy? She seemed completely smitten with him. Was he planning to dump her and move on whenever he was done here? Was he two-timing her with another girl? Did Amy have any idea? Could Clay do something like that? He'd never been the kind of person to intentionally hurt someone. Could he possibly have changed that much?

But a drug addiction could change people completely, make them do things they wouldn't normally do. . . .

A floorboard squeaked, and I jerked back. My mother was in the doorway. She looked from the cell phone to me, as if *I* were the one doing something nefarious.

I didn't bother defending myself. We'd played enough verbal chess already. "Who's Tara?"

She blinked, remaining silent for a moment, then shrugged, indicating that she had no idea.

"You'd have to ask your brother, I guess." A curious glance angled toward the drawing pad I'd unearthed upstairs.

"Clay's not answering any questions right now." I glared at him in a way that should have fried him on the spot. "He was out all night. With Amy."

Mom only smiled pleasantly, rolling her eyes a little, as in, *Boys will be boys,* then she gave Clay an adoring glance, indicating that he could do no wrong. "He *is* an adult, Heather." Another glance targeted the drawing pad with a hint of suspicion.

I flipped a hand in the air, frustration taking over. Again. "You know what, I've got to get out of here for a while." I wasn't about to show her the sketch of the girl in the floral dress. In a game where everyone seemed to be one step ahead of me, there was a small but perverse nugget of satisfaction in the fact only I knew about Ruth's request. "I'll see you later."

An idea popped into my mind, lightning fast and strangely alluring. Amy was Blaine's cousin. Blaine was probably at work at the bank. How much did he know about Clay and Amy's relationship?

Mom's lips pursed, as if she suspected that I was up to something. "Where are you going?"

What do you care? I wanted to answer, but instead, I just said, "I have some things to do, and then I'm eating lunch at Ruth's." I vacated the room without giving her a chance to

265

formulate any more questions, then moved through Uncle Herbert's office, the kitchen, and the utility room at a good clip. I didn't stop until I'd commandeered a funeral sedan and rolled out the driveway, leaving Mom and Clay to continue their codependent dance without me.

If Mom wasn't willing to be forthcoming about Clay's issues, other sources of information would have to fill in the blanks. A little background about Clay's previous visits to Moses Lake and his relationship with Amy might be helpful. How long *had* they known each other? How often did he visit? What did he do when he came? What was his motivation for visiting?

A sickening possibility nibbled at my mind. Even back when we lived in Moses Lake, Chinquapin Peaks and the remote areas along the river were known drug havens. Far from any paved roads, up in the timber country, marijuana patches grew in secret and meth labs operated in the woods. Maybe Clay was coming to the area for . . .

Stop it. Just stop. That's ridiculous.

I had to quit jumping to conclusions. My sources of information in Moses Lake being few, Blaine was a logical choice. Surely, Blaine wouldn't want his cousin setting herself up for heartbreak. He would want to protect her, wouldn't he?

Aside from the need for information, the idea of

seeing Blaine was alluring in a way I didn't want to contemplate. It wasn't until I reached the bank that I realized I had no idea what I was going to say or how I'd broach the subject. I couldn't just walk into Blaine's office and blurt it out. Somehow I had to work my way around to it. Delicately. Tactfully.

Was there a tactful way to say, *My brother is cheating on your cute little cousin, and I found what looks like drug paraphernalia in his pocket, and I'm wondering if she's involved, too?* Blaine would think I was some sort of a paranoid crazy person, obsessed with my brother's life.

I tried to come up with an opening line as I walked through the lobby and tracked down Blaine's office. The blinds were closed over the tall plate-glass windows with his name painted in gold letters, and the blonde who'd been whispering in his ear at church sat poised behind a desk in front of his door. *Marilyn*, the nameplate read.

Marilyn's face narrowed in a way that told me she knew who I was, even if I couldn't place her. Folding her nicely manicured hands on the desk, she gave me an unhappy look when I asked to see Blaine. "He's in a meeting." After tongue-swiping her teeth for lipstick, she flashed a quick, plastic smile, her gaze sliding toward the exit and back, as if to sweep me through the lobby and out into the street like a stray dust bunny. "Do you have an appointment?"

"No, but I'll wait." I moved to one of the maroon-and-gray tweed chairs opposite her desk.

My continued presence rated an eye roll, her irises forming unnaturally blue half moons beneath her lashes, which were unnaturally blue, as well. I remembered the blue mascara and the peeved expression from high school algebra class, and suddenly the name clicked, too. *Marilyn Hill.* When I was at Moses Lake High, she was a second-year senior who'd transferred in from some other state to live with her grandparents. She was finishing up a few credits in order to graduate. She was tall, blond, and well developed, even then. All the boys were fascinated with her, including the algebra teacher. Marilyn didn't like algebra. The teacher cut her a break every chance he got, which I found irksome at the time.

"I'll tell him you stopped by." She wagged a finger in my direction, as if to indicate that she was searching her memory banks for my name. "Uhhh . . . Don't tell me. I know it starts with an H. . . ."

The door opened behind her, and both of us jerked toward the sound. Blaine poked his head out, saw me there, and smiled, seeming not the least bit surprised by my presence in his bank. "Well, hey," he said.

A fluttery feeling flitted around my chest, touching here and there at random, like a cleaning lady with a feather duster. I forgot all about my brother. "Hey, yourself." The words came out sounding throaty, flirtatious. Embarrassingly familiar, actually.

Marilyn drew back in her chair, her chin tucking into her neck, creating an accordion of flesh that looked like it belonged on someone much older. Clearly, she liked me even less now than she had a few minutes ago.

Leaning out the door, Blaine handed her a folder with papers askew inside it. "Make sure Charlotte gets these."

Marilyn's long, red fingernails closed over the file, her fingertips brushing his in a way that indicated . . . well . . . something. "All right." The words came with a scrunchy playful sneer. "But you'll owe me."

"Always do." He was smiling when he said it, but there was a hint of weariness in the undertone, as if he was tired of whatever game she was playing.

Blaine turned his attention my way. "You here to see me?" He blinked, his eyes brightening with curiosity, and for a minute, all I could think about was what gorgeous brown eyes he had. I couldn't even remember why I was there.

Brother. . . . What brother?

"Ummm . . . well . . ." *Yes. Yes, I am. Either that, or I stopped in to see Marilyn, since she likes me so much and all.*

He knew I was there to see him. He just wanted to hear me say it, or else he wanted me to say it in front of Marilyn. Maybe the two of them had a thing going. Were they dating in high school? I couldn't remember for sure.

"I just had a quick question. If you're not busy." I craned to the side slightly, trying to see whether there was someone in his office. He was "in a meeting," after all, or so I'd been told. I could feel Marilyn's gaze making a radar sweep back and forth between Blaine and me, trying to discern any hidden connection between us. Rumors would probably be all over town about two-point-five seconds after I vacated Marilyn's space.

"Nope. Not at all." A push opened the door wider, and a friendly hand motion invited me to enter his office. "Come on in."

Marilyn showed her irritation with a soft, passive-aggressive snort as I circumvented her desk. I pretended not to notice, but trailing along behind me was the feeling that coming to the bank had been a bad idea in more ways than one.

If Blaine was worried about his secretary spreading information around town, he didn't show it. Offering me a chair slightly larger and more cushy than Marilyn's maroon-and-gray tweed ones, he shut the door, then hooked a leg over the corner of the desk. He sat-stood, his arms crossed comfortably over an open blazer with a pink polo shirt underneath. It takes a confident man to wear pink. "So what's on your mind this morning?"

If he only knew. Right now, I was looking at him, propped there in his starched jeans, blazer, and cowboy boots—a strange outfit for a banker, but I had to admit that it really did work—and I was thinking, *Is he trying to flirt with me, or am I imagining that?*

The imagination scenario seemed more likely, but I found myself hoping for the first idea.

"Well, first of all, I wanted to say thanks for the firewood and the heater. That was really thoughtful." *Am I blushing a little or is it just hot in here?*

"Least I can do for a good customer." He winked. "Let me know if you change your mind about those cricket-killers."

"I'm still considering it, but . . ."

The door rattled in its frame just as I was thinking about playfully haggling the price. The movement was probably just caused by pressure equalization when someone came or went through the street entrance, but I pictured Marilyn leaning against the wood with a coffee cup to her ear, or perhaps listening in on an intercom.

"Can she hear us from out there?" I nodded toward the door. The transom over it was open, for one thing.

Blaine blinked, his lips forming a quirky, slightly startled twist, as if he thought I might be suggesting a need for closed doors and privacy. A need of the intimate sort, so to speak.

The flush pushed upward and outward, toward my ears and my forehead. All of a sudden the room felt close, and he seemed way too near. I could smell his cologne—something leathery, musky, slightly woodsy. Nice.

Leaning back in my chair, I tried to clear my thoughts. What in the world was wrong with me? I couldn't remember the last time I'd lost my head and stumbled all over myself around a guy. Sometime shortly after leaving Moses Lake and the high-school me behind. "I mean, I had something I needed to talk to you about, and I wouldn't want it all over town." *Ooch.* That sounded bad, like I was accusing Marilyn, whom I really didn't even know anymore, of being a gossip. Not too nice of me, considering that she sat right up front in church on Sunday.

Smooth, dark brows knotted in Blaine's forehead, and he traded the relaxed posture for one somewhat confused and slightly suspicious . . . with perhaps a hint of disappointment. Had he been hoping this was purely a social call?

Twisting to swivel the phone around on his desk, he punched the button, said, "Marilyn, can you go ahead and take those loan applications over to Charlotte now?"

I heard what sounded like footsteps and shuffling outside the door, then the squeak of a rolling chair as a backside settled into it. "Charlotte's gone to career day at the school this morning. I won't be able to give them to her until after lunch."

Snapping his fingers, Blaine grimaced playfully, then stood up and grabbed his coat—the canvas western sort that says *I'm all man.* "Let's walk across the street and grab a cup of coffee."

A warm, prickly feeling slid over me, as if I were diving into the coffee rather than talking about getting a cup. "Oh, hey, I don't want to interfere with your day." Why I said that, I wasn't sure. It bothered me a little, Blaine's smoothness, his confidence, the fact that he didn't ask if I wanted to go for coffee; he just assumed. Admittedly, I was probably splitting hairs, but then, splitting hairs was what I did best. Architecture is all about the minute details. And something about the minute details of Blaine Underhill just didn't add up.

Why was this guy, who undoubtedly had smitten- small-town girls fighting to wrap themselves around his little finger, trying so hard to put the moves on me? What could possibly be the purpose, considering that I wasn't his type and he wasn't mine, and we both knew I'd be leaving Moses Lake sooner rather than later to return to someplace where things actually made sense. "But . . . ummm . . . I do need to pick up some bratwurst at the Waterbird." Close door.

Open door. What a basket case I was.

"Not a problem. The coffee's good there, too." He circled the L-shaped desk, tapped his computer mouse, and scrolled upward to close the window on the screen. Just before it disappeared, I caught a glimpse of what looked like . . . a video game?

"Ummm . . . you're playing video games?"

He shot a sideways grin, a little boyish, a little devilish. "Investment opportunity. Looking it over."

"Yeah, right."

"Software company." He moved to the door, then opened it and stood back, waiting for me to pass through. "Seriously."

"Like I believe that." I was just bantering, really. It didn't matter whether I believed him or not.

Marilyn glanced up from her computer as we exited the office. She gave the coat on Blaine's arm a wary, somewhat unhappy look. "The guy from the software company called."

Blaine swept me the platter-hand, as in, *See, I told you so.*

"The bank in Moses Lake invests in software companies?" I inquired as we crossed the lobby. Was it my imagination, or were all three tellers sending out the hawkeye?

"We're trying to diversify," Blaine explained. "Trying to convince my dad to grow with the times. In this business, you either get innovative, or you sink."

"How *did* you end up in this business?" As I recalled, Blaine was headed to a midsized college in West Texas to play football and major in . . . coaching, or something. I couldn't quite remember. His father, a big man with alligator-skin boots and an even bigger cowboy hat, was so puffed up about the scholarship, he'd erected a giant *Congratulations, Blaine Underhill* billboard in front of the hardware store. The family threw a huge graduation soiree at his grandparents' cattle ranch outside town. My mother, Clay, and I were not invited, of course.

Now, considering what Blaine had told me during our walk through the woods yesterday, I wondered how he felt about that scholarship, and the billboard, and carrying the whole town's expectations on his shoulders. He claimed he never even liked football. It was hard to assimilate that information with the got-it-all golden boy I remembered from high school. Amazing how you could be so wrong about someone. He hid his feelings well at the time. Maybe he still did. That was one of the things that both concerned me and drew me in. I wondered who he really was.

"My dad had a heart attack my junior year in college." He slipped his coat on as we left the bank building and proceeded toward his pickup nearby. "I had to come home to help take care of things. I didn't mind it, really. By then, I was a redshirt on the college team with a blown tendon, and I'd had my bell rung a few too many times. I was okay with coming back to Moses Lake for a while. Dad was in bed under doctor's orders, my stepmother was a wreck, my sisters were just starting high school, and Mama B had started showing up at Dad's office, trying to run the place and driving everybody crazy. I just kind of . . . fell into taking over the bank—there wasn't any way my stepmother could handle that, Dad's rehab, the hardware store, and the ranch at the same time. She can't even keep the books straight at the hardware store, really. I went ahead and finished a finance degree by commuting over to Stephenville. The music major didn't seem too practical anymore, at that point."

"You were a *music* major?" I queried, as he started the truck.

He waited until he'd backed out of the parking place to answer. "Yeah, you know, I was gonna head for Nashville and make it big if football didn't work out." A soft laugh seemed to dismiss the idea as comical now. "Funny, the dreams you have at eighteen."

A memory teased the dust moats of my mind. I was sitting in the back row of the school auditorium. Our English teacher had dragged us over there to watch the dress rehearsals of the talent show. I just wanted to go home. The cheerleaders had finished doing some dance in spandex, and then Blaine walked on stage. Just

Blaine and his guitar. "I remember you in the talent show rehearsals," I said, drawing a breath. "You were good."

"Well, you know, you grow up and life gets in the way." He paused, seeming to reassess whatever he was about to say. "Sometimes what you've got in mind and what God's got in mind aren't the same thing. They needed me here. I got to help look after my grandpa the last couple years of his life. My stepmother couldn't have done it alone. She had all she could handle with Dad's heart attack, and Mama B was wearing herself out, trying to take care of everything and everyone. I moved in at my grandparents' ranch and kind of fell in love with home all over again, you know? Decided I wanted to stay. Your priorities change. You grow up and leave some things behind."

Main Street rolled by as I contemplated priorities while watching our reflection paint a wavy spill of color against the old plate-glass windows of the hardware store, the dime store, a couple of antique stores, the chamber of commerce. I'd never believe that Moses Lake could be anyone's dream. "Guess that's true. Things happen. You could still do it, though. Strap your guitar on your back and head for the big city."

"Nah, I'd miss my boat too much." A glance toward the lake seemed to say that he was already fishing in his mind. "It's good here. I can leave the ranch and be at work in ten minutes—fourteen if I get caught behind the school bus. No sitting in traffic for hours on the way to work. You city folks don't know what you're missing."

"No theater, no museums, no five-star restaurants . . ." I retorted, but I was just teasing, really. Blaine seemed so completely at home in Moses Lake, so completely at peace with himself. I envied that.

"We've got Catfish Charley's," he countered.

"No shopping mall . . ."

"Thank goodness," he answered, and both of us laughed. The rest of the way to the Waterbird, we talked about Seattle and my job. He actually seemed somewhat impressed when I mentioned the national and international clients for whom we'd designed commercial buildings. My job had taken me all over the world. I didn't mention that on most trips I'd seen little more than the insides of hotels.

"Sounds exciting," he said as we parked at the Waterbird. Neither of us moved to exit the truck.

"It can be," I admitted. "Mostly, it's a lot of details and a lot of chipping away at a project, but when you see the steel going up, it's like watching something from your imagination come to life on a massive scale. It's an amazing feeling, even with the stress factor. Projects never go exactly the way you plan them."

"I've financed enough construction to know that." He rested an elbow on the window frame, seeming content to sit there talking.

I sensed an open door to opportunity. I needed to bring the conversation around to Clay, Amy, and the issues in Moses Lake. "I imagine you have to be careful about what kinds of investments you take on, being a small bank, I mean."

"Yes we do." His attention veered off as the little dark-haired girl who'd served us pretend tea on my last visit to the Waterbird stepped out of the building. This time an old man was with her, and both of them were carrying fishing poles. They crossed in front of our truck, hand in hand.

Blaine opened his door and waved. "Hey, Birdie, you taking your granddad fishing?"

"Yeah-huh." The little girl smiled enthusiastically. "Gonna get a big bass."

"There a school vacation today?" Blaine leaned farther out the door, and both the old man and the little girl gave him sheepish looks.

"Had to ugg-go to the udd-doctor today," the old man answered, his speech strange and slow. "Purdy udd-day fer fishin'. Udd-don't tell the uhhh . . . school ubb-board."

Blaine chuckled and waved. "I won't say a word. I promise." He watched them disappear across the parking lot. "See, that's the beauty of doing business in a small town. We helped old Len get the money to finish fixing up his house, so

279

he could raise that little granddaughter of his. The man's a military veteran, injured in combat in Vietnam. He ought to have a decent roof over his head. He deserves a road to live on that's passable in the wet weather, so he can get little Birdie to school, too. When it rains, Len has to take her three miles to the bus stop on a mule, or bring her across the lake in a boat, in the rain. That's just not right. People wouldn't put up with it over on this side of the lake, but the folks with money really don't care what happens up in Chinquapin Peaks. That's one of the reasons I put my name in the hat for county commission. Some things just need to be different, you know?"

"That does sound wrong." I found myself trying to jibe the mental image of the guy who was trying to steal my family land with one of this guy, who wanted better treatment for families in Chinquapin Peaks. Even I knew that the undeveloped side of the lake was like the Land that Time Forgot. That was one of the reasons I felt good about helping to bring in the new Proxica facilities. "The real solution is jobs, though. If people have income, they're not at everyone's mercy."

Blaine turned my way, gave me a long, appraising look, his brown eyes intense. I realized I'd strayed too close to the real reason for my visit here. For an instant, I wondered if he knew, but then his intensity lessened. "You're not thinking of throwing your hat into the commissioner's race, are you? Because I've already printed my signs."

I pretended to consider it. "I think you're safe. I couldn't get elected trash collector in Moses Lake, anyway."

He caught my gaze again. "Don't be too hard on yourself. You're not so bad after a while." He grinned, and a laugh convulsed from my lips.

I liked Blaine Underhill a lot better than I wanted to.

The realization both tempted and worried me as we exited the truck and went into the Waterbird. Uncle Charley, Uncle Herb, Burt Lacy, and Nester Grimland were playing dominoes in one of the back booths. They registered surprise as we walked in, and I quickly realized that coming here probably wasn't the best idea. It would soon be common knowledge that Blaine and I were out for coffee. His stepmother would probably come after me with a wooden stake and a sledgehammer.

Blaine didn't seem the least bit worried. He chatted with the coffee club and the woman behind the counter, Sheila, as we procured coffee and doughnuts, and then took a booth as far as possible from the ongoing domino game. To restart the conversation, I asked how long my brother had been dating his cousin. I tried to make it sound like an innocent question.

"A while, I guess," Blaine replied vaguely.

"Do you think it's serious?"

He scratched his head, brown curls sweeping off his forehead, then falling into place again. "Feeling protective? Amy's a nice girl. I promise."

They just pulled an all-nighter, and then he got a sexy text from Tara, was on the tip of my tongue, but I didn't say it. Ears were straining our way from the domino booth, for one thing. I wasn't sure how much they could hear. I sipped my coffee and tried to decide what else to say.

We made small talk about the wall of wisdom for a few minutes. Blaine's favorite entry was *May the holes in your net be smaller than the fish in it—Irish blessing.* He and his grandfather had written it on the wall in 1985, a bit of homage to the old country.

"My dad and I wrote one together, too," I said, feeling a kinship.

"Well, it's kind of a tradition, bringing your kids here to sign the wall." His cell phone rang in his pocket, and he pulled it out, sneering at the screen. "Now you see why I don't carry one of these things in the evenings." He answered the call, and it was clear from the conversation that he was needed back at work. While he finished talking, I bought a batch of the Waterbird's famous bratwurst and then we returned to the bank.

"Raincheck," he offered, walking backward as we parted ways in the bank parking lot. "How about we finish the conversation over dinner?"

"Sure" was out of my mouth before I even had time to think about it. It made sense, though, considering that I hadn't been able to roll the conversation around to my brother, Amy, bank loans, and substance abuse. How did one smoothly bring up such subjects, anyway? Blaine flashed a smile, and even though I knew that agreeing to have dinner with him might not turn out to be one of my better ideas, I suddenly wasn't sorry.

After watching him disappear into the bank, I picked up my laptop from the gardener's cottage, then went to the Chinese food convenience store and agonized over composing an email explaining my situation to Mel. What I ended up with was a jumble that intimated some sort of impending, but unspecified, family disaster. After promising to check in daily, I pushed Send, released my excuses into the ether, and cracked open a fortune cookie. The fortune was one of those generic types that could apply to many situations. *From unlikely sources come unlikely surprises.*

I glanced toward the bank and thought, *Blaine Underhill just invited me to dinner. Did that really happen?*

I found myself mulling it over, trying to discern his reasons. Was he a nice guy, a sensitive type who wanted to be a musician but grew up amid the pressures of a sports-obsessed family? Or was he a small-town playboy, just looking to score?

Why would Blaine be interested in someone like me? We had absolutely nothing in common. Not one thing, other than my brother, and you didn't have to be a genius to know that Blaine started mincing words every time I even tried to lead the conversation around to Clay. Which raised another question. Why would Blaine be keeping Clay's secrets, if he knew them? Because Clay was dating Blaine's cousin? What would happen when Blaine found out that Clay had interests, so to speak, somewhere in Fort Worth?

The whole thing made my head spin to the point that I finally had to just give up thinking about it and leave for Ruth's. I'd always been far too skilled at coming up with *what if*s, at anticipating the worst. Predicting all potential forms of failure and disaster made me a good architect, but not always so winning as a person.

The tension in my shoulders eased as I drove through the rolling hills near Gnadenfeld, passing miles of green winter wheat. Horses, cattle, and sheep grazed happily, and tall, white farmhouses built for large families languished in the winter light. On the seat next to me, the cover of Ruth's sketch pad fluttered in the breeze from the heater. I flipped it up, looked at the drawing of the woman in the blue floral dress. She was beautiful, her long hair floating about her in a swirl, loose and free, her lips parted slightly, smiling, her eyes holding a startled but confident look, as if she'd been caught by surprise but wasn't worried about it.

Who was she? When had Ruth drawn her portrait, and why?

The cows were dozing happily in the pasture when I reached the dairy. In the barn, Ruth's relatives were processing the morning milk. The wind carried a strong whiff of cow barn as I exited the car. That smell, and the complete absence of television on the place, were two things I'd never envied about the lives of the dairy kids. Operating a farm was hard work. The kids woke early and did chores, and then many of them headed off to the public school in Gnadenfeld, where they would get a reception similar to the one I had received daily in Moses Lake.

For the most part, the Mennonite kids in Gnadenfeld had lacked the essential coolness revered in high-school social circles. The fact that there were plenty of them, living various levels of an old-fashioned, conservative life-style, didn't seem to matter. The whole group fell fairly low on the popularity spectrum, which was probably why the dairy kids had liked me. They thought I was cool—a strange dresser—but cool. They taught me some valuable lessons about grace, as well. Despite the ways in which the world was unkind to them, they didn't return what they got. They were taught to give to the world what was right and godly—kindness and tolerance. Sometimes after a visit with Ruth's family, I wore that mantle of grace for a day or two. But it was so much easier to simply hate all the kids who hated me, to hate the church ladies for trying to reform me into a proper little Southern belle, to hate my mother for failing to take care of us, to hate my father for leaving, to hate Moses Lake for being the place where he died. ....

As I closed the car door, Mary and Emily appeared in the barn doorway, each dangling a puppy under one arm. When they figured out who I was, they bolted across the lawn, the puppies' plump bottoms swinging back and forth against billowing skirts. Both girls stopped a few feet away. Emily cuddled her face against her puppy, eyeing me shyly, while Mary stepped forward and offered to share.

"I got the big one," she informed me, holding the puppy out and trying to peer into my vehicle. "He's just precious."

"I can see that." The loaner puppy groaned as I accepted him into my hands. His eyes rolled upward in a way that said, *When you're done with me, please don't give me back. Hide me some- where.* He grunted and rooted around as I snuggled him under my chin, taking in the sweet scent of puppy breath. "I think he wants his mom."

Mary's brows drew together as if, perhaps, she'd been told a few times before to let the puppy have a break. Emily chewed her lip and looked over her shoulder toward the barn with a hand-in-the-cookie-jar expression. "The mama's busy," she whispered, her voice disappearing into the puppy's dark fur as she rubbed her cheek back and forth over its head. Her soft red curls brushed the puppy's nose, and it sneezed. Both girls laughed.

"I brought some bratwurst for your Aunt Ruth." I scratched my puppy's tummy, and its little foot paddled wildly. "Want to come in and help us cook lunch? You could put the puppies away for a nap." The puppies would thank me for this, I felt certain. During childhood visits to Moses Lake, I was always in trouble for overhandling whatever baby animals were around the farm at the time. *Now let's stop wartin' the babies,* my grandmother would say gently, and instruct me to release my prisoners.

Emily squeezed her puppy reluctantly, but Mary nodded with enthusiasm, reaching for the one I was holding. As the girls dashed for the barn, I retrieved the bratwurst from the car. Then the three of us proceeded to the house together, Mary carrying the bratwurst, and Emily's little hand in mine, making me feel welcome.

We found Ruth in a kitchen chair kneading bread dough, working alongside Mary and Emily's mother. She was dressed less conventionally than Ruth, in a jumper that was conservative but looked like it might have come off the rack,

287

and tennis shoes. Her hair was pulled into a bun, covered with a scarf much like Ruth's. She fawned over the pile of bratwurst as if I'd brought her gold nuggets. The residents of Gnadenfeld generally loved food, especially high-quality German fare. Mary and Emily followed Ruth to the cutting board to watch her unwrap the package and separate the links.

"I found one of your drawing pads," I said to Ruth. "There was only one page in it, though. Just one drawing. I ransacked the upstairs, and it was all I came up with."

A twist of Ruth's lips formed a dimple in her cheek. "Your uncle hid them away in strange places. If you keep looking, you may find another. You can bring it tomorrow."

I smiled, but didn't say anything. With Ruth, there was always a reason for another visit.

Her eyes sparkled with anticipation as she wiped her hands on her cook's apron, then told the niece that we were going to the sun porch to visit and watch the cows graze. The niece waved us off, saying she would put the bread in and call us when the food was finished cooking. She and the girls were singing in the kitchen as we wandered through the quiet old house with its odd collection of antiques and salvaged items that looked like they'd been rescued from someone's curbside castoffs.

On the sun porch, Ruth lowered herself into a

chair and reached for the pad. "Who have you found?" she asked. I didn't answer, but let her turn back the cover and discover the woman for herself.

The blue eyes captivated me again as I sat on the settee and leaned over the end table so that I could see the drawing. Ruth breathed long and deep, studying the sketch.

"I remember her," she whispered, running a finger along the paper, tracing the woman's hair, then looking at the smear of charcoal on her fingertip.

"Who is she?" My chest filled with anticipation. I wanted to know the woman's story.

"I never learned her name, but I knew her." Ruth's eyes softened, going unfocused, as if she were looking beyond the drawing, as if she could see more in it than I could. "She walked with them, with three German officers. She was smiling and laughing as they went along the road from town. She was bold. Can you see that in her? And she was beautiful. So beautiful. She wore a blue flowered dress. As blue as her eyes. She turned to look at us, the poor, huddled mass of us, marching away with the Nazis as they retreated. What did she think of us, I've often wondered. What did she make of the tired, ragged lot of us?" Ruth turned the sketch toward me, as if she wanted me to understand the deeper history of the person pictured there. In my imagination, she began to come to life as Ruth continued her story.

"She was glad to see us leaving Russia, no doubt. Catherine the Great had given the Mennonites land there many, many years before. The Mennonites had a reputation for being good farmers. The intention was that they would improve the land, making it more valuable to Catherine and the country, but the Russians didn't like having foreigners as neighbors. The Communists had taken everything from the Mennonites by the time of World War II. They'd left our population sick, and starving, and dying; had sent the young men off to work camps. My father was glad to see the Germans take ground in Russia, and later, when the Russian forces drove the Germans back, those who were left in our community followed the German army in retreat, for fear of what would happen to us when the Russians returned. We were German by heritage, of course."

Looking away from the drawing and then back, she shook her head. "They knew who this woman was, the Germans. They knew that she had reported German troop movements to the Russians. I suppose she thought her beauty would cause her to be spared. I suppose she thought no man could destroy something so lovely, so young. Even going up the hill, she seemed unafraid. She walked to her death without stopping. I have always wondered if she really was unafraid. . . .

Or if she was only hiding her fear. I have wondered if she had a faith, if she knew God, or if her beauty was her god." Her eyes moved from the paper, cut slowly toward mine. "It's the difference, you know. Faith. It's the difference between hiding fear and mastering it."

Ruth's gaze settled on me, and even though I felt it, I didn't meet her eyes. I was looking at the woman in the floral dress, studying her face, trying to decide.

Was she smiling because her life meant nothing to her?

Or was she smiling because she knew there was nothing mere men could do to take away the life that mattered most?

Love is the only water
that can quench the heart's thirst.
—Anonymous
(*left by Agnes and Fred,
70 years together, happily wed*)

≈ Chapter 13 ≈

Reasons why accepting a dinner invitation from the guy you always dreamed about in high school, while on a trip back home, is a bad idea? Let me count the ways: *One*—you have nothing to wear but the three completely uninteresting outfits in your carry-on bag and sweatshirts from the hardware store. *Two*—you quickly realize there's no way to do this without the entire family knowing about it. *Three*—you can just imagine what the family will say. *Four*—unless you leave town for the date, everyone else will know, but if you do go out of town, it implies something more than just a let's-do-a-little-catching-up get-together. *Five*—you'll feel like you're in high school again and be so nervous you'll spend an hour fixing your hair, then hate it, and change in and out of your three possible outfits a dozen times. *Six*—what's the point anyway, since you live halfway across the country? *Seven*—upon spotting your date on the porch, one of your uncles will invite him in, and the two of you will end up side-by-side on the sofa in the funeral parlor, with your mother looking on and the uncs acting parental and protective, asking where you're going and when you'll be home.

Technically, the last one would only happen to those who have nosy uncles and a funeral parlor in the family, but it's nonetheless mortifying (no play on words intended). Fortunately, Blaine was a good sport, if somewhat evasive in answering their questions. I still didn't know where we were going, but Blaine was laughing as we walked out.

"Looks like I'd better watch my back," he said and grinned, his mirth illuminated by gas-powered yard lamps that gave the driveway the look of a landing strip at twilight.

"I'm sorry." The evening air nipped at the burn on my cheeks. "I should've sneaked through the memory garden and met you at the driveway."

"Now, how much fun would that've been?" Blaine stopped at the *T* where the front walk met the driveway, but there wasn't a vehicle anywhere in sight. Surely we weren't going to walk to dinner. The only place open winter evenings in downtown Moses Lake was my favorite Chinese convenience store. Surely I hadn't paced the bedroom for an hour and changed clothes countless times so that we could eat Chinese in the convenience store.

Aside from the ambiance issue, there was the

fact that, for the sake of fashion, I'd put on the suede boots. Even though it was a surprisingly mild evening for February, the winter chill was already starting to press through the too-thin soles of the boots. If we were walking, I needed to detour to the cottage and change footwear.

"So, where are we going?" I looked around for a vehicle. Maybe he'd parked out back by our cars.

"Good question." He made a show of standing beside me and looking up and down the driveway, as if he didn't know, either.

"No . . . seriously. Should I change shoes or grab an extra coat?"

Cocking his head, he pointed a finger at me. "You know, you worry ahead of yourself a lot."

It almost felt like an accusation. "I like to be prepared. I mean, I don't like surpri . . ." Wow, that sounded bad. *I don't like surprises.* Talk about a euphemism for *I'm no fun.* "Okay, that's not what I meant. I like to anticipate . . . possible contingencies, that's all." *Which makes me great at my job, by the way.* "I mean, that's the business I'm in. You have to think of everything.

"Look at those new Ambrosia Resorts, for instance. The back of the building is concave and it's west-facing. Guess what happens when the afternoon sun hits it? The building acts like a giant magnifying glass. Nicely focused solar energy aimed right at the pool. Can you say, southern-fried tourists?" I realized that I was babbling. I couldn't help it. All of a sudden I was as nervous as . . . well, a schoolgirl on a first date.

Blaine stroked his chin, thinking about the southern-fried tourists perhaps, and then he chuckled, his breath coming out in a little puff of vapor. "You know, I can never quite get a grip on where you're going next with the conversation."

It was impossible to tell from the tone whether that was a good thing or a bad thing, in his view. Probably bad. Things were so much easier with Richard—predictable. We could drone on about business through an entire date, and that was fine. Both of us expected it, in fact. Nobody analyzed anybody else's personality. Which was probably because there was very little personality involved. The idea was a small, silent blow to my already flagging confidence. Maybe I didn't have much personality. The only thing I had to talk about was work, and some people didn't want to hear about that.

I had a sudden sense of panic about the date . . . errr . . . dinner . . . whatever it was. The evening would be a disaster. And what was the likelihood I'd be able to ferret out anything about the situation with Clay, anyway? Blaine had been uncooperative so far.

I needed to find a way out of his dinner invitation. Now.

"I'm sorry. I'm really not fit company tonight.

My boss dumped another project on me, and I should probably just go get started on it. I won't be any fun, anyway. I've got such a headache . . . a migraine, really." *Lie, lie. lie.* Lightning would probably strike me any minute. I moved a step toward the cottage, halfway tempted to pull a Cinderella and just bolt from the scene. I pictured myself curled up on the sofa instead of standing in the middle of the lawn freezing and feeling stupid. It sounded good, really. Safe. Maybe Roger would come around, and we could hang out together. . . .

Just me, myself, and I . . . and Clay's stupid dog. Now there was a pitiful picture.

Blaine caught my hand, as if he knew I was thinking of making a run for it. He leaned close to my ear, his breath warm against my ear. "Come on. You're not going to balk at a little adventure, are you?"

A tingle slid over my skin from head to toe, and suddenly the night was thirty degrees warmer. "Ukh . . . no," I coughed out. "It's not that I'm balking. It's just that . . ." He leaned back and watched me again, and I completely lost my train of thought. "I don't want to fry any tourists." I blinked, covered my mouth. Where had that come from?

Blaine laughed. "I promise you, there will be no fried tourists on this trip."

"Oh, well, then, okay," I said to save face. I'd

provided humor, at least. That was charming in its own way, right? Maybe I could work toward making him laugh so hard that, in a fit of hysteria, he would finally reveal whatever he was keeping from me about my family.

His face straightened slightly. "Trust me." His voice was soft and low.

That's just it. I don't . . .

A movement inside the house caught my attention. Checking over my shoulder, I realized there was an audience peeking around the heavy velvet curtains. If I didn't go on the date, they'd be all over me, wanting to know what happened. If I went, I could later quell the family banter with a bland report like, *We went to dinner. It was nice to catch up.* End of story. "At least tell me if we're walking somewhere."

"Not exactly . . . but sort of."

"Do I need my combat boots?" I shifted from one foot to the other. The little cold prickles were already starting. Fashion be hanged, these boots were going in the suitcase until I got back home.

"Probably a good idea" was all Blaine would divulge, so we proceeded toward the cottage, leaving our audience behind.

After a quick change of footwear, we were off. I followed Blaine down to the lake, and from there, he turned left, walking up the shore toward town.

"Where are we going?" I felt like I might explode if I didn't get some details.

"You'll see."

"Well, how *far* are we walking?"

"Not far."

"Because it's cold out here, and . . ."

He turned my way, his face shadowy in the twilight. "You know, just because you haven't been apprised of the plan doesn't mean that a plan doesn't exist." He shrugged toward the horizon. "Beautiful sunset, huh?"

I let my gaze drift across the water to where the hills had all but vanished into dusky hews of purple and lavender. Overhead, the last rays of sunlight outlined the long, wispy winter clouds, drawing bold strokes over the deepening sky. Not five feet from where we were walking, the water lapped rhythmically at the shore. A dove called, its voice floating in the cool mist, low and peaceful. I realized that I hadn't noticed any of it until that moment. I'd missed it all. "It's beautiful out here," I said, but then I couldn't resist adding, "Has anyone ever told you that you're just . . . disgustingly serene, though?" I had to wonder at this point, if anything, including the land deal with my brother, ever rattled Blaine.

He laughed softly, unconcerned. "No. Has anybody ever told you you're really . . . tightly wound?"

"No," I countered. In terms of architecture,

where fractions of an inch meant millions of dollars, there was no such thing as being too tightly wound.

"Then we're both learning new things about ourselves, aren't we?" He pointed to a dock, and we steered our trajectory toward it. To our left, the path ran uphill, through the church picnic grounds and into town. Apparently, we weren't headed for the Chinese pizza place.

"Either that, or we bring out the worst in each other," I joked.

He shook his head good-naturedly as we walked to the dock and then along it, his boots making a hollow echo that glided over the water. Blaine's black-and-silver boat was tied to the end. Apparently, wherever we were headed, we were going there via the lake. . . .

We ended up at, of all places, my uncle's restaurant, Catfish Charley's. A warm, homey feeling flowed over me as we pulled into one of the boat stalls there. Several spaces were occupied, and onshore, where a floating walkway led to a gravel parking lot, a couple dozen cars lounged idly as stars twinkled to life overhead. I'd always loved this place because my father had loved it. A visit to Moses Lake never passed without a trip to Catfish Charley's to say hello to my uncle's hundred-pound pet fish, Charley. Dad, Clay, and I would grab an ice cream cone, then sit on the dock to fish, or stay inside and partake of Uncle Charley's famous fried catfish and corn pups.

I'd been afraid to come back because I wasn't sure how I'd feel about it, but it felt good. "Looks like the place is hopping," I observed as we departed the boat and walked along the dock. "I thought Uncle Charley was only keeping it open on the weekends now."

"Friday through Monday," Blaine explained. "Live music on Monday nights—helps bring in a crowd."

"Looks like it's working." Now that he mentioned it, I could hear music wafting from the gaps in the old building, riding the fumes of fry grease and onion rings, like steam from a boiling kettle.

"There's still a lot of life in this little juke joint. It's a landmark, you know—the only thing on Moses Lake that was actually on the river before the lake was built. History like that shouldn't be lost." He patted the weathered railing as we walked by, his action showing obvious affection. "Bringing back the live music was a good thing. That was a big draw here in the forties and fifties. My folks used to talk about it. Your grandfather and your great-uncles had a jazz quartet with my granddad. Entertained the ladies." He fanned an eyebrow at me in the orange light of the dock lamps.

"Really?" It was odd to think that other people

in this town knew more about my family than I did. . . . Strange to realize that my father had left those connections behind when he married my mom. What kind of love would cause a man to abandon everything he'd always cared about? What kind of selfishness would it take for a woman to force the man she married to all but sever the ties with his family, with his history? Couldn't my mother have just gotten over herself and gotten along? Why had she felt the need to cause us to hate this place? Why, now, did she feel so differently?

We entered the building, and as we waited to be shown to a table, it was like old home week. I recognized several of the patrons from my high-school days: the track coach who was married to the English teacher; the cheerleader with the red hair and the high, squeaky voice you could hear all the way across the stadium; the postman; the kid who showed championship swine and always smelled like it; the man who handed out the bulletins at church . . .

My brother and Amy?

They were seated in a booth near an area of raised decking along the back wall, where I recalled that there had once been tables. Now the tables had been cleared, and the decking was a stage built to look like an indoor pier. A four-piece band of middle-aged guys in fishing hats was plucking out a tinny waltz. Behind the stage, a wall of windows looked onto the outdoor deck, where torches and tall propane heaters burned away the winter night. A young couple was dancing under the stars. A waltz. I recognized them in silhouette. Reverend Hay and his fiancée. Her head rested on his chest, tucked safely beneath his chin. There wasn't an inch of space between them.

I found myself watching, imagining the feel of that moment, yearning for something, until finally I pulled my gaze into the room again. At the corner table, Clay and Amy were talking intently, completely oblivious to everyone else in the room. Clay drew something on a piece of paper, pointed to it with his pencil. *Tap, tap, tap.*

I wondered if he was breaking up with her, maybe telling her the truth, finally. The communication there definitely didn't look romantic, but neither did it look adversarial. I wasn't sure what to make of it.

The waitress grabbed menus and motioned for us to follow her to a table. Blaine said hello to my brother before I could get close enough to see what Clay was writing. Quickly flipping the place mat over to the preprinted side, Clay stood to shake Blaine's hand in greeting. Amy tackled Blaine with a hug, and he kissed her on the top of her head. I was weirdly jealous, which seemed almost perverse. Amy hugged me next, and I felt like a heel. I couldn't help thinking about Clay's text message from Tara.

I should tell her, I thought. *Someone really should tell her. . . .*

The opportunity seemed to present itself a short time later. Just after Blaine and I had ordered catfish platters, Amy left Clay's table at the same time that the postmaster came by our booth and pulled Blaine into a conversation about the roads in Chinquapin Peaks, mail delivery, and the upcoming debate in the county commissioner's race.

I excused myself and crossed the dining area to the rest room line, where Amy was standing alone.

"Well, hey," she said, in a way that instantly made me feel guilty for arriving with the intention of bursting her bubble. Maybe I should just let things happen on their own—take Blaine's advice and relinquish control to the powers that be.

Then again, if I were Amy, I'd want to know.

"You and Clay look like you're having a good time." Actually, they didn't. I'd been watching from the corner of my eye for a while, and for the most part, their dinner looked like a business meeting.

"We were talkin' about the restaurant," she said, quickly enough that the response didn't ring true. "He's got big plans." She nodded along with the words, as if to give them substance.

I wasn't sure what to think. "Oh. Seems like what he'd really need to be doing is actually working here. You know, learning how to run the place."

Amy fidgeted. "I guess he does that during the day when I'm at work."

"No. He really doesn't."

Amy blinked, her blue eyes wide, earnest, painfully clueless. She cut a nervous glance toward the bathroom door. I heard the toilet flushing.

"I imagine he's got it all figured out." Amy shifted a step closer to the rest room. "I love this place. My pop-pop and my nana met here, right after World War II. It was love at first sight. First dance, really. She was the only one he ever met who could follow his lead like that."

An acidic feeling drained from my throat to my stomach. *Please don't tell me you're in love with my brother. He has a girlfriend in Fort Worth. . . .*

I bit down on the words, unable to say them. The bathroom door opened, and the front-desk nurse from the rural medical clinic came out. Her hair was gray now, but her face hadn't changed. Amy bolted for the door like she'd been catapulted from a crossbow.

I returned to my table, where the catfish platters had arrived. Blaine and I chatted as we ate, and I was once again trying to steer the conversation around to the subject of Clay and Amy when the band returned from a break. We paused to clap along with the rest of the crowd, welcoming the band back to the stage. They weren't half bad, the music a combination of country and Cajun, the perfect atmosphere for a floating catfish joint. My gaze drifted to the deck, where couples were dancing again—the pastor and his fiancée, an elderly couple, a guy in a uniform—probably a park ranger or game warden—and a dark-haired woman. Clay and Amy were out there, too. I remembered the story about Amy's grandparents. Love at first dance. What would that be like? How would it feel?

I wanted to know. I was afraid I never would. I was afraid I didn't have it in me.

"Want to dance?" Blaine offered, perhaps misinterpreting my dewy-eyed look as a desire to hit the outdoor dance floor.

"I don't know how." I hated to admit that, but it was the truth. While kids like Blaine were scooting a boot at the rodeo dance or having parties at backwoods hangouts, I was home cooking supper, taking care of my little brother, washing clothes for school, or helping set up for funerals at Harmony House so that I could earn a little money to keep us from being total freeloaders until the insurance company paid off my father's policy.

"It's just a two-step," Blaine pointed out, finishing the last bite of his coconut cream pie. "It's not that hard. One-two-three, one-two. You're the math genius, remember?"

I studied the deck again, pushing the remains of

my dessert away. A part of me, the girl who'd sat home on Saturday evenings dreaming of a moment like this, wanted to be out there under the stars, twirling off into the night. But the woman who practically lived in her office spoke up instead. "No way I'm dancing in front of everyone."

Blaine's gaze tangled with mine, and I felt the two of us toying with the ends of the rope in a playful tug of war. "C'mon . . . where's that sense of adventure? What are you afraid of?"

"Ummm . . . let's see . . ." I sifted for an answer. *Looking like a dork in front of everyone,* was on the tip of my tongue, but I was reaching for something more clever, more . . . charmingly coy.

The man in uniform and his dance partner came in the back door and stopped at our table, and Blaine introduced me. Mart McClendon, the local game warden, and his girlfriend, Andrea. Blaine asked about Andrea's broken wrist, and she held up a pink cast, offering a wry smile and saying she would never again let her son talk her into skateboarding down the driveway. The conversation went on from there, but I lost track of it. I was watching Blaine and marveling at the fact that he seemed to have a rapport with everyone in town. Not only did he have rapport, but he knew about their lives. He asked after their health and well-being. Either he was a natural-born politician, or he genuinely cared. It was no wonder

Clay liked him. He was incredibly charismatic.

As he was wrapping up the conversation, I glanced at the takeout counter and spotted someone familiar. My stomach sank, lead-lined all of a sudden. Blaine's stepmother had just finished putting in an order. She was turning around, her gaze slowly sweeping the room from left to right. She offered finger waves here and there. I sank in my seat, working toward invisibility, but the game warden moved away just in time to leave me directly in her line of sight. She stiffened immediately, her chin coming up. In my head, I heard the sound that alley cats make when they meet in the night—an unholy noise between a scream and a growl. One of Mrs. Underhill's eyes narrowed more than the other, squeezing almost closed as if she were sighting down a rifle at me. Good thing she didn't have one in her hands.

Blaine, completely unaware that we had gained an audience, leaned across the table, pat-tapped me on the shoulder, and said, "C'mon, let's go. I've got an idea."

I was fully in agreement with the *Let's go* part, except for the fact that Blaine's wicked stepmother was standing by the door. "Let's head out the back way," I suggested, nodding toward the exit onto the deck.

"Let me get the bill first." Before I could stop him, he started across the room. I vacillated between following and staying put, then finally proceeded to the counter. I wasn't letting that woman put me in a corner anymore. I was no longer some shy, messed-up teenager. I was Heather Hampton. I could travel the world, handle demanding clients, bridge cultural barriers, mediate difficult situations, find solutions, impress the bigwigs, create tall buildings with a single stroke of an electronic tablet. Surely I could handle an aging small-town belle with an attitude.

"Heather." My name appeared to have a bad taste to it at first, then she forced a smile. "I'm surprised to see you here."

Blaine cleared his throat and sent her a warning glance over his shoulder. I had a sense that, in the few moments I'd been deciding whether or not to cross the room, they'd had a conversation about me. Mrs. Underhill pressed her lips together, wrinkles forming around the edges. "I meant to say that I thought you wouldn't be in town for long."

"I don't plan to be." With some luck, I could allay any reason she might find to either give my family trouble or sic the casserole ladies on me. They undoubtedly loved Blaine as much as everyone else did. They wouldn't want to see him out to dinner with me, of all people.

I had the sense of being watched from behind. Perhaps some member of the casserole mafia had called Blaine's stepmother when Blaine and I showed up at Catfish Charley's together, and that was why she was here—doing recon, so to speak.

"Just a little longer than I thought," I added lamely.

"Oh." Another pucker-lip punctuated the response. "Well, have a lovely trip home, if I don't see you again."

In other words, *Don't let the door hit you in the backside on the way out.*

A gush of water-laden night air pushed past us, and when I looked up, Mama B was working her way in the door, the hood of her pink sparkly jacket blowing over her face. Pushing it back impatiently, she spied Blaine at the cash register. "Well, hi, darlin'! What're you doin' here?" Without waiting for an answer, she swept him into a hug and rocked him back and forth before letting go.

He actually blushed a little, which was cute. "Just having catfish, Grandma." He glanced my way, and Mama B honed in, her gaze traveling back and forth between Blaine and me. "Well, my lands, are y'all out on a date?"

Blaine's stepmother gasped, horrified at the concept. "Of course they're not. I'm sure Heather just wanted to see the restaurant before she *went home.* To *Seattle.*"

Mama B scowled at her. "Oh, for heaven's sake, Claire Anne, mind your business. The boy needs to meet some gals he hasn't known since kindergarten. Maybe he'll get interested."

The wash of color in Blaine's face crept down

his neck, giving him the look of a little boy having his cheeks pinched by the old ladies in church. A laugh tickled my throat, and I coughed to cover it up. Was it my imagination, or was Blaine in a remarkable hurry to get his wallet back into his pocket? The teenage checkout girl tried to suck him into a conversation, and for once he didn't respond. He turned back to me and said, "Ready?"

I definitely was. Mama B patted my arm and gave it a little squeeze. "Y'all have a good time this evenin'. Go look at the stars or somethin'." Then I exchanged a lemon-juice good-bye with Blaine's stepmother and hit the door before Blaine could even open it for me. An awkwardness descended over us, and as we climbed into his boat, I couldn't help asking myself what I was even doing. What could I possibly hope to accomplish?

I'd be better off back in the cottage, curled up with Roger. At least a half-dozen times during dinner, I'd tried to bring up the subject of my brother, and Blaine had deflected the conversation every time. Now he turned the boat away from Harmony Shores, rather than toward. "Where are we going?" I bundled my coat tighter and sank down into the furry collar.

"Just across the cove."

I knew what was across the cove—the legendary Blue Moon Bay, a little inlet with an old campground where the teenagers probably still congregated on summer weekends. Not much ever changed in Moses Lake. I'd never been to the Blue Moon, except in a few ridiculous teenage dreams.

"You're taking me to the Blue Moon?" I didn't have to work at it to sound incredulous. The Blue Moon was also known as the place where kids who were fortunate enough to have access to a waterborne vehicle went parking.

"Ever been?" His tone was intimate, slightly suggestive. It flowed over me like warm water, raising goosebumps on my skin.

"Oh, sure, lots of times."

He knew that wasn't true, of course. The trouble with spending time around someone who remembers you from high school is that you can't gloss up the past. In Seattle I had total anonymity. I thought I liked it that way, but now there was something alluring, even freeing, about not having to hide.

I tried not to focus on it too much as we crossed the cove. The night and the location seemed too perfect to be tainted by worry. Overhead, the winter moon hung large and heavy, casting a soft light that reflected off the quaking leaves of the live oaks, making them wink and shine as if each leaf had been freshly washed just for us. The air smelled cold and sweet, and Blue Moon Bay, with its overhanging cliffs and ancient, gnarled trees was, indeed, as beautiful by moonlight as I'd always imagined it would be.

"They have a private dance floor here, you know." Blaine's voice held just enough volume to be audible over the low rumble of the boat, as if he were taking care not to disturb the peace of the night. When he cut the motor, I could hear the twangy rhythms of music drifting over from the dancing deck at Catfish Charley's.

"A private . . . wha . . ." I stammered as we floated up to the wide, flat rock shelf where tiny crystals reflected the moonlight like a sprinkling of sugar. I gathered his meaning as he grabbed a scraggly cedar to tie on. "You realize that would be, like, taking your life in your hands?" I imagined our feet tangling, and the two of us tumbling off into the lake, potential hypothermia only minutes away.

"I'm not worried." He climbed out of the boat in three agile steps—one on the seat, one on the side rail, and one on the rocks. He made it look easy enough.

"You know, I'm seriously not one of those girls who hung out at the rodeo and learned to scoot a boot at the street dance." I kept my seat, but I was only teasing now, really. I knew I would be going over the edge soon enough. There was a private dance floor waiting, after all. The idea was heady, thrilling, exciting in a way I wasn't prepared to defend against. Nothing like this had ever happened to me. I'd wanted it to, but it hadn't.

312

"That was my mistake," he murmured, and I was hopelessly lost. I stood up, moved toward him, took his hand when he stretched it out. The boat shifted underfoot as I stepped onto the seat, then tried to decide whether to step on the railing or go straight for the rock. Below, I saw a narrow, black slice of water reflecting the glow of the boat's running lights. A chill slid under my coat, a pinprick of fear coming with it. The boat was drifting farther from the rocks now, the watery crevice widening.

I thought of Ruth's story, of the girl in the blue floral dress—bold, certain, unafraid.

I wanted to be the girl in the blue dress.

One jump from the boat suspended me in space, Blaine's hand pulling me in, guiding me until I landed safely on the rocks. Momentum carried me forward, so that I was pressed against his chest, my free hand clutching his coat. I wondered if he could feel my pulse pounding through the tips of my fingers as his face dipped near mine. I looked up and knew he was planning to kiss me. "I thought we were dancing," I said, but the words were an invitation.

"We are," he whispered close to my lips, his arm sliding around my waist, his fingers, cool from the trip across the cove, trailing over the wind-reddened skin of my cheek. "Dancing." The words were barely a hint of sound. His lips found mine, and I felt the dance begin.

• • •

By the time the chill of the night forced us to return home, I knew two things. The waltz and the Texas two-step weren't as far beyond my reach as I'd thought, and I'd never gotten over my high-school crush on Blaine Underhill.

I came home feeling buoyant and giddy. Unfortunately, right after Blaine delivered me to the cottage door, I discovered that I had locked myself out during my earlier rush to change footwear.

"Here, let me try," he said, as if somehow locked doors would open for him when they would not open for me.

"It's really locked," I assured him, but he tried it anyway, then bent down and gave the knob a good look, trying to peer through the old keyhole.

"It's locked," he concluded.

I shook my head, chuckling despite the fact that I was stuck out in the cold. "I can get a key from the main house." Both of us looked up the hill. The windows were dark, everyone obviously in bed.

"I'll drive you up," he offered.

"We came in a boat."

"Good point. I'll walk with you." Considering it was after midnight, Blaine was amazingly upbeat. He didn't sound the least bit cold or tired.

"No, it's okay, really." The last thing I wanted was to create a bunch of commotion that would wake everyone so they could take note of what time I'd arrived home and whether I had a tell-tale flush on my cheeks. I was fairly sure I did, but I was better off keeping that to myself. The evening had already traveled far, far beyond anything I'd planned.

Blaine stood in front of me, blocking the steps, his head tipping to one side, dark curls bunching in his collar. "My grandma raised me better than that. What kind of gentleman would let a lady go tromping around in the dark by herself?"

The kind I usually date. "I don't know. What kind?"

He walked backward down the steps, his lips spreading into a grin as he gave a quick, sideways jerk of his head, motioning toward the big house.

I felt myself wavering. Was there any way this guy could possibly be for real? I mean, it had to be an act, right? Anybody that perfect would be married to a former beauty queen and the father of two-and-a-half kids by now.

"Not this kind, darlin'," he said, his voice throaty, the words hanging in the air in a puff of vapor.

I melted into a little ball of goo right there on the porch. *I give up. I'm putty in your hands,* I thought as I followed him onto the lawn. We walked up the hill toward the house without talking, our feet making trails in the white-tipped grass amid the moon shadows of the winter-bare trees. At the top of the hill, the house towered imposingly, the tall, wood-paned windows unevenly reflecting the glow from outdoor gas-lights, creating the haunting appearance of movement.

Blaine tucked his hands into his coat pockets. "Man, I can see why this place was a double-dog dare at night."

Was it my imagination, or was he slowing up a little? "You're not scared, are you?"

He scoffed indignantly, "Uh, no . . . Do I look scared?"

I pretended to check him out as we passed by one of the yard lights. "Well . . . yeah, kind of."

"I just didn't want *you* to be scared." Climbing the steps to the veranda with me, he studied the house.

A chill slid under my collar as I moved carefully across the slick, frost-covered decking. "I used to live here, remember? Anyway, they can smell fear, you know? The ghosts. It wakes them up."

"Thanks a lot." He stood to one side and waited while I reached for the utility room door, which I quickly determined to be locked. "Uh-oh." It was a fairly certain thing that, if this door was locked, all of the doors were locked. Back when the funeral home was in operation, Uncle Herbert had always been somewhat meticulous about that, as combinations of money, personal effects, and treasured loved ones could be stored in the house at any time. Old habits died hard, I supposed.

I turned around and started back across the veranda. "We'll have to go in through the cellar door." For those who knew the way around Harmony House, the ground-level doors that led to the basement were easy to jimmy.

"The place with all the old coffins in it?" Blaine wanted to know. "That basement?" His cowboy boots slid on the decking, and he did a fairly agile ice-skating maneuver before grabbing the railing.

"I thought you weren't scared." Despite my show of bravado, a shiver ran over me, making the shadows on the side of the house and the vapor puffing from our mouths seem unusually eerie. I had never liked Harmony Shores at night, but if the alternative was to wake everyone up and have a date discussion—which we would, because Uncle Herbert, having been in the funeral business, was hospitable at any hour of the day or night—I'd take my chances on the basement. I was glad, however, that I didn't have to do it by myself.

"I'm *not* scared," Blaine assured. "I was just worried about you."

"Hey, I did the two-step next to an icy lake. It's all downhill from there." The comment won a chuckle just before we reached the cellar door. I leaned over to grab the handle, and the bite of the frosty metal caused me to jerk my fingers back, pulling them into my sleeve.

"Here." Blaine took a pair of leather gloves

from his coat pocket, put them on, and lifted the door.

"I don't suppose you have a flashlight in that pocket, too?" I asked, peering down the steps. The blackness in there was so thick that the cellar seemed bottomless, only small, faint circles of light coming from the wavy glass windows at ground level. I knew exactly where the light switch was—on the other side of the room.

"Actually, yeah." He produced the boat keys with a little pinch light on the end of the chain. The faint glow was just enough to allow him to proceed into the basement. Apparently, he wasn't the kind of gentleman who would let a lady descend into a dark, scary subterranean lair first, either. I didn't argue with him about it. I just grabbed a fistful of his jacket and followed along.

The penlight died when we were halfway across the room, blowing out like a candle and leaving us huddled together in the darkness like Shaggy and Scooby-Doo. "Well, that's not good," Blaine muttered. I felt his coat stretch as he reached ahead, trying to feel his way along. He collided with something, and I collided with him, knocking him forward.

"I think that's a coffin," he observed, jerking back.

"I don't even want to know." I was happy enough to take his word for it as he clumsily circumvented the obstacle, and I followed. In the dim light from the windows, shadows shifted at chest level, painting strange shapes and swirls, leaving the territory below murky and impossibly black.

A chill brushed my cheek and slipped over my skin, causing me to do a full-body shudder. A moaning whisper circled the floor joists overhead. I clutched Blaine's coat in two tight fists.

His foot hit something else, sending an unknown bit of cellar flotsam skittering across the floor to a corner, where it collided with a hollow metal object. I heard what sounded like a note of music, and then the faint melody of a woman's singing drifted overhead.

"Do you hear that?" I whispered, thinking of the girl who was rumored to have killed herself in the house, and of all the generations of people who had lived and died there.

"I hear it," Blaine answered in a hush.

I do not believe in ghosts. I do not believe in ghosts. I do not . . .

The singing grew louder, seemed to be coming from everywhere, all around us.

Blaine tripped over something again. It collapsed and clattered to the floor. I squealed, trying to decide whether to stay put or make a run for the door.

Footsteps echoed through the basement. They were coming closer. A door creaked slowly open. I caught a breath.

Light flooded into the room, and a voice hollered, "Hey, down there!"

When I looked up, Uncle Charley was at the top of the interior stairs. "What're ya'll doin' sneaking 'round the cellar way? C'mon up. We got *The Sound of Music* on late-night TV!"

For with thee is the fountain of life;
in thy light shall we see light.
—Psalm 36:9
(*left by Ron, still climbing highline poles
to keep the power on*)

≈ Chapter 14 ≈

Mary and Emily were helping their mother to prepare *verenike* and cream gravy when I arrived for my next visit with Ruth. I'd found another of her drawings, not in an art pad this time but just on a piece of paper that had been torn out. I'd discovered it in an antique serving buffet in the vestibule, where prayer cards and pictures of the deceased were traditionally displayed. Ruth's drawing had been tucked into the drawer haphazardly among leftover funeral programs dating from at least three different decades.

The day was blustery and gray when I arrived at the dairy, so Ruth and I sat in the main room of the house next to a crackling fire, Ruth in a simply-made rocking chair that looked well-worn, and me on an aging gold velvet sofa that had probably been rescued from someone's discards. The sofa wasn't in bad shape—just out of style. One thing about Ruth's family, they could squeeze a dime until you could see through it. As a rule, they didn't believe in waste. Fashion not being of high concern either, they found other people's junk to be perfectly useful. During my high-school year at Moses Lake, I'd learned to be careful of hitching a ride with Ruth when she went out on an errand in one of Uncle Herbert's vehicles. More than once, we had ended up on the side of the road, digging through the castoffs in curbside trash piles. During these unplanned detours, we not only rescued things Ruth wanted, but anything and everything she thought she could give to other people. We cleaned up the treasures—soaped them and polished them—and she presented them to neighbors and friends, either Mennonite or non-Mennonite, depending on the item. Ruth was not above rescuing clothing or toys, and after a washing and mending, she pronounced them good-as-good (not good-as-new, which would have indicated that new stuff was in some way inherently superior to things that were nicely preloved).

Clay adored playing the treasure-dig game with Ruth. It was entirely possible that was why his fashion train still stopped at Goodwill. I, on the other hand, was horrified by the idea of germs, and dead skin cells, and other people's hairs, as well as the possibility of being seen on the side of the highway, should someone from school drive by. I was already weird enough.

I laughed now, stroking the sofa, thinking that

some of the best things in life are the ones you're dragged into kicking and screaming. Those treasure hunts with Ruth were good times. She'd probably be pleased to know that much of the décor in my apartment centered on found items from thrift shops and eBay. There were no harvest gold sofas, but I had discovered an egg pod chair and an Oscar Tusquets vintage table that gave the place a serious Jetsons-era look.

Ruth's eyes twinkled as I set her sketch on the sofa beside me, face down. "I found another one," I said, smiling because I knew she would be pleased. "Sort of stumbled upon it, actually. But anyway, here it is." I lifted the paper to hand it to her, but she motioned for me to leave it where it was, upside down on the sofa cushion.

Lacing her fingers in her lap, she indicated no hurry to look at the drawing. Ruth's patience had always been surprising and difficult for me to relate to. "They are probably hidden all over the house. Your uncle was terrible about rescuing them from the trash and hiding them where I wouldn't come across them and throw them away again."

Curiosity nibbled. "Why not keep them? Your drawings are beautiful. It seems like a waste not to frame them." I thought of all the times I'd watched her sitting on the porch with her pad at the end of the day, when she was waiting for her carpool friends to pick her up. The older

Mennonites of Gnadenfeld, while not opposed to car ownership like the Amish, still seldom drove anywhere by themselves. To do so would have been less than frugal, and a lack of frugality implied ingratitude for the resources God provided. In a de facto sense, they were green before green was in vogue.

My aunt Esther had a hard-and-fast rule about our bothering Ruth, or any of the help, after working hours were over. We were strictly not allowed, but I often watched Ruth from a distance while she sketched. I never knew her creations were destined for the trash. She must have thrown them away in the funeral parlor, where I never went unless I had to when I was working for Uncle Herbert.

"They weren't for framing. Not for anyone else to see." Ruth's fingers twitched against her floral print skirt.

"But why not?" It occurred to me that Ruth, who in her spare time sold home-canned and baked goods, could have more easily sold her drawings to produce income. "It's okay if you don't want to answer."

"It would have been vainglorious, I think." She shrugged slightly, as if shedding the compliment, but I suspected that the vaingloriousness of artwork was something she didn't quite believe in. "Besides, I would not have wanted to look at them again. Not all of them, anyway."

I thought about the story of the girl in the floral dress, and Ruth's behavior made sense. Her drawings were like diary entries—some painful, some beautiful. "I understand." I did, really. There were boxes in Uncle Herbert's cellar, according to my mother. Boxes that had been packed away since we left the little stone house at the family farm and moved into the gardener's cottage at Harmony Shores. Neither Mom nor I had brought up the issue of the boxes since the phone call that hastened me back to Moses Lake. I hadn't gone looking for them, and I didn't have a desire to. I would come and go from Moses Lake without seeing them, unless I was forced to sort through them with my mother. I knew exactly what was in those boxes. I'd watched Aunt Esther and her church ladies pack them. They were filled with videotapes, photo albums, the framed pictures that had always hung in the halls of my childhood. Images of life as it once was—soccer practices, Halloween parties, picnics by the ocean, my dad and I in line for Mr. Toad's Wild Ride at Disney World.

I understood why Ruth threw away her drawings. Some things are too painful to revisit.

"What is that one?" She wagged a finger toward the drawing.

"Children playing, and a horse," I said, but I didn't turn it over. "We don't have to talk about them if you don't want to. There was a story you were going to tell me. Something more about my family, maybe? You said you wanted to tell me about my grandfather. We never got to it last time, because we were talking about the girl in the blue dress."

I wasn't sorry to have learned about the girl in the blue dress yesterday, but I did want to hear about my family. Even though Ruth was already assuming that I would be back tomorrow, there was no telling how many more times I would be able to visit before I had to leave Moses Lake— work, family, or the Proxica deal could change my circumstances at any time. I'd checked my email on my way to Ruth's, and even though Mel had grudgingly allowed me to take a few personal days, he was not happy about it. He wanted me to know I was *on notice* and would be called back immediately if anything critical came up.

Right then, sitting by the fire with Ruth, the office seemed a million miles away. I'd never had much interest in family history or stories about the pioneering days in Moses Lake. When my grandmother and grandfather brought up those things during our occasional visits, the information had seemed fairly unimportant. I suppose I'd always felt that there would be time to reconnect if I ever wanted to—maybe someday after I'd found Mr. Right and the two of us had created a couple of surprisingly perfect and multi-talented offspring. Now, with the prospect of selling off the old family places, I felt the need to carry at least a little bit of that history with me. Who could say if I'd ever see the uncs again after they moved to the retirement community in Oklahoma? Their lives would be filled with Donny and the grands and great-grands.

Ruth motioned to the paper, her gaze drifting toward the fire. "Look at it and tell me what you see."

I turned the sheet over and did as she asked, even though I didn't need to. I'd studied the sketch previously. It was a collage of sorts— several children playing in the grass and a teenage girl standing on the back of a farm horse, balancing with her arms out, her legs clad in long, black stockings. Her bonnet had slid back, so that tendrils of hair whisked around her face, swirling like the horse's mane. She'd tucked her chin slightly and rolled her gaze upward in a way that seemed coy and confident. Her lips held a precocious smile, as if she knew she was doing something she shouldn't, something dangerous, but she didn't care. Her eyes were green, the only bit of color on the image, except for the wildflowers beneath the horse's feet.

I described her to Ruth, but I couldn't put into words the expression on her face.

Ruth gave a small, private smile, as if she were imagining it anyway. "That is my sister." Taking in a long breath, she seemed to drink in the scent of the picture, the lingering of graphite and pastel, the fragrance of the wildflowers, bright and alive in a world that was otherwise gray. "She was not afraid of anything, Lydia. Not then. That was before."

"Before what?"

"Oh . . . before . . ." Ruth drifted off momentarily, then turned her head to the sound of the front door opening. A boy, perhaps seventeen or eighteen wearing jeans and a blue chambray shirt, stepped in and dusted his boots on the rug.

"Is that John?" Ruth called without turning around.

"No, it's Hosephat. Gee Hosephat," the boy said, smiling slightly at his joke but remaining reserved. Ruth's family had never known what to make of mine. The Mennonites worked any number of places around the area, but the more conservative they were in their views, the more they tended to socialize amongst themselves. Close connections like the one Ruth had with my uncles weren't all that common.

Ruth shook her head at the boy. "Lunch is almost ready, Mr. Gee Hosephat. I know that must be why you came."

The teenager cast a hungry look down the hall. "I thought I smelled something." He crossed the room to greet both of us before proceeding on to the kitchen.

After he was gone, Ruth shook her head. "John

is a grand nephew, Mary and Emily's cousin. One of my sister's grandsons."

"The sister in the picture?" I asked.

"No." Taking a long breath, Ruth let her lashes drift downward until she was gazing into the fire, her eyes unfocused. "John's grandmother went to be with the Lord last year. I miss her. Every day of our lives, we cooked together, did our ironing and mending together, and prayed together. I couldn't have children, you know, but Naomi had seven, so there were plenty to share. Naomi was a good, quiet woman. Obedient to the Lord. Plain in her appearance, as I am plain." Pointing toward the paper, she shook her head. "But this one, Lydia, she was not the same. We were eight, in all; our mother, father, three brothers and three sisters. Most of us were plain and pale, quiet in nature, but Lydia came into the world with her dark hair and her confident ways. She was second in line, behind John, but you would have thought Lydia was the eldest. Then there was Matthew, then Naomi, and I was younger, and finally the baby."

Pausing, she cradled her arms, as if she were holding the baby now. "He was such a fine, fat little one. My grandfather had built a beautiful home in the Ukraine on the land allotted to the family years before. So many of the Mennonites had beautiful farms in the villages between the Black and Caspian seas, but after the revolution, the land and what it could produce belonged to the

Communists. They were suspicious of Mennonite people and their low German and Plautdietsch speech. I remember men and boys being sent to work camps, the *gulags*, and never coming home. Of course, you prayed that it wouldn't happen to your family, but they took away my eldest brother, and then Matthew. . . . He was only a child. Just a bit over ten years old. My father sat at the table with his back straight against the chair. He did nothing to stop them. Lydia was angry about it. She was about thirteen, then, I think, but older than that in her mind. She had seen things. I was young, but I had seen things, too. Always we were afraid that Stalin's secret police would come to the village and put us on a train. Always we were hungry, but if you were caught stealing food or trying to hide what you had produced, terrible things could happen."

Shivering, Ruth pulled her knitted shawl closer around her shoulders. I stood up, took a log from the woodbox, and added it to the fire, then returned to the sofa and waited for Ruth to begin again. Lydia, the girl with long waves of dark hair, the one who was different from everyone else, was coming to life in my mind.

I waited for Ruth to tell more of her story. Finally, she pressed a hand to her lips, laughing privately. "But there was joy, too. Children will always find joy, somehow. Lydia wanted to run away and join the circus before the war. We went sometimes to the Russian villages to beg for food, and once there was a circus. Lydia peeked under the tent. She told us of it in whispers, when she knew my father couldn't hear. She told us she would have those glittering costumes with the crystal beads and the gold threads sewn into them, and she would ride a white horse. I could not imagine such a thing. To entertain the idea, even!"

Pressing three fingers to her lips, Ruth leaned forward to look at the drawing of her sister. "My mother and the baby died when cholera came. My father was weak, especially after the illness. The Second World War had begun by then, and I was just beginning to become a woman. There was even less food than before. The Russians prevented us from travel, so it became more difficult to go begging in the villages. My father admonished us to have faith through all of this. He told us that the Germans were drawing closer and when they came, because of our German heritage, we would fare better."

Leaning forward, Ruth pointed to one of the girls playing in the grass at the horse's feet. "My sister Naomi clung to my father's faith. But Lydia grew tired of it. She was sixteen then, prideful, beautiful in a way that was noticed, that was rewarded by the few men and boys remaining in the villages when we could go begging. There was a bit of extra bread here, a cup of milk there.

Lydia turned against my father. She was not modest. She uncovered her hair. She said, if she were not to do it, we would all starve to death. 'Who is going to feed us?' she asked my father as he lay in his bed, too weak to punish her. 'You? Naomi? You only lie there. You only lie there, waiting on the Lord while we go hungry. If this is what the Lord asks of His people, then I do not want it.' "

Ruth turned to look at me then, moving her gaze slowly away from the contrasting images of Naomi and Lydia on the paper. "You may wonder which of my sisters was right—the one who honored my father's instruction, or the one who turned away. Terrible things had happened to us, after all—death, disease, hunger, our family torn asunder, abuses I cannot even speak of. How could a God who loves us allow such things, you might wonder?"

She seemed to be waiting for an answer, but I didn't have one. A log popped in the fireplace, a spit of flame tearing away and floating upward. *I have wondered. I've needed that answer all these years, but there is no answer.*

Ruth shifted in her chair, her breath coming in labored grunts as she tried to reposition the bed pillow tucked behind her back. "I cannot tell you the answer. There is none on this side of heaven, on the dark side of the glass, I think. The Germans came, and there were rewards for those who would help them in their battle. The Mennonites would not agree to fight, of course, but some were forced and some gave information. Some told who in the Russian villages had helped the Russians, who might be helping them still.

"Lydia told what she knew. The Russians were, after all, the very people at whose hands we had suffered. 'It is only justice,' she said. I have wondered if she was aware that those people would be walked up the hill, like the woman in the blue dress, and positioned at the edge, so as to fall into a grave with so many others. I sometimes think Lydia must have been unaware. It is easier to believe that."

My stomach roiled at the thought of mass graves and people being walked up a hill, knowing they were walking into death. Looking at Ruth, it was hard to imagine that she had seen these things, that to her these were not just pieces of history, images from some sad newsreel. This was her past. She'd lived it. "Did Lydia report the woman in the blue dress? Was it your sister who told?"

Ruth answered with a long, sad look. "I have never known. I don't want to. Naomi told me never to ask, and I didn't. But Lydia was not the same after the killings. She lost her laughter. Even when we followed the German army in its retreat from Russian soil, she was hollow and angry. Her revenge had fed her for a day, but it was a meal that emptied her afterward, and there seemed to be nothing that could fill her again. She married a German man as the war was ending, but her life was never happy. Naomi and I came here to America. Naomi had seven children and lived well all the rest of her life until the Lord called her home. But that story is for another day."

"I'd love to hear it," I said, but I could tell Ruth was wearing down, getting tired. She'd sagged against the pillow, her body cocked to one side in a way that looked uncomfortable. Once again, we hadn't gotten to the story about my grandfather.

"You come back again tomorrow." She smiled at me, her withered fingers patting the arm of the sofa as if she were patting my hand.

"I will."

"Which of my sisters did the right thing?" Ruth stared into the fire again, her head drooping forward. "The one who fed our stomachs but was faithless, or the one who kept our faith but let us go hungry?"

"I don't know," I admitted, though I suspected that wasn't the answer she wanted.

"I sometimes think both of my sisters are inside us." Her eyelids were sinking now, silver lashes brushing her cheeks. "I have always thanked God that I was younger. It did not fall on me to make the choice between the two paths."

She sighed, her eyes closing, her breaths lengthening. I tiptoed away quietly, leaving her there to rest. Lunch was ready in the kitchen, and

I stayed to share the meal at a long table with Mary, Emily, John, and various members of Ruth's family. The prayers settled over me as grace was offered, and for the first time in a long time, I felt grace. I'd always thought of my life as irreparably marred by tragedy, but now I could see that we all have marks of some kind, scars we'd rather not live with. It's what we do in spite of them that matters.

After the meal, Mary and Emily walked me out, and we visited the puppies in the barn. I watched the girls take them to the barnyard and try to corral them against the wall.

"You shoulda brought Roger," Mary pointed out, running after a chubby puppy to put it back in the puppy containment area.

"Rod-er likes the puppies," Emily added.

"Yes, he does," I agreed. Watching Mary and Emily, I couldn't help contrasting their lives with those of the children in Ruth's drawing. They were growing up in completely different worlds. "Maybe I'll bring Roger back next time. You two have fun today." I hoped Mary and Emily's world would always be this gentle, this welcoming and sweet.

As I walked to my car, I thought about Ruth's story of the two sisters. Ruth had made the choice, whether she realized it or not. She'd witnessed terrible things, suffered hunger, disease, watched her family be torn apart while God seemed to do nothing to stop it. Yet she still believed in love and mercy.

I wanted to believe. I needed to. There was a hunger in me that couldn't be filled by anything I'd achieved or purchased or invested my time in. I was like Lydia. For everything that was beautiful about her on the outside, there was a piece on the inside that was broken, jagged, dangerous. She curled inward, protectively around herself, until finally she bled herself dry.

I was living Lydia's life, but I wanted Naomi's. I wanted peace. I wanted hope. I wanted the joy of those two little girls playing in the grass.

Low clouds gathered overhead, and the scent of freshly baked bread hung heavy in the air as I left the dairy and drove through Gnadenfeld. My mouth watered, drawing me toward one of the bakeries, my justification being that I'd just take a few things home as a treat . . . for the uncs, of course. A little comfort food.

I needed some comfort at the moment, and even though I fully understood the wisdom of not having Mennonite baked goods around the house—I'd gained ten pounds my senior year in high school and gone from stick-thin to curvy—I went into the remodeled Texaco station, anyway.

The interior smelled like heaven. Behind the counter, a teenage girl in a soft mauve dress with a mesh prayer covering pinned over her bun was working on math homework. She set her pencil down and looked up at me. She had beautiful eyes. I thought of Lydia in the drawing. Lydia as drawn by Ruth probably wasn't any older than this girl, yet she had seen unspeakable things, experienced horrors of a sort I couldn't even imagine.

A lump swelled in my throat and I swallowed hard, then ordered some treats, feeling foolish. The girl behind the counter probably thought I was off in the head.

Leaving the bakery, I stood on the curb a moment, took in a long, slow breath, and smelled the faint scent of emissions from the Proxica plant, held low over the ground by the cloud cover today. Something familiar on the street caught my eye. An old white Toyota pickup. The Ladybug. It turned just past the building across the street and disappeared into an alley. I walked down the curb a few steps to catch sight of it again.

Clay was parked in the alleyway. I started to call to him as he got out of the truck, but something in his movements stopped me. He was looking around, checking over his shoulder to make sure no one was watching. A man came out the back door of the building, handed something to Clay in a brown paper sack. My brother tucked it under his jacket, hurried back to his truck, and was gone.

My stomach rolled as I stood on the sidewalk, watching his taillights disappear around the back of the building. Suddenly the smell of the baked goods in my arms seemed off-putting. Despite everyone's assurances that my brother was fine, the body language of that alley meeting was impossible to misread. I knew what kinds of packages had to be picked up via the alley doors of buildings, in secret.

Siddhartha looked into the river
and saw many pictures in the flowing water.
—Herman Hesse
(*Left by an artist, who painted
the day away by the shore*)

≈ Chapter 15 ≈

When I returned to Uncle Herbert's place, Mom and the uncs were down by the old barn, where Clay's collection of partially-repainted canoes still languished on the lawn. Uncle Herbert, Uncle Charley, and Mom were walking around the barn, pointing and talking. Perhaps they were making plans for future hoedowns to entertain the throngs of bed-and-breakfast customers looking to stay in a former funeral home? Whatever was going on, they seemed to be deeply engaged in it, the three of them looking up at the roof while Uncle Herbert pointed and talked, and Uncle Charley shook his head, disagreeing. They didn't notice me driving in, so I closed the car door quietly and went into the house, my mind still on Clay.

Inside, a laptop computer sat idling on the kitchen counter. I bumped it accidentally-on-purpose while setting down my supply of bakery goods, and the screen came on. Two windows popped up side by side, and I paused to look at them. One appeared to be an email containing a series of instructions for a graduate student or fellow professor who was covering Mom's classes. She'd asked him to give her freshman composition students an assignment—the dreaded term paper, a social criticism of *Sonny's Blues* by James Baldwin. Scanning down the page, I read the last line, a final note to her colleague.

Thank you for your understanding, Andrew. I could be gone on family leave for a couple weeks yet but should return well before finals. Sorry to miss Valentine's Day, but we'll make it up in style—dinner and a theater night, perhaps? You pick . . .

The note stopped there, as if she'd been interrupted before finishing it. In the window beside the email was a drawing—an attachment she'd downloaded, apparently. The sketch was someone's crude attempt to create a 3-D walkthrough of a living room interior, using AutoCAD. Whoever had done it didn't know the software well. The representation was rough, and from the notations, it looked like someone wanted to design a room based on knobby cedar poles, hand-hewn beams that fit together with wooden pegs, and barn wood.

Barn wood . . .

I looked out the window at my mother and the

uncs, who were now investigating the framing around the big sliding doors that, when there were farm fields nearby, had been designed to admit wagons mounded with freshly-harvested cotton. Maybe Mom was planning to tear down the barn—sell it off to someone who wanted to use the rustic materials inside a house or cabin. It seemed a shame to do that. The barn was part of the history of this place. Even though it was over a hundred years old and needed some work, it wasn't beyond saving.

Aside from that there was another question, one even more perplexing. Mom had someone back at Berkeley waiting for her to return, planning a belated Valentine's dinner and teaching her classes? *Thank you for understanding . . . gone on family leave for a couple weeks yet . . . Sorry to miss Valentine's Day, but we'll make it up in style . . .*

That was even stranger than Clay's text message from the girl with whom he was apparently two-timing Amy. Why would my mother be stringing along some poor guy in California if she intended to move to Moses Lake for good? Why would she lie to him? She had to be lying to someone—she couldn't move to Moses Lake and return to California at the same time. Had she been lying to the uncs? Did she intend to go back to her teaching position? Why come here and build up the uncs' hopes with talk of settling down in the country? To what purpose?

Would she do that so Clay could secure bank loans? Was Mom pretending to be a future partner in Clay's business ventures so she could set him up in Moses Lake, and then leave? It wouldn't be the first time. When Clay was in his last year of high school, she'd accepted a fellowship in Paris without telling anyone. Out of the blue at Thanksgiving, she'd announced that she'd be boarding a plane four months before Clay's graduation, but there was nothing to worry about, because the rent on the house was good until the end of May. She'd asked the neighbors to help Clay out if he needed anything.

I still remembered the wounded, confused expression on Clay's face. He looked like an abandoned house pet that had just been booted from the car on the side of some lonely highway. Surely she wouldn't do that to him again. Maybe she was lying to the guy back at Berkeley— Andrew, whose name had never come up in conversation before, but with whom she was apparently close.

Was she lying to Clay, or were she and Clay lying to me . . . to everyone?

The phone rang just as my thoughts were melting into a slag heap of molten theories too corrosive to handle. A scenario was forming, and I couldn't face thinking about it. The idea clarified and hardened as the phone rang a second time and a third, until finally Uncle Herbert's recorded message echoed from his office. On the message, he was using his funeral voice, smooth, low, and soothing. "Hello, you've reached Harmony Shores Funeral Home. We're no longer offering services, but if you'd like to leave a message . . ."

I listened until the caller began recording a response. "Hi, Dad, this is Donny." I pictured Uncle Herbert's eldest son, Donny. He and his family had come down for my father's funeral. Even though they were only cousins, Donny reminded me so much of my father that it hurt just to be around him. Same laugh, same eyes, same tall frame and broad shoulders, same receding hairline.

I sidestepped toward the kitchen phone, my ear still cocked toward the message. "So, listen, Dad, I just wanted to check in and see how everything's going. The Craigslist guy should be there to move the stuff out of the basement a week from tomorrow. He says he'll just warehouse all of it until it sells, no problem. Who knows, maybe there'll be a rush of vampires looking for places to sleep, and the display coffins will sell off in a hurry. Anyway, be sure you've got the red tags on anything down there that you don't want him to haul off, okay? All of that stuff is going to do better on Craigslist than in an estate sale, and this way you won't have people tromping all through the place. Remember, the furniture stays unless it's something that's got sentimental value. They want the rest of it left where it is. Anyway, I'll call back later and . . ."

I grabbed the kitchen phone and pushed the button for the funeral home line before Donny could hang up. "Hi, Donny, this is Heather. Your dad is down the hill with Uncle Charley and my mom."

Donny hesitated long enough that I thought maybe he'd hung up. "Oh . . . Heather," he said finally. "Well, I didn't know you were down there."

Why am I not surprised? Wait until I tell you what else you didn't know. It occurred to me, then, that Donny didn't seem surprised that my mother was at Harmony Shores. Apparently, he already knew. "I've been in town for a few days. Ummm . . . has anyone told you what is going on here?"

"Going on, as in . . ." Donny's lead-in was strangely cautious, as if he were concerned about where I might be headed.

"With the land sale, the estate sale. Everything. The broker offer expires soon. We were supposed to have signed and executed it last week in Seattle, but my mother didn't show up to do the paperwork, so I came down here. What's weird is that no preparations have been made here. Everything, and I mean everything, is just the way it's always been. It doesn't look to me like Uncle

Herbert and Uncle Charley are planning on moving anywhere, and all of a sudden my brother is talking about taking over the catfish place, and my mother thinks she's going to open a bed-and-breakfast in the funeral home." *I know, I know. Go ahead and laugh. It sounds really ludicrous when you say it out loud.*

"Hmmm," Donny muttered. Even for a straight-laced electronics engineer, it was a strangely flat response. He hesitated for a long time afterward. "Well, I'm sure it's fine, Heather. Dad and Uncle Charley just sent their deposit check for the new condo. They're looking forward to living the retirement life with all those hot senior babes. I think most of the furniture stays with the house there at Harmony Shores. Don't worry about it, all right? The moving company will be coming in to pack Dad's personal belongings for him. He's supposed to red tag anything he wants to hang on to. When I took the deposit check to the retirement village last week, I measured his condo, so he could make some more decisions about what furniture to take and what to leave behind."

My mind tripped and stumbled. An actual check had been sent to Donny? My understanding had been that Herbert and Charley needed the money from the broker offer to pay the thirty-thousand-dollar deposit on their retirement condo, which was why the broker offer was such a godsend.

If Uncle Herbert had sent money to Donny, that

meant that actual cash had already changed hands between my mother, my brother, and the uncs. But if Uncle Herbert intended to stay in Moses Lake, then why was he making the down payment on a condo in Oklahoma?

"Donny, listen, I think you'd better come here. We need to all sit down in one room"—*lock the doors*—"and get to the bottom of this before it's too late."

"Hang on a minute, Heather." I heard someone talking in the background, and the scratchy sound of Donny putting his hand over the phone.

Donny came back on the line. "Listen, Heather, I'm headed to a meeting. Don't worry about it anymore, all right? Everything's fine. Dad's got it under control. Good talking to you."

"No . . . wait, but . . ."

He hung up. I held the phone away from my face and looked cross-eyed at it, my mouth hanging open. "He hung up on me. . . ." The words were for no one but the ghosts in the house, and they didn't answer. I quickly pushed *69 to dial back Donny's number. He didn't answer. I tried three more times. No luck.

"Ohhh, that is just . . ." I didn't even have words for it. Finally, I smacked the phone into the cradle and paced the kitchen, thinking, *Apparently his meeting matters more than his family, and . . .*

The strangeness of that thought struck me. Talk about the pot and the kettle. Was this not exactly the personality flaw my mother and Clay had accused me of? Their complaint about me? Richard's complaint about me? Even Trish's, when I got right down to it? I was so over-burdened with my own issues, I didn't have time for anyone else's.

That's not who I am, I thought. *It's not. That's not me.*

Not this time.

Whether the Proxica deal worked out or fell completely apart, I was going to make sure my family came out of this in one piece, and the basement was as good a place to start as any, whether I wanted to go down there or not. If I could find any evidence of items that had been packed or red tagged for moving, that would at least be proof of something. Proof I could use to confront my mother and force her to tell me the truth.

I was still muttering to myself as I turned the corner to cross through Uncle Herbert's office. The rustling of papers caught me off guard, and I stopped short, slapping a hand to my chest, a breath hitching in my throat.

There was a strange man behind the desk. He was young, maybe in his twenties, dressed in a sport coat and slacks. He seemed to be making calculations, using a graph paper and an antiquated adding machine. Apparently he was unconcerned with my passing.

I had the fleeting thought that he was a ghost. A fully solid ghost whose breath ruffled the adding machine tape, as he peered at the numbers. A ghost who chewed Juicy Fruit. I could smell it.

I stopped just past the desk and turned to look at him. "What are you doing in my uncle's office?"

He glanced up, seeming surprised that I had addressed him, but not alarmed. "I'm with the auction company."

"For the estate sale?"

"Right." He turned back to his work, indicating a lack of interest in engaging me. He punched in a few more numbers, studied them.

"You're getting stuff ready for the estate sale?"

"Right."

"My uncle knows you're here?"

"Right."

The one-word answers fanned the burn in my stomach. With the exception of the visit to Ruth's, it had been another upside-down and backward, down-the-rabbit-hole day, filled with events that, lumped together, made no sense. "The estate sale, which is . . . when, exactly?"

He punched in more numbers, snorted softly, erased something on his graph paper, rewrote in the spaces. "You'd have to talk to Herbert about that, ma'am."

"But I'm asking you." My inner dragon lady, the one who sent interns scurrying against walls, was rapidly coming to the surface. I'd been way too

348

much of a wimp since my bedraggled arrival in Moses Lake.

"I don't have any information. Your uncle would be the one to talk to." He began furiously punching numbers, muttering, "Mmm-hmm . . . mmm-hmm," to himself, as if I were no longer in the room.

"Might I ask what you're doing, exactly?"

"Calculating." The answer was flat, intentionally off-putting, meant to let me know that he wouldn't be divulging anything.

Clenching my teeth over a snippy retort, I continued on toward the basement. The red tags, if they were there, would at least be proof of something. I wasn't exactly sure what, but . . .

Outside, a pickup truck was coming up the driveway. As it popped over the hill, a soft, sweet feeling, like a dusting of powdered sugar, fell over my churning inner self. Blaine. I needed a friendly face at that moment.

But in reality, I had no solid reason to believe Blaine was a friend. However interesting, different . . . all right, even magical last night's dance at Blue Moon Bay had been, Blaine was somehow wrapped up in this business with my mother and my brother, and he wasn't willing to divulge any secrets.

Maybe if I told him what I'd seen today in Gnadenfeld, it would make a difference. Blaine really appeared to be a decent guy. Surely he had just been taken in by Clay's enthusiasm and the high energy of Clay's current manic interest in Moses Lake. All I had to do was make Blaine see the truth.

Grabbing a jacket, I hurried out the front door as his truck tooled into the circle in front of the house—moving rather fast, actually. Gravel flew as he skidded to a stop, and I hung back until the dust died down. Blaine leaned across the front seat to throw open the passenger door. "You up for a little adventure?"

I hesitated at the base of the porch steps, the voice in my head saying, *Who cares about the land deal, the family's financial stability, or the future of your career. Get in the truck with the hunky guy.* "Where are we going?"

"Just trust me. This'll be worth the ride."

"That's what you said last time." I moved a few steps closer.

His smirk broadened into a devil-may-care grin, unabashedly confident. "And was it?"

Heat traveled from my head to my toes. There was only one answer to that question, and we both knew what it was. Call me coy, but I couldn't quite bring myself to admit to it. Grabbing the door, I dragged myself into the passenger seat, trying to appear reserved so as to not make evident my inner voice cheering, *Yee-haw! Let's go, cowboy!*

Moving his foot from the brake to the gas, he

grinned, his eyes sliding over me in a way that made my stomach flutter. All thoughts of my brother and my frustrating afternoon flew out the window. I remembered last night's dance and the kiss.

Never in my life had a kiss brought such an onslaught of emotions that I couldn't even think straight while it was happening. That kiss wasn't like any other kiss. I still wasn't sure why. Maybe it was the night, or the magic of Blue Moon Bay.

Or the dance.

Or maybe it was the man.

That prospect bothered me. I reeled my mind in like a Macy's balloon, pulled too high by a stiff wind. If I was going to hang out with Blaine, I had to be smarter this time, more in control.

That thought took wing as Blaine glanced over at me, a little dimple forming in his cheek when he checked for traffic before pulling onto the road, and turning left, away from town. "Don't look so worried. Last night's surprise worked out all right, didn't it?"

I felt hot, despite the relatively cool air wafting through the vents. "Maybe I was just playing along to make you feel good." My cheeks twitched upward, making it tough to keep a straight face.

A knowing smirk answered. "Tell me you're not the kind of girl who would mess with a guy's heart."

Tell me, I thought. *Tell me you're not that kind of guy.* But I felt my little balloon head floating up and up and up. I wanted to lose myself in the moment again, throw caution to the wind, abandon all sense of reason, gamble like a high roller.

"Last night was nice." The admission surprised me. It felt vulnerable and raw. Whatever else happened, I would carry that dancing lesson with me. My chance to finally visit the Blue Moon on a dream date. It had only taken me sixteen years. "Never know when the two-step will come in handy, back in Seattle."

His face straightened, as if the mention of my going home bothered him. Maybe I was just imagining it. Wanting it. It was silly, of course. Leftover high-school emotion, more than anything.

"Hang around awhile. I'll teach you a few more steps."

My heart tumbled, pressing against my chest. I let my eyes close for a moment, tried to collect my thoughts. "I wish I could." The words were just a whisper. I didn't realize I'd said them out loud until I heard them.

"They construct big buildings in Texas, too," he pointed out quietly.

I didn't reply. I didn't know what to say. Everything was so up in the air. Depending on what was going on with Clay, I might be around for a while. If I couldn't convince him to face the problem and go back to Seattle with me to seek some kind of treatment, I'd have to take an extended leave of absence from my job and stay in Moses Lake. What would Mel say? He would have to replace me with a new second in command. Temporarily. But temporary could quickly become permanent. I'd become Mel's second when his last right-hand man had taken off to nurse his wife through cancer. All I'd seen at the time was my opportunity.

There were dozens more just like me, waiting in the wings. Looking for a big break.

If Mel doesn't understand, after all you've done for him, after all you've put in, then forget him. There are other places to work.

Were there? Would I really do something that drastic?

If Clay was willing to consider some kind of treatment here, I could look for a position in Texas—Dallas or Austin—maybe help get myself into a firm by telling them I had a line on designing a group of dental clinics in the area. . . .

I felt the colors bleeding outside the lines, racing in directions I never thought they'd go. Texas? Staying in Texas?

Outside the chaos in my mind, I heard the grinding of the tires on the pavement, a rattle in the air conditioner fan, the keys jingling as we passed over a pothole. I realized how quiet the truck had become. Had Blaine somehow picked up on the crazy track my mind was taking? Could he see it, just by looking? When I glanced over at him, he was focused on a trailer load of new speedboats passing by. Oblivious, thank goodness.

"Blaine, I have to ask you something, and I just . . . really need the truth right now." Breath cramped in my chest, feeling solid and painful.

"All right." His tone was wary. "I'll answer, if I can."

I pulled in air, then let it out with words laced into it. Dangerous words. Words that could change everything. "Do you know what's going on with my brother? Do you know what kind of a . . . a problem he has?"

"Problem?"

There was no choice but to lay it out now. "Drugs, Blaine. I found . . . things in his clothes, paraphernalia. A vial, a ziplock bag that had some kind of powder in it. Then today I saw him sneaking around in some alley over in Gnadenfeld . . . making a transaction of some sort. He knocked on a door, and someone gave him something, and he hid it in his coat."

Blaine didn't look at me but remained focused on the road as he piloted the truck into a scenic turnoff high on a bluff overlooking the lake. "Heather, I don't think . . ."

"Do you *know*, Blaine? Do you know what he's into—what he's using?"

354

I felt the truck settle into Park, heard the engine die. Blaine's hand slipped over mine, his fingers a warm, reassuring circle. Meeting his gaze, I searched for lies and secrets, but I couldn't see any. There was only the soft brown of understanding, of kindness and concern. "Heather, I can promise you that your brother's not on drugs."

"But how . . . I . . . I found things . . ."

He swiveled toward the front window before I could repeat myself. "There they are." He motioned to draw my attention, and I turned just in time to take in something so beautiful it chased away all other thoughts. Silhouetted against the bluffs, two bald eagles floated on the mingling air currents over the lake. They moved effortlessly, rising and falling, circling one another and cartwheeling through the sky, consumed by the joy of the moment and the freedom of flight.

Blaine exited the truck silently, and I followed, even the soft click of the door seeming too loud. The eagles dipped out of sight, and Blaine moved toward the edge of the overhang.

"C'mon," he whispered, stretching a hand toward me. I slipped my fingers into his, and he led me through a tangle of cedars, the two of us creeping one step at a time, like photographers stalking the perfect shot in some remote Discovery Channel location. Overhead, the eagles' shrill cries sliced the crisp winter air, sending a primal shiver over my skin, the instinctive reaction of predator and prey. They seemed closer now, as if their wings were beating the air just above the cedars. Blaine continued to pull me with him until we were crouched side by side on the edge of a bluff, an arch of thick, green cedar surrounding us.

The eagles swooped past, so close I drew back out of reflex and caught a breath. Blaine glanced at me and winked as the birds dipped near the water, then soared upward in tandem, their massive, powerful wings pumping long, even strokes as they rose against scattered winter clouds.

"That's amazing," I whispered, exhilarated and at the same time feeling a lump in my throat. I'd been all over the world, had helped to design buildings that seemed to defy gravity and meld into the surrounding expanse of sky, but I'd never seen anything so incredible as the eagles in flight over the lake. Nothing man-made, no feat of engineering could even begin to compare to this.

At the apex of flight, the birds circled, then seemed to hesitate, almost suspended in midair.

"Watch." Blaine squeezed my hand, leaning close to me so that he could see around the fringe of cedars. I felt his nearness. The sensation and the spectacle overhead sent electricity surging through me, bringing to life every inch, every fiber of my being, capturing every thought and breath into the moment.

"What are they doing?" I whispered.

"They like each other." Blaine's breath rustled my hair. I felt myself tumbling over the edge of the abyss, floating and swirling. "It's a courtship dance."

I thought of last night, of gliding across the rocks at Blue Moon Bay in Blaine's arms, the two of us moving as one to the tinny strains of music drifting across the water. That moment was like this one—an instant of being completely present, swept into an experience so powerful that nothing else could compete with it.

I'd never been drawn in that way before. It was at once impossibly alluring and frightening.

"There they go." He stretched a hand up, pointed, and in one sudden, powerful collision, the eagles locked talons and spiraled downward, their bodies whirling, the white feathers on their heads glinting like the fins on a windmill, spinning impossibly fast. The velocity increased as they tumbled downward in free fall, spiraling toward the ground. I'd heard of eagles locking talons in a death spiral before, even seen it once on the nature channel, but I'd never expected to witness it in person.

I felt myself spinning along with them, felt the fear and the elation of something so free, so dangerous, so wild. Every muscle in my body tightened. I realized I was holding my breath, clutching Blaine's hand, afraid to watch but unable to stop as the ground raced closer. They surely wouldn't survive the fall. . . .

A burst of air escaped my lips, then a laugh as the eagles released one another within inches of the bluffs and swooped upward. I slapped a hand to my chest, catching my breath. "Oh, wow. I've never seen anything like that in my life. That was . . . was . . ." Emotion stole away the words. Moisture welled in my eyes, pooled and spilled. Some moments are beyond the capacity of words, beyond the measure of any earthly comparison.

I turned to Blaine and saw a reflection of everything I was thinking, a mirror of everything I was feeling. His eyes, his smile seemed to tell me, *You don't need to say anything. I get it.*

I kissed him, or he kissed me. It didn't matter. The feeling of being there with him, of sharing something so profound, carried me away from myself.

When our lips parted, he reached up and gently wiped the trail of moisture from my cheek with the backs of his fingers. Then he let them sink into my hair and trail down my arm until he was holding my hand again. The mat of last year's leaves rustled underneath him as he shifted, resting on one elbow and looking at me. I wondered what he was seeing, what was in his mind. I wanted to know everything. I wanted to tell him everything.

"I used to think about you, you know," he said,

then cleared his throat and looked away, as if the words made him too vulnerable.

"What?" I had to know what was behind the revelation. "When?"

"Back in chemistry class." Smirking a little, he picked up an acorn and tossed it over the bluff. "I used to think about you."

"You did not," I teased, but I wanted to believe it was true.

"Second row from the wall, second seat from the back. I remember." A little twist of his head added, *Yeah, take that.*

I tried to recall where I'd sat in chemistry class. He was right, actually. "You never said anything." I couldn't blame him, but I wished he had. It wasn't his responsibility to save me from myself during those dark months, but someone like him could have made such a difference. I needed a friend back then.

"I should have." His chest rose and fell in a sigh, like he was admitting to something he was ashamed of. "I wanted to. I mean, I was little when my mom died. I didn't remember that much about her, but I still knew what it was like to miss her, to wish she were here. Every time I saw you around school, I felt like I should tell you that. I was just . . . embarrassed to say it, I guess. I shouldn't have been. Ever since I was little, Mama B told me stories about how my mother was always headed someplace or other to help someone out with food, or offering to babysit somebody's kids, or staying up at the hospital to look after folks, or starting a prayer chain. I always felt like she'd expect me to do the right thing for people, but to tell you the truth, it was easier just to keep my head down and stay off my stepmother's radar."

My perspective shifted, new depth filling the profile of Blaine Underhill, like one of Ruth's drawings suddenly becoming real, taking on three dimensions from two. I'd never even considered that he and I had something in common—then, or now. I'd never considered that anyone could understand the pain I felt after losing my father, or that maybe, growing up in a blended family, he felt like a bit of an outsider himself. I'd never seen him as someone who might have an empty place inside, just like I did.

"Thanks," I said, toying with his fingers, watching his skin against mine. "But I don't blame you. I didn't exactly try to be approachable. I know I wasn't Miss Congeniality."

"What . . . you?" Both eyebrows shot up into the curls over his forehead.

The deer-in-the-headlights expression pulled a snicker from me. "I wanted to be one of those life-of-the-party girls. I just wasn't." I'd never admitted that to anyone until now.

"Yeah, me neither." His chin dipped downward, his lips curving into a little smirk.

"You can't even say that with a straight face," I pointed out, swatting his arm, almost like one of the fun girls. He made me feel like one of those giddy, silly types. Like Marilyn in algebra class, knowing she had everyone, including the teacher, hanging on her every pout and twist of the pinky finger.

Blaine tossed another acorn into the abyss, then flashed a look at me from beneath thick, dark lashes. "Looks to me like you turned out all right."

A hot flush started in my cheeks and seeped over my body.

The funny thing was, I'd been thinking exactly the same thing about him.

> A little water clears us of this deed.
> —Shakespeare, *Macbeth*
> (*Left by Dustin Henderson,*
> *writing an English paper on the run*)

≈ Chapter 16 ≈

I was walking barefoot along a dock, the day quiet and peaceful, the weathered decking radiating the leftover warmth of a waning afternoon. In the distance, eagles flew against the sun, their shadows sailing over the water, larger than it seemed they should be.

A sundress swished softly around my knees, caught the breeze and flipped upward. I stopped to smooth it. High overhead, the eagles locked talons and spiraled downward, their bodies whirling toward the water.

I stood frozen where I was, holding my breath, watching the spectacle with fear and awe.

The eagles spun faster and faster, bound in their dizzying embrace, the water's surface rushing closer.

"No!" I screamed. "Stop!" But the wind whipped my voice away.

In a fury of movement and sound, the birds disappeared below the edge of the dock, struck the water and plunged in. The surface turned placid and silent. I moved forward slowly, one step, then another, another, trying to gain a view.

Were they there? Were they alive?

Suddenly I was running toward the doors—the white ones that led to the chapel room of the funeral home. The ladies were filing through, crowding the entrance in their dark dresses and matching gloves. I stretched upward to see over the wall of hats and hair and mesh.

"Who is it?" I asked. "Whose funeral?" But the organ was playing so loudly that no one seemed to hear.

"Who?" I yelled louder, reaching for the woman in front of me. My hand was clothed in a black kid-leather glove, a floral pattern of beads at the wrist. I drew it back slightly, surprised, then realized I was looking through a mourner's netted veil. I shook the woman's shoulder, but she only continued moving along with the crowd, her wrist raising her veil slightly as she wiped her eyes. Amy?

"Amy? Amy, whose funeral?" I begged, but the crowd was pulling her away. Her shoulder slipped from my hand, a length of her veil trailing through my fingers. I tried to cling to it, but I couldn't. The ladies were pressing all around me now, squeezing past, pulling me into the chapel room. I didn't want to go. I remembered my father's body in the casket, my mother sitting numbly in the front pew, Clay in a black suit that was a miniature of the ones my father wore to church on Sunday. Clay's blond hair had been carefully combed by Ruth. Tears slowly streaked his sunburned cheeks.

The crowd was forcing me in, lifting me from my feet as I tried to turn and run. Behind me, I saw Ruth's family coming in the door, their heads bowed, the women's faces unveiled, sober beneath their tightly-bound hair, mesh prayer caps, and scarves. They were carrying food—heaping platters filled with *fleischballe* and *apfelsalat*. They stopped in the entry hall, seeming unwilling to enter the chapel area.

"Ruth!" Twisting, I reached for her, but she didn't respond. "Ruth!"

I was in the chamber then. The crowd parted and the doors began closing behind me, people fanning into the room, the old oak pews groaning softly as mourners selected seats. I tried for the door, but my body was heavy, filled with stone. The sundress from the dock had turned to thick, black wool, binding my legs so that I could barely move. The latch clicked into place as I grabbed the ornate brass handles and tried in vain to return to the vestibule. Outside, the Mennonite women sang a hymn, silverware clinking and plates rattling.

Inside the chapel there was silence, utter and complete—absent of coughing, sniffling, or the comforting words of a service. I turned slowly and realized the crowd was waiting for me, everyone motionless, expectant. In the front row my mother lifted a hand, palm up, indicating that I should file past the casket. I remembered the day of my father's funeral, when they'd forced me to stand beside his body as the mourners moved through. I'd felt sick. I couldn't look at him in that box, pale and gray, artificially painted with life. It seemed so impossible that he could be gone. Forever. That there was nothing I could do to bring him back.

I was angry with him for leaving us behind. I was angry with my mother for fighting with him, for making him so upset that he walked away from her and headed down to the basement to decompress. I'd heard the fight, but I didn't know what it was about. Was it worth his life?

I felt myself moving toward the casket now, not willingly but as if the floor were shifting under my feet to bring me to the front of the room, past the pulpit, where Reverend Hay stood silent and stoic, scarecrow-thin. His long face turned my way as I moved up the steps to the coffin.

Every eye in the room focused on me, following me to the casket, forcing me to gaze downward at the dark, freshly-polished shoes, the black slacks, the suit coat, the blue tie, the broad, muscular shoulders, and then the face.

"Clay?" I whispered, and in the gallery, a single mourner let out a long, animal-like wail. I collapsed on the floor, my legs suddenly uncooperative, refusing to keep me by Clay's side. I wanted to shake him from his slumber, tell him this wasn't funny. This was a twisted, sick joke.

Uncle Herbert and Uncle Charley, dressed in dark jackets, moved forward, slowly closing the casket. I crawled to the base, reached upward, clawed the wood, tried to scratch my way through. Another mourner put forth a long, loud wail, piercing the silence. . . .

Snapping upright, I took in a gush of air, felt my heart pounding as the chapel room, the mourners, and the image of my Clay in the coffin disappeared like a whiff of smoke. Only the scratching and the keening remained. I realized that Roger was outside the cottage, trying to get in.

For once I was thankful for Clay's hapless dog. Anything that could vanquish such a horrible dream had to be a gift. How could my mind come up with such terrible things—the eagles dead in the lake? Clay in my father's place, in the coffin? What kind of twisted, subconscious conjuring could create that?

Rubbing the sleep from my eyes, I scooted to the edge of the bed. The chill in the cottage slid over my skin, raising gooseflesh. Poor Roger was probably freezing out there. It was colder again tonight, and apparently I'd set the damper on the wood stove too low. My slippers were like ice on my feet. Frigid slices of air pressed through the pine floorboards, knifing at my legs as I moved through the interior of the cottage, dim except for the glow of the moon and the yard light, drifting through the windows. On the kitchen clock, the hour hand ticked into place with an electronic click. Four in the morning? Clay had left his poor dog outside overnight again, apparently.

On the porch, Roger heard me coming. He yipped, then furiously clawed the stoop, trying to dig his way through. The door rattled on its hinges as I reached for the latch. "Hang on, Roger." I pushed, then pulled the door, performing the magic combination that had always caused the latch to release. A blast of frigid night wind slipped through the opening, and I stood back, expecting the dog to barrel through in a flurry of hair and movement, but nothing happened.

"Come on, Roger," I called, impatient with the cold air rushing in. "Roger, *come on!*"

His toenails clattered on the frosty wood outside as he scampered down the steps. Apparently, he didn't want to come in; he wanted to play. At four in the morning.

When I poked my head around the door and looked out, he was standing in the glow of the yard light, watching me expectantly. Leave it to Clay's dog to decide the middle of the night was an opportune time for a game of catch-me-if-you-can.

"Roger, get in here." The sleepy voice had been replaced by the parental voice—the one employed only on rare occasions when I acted as an emergency babysitter for Trish's kids. Unfortunately, it didn't seem to be working on Roger. He stood his ground on the lawn. "All right, then. Stay there, if that's what you want." That always worked with Trish's kids. Once they knew that not all adults will chase you around the house with a peanut butter and jelly sandwich and beg you to eat it, the game was up. I got along really well with Lila, Laura, and little Nat. We had fun, even.

Roger needed to learn the Lila, Laura, and Nat lesson.

"Closing the door now," I warned, then followed through, and just as I'd expected, Roger returned to the porch and repeated the whimpering and scratching. After leaving the door shut long enough to make my point, I opened it again. "See, Aunt Heather really will leave you out there in the cold."

Once again, no Roger. I leaned out, poking my face into the chilly air. Roger was back on the lawn, barking and looking excited.

It occurred to me that I was playing mind games with a dog, and losing . . . at four in the morning. Which made it doubly stupid. Clearly, Roger wasn't in danger of freezing to death. He was too busy having fun. "All right, you're on your own."

After closing and latching the door, I trundled back across the living room, adjusting the stove damper on the way. With a contented sigh, I was back in my bed, burrowing beneath the quilts by the time Roger clattered onto the porch again. Tomorrow, I'd have to tell Clay in no uncertain terms not to leave his dog outside at night. It was just cruel, irresponsible, and the dog was bothering other . . .

He was scratching at the door again, ready to continue our fun little game.

"Go away, Roger! Bad dog!" I nuzzled in deeper and pulled the covers around my ears. He'd give up in a minute or two. If I could outlast Lila and Laura, I could outlast Roger.

Roger scratched, whined, yipped, then knocked something over on the porch. Something heavy. It clattered down the steps.

"Stop it, Roger!" I yelled.

Another object tumbled off the porch. Firewood. Roger was unstacking my firewood. Ohhh, I was going to have something to say to Clay about this in the morning. In fact, if that dog didn't vacate my porch pretty soon, we weren't even going to make it until morning. I wouldn't be responsible for what happened if I had to go out there again. I really wouldn't.

Even the pillow mashed against my ears was no match for Roger's canine determination. The cottage walls were paper-thin. He might as well have been scratching at my bedpost.

369

"All right, *that's it!*" The covers flew off and I staggered from the bed, feeling fairly certain that, had anyone gotten in my way, I could have done the Medusa thing and created a pillar of stone. Stalking to the front door, I clumsily put on my coat, then staggered around while trying to cram my feet into the nearest available footwear—my suede boots. I was going to hunt that dog down, grab him by the collar, take him up to the house, and dump him on Clay's bed. I . . .

For the first time, I noticed that Roger's bark was different somehow—not the playful squeaky yip I'd become accustomed to, but a low, demanding sound. Barking, then silence, then barking again—as if he were pausing to see whether anyone was listening. What if he wasn't playing? What if something was wrong? What if he was actually delivering a warning? Every once in a while, there was a story on the news about some trusted pet awakening a family, saving them from a house fire or carbon monoxide poisoning.

I sniffed the air. No smoky smell . . .

Could you get carbon monoxide poisoning from a wood stove? Probably. Maybe Roger had detected something. I didn't feel sick. Didn't people have headaches or other symptoms if they were breathing carbon monoxide?

Roger barked again, this time from somewhere near the corner of the cottage on the side that faced the main house. Was something wrong up there?

My mind conjured horrible images of Harmony House engulfed in flames, and I hurried to the kitchen window to check. Everything seemed normal, but my heart was fluttering unsteadily in my chest, my nerves on edge—such a far cry from the comfortable, sated feeling I'd had after visiting the eagle's nest and then going to the Waterbird to have a sandwich with Blaine. We'd sat there talking forever—not about anything particular or anything important. We'd talked about high school, my life, his life. I'd tried again to bring up Clay. *Let's not hash over family stuff tonight,* he'd said.

He'd walked me down to the cottage after he brought me home. Smiling, he lamented the fact that he couldn't take me out for another dancing lesson. He had a school board meeting at eight o'clock. He'd invited me to the big Valentine's soiree tomorrow night at the school, then kissed me, and I'd walked inside, floating on air. The lights were off in the big house, so I'd stayed in the cottage reading old copies of *Field and Stream* and watching for Clay to return. In spite of Blaine's vague reassurances, I wanted Clay to explain what I'd seen in Gnadenfeld and what I'd found in the truck. Unfortunately, my brother seemed to be making himself scarce. I'd finally fallen asleep on the sofa. Clay's truck still wasn't in the driveway later, when I moved to my bed.

Maybe that was why I'd had the dream. I was worried about him.

Maybe my dream was a warning. If Clay was mixed up in something, he could be keeping Blaine in the dark, just like all the rest of us. . . .

Stop, I told myself as I stumbled back to the door, my legs clumsy and uncooperative. *Stop letting your imagination get the best of you. Just go make sure everything's okay up at the house. It's probably fine.*

While I was up there, I'd leave a note in my brother's room, tell him we needed to talk before he left in the morning. Period.

An icy, watery wind slipped in the door as I opened it, the sharp sensation slicing away the last remnants of sleep with one quick stroke. Roger was standing between the cottage and the barn. He remained motionless, silent as I walked out.

"Roger?" My voice was hoarse, but the sound rebounded against the buildings and the frost-tipped woods.

Roger glanced my way, growled, then walked toward the center of the yard, out of view. Tugging my coat tighter around myself, I crossed the porch, moved down the steps, and instantly felt the cold ground penetrating my shoes. "Roger?" I called again. "Roger?"

A chill pressed over me, but it had nothing to do with the temperature outside. A branch crackled in the woods, and I had that eerie feeling again—the one that told me someone was nearby, watching. Fine hairs rose on my skin as Roger's barking drew me around the end of the cottage, until I could see the lower half of the yard. Roger was waiting halfway down the hill, near the ring of light from a gas lamp. He looked at me, barked, then turned toward the big house, barking twice more. A gust of wind whipped off the lake, driving me backward a step before I moved into the open, checked the main house, and then began a slow, visual sweep of the yard. Nothing out of the ordinary. Maybe Roger had spotted a possum or a raccoon marauding in the trash cans or . . .

Near the center of the gas lamp's glow, I saw what Roger wanted me to see: Clay's truck was there in the yard, not more than a hundred feet from the lakeshore. It rested at an odd angle, high-centered on the fig tree, the driver's side door hanging slightly ajar, the dome light giving the branches an eerie luminosity. I looked back and forth toward the house, scanned the set of tire tracks in the frost.

No wonder Roger was barking. Apparently Clay's truck had somehow rolled off the edge of the driveway and gone rogue. It seemed to be empty, and there was no sign of activity around it—no tracks other than Roger's. Maybe the impact had caused the door to pop open on its own?

Roger followed me to the truck and around the back of it, stood waiting as I checked the cab, then leaned over to look underneath. The Ladybug was beached like a whale on a sand bar, and it didn't look like it was going any farther without the help of a tow truck or maybe a crane to extricate it from the remains of the scraggly fig tree. Closing the door, I looked up the hill again. The windows in the house were dark, everyone apparently having slept right through the Ladybug's midnight rampage. Really, it was pure luck that it hadn't ended up in the lake.

Catching Roger's collar, I rubbed between his ears, feeling like I owed him an apology. He'd actually had a good reason for rousing me. Nothing could be done about this mess tonight, but it would be quite the source of family conversation in the morning. The uncs would have an exciting tale to share with all their buddies at the Waterbird. "Good boy," I told Roger. "You're a good boy. C'mon, let's go back inside now." Giving the Ladybug one last perplexed glance, I started toward the cottage.

Roger twisted against my grip, pulling backward and shaking his head, trying to wiggle out of the collar.

"Roger, stop!" I dragged him a little farther.

He yipped and fought like an animal possessed, squealing and gagging when the collar twisted tight. The chain pinched my finger, and I let go out of reflex. Roger was gone in an instant, bolting through the dim circle of light and disappearing on the other side of the truck. His insistent barking beckoned me to follow, and as I circumvented the vehicle my mind flashed back to the dream, to the chapel steps, each one bringing me closer to knowing what was inside the coffin, to seeing something I didn't want to see.

In front of the truck, Roger was sniffing the ground, digging at a mound of dirt, or trash, or . . . something . . . No, not trash . . . clothing . . . a coat . . .

I squinted, trying to make out the mass in shadow. Someone was lying face down in the frosty grass. . . .

My heart flipped unevenly. "Clay?" I ran the last few steps. A soft moan stirred the frosty air as I dropped to my knees.

"Clay!" I gasped, rolling him over, supporting his head. My fingers touched something warm and wet . . . blood?

"Clay, what happened?" Leaning closer, I searched for answers, thinking of the day I'd found him on the settee in the parlor, crashed after his all-nighter with Amy. Maybe he wasn't just tired that day, either. Maybe he'd passed out. Had he come home tonight not fully within his faculties, passed out in his truck, and let it roll down the hill? Had he hit his head when the truck crashed, or afterward when he was trying to get out? "Oh, Clay," I whispered. If not for the fig tree, he could have ended up in the lake. He *would* have ended up in the lake. I'd be calling the police right now, watching them pull my brother's body from the frigid water. . . .

"I'll go get help." I moved the hood of his jacket so that I could lay his head on it. His hand flailed clumsily, catching my arm just above the wrist. His fingers were as cold as the frost-tipped grass, barely able to cling.

"Nnn-no," he whispered, his face hidden in the shadow my body cast over him. "Just . . . the cot . . . cot-tage."

"Clay, you need to be looked after. We need to call a doctor. You shouldn't try to get up until someone checks your neck."

His grip tightened, and he shook violently. Rolling to the side, he pulled his knees under himself in an attempt to gain his feet. A violent cough racked his body, and his arms quivered inside his coat as he struggled to brace himself up.

"Unn-no, Hess . . . the cot . . . cot. . . tage. Just help . . . meeee . . ."

I understood his plea, even though I didn't want to. He was desperate to avoid having everyone else see him like this.

I knew it wasn't the best course of action, nor the safest, but I helped him up. Tremors wracked his body, and he swayed against me, leaning hard on my shoulders as we dragged trails in the frost, one unsteady, labored step, then another, across the hillside, the distance seeming an impossible barrier. In our wake, Roger followed quietly.

My lungs were burning by the time we reached the porch and climbed up. My knees buckled and shook under the strain of lifting Clay's weight up each step and then finally through the door. The night chill followed us inside, clinging to us, and I laid my brother on the couch, then went back and closed the door. Roger trailed me nervously as I opened the damper wide and grabbed the quilts from the bed, piling them on top of Clay. His face and hands were white, icy cold. Turning on the lights, I saw the blood-streaked hair on the side of his head and bent to check it. The cut wasn't that large, but it had bled quite a bit, and the flesh around it had swollen into a nasty lump. Roger sat beside Clay and watched with concern as I made an ice pack and wrapped it in a kitchen towel. Moaning, Clay rolled onto his side and curled into a ball, his body trembling when the towel touched his head.

"Shhh," I soothed, looking under the towel, then carefully placing it back on my brother's hair. This wasn't an unfamiliar position for us. As a kid, Clay was always falling out of trees or having wrecks on his bike and coming home with injuries. "You've got a pretty good bump under there." The blood in his hair was crusty and tipped with ice. How long had he been out there?

How much longer would he have made it in the cold, if Roger hadn't come looking for me? Roger might have saved his life.

Clay could be gone right now. We could be one of those families, huddled together in some hospital in the middle of the night, telling a police officer that we didn't know Clay had a substance abuse problem.

Despite what Blaine had told me, what he'd promised, was there any other possible explanation for Clay's behavior, for what had happened tonight? I wanted to come up with one, but I couldn't. How could Clay do this? How could he be so irresponsible? How could my mother have let it go on? Clay could have killed someone on the road. He could have killed himself.

"What happened to you?" I leaned over to him, tried to pry his eyes open, to tell whether his pupils were dilated. "Where were you tonight? What were you doing?"

Groaning softly, he batted my hand out of the way, taking over holding the ice pack. "G-guess . . . I . . . uhhh . . ." His brows squeezed, and his lips drew back, his teeth clenching as he changed positions slightly. "I'm . . . so c-cold." Another round of shivers racked his body.

"Clay, where were you tonight?" I sat on the coffee table, an ache spreading inside me but my voice surprisingly level, my mind still racing. *Should I call 9-1-1? Go wake up Mom and the uncs? Drive him to a hospital?* "What happened?"

His free hand dragged the quilts higher, then investigated the head wound, his fingertips quivering at the hairline, slipping under the ice pack slightly, then pulling back. "I bump . . . g-guess I bumped my head-d-d. . . ." He opened his eyes, then let them fall closed again.

"Clay!" I snapped, in the bossy, impatient big-sister voice from days gone by. "Clay, don't you dare go to sleep. You tell me what happened. Now. How did you end up out there?"

Slowly, he shook his head, the frosty tips of his hair melting into little round pools, some clear, some reddened with blood. Roger climbed onto the opposite end of the sofa and belly-crawled forward, resting his chin on Clay's leg. "Hey, bud-d-dy." Clay reached for the dog, but then just let his hand fall and sighed. "Got home . . . from . . . from Amy's, I th-think. The truck . . . rolled down . . . maybe. What . . . what time is . . . ?"

I glanced at the clock by the stove. "It's four thirty-five in the morning. It's freezing. What were you doing, sitting out there in your car?" Had he come home, parked the car, and passed out, or had he arrived home so messed up that he'd driven right off the end of the driveway? Had he gone out there to maybe take a hit of something where he wouldn't be seen? What? "Clay,

379

what were you doing sitting in your car in the middle of the night? When did you get home? What time?"

Dragging his eyelids upward again, he moved the ice pack away from his head, the white towel now pink with watery blood. "I'm not . . . don't remember . . . coming. Here . . . take this. It's-s-s cold." He set the ice pack on the table and bunched the blankets under his chin. Roger looked at me, brows wrinkling, as if he were doing the same thing I was doing—trying to piece together the evening's events. Clay had been out on a date with Amy, come home and . . .

"You've been outside a long time, Clay. What were you doing in the truck? Why didn't you go in the house when you got home?"

"*Ummmph* . . . don't remem . . . ber," he muttered, turning his head away as if I were disturbing him. "Fell asleep . . . I guess. I was . . . listening . . ." His voice drifted off as he sank deeper into the pillows. ". . . to a song . . . I think."

"So you were listening to a song, and you fell asleep, and the truck rolled down the hill. Is that right?"

"Umm . . . maybe. Yeah-h-h. I g-guess."

He shivered again, his knees curling upward. I wanted to grab him and shake him, yell at him, *You know what, if it weren't for the fig tree, you'd be in the lake right now! If Roger hadn't been outside, you might have frozen to death! What is wrong with you? What are you doing to yourself?* "All right, listen. I'm going to go wake up Mom and the uncs, and we're taking you to the hospital. You need an MRI or something to check for a concussion." *And a toxicology scan, too.* We could kill two birds with one stone, and with a hospital report to back me up, we'd finally be able to face whatever Clay was dealing with. There would be no more room for denial, on anyone's part.

I put my hands on my knees to push to my feet. My legs were stiff and logy, like I'd just run a marathon.

Clay caught my wrist, holding me in place, his eyes opening, suddenly more alert. "No."

"Clay, you need help."

He blinked hard, pushed against the sofa, and lifted himself slightly, as if he intended to get up and stop me from leaving. "I just fell . . . asleep. I'm fine."

I couldn't say why I gave in to the pull, but I sank onto the table again, weary, confused, drawn in by the sudden intensity in my brother's face. "You're not fine, Clay. People who are fine don't fall asleep in the car and almost end up in a frozen lake. People who are *fine* don't carry vials and ziplock bags in their pants pockets. They don't sneak around in alleys, making secret pickups through back doors. You're not *fine*. You're on something, and that's why you passed out in the truck tonight, isn't it?"

"On some . . . thing?" His lip curled, flashing an eyetooth, and he blinked again, seeming alert but genuinely confused.

"Drugs, Clay." Finally, the chance to spell it out, to confront the problem at the source, and with evidence to back me up. "Drugs. How stupid do you think I am? How long have you been doing this? Does Mom know you're using? Do the uncs?" *Does Blaine? He promised me you were fine, that there was nothing to worry about. Was he fooled like everyone else? Would he lie for you?*

I jerked my arm back, but Clay's fingers squeezed tighter. "There's not . . . There's n-nothing to know." He forced a lopsided, wavering smile before a shiver coursed through him. "I'm not on dr-drugs, Hess. I was just . . . tired. Too m-many late nights."

"With Amy? With Amy, whom you're so crazy-serious about that you're texting with some chick from Fort Worth? Tara somebody? What's going on with you, Clay? That's not even like you. You've never been this way with people—lying, cheating, this whole line about taking over the restaurant, but you're never there. You're not exactly working yourself to death learning the business. If all of this is some sort of scam, you have to come clean. Now, Clay. Before things get any worse. You could have died tonight."

Tears pushed into my eyes, blurred my vision of him, spilled over. He met my gaze, and through the sheen of water, I saw the little brother who had been my only reason to keep moving forward through the most violent storm of my life.

The words I hadn't been able to find then came to me now. "I love you, Clay." I realized it had been years since I'd said that to anyone, since I'd allowed myself to feel the raw vulnerability of love. A tomb inside me cracked open, a slumbering spirit rising like Lazarus. I remembered how it felt to really love. "I don't want anything to happen to you."

His fingers slid down my wrist, and he took my hand in his, pulled it toward him, tucked my fingers under his chin like he used to when he was little. Fresh tears filled my eyes. I remembered all the nights I'd sat by his bed, comforted his hurts. All the times we'd walked in the woods together, when I'd played along with his games of Robin Hood and Star Wars.

"I love you, too, Hess," he whispered, his eyes earnest, compelling, tender, seeming completely lucid now. "I just fell asleep . . . and the p-parking brake . . . it's old. That's all. I promise . . . I'm not on dr-drugs, all right?"

"All right," I answered. Then I just sat watching him, trying to decide what should come next.

The river reveals its mysteries in its own time.
—Anonymous
(left by Herbert Hampton,
undertaker, Moses Lake)

≈ Chapter 17 ≈

Valentine's Day dawned bright and sunny. Clay was still sleeping on the cottage sofa when I walked up the hill for breakfast. I'd checked on him several times, and he seemed to be fine, just exhausted and embarrassed about what had happened. His admonitions not to worry Mom and the uncs swam in my head as I crossed the veranda. What possible good could come of my keeping it a secret that, if not for Roger, Clay might have drowned or been found on the lawn this morning, hypothermic or worse?

But in the back of my mind, there was a still, small voice. A memory of the look in Clay's eyes when he begged me not to tell. If I outed him to the family, would he do what he had often done in the past when one of his card castles came tumbling down—simply take off for parts unknown, disappear into the wide, wide world until he decided he was ready to turn up again? What if this time, he disappeared forever?

But did I really have it in me to tell Mom and

the uncs what Clay wanted me to tell them—that the Ladybug was marooned on a fig tree because it had rolled down the hill unoccupied? They would never know the difference, of course. Morning sun had caught the lawn. The frost was already melting off in glistening, watery patches, Clay's footprints and mine bleeding together in an indiscriminate slug trail. Slipping through the back door, I took one last look at the truck, listing like a shipwreck as moisture drew streaks in the layer of grime. What was the right thing to do?

Inside the house, Mom and the uncs were gathered on the sun porch. Snatches of an ongoing conversation floated in the morning air, but the flow stopped abruptly when they heard me in the kitchen.

"Is that Heather?" Mom called.

"It's me." I leaned back from the counter to see if she was coming into the kitchen. When she didn't appear, I poured a cup of coffee and headed for the sun porch, glancing into Uncle Herbert's office as I passed. The desk was stacked with carefully-arranged piles of what looked like papers and receipts, and on the overhead shelf, an old mantel clock had been wound, its steady *ticktock* the only noise in the room.

Everyone turned my way in unison when I entered the sun porch. They were gathered around the wood stove, avoiding the winter chill at the edges of the room. The white shutters were closed on the back windows, barring the low-angled morning sun off the lake, which explained why Clay's marooned truck hadn't yet been noticed. I had the distinct feeling that I was interrupting something, though.

"So what's the deal with the guy working in the office?" I asked, stalling for time, trying to decide what to say about Clay. I couldn't just pretend I hadn't seen his vehicle balancing at a forty-five degree angle in the backyard.

Mom's lips curved upward. She was trying to look cucumber-cool this morning, but she wasn't. There was something haggard and haphazard about her appearance. She hadn't combed her hair and plaited it in the usual braid. It hung loose around her shoulders, and mascara circles rimmed her eyes, as if she'd gotten out of bed in a hurry and come straight downstairs. "He's just going over Uncle Herbert's books from the funeral business—you know, getting everything ready for the sale."

"The sale to you and Clay?" I was determined to pin her down. "Why would the books from the funeral home have anything to do with that? I thought you were buying the house so you could open a bed-and-breakfast, not a funeral home." I stressed *bed-and-breakfast,* so as to let her know that I didn't believe any of it. The entire time I'd been at Harmony Shores, I hadn't seen Mom working to refit the house for use as a bed-and-breakfast any more than I'd seen Clay frying catfish.

Mom squirmed in her chair. "We just want to get everything squared away." Scooting forward, she glanced out the side window toward the driveway, where the funeral sedan and the hearse were parked right now. "Have you seen Clay today?"

It was my turn to be uncomfortable. I felt the moment of truth upon me. To tell or not to tell? *Tell,* a voice insisted in my head. *Tell them about last night.*

But I remembered the way Clay looked at me— just the way he used to when the kids at school had picked on him or passed him over for a dodge ball game, or he'd forgotten to do some assignment and received a bad grade. Disappointing everyone and admitting failure, when he finally had to stop pretending and face it, was almost more than he could bear. All his life one big plan after another had come tumbling down upon him, like buildings constructed on sand. "He's down in the cottage, asleep. He locked himself out last night," I heard myself say. Guilt slipped over me, heavy and itchy. "His truck rolled down the hill. It's stuck on the fig tree."

That revelation, of course, was enough to end the morning conversation. Mom and the uncs hurried out to see about the truck. There was some discussion about waking Clay, but as usual, everyone was weirdly sympathetic to the fact that he'd kept himself out all night. They decided it would be just as well to let him rest, since there was really nothing he could do about moving the truck, anyway. In short order the uncs had made a few phone calls, and we were waiting for Blaine to show up with a tractor. He soon arrived wearing a faded barn jacket and jeans that were haphazardly tucked into the tops of muddy cowboy boots. The well-used boots called up a memory that unfurled, full and clear in my mind.

My father and I were at the farm when I was little. The barnyard was muddy, but he carried me over it, his feet sinking into the muck, his jeans tucked into the tops of his boots.

Closing my eyes now, I could smell the fresh scents of hay and Irish Spring soap. Dad set me on the tractor seat, then walked through the mud and opened the gate while I played with the steering wheel and the levers, pretending to drive. Finally, he climbed onto the seat behind me, and I half sat, half stood between his arms, my hands wrapped on the wheel next to his as the tractor chugged out of the barnyard. After we passed through the gate, we turned the wheel, pointing the tractor down the dusty lane that led past scrappy fence-rows overgrown with mustang grapes and wild roses. The remaining animals on the farm were old and tired, seemingly unmotivated to challenge the ragtag barriers. My grandfather was known for being frugal to the point of patching the fences together until they were as threadbare as a hobo's pants. Inside the pasture, the grass was short, the cattle shearing it down near the soil.

I pointed to a broken place where only one wire and a cedar tree kept the little herd of Angus cattle from making their way to the lane, where high grass awaited.

"They could get out," I said, gazing back at the pasture. The bull looked massive and mean. I didn't know much about cattle, but my grandmother had warned me many times to stay out of the cow pasture because the bull liked to chase people.

"They won't get out," Dad assured me. "There's always been a fence there."

"But there's not a fence there now. Not really." Even at nine years old, I was inquisitive, prone to questioning—a kid who liked science fairs and wanted electronics kits for Christmas when my mom insisted on buying me sets of watercolors, blank journals, classic novels, musical instruments, and weaving looms, trying to bring out my sadly anorexic whimsical side. The truth was that I wanted to be like my dad, to align myself with him, not with her. My dad's world was measured, secure, reliable, while hers seemed unpredictable, like waves on a stormy sea.

In a weird way, I had a feeling that the very thing I disliked about her was what drew my father in. She ignited a different sort of passion in him, tossed glitter and spatters of bright color over his black-and-white life.

Then again, he was gone on business at least half of the time. He didn't have to deal with the parties she threw to keep herself occupied when he was away. On those nights, there might be strangers in the living room discussing art-for-art's-sake or rehearsing lines for community theater at all hours of the night, seemingly oblivious to the fact that there were children nearby who needed a snack and a bath, or a fresh diaper and a bedtime story. By eight years old, I had assumed responsibility for the practicalities of caring for Clay. Unless my father was there, I took care of baths, baby food, and read *Cat in the Hat* a million times.

That day on the tractor, Dad had rested his hands over mine on the steering wheel, forming a physical connection between us. "I want you to listen to me, Heather. A lot of people out there are like those cows, and they can go along that way their whole lives. They get comfortable in one place, even when it's small and dirt bare, like that pasture. You know why they do that?"

I shook my head, thinking, *Because cows are stupid?* But I knew he was probably looking for a better answer than that.

"Because they don't use their minds," my father said. "Because they make assumptions. Those people don't change the world, Heather. They just live in it. They're like those cows who'll stand all their lives behind one strand of barbed wire, not because they can't get out, but because they're convinced they can't. You keep your mind sharp, all right? Always look for yourself. Never let other people tell you where the fences are."

"Okay, Dad," I answered. My nine-year-old mind only grasped the fringes of meaning behind his comment, but I understood the thing that mattered most. My father thought I was capable of great things. He believed in me.

When we started down the lane again, he put my hands on the wheel and pulled his own away, resting them on his knees, so that his arms were like steel bars on either side of me, holding me in place. "You drive," he said. "You're big enough."

All of a sudden, I felt ten feet tall.

That was one of the things I missed most about my dad, I realized now. He'd made me feel like I was capable of anything. I wished he were here now. I wanted him to tell me what to do about Clay, to make me believe that I could somehow solve the problem and have everyone in the family come out of it in one piece.

Watching Blaine on the tractor, I tried to conjure up that connection to my dad, to decide what he would be thinking, what advice he would give if he were with me. He loved Moses Lake so much. When we'd moved so he could bring the new Proxica plant online, he was so happy. But the longer we stayed, the more he'd been preoccupied, distant, lost in his own thoughts. Something was very wrong those weeks before he died. Moses Lake was wrapping itself around him, dragging him down in a way I couldn't understand.

Was history repeating itself? Was this place trying to claim my brother, as well?

Blaine glanced my way as he jumped down to unhook the chains from the Ladybug. He did a double take, cocking his head to one side as if he wondered why I was staring grimly into space. "Want me to drive the truck up the hill for you?" he asked Uncle Herbert.

Uncle Herbert shook his head. "Naw, that's all right. We'll get it. Doesn't look like too much damage done, except to my fig tree. Can't imagine how this truck ended up rolling off like that, though. Lucky it didn't make it to the lake."

I shuddered, thinking of my brother plunging into the icy water, sinking below the surface, passed out, unaware, trapped in the car. I remembered the dream that had awakened me last night. I saw Clay's face pale and gray, his body in my father's coffin. Even the warmth of the midmorning sun couldn't keep the chill off my body as the uncs studied the front of the truck like a couple of golfers gauging a putt, and Mom checked the inside of the cab, looking for something. *What?* I wondered, but there seemed to be no point in asking, so I started up the hill toward the house, instead. I needed a cup of coffee and a chance to clear my head.

The tractor passed by me on the way to the house, and Blaine parked on the pavement, then cut the engine. He was waiting when I reached the top of the hill. We went into the house for coffee.

"You all right?" he asked, leaning against the counter, his hands wrapped around the steaming cup. "Where's Clay, anyway? Seems like since he's the one responsible for the truck, he ought to be out there with the rest of us."

"He's still sleeping." I felt myself sneering when I said it. "And no, I'm not . . . all right. I . . ." My voice trembled, the admission cutting close to the core. "I don't know what to do, Blaine. I really just . . ." Tears pressed harder, and I blinked, stuffing down the emotion. Crying wouldn't do any good. What I needed to do was think. Think of a way to solve the mess my family was in. I needed help.

Blaine's hand slid up my arm, into my hair, offering comfort, solace, sympathy of a sort that made me want to fall into his arms and give into the need to lean on someone. "Hey, what's going on?"

I stiffened against the tears—not against his touch, but against the helplessness of the situation. My brother was in trouble, and I couldn't fix things. "That truck didn't roll down the hill on its own, Blaine. Clay was in it. He begged me not to tell anyone. He's lucky he didn't end up in the lake."

Blinking, drawing back a little, Blaine looked out the window. "Did you ask him how it happened?"

"I asked him, and he says there's nothing wrong, that I'm out of my mind for thinking he passed out in the truck because he was stoned or drunk when he came home. He says I'm crazy for wondering if he has a problem. Mom told me the same thing. Everyone just acts like I'm nuts." *Even you.* "But a normal, healthy, sober person doesn't fall asleep in a truck, in the cold, and roll down a hill. He passed out. He must have."

Blaine squinted toward the cottage. "Your brother's an adult, Heather. If he says . . ."

"Ffff!" I spat, rolling my eyes. "You don't know Clay very well. He's an overgrown adolescent, and every time he flakes out, my mother comes to his rescue. She makes excuses for him over and over again. That's why he is where he is right now."

"You don't give your brother much credit."

The frayed thread that had been holding my composure in place snapped with a twang, and my emotions rushed forth in all directions. Anger took the lead. "You know what—I'm tired of everyone making me out to be the bad guy! I'm not some kind of harpy with a sibling-rivalry issue, trying to pick on poor Clay. I love my brother. I'm worried about him."

I flailed a hand in the general direction of the path that the vehicle might have followed, if not for the fig tree, and thank God for that. There was no other way to explain the series of events that had saved my brother's life last night. Divine Providence had intervened, sparing Clay and all the rest of us. Watching Blaine move the truck, I'd also become aware that there was a gas lamp to the left of the fig tree and a gas meter to the right. If the truck had run over one of those on its way down the hill, the whole place could have gone up in a fireball. I wasn't even ready to put forth that possibility. "We could be fishing my brother out of the lake right now. Dead. We're just lucky we're not."

The vision from my dream came back, and all of a sudden I couldn't stand there any longer, thinking about what could have happened. "You know what, never mind." I pulled away, hurt that even Blaine didn't seem to be on my side.

"Heather, wait." He stepped toward me, but I moved out of reach, raising a hand to stop him.

"No. I'm tired of waiting for someone to finally tell me the truth around here. Whatever game they're playing, and whatever game you're playing, I'm sick of it. I don't want any-thing more to do with it. I'm done. I quit." I spun around and headed out the back door, hoping he wouldn't follow and perversely wishing he would.

He didn't, which was undoubtedly for the best.

Roger bounded off the front porch when I turned the corner to the cottage. Taking one look at me, he ducked his head and veered toward the woods, no doubt perceiving that a storm was underway. My anger dulled to a slow boil as I climbed the steps, and exhaustion followed, along with a sense of dread at the idea of talking to Clay again. After last night, I lacked the energy for sorting through more of his excuses. I wanted to curl up in a dark corner somewhere and forget it all. I wanted to get on a plane and go home and leave every bit of it behind.

Something collided with my toe and skittered across the decking—one of Roger's finds, no doubt—a stick or a bone. Opening the door to the cottage, I glanced down, stopping in midstride. In a ball of leaf-covered goo lay a small, square object that looked suspiciously like . . . my cell phone? I extricated it from the leaves and stared at it in awe. It *was* my iPhone, and thanks to the heavy-duty OtterBox case that Richard had given me for Christmas, it appeared to be in remarkably good shape. Awed by its reappearance, I stepped inside with an inordinate sense of relief, as if this were an omen of sorts. The connection to my normal existence had come back at the most opportune of times, reminding me that my mother, my brother, and Moses Lake had done just fine without me for years. Real life—a life I could predict and control, measure and plan—was just the touch of a button away.

In the space of a few minutes, I could book a flight home. I could tell Clay that, whenever he was ready to talk, I was ready to listen, but I couldn't play this cat-and-mouse game anymore. Maybe he would wake up. Maybe he would finally understand how serious his situation was.

But when I turned toward the sofa, it was empty. The shower was running, steam seeping underneath the bathroom door and dancing in the hallway light. Apparently Clay was up. He was doing better than I thought he'd be. Hopefully I could get some more coherent answers while I had him here alone.

Even as I thought it, I was afraid the answers would be the same today as they had been yesterday. Wherever the truth lay, I was powerless to bring it into the open. Ultimately, you can't help someone who doesn't want to be helped.

I wiped off Roger's latest treasure in the kitchen and then went to the bedroom to unearth my charger and plug it in. When I did, the phone came to life as if nothing had ever happened. The sound of its awakening was music to my ears. Some measure of sanity returned to me as I scanned through the list of missed calls. Scores from Mel and a couple from Trish. Nothing from Richard. Mel had called five times this morning, already.

Something must be up. I did a dial-back on the last call and looked out the window while I waited for Mel to answer his cell.

Oddly enough, Mel's newest underling, Rachel, picked up instead. She breathed a sigh of relief instead of saying hello. "Oh, Heather, thank goodness!" Rachel was twenty-nine years old, fresh out of a mini-cubicle in the design department, and hungry. Right now she sounded uncharacteristically frantic.

The tone of her voice made hairs prickle on the back of my neck. "Rachel, what's up? Why are you answering Mel's cell phone?" Typically Mel and his phone were never more than two feet apart. As far as I could tell, he slept with the thing. Even I didn't touch Mel's phone.

"He's been in the hospital, but he got out this morning. He went home to shower and pack some clothes," Rachel rushed out. "Itega wants another meeting, at their headquarters in Tokyo this time. Mel says for you to get your rear on a plane, tonight. He'll leave a package for you at LAX with your passport and anything else you need. I've already checked flights for you. It looks like the nearest airport is in Waco, right? I think I can get you out of there around five o'clock. I'll call you back with a flight number. Mel's leaving as soon as he can get packed. I just emailed everything to you for the Itega meeting. . . . Is there anything else you can think of?"

Is there anything else you can think of? I couldn't think at all. The world outside the window went out of focus. "Mel was in the hospital? What's wrong?"

Rachel snorted impatiently. "Something about blood sugar and ketoacidosis. But anyway, he says if you want to be his second on the Itega project, you better get out of Toad Waller, Texas, and show up in Japan by tomorrow. That's a direct quote, by the way." She breathed the words *second on the Itega project* with obvious awe and a back draft of envy that said *Yeah, I'd jump into your shoes in a heartbeat.*

Tossing my carry-on suitcase on the bed, I started grabbing clothes off the wooden chest and tried to propel my mind out of Moses Lake, to the airport, onto an international flight. "Well, but is it okay for him to travel? All the way to Japan?" I passed by the bathroom door, heard Clay drop something in the shower, felt my concentration veer off.

"Guess so. Must be," Rachel answered blandly, her tone seeming to say, *How is that my problem? There's a project at stake, for heaven's sake.* "Anyway, he didn't say. His mind's on the deal, *of course.*" She stressed the last words, silently pointing out that my mind should be on the deal, too. "Okay, you're confirmed for the flight. I'm texting you the information. What do you need me to send with Mel?"

Rachel's words, her complete lack of interest in anything but the deal, made me stop for an instant. I heard an echo in the words, had a sense of déjà vu. They reminded me of someone. *Was that me? Is that who I've been?*

The shower turned off across the hall as I told Rachel to grab a couple of clean suits and blouses from the stash of I-slept-at-the-office clothes in my closet there. After making a list and promising to send everything with Mel, Rachel reiterated the flight time and hung up. My mind sputtered, refusing to fully kick into gear. A flight to Japan on the red-eye. I'd go to sleep on this side of the world and wake up on the other, thousands of miles from Texas. Maybe that was the best thing. Maybe it was a blessing in disguise. I was driving myself crazy in Moses Lake, getting nowhere, hopelessly outnumbered.

Every muscle in my body tightened, adrenaline streaking through me like an electrical current, making my breath come in fragments and my pulse speed up as if I were preparing for a race. Bracing my hands on the bed frame, I took in moist, cool air that smelled of lake water and damp wooden window frames, the scents pulling me back to the here and now. The flight out of Waco wasn't for hours yet. I could at least try to talk to Clay one more time.

I heard the bathroom door open as I was zipping my suitcase, and a moment later Clay poked his head into the room, his chin dropping when he saw me lowering the carryon to the floor and clipping my laptop case in place. "Listen, Hess," he said. "About last night. It was no big . . ."

I lifted a hand, held it out like a stop sign. "Don't. Okay? You know what, Clay? I love you. I can't even really express how much, but if you won't face the truth, if you're not ready to admit that you've got a problem, there's nothing I can do. You need help, and you need it now. Before something terrible happens."

Combing wet curls from his face, he gave me an earnest, perfectly sober look. He'd washed the blood away, smoothed his hair over the cut to hide it. Everything looked perfectly normal. "It's not like that. I promise. I just fell asleep—burning the candle at both ends too much lately. I'm sorry I scared you. Don't go, all right?"

I closed my eyes, turned away, then grabbed my wallet and stuck it into the computer case. "I have to go. I'm flying to Japan this evening." My thoughts sped forward through the day, demands and expectations pulling and tugging, at war with emotions and needs. I tried to focus on the practical. "I want to go over and visit Ruth before I leave. I'll cut over to Waco from there and leave the car locked at the airport with the keys under the seat. You and Mom can just bring an extra key and pick it up, okay? That will be easiest." I didn't want some long good-bye. I couldn't handle it.

"Okay, sure, but Hess . . ."

A long breath spilled from me as I looked at my brother and saw all the years and experiences, heartbreaks and changes we had experienced together. Tears welled, and I swallowed the sentiments before they could seep out. "You need help, Clay. When you're ready, call me. I'll do whatever it takes to get you what you need. I'll pay for it. I'll arrange it. I'll help you find the right resources. Anything. I want you to be okay. I need you to be, but I can't do it for you. Please, please, whatever's going on, don't drag the uncs into it. They don't deserve that. They're too old to recover from it. Just think it all through, Clay, all right? I'm only a phone call away. Tell Mom and the uncs I'll be in touch in a day or two. Hopefully we can still figure out something about the property deal."

Even though I told myself I was doing the right thing, guilt burned in every part of me. I pushed it back, hugged my baby brother, held on until it was too painful to cling any longer, and then gathered my things and walked out the door.

Clouds gathered on the horizon as I hurried up the hill to the driveway and loaded my things into the sedan I'd driven the day before. Inside the house, the family was probably having breakfast, but I didn't go in to check. I couldn't handle some emotional scene if they tried to talk me out of leaving. I also had the sense that it would be even worse if they didn't. Suspecting that your family doesn't want you around is much better than actually knowing it for sure.

It's better this way, I told myself as I started the car and rolled down the driveway. *We all know it, really. I don't belong here.*

I'd call later, after I'd left Harmony House behind. *No hard feelings,* I'd say. *A project came through at work. I had to fly to Japan. . . .*

I'd try, long distance, to convince Mom that Clay needed help.

Maybe that would be enough. I couldn't keep beating my head against a brick wall any longer while my life, my career, went down the tubes. It was too painful. Beyond that, it wasn't logical. Sooner or later, when a design isn't going to work, you have to scrap it and start over.

Could you scrap your family, leave behind the places you came from?

I tried to convince myself that it was possible as I passed the Moses Lake sign.

Welcome to Moses Lake.
If you're lucky enough to be at the lake,
you're lucky enough.
Come back soon!

I wouldn't be back soon. Or ever. This time it was really good-bye. The thought lay like a lump of stone in my chest.

How about a pair of cricket killers? Blaine's voice whispered through the car, flowing over me like the draft from the heater. *We got your steel toes, your stacked heels, your Mary Janes, flip-flops, wool socks, boat shoes, whites, browns, and blues. What's your pleasure?*

The heavy feeling slid slowly to my stomach, like a swallow of something too warm. My throat swelled and prickled.

I'm not going to cry. This is stupid.

I reached for the iPhone, punched up the text messages. Mel, Mel, Mel, Mel . . . Gary the dentist . . . Mel, Mel . . . Richard. Only one from Richard, in all this time. Judging by the first couple of words, it looked like he was checking in about the real estate contracts. Just business.

I was hurt, but in a strange way, not disappointed. At some point during the last few days, I'd gotten over wishing that Richard was *the one*. And if I really let myself admit it, I knew why. That night with Blaine, dancing beneath the stars at Blue Moon Bay, had made my relationship with Richard seem inconsequential. Richard was absolutely right in wanting the kind of passion that made you remember someone's birthday, that made thinking of that person as natural as breathing, little puffs of memory coming in the course of normal events, life-giving, like oxygen—a smile, a laugh, the color of an eye, the touch of a hand, the sound of a voice.

I couldn't even describe the exact color of Richard's eyes—grayish, I thought.

Blaine's eyes were the color of warm earth. They sparkled like topaz when he laughed.

But Blaine wasn't *the one*. He wasn't the one, but I wanted someone . . . like him. Someone who fit into my life plan. Someone who wasn't helping my brother keep secrets and lying to me about it. . . .

My mind swirled with questions as I wound along the quiet highway, shards of sunlight and thready winter shade slipping soundlessly over my car, dry amber grasses bending and waving in the wakes of other vehicles. When I passed by the gate to the family farm, I looked the other way. I didn't want to reminisce about the place or to admit to myself that I'd let this trip come and go, and I still hadn't faced the cellar door that had haunted my nightmares. I supposed I never would. After this meeting in Japan, I'd go back to my life. The farm would be sold—either by some miraculous resurrection of the broker offer, or through Clay's arrangement, whatever it really was. If Clay managed to pull it off, the property would eventually end up in the hands of the Underhills, perhaps. Blaine's father had become land wealthy over the years, taking on property and buildings when the mortgages were in arrears. . . .

I tried not to think about it the rest of the way to

Ruth's. It was too painful to consider. Maybe Clay would come to his senses. Maybe he'd call me and ask for help.

Turning into the dairy, I waited for the quiet peace of that place to slip over me, to soothe away my hesitations, but all I could think was, *This might be the last time I see Ruth. It probably is the last time. . . .*

It would be, of course. I wasn't coming back. Once I got home, I'd be busy with all the normal things, consumed as usual. Maybe I'd try to do a little better job of maintaining connections, in the human sense. I could make more time to get together with Trish, go with her to take the kids to a playground or the zoo. Maybe I'd join a gym, get involved at a church—start going more than a few times a year.

My visit to Moses Lake had brought one realization at least: I wasn't really accomplishing anything by hiding from God and from my past. All these years of being angry hadn't brought my father back or changed what had happened. I'd only succeeded in making the past part of the future, spreading it like oil, a slick, sticky coating over everything. I'd allowed my father's death to claim my life, as well. I was like Ruth's sister, Lydia, bitter and old before my time. I couched it under the guise of being dedicated to my career, but deep inside, I knew the truth.

When I got back to Seattle, I was going to

change things. Be more open, have a talk with Mel about his health and the ridiculous hours we were keeping. . . .

The ideas were still cycling in my head when I knocked on the door at Ruth's, and Mary and Emily let me in. Ruth was surprised to find me there much earlier than expected. I explained to her that I had a flight out today; I had to get back to work. She only frowned, as if she were looking through me, seeing all the things I'd kept hidden, even from myself.

She didn't question me, though. Ruth was never confrontational. It wasn't her nature. She only watched me as we moved to the sun porch and sat down, Mary and Emily trailing behind us.

Emily whispered to Mary, and Mary moved to my chair, cupping a hand near my ear to ask where Roger was.

"Oh, Roger couldn't come," I admitted apologetically. "I'm sorry. I couldn't bring him today."

Emily's lip pooched, her jumper bunching on her shoulders as she reached up to smooth escaped corkscrews from her face. "How come?"

"I'm not going back to Moses Lake from here, so Roger wouldn't have a way to get home." I felt like a heel, a fun-killer, a promise-breaker for failing to bring Roger to visit again. Beyond that, there was the tug that seemed to haunt me when I looked at these two little redheaded girls in their starched dresses, their smooth skin like china-doll porcelain. They were adorable and sweet, and they made me feel like the most interesting person in the universe, as if they were certain I had the answers to all the important questions. I loved that feeling. I loved the touch of Emily's hand on mine, the inquisitive look in Mary's bright hazel eyes.

I wanted to be somebody's mom someday, to have a family of my own, to bake bread and talk about puppies and go for long walks along a riverbank somewhere. I wanted first days of school and summer vacations, first cars and graduations. But the possibility seemed so far away.

"Can Roger come next time?" Mary pulled an escaped strand of hair over her nose and twisted it into a rope, her eyes crossing as she watched it.

The questions and Ruth's unwavering regard hemmed me into an uncomfortable position. "Maybe Clay can bring him next time."

In the corner of my vision, Ruth laid a finger alongside her lips, then shoed the girls from the room, so we could talk. "I'm glad you've come by," she said, but there was a melancholy tone in the words. I wasn't accustomed to seeing Ruth like that. Even sick with cancer, she had an upbeat, peaceful quality that I admired . . . craved, really. I wanted to be more like Ruth, more serene, more certain that God was laying the path, watching over my shoulder, guiding each step. Planning to give me what was best for me in the future.

Ruth was good at faith in the way that I was good at my job, I realized. She worked at it. *Nothing worth doing comes easily,* had always been one of her favorite sayings.

"I didn't find any more of your drawings," I told her. "I'm sorry. I never made it down to the basement to look. I'll send Clay a text and ask him to search the rest of the house."

Ruth shook her head. "No matter." She leaned across the arm of her chair—an aging leather recliner with a crocheted afghan over it. "I only wanted them for you to see. You always asked me about them, but I was never ready to tell those stories. Do you remember?"

"I remember." How many times had I secretly watched her as strokes of charcoal became figures, and figures became people? "I used to peek from the window sometimes, when you were out on the porch. I remember watching you draw the circus performers. I guess those were the ones Lydia saw when she decided she wanted to run away."

Ruth smiled and nodded. "I never saw the circus people, but Lydia told me about them—every detail she could remember. I was on the hillside when she sneaked down and peeked under their tent. I stayed there with Naomi and the other girls, because I was too afraid. Of all of us, Lydia was the only one who saw the circus. She was the only one who had the courage. After that, we played circus on the old farm horses, but we had to go on Lydia's say. She was the one who knew how the circus looked, so she became the master of us all in the circus game. We did her chores for her, so that she would let us play circus. It is easy to do that sometimes—let fear make hostages of us, don't you think?"

"Yes, I guess so." I was uncomfortable again. Ruth was pushing harder than usual, perhaps because she knew that I was leaving. She had a point she wanted to get across, but she would never come right out and say it. In general, the Mennonites I'd met in Gnadenfeld were unfailingly polite, gentle, and unassuming in a way that most people are not

"Why do you think we let fear hold us prisoner?" She turned her attention to the magazine rack on the floor, looking for something. "Our pastor spoke on this last Sunday. I've been pondering it since then."

I didn't have to consider the answer too deeply. It was on the tip of my mind already. "It's easier that way—to do what's safe, what you think you're supposed to do," I admitted.

"I believe that may be right." She nodded solemnly, her lips forming a downward arc, as if she were acquiescing for the both of us. "But then you never see the circus."

"True." I let out a laugh-breath to break the tension, and Ruth smiled.

"You can regret it all your life, not seeing the circus." She wagged a finger at me. "Your sister might make a slave out of you."

"If there were a circus nearby, I'd take you to it, Ruth."

She checked the doorway before answering, "At this point in my life, I'd go."

We laughed again, together this time, and then Ruth resumed digging through the magazine rack, searching for something among local newspapers saved for fire starters. "Well, I can't find it just now," she admitted, sinking back in her chair, breathing more heavily. The shallow sound of it reminded me of how sick she was. I considered asking about her prognosis, but I didn't want to dampen our last visit.

"I had a drawing for you. I unearthed it upstairs with some of my old things. Perhaps Mary and Emily have run off with it." Frowning, she patted the arm of the chair and craned toward the doorway, as if she were considering calling for the girls. "Well, when I find it, I'll send it to you. You should have it."

"What is it?" Resting my elbows on my knees, I leaned toward her and looked at the magazine rack, hoping to spot a bit of art paper peeking out. Maybe she'd missed it in there. "What is it a drawing of?"

"Soldiers," she answered, and I felt the slightest twinge of disappointment. I was hoping for the one of Lydia, as a reminder, perhaps. I felt a connection to Lydia, but I still wanted to be Naomi.

"Soldiers? I remember seeing you draw soldiers, more than once, actually." I'd seen soldiers, nuns, other children, a priest. I'd always suspected that at least some of the drawings were inspired by Ruth's past. While we worked in my uncle's kitchen, Ruth had told me stories about her arrival in New York, along with a group of orphans permitted to immigrate from Germany after the war. They were housed in a tall, dark building that was drafty, cold, and undersupplied, but the nuns and a priest were kind to them. There was no place to play, but when the weather was nice Father and the nuns took them to the park. Some of the people there gave them harsh looks, because they spoke German, Yiddish, and Plautdietsch, the only languages they knew.

"These were special soldiers," she said. "You would recognize them, I think, if you saw them. Did you know that your uncles and your grandfather saved Naomi and me? In order to come to America after the war, orphans required a sponsor, one who would guarantee that expenses for the child's care would be arranged for, and that the child would not be consuming public funds. Your grandfather was in America at the end of the war. I'm sure you know that he was injured at Normandy and sent home to his parents' farm, while your uncles continued to serve with the occupation forces in Europe. Your uncles arranged for Naomi and me to leave Germany with a group of orphans and come to the United States. Your grandfather was our sponsor here. He knew we were Mennonite girls, of course, and some of his neighbors were Mennonites. He felt that he could find a place for us among those of our own faith, and he made it his business to do so."

"He did?" My father hadn't talked much about his family history, nor had my grandfather, who never fully recovered from his war injuries, emotionally or physically. I always knew that my grandfather was a good man, a good farmer and a hard worker, but he was largely a stranger to me. "No one ever told me any of that."

Ruth didn't seem surprised. She glanced over the edge of the chair again, as if she were wishing for the drawing. "We never talked about it after we came here and were adopted into a Gnadenfeld family. Oh, your uncles looked in on us. They made certain we were faring well, but they never spoke about how they found us. I suppose they wanted to forget the things they saw in that war, and they thought it was better for us to forget. I suppose they believed it best not to remind us."

"Remind you of what?" I probed, carefully.

Ruth seemed to consider whether she should answer, then she relaxed in her chair, her fingers steepled in front of her like knobby hackberry

413

branches growing together. "There was a man in Berlin. He took in children, orphans like us, and gave them shelter. Lydia had married by this time, but her husband was German, just coming home from the war, and he had nothing. He could not even provide for himself and Lydia. He told us he'd heard about a man who took in orphans, and we went there, Naomi and I. The man was Russian. He seemed kind enough. There were beds and food, other young people, parentless like us. We felt that the Lord had delivered us, that our prayers had been answered. We had no way of knowing what he expected in return for our care."

Ruth's gaze lifted slightly, met mine, her blue eyes narrow and intense, drawing me forward in my seat. "We were Mennonite girls from a tiny village. We had never known of such a thing, but after a day or so, we began to hear of it from the other children. We would have to do what the man wanted, they said. Bad things would happen if we didn't, and then we would be left on the street to starve, to suffer in the cold. We were so afraid, Naomi and I. It is a terrible choice between your soul and your stomach. A frightening choice for a child. We sneaked out on the fire escape after all the children were asleep, to pray, or to run away, but the ladder had been taken off. We could only go down so far, and below was concrete."

Pausing, Ruth peered over the arm of her chair, as if she were remembering. I imagined her and

Naomi, young teenagers, innocents, trapped and desperate for a way out. "We sat and we prayed, and then we heard voices, American voices. When I opened my eyes, there were men looking at us, American soldiers, four of them. One of them spoke to us in very bad German. 'Are you a little Mennonite girl?' he asked and pointed to our prayer caps. We nodded and told him that we were. 'Come down here,' he told us. 'You don't belong in that place.' We told him we couldn't get down, and he said, 'You jump and we'll catch you in my overcoat.' "

Wagging a finger in the air, Ruth met my gaze. "I have relived that day many times since then, that moment of decision. I think it is appropriate that we were on the fire escape, don't you? God walks with us through the fires of life, all of them. Even this latest one, this cancer. Some good will come of it. It brought you here, for one thing."

Moisture gathered in my eyes, and I blinked hard to keep it from showing. How could Ruth believe that good could come from the disease ravaging her body? How could she say that my visits in any way compensated for what she was going through?

A chuckle broke the silence, and her eyes sparkled with a thought she kept private at first, then revealed. "Your uncle Herbert was the strongest man I ever met, and the most handsome. I fell in love with him that day, when he took us

415

away. A girlish sort of love. I was so young."

I blinked, shocked. I'd never known there was so much history between Ruth and my uncles, and certainly not that sort. "Did you ever tell him?"

She adjusted the scarf covering her hair, looking flustered, as if she'd gotten caught up in the moment and blurted out something she hadn't meant to. "Oh, of course not. I was so young, and I was afraid. I kept those feelings to myself, and he married after he came home, and eventually so did I. I did what was expected and married within the Mennonite faith. The family who adopted Naomi and me had been good to us. I wanted to please them. I wanted to live a life that was humble and plain." She laughed to herself, swatting a hand in the air as if to wave away an alternate past, like smoke.

"You never told him in all these years?" Suddenly I had a greater understanding of Ruth's devotion to my uncles, of the special relationship between the three of them. I understood why Uncle Herbert saved Ruth's drawings, why she went out of her way to bring canned goods to him or to bake the German foods that he loved, even though my aunt hated the smell of vinegar and sauerkraut in the house. Ruth loved him, and in some capacity, that affection was mutual.

Watching her now, I understood the way I'd caught her looking at him on the porch the other day. I'd always thought that his reserved nature, his lack of interest in communication frustrated Ruth, but in reality, the emotion in her eyes had been longing, the regret of an opportunity missed, a desire that would never be fulfilled.

Uncle Herbert had never seemed fully happy in his marriage to Aunt Esther, even though the marriage had provided him with a position in the community and a big house in which to operate his business. Aunt Esther had run his life with an iron fist, fussed about pomp and circumstance and their social standing. Ruth, I suspected, had never been close to her husband, who was considerably older than she. How might their lives have been different, if they'd chosen each other instead?

"Fear can cause you to miss more than just a peek under the circus tent." Ruth pointed at me as if she knew what was in my mind.

Mary and Emily came in the back door then, and the moment was gone. We talked and watched them play for a while before sharing a small lunch with the family. Ruth was tiring when we finished, and I felt the flight time closing in on me, as well.

"I'd better go," I told her. "Thanks for lunch and . . . well, for everything." My throat burned as we walked to the door, Mary and Emily trailing along. Ruth wrapped her arm in mine, leaning on me, her steps unsteady.

We were walking together for the last time, and both of us knew it.

"You are always welcome here anytime," she offered, as if to deny the fact that this was really good-bye, probably forever. "You could put off your flight and stay a few days. Wherever you are headed isn't going anywhere. There's no need to run off."

I wanted to accept her offer. Everything in me yearned to slow down, take some time to think, to call Mel and tell him he needed to go back to the hospital and look after his health—and by the way, I wasn't coming home. I'd decided to become a Mennonite. Take up milking cows and baking zwieback, maybe design a few dental clinics on the side for extra cash. But instead I said, "Oh, I'm not running. I'm just going on this trip for work, and then back home."

"I suppose it depends on your definition of the word." She squeezed my arm, then watched the girls dash onto the lawn to play horsey on a live oak branch that dipped near the ground. "Home."

I patted her hand but didn't answer. What was I supposed to say? *Moses Lake isn't home. I've always hated this place. . . . But there was this one night out at Blue Moon Bay . . . and this trip to the bluffs to watch the eagles fly . . . and this moment in the shoe department of the hardware store. . . .*

We hugged good-bye. She held on to my hand for a moment afterward, as if she meant to lecture me again. I halfway wanted it to work this time.

"Oh . . . I've remembered where the drawing

of your grandfather and your uncles disappeared to." She let her head fall back, silently scoffing at herself. "I gave it to your brother yesterday evening. He came by here to borrow a shovel and a few canning jars." Fanning a hand by her head, she rolled her eyes heavenward. "Goodness! My mind these days. I think the medications might be worse than the disease."

I stopped where I was. "Clay borrowed a shovel and jars from you? Last night?" What in the world did that add up to? "Why didn't he just get those things from Uncle Herbert's place?"

Ruth's brow creased. "He was doing something out at your grandparents' old farm, I think. He said there wasn't a shovel out there and it was closer to come here and borrow one. He didn't have time to go back to Moses Lake before dark. I gave the drawing to him, so he could bring it to you. I wasn't feeling well, and I thought I might not be able to visit with you today, but the Lord is good. I woke feeling quite chipper this morning. Your brother hasn't given you the drawing, then?"

"No. Not yet. He got in late." No sense in worrying Ruth about last night's fiasco with the Ladybug. "It's probably still in his truck. I'll ask him to mail it to me."

I turned to leave, then paused again. "Are you sure Clay said he was working out at the farm? There have always been plenty of tools out there. As far as I could tell when Clay and I stopped

419

by there for gas the other day, not a thing has been moved or sold off. . . ." *Leave it be, leave it alone, Heather. Don't get involved. Head for the airport. Don't get sucked in again.*

But even as I thought it, I felt like that little Mennonite girl standing on the hill above the big top, trying to decide whether to play it safe or go take a peek at the circus.

You either think on your feet,
or sink on your feet.
—Dale Tazinski, LPC
(*Fifty pounds lighter on his feet,
after joining Weight Watchers*)

≈ Chapter 18 ≈

The airport in Waco was quiet and easy to deal with. Short-term parking was free, so leaving the car wouldn't cost a thing. My exit from Texas was growing simpler by the minute, as if heavenly blessings were raining down upon it. There was even a bit of Proxica PR on the airport wall. *Feeding a New Generation*, the lighted sign read.

I found my gate and sat in the waiting area, my thumb rubbing slow circles over the slick plastic iPhone case. The broker offer was set to expire tomorrow. The day after Valentine's Day. I needed to call Richard, see if there was any possibility of having the offer extended a week, or even two. By then Clay would probably have lost interest in Moses Lake. Hopefully if I kept trying, I could convince him to admit that he had a serious problem and needed help.

What if he doesn't? What if something terrible happens, like last night but worse? The question was uncomfortable and confining. Inconvenient.

Maybe I was wrong to be leaving. I could still tell Mel he'd have to handle Japan on his own. Maybe I should stay and keep fighting. But how? No one in my family would listen. They were all fully determined that I was the one in the wrong, the pariah taking my sibling-rivalry issues out on poor Clay. Even if I told them everything that had happened last night, Clay would counter with his story about having fallen asleep in the car, and they would believe it because it was easier to believe, more pleasant.

I dialed Richard's number, put the phone to my ear and sank in the chair, letting my head fall back against the wall, my eyes closed.

Richard's voice was all business. "Richard Lawson."

"It's me." For an instant I wished I could rekindle the intimacy that had been between us. It was Valentine's Day, after all. How was he planning to spend the evening?

Maybe I didn't want to know.

"Heather?" He sounded as if I'd been gone for a month, and he wasn't sure who *It's me* might be. I waited for him to ask how I was, how things were going. I wanted to pour out the whole story to someone. I wanted someone to be waiting for me at the Seattle airport whenever I finally made it home from Japan. I thought of Gary the dentist and his family. I wanted my return to be like his.

The longing hurt.

"What can I do for you?" Richard's tone conveyed that he was pressed for time.

I swallowed my disappointment and moved right to the heart of the matter. "Any chance of getting the broker to extend the offer on the property—a week, maybe two? I think this thing will work itself out, given a little time." As soon as I had a moment to collect my thoughts, I'd get in touch with Donny and let him know in no uncertain terms that he needed to extricate his father and Uncle Charley from the mess my mother and brother had created.

"I don't see that happening." Richard's answer sent my hopes spiraling downward. "Proxica needs to seal the deal immediately to minimize any chance of information leaks. It's hard to keep things under wraps in a small town. I know that the broker is working an offer on another piece of property nearby. They'll ink that immediately after this offer expires. They're getting nervous, with the AP picking up the Kentucky story."

"The AP . . . What? What Kentucky story?" Not only was I out of sync with my family, but now Richard was speaking in riddles, too.

"The pesticide case. There's a class-action suit against them in Kentucky—the thing about that pesticide, Armidryn. Proxica was using it widely on their farms until about the midnineties, when there were some court cases about a similar pesticide in Europe—they say the chemicals show up in water wells, farm produce, cow's milk, that sort of thing, and cause health problems. That it stays in the soil for years.

"Anyway, at the time, Proxica denied that Armidryn was similar to the European pesticide, and they produced lab results and chemical specs to prove it. They did quietly quit using Armidryn on their farms and around their production facilities, though, and they patented a new formula, Armidryn II, that was supposed to be even safer. But some recent soil and water tests in Kentucky have shown high residual concentrations on some Proxica farms.

"The suspicion is that when Proxica needed to quickly and quietly get rid of their stores of Armidryn I, they may have buried it on some of their farms. There are also some accusations that either they continued shipping Armidryn I but claimed it was Armidryn II, or that Armidryn II isn't as biodegradable and safe as Proxica claimed. None of it has been proven, though. Chances are, it'll be tied up in court for years. Proxica isn't about to just knuckle under. They can't."

He paused, talked to someone on his end of the phone, then came back. "But you can see why they wouldn't want to be trying to close land deals for future expansion after the court-case story goes national. The paranoia over something like that could cause all kinds of protests,

424

problems with zoning, trouble with the locals and so forth."

Trouble with the locals . . .

I sat up, opened my eyes, stared numbly at the windows, where the day was dimming as planes came and went. Everything seemed to stop, growing dark around the edges as I looked down the hall, taking in a skewed view of the illuminated Proxica sign.

Feeding a New Generation . . .

My father was so proud of that slogan, of Proxica's commitment to healthy foods and to providing jobs for rural families. Were the facilities in Kentucky anything like the ones that would be built in Moses Lake? Anything like the ones that were already in Gnadenfeld? Had they been shipping this chemical . . . this Armidryn II to farms in our area? Could some of the original Armidryn stores have been buried here?

"What kind of health problems?" The fluorescent lights behind the sign flickered. A mother and a little girl walked past, pushing an old woman in a wheelchair. I thought of Ruth. She and her husband had lived on a Proxica farm for years, ever since the plant and the farms went in. My father helped Ruth's husband get the job. "What kind of health problems do they think Armidryn causes, Richard?"

"I didn't read up on it too extensively. My paralegal pulled a few things while she was getting the file together for the land deal. I skimmed it. Try Google. The conspiracy theorists are all over it. You'll find what you need." His answer was bland, matter-of-fact, giving no indication that he had any concept of the string of Black Cats exploding inside me. "Listen, Heather, I'm headed into a last-minute mediation. I'm going to have to sign off."

I stood up as if to run after him. My carry-on bag fell over, hitting the floor with a smack. "Wait. Wait a minute! You knew about this? You were aware of this lawsuit, this . . . issue when you were putting the deal together? You never said anything to me?"

"I figured you knew. You usually do your homework, Heather." He was getting impatient now. I wanted to reach through the phone and grab him by that perfectly-pressed collar of his. "Besides, you and Mel both have more connections to Proxica than I do."

I slapped a hand to my throat, swallowing a ball of ashes. "You figured I *knew?* You figured I *knew,* that I just didn't care if a company that's under a class-action lawsuit moved into my father's hometown? On land that's been in my family forever?" What kind of a horrible, disgusting mercenary did he think I was? How could he, the man I was dating, the man I thought I wanted to marry, think that of me?

The answer was clear enough. I hadn't given

him any reason not to. He'd only seen me as the person I appeared to be.

Maybe as the person I was?

Ruth had cancer . . . "How could you think I would be okay with that?"

He responded with a harsh, cynical sound, something between a laugh and a hiss. "Oh, come on, Heather. You couldn't wait to get rid of the place. You hated it. You wanted to stick it to your family and the whole town."

I squatted down to pick up my carryon, stayed there with my head resting in my hand. "I would never . . ."

"Mel knew about the Kentucky lawsuit. He wasn't worried about it. By the time anything happens in terms of a court case, the facility in Moses Lake will be a reality, and your firm will be out of the loop. You're going to tell me that Mel never said anything to you? You're going to tell me the Kentucky issue never came up?"

"No, it never came up. Mel didn't mention anything like that. I would never help some . . . some corporate entity that's hurting people— that's *poisoning* people. Who would, Richard? What kind of a person would do that intentionally?" Was this the sort of life I'd built for myself, a thief among thieves, a person who would do whatever it took to turn a profit?

"Listen, I've got to go," he repeated. "I'm due in the meeting."

"You know what . . . ? Good-bye." This time I meant it with every fiber of my being. I hoped I never saw Richard's face again. Or Mel's. The idea of spending time in the same room with either one of them disgusted me.

The walls of the airport dissolved in a blur of movement as I grabbed my things and hurried toward the door. Passing the Proxica sign, I wanted to pick up my suitcase and smash the plastic, obliterate the innocuous-sounding slogan.

After throwing my belongings into the car, I stopped long enough to text Mel and tell him I wouldn't be making it to Japan—today or any-time. I ended by letting him know exactly how I felt about the class-action lawsuit against Proxica in Kentucky. Before I could change my mind, I took a breath, pushed *Send*, and set down the phone.

My thoughts rushed ahead, forming connec-tions, the events of the past few days coming together like pieces of a puzzle as I pulled out of the parking lot and started toward Moses Lake. Everything that had confused me solidified into a scenario that made perfect sense. Shovels, ziplock bags, vials . . . Clay's hint that he knew the broker offer on the property had something to do with development, the fact that he just happened to be dating a girl who worked at Proxica's Gnadenfeld plant, his sudden interest in Moses Lake . . .

All along, even in the face of overwhelming evidence that seemed to indicate it, I couldn't quite picture my brother succumbing to a drug problem. It just wasn't like Clay to get involved in something like that.

But it was like him to take up a cause.

A cause that may have turned dangerous. . . .

What if, all those times I'd felt like someone was watching us at Harmony House, someone really was? Maybe I hadn't been turning shadows into ghosts but had been seeing people lurking. People who were trying to figure out how much my brother knew, where he was hiding the proof, and who he'd told.

I had to find out the truth, and if I was right about what Clay was doing, I had to stop him before something terrible happened.

When I made it back to Moses Lake, the high-school gym was lit up like a Christmas tree. Western swing music poured from the gaps around the windows of the WPA-era stone building. Under the portico hung stars made of rebar framing and red Christmas lights with the paint partially scraped off, so that portions of the stars twinkled a gaudy combination of red and white. The sight of them brought back memories. They had been a fixture at every high-school dance and community gathering I'd missed out on during my senior year. I'd seen them hanging in the eaves, sitting on the stage, poised in the bleachers, or out front under the portico, as I hurried through the gym from one building to the other. Cheerleaders hauled them back and forth while decorating for pep rallies and socials, giggling and working in pairs to lug the stars around the gym and decide where to position them.

I'd hated those stars. They were one more reason to be angry with my father, to hate what he had done to me by taking the job at the Gnadenfeld plant and moving us to Moses Lake.

After he was gone, the fact that I'd barely spoken to him the last three months of his life, the fact that I'd hated him, was one more reason to hate myself. The stars reminded me of all of that.

Tonight, Reverend Hay was standing under the portico with the high-school principal from back in the day, Burt Lacey, along with Uncle Charley, and Mr. Hall, who'd been president of the school board when I graduated and probably still was. They stopped me before I could get to the door, but I couldn't focus on their greetings. My mind was awash in thoughts and questions, coming in short, rapid fire bursts. *Armidryn, cancer, Proxica. Did Dad know?* I wanted to find my mother, to force her to tell me exactly what was happening that last week before my father died. Did he know what Proxica was doing? Did he suspect that something dangerous had been buried as the facilities were being built? Had he found evidence? Was that why he had been acting so strangely before the accident?

Accident . . . Was there a chance that my father's shooting wasn't an accident or a suicide, but a murder?

"Couldn't get a plane out tonight after all, huh?" Uncle Charley stretched out an arm, pulling me in for a shoulder hug. "We've been having us a little school board meetin', right here during the community Valentine's shindig . . . sorta on the sly, so to speak. There's a bond issue about to pass, and we gotta figure out how to get Moses Lake ready for the twenty-first century without letting Claire Anne Underhill tear down this old place and put up some glass-and-metal cracker-box. Kids shouldn't go to school in something that feels like a hospital. A place oughta have history, and this old building's strong. It'll go another hundred years, if we treat it right."

Lips curving upward contemplatively, he gazed into the eaves, small puffs of steam floating from his nostrils, the stars reflecting off his glasses. "Young boys mustered up to go to war in this old buildin', danced a last dance with their best gals, said good-bye to their folks, stole a kiss from their sweeties behind the bleachers. You can't replace history like that."

I shifted impatiently from one foot to the other, Uncle Charley's arm weighing heavily on my shoulders, his vision clouding my mind. I pictured young men with duffel bags—a change of clothes, clean socks, and their parents' fears packed inside—their dreams on hold. I pictured Ruth and her sister coming to this school, the ladies of the community gathering around them, taking in those frightened, damaged Mennonite girls, telling them they were safe within these walls. I pictured my father and his friends running across the gymnasium during pep rallies, their blue-and-gold Moses Lake football jerseys loose with no shoulder pads underneath as they tore through paper signs reading *Smear the Spartans!* or *Beat the Bulldogs!*

The images haunted me like unwanted ghosts, even as I tried to push them away. I couldn't think about that now. "Uncle Charley, there's a lot involved in rehabbing a building of this age. The existing structure would have to be closely studied and assessed, and plans drawn up to provide for an expansion that would blend with the historic structure. It's not impossible. The right person could do it. When I get back to Seattle, I could help you find—"

"We think you're the right person," Uncle Charley interrupted, squeezing my shoulders and hanging on in a way that insisted I stay there. "We got a majority of the school board standin' right here. A quorum, so to speak. We wanna hire you. You got history here, and family. You know what this old buildin' means. Somebody who's not a Lakesider won't understand that."

I was momentarily stunned silent, my mental

dialog flowing in a half-dozen different directions. *Stay longer in Moses Lake? Design the new high school. Armidryn . . . Proxica . . . Did Dad know? Ruth has cancer. . . .*

Inside the door, people passed by, a woman laughing as she tried to loop a chef's apron over the neck of a man carrying a bag of charcoal. He waved her off, ducked and turned, but I didn't have to see his face or hers to know their identities: Blaine and his secretary, Marilyn, having a little fun at the community Valentine's gathering.

I spotted my mother crossing the empty space in the center of the gym. My focus narrowed again. "I . . . I have to catch Mom right now," I murmured, and then twisted out of Uncle Charley's grasp. I couldn't think about anything beyond the moment. I had to find out what Clay was into and figure out how to keep him from putting himself in danger.

Uncle Charley and the rest of them gave me strange looks as I turned and hurried to the door beneath the red glow of a Christmas-light star. Mom was walking toward the back of the gym, moving with a look of purpose as she disappeared behind a line of milling high-school kids at a carnival-style basketball-toss game. A tangle of women at the cakewalk, decked out for Valentine's Day in red sweaters and jackets appliquéd with fabric hearts, blocked my path across the floor. I recognized Blaine's stepmother among them. Unfortunately, she spotted me, too. I didn't have time for a catfight, but I could tell one was headed my way.

"Have you seen my mother or Clay?" I asked, trying to sidestep her as she moved to block my exit. I caught myself looking around the room for Blaine. Where was he, anyway? Marilyn was walking back across the gym now, looking bored and disappointed.

Mrs. Underhill's lips pursed, her perfectly penciled eyebrows arching together in an expression of sympathy and concern that surprised me. She turned a shoulder to the cakewalk activity, her hand coming to rest lightly on my arm. "Heather, I suppose you've heard about this silly plan of theirs."

"Plan?" Did she know about the issues with Proxica?

"This foolishness about taking over Catfish Charley's and Harmony Shores." She batted her free hand in the air, then fanned herself with it. "I mean, really. A bed-and-breakfast in a *funeral home*. Who in their right mind would want to stay there?"

I fidgeted, looking past her, trying to spot my mother. "Mrs. Underhill, I don't know what my family's plans are. I really don't have time to talk right now. Do you know where I can find my mother or my brother?"

A cursory look over her shoulder and a shrug answered my question, and then she homed in on me again. "You know, life in a remote place—a place like Moses Lake—isn't for everyone." Her voice grew louder as a band warmed up on stage. Around the room, the carnival games were being taken down to allow a dance to begin. "Oh, people think it *seems* wonderful. Move to the lake, get away from it all. But things aren't always easy in a small community. It doesn't suit some people."

"I'm sure it doesn't." Where had my mother gone?

"Your father knew that. Goodness, he didn't want to admit it, of course, but he knew this place was wrong for your mother—too quiet, too slow-paced. That's why he never brought her back here to live after they married. He was afraid something would happen like . . . well . . . what happened."

Suddenly she had my full attention. "What do you mean, *what happened?* Mrs. Underhill, if there's something you'd like to tell me, please just spit it out."

She turned her face away slightly, touched manicured nail tips delicately just above her mouth, careful to avoid her lipstick. "I shouldn't say . . . but, well, there were rumors, of course. It was all over town. She wasn't very discreet."

"Discreet about what?"

Her eyes darted from side to side, checking the perimeter. "Well, the man she was carrying on with, of course. Some out-of-towner staying in the rental cabins below the Waterbird. Your mother was seen around town with him back then. Your father found them out. The teller at the bank heard your parents fighting about it. There is an intercom in the drive-through lane, after all."

She patted my arm, and I backed away from her, horrified. I didn't need this right now. I had to focus on the present, to dissuade Clay from his reckless need to save the world single-handedly.

Mrs. Underhill clucked her tongue. "Oh my. I can see that you didn't know *any* of this. I should have kept it to myself. It's ancient history now, isn't it, sugar? I only meant to help you see that this place isn't . . . healthy for your mama. Your uncles are such sweet men, but they don't need to be burdened with . . . hangers-on."

I couldn't listen to any more. Pulling away, I crossed the room to the punch bowl to ask one of the fishermen from the Waterbird if he'd seen my mother.

"She was here a minute ago." He glanced at the game warden, who was standing beside him in uniform. "You see where she went, Mart?"

The game warden nodded toward the folded-up bleachers. "I think she went with Andrea and Dustin to put some carnival games in the storage closet. They're probably back there behind the bleachers."

I thanked them and walked down the sideline of the basketball court, then rounded the wall of folded-up bleachers. My mother was at the other end of the cavernous, shadowy space where exercise pads, stacks of chairs, and gym equipment had been stored. I could see her standing at the end of the long hallway that led to the locker rooms. The hallway was dark, but by the angle of her body, I could tell she was talking to someone on her cell phone.

My feet fell silently as I hurried along the side wall toward her, passing the storage room, where people were moving boxes. Something fell inside the room, and I hitched a step, the toe of my shoe squeaking on the wooden floor. Mom turned around quickly, uncrossed her arms, snapped her phone shut, and dropped it into her pocket, as if she'd been caught at something.

"Heather," she said, smoothing her shirt self-consciously as I drew closer. "Clay said that you'd left for the airport."

Under other circumstances, I might have been hurt by the fact that she was disappointed to find me there, but at that moment I didn't care. In addition to the issues with Proxica and Clay, Claire Underhill's revelation was now whipping my thoughts into a froth. She'd confirmed one of my greatest fears: My mother had been cheating on my father. The man I'd seen her with all those years ago was her lover, and my father had found them out. He'd died knowing that his wife had betrayed him. Maybe he'd even died *because* she'd betrayed him. . . .

"I left for the airport, but I came back. I need to see Clay. Where is he?"

"He and Amy haven't made it here yet." She cast a worried look toward the front door, then tried to cover it up. "They must have decided to go somewhere else for a Valentine's date."

Irritation stiffened every muscle in my body. "You know and I know that's not true. Where are they, and what are they doing?"

She lifted her chin, seeming offended that I had confronted her. "What is it that you're asking about exactly, Heather?"

"Clay's whereabouts. And while we're on the subject, why don't you tell me what he's up to?"

Mom's lips pressed together in a tight, stubborn line, and a retaining wall inside me cracked. Everything I'd been holding back since my father's death burst free. "You know what? Come to think of it, I want the truth. I want you to tell me what happened to Dad. I want to know why you ended up in police custody that night. I want you to tell me what was going on with you and that man. I saw you with him, you know."

Finally, after so many years, I'd found the courage to just come right out and say it. "You were having an affair, weren't you? You were cheating on Dad. That's why he was so upset. That's why you two were fighting the day he died."

Mom's eyes went wide. "For heaven's sake, Heather. Of course I wasn't having an . . . How could you even say something so reprehensible to me?"

I shifted away, felt the heat rising on my anger, the pot boiling. Of course, this was somehow all about her, all about the ways in which I was causing her pain by trying to get at the truth. "Why the suitcases, then?"

"Suitcases?" Blinking, she cocked her head to one side.

"The suitcases. There were suitcases packed, waiting by the bedroom door upstairs. The day Dad died."

Her hand stretched out and rubbed up and down my arm, bunching the sleeve of my jacket. "Heather, you were so traumatized that day. You don't know what you—"

"Don't tell me what I saw!" My voice rose just as the music stopped. Through the cracks in the bleachers, I saw heads turning our way. Clenching my teeth, I swallowed hard, balled my fists at my sides, and shrugged her hand away. "Don't you *dare* tell me what I saw. I know what I saw. I know what was going on when he died. I saw you with a man. I saw him drive up, and I saw you get in his car. I know Dad was upset about it. Did you realize that the teller at the bank heard you fighting about it? That it was all over town?"

Mom shifted nervously. "Heather, it wasn't what it . . . I wasn't . . ."

"You weren't what? Meeting with your lover? Planning to run out on us?" I tried to imagine how my father must have felt, but I couldn't fathom it. He loved my mother, worshiped her, supported her art, defended her, chose her over his family. He gave up everything for her, and she had repaid him with betrayal.

Tears pressed my eyes and brimmed on the bottom, giving my vision a watery rim. I swiped them away impatiently. "I *saw* you with him. I saw you sneaking around by the barn with that man."

Her eyes flashed wide. "It wasn't an affair."

Her denial only poured acid in old wounds. Even after all these years, she didn't love me enough to give me the one thing I needed most— the truth. "Was Dad . . . ? After he found out, was he . . . ?" I couldn't bring myself to say the words *depressed* or *suicidal*. "Was it an accident, or was it on purpose? Did he mean to do it? Was that why it took the life insurance company so long to settle the policy? Was that why the police questioned you? Or did they think you and your lover planned it?"

Mom's mouth dropped open. She pulled in air.

"Now listen here, Heather . . ." I sensed that I'd crossed some invisible line, stepped into territory from which there would be no graceful retreat. I didn't care.

"I need to know what happened to my father." Tears spilled over, drew trails down my cheeks—hot, then cold. A sob wrenched from me, and I pressed a hand to my lips to stop the trembling. "I have a right to know."

She closed her eyes, sighed, then finally looked at me again. "Heather, I should have told you a long time ago, but it was just so hard, coping with everything . . . after."

"Hard?" I wiped my eyes impatiently, frustrated with myself for breaking down in front of her. "Hard? How do you think it was for Clay, for me? He was our dad."

"And he was my husband," she countered, as if to measure my grief against hers. "And we may have had our issues. We were two very different people who fell in love when we were practically children and ran away together on a whim, but we were trying to make it all work."

I thought of the countless times, even before my father's death, that she had made our lives difficult, with her flightiness, her need for constant change, her insistence on running off to symposiums, poetry conferences, and music festivals, leaving my dad with the problem of arranging for our care and paying for her antics.

"My father gave everything to you. Everything he had. Everything we had," I hissed.

Her jaw formed a hard line, the muscles clenching with determination. This had always been the way with my mother and me. At each other's throats, in each other's sore spots. "That man, the man you saw me with, was not who you think. He was an agent with the Department of Justice. He told me that if I didn't cooperate, they'd send your father to prison. I was terrified, Heather. Where would we have ended up then? I didn't have any way of supporting two children, of paying for lawyers and dealing with a husband in federal prison."

"Federal prison?" My voice rose again, a sardonic laugh following the words. What kind of story was she coming up with now? What kind of nonsense? "My father never did anything that would have gotten him in trouble with the government or anyone else." My father was the most honest, upright man I'd ever known. His faith and his principles ran deep.

"He worked for Proxica." Mom's gaze darted around, checked the storage room door cautiously. "They were investigating Proxica for disposing of chemicals illegally on their farms, and I don't even know what else. The workers on Proxica farms had no idea what they were handling, what they might be living with right around their homes, underneath the yards where their kids were playing. What could be getting into their food and water. The Justice Department thought your father was taking money to keep quiet. He'd gotten a bonus for bringing the Proxica operation in Kentucky on line in record time. The Justice Department wanted me to provide documents—look for things in your father's briefcase.

"I was scared, Heather. I didn't know what to do. I cooperated for a while. I thought I could give them what they needed, and your father would be cleared. I knew he wouldn't willingly participate in something that was hurting people, especially so near Moses Lake. I thought I could clear his name, and then, other than looking for a new job, our lives would go on as normal. What choice did I have? You were about to go to college, but we had Clay to raise. Your father was dealing with losing his parents. I thought I could . . . get us out of this mess. I could do what the Justice Department wanted, and it would all go away."

"But it didn't." My mind tripped and stumbled, dropping over a precipice, ending in a place I'd never anticipated. "It didn't go away, did it?"

Gooseflesh rose on her arms, and she rubbed it away. "No, it didn't. Your father heard rumors in town. He heard that I'd been seen with someone—a man. He confronted me about it. I had to tell him the truth. I begged him to pack up, to take us out of Moses Lake. If he wasn't working for Proxica anymore, he wouldn't be of use to the Justice

Department, I thought. But your father wouldn't do it. He wanted to stay here, look into it himself, gather evidence, see if his bosses knew what was going on, see if there really were barrels of chemicals being buried.

"Someone ran your father off the road one night on the way home from work, and he was afraid it wasn't an accident. That's why he got that stupid shotgun out of the closet. That's why I packed the suitcases. That's why we were fighting before he died. I wanted to just get in the car and go, all of us. I told him if he wouldn't leave with us, that I'd take both of you and I'd leave him.

"I didn't mean it. I just wanted him to come with us. I just wanted us to run." She looked away, concealing whatever emotions she felt.

I stood mute, scrambling to assimilate the tidal wave of information, to blend it into what I knew about my life. What I thought I knew. "Why did the police take you away right after he died? Why were you gone overnight? If all this is true, why keep it a secret for so many years? Why didn't you tell me?"

Her shoulders quaked as though a shiver had rattled her, and she hugged herself tighter. "They put me in a room, and they told me that if I said anything about what had happened, if I did anything to hamper the government's case, they'd see that I was prosecuted for murder. I didn't care by then. I didn't care about anything. I just wanted to . . . crawl into the casket with your dad. I didn't know how I was going to survive, how I would take care of you kids. I didn't know if whoever ran your father off the road might come after us. I didn't know where to go or what to do. I was so lost without him. All those months afterward, I couldn't breathe. I couldn't function.

"By the time I started to take in air again, the issue with Proxica had been swept under the rug. I never heard from the agent again, and life went on. Your father's bosses played golf with governors and congressmen. Who knows what happened? Who knows how many payoffs they gave out? I couldn't fight it. I could barely keep my head above water."

I pressed my hand over my eyes. On the dance floor, the song changed to a polka melody that seemed incongruous with the tension between my mother and me. "This is what Clay is into, isn't it? That's why he's here, and that's why you're here. You two are trying to finish what Dad started."

"Yes," she admitted. "A few months ago, when we were initially talking about selling the land, things began coming up. I heard that Ruth had cancer, and that her husband had died of cancer, and that one of her nephews had leukemia. Clay and I started talking to the uncs more about it, and we began putting it all together. All of us wanted to do what we could to see Proxica punished."

"All of us?" I rubbed my fingers over a rush of

blood that made my forehead seem to swell painfully. "Everyone? The whole family? The uncs, you, Clay. You were all in on it?"

She nodded. I watched her in narrow slices through my fingertips. She was looking at the bleachers, not at me. Words wedged in my throat, then came out all at once. "And none of you thought you could trust me? None of you had the confidence in me to tell me what was going on and why?"

"You were connected to Proxica, Heather. Richard let something slip during our talks about the real-estate deal—something about the broker having a corporate buyer in a hurry for the farm property that was zoned for a commercial operation, which ours was, because the family had run the dairy there years ago. Between that and things Amy had overheard at work, we could see what was happening. It will be over my dead body that Proxica puts so much as a tire track on any land we own."

I shifted from one foot to the other, vacillating between anger and shock. "You should have told me. You should have *trusted* me. I loved my father. I would have done *anything* for him. It killed me when he died, and now you've put Clay in the same danger. Do you realize that he could have died last night? He was in that truck when it rolled down the hill. He almost ended up in the lake. Where is he? Where is he right now?"

Kneading her hands in front of herself, she looked toward the door. "He and Amy were going to get into the Proxica plant tonight to see if they could find some old records about the Armidryn and where it might have been disposed of. Amy said there would only be a skeleton crew there right now, with it being second shift and Valentine's Day. She and Clay were planning to take whatever they found out to your grandparents' farm after that. Clay has been working out there." Her lips formed a worried line as she checked her watch.

He's been working out there. Everything made sense now, including Clay's disappearing acts that seemed to have nothing to do with learning to run a catfish restaurant.

"I'm going out to the farm," I told her, but the idea of revisiting that place, the place where my father had died, sent a wave of nausea through me, created a foreboding that rooted me where I stood. I didn't want to go there alone. For some reason, I thought of Blaine. "He knew, didn't he? Blaine knew what you and Clay were doing. He was in on it, too."

"Yes," she admitted. "He knew, but . . ."

I'd heard all I needed to hear. Without waiting for anything more, I turned away and left her there, then headed for the door. Somehow, I had to get my brother out of this mess. Tonight. Before tragedy struck our family a second time.

The more silent the surface,
the deeper the water.
—Fisherman's proverb
(*Left by Jim Shivers,
an angler watching rain make rivers*)

≈ Chapter 19 ≈

The tires squealed and the back end fishtailed as I rounded the last few curves on the two-lane road, headed for the farm. I had to get Clay to end this crazy plot before it blew up in his face. If someone connected to Proxica had run my father off the road when he drilled too close to their secrets sixteen years ago, why wouldn't they come after Clay now? Whatever information my brother had discovered should be turned over to the authorities, and the sooner the better.

If, by interfering with the family's plan, I angered them and none of them ever spoke to me again, I'd gladly live with that to know that Clay was safe. Had it never occurred to him that there were state and national agencies—actual branches of law enforcement—charged with regulating companies like Proxica, with protecting the public health? Hadn't he thought about the fact that, by digging into the situation himself, he might actually be contaminating evidence or worse yet, putting Proxica on alert so that they could further conceal their crimes before a government agency could investigate? If Clay had proof of this Armidryn thing, why was he still playing vigilante? Why were the rest of them going along with it? Why were the uncs, my mother, even Blaine willing to let Clay put himself at risk?

Blaine . . .

I couldn't even think about him right now, about what he'd done. Was it his job to distract me, to give the rest of them room to maneuver, to convince me that there might be something special for me in Moses Lake, a chance at everything I'd always wanted but couldn't find— family, a connection, a history . . . love?

I pushed the word away, not even knowing what it meant anymore, what it should mean. Maybe I was too damaged, too messed up to ever find it. Maybe I just wasn't meant for family life. The people you loved, the people who loved you were supposed to be the ones you could trust, the ones who trusted you. Yet everyone here assumed that I knew what Proxica was doing, and I just didn't care. They thought I was the kind of person who had no personal code to live by, who would do anything to come out ahead in business.

My boss saw that person when he looked at me, and so did Richard.

What kind of people assumed the worst of you? Not people who care about you. As Reverend

Hay had put it, *Love sees in you the best possible version of yourself.*

Emotion rose in my throat, and I pushed it away impatiently. I just needed to settle things here and get away, to go home to Seattle and really think. Maybe Seattle wasn't even the place for me, but there had to be someplace where I would fit— somewhere I could combine work and meaning. I had money in the bank. I could take some time off, start looking, send resumes all over the world— perhaps land in an exotic location. Paris or Milan. Istanbul.

There were no ties to bind me. None at all. I could move to the far side of the world, and if Proxica did expand in Moses Lake, I would never even know it.

The idea pinched, bringing a painful little nip as I rounded the final bend in the road and the farm gateway materialized at the edge of the head-light's glow. My father had risked his career, maybe even his life, to stop Proxica sixteen years ago. If they expanded to the family farm, it would be as if the concrete and steel were being laid over his grave. As if his life, his sacrifice didn't matter. Proxica had won once, and if I had come to Moses Lake for no other reason, perhaps that was it: Maybe I'd been brought here for an atonement of sorts. Perhaps I was meant to help finish what my father started. Perhaps the one way I could finally make peace with his death was to protect my family and this place my father loved.

Determination filled me, feeling hot, solid, and righteous as I skidded into the driveway and careened up the lane. If Clay was still here, we were going to have a serious talk, and if not I would figure out exactly what kind of evidence he'd been collecting and storing, how long he'd been doing it, and what kind of laws he was breaking. Hadn't it occurred to him that he could end up in jail for sneaking into Proxica facilities? Was that what he was doing last night before the incident with the Ladybug?

Another possibility struck me, the impact sudden and startling. What if someone had tried to bash his skull in last night and that was why he didn't want the family to know about the accident? Was he afraid Mom or the uncs would blow his cover if they found out? Was he worried that they'd call an end to this thing?

Goose bumps prickled under my sweater. Leaning close to the window, I scouted the growth of trees along the lane, dark and silky in the moonlight, thick enough to hide anything, anyone.

My heart fluttered in my neck as the car rattled over a cattle guard at the low-water crossing, then kicked up gravel in the washed-out ruts on the other side. Could those same people have followed him tonight, could they have caught up with him at the Proxica plant? Was that why he and Amy hadn't shown up at the dance?

A cold feeling settled over my skin as I topped the hill and the trees parted, revealing the farm-yard. The two-story house my grandparents had built was silent, the curtains drawn, the windows black, the porch steps littered with pecan shucks and fallen branches now that the renter had moved away. No vehicles were parked out front, but in the small turn-of-the-century stone house next door, a light shone. Would Clay have been doing his work in there? In the house where we'd lived during those months before everything in Moses Lake went terribly wrong? The house where my father died?

I let the car roll to a stop in front of it, sat behind the wheel, the burn of my anger abandoning me when I needed it most. As far as I knew, the stone house had been locked since my father died. How could Clay bring himself to go inside? How could he spend time there? What happened in that place sixteen years ago was the end of everything for us. The end of our family. The end of the laughter and the gaudy Crayola-colored days of childhood. The small, brown door in my nightmares was there.

Even in my dreams, I didn't have the courage to step through that door.

I closed my eyes, tried to imagine it, tried to see myself turning the handle, passing through, finally reaching the other side, finally remembering whatever had happened in the minutes after the gunshot exploded through the little house. All these years, those moments had been blank. I remembered the thunderous sound, the cellar door, and then the memory jumped forward, skipping like film that had been spliced, a broken piece cut out. The next thing I knew, I was bolting through the kitchen, looking for Clay, wanting to save him from seeing . . .

From seeing what?

What had I witnessed that day?

My mother said she had run into the cellar from the subterranean steps on the back of the house, stopped me before I could get down the stairs, before I could view the horrible scene below.

But there was blood on my hands. I remembered it now. I could see it in my mind, see my hands underneath the water at the kitchen sink, rubbing, trembling, a voice—my own voice—keening in my ear.

I'd rushed to wash the blood out of the sink as Clay came up the hill—just a little blond-haired boy, carrying some sort of treasures bundled in the front of his shirt. He stopped to playfully kick a soccer ball and watch it, having no idea that life had gone terribly wrong while he was playing in the woods. I turned off the water, then ran out to stop him, in case he was headed for the cellar door to show his treasures to Dad. I didn't want my little brother to see . . .

Closing my eyes, I pushed the memory away, stuffed it into the quiet, tightly-wrapped place where the other side of the door had stayed all these years. I didn't want to think about whether my father's death was an accident, or whether everything that was happening, his whole life tumbling down at once, was simply more than he could handle. The depth of my fear was too staggering. It drilled to the center of my soul, carved a clean, round path, like the massive metal bits that cut through soil and rock to take core samples, testing the stability of building sites before structures go up.

If my father had left us on purpose, if he'd meant to do it, it would be as much my fault as anyone's. I'd turned on him during those months in Moses Lake, abandoned him when he needed our love and support, as he planned my grandmother's funeral, then watched my grandfather wither away. I'd been so angry with my dad for moving us to Moses Lake that I'd never even considered what he was going through, losing both of his parents in such a short span of time.

The last words I'd said to him were, *I can't wait to get out of this house, and when I do, I'm never coming back.*

If I could have five minutes with him now, I would tell him I didn't mean those words. But there were no more chances to talk to him, to open up and throw my arms around his broad shoulders and have him lift me off my feet in a bear hug.

I didn't want to return to this house, where all

those future opportunities had been whisked away. Whatever happened in that basement was stronger than I was. It had been winning the battle for sixteen years. How could I possibly believe that I could defeat it now?

Love is both a sword and a shield, Reverend Hay's sermon whispered in my mind. *It is all the armor we need.*

I did love my family. I loved my father. In some hollow, wounded part of me, I'd been wandering since the day he died and our family fell apart. I'd tried to fill the emptiness with substitutes—work, success, nice clothes, a career that provided the achievement of designing massive structures that would stand for generations to come. I'd tried to pack inanimate things into the gaping hole. But brick and mortar, lines on paper, accolades and achievements, all the things money can buy can't fill the soft, tender place where people should be.

I thought of Ruth and her sister, Naomi, praying on the fire escape, trapped by an evil they couldn't even begin to understand. *God walks with us through the fires of life,* she'd said, her conviction filled with such faith. Deep inside I knew, I'd always known, that there was no way to the other side of this pain but through the fire. There was no way out for me but through that house.

Opening the car door, I stepped out, and started across the yard. On the porch, the swing rocked in

455

the breeze. I remembered sitting there with my father when I was little. I was wrapped in a quilt, curled against him as he talked about growing up on the farm—something about a horse that belonged to a neighbor and my father sneaking out to the barn with the intention of riding it. He had no idea that the horse had just come off a racetrack and didn't know how to stop or turn, only how to run like the dickens. . . .

My lips quivered at the memory, and I was caught between laughter and tears as I crossed the porch and tried to peek in the windows. The curtains were drawn, but the door fell open before I touched it. I wasn't surprised. One of the things that had driven my mother crazy about this house was that, if you slammed the door too hard, it would pop back open. Clay always slammed the door. My mother had scolded him for that over and over. Dad had only laughed at Mom and called her a city girl. *Who do you think's going to break in, a grizzly bear?*

Her eyes had widened. *There aren't really grizzly bears around here . . . are there?*

Just one, he'd said, then lifted his hands like claws and chased her and Clay around the room.

A puff of laughter caused my breath to plume in the night air as I stood on the threshold between past and present. Warmth flowed out of the house, chasing away the vapor and the laughter. Someone had been spending time here. The heat was on.

456

Clearly, Clay was either here now or intended to return yet tonight.

Stepping in, I pushed the door closed behind me, softly, so that the latch clicking into place was almost soundless. If Clay was in the house, I didn't want to provide any advanced warning that would allow him to hide whatever he was doing. I spotted his backpack on the table in the dining room, to the right of the entryway. A floorboard creaked under my feet as I moved closer, the scent of dust and stillness filling my nose. A laptop computer sat beside the backpack, the screen in snooze mode, a laser light show twirling idly on the monitor, sending flickers around the dimly-lit room.

Papers, books, ziplock bags with soil and bits of plants inside littered the table. I flipped on the light, moved closer to look at them, found stacks of pictures of Proxica farms, each photo carefully labeled with the location and corresponding notes that seemed to be written in some sort of code. Beside the pictures sat an official-looking black folder, the results from chemical tests on water samples run at a lab in Houston. Tucked in the side pocket, a similar document appeared to be an analysis of several soil samples. In another file, there were names and case histories of people who'd worked on Proxica farms or in the production plant—their ages, their health problems. Ruth and her husband were listed.

Behind the documents about human illnesses were photos and papers detailing unexplained problems with livestock—cancers, birth defects, lack of weight gain, mysterious deaths, pictures of dairy cows with cancerous growths on their skin and protruding from their eye sockets. An autopsy of a dog.

A file that had clearly been stolen from the Proxica offices had been hidden inside Clay's backpack. It appeared to contain some sort of old log sheets for various Proxica farms in Texas, Kentucky, and several other states, many dating back to the seventies. Clay had marked columns of numbers and written other numbers beside them in red.

"Oh, Clay," I whispered. No matter how valid the cause, breaking into the offices of a corporation and stealing property was illegal, not to mention dangerous. With the money and connections Proxica had, Clay could end up in prison. I needed to be careful about how I handled this, who we turned the information over to. We'd have to find someone who would listen, with whom we could bargain for a promise of amnesty for Clay. But whom? I had no idea where to even begin looking.

I couldn't just call the local police department for something like this. Clay would be prosecuted so fast it would make his head spin—and potentially for more than just stealing the documents. With all the terrorism scares these days, there was no telling what the charges might be. Vast stores of ammonium nitrate and anhydrous ammonia were kept at Proxica facilities— fertilizer in the right hands and a powerful bomb-making material if procured by criminals, as well as an ingredient used for the manufacture of methamphetamine in backwoods drug dens of Chinquapin Peaks. Proxica's lawyers could accuse Clay of all kinds of things.

I touched the computer to wake it from sleep mode, leaned close, and scanned the contents—a newspaper article about the class-action lawsuit in Kentucky. There was a jump drive attached to the computer. The article had been saved there. I pulled the jump drive out of the slot, tucked it into my pocket. The computer chimed, the noise seeming inordinately loud in the silent house.

A cabinet door closed in the kitchen. I jerked back. "Clay?" I whispered.

No one answered.

"Clay?"

Something fell and hit the kitchen floor with a smack that reverberated through the house like a gunshot. Closing the computer, I took a step backward, my heart bounding into my throat. The floor creaked just around the corner. Maybe Clay was here, after all.

Maybe someone else was here. . . .

Possibilities raced through my mind as a

shadow wavered in the rectangle of light from the kitchen. I heard a rhythmic clicking sound. The shadow lengthened, began to take on a shape.

"Roger," I gasped as a nose and a lolling tongue rounded the corner, followed by the rest of Roger. He trotted happily across the room, and I patted him on the head. "You goofball," I breathed, my heart still hammering. "You stupid dog. Where's Clay? Is he here?"

Roger rolled a look at me, as in, *Beats me.* We crossed the dining room and turned the corner into the kitchen, but there was no sign of Clay. On the opposite end of the room, the doorway to the living area was dark, no lights burning in the rest of the house. Apparently, Roger had been left here for safekeeping while Clay and Amy proceeded with tonight's clandestine visit to the Proxica plant.

Please, God, just let them be all right. Just bring them home safely. The prayer whispered in my mind as I hurried back to the dining room, stuffed everything into Clay's backpack, looped it over my shoulder, and grabbed the laptop. I would take it all for now, put it somewhere safe until I could find Clay to talk some sense into him. If we put our heads together, we could figure out a way to reveal the information about Proxica without putting Clay in legal jeopardy, and then—

A noise pressed through the cracks in the floorboard. A voice . . . no . . . someone coughing? Downstairs. In the cellar.

Time seemed to bend and twist as I set the laptop back on the table and crossed the dining room, then the entryway, moving toward the small, wooden door that lay in shadow at the other end. The vision from my dreams flashed in my mind, the entryway stretching, becoming impossibly long, the door always out of reach.

Fear and need intertwined, an impossible web, pulling me closer, screaming at me to run, to be anywhere but here.

I'm not running. I will not run this time.

I stopped in front of the door, listened. Roger bumped my legs. Laying a hand on his head, I sought comfort, listened for the voice. I couldn't hear anything. Maybe it was only my imagination, just the joists groaning and settling.

I already had the backpack and the jump drive. I could just leave and . . .

Memories of my last day in this house permeated the door, pressing through cracks, smelling of must and aging wood, blending today into yesterday, yesterday into sixteen years ago. The past, all the moments that had been blank, came rushing back like flames bursting through a firewall. My mother had screamed at me, told me not to come down the stairs, but I'd seen. I'd seen his legs, his feet splayed out behind the desk. He was wearing the boots he liked to wear when it was muddy. His *farmer boots,* we called them.

I'd moved to the bottom of the stairs, touched

the banister, felt something warm and wet, a spatter that didn't belong there. I heard him heave a last gush of air, the long rattling sound of it, and then silence, a seep of red running from beneath the desk in a narrow river. I'd rushed toward him, looked down, seen him lying in a pool, his lower torso coated in blood, his legs contorted unnaturally, nerves causing them to jerk before going still.

Mom blocked my path, screamed at me again, told me to find Clay, to keep him out of here. She was grabbing the phone, my father's blood smearing the receiver. . . .

The moments sped after that—running up the stairs, washing off the blood, looking for my brother, the paramedics coming. The awful realization of what had happened.

If I didn't do this now, if I didn't go into that cellar, I never would. I'd be trapped on this side of the door forever.

My fingers trembled on the knob as I turned it. I swallowed the pulsating lump in my throat.

Please make me strong enough. Please.

The scents of must, damp limestone, and soil solidified in my chest as the door creaked open. I clutched Roger's fur, and we started down the steps together. The dog didn't try to bolt ahead, but moved soundlessly with me on the hollow wooden stairs—one step, two, three, and then another.

There was a light at the bottom, a dim glow illuminating boxes, paint cans, gardening tools covered in dust. The workbench where my father liked to create things from scraps of wood was laced with filmy cobwebs. I still had a jewelry box that he'd made for me. *For Heather's treasures,* the inscription read under the lid.

My father had always wanted me to be happy. He would want me to do this, to walk through this fire.

I'm not alone. I'm not.

A circle of light shone around the corner of my father's desk. The dull *clink-clink* of a moth battering itself against the bulb wrinkled the silent air. Descending another step into the darkness, into the past, I slowly squatted down, clutching Roger for support as the desk chair squeaked, testifying to the fact that someone was in it. My gaze traveled slowly over a hand, then the arm of an overcoat, upward until I could make out the form of a man with his back toward me. He'd leaned over the file cabinet on the other side of the desk, his form bisected by the circle of light, so that he was halfway inside it and halfway in the shadow beyond. His short, dark hair, the sunbaked wrinkles on the back of his neck, the way he towered over the chair was familiar.

Past melded with present, and my mind stumbled from one into the other.

"Dad?" I whispered.

But at your rebuke the waters fled,
at the sound of your thunder they took to flight;
they flowed over the mountains,
they went down into the valleys,
to the place you assigned for them.
—Psalm 104
(*via Jake Moskalak, game warden,
north end of the county*)

≈ Chapter 20 ≈

He swiveled toward me, the chair's squeal splitting the air, the moment seeming to move in slow motion, too bizarre to understand. That couldn't be my father. I knew it in some practical, concrete way, yet an illogical hope floated with the dust, hovered there, then died as the lamplight caught the man's face, illuminating his profile—a long, thin nose, an earlobe that belled outward slightly, a square, chiseled chin with a cleft in the middle. Not my father's face, but I knew him. . . .

I scrambled through memories, trying to place his features, my thoughts sliding on ice, my body suddenly cold. It was *him*. The man I remembered. The man I'd seen with my mother all those years ago—either her partner in an affair, or an agent with the Justice Department, depending on whom you believed. The man who was, in some way, culpable in my father's death.

Without him, everything might have turned out differently. Without him, my father might still be alive.

A firestorm of anger and hatred swirled from that hiding place within me—the place where I'd stuffed all the unanswered questions, all the resentments toward my mother, all the fears and needs and unspoken grief. There wasn't time for it during those terrible months after the funeral. But now I felt the shell cracking, the contents still molten under the surface. How dare he come here! How dare he touch my father's things, sit in my father's chair! Did my mother know? Had she told him he could come here?

"Get out!" I heard myself growl, the sound deep and guttural, animalistic and instinctive in nature. Rushing down three more steps, I grabbed at the antique tools that hung on the stairway wall, and came up with a rusty machete-like potato knife. I raised it like a weapon, the sharp, rusty spike on the end sending an ominous message. Roger barked and tried to squeeze past me. "Roger, no!" I scolded, pinning him against the wall with my knee. "Get back."

The man behind the desk rose slowly, his face moving out of the light, a long, dark overcoat falling around him, making him little more than a shadow.

I should have been afraid, but there was no

space inside me for fear. There was only rage, white-hot and molten.

He lifted his hands, his palms raised in a surrender position.

"How dare you come here," I growled. "How dare you touch my father's things. You have no right to be here." I descended another step. Why was he in the cellar? What was he looking for in my father's file cabinets?

His coat caught a sheet of paper on the corner of the desk, sent it floating downward like a falling leaf. My mind rushed back. I remembered a leaf skipping across the floor the day my father died. It was vibrant and red, tumbling along with a smattering of lacy white petals from a late bloom of crape myrtle, snow-like, innocent, beautiful, then trapped in a pool of my father's blood. . . .

I blinked now, trying to banish the past and focus my mind into the present.

"It's best that you leave." The stranger was calm, his voice measured. "Go back up the stairs and get in your car." He shifted in the dim light, glanced over his shoulder, then back at me. "This place isn't safe tonight." The request was authoritative in a way that made it seem almost reasonable, yet I wanted to charge at him with the knife, to bring it slashing down, to let it carry all the anger that had been living inside me, undirected, misdirected, constantly circling in on itself in a confined space.

"I'm calling the police, but first I want to know who you are. Why are you here? What happened between you and my mother before my father was killed? What did you do to him? Did you threaten him?" I couldn't ask the last questions thundering in my head: *Did you push him to the breaking point? Was his death an accident or did he do it on purpose?*

The stranger's long, thin fingers flexed and then straightened, his body language still indicating that he didn't intend to try for the knife. He seemed either unwilling to provoke me or confident that he could overpower me, if I came at him. "I promise you, Heather, that the truth will come out soon enough. But you need to go back to your uncle's house. Lock the doors. Make sure your brother and Amy stay there, and the rest of your family, as well. Our cover may have been breeched. I'm not sure who we can trust."

His words and the mention of Clay and Amy swirled anger into fear. He knew all of us. He knew everything about us. Had he been the one watching us?

At the top of the stairs, the door between the cellar and the house groaned softly and then blew shut. I jerked at the sound, my heart lurching, then settling into place again. "Who are you and how do you know so much about my family?"

"It'll all be out in the open soon enough. Right now I need you to lea . . ."

A floorboard creaked overhead. He lowered his hands, took a step sideways, the bottom half of his face coming into the light again. Placing a finger to his lips, he whispered, "Shhh." He motioned toward Roger, who had turned at the sound of footsteps.

Clay, was my first thought, and I felt comforted. But the sensation quickly evaporated, leaving uncertainty. Roger growled low in his throat. The footfalls upstairs were heavy, the hollow sound of boots on wood. That wasn't Clay.

The stranger motioned for me to come down the stairs, then he doused the light. I hesitated, not knowing which way danger might lie.

Something crashed overhead. Glass shattered.

Roger cowered against my leg in the darkness. I circled my fingers around his collar, held him close, and crept down the stairs, Clay's backpack sliding on my shoulder. The stranger caught my arm when I reached the bottom step, pulled Roger and me into the immeasurable blackness beneath the stairway. I felt the man's body against mine, the backpack pressed between us, his arm encircling me just below my neck. He leaned close to my ear, murmured, "Keep quiet."

"What's happening?" I whispered, terrified.

"Shhh," he hissed. His arm tightened, pulled me farther into the darkness. My body went stiff. As the door opened at the top of the stairway, I fought the urge to pull away, run, scream. A partial sentence drifted downward with a flashlight beam.

". . . you wanna do with the little whistleblower and her boyfriend? How 'bout we toss them both down here and throw in this can of diesel with 'em? This place'll go up like a tinderbox. We'll get rid of that computer, whatever other proof they think they got, and the two of them all at once. Time the fire department gets way out here, there won't be nothin' left to find. Ain't nobody gonna know nothin'."

"You're as dumb as you look, Frank." The second man's voice was gravelly and rough, chilling in its lack of emotion. "It's gotta look right. Think about it—if her and her boyfriend was out here cookin' a little meth with some anhydrous they stole from the Proxica plant, and it blew up on 'em, they wouldn't be down in the basement, now would they? Dump that diesel can down the cellar stairs and leave the cellar door open. I'll go set things up in the kitchen, then we'll get Hampton and his girlfriend outta the trunk and put 'em in there. Them fumes'll start a flash fire quick enough, and that diesel on the stairs will suck it right down into the basement, too. The whole place'll go, but it'll all just look like an accident—like he got sloppy. Ain't gonna be as excitin' as if that boy's truck had rolled over that gas meter last night. Man, I had that thing set to blow, too. Just a little tap's all woulda took, and we'd have had us some real fireworks. It's cleaner this way, though. Now that we know his girlfriend was in on it, we can do 'em both at once."

Terror raced through me, and I caught a breath. They had Clay and Amy outside? They'd rigged the gas meter at Harmony House? If Clay's truck hadn't veered into the fig tree last night and missed the gas meter, we would have all been dead.

I shifted toward the stairway, but the man behind me held tight as the plans continued overhead.

"Don't let it splash too far from them stairs, but make sure the diesel gets all the way to the bottom. We don't want to do nothin' to make the fire marshal suspicious when he checks this place out, afterwards. It's gotta look like that diesel can just fell over down there and spilt accidental-like."

Frank laughed appreciatively. "Yeah, all right." The top stair creaked under his weight, dust sifted downward, and the man behind me slid his fingers over mine on the handle of the potato knife. I let him take it from me.

The second step creaked and the light came on, the bulb swinging on a single, narrow cord. Diesel splashed in the can as he unscrewed the lid. Fumes filled the air. A cough convulsed in my throat, and I pressed a hand to my mouth to stifle it, then pulled my shirt over my nose, gagging on the smell of diesel as Frank passed just inches from our heads, then splashed the bottom of the stairs and began working his way up. Thoughts raced wildly in my head, the urge to bolt becoming almost too strong to control. I wanted to run for the door across the room, scramble up the old stone stairs that had been chiseled from the hillside in back of the house, and burst into the fresh air. Closing my eyes, I willed myself to be still, not to move. *He'll leave in a minute. He'll leave in a minute. . . .*

I didn't want to die here in the darkness, in this cellar that had swallowed the last moments of my father's life.

"Frank, we got comp'ny! Someone's comin' up the driveway! Turn out that light down there!" Frank stopped, his feet just above my head.

A string of curses followed him as he climbed the stairs again, doused the lights, then set the diesel can on the top step. I heard the click and slide of metal against metal. The cartridge of a gun.

Roger growled low in his throat. I closed my eyes, slid a hand over his muzzle.

Who was coming now? Another accomplice? Someone else? Maybe Mom or the uncs, showing up to check on us?

Terror balled in my chest. Anyone arriving now would have no way of knowing this was a trap. Overhead, Frank kicked over the diesel can before moving through the door into the house. The acrid smell of fumes floated on the air.

The stranger let go of me, and I stumbled from under the stairway, still clinging to Roger's collar. "We have to get away from here."

"Go through the outside door." His voice was measured but insistent. "Don't stop anywhere near the house. Hide in the brush, and no matter what happens, stay put." He rushed up the steps, then slipped soundlessly through the door at the top. When it closed behind him, only inky darkness remained. Feeling my way with one hand and clutching Roger's collar with the other, I moved forward, fumes filling my lungs, making me lightheaded and sick. I couldn't get my bearings. Which way was the door that led up the steps to the yard? Which way? The ventilation windows at ground level were tiny and dirt-covered, allowing almost no light.

Overhead, the house had gone silent—no movement, no voices, no footsteps. What was happening?

My head floated and spun. I felt like I was falling. Roger tugged at his collar, pulling me sideways, causing me to stumble against something solid. I pressed against it, coughing, my lungs burning. I couldn't get my breath.

Clutching the desk, I tried again to gain my bearings, to feel my way. Which way? Which way? Something caught my leg, and I lost my balance again, tumbling over Roger. We fell against the desk chair, tipped it and crashed to the floor with it, the sound reverberating through the cellar. I scrambled to my feet again, Roger barking, my heart hammering in my ears.

Beyond the pounding, I heard something, then strained toward the sound.

Someone was calling my name—beckoning me. Not upstairs . . . outside.

Blaine?

A rush of relief came with his voice, and then fear. Where were Frank and his accomplice? Outside? In the house? Were they waiting to see if Blaine would leave, trying to figure out if he was armed? Was a gun pointed his way right now?

Sifting through the darkness with my hands, I found the wall and moved toward a ventilation window on the side of the house, closer to Blaine's voice. Boxes, buckets, and bits of furniture caught my feet and legs. Old tools, rakes, and shovels resting against the wall skittered sideways, each noise sending my heart into my throat. Was anyone upstairs? Could they hear me? Grabbing the handle of a hoe, I held my breath and tapped the glass of the ventilation window. *Please, please let it be Blaine who hears.*

There was no response. Upstairs, someone was moving, the footsteps careful, almost soundless, one floor joist crackling, then another. Someone was still in the house, heading toward the front door, toward the sound of Blaine's voice. I had to do something. Turning the tool over, I swung and hit the glass hard, threw an arm over my face as shards rained down around me.

Blaine's voice pressed through the opening as the sound died. "Heather?" He was outside the window now, his body silhouetted against a blanket of stars. A flashlight beam blinded me momentarily. "Heather?" he asked again.

"Blaine, get away," I whispered, trying to climb onto a box to get closer but quickly sinking through the lid onto the soft contents. "Get away. There's someone in the house. Two men. I think they have guns. They're going to burn the house and—"

Something crashed upstairs. Roger barked behind me, and the explosion of a gunshot split the air, followed by another sound, like the *whoosh* of a campfire bursting into flame after a dousing of lighter fluid. A scream ripped from my throat, and I spun around, tripped over Roger, then climbed to my feet and stumbled across the basement, tripping, falling, scrambling over old bicycles, stacks of buckets, gardening tools, boxes, and crates.

In the darkness, Roger barked, then clawed at something wooden—the outside door, I hoped. I made my way toward the sound until I reached the far wall and the door handle. A tangle of spider webs melted over my fingers, sticky and filmy, as

I grabbed on and pulled, but the wood, swollen from so many years of disuse, wouldn't budge.

"Heather, move back," Blaine was on the other side now. "Get out of the way." He threw himself against the door as the fight continued overhead.

A piece of furniture crashed near the cellar stairway, rolling and hitting the door hard, rattling it on its hinges as a series of gunshots exploded. Smoke seeped in from the ceiling, tinging the air with a combination of ashy scents and diesel fumes waiting to burn. Terror raced through me. A bullet splintered the floorboards and struck a joist. Roger clawed at the stones underneath the threshold, trying to dig his way through. Blaine's weight collided with the door again, causing it to give a few inches. Wrapping my fingers around the weathered wood, I pulled. How long before the diesel fumes would catch the flame and draw the fire down here? How long? Another gunshot rang out. Something or someone hit the door at the top of the stairs. Another scream wrenched from me.

"Move back." Blaine's words were ragged and urgent, commanding. "Get out of the way, Heather." Through the gap in the door, I saw him move back a step and prepare to kick his way through. Dragging Roger with me, I pressed close to the wall, Clay's backpack bunching against the stone.

Overhead, the noise stopped suddenly. Blaine

kicked the door, and it broke loose from the hinges, tumbling inward and landing on the floor with a thunderous crash. He reached through, grabbed my hand, pulled me against the stone wall of the cellar steps, wrapped me in his arms. "Are you all right? Heather, are you hurt?"

"I'm okay. I'm okay, but it's Clay. They've got Clay and Amy—in their car, I think. There was another man here. He was trying to stop them."

Pushing away, I bolted up the cellar stairs and into the yard. Roger scrambled past me as I coughed, wheezed, and gulped in air. Blaine caught me, grabbed my arm, and we cleared the corner of the house. Across the farmyard, a car barreled from the barn, crashing through the corner of an old wooden fence, then flinging gravel and going airborne as it sped over the earthen terraces, heading for the driveway.

"They've got Clay and Amy!" I screamed. "Blaine, we can't let them go!"

A second engine revved to life in the orchard behind the house. The glow of headlights ping-ponged across the yard, and a dark sedan fishtailed from the orchard lane into the drive-way, speeding after the first car. Inside the house, the fire roared, moaning like a giant beast awakening, hungry and powerful. Smoke billowed through the front door, heat flowing outward, causing us to shield ourselves with our arms. Glass buckled and shattered, the panes in the wooden windows exploding, one, then another, and another.

Blaine ran for his truck, and I spun around and rushed after him, Roger on my heels. Moments later, we were racing down the driveway, but both vehicles had disappeared from view. When we reached the county road, darkness lay in either direction, curves and hills cloaking everything, making the cars vanish like props in a magician's trick.

"Which way? What now?" Blaine demanded.

My mind spun in panic. I raked my hair out of my face, then coughed on the sooty cotton in my throat. "Harmony Shores," I gasped out as I shed Clay's backpack into the floorboard. "They did something to the gas meter there. We have to get everyone out of the house." *Please don't let anything happen. I was wrong. I was wrong to act like I didn't care. . . .*

The prayer cycled in my head, blanketing panic with hope, but also with the terrifying realization that the future wasn't a given. At any moment—tonight, tomorrow, five minutes from now—my time with the people I loved could be gone.

Blaine pressed something into my hand. A cell phone. "Start calling 9-1-1. Keep trying until you get reception. Send someone to Harmony Shores and get the fire department to the farm. Give them a description of the cars and tell them we don't know which way they went or where they're headed, for sure."

My hands shook as I dialed the phone, then pressed Send. *No service.* I tried a second time and a third, hoping and praying as Blaine's truck squealed around curves and popped over hills, catching air, then landing again. *No service, no service, no service.* "Hurry, Blaine!" Tears cloaked the words, the phone blurring as I dialed again. "Please hurry."

Blaine's hand caught mine, squeezing for a moment before he reached for the steering wheel again. "We'll get there. Keep dialing. Any minute now, it'll . . ."

"I've got a signal!" I blurted and pressed the Send button. Static hummed, the signal zigzagged from tower to tower, trying to find a connection. The moment seemed impossibly long. I imagined Harmony House in flames. I imagined my family, trapped in that monstrous structure, the uncs moving in their labored shuffle-steps, too slow to get out.

The call dropped, and my stomach plummeted with it. "No!" Frustration threw me back against the seat. "No, no, no!" I dialed again, pushed Send, listened to the tides of static, the endless clicking. . . .

"9-1-1, what's your emergency?" The voice was faint, almost lost, but it was there.

"We need help. We need help at Harmony Shores Funeral Home in Moses Lake. There's a gas leak in the yard . . . the meter. Get everyone out of the house. Please get everyone out. . . ."

"Ma'am, ma'am," the operator interrupted. "I need you to slow down. I can barely hear you. Did you say a gas leak?"

"Yes, please . . . at Harmony Shores Funeral Home. Moses Lake . . ." The call went dead, and the operator was gone.

By the time I was able to connect another call, a sheriff's deputy had already been sent to Harmony Shores. Blaine took the phone to report what had happened at the farm and to describe the cars we'd seen speeding away.

Fists balled in my lap, I collapsed against the seat, tears flowing over my cheeks. "It's okay. It has to be okay." One miracle could lead to two. Clay and Amy could be found, alive and well. I wouldn't allow myself to believe anything else.

"It will be," Blaine whispered, and I felt his hand on my hair, smoothing it away from my face. I leaned into his touch, took comfort from it, tried to let his assurance travel into my body, to become reality as we drove the final few miles, and the lights of Moses Lake appeared ahead.

When we turned into Harmony Shores, my mother and the uncs, still drowsy and confused, were moving onto the lawn with a sheriff's deputy. The deputy checked with dispatch to see if anything had been reported about the cars, but he seemed skeptical, as if my story of what had happened at the farm were too farfetched to be believed. He seemed to be of the opinion that I'd invented the whole thing about the two men breaking into the farmhouse and setting it on fire. The revelation about the strange man in the basement was completely beyond what he was willing to accept, and he forced me to repeat it several times before he could keep it straight.

"Why don't you do your job?" Blaine snapped. "I saw the cars leaving that place, too. I heard the gunfire." He towered over the deputy, and for a minute, I thought he was going to lay the guy out on the lawn. "Get the call out to the highway patrol, the park rangers, and the game wardens. That car could be a long way from here by now. They might try to hide out up in the hills or in the state park."

My mother was frantic, and the uncs were trying to comfort her. "It wasn't supposed to happen like this," she kept muttering. "This wasn't supposed to . . . Oh, Clay. Where's Clay? Why can't they find him?"

A van from the utility company arrived to shut off the flow of gas to the meter. We waited while they went through procedures, then checked the house and reported that there was evidence of tampering around the gas meter. "You breathe too hard on that thing, it'd go sky high," the technician reported, wiping his forehead. "We'll get out here in the mornin' and fix it. Till then, everybody should keep away from the house, even though the gas is off now. All the piping oughta be checked, too. Somebody's been messin' with things—that's for sure."

The deputy looked embarrassed then. He got in his car to make some more calls and ramp up the alert level.

Blaine threw his hands in the air and started toward his truck. "I'll be back. I'm going to do some looking around. One more set of eyes can't hurt."

"That's just what I was thinkin'." Uncle Charley shuffled toward the vehicle, pajama pants fluttering in the breeze as he moved across the gravel in his house shoes and bathrobe. "C'mon, Herb. No sense in us sittin' here doing nothing."

"I'm going with you." I started after Blaine, leaving my mother alone by the cruiser, shivering and staring off into space.

Blaine caught my arm gently. "You need to stay with your mom." Even though he didn't say it, I could tell what was in his mind. *You need to stay with your mom in case it's bad news.* He walked back to the cruiser and told the deputy to take us up to the church, where it was warm, then he returned to his truck, where the uncs and Roger were already waiting.

A shiver coursed through me as they drove away, the taillights turning the corner at the end of the driveway and disappearing into the night. Finally, I rejoined my mother, slipped my arm around her shoulders, and guided her into the backseat of the cruiser, the action more muscle memory than anything else. For months after my father's death, I'd moved her around the house as if she were a rag doll, relocating her from the bed to the sofa each day, misguidedly hoping that maintaining some sort of routine would make things normal.

"This wasn't supposed to happen," she whispered as we waited for the officer to secure the scene.

"Clay's going to be all right." I was torn between the urge to comfort and the need to be angry. Finally, I just held her hand. What good would it do to be angry now? What would it accomplish? What had it ever accomplished? "He'll be all right, do you hear me? You know Clay. He always lands on his feet."

"He just . . . He needed to do this. For your dad." Her head dropped forward, her hands wringing in her lap. In the uneven light, her hands looked old, the veins pronounced, her fingers thin. She seemed frail and vulnerable, not entirely prepared for the world outside her poems and her literary analyses of classic novels. In so many ways, she had always been this woman, and I'd always kept myself apart from her, waiting for her to become the mother I wanted her to be, waiting for her to fit my expectations. But I was asking for some- thing she didn't have to give. She hadn't changed,

I realized now. She wouldn't change. She would always be flighty, artistic, introspective in a way that allowed her to shut out the world. I could either love her the way she was or not love her at all.

The second choice was more painful than the first. There were connections in this life, a history that I would never have with anyone but her. "We'll be all right," I said quietly, holding her close for the first time in years. As we drove to the church, she let her head fall sideways until it rested on my shoulder. For a moment, there was just the two of us, clinging to each other as the world spun off-balance.

When we reached the church, Reverend Hay was waiting at the fellowship hall door. There were people with him—two men, several of the church ladies, and Mama B. Even Blaine's stepmother was there. They'd started a prayer chain to bring Clay and Amy home safely.

"Callin' circle's underway," Mama B said, sounding like a mission commander in the throes of a full frontal assault. "We're gonna get our kids back safe. People are up prayin' all over town." Slipping one arm around me and one around my mother, she guided us toward a sagging sofa in the opposite corner of the room. "Y'all just come on in and sit down, now," she urged, looking over her shoulder as we passed the kitchen, where

Blaine's stepmother was huddled with another woman, talking in hushed tones while surreptitiously watching our entrance. "Claire Anne," Mama B barked, and Blaine's stepmother stood at attention. "Get some coffee out here. We're gonna need it. And somebody bring me a blanket. These gals are chilled to the bone."

As church members gathered around us, offering comfort and soft, faded quilts, I felt their presence, their kindness, settling over me and seeping deep inside, easing the wild pulse thrumming in my ears. Even Blaine's stepmother seemed to be trying to help, moving around the fringes of the room in a ruffled apron, offering coffee cups and refills. She set one beside my mother without asking, then awkwardly touched my mother's shoulder before whisking away. Mom didn't respond, other than to pull in a tattered breath and clutch the quilt high around her neck.

Leaning close, Mama B forced eye contact. "Hon, now I want you to drink some of this coffee, y'hear? You want cream and sugar in it? Hon, you want cream and sugar?" Somehow, the request brought my mother out of herself. She nodded, her watery eyes fixed on Mama B.

"Claire Anne, get us some cream and sugar." Mama B's voice rattled the ceiling panels, and Blaine's stepmother scurried off to the kitchen, where she received a sympathy eye-roll from one of her friends. "And a piece of that pound cake," Mama B called after her, then returned attention to my mother. "Now, hon, you listen at this here. We're not doing any more of this cryin'. We're gonna have faith and keep praying, and believe on that prayer. That's my little granddaughter out there with your boy, and she may be tiny, but I know for a fact she's tough as a boot. She'll figure a way to come out of this all right, and so will your boy. My family pioneered this land. Some lowbrow, two-bit criminal's not gonna come in here and get the best of us. You hear me?"

Mom nodded.

"You drink some of that coffee now." Mama B pointed at the cup insistently, and my mother released the quilt, letting it slide from her shoulders. Peering around me, Mama B noted that there was no coffee on my end table. "Claire Anne! Bring another cup for Heather. She looks like she's about froze to death." In the kitchen, Blaine's stepmother was gathering things on a tray, her back stiffening every time her mother-in-law called her name.

Watching Mama B comfort my mother now, I couldn't help wondering if things might have been different all those years ago, when tragedy first touched our family. If we had reached out instead of retreating into ourselves, would these people have received us this way? If I had allowed myself to fall into this community that had so loved my father, would they have caught me? Was my stubbornness, my pride, my resentment, and my guilt more the cause of my suffering than these people were?

Maybe I'd been wrong about Moses Lake. Maybe I'd been wrong about so many things in my life. It shouldn't have taken something like this—the prospect of losing my brother—to make me assess myself, to lift the veil from my eyes. In keeping my defenses high, in striving to maintain a self-sufficient, ordered, controlled life that contained minimal risk, I was missing everything that mattered most. A well-lived life, an authentic life, involved risks—and faith allowed you to take those risks. That was what Ruth had been trying to tell me, the very thing she'd understood as she balanced on that fire escape. The great leaps in life are not made in the absence of fear, but in the presence of faith.

Mama B rested a hand on my knee and patted gently. "Blaine's out there, too. He's out there looking for them, and there's nothing that boy can't do. He was the first one to hold Amy when she was born. Bet you didn't know that. It was a snowy night, and Amy's daddy was out of town, so Blaine stayed over at his auntie's house to watch after her. Lands if she didn't have the baby right there on the kitchen floor with Blaine helping her. He'll find Amy. You watch. Good gravy, where is that coffee?"

Mama B left to check on things in the kitchen. I reached across the space between my mother and me and held her hand. Twenty minutes passed, thirty, then forty-five as the prayer chain grew and took on a life of its own, cell phone calls coming in, information going out. I tried not to imagine where Clay was now.

The clock in the church office chimed once, a solitary note weaving from the quiet shadows of the hallway. One in the morning.

One fifteen.

One twenty.

The old hardwired phone on the wall rang. Reverend Hay snapped upright, sending his folding chair skittering sideways. Every eye in the room followed him as he answered the call, pacing back and forth at the end of the coiled cord. The room grew silent, other than the faint sound of a voice on the other end of the phone, and Reverend Hay's answers. "Mmm-hmm . . . mmm-hmm. That's good news, Mart." Pumping a fist in the air, he gave us the thumbs-up sign. "That's the best news. Praise the Lord!"

A smile split his thin face, causing his eyes to crinkle around the edges as he slapped the receiver into the cradle. "They've been found, praise be! The sheriff's office received an anonymous call to send an ambulance to a car in the ditch on a county road, and when they got there, they found Clay and Amy in the trunk. No sign of the driver or anybody else, and they don't know who made the call. The paramedics think Clay and Amy might've taken in some carbon monoxide. They're in an ambulance, on their way to the hospital in Gnadenfeld."

Love is the mystery of water and a star.
–Pablo Neruda
(*Left by an anonymous tourist
who visited unnoticed*)

≈ Chapter 21 ≈

Clay's visitors came and went as night faded into morning, while next door Amy's parents, Blaine's family, and Mama B sat vigil around her room. Ruth arrived with the morning light, leaning on the elbow of her favorite nephew. In the doorway, she held Uncle Herb's hand, patted it between hers, smiled at him, and nodded. "We've done it," she said, and then crossed the room to stand over my brother's bed and point the no-no finger at him. "Never, never again, anything like that. To live peacefully is to live well. You remember that from now on."

Clay's grin was tired and lopsided, his lip swollen and bruised on the left, the oxygen tube bumping awkwardly under his nose. He waved at Mom and Uncle Charley, who were exiting the room to make space. "I think I've had . . . enough. . . . adventure . . ." His words grew raspy and trailed off. He swallowed, wincing with the effort, a little mischief twinkling in the eye that wasn't swollen shut. I was almost glad to see that the mischief was still there, even after the beating he'd taken and the carbon monoxide inhalation in the trunk of the car. ". . . for a while," he added, and I wanted to smack him one.

Lips pressing into a line, Ruth turned to me. "You should talk some sense into him."

"We could tie him to the bed," Uncle Herb suggested. "Charley's got an old lariat rope in his truck."

We laughed together, eager to diffuse the tension in the room. For an instant—just an instant—I saw the image of Clay from my dream. We'd come so close to really losing him. We could have lost him. Watching him laugh now, then draw his eyebrows together, wincing, then give in and laugh again, I regretted all the petty thoughts, resentments, and fears that had kept me away from him, from my family for so many years. Our time together as adults almost ended before it began, and if it had, it would have been my fault as much as anyone's.

I'd been so busy focusing on my self-determined parameters of what I felt my family should be, that I'd missed the beauty of what they actually were—fragile, flawed, heroic, imperfect, champions of lost causes. Each with things to learn and things to teach. God had knit us together like plantings in a garden—wild and unique above ground, blooming in different ways at different times, the roots intertwined deep beneath the soil. No matter who else passed through my life, no one would take the place of my brother. He would always be the only one with whom I shared the quiet beginnings of life, the awkwardness of growing up, the secret hiding places of childhood, the early hours of Christmas mornings waiting for Santa Claus, the arguments over space in the backseat of a car, the walk to school on the first day, and the rough times after things didn't go so well.

I looked at him now, his scruffy blond hair in unkempt curls against the pillow, and I saw all of those things. He winked at me and smirked, embarrassed by all the attention as Ruth fawned over him some more, covering him with a knitted afghan she'd brought for him and telling him a story about a stray dog that had wandered into the dairy and wreaked havoc the day before. Mary and Emily were convinced that the dog was Roger.

Clay chuckled wearily and said it was a good thing there weren't two Rogers, and then Ruth ordered him, in no uncertain terms, to rest and get well, before finally hugging him good-bye.

I walked her out, moving slowly to the end of the hall with her as her nephew tagged along behind. "Our Clay is a good boy," she said, adjusting her prayer covering and smiling at me.

"A good man," I corrected.

"There's a strong heritage in him. A heritage of men who are not afraid."

I only nodded, thinking that I wished Clay would knuckle under to fear a little more often. I was already dreading waving him off on his next adventure, whatever it might be. The idea that he wanted to settle down in Moses Lake had never been believable, and now that I knew why he'd come here, I knew he'd be moving on as soon as he was well enough.

"It's in you, too," Ruth pointed out, her fingers circling mine, squeezing and shaking gently. "Don't be afraid to live your life, Heather. It comes and goes more quickly than you'd imagine."

"I've been thinking about that," I admitted. I wasn't sure what was next for me, but I did know that I wouldn't be returning to my old life, to the people with whom I'd surrounded myself. That box seemed too confining now, too limiting. My time in Moses Lake had grown me in ways that wouldn't allow me to fit back into the same container.

We stopped at the elevator door, and Ruth's nephew pushed the button, then stood politely, pretending not to be listening to our conversation. The chime sounded, and the light flickered. We waited while a nurse wheeled a woman with a new baby off the elevator, as the husband followed behind, carrying a suitcase and a balloon bouquet, his face all smiles. I felt the sting of yearning again, but also the vague chill of uncertainty. Did

I really have it in me to step from behind the clean glass and steel walls I'd constructed and take a risk on something that couldn't be measured or calculated or planned? Was Blaine *the one?* Was there really something special between us, or was I just trying to see what I wanted to see? Was I as wrong about him as I had been about Richard?

"You'll come visit me in a day or two, and I'll tell you more stories." Ruth's comment tugged at my thoughts, but the deeper questions continued churning, a miniature whirlpool of conflicting emotions.

"If I'm here," I answered. "I mean, I think I will be . . . for a while . . . until Clay's well, at least." Suddenly I felt lost, out of sorts, overwhelmed by the unsettled, unplanned nature of the future. "I quit my job . . . I think."

But now that the Proxica scandal was about to be made public, Mel would be glad we hadn't ended up being officially tied to the company. If I called him, he'd probably act like the whole take-this-job-and-shove-it text message never even happened.

Ruth's fingers released mine as her nephew moved to hold open the elevator door. "Get a good night's sleep before you decide," she advised, shuffling into the elevator. "A tired mind doesn't think well, you know."

"I know."

"And eat something. Whole food, not the processed sort."

I chuckled. "I will." Actually, a trip across the street to the bakery sounded like a good idea about now.

Her brows arched in a way that caused me to see the little girl who had yearned to peek under the circus tent. "You should think about that riddle. The one the tinker wrote at the Waterbird. We German folk are good with riddles. The Irish think they have the market, but they don't. If you have the answer, tell me tomorrow."

I nodded, but in reality, my tired mind was hardly in the mood to contemplate ancient wisdoms. It was just like Ruth, though, to try to use this as a teachable moment.

I rubbed my eyes as I walked back toward Clay's room. In the hallway ahead, my family was exiting the room en masse, stealing nervous looks over their shoulders. I quickened my steps, forgetting about the riddle.

"We're heading to the cafeteria," Uncle Herb offered, shrugging in an indication that I should turn and follow.

"C'mon down there with us," Uncle Charley added as he moved past me. "Your brother needs a little time alone right now." Circling his lips, he flashed a wide-eyed look over his shoulder and sucked in air.

"What's wrong with Clay?" My anxiety

ratcheted up. The doctors had said that, while bruised and battered, Clay would be fine.

"Nothin' that ain't his own doin'." Uncle Charley shuffled around and kept walking. "But that could change after she gets ahold of him."

"She . . . who?" I turned to my mother, who was carefully closing the door to Clay's room, leaving it ajar only a few inches before she stepped away and wheeled a hand in a *let's-move-on* sort of way.

"His fiancée," she whispered.

Taking several sideways steps, I peered through the gap and into the room. Someone was standing beside Clay's bed. I could see the back of a pair of faded Levis and a sweatshirt. "Amy?" Surely Amy couldn't be on her feet already. She'd been in worse shape than Clay. Just a couple hours ago, when I'd looked in on her, she was still on oxygen, and they were making plans to take her down to X-ray to discern the best course of action for a separated shoulder.

A little nudge to the door opened it a bit wider, increasing the view of Clay's room. Behind me, Mom grabbed my sweatshirt and tried to pull me away.

Some . . . woman was hugging my brother. She was tall and slim, her medium-length brown hair pulled back in a simple ponytail. She'd curled herself against Clay's chest, sobbing into the sheets as he rested his chin on her head.

I staggered backward, snapping toward my mother's tug like a slinky, stretched too far. *Who's that?* I mouthed, pointing.

Mom's steepled hands touched her lips before carefully measuring her next words. "There are a few things we haven't told you."

I wasn't sure how to answer. Having already felt the world rock off kilter once that day, I didn't know if I wanted to hear the rest of the family secrets. Suddenly my brother's sexy text messages from Fort Worth made sense. There really had been someone else, all along. Was Clay's supposed relationship with Amy all a ruse? An excuse to be hanging around Moses Lake and Proxica? Obviously my mother knew the answers, so I started down the hall with her. Ahead, one of the uncs was holding the elevator for us. "Was Clay stringing Amy along, or was there never anything . . . I mean, did she know it was all an act?"

Mom quickened her pace, jogging the rest of the way to the elevator, forcing me to run-walk or be left behind. Once we were inside, she tried to placate me. "Let's get some coffee, and we'll explain the whole thing."

Frustration, exhaustion, uncertainty, and the remnants of a terrifying night welled up in me, and I smacked the *Stop* button, causing the elevator to jerk to a halt. "You know what? I just want the whole story all at once. I need to know what's true."

Mom and the uncs flicked sideways glances at each other, and Mom laid a hand on my shoulder. "Heather, just calm down. You've had quite a traumatic night, too, and . . ."

"Don't mollify me!" I jerked away from her. "Just tell me all of it. Please! Clay was never involved with Amy, was he? That was all an act, right?" My entire family had been putting on an act, and I'd been left in the audience, with everyone else.

"They needed someone on the inside . . . someone who wouldn't be suspected."

"They, *who?*" I pressed. "Whose idea was this whole thing?" The connections were tangled in my mind. "Who came up with all that malarkey about Clay taking over Catfish Charley's and you opening a bed-and-breakfast in the funeral home?"

"We had to make it look convincing," Mom defended. "To have an excuse to be in town while Clay put his case together."

Uncle Charley nodded enthusiastically but remained as far from me as the elevator would allow. "We had to get the drop on Proxica, see? Bait those slick suckers into the trap and shut the door before they knew what was comin'. Them Proxica folks got powerful friends in the government—state and national. It's a big company. Every time someone's tried to go up against them, a few phone calls get made, and that's the end of it. Meantime, they're makin' money and they got poison leaking into water wells around here, and they know it. They've known it for a long time.

"Your dad figured what was happening years ago—how they were getting rid of that Armidryn. Your brother looked at some of your dad's old papers in the cellar out at the farm. He also did some checking online and read about that lawsuit in Kentucky, and he started to put two and two together—Ruth's husband dying from cancer, and then Ruth getting sick, and others around Gnadenfeld. He started talkin' to folks and lookin' into it some more. You done good getting out of the farmhouse with his backpack, too. They might've burned Clay's computer in that fire, but there's enough evidence in that backpack to prove it all. Everything it'll take to bring them sorry suckers down."

I turned to my mother, feeling as if someone had cut the elevator cable and we were careening downward, headed for a crash. "So it's all true? About Dad . . . about the Justice Department? How could you let Clay get involved in that, after what happened to Dad?"

Mom braced her hands on her hips, her chest rising and falling. "He's your father's son. I couldn't convince him to run away, any more than I could convince your father. All I could do was be here and try to keep him safe. By the time I found out what your brother was doing, he'd already been in touch with the investigator who'd worked on the case sixteen years ago. After what happened to your father, I never wanted to see that man again. I didn't want him to have the chance to ease his conscience, to make things right. He was the one who pushed your father. He was the one who promised to protect your father, and then your dad was gone. One minute I had everything, and the next, everything was gone."

My eyes welled, and I felt the heat of tears on my cheeks. "You had us. You still had us, and we needed you." The little girl in me, the one who'd been locked away during the months following my father's death, broke free, filled with desperation, unanswered questions, and unfulfilled needs.

"I couldn't find my feet," Mom whispered, her face flushed and red, the tendrils of hair on her cheek damp now. She smoothed them away impatiently. "I couldn't find my feet, Heather. I was never strong the way you are, the way your father was. And Clay . . . he's like you in that way. He's like your father. When Clay came here, I didn't know what else to do but come along and help him put this case together."

I swiped tears away impatiently. "What case? What happens now, exactly?"

"They bring the case against Proxica. A class-action suit," Uncle Charley chimed in, as if that much were elementary. "Your brother and that law firm he's with are gonna make Proxica pay for all the people like Ruth, who're sick because of the chemicals. Looks like the Justice Department is gonna get involved, too. Amy and your brother could get a big chunk of money from the whistleblower law. Proxica has a whole lot to answer for and a lot of cleaning up to do around here."

"Clay is with a *law firm?*" Of all the information that had just come my way, that was the only bit I could really grasp.

I heard my mother sniffling, and Uncle Charley offering his hankie. "Yer brother passed the bar three months ago. He didn't want anybody to know it, on account of the case."

Something soft touched my hand, and Uncle Herbert said, "Here, dry your eyes now." He pressed a button on the panel, and the elevator jerked and rattled as it resumed motion.

I was too exhausted for coffee, too exhausted to think anymore. I caught my breath and turned to Uncle Herbert as the elevator settled into position on the bottom floor. "So nobody is moving to Moses Lake, and you and Uncle Charley are actually looking forward to living in the retirement villas in Oklahoma? You're selling everything?" Suddenly my musings about staying for a while in Moses Lake made little sense. The family was leaving, scattering to the wind.

"Well, we got a buyer for the funeral home, and Clay said he'd help us put the restaurant up for sale online," Uncle Charley stated. "No way I'm sellin' it to some broker, after this last mess. That restaurant has history. I want to pick the buyer so I know it goes to somebody that'll take care of it."

Uncle Herb nodded, indicating his complete agreement. "We thought we'd keep the old farm— bring the grandkids down sometimes. And maybe Clay would want to visit, since he's working up in Fort Worth. It'll be a family place, like it's always been—for your brother, and our kids, and for you, if you want it. The little house is gone now, of course, but the two-story is still there.

"And when we asked you about doing the architecture work for the new school, that wasn't a smokescreen, either. We meant it. The fella who bought the house at Harmony Shores might need some work done, too. He took it on as an investment—wants to turn it into a wedding parlor and make the barn and the gardener's cottage into a bed-and-breakfast. Guess that old house has at least one more life in it, yet. Moses Lake isn't that far from Dallas. You could hang out your shingle up there and live down here, drive back and forth when you need to. There's the new fellowship hall at the church to build, too. They're gonna need an architect for that."

Shaking my head, I stepped off the elevator, trying to imagine myself staying here with all of them gone. "Why would I stay in Moses Lake? Everyone else is leaving."

Uncle Charley laid a hand on my shoulder, stopping me before I could turn toward the cafeteria. "Not everybody. Matter of fact, you might know the man who bought the house at Harmony Shores—some fella by the name of Underhill. He's had his man there all week, cataloging things in the house and running the calculations." He motioned toward the chairs outside the reception area in the lobby, where a familiar pair of cowboy boots was sprawled across the green flecked tile, the jeans leading upward to a tall, lanky body crumpled in a vinyl chair, the face hidden beneath a felt cowboy hat that looked like it had seen better days. "It don't appear like he's goin' anyplace."

I stood looking at Blaine, and my heart did that strange, queasy, fluttery flip-flop that was irrational, unpredictable, and completely undeniable. In spite of all the ways we were different and all the complications, the fact was that every time I looked at him, my pulse sped up and I couldn't catch my breath. He made me want to believe in all the dreams I'd been too careful to allow, too afraid to hope for. With him, I wanted to risk myself, to let go, to believe in the romantic notions of fairy tales. He had, after all, done what heroes do. He'd kissed the girl, asleep in her own life, and awakened her to a world she'd never seen before. He stirred, as if sensing we were there, and Uncle Charley leaned close to me, whispering, "We'll leave y'all alone to talk." Then he gave me a nudge in the back, pushing me forward a few steps before he, Uncle Herb, and Mom continued on to the cafeteria.

Blaine yawned, clumsily lifting the hat from his face and blinking against the morning light streaming through the glass doors. For a moment, he seemed surprised to find himself in the hospital lobby.

"Hey," I said, and he turned to look at me, his eyes warming.

"Hey, yourself," he replied, stretching his neck side-to-side and sitting up in the chair. "Everything okay with your brother?"

I nodded, a smile tugging from the inside out. "Everything's fine." For the first time in my adult life, I felt the truth of that. I felt like that little girl, leaping from the fire escape, filled with a faith that strong arms would catch me. "Everything's really . . . good."

I sat down in the chair next to him. "Is Amy doing all right?"

Hanging his cowboy hat on his knee, he rolled his head toward me, still resting against the wall. His dark hair was saluting the new day in several different directions—evidence that he'd been sleeping in the chair awhile. "She's a little better this morning. Mama B finally kicked us all off the third floor so Amy could get some rest. She put up a pretty good fight when those guys hauled her and Clay out of the Proxica plant and put them in the car. She got away for a minute, but the guy caught up to her and knocked her down a flight of stairs. If I'd had any idea she and your brother were planning to sneak into Proxica last night, I would've put a stop to it. I never would have agreed to either of them taking a chance like that, even as bad as I wanted to see Proxica stopped."

Even as bad as I wanted to see Proxica stopped. When he said it, I could see the passion, the burn behind the words. It bothered me that he'd kept that hidden from me, that there had been a wall of secrets between us. What other secrets lay hidden? "I wish you'd told me what was going on."

The soft, earthy brown of his eyes pulled me in. I wanted to fall, to let all the questions fade away, but if the last sixteen years had taught me anything, they'd taught me that the questions you don't resolve are the ones that hold you prisoner. "You made it hard not to," he admitted. His hand lifted from the chair and the backs of his fingers brushed the side of my face. "But it wasn't my secret to tell. I made a promise, and I don't make promises I don't intend to keep. I never wanted to hurt you, Heather. I didn't set out to lie to you, or sidetrack you, or anything else."

"What did you set out to do?" I tried to make it sound like a quip, but I felt myself hanging in air, waiting for the answer. Some small part of me was still afraid, still clinging to the past, still convinced that Blaine Underhill was too perfect to be real. Too good to be meant for me.

His fingers slid over my cheek, into my hair. "Just to spend time with the girl I missed out on in high school."

My mind swirled with a heady mix of emotions. I knew he was going to kiss me, and I wanted him to. "I'm not that girl anymore," I whispered against his lips, and in that instant, I knew it was true. This journey back to Moses Lake had brought me full circle, broken me open in a way that made all things possible.

"You're better than that girl." Blaine's words slid over me, and then his lips met mine. The kiss transported me from the hospital, to a rock ledge by the water, and for a moment we were dancing.

When his lips parted from mine, I laughed softly.

Blaine's eyes narrowed, those thick, dark lashes forming a narrow slot. "What's that look for?"

"I was thinking about the Blue Moon," I admitted. "About the two-step."

"We could do it again sometime." He grinned.

"Okay." A tingle of anticipation lit up my body, chasing the weariness away. "I will if you will."

A movement in the corridor, then a quick flash of darkness against the morning sun pulled at my attention. I looked up and saw a man in a dark coat crossing the hall to the stairway door. Even from this distance, something about him was unmistakable.

I stood up, moved a step closer to gain a better view against the light. My thoughts lost their misty edges, coming quickly into focus. Why was he here? What did he want? What questions could he answer?

"Heather?" Blaine shifted in the vinyl chair.

"I'll be right back." My heart sped up and I hurried down the hall, walking, then running as the stairway entrance slowly closed, the hydraulic cylinder hissing softly. I caught the knob just before the latch could click into place.

"Wait," I called, pulling back the door. "Wait. I want to talk to you."

The man paused at the bottom of the half-flight of stairs, his thumb and fingers resting on the handle that would allow him to exit. For an instant, I had the sensation of being with my father, but I knew it wasn't him. The stranger turned slightly, so that I could see the profile of his face beneath the shadow of his baseball cap.

"Everything's taken care of," his voice echoed against the stairwell. "The men who took your brother and Amy will be prosecuted, and Proxica is finally going to get what has been coming for a long while. It won't matter how many congressmen their CEOs take on island vacations. They're not getting out of this one."

"You caught those men—the two from last night?" I asked, anxious to confirm that the men who had come after my family were locked away somewhere. "Are we safe now? Is my brother safe?"

He nodded, his fingers relaxing on the door handle. "Your brother did a good job. Your father would be pleased. This was what he wanted."

The mention of my dad left me numb. "I saw you the day . . . when my father was killed. You were there with my mom, earlier that day."

His head dropped forward, his cap and the collar of his coat hiding him again. "I shouldn't have let it go as far as it did. I wanted to crack Proxica. I was driven, ambitious. I just needed a little more. He wanted out, you know—your dad. He wanted out that last day. He was a family man. Said his wife and his kids came first. I should've just let him go, but we needed someone on the inside, so I squeezed a little harder. I told him there wasn't any way back to the life he had before—the only way out was through Proxica. Then, of course, we lost him, and we lost Proxica."

The question that had plagued me for sixteen years pressed to the surface. "He didn't . . . Did my father . . . ? It was an accident . . . wasn't it? He didn't mean to . . ." Air seared my throat. I heard each heartbeat inside me, the tempo seeming to slow, bending the seconds into impossible, painful spans of time.

The latch on the street door clicked, and the

stranger pulled it open, letting in a gush of winter air. "Like I said, your father was a family man. He wanted to do what was right, but you kids mattered to him more than anything else. He was just trying to keep all of you safe. He wanted to protect you, and that's why he had the shotgun. What happened in that cellar wasn't intentional. Just a tragic accident, but it was my fault it got to that point. It was my case."

He opened the door then and stepped out, his words playing again in my head as he disappeared against the glare.

My body felt light and numb as I turned to walk away, uncertain how to process, after all these years, the answers I'd waited so long to hear. My father had loved us more than anything else. He'd only been trying to protect us. His death was an accident. Neither I, nor my mother, nor his job had pushed him to it. In spite of the ways I'd been difficult, immature, self-centered, and unkind, he'd loved me and was willing to sacrifice anything to protect me. He wouldn't have left us willingly, no matter what.

Looking up, I saw Blaine coming from the lobby, closing the distance between us in confident, even strides. I moved toward him one step, then two, then three, freedom settling over me with each one—as if the burden I'd carried for so many years was being cleared away, like a cache of debris trapped in an inlet along the lake, swept clean when a good rain finally comes along. At last I'd found the answers I needed. God had brought me to them, to Moses Lake, to the only place where He could lead me through the fire into everything that lay beyond.

"Who were you talking to?" Blaine craned to see through the stairwell window as we met.

"Just someone who knew my dad," I answered, waiting as we turned to walk back up the hall. Slipping my hand into Blaine's, I felt myself walking into life, a new life that was like nothing I had ever imagined. Suddenly I knew the answer to the tinker's riddle. I understood it in a way I never had before.

The future is a blank page, but not a mystery.

The truth of that small phrase, of that plain-spoken proverb from the wall of wisdom was so clear to me now. Though we only read the story in due time, the books of our lives have been already written. God has drawn us in shades of charcoal and pastel, known our hours, seen our days, laid down our paths, created each of us as unique and uniquely loved. Our lives come as a blank canvas only because we cannot see as He sees. Before we can conceive our stories, He has watched them in His mind's eye, and not the stroke of a pen happens at random.

Above the book, the Architect watches with a broader eye, a greater plan. He knows what is to be written on every page.

≈ Acknowledgments ≋

In returning to the little town of Moses Lake, I'd like to thank a few people who helped to make this trip possible. Every book is an adventure that begins long before bookshelves and book covers—usually with a writer tapping on the doors of friends and strangers, trolling for research material.

First and foremost, thanks to long-distance friend, BJ Holley, for answering questions and sharing a few funny stories about owning a family funeral home. You helped to bring that big white house at Harmony Shores to life. Thank you to Kathy for letting me pick your brain about real-estate development issues while sharing ice cream in the Free State of Menard. Teresa and I are still laughing over the story about headlights in the pasture. Thanks again to my favorite Wingate fisher-boys for answering fishing questions and lending funny fishing phrases to the wall of wisdom at the Waterbird Bait and Grocery. You're welcome to stop in for a game of dominoes with the Docksiders anytime.

As always, I am grateful for the loving,

supportive family God has blessed me with. Thank you to my mother for being a right-hand man . . . errr . . . woman, who can aptly critique a manuscript but will still tell me to eat my vegetables. Thank you to my sweet mother-in-law for helping with address lists and feeding my big boys when I'm away on book trips. Thanks also to relatives and friends far and near for everything you do to make me feel loved and nurtured, and for stopping people in the checkout line and at the doctor's office to talk about books. I'm incredibly grateful to my favorite digital designer Teresa Loman for being such a sweet-spirited soul sister and gal pal, and to Ed Stevens for constant encouragement and help with all things technical. The world needs at least five million more of both of you. Thanks also to my friends and fellow Southern gal bloggers at *www.SouthernBelleView.com*. What a hoot to be sharing a cyber-porch with you and blogging about all things southern. Thanks also to all those who stop by the blog and share your stories. It's amazing these days, how big a front porch can be!

In terms of print and paper, my undying gratitude, cheers, and shout-outs go to the incredible group at Bethany House Publishers. To Dave Long and Sarah Long, thank you for being such talented editors and just plain fun to work with. Julie Klassen, I will miss you as an editor, but I look forward to many more of your wonderful books. To the crew in marketing, publicity, and art, thank you for everything you do. Without your vision and hard work, books would be loose leaf pages in black-and-white, sitting on a desk somewhere. To my agent, Claudia Cross at Sterling Lord Literistic, thanks again for all that you do.

Last, but not least, I'm so very grateful to reader-friends everywhere, who filled the fictional town of Moses Lake with life and laughter last year when *Larkspur Cove* hit the shelves. Without you, the stores would be boarded up and the coffeepot at the Waterbird would go dry, and then who would the Docksiders tell their stories to? Thank you for sharing the books with friends, recommending them to book clubs, and taking time to send little notes of encouragement my way via email and Facebook. I'm incredibly thankful to all of you who read these stories and to the booksellers who sell them with such devotion. You are the fulfillment of a silly little dream my first-grade teacher sparked in me when she wrote on my report card, "Keep that pencil moving with that great imagination. I'll see your name in a magazine one day." God has blessed that dream and stretched it in ways that only He could have conceived, and I am so very thankful.

I hope you have fun on this visit to Moses Lake. The local folk have been asking about you, by the way. They want you to know they love it when you stop by, and you're welcome to stay as long as you like. Sit back, dip a toe in the water, and watch the eagles ride the warming afternoon air. Your presence is a joy and a blessing that no words could aptly describe. Welcome!

⮘ Discussion Questions
⮚

1. In returning to Moses Lake, Heather is coming home to a place that was special to her as a young child, even though the memory was later marred by tragedy. Do you remember a special childhood place? What makes the places of our childhood live large in our memories?

2. Heather and Clay have vastly different personalities—Heather being more like their father and Clay being more like their mother. Do you think we're always more like one parent than the other? How do our connections or missed connections with our parents shape us?

3. In spending time with her brother again, Heather realizes that there are memories and experiences we only share with our siblings. How are our sibling relationships different from any other relationships? Have you experienced sibling strife in your family at various times? How can we cultivate healthy relationships with our siblings?

4. Heather resents the past efforts of her aunt and the bridge-club ladies to coach and reform her so that she could fit the parameters of Moses Lake. Why do you think they were so intent on this? Did they mean well, or not?

5. Heather recalls her past crush on Blaine shortly after she returns to Moses Lake, but when she meets him again, she learns that he isn't the person she thought he was. Have you ever gotten to know someone you had only observed from a distance, and been surprised at the person inside?

6. When looking into the past, Heather idolizes her father, while her brother finds fault with him and is more understanding of their mother's position. Where do you think reality lies? Is it common for siblings to have different views of family history? Have you ever experienced this in your own family?

7. As she spends time in Moses Lake, Heather begins to recognize that the tragedy in her past has limited her openness to relationships in the present. How does loss in childhood change us and shape us in adulthood? Have you seen evidence of this in people you have known? How can we move beyond past experiences that are painful?

8. When Ruth tells the story of her sisters, Lydia and Naomi, she ends with the dilemma of which one chose the right path—the sister who compromised herself to feed them, or the sister who clung to her faith. What are your thoughts on the paths chosen by the two sisters? How do you think you would react, if faced with such a dire situation?

9. In recounting her family history, Ruth says, "Terrible things had happened to us, after all—death, disease, hunger, our family torn asunder, abuses I cannot even speak of. How could a God who loves us allow such things, you might wonder?" What is your answer to this question?

10. In spite of her cancer and the tragedy in her early life, Ruth is peaceful in her spirit. In what ways, surrounded by a troubled world, can we cultivate a spirit of peace and abundance?

11. Because Ruth's sister, Lydia, was brave enough, she was the only one who saw the circus. Ruth seems to regret that her fear kept her on the hill with the other girls. Has fear ever kept you from doing something that you later wished you'd done? If you had the chance again, would you do it?

12. Heather eventually concludes that she can either love her quirky family the way they are, or not love them at all. Do you think this is true? Should we learn to accept people exactly the way they are, even if we don't agree with some of the things they do? Why or why not?

≈ About the Author ≈

Lisa Wingate is a popular inspirational speaker, magazine columnist, and national bestselling author of several books, including *Tending Roses*, *Talk of the Town*, *Good Hope Road*, *Dandelion Summer*, and *Never Say Never*, winner of the 2011 Carol Award. Her work was recently honored by the Americans for More Civility for promoting greater kindness and civility in American life. Lisa and her family live in Central Texas.

Visit *www.lisawingate.com* to sign up for Lisa's latest contest, read her blog and excerpts from her novels, get writing tips, contact her, and more.

Center Point Large Print
600 Brooks Road / PO Box 1
Thorndike ME 04986-0001 USA

(207) 568-3717

US & Canada:
1 800 929-9108
www.centerpointlargeprint.com